A TRIO FOR LUTE

DAMIANO
"A treasurable read."
—Anne McCaffrey

"A brilliant tale of magic and faith."
—*Hamilton Spectator*

"A charming, delightful, original fantasy. I recommend it
to you heartily."
—*Analog*

DAMIANO'S LUTE
"MacAvoy is clearly a writer with immense gifts and not
improbably one of the future giants of the sf/fantasy field.
This book cannot be too highly recommended."
—*Booklist*

"Absorbing . . . The author's ability to bring to vivid life
the general background of this period of history, and yet
interweave it with the type of fantasy which was actually
accepted in that day is truly amazing."
—Andre Norton

RAPHAEL
"She concludes the story already related in *Damiano* and
Damiano's Lute with surprising innovation—something that
I believe is becoming her trademark."
—*Fantasy Review*

D0029316

Bantam Spectra Books by R. A. MacAvoy
Ask your bookseller for the titles you have missed

THE BOOK OF KELLS
THE GREY HORSE
TEA WITH THE BLACK DRAGON
A TRIO FOR LUTE:
DAMIANO
DAMIANO'S LUTE
RAPHAEL
TWISTING THE ROPE

A TRIO FOR LUTE

DAMIANO
DAMIANO'S LUTE
RAPHAEL

R. A. MACAVOY

SPECTRA

BANTAM BOOKS
TORONTO • NEW YORK • LONDON • SYDNEY • AUCKLAND

A TRIO FOR LUTE
A Bantam Spectra Book / July 1988

PRINTING HISTORY
DAMIANO copyright © 1983 by R. A. MacAvoy
DAMIANO'S LUTE copyright © 1984 by R. A. MacAvoy
RAPHAEL copyright © 1984 by R. A. MacAvoy

All rights reserved.
Cover art copyright © 1988 by Gary Ruddell.
No part of this book may be reproduced or transmitted
in any form or by any means, electronic or mechanical,
including photocopying, recording, or by any information
storage and retrieval system, without permission in writing from
the publisher.
For information address: Bantam Books

ISBN 0-553-27480-5

Published simultaneously in the United States and Canada

Bantam Books are published by Bantam Books, a division of Bantam
Doubleday Dell Publishing Group, Inc. Its trademark, consisting of the
words "Bantam Books" and the portrayal of a rooster, is Registered in
U.S. Patent and Trademark Office and in other countries. Marca
Registrada. Bantam Books, 666 Fifth Avenue, New York, New York
10103.

PRINTED IN THE UNITED STATES OF AMERICA

O   11 10 9 8 7 6 5 4 3 2 1

A TRIO FOR LUTE

DAMIANO
DAMIANO'S LUTE
RAPHAEL

DAMIANO

What thou lovest well remains, the rest is dross
What thou lovest well shall not be reft from thee
What thou lovest well is thy true heritage
                    Ezra Pound, The Pisan Cantos, LXXXI

This novel is dedicated to Pierre Bensusan, the musician, whose face on an album cover inspired the character of Damiano and whose music could inspire Raphael himself.

CHAPTER 1

A string buzzed against his fingernail; the finger itself slipped, and the beat was lost. Damiano muttered something that was a bit profane.

"The problem isn't in your hand at all. It's here," said Damiano's teacher, and he laid his ivory hand on the young man's right shoulder. Damiano turned his head in surprise, his coarse black ringlets trailing over the fair skin of that hand. He shifted within his winter robe, which was colored like a tarnished brass coin and heavy as coins. The color suited Damiano, whose complexion was rather more warm than fair.

"My shoulder is tight?" Damiano asked, knowing the answer already. He sighed and let his arm relax. His fingers slid limply across the yew-wood face of the *liuto* that lay propped on his right thigh. The sleeve of the robe, much longer than his arm and banded in scarlet, toppled over his wrist. He flipped the cloth up with a practiced, unconscious movement that also managed to toss his tangle of hair back from his face. Damiano's hand, arm, and shoulder were slim and loosely jointed, as was the rest of him.

"Again?" he continued. "I thought I had overcome that tightness months ago." His eyes and eyelashes were as soft and black as the woolen mourning cloth that half the women of the town wore, and his eyes grew even blacker in his discouragement. He sighed once more.

Raphael's grip on the youth tightened. He shook him gently, laughing, and drew Damiano against him. "You did. And you will overcome it again and again. As many times as it crops up. As long as you play the instrument. As long as you wear flesh."

Damiano glanced up. "As long as I . . . Well, in that case may I fight my problem a good hundred years! Is that why you never make mistakes, Seraph? No flesh?" His toothy smile apologized for the witticism even as he spoke it. Without waiting for an answer, he dropped his eyes to the *liuto* and began to play, first the treble line of the dance, then the bass line, then both together.

Raphael listened, his eyes quiet, blue as lapis. His hand still lay on Damiano's shoulder, encouraging him. Raphael's great glistening wings twitched slightly with the beat of the music. They caught the cloudy daylight and sent pearly glints against the tiles of the wall.

Damiano played again, this time with authority, and smoothly passed the place where he had to change the meter—two strokes, very fast, plucked by the middle finger. When he was done, he looked up, his face flushed with success, his lower lip red because he'd been biting down on it.

Raphael smiled. His wings gathered forward and in, making a sort of private chamber within the drafty Delstrego hall. "I liked that," the angel said. "—The way you played it, too, first each line, then both."

Damiano shrugged and flicked his sleeves from his hands, his hair from his face. Though his expression remained cool through this praise, he squirmed on the bench like a child. "Oh, that was just to warm up to it. I wouldn't perform it that way."

"Why not?"

"It's too simple. There's nothing to it, just playing the one line, without even any trills or ornament."

The archangel Raphael took the little wooden instrument out of Damiano's hands. He edged away along the bench, and his wings swept back in a businesslike manner. His face, as he retuned the strings, was chiseled perfectly, almost harsh in its perfection, unapproachable, forbidding. But the high B string rang flat (the pin tended to slip), and his left eyebrow shot up in theatrical shock, along with his left wing. Damiano smothered a laugh. Slowly Raphael began to play the melody "Ce fut en mai," which is a very simple tune, one he had helped Damiano to learn three years previously. He played it a number of times through, without trills, without ornamentation, without counterpoint of any kind. He did, however, play it differently. The

first iteration was jolly; the second, sad. On the third trip
through, the song bounced as though it were riding a
horse, and the fourth time the same horse was being
ridden into battle. The fifth became a dirge, and when it all
seemed over for good (like an eventful life—that song—
now over for good), he played it through again like the
dance it was. Damiano listened, his amusement turning to
awe.

"I'll keep my mouth shut from now on," muttered the
youth.

"I would be sorry if you did that, my friend," said the
angel. "I like to hear you talk." The smile he turned on
Damiano was terrifying in its mildness, but Damiano was
used to Raphael's smile. He grinned back.

"Please, Seraph, while you have the lute, play me again
the French piece from last week. I can't grasp the cross-
rhythms."

Raphael lifted his golden gull-wing brow again, but as
no musician needs to be asked twice, he began to play.

Damiano watched and listened, thinking: I am privileged like no other man on earth. I can never deserve this,
not though I transmute lead to gold and flesh to fire, not
though I keep my chastity for life.

It then occurred to him that perhaps not every young
man in the Piedmont would consider it a reward worth
remaining a virgin for—hearing an angel of God play the
lute of four courses. Even Damiano himself had his
moments of dissatisfaction (with virginity, that is, not with
Raphael).

And then angels were not a popular object of study,
even among the order of alchemists, since they had no
material power to offer and were more apt to tell the truth
than tell the future. Even Damiano's father, who had been a
witch of great repute, had never tried to summon an angel.
Other sorts of spirits he had contacted, admittedly, but of
that Delstrego had repented.

At least Damiano hoped his father had repented. It was
quite possibly so, since Guillermo Delstrego was a good
while dying.

While Raphael played the pastorelle, Damiano attempted to follow him, knowing the music. But soon the
angel burst the confines of the French piece, as his student
had known he would, and drifted away into melodies and

rhythms suggested or invented on the spot. Raphael had a trick of running his lines together until, like the triune Godhead, they were united into a single being. Then, when Damiano had almost forgotten what he was listening for, the different lines sprang apart again. There were four, no five of them. Six?

Soon Damiano was utterly lost, as the angel struck the strings all together in what should have been a dissonant crash but was not. Raphael brushed the strings lightly, as though with his wings, and his left hand fluttered over the smooth black wood of the lute's neck. The sound was no longer music at all—unless water was music or the scraping of wind over the grass.

Damiano heard silence and noticed Raphael's eyes on him. The angel's face was perfect as silver, as a statue, and his gaze was mother-shrewd. He waited for Damiano to speak.

"Am I ever going to play like that?" the young man mumbled, nudged out of a waking dream.

White wings rustled on the floor. Raphael seemed surprised by the question. "You will play like—like Damiano, as you do already. No one can do elsewise."

"That's all? As I do already?" His disappointment dissolved in the intensity of the midnight gaze.

"More and more, your playing will become *Damiano*. As your life takes its form, so will your music."

Damiano pursed his bee-stung lips. His eyes, avoiding Raphael's, slid around the great hall with its cream-colored walls, floor of painted flowers, and assorted alchemy bric-a-brac scattered on the acid-stained oak tables. He focused on the black kettle hanging over the central hearth.

"Damiano jerks and stutters. He has the smooth articulation of a sore-footed cow. And as for his life—well his life is to take lessons: in magic, in music. He has done that for twenty-one years."

Raphael didn't smile. "You are very hard on yourself. Remember that the harshest critic on earth is my brother, and his specialty is telling lies. Personally I like Damiano's playing." He extended the *liuto*. Damiano took it and fondled it absently. He always felt uneasy when Raphael began to talk about his brother the Prince of Darkness.

"If you continue to study," added the angel, "I expect you will develop the ears to hear yourself as I do."

"I knew there was some reason I was studying," he muttered. "So it's just so I can hear myself without wincing?"

His grumble died away, and Damiano lifted his eyes to the echo of siege engines, distant and ghostly, resounding in the hall. The iron lids of the many pots on the hearth rattled in reply.

The angel didn't seem to hear. "I thought that was done with," muttered Damiano, furrowing his forehead. Rough brows met in a straight line. "Last Tuesday the men of Savoy crept out of Partestrada, between midnight and matins. The citizens they abandoned are in no position to fight."

Raphael seemed to contemplate the bare hall. "It's not really . . . battle that you hear, Dami. Pardo's rams are knocking down walls outside of town."

"Walls? Whose? Why?" Damiano shot to his feet and wedged his shoulders into the narrow crack of a window. A man of more substance would not have been able to do it. The wall was almost two feet thick, for the Delstrego house had been built as a fortress.

Damiano craned his head left and peered along the main street of Partestrada. From this particular window, if he twisted with a good will, he was able to spy around one corner to the front of Carla Denezzi's house, where in good weather she sat on the balcony, doing her complicated needlework. Damiano was practiced at making this particular neck twist. What it told him often decided whether he'd bide his time at home or venture out.

Today the balcony was empty; and its wooden shutters, drawn. The street below, too, was empty, totally empty. Not a man or a woman, not an ox wagon or a wandering ass to be seen. The town didn't even smell right, he thought as he inhaled deeply through his nose. It didn't stink of urine, peppers, pigs, sheeps, men's or horses' sweat—none of the comfortable smells that meant home to him. The streets smelled burnt, like the air surrounding a forge. He lifted his eyes to the distant fields and forests beyond the town wall, which faded from brown to gray to blue in the November air. Damiano squinted—his far vision was not the best. Out of habit he reached back along the wall, his hand scrambling over the slick tiles till he grasped his staff.

It was not the traditional witch's stick, not being brown, branchy, or picturesquely gnarled. Damiano's staff was ebony and lathe-straight, ringed in three places with silver. Knobbing the top was a silver crest set with five topazes and a rather small ruby (red and gold being the Delstrego colors). It had been given to Damiano by his father when the boy was twelve—he then stood only as high as the second silver band. Now, nine years later, the staff was still a bit taller than he was, for Damiano had not grown to Delstrego's expectation.

The staff was as important to Damiano as crutches were to a lame man, though young Damiano had two limber and useful legs. It was his spelling-instrument, and upon its black length he worked with more facility than he did on the lute. Also, although he had never worked a spell toward the purpose, Damiano believed he could see better holding the staff. He held it now.

"The wall belongs to a man named Francesco Alusto," answered the angel, his quiet voice cutting easily through the stone wall to Damiano's ears. Damiano weaseled back into the room, his cheeks flushed, his eyes bright with worry.

"Alusto? He owns the vineyards, such as they are. But why? What will they do when they get in? Isn't it enough that they control the town?"

There was an indefinable reproach in the angel's eyes. "Why? Because Alusto became a wealthy man under Savoy patronage. Although his being a wealthy man might be enough. What will they do? Damiano! They will rape and kill, take what they can carry or haul, and then march away. Perhaps they will burn the place as they go.

"But I am not here to instruct you in the customs of war—that would be a bad education, I think, and more easily gotten elsewhere." He spoke without heat, yet Damiano dropped his eyes to the pattern of the floor. Against his better judgment, almost against his will he found himself saying, "Don't you care, Seraph? Don't you hear the cries of men dying? The weeping? It rang in my ears all of last week when they fought beside the city wall. The good God knows that since the Plague there are few enough men left in all the world."

The angel's expression might have been called ironical, if irony were a thing that could be built on a foundation of

pity. "I know you hear them, Dami. I almost wish you did
not, for when the ears are open, the rest of the soul must
follow, to its own pain. But I hear men suffering. I too. The
difference between us is that you hear them when they cry
out, whereas I hear them always."

Damiano's startled glance flew upward to his teacher's
face. He saw the pity, not directed only toward suffering
humanity but also toward Damiano himself. He stood
confused, not knowing why Raphael should waste his pity
on Damiano the alchemist, who was young and wealthy,
and in good spirits besides.

"What would you have me do?" the angel continued.
His wing feathers gathered up like those of a bird in the
cold. "I can't change the heart of man or the history he's
making for himself. I am not"—and here he spread his
hands out before him and his wings out behind him in a
sweeping gesture that took in the entire arc of the
compass—"in truth a part of this world. I have no calling
here."

Damiano swallowed hard. "Except that I called you,
Raphael. Don't—give me up. Please. If I speak offensively
in your ears, remember I'm only a mortal man. Tell me my
fault. I would take a vow of silence rather than have my
words offend you." He reached out and slapped the angel's
knee, awkwardly and with rather too much emphasis.

"A vow of silence? That's a rigorous promise, Dami,
and there are few people I have met less suited to it."
Raphael leaned forward, and yellow hair fell gently curling
around his face. "I will not give you up, my friend.
Compared to mankind, I am very patient. I have the time,
you see. And I am not as easily offended as you might
think. But you must not ask me for answers that are not
revealed to men." The golden eyebrow rose further, and
one wing scraped the flat ceiling. "—It may be that they are
not revealed to me, either."

The wing descended, obscuring the window light like a
filter of snow. "Besides, Damiano, the important questions
involve not the intent of God toward us but the soul's own
duty, and you know that clearly, don't you?"

Damiano did *not* know it—not on certain issues, anyway. Behind Damiano's teeth, white and only slightly
uneven, trembled the question that had waited in silence
for three years, ripening—the terrible question about the

necessity of virginity. Surely now was the time to broach it. Raphael had practically asked for such a question—it was not something unrevealed to men, after all, but only knotty. Such an opportunity would not knock again.

He heard a scrabble and panting on the stairs, and his dog tore into the hall, calling, "Master, Master, there's a soldier at the door. With a spear!"

She was a small dog, knee-high, very heavy in the head and shoulders, and bandy-legged. Ugly. Her color was white, except for a saddle mark over her shoulders, and so she was called Macchiata, which is to say, Spot.

"With a spear?" echoed Damiano, feeling the moment for his question dart off like some small animal that, once frightened, will forever be harder to approach. He stood, indecisive, between the angel and Macchiata.

"*Pax tecum*," whispered Raphael. His wings rose and glittered, and he was gone.

Macchiata blinked at the disturbance in the air. She shifted from leg to crooked leg, and her ruddy hackles stood out like the quills of a hedgehog. "Did I scare him away, Master? I'm sorry. I wouldn't scare Raphael on purpose.

"—But there's a soldier . . ."

"With a spear," added Damiano disconsolately, and he slouched down the stairs after Macchiata.

CHAPTER 2

The second floor of the house was broken up into smaller rooms. Damiano passed through the vestibule with its florid tiles and heavy, glinting hangings, where the hearth sat smoldering through the short autumn day. The door was made of oak panels layered with the grain in different directions and studded with iron. It stood ajar, as always, for the convenience of Macchiata.

The sergeant watched Damiano advance through the dimness. It was a boy, the sergeant thought—a servant. Beasts with human tongues were bad enough—more than bad enough. That bitch made his honest, though thinning, hair stand on end. He would not now be pushed off on a servant. Not though Delstrego could give a man boils with his stare, as the townsfolk said. Pardo could do worse to the man who did not follow his instructions.

Then Damiano stood in the light.

Not a boy, quite. But spindly as a rail. Girl-faced too. Damiano blinked against the sudden brilliance.

"I want your master, boy," growled the soldier. He spoke surly, being afraid.

"You will find him in the earth and above the sky," answered Damiano, smiling. The sergeant was surprised at the depth of the voice issuing from that reedy body, and though he did not trust the words, he involuntarily glanced upward.

But Damiano continued, "*Dominus Deus, Rex Caelestis:* He is my master and none other."

The sergeant flushed beneath his bristle and tan. "I seek Delstrego. God I can find on my own."

Insouciantly, Damiano bowed. "Delstrego you have found," he announced. "What can he do for you?"

The sergeant's left hand crawled upward unnoticed, prying between the leather plates of his cuirass after a flea. "I meant Delstrego the witch. The one who owns this house."

Damiano's unruly brows drew together into a line as straight as nimbus clouds. "I am Delstrego the alchemist: the only Delstrego dwelling in Partestrada at this time. This house is mine."

Snagging the flea, the sergeant glanced down a moment and noticed a patch of white. That hideous dog again, standing between the fellow's legs and half concealed by the robe. Her teeth shone white as the Alps in January, and her lips were pulled back, displaying them all. Perhaps she would open her mouth in a minute and curse him. Perhaps she would bite. Surely this Delstrego was the witch, whatever he looked like or called himself.

"Then it is to you I am sent, from General Pardo. He tenders his compliments and invites you to come and speak with him at his headquarters." This was a prearranged speech. Had the sergeant chosen the words himself, they would have been different.

But Damiano understood. "Now? He wants to see me now?"

"Certainly now!" barked the soldier, his small store of politeness used up. "Right now. Down the street in the town hall. Go."

Damiano felt Macchiata's rage vibrating against his shins. He restrained her by dropping the heavy skirt of his robe over her head. "All right," he answered mildly. "I'm on my way." He stepped out onto the little, railless porch beside the sergeant. A twiglike, white tail protruding from the back of his robe pointed stiffly upward.

The sergeant noted the gold and scarlet velvet of the robe and its foppish sleeves. Inwardly he sneered. He further noted the black wand, man-high, ornamented like a king's scepter. "Not with that," he said.

Damiano smiled crookedly at the soldier's distrust. "Oh, yes, with this especially. Pardo will want to see this." He spoke with great confidence, as though he, and not the sergeant, had just left the general's presence. Glowering but unsure, the sergeant let him pass.

"Aren't you coming along?" inquired Damiano, turning in some surprise halfway down the stair. The sergeant had stood his place at the open doorway, his ruddy bare knees now at Damiano's eye level. "—To see that I don't play truant by darting over the city wall or turning into a hawk and escaping into the air?"

"I am to guard the house," answered the soldier stolidly.

Damiano stared for a moment, his mind buzzing with surmises, then he continued down the stairs.

Under the arch of the stairway, beside the empty stables, stood another of Pardo's soldiery: a tall man with a scar running the length of one leg. He too watched Damiano pass and kept his place.

The street was not so bare as it had appeared earlier. It was scattered with swart-garbed soldiers, who stood out against the dust and stucco like black pepper on boiled frumenty. Damiano had never been able to abide boiled frumenty. No more did he like to see the streets of Partestrada dead like this. He was quite fond of his city.

Damiano could feel, using a little witch-sense—which was nothing like sight or sound, but rather like the touch of a feather against the face or, better, against the back of the palate—that there was no one at home in any of the square plaster houses around him. He gripped his staff tighter and strode forth, immediately stumbling over Macchiata.

"Get out of there," he grumbled, lifting his skirts and giving the dog a shove with his foot. "Walk before, behind or beside, but not under."

Macchiata laid back her ears, thin, white, and folded like writing paper. "You put me there, and I couldn't see."

Damiano started forward again, hoping no one on the street had noticed. "That was to keep you away from the soldier. He might have spitted at you in a moment, and there's nothing I could have done about it. Then where would you be?"

The dog did not respond. She did not know the answer.

Someone *had* noticed. It was old Marco; even war and occupation of the city by the enemy could not keep him from his place beside the well, squatting on his haunches with a bottle of Alusto's poorest wine. Damiano, at this distance, could not make out his face, but he knew it was Marco by his position and by the filthy red wool jacket he wore. Damiano would have to pass right by the old man, and he would have to speak to him, since Marco had been one of Guillermo Delstrego's closest friends. Perhaps his only friend.

Marco was, however, insufferable, and as Damiano passed he only bowed in the general direction of the well and called, "Blessing on you, Marco," hoping the old sot had passed out already. Quite possibly he had, since it was already the middle of the afternoon.

"Hraaghh?" Marco had not passed out. He jackknifed to his feet and strode over to Damiano, holding the wine bottle aggressively in one sallow hand. Macchiata yawned a shrill canine yawn and drooped her tail, knowing what was coming. Damiano felt about the same.

"Dami Delstrego? I thought you had flown to the hills three days ago, just ahead of the Green Count's army."

Damiano braced his staff diagonally in front of him and leaned on it. "Flown? Fled, you mean? No, Marco. You haven't seen me for three days because I've been tending a pot. You know how it is in November; people want my father's phlegm-cutting tonic for the winter, and when I say I'm not a doctor, they don't hear me.

"Why did you think I'd run away?"

Marco waved his bottle expansively, but very little of

the contents splashed out. "Because they all have. Every man with any money in the village . . ."

"City, not village," corrected Damiano under his breath, unable to let the slight pass, yet hoping Marco would not hear him.

"And every young fellow with two arms that could hold a spear, and all the women of any age, though some of those old hens are flattering themselves, I will tell you . . ."

"Why did they leave, and for where?" Damiano spoke louder.

"Why?" Marco drew back and seemed to expand. Damiano sighed and cast his eyes to the much disturbed dust of the street. Nothing good had ever come from Marco swelling like that.

"Why? You juicy mozzarella! To save their soft little lives, of course. Are you so addled with your books and your devil's music that you . . ."

"What do you mean, 'devil's music'?" snapped Damiano in return, for nothing else Marco could have said would have stung him as sharply. Macchiata vocalized another yawn and flopped upon her belly on the ground.

"Maniac, pagan . . . The church fathers themselves called it cursed."

Damiano thumped his staff upon the ground. Its vibration, smooth and ominous as a wolf's growl, brought him back to reason. "They did not. They only said that contrapuntal music was not suitable to be played in the mass. But that too will come," he added with quiet confidence, thinking of the hands of Raphael.

Marco listened, sneering, to Damiano's words. To the deep humming of the staff, however, Marco granted a more respectful hearing. The old man plucked absently at his felt coat, from which all the gold embroidery had long since been picked out and sold, and he raised his bottle.

"Well, boy. You should still get out. You have two arms and two legs and are therefore in danger of becoming an infantryman. And Pardo isn't from the Piedmont; he may not be intimidated by your father's name."

"I thank you for your concern, Marco. But I am much more valuable as an alchemist than I would be as a soldier. If Pardo is a man of vertu, he will see that."

The bottle did not quite drop from Marco's hand. He

stared at Damiano slack-jawed, all the stumps of his front
teeth exposed. "You will go over to the monster?"

Damiano scowled. "The monster? That is what for forty
years you called Aymon, and then his son Amadeus. He
was no friend to Partestrada. He ignored our city, save at
tax time—you yourself have told me that, and at great
length."

"The old tyrant grew softer once he'd filled his belly
from us, and his son at least is mountain born," snorted
Marco.

"Perhaps Pardo will be different. Perhaps he is the one
who will realize he can ride to greatness along with the city
of Partestrada. If he has a mind, and eyes to see, I will
explain it to him." Damiano spoke words he had been
rehearsing for the general's ears. Marco cleared his throat,
spat, and turned his back on Damiano to shuffle toward the
sun-warmed stones of the well.

"Wait, Marco!" called Damiano, hurrying after. He
grabbed the greasy sleeves of Marco's jacket. "Tell me. Are
they all gone? Father Antonio? Paolo Denezzi and his
sister? Where is Carla? Have you seen her?"

Marco spun about, vermilion-faced. "Tell you? That
would give you something else you could explain to
General Pardo." Without warning he swung the clay bottle
at Damiano. The staff took the blow, and the bottle fell in
purple-stained shards at his feet. Only a swallow had been
left in it.

"Your father," called Marco, stomping down the street
in the direction from which Damiano had come, "was an
honest witch. Though he burns in hell, he was an honest
witch."

Damiano stood staring at the drops of wine beading the
dust, till Macchiata laid her triangular head against his leg.
"He shouldn't have said that about your father," she said.

Damiano cleared his throat. "He wasn't insulting my
father. He was insulting me.

"But I can't believe Marco thinks I would betray my
friends, let alone my city. He is just old and angry."

Damiano shook his head, took a deep breath, and
jerked his sleeves from his hands and his hair from his
eyes.

"Come," he said. "General Pardo is expecting me."

* * *

Damiano hated being reminded about his father, whom he had last seen dissolving into a green ichor. Guillermo Delstrego had died in pain and had stained the workroom tiles on which he lay. Damiano had never known what spell or invocation his father had been about, for there were many things Delstrego would not let young Dami observe, and that particular invocation Damiano had never had any desire to know.

Guillermo Delstrego had not been a bad father, exactly. He had certainly provided for Damiano and had taught him at least a portion of his arts. He had not beaten Dami often, but then Damiano had not deserved beating often, and now it seemed to Damiano that his father would have liked him better if he had. A mozzarella was what Marco called him. Delstrego probably would have agreed, being himself a ball of the grainiest Parmesan. But after their eighteen years together, and despite Damiano's quick sensitivity to people, the young man could say that he'd scarcely known his father—certainly not as well as old Marco knew him.

Damiano was like his mother, whom Delstrego had found and married in Provence (it was said no woman in the Piedmont would have him), and who had died so long ago she was not even a memory to the boy. He had her slimness, small face, and large eyes. And though his nose was rather larger than hers had been, it was nothing like the strongly colored and very Roman appendage that Guillermo Delstrego had borne. Yet Delstrego had had to admit the child was his, because witchcraft did not run in his wife's family, and even as a baby Damiano had given off sparks like a cat.

Was Delstrego in hell? There was gossip that said a witch was damned from birth, but the Church had never yet said anything of that sort, and Damiano had never felt in the slightest bit damned. He attended the mass weekly, when work permitted, and enjoyed involved theological discussions with his friend Father Antonio of the First Order of San Francesco. Sometimes, in fact, he felt a little too sure of God's favor, as when Carla Denezzi let him sort her colored threads, but he was aware of this fault in himself and chided himself for an apostate whenever the feeling got out of hand. His father, though, who died invoking the Devil, alone knew what . . . Who could be

sure about him? When he asked Raphael, he was told to
trust in God and not to worry, which was advice that,
although sound, did not answer the question. Damiano
prayed both at matins and at vespers that his father was
not in hell.

It was quite frosty, even though past noon. Cold
enough to snow. The sky was heavy and opaque, like a
pottery bowl tipped over the city, its rim resting on the
surrounding hills and trapping all inside.

Except it had not trapped anyone, anyone but old
Marco and himself. Where had the people gone? Where
had Paolo Denezzi gone, taking his whole family? It was
not that Damiano would miss Denezzi, with his black
beard and blacker temper. His sister, Carla, however . . .

The whole city was one thing. An undifferentiated mass
of peasants and vendors and artisans called Partestrada; to
Damiano it was all that Florence is to a Florentine, and
more, for it was a small city and in need of tending.
Damiano was on pleasant terms with everyone, but he
usually ate alone.

Carla Denezzi was another matter altogether. She was
blonde, and her blue eyes could go deep, like Raphael's.
Damiano had given her a gilded set of the works of Thomas
Aquinas, which he had gone all the way to Turin to
purchase, and he thought she was the jewel around
Partestrada's throat. Damiano was used to seeing Carla at
the window of her brother's house or sitting on the loggia
like a pretty pink cat, studying some volume of the desert
fathers or doing petit point. Sometimes she would stop to
chat with him, and sometimes, if a chaperon was near and
her brother Paolo was not, she would permit Damiano to
swing himself up by the slats of the balcony and disturb
her sewing further.

In his own mind, Damiano called Carla his Beatrice,
and if he was not being very original, it was at least better
to liken her to Dante's example of purity rather than to
Laura, as did other young men of the town, for Petrarch's
Laura had been a married woman and had died of the
plague, besides.

Now Damiano passed before the shuttered Denezzi
house front and he felt her absence like cold wind against
the face. "Where are you, my Beatrice?" he whispered. But

the bare, white house front had no voice—not even for him.

The town hall had no stable under it, and it was only two stories high. It was not a grand building, being only white stucco: nowhere near as imposing a structure as the towers of Delstrego. It had not been in the interest of the council to enlarge it, or even to seal the infected-looking brown cracks that ran through the wall by the door. Except for the weekly gatherings of the town fathers, discussing such issues as the distance of the shambles from the well and passing judgment on sellers of short-weight bread loaves—such were commonly dragged on a transom three times around the market, the offending loaf hanging around their necks—the town hall had been occupied by one or another of Savoy's captains, with the half-dozen men necessary to keep Partestrada safe and in line.

Damiano knew what Savoy's soldiers had been like: brutishly cruel or crudely kind as the moment would have it, but always cowed before wealth and authority. No doubt these would be the same. It was only necessary for a man to feel his own power . . .

His confidence in his task grew as he approached the open door of the hall, which was guarded by a single sentry. His nod was a gesture carefully tailored to illustrate he was a man of means and family, and a philosopher besides. The soldier's response, equally well thought-out, was intended to illustrate that he had both a sword and a spear. Damiano stopped in front of him.

"I am told that General Pardo wants to see me," he began, humbly enough.

"Who are you, that the general should want to see you," was the cold reply.

A bit of his natural dignity returned to Damiano. "I am Delstrego."

The sentry grunted and stepped aside. Damiano passed through, leaning a bit on his staff, allowing any casual observer to believe he was lame.

"Not with that," spoke the soldier, and Damiano paused again. He could not lie barefacedly and tell the man he needed the stick to walk, but he was also not willing to be parted from it. He squinted nearsightedly at the guard, mustering arguments. But the guard pointed downward. "The general doesn't want to see your dog."

Macchiata's hackles rose, and she growled in her throat. "It's all right," Damiano said softly to her. "You can wait outside for me. And for your sake, do it quietly!" The dog lumbered out the door, watched by the amused guard, and Damiano proceeded into the hall.

General Pardo was the sort who looked good in black, being hard, neatly built, and of strong color. His height was impossible to judge as he sat slumped in the corner of an ornate bench-pew, his legs propped on a stool beside it. He was dusty, and his face sun-weathered. He regarded Damiano in a manner that was too matter-of-fact to be called arrogant. Damiano bowed from the waist.

"You are the wizard?" began Pardo. To Damiano's surprise, the general addressed him in a clear Latin.

The young man paused. He always corrected people who called him witch, though everyone called him witch. No man had ever before called him a wizard. The word was one Damiano had only read in books. It rang better than witch in the ears, but it also sounded pagan—especially in Latin. It did not seem right to begin his conversation with General Pardo thinking him a pagan, and yet it wasn't politic to begin matters by correcting the general. "I am Delstrego," he replied finally, knowing that at least his Latin accent was above reproach.

"Not a wizard?" The question was sharp.

"I am . . . an alchemist."

Pardo's response was unsettling. His mouth tightened. He turned his head away. It was as though something nauseated him. *"Deus!* An alchemist," he muttered in southern-accented Italian. "Just what I need."

Damiano leaned against his staff, puzzled. He also dropped into Italian: the Italian of the Alps, heavily flavored with French. "An alchemist seeks only to comprehend matter and spirit, and to raise each of the highest level, using the methods of Hermes Trismegistus . . ."

"DON'T," bellowed the general, "TELL ME—" He took a deep breath. A soldier clattered into the room, then seeing it was only the general exploding, he backed out.

"—about Hermes Trismegistus," finished Pardo. Damiano stood pale and staring, like a man who has broken through ice into cold water.

"Why?" he asked in a small voice. "Why not Hermes?"

The general shifted in his seat. A smile spread across his features. "Because, boy, I have heard enough about Hermes Trismegistus and the quest of alchemy to last me three lifetimes. Florence is riddled with fusty old men who claim they can turn lead into gold. Venice is almost as bad." He turned a gray-eyed hawk glance on Damiano. "Avignon . . . is beyond help.

"You are too young and healthy to be an alchemist, Signor Delstrego. Also too clean. Can you turn lead into gold?"

"Not . . . in any great quantity," answered Damiano, embarrassed.

"Can you at all?" pursued the general.

Damiano sighed and fingered his staff. It was his burden that many of the goals of alchemy he found easier to accomplish using the tools of his father rather than those of the sainted Hermes.

"My methods are not pure"—he temporized—"and the amount of labor involved is . . ."

Pardo swung his legs down from the stool and glared at the youth in frustration. "What I want to know, boy, is HAVE YOU POWER?"

Pardo had an immense voice and was used to commanding large numbers of men on the battlefield. But Damiano was no longer used to being commanded. The bellowing raised in him an answering anger. His fingers tightened upon the black wood of his staff.

Without warning the air was filled with booming, as every door and shutter in the building slammed back upon its hinges. Sparks crackled in the folds of Damiano's woolen robe. The light wooden door of the audience chamber trembled for half a minute. A cloud of plaster dust fell.

Pardo regarded it calmly. "I could feel that," he remarked, "in my ears."

Damiano kept his mouth shut, feeling he had done enough, and knowing that slamming doors would not protect him from a regiment of swordsmen. Besides, he was tired.

"That's what I was trying to find out," added the general conversationally, as he nudged the stool in Damiano's direction. "Sit down, Signor Delstrego. I want to talk to you."

"Thank you, General." Damiano lowered himself gratefully onto the cushion. "I also, was wanting to speak with you."

"Ahh?"

Uttered by a Piedmontese, that single, interrogatory syllable would have echoed in the back of the throat and in the nose, like the crooning of a mother cat. At the most a Piedmontese would have glanced at his companion as he spoke to show him it was to him the inquiry was addressed. But General Pardo was a Roman by birth. Both eyebrows shot up and his lips pulled back from his teeth. The intensity of interest revealed by the single syllable of "Ahhh?" seemed in Damiano's eyes excessive: a thing too, too pointed, almost bloodthirsty. It was of a piece with the general's appearance and his snapping temper.

These Italians, Damiano thought—not meaning to include the Piedmontese—they are too hot and too cold together. Passionate and unreliable.

"To speak with me? I expected as much," concluded Pardo, with some satisfaction. "Well be my guest, Signor Dottore. I slept in a bed for the first time in a week, last night, and now am disposed to listen."

Damiano spared only a moment to wonder whose bed the general had slept in, and whether the original owner of it now slept on a straw pile or in the hand of God. Then he put his mind to the task.

He leaned forward on his stool, his legs crossed at the ankles, each knee draped in gold cloth like the smooth peak of a furrowed mountain. His staff was set between his feet, and it pointed at the cracked roof and the heavens beyond. Against the ebony he leaned his cheek, and the wood was invisible next to unruly curls of the same color. His eyes, too, were black, and his mouth childishly soft. A painter or a poet, seeing that unlined face, might have envisioned it as springtime, a thing pretty enough in itself but more important in its promise of things to come.

General Pardo looked at Damiano, but he was not a painter or a poet. He noticed the huge hands, like the paws of a pup still growing, and he saw Damiano, like a pup still growing, as a bit of a clown.

"It is about this city," Damiano began, and was immediately interrupted, as Pardo inquired what city he meant.

"Partestrada," replied Damiano, wondering how the general could be so slow. "Partestrada has been under Savoy governance for many years."

"If you can call it governance," introjected Pardo.

Damiano paused to show he had heard the other, then continued. "In that time the city has grown from a town of four hundred families into the only place of any note between Turin and Aosta."

"Of any note . . ." echoed Pardo doubtfully.

"Her people are healthy, her surrounding croplands flourish. She supports two silversmiths and a . . ." Damiano decided not to mention the vineyard at this time. ". . . and she is located on the Evançon, a river that is passable almost its entire length. She has grown like the child of the mountains that she is."

"And you would like her to continue in the same fashion?" asked the general dryly. "Without interference."

Damiano lifted his eyebrows in a gesture that, though he did not know it, was the mirror of that which he had distrusted in Pardo. "No, Signor General, that is *not* what I want for my city. All this she had accomplished on her own, unguided, like a peasant virgin, beautiful and barefoot. What would she be under the protection of a great man?"

Pardo leaned forward, uncomprehending. "I am not in the habit of protecting virgins, peasant or otherwise," he said simply.

Damiano felt his face growing hot. He had picked the wrong metaphor to use with a soldier, certainly.

"What I mean is," he began slowly. "We need the presence of a man of wealth and culture, in whose house the arts will flourish, and whose greatness of soul can inspire Partestrada with a similar greatness . . ."

"It's the pope you want," suggested Pardo with a white smile. "Go to him, Signor Delstrego, and tell him to move from Avignon to Partestrada, where the air is better."

Wit is cheap, thought Damiano, yet reason cannot best it. He dropped his eyes, accepting the humiliation as he had accepted it from his father daily in his childhood. This general reminded him of his father in more ways than one.

For the sake of his city, he tried once more.

"General Pardo, it would not be bad for you to join yourself to Partestrada and to grow with her. By her placement and her people she is destined for greatness. You could be the tool of her greatness. She could be the tool of your own glory. Like Visconti and Milan."

Pardo's nostrils had flared, but he had let Damiano continue until he heard the name of Milan. "Milan!" he barked. "When I marry a city it will be one with a greater dowry than Partestrada! Why do you think I am up here, sweeping your little hill towns like a housewife with a broom, if not in preparation for Milan? I need money and power, and my army needs experience. I will get what I can from the crumbling House of Savoy, while Amadeus is busy with his new wife and the stupid wars of Jean le Bon. When that great one turns to bite the flea on his leg I will be gone.

"But I will come again. And again. And each time I will harvest this miserable, cold cloud-land, until I am rich enough and have men enough, and then I will move on Milan. If I cannot buy that city's love, I will take it by force."

Damiano's face tightened painfully, but he spoke what was to him the obvious. "Milan has been in so many hands. You will not be remembered in history by taking Milan."

"HISTORY IS SO MUCH DOG SHIT!" bellowed the general, pounding his fist against the wooden back of the pew. "Milan? That is something else. Passed through many hands? Well the whore is none the worse looking for it.

"Boy, have you SEEN Milan?"

"Many times," answered Damiano, meaning three times, once with his father and twice since, buying books. "It is a beautiful city, although very flat."

Now it was Pardo's turn to lean forward and stare. "I don't want you to take this as an insult, Signor Delstrego, because I think I could like you. You have loyalty and enthusiasm. Also a very useful talent, if that business with the doors was any guide.

"But your provincial upbringing has colored your thoughts. You have read about Florence and Rome, and you think they are no different from your little town in the hills, where your family has a certain . . . reputation. It seems to you better to devote your time to making the little town bigger than to risk all by starting anew in a place where there are more possibilities, but you have no reputation at all."

Damiano frowned perplexedly and shook his head, but
Pardo continued. "My advice—and I am a man of some
experience—is to risk it all and leap for what you want.
Most men are less than they seem. It is nature; their fate is
to feed the few who have vision and courage. Most cities
exist to be plundered, and it is out of that plunder we
create the glory of Rome, of Florence, and of Milan."

Pardo smiled, with a too-knowing smile—with Guillermo Delstrego's smile, in fact. And he was speaking in sly,
comradely fashion, as Damiano had often heard his father
speak to some low companion, the two sitting side by side
in the empty stable, away from the light of the sun.

"Alchemists are all posers," Pardo said. "And real
magic—black magic—is very rare. But it exists! I am sure in
myself that it exists!"

Damiano shook his head more violently. "Not for me,"
he protested. "Never black magic."

"Your father was not above cursing an enemy," Pardo
contradicted equably. "And I'm told he did it effectively."

"Who told you? That's heresay. You mustn't believe it!"

"An old man named Marco told me," answered the
general. "At the same time that he told me where the
inhabitants of the city were hiding in the hills."

Damiano rose from his chair, his face draining. "Marco?
He betrayed the citizens?"

With one hand Pardo waved away Damiano's shock.
"Don't worry. I'm not going to butcher them all. There's no
value in that. It is what they took with them that I want,
and any villager who is willing to die over a purse or a ring
of gold deserves what he gets.

"But it's what Marco told me about your father and
yourself that I found most interesting. He said your father
was the most powerful witch—I mean, rather, wizard—in
the Italies."

"He was a witch," said Damiano, dully, "and not the
most powerful, by his own admission. He always said that
Saara of Lombardy . . ."

"Good enough," interrupted Pardo. "He also said you
were almost your father's equal in power, though too
faddish and delicate-minded for your own good."

"A mozzarella," murmured Damiano, staring at the
floor. Marco betraying the city. Soldiers with hairy knuckles
ripping the gold from around Carla Denezzi's neck. The

gold and what else? He became aware that Pardo was still talking.

"—with me," the general was saying. "I am not proposing a marriage, like that which you were so willing to arrange between this town and myself, but I am not a bad man. I am educated and a Christian. I kill no man for pleasure. Turn your skills to my service, and I promise you I will reward you well."

Damiano stared through Pardo. "What did you give Marco, for his services?"

Pardo's smile was crooked. "I have granted him the vineyard outside the gates," he replied. "But Marco is an old sot and a traitor as well. I could be much more generous to a man of skill, whom I could trust."

Damiano found his tongue. "You will have no need to be generous with me, Signor General."

Pardo rose slowly from his bench. "You refuse me outright?" Like a cat, which begins its attack with a single step, the general advanced on Damiàno. "Outright?" he repeated.

"It doesn't come to that," answered the youth, standing his ground. "You see, I would be of no use to you. The abilities I possess—or even those of my father—do not make good weapons of war. If they had, I think he would have used them so."

General Pardo stood facing Damiano. They were almost of a height. "Explain," barked the general.

Damiano leaned forward upon his staff. He gazed at the red tile floor, thinking. At last he began.

"Works of magic are no different from ordinary labor. One starts with material and adds the strength of one's own power, and in the end you have made something. When I threw open all the doors and windows of the building, I used the air as my tool and hammered it according to a design I had learned. In the end I was more tired than I would have been had I run from door to window and swung them open by hand."

"But the windows in rooms that were bolted you could not have touched at all without wizardry. Am I right?" The general sought in Damiano's face some sign of subterfuge or evasion. Damiano met his glance.

"Ah, yes. But that is another element: the moral element, and that is a very real thing in magic, real and dangerous. If I open a door that you have locked against me, or cause it to open as you are walking by, with the intention of hitting you with it, then my deed is a wholly different thing than a mere opening of doors. Magic worked in malice will almost always spring back against the worker; that is why purity of heart is important in a witch.

"You may well laugh," added Damiano, for Pardo *was* laughing, "but so it is. Being a channel of this power, I must be careful of my desires. If I grow angry with a tradesman and feel in my imagination my hands around his neck, then I will carry the seed of strangling around in my head and may well feel demon fingers at my own neck in the middle of the night."

"Still," introjected the Roman, "curses are pronounced, so someone must dare to pronounce them."

Damiano shrugged. "A witch can be able without being wise. Notice how many with the power are poor and diseased, worse off than the unfortunates they have cursed. Some carry such hatred that they would rather do harm than remain well themselves. Some have learned the skill of putting off all their payment until some time in the future, trusting they will die before the bill falls due."

Damiano sighed deeply. "But I don't think by dying one can escape that particular sort of debt." Again he found himself thinking about his father. "Still, even if I could murder and escape unscathed, it would be a sorry sort of killing, because in the time it would take me to strangle one man through witchcraft—one man, I say, for I don't have the power to destroy a regiment—I could be run through ten times by a simple soldier with neither mind nor magic."

Pardo's gaze was eager and predatory. "This is interesting. Very. And convincing, since it is my intuition that nothing in this life is free. Yet, Signor Delstrego, you are not a military man, and therefore you don't know what things can be valuable in war. You need not kill a regiment to destroy it; merely let them see their commander fall from his horse, gasping and turning purple. Let me tell you what things I have seen ruin an army: flux from bad water, the prophecy of a crazy old whore the night before a battle, three crows sitting on the corpse of a black heifer. Things as silly as this make the difference between loss and victory. And it will always be so, as long as armies are made of

men. Think what it will mean to my men to have the
wizard Delstrego riding with them into battle. Think what
it will mean to the enemy!"

In General Pardo's gray eyes sparked enthusiasm, and
Damiano was not immune to it. Certainly no man before
had ever expressed exhilaration at the thought of having
him at his side in battle. The wizard Delstrego. . . .

But even as he felt these things Damiano also felt his
staff thrumming quietly in his hands, a private voice of
warning. He reminded himself that he had come here to
argue for his city, and that Pardo had refused him. And
Pardo was a Roman, so obviously could not be trusted.
Besides, he reminded Damiano of his father, and what
could be less inviting than that?

Suddenly he was aware of noises in the hall outside the
audience chamber, and the room itself grew dimmer as
bodies blocked the light from the door. Pardo was hedging
his bet.

Damiano smiled vaguely at the general, and his fingers
tightened over the second silver ring on his staff. He
opened his mouth as though to speak, but instead he
disappeared.

General Pardo blinked. His eyes darted right and left.
"FIND HIM!" he bellowed at the men who poured into the
small, square chamber.

For a moment the doorway was empty, and Damiano
stepped through on tiptoe, holding the shoe of his staff off
the tiles. He paced the hall, trading stealth for speed as he
approached the arched door that gave onto the street.

Macchiata sat in the dust with an attitude of martyred
patience. Her nose worked, sensing him near, and her
head turned expectantly toward the entryway. The single
sentry stood oblivious to Damiano, his helmeted head
craned over his shoulder as he attended to the rising
hubbub from the general's quarters.

Damiano touched his dog on the back so lightly she did
not feel him. He whispered two words. She yelped and
started.

"Oh, there you are," she gasped, and her inadequate
little tail wagged stiffly. In answer Damiano put his hand to
his mouth and gestured for her to follow.

"I am invisible," he hissed, springing lightly along the
bare street, where aimless flakes of snow had begun to fall.

"But I can see you, Master," the dog replied following in more cumbrous fashion.

"You are invisible, too." Damiano paused, staring.

Against the well sprawled old Marco, snoring, a powder of snow, like dandruff, across his felt jacket. He looked the same as ever: dirty, slack, disgruntled, even in sleep. Had he really betrayed the people of Partestrada to Pardo? If so, why was he still sitting out here in the snow, instead of throned in relative splendor at the house that until today had belonged to Cosimo Alusto? Pardo must have been lying. Yet what he had repeated concerning Delstrego and his son was every inch old Marco.

What did it matter? Damiano bent down and shook Marco by his greasy ears. "Wake up Marco," he whispered. "Talk or I will turn you into a pig and you will talk no more! Wake up now."

Marco came awake gasping at the air. He gasped, "What? Who is it?"

"It is Delstrego, old man." Let Marco figure out which one himself. "Where have the citizens gone? Speak or be sausage."

Marco clutched at the wrists of invisible hands that in turn were clutching his lapels, slamming his head against the stones of the well. Feeling their solidity did not reassure him.

"Guillermo? Do me no hurt, old friend. They are in the vetch field, where the sheep are summered. Pardo said he will offer them no violence, except, of course, for Denezzi, and I knew he was your enemy, so I told the general he had gold—more gold than he has, you know . . ."

Marco giggled ingratiatingly. In horror, Damiano stood, letting him drop back against the well. He turned on his heel and darted off. Behind him came a snap and a yowl of pain, then he heard Macchiata panting at his side. "I always wanted to do that," she growled contentedly. Damiano only hushed her.

The tall, scarred soldier still stood beneath the arch of the Delstrego staircase. Peering upward, Damiano could see the door was open. He stopped and pulled off his boots. His breath was beginning to steam; he hoped it was not obvious. Barefoot he climbed the stairs, with Macchiata behind him. Her nails clicked against the stones, and he glared back at her.

In five minutes he was out again, still invisible, with an invisible sheepskin sack slung over one shoulder and the *liuto* over the other. In the sack he carried wine, cheese, money, and phlegm-cutting tonic. In his heart he carried purpose. He lifted his eyes to the northern hills, where the sheep pastures flanked the Alps.

Damiano padded noiselessly past the guard and down the open stairs. Once at the bottom he turned and looked about him, missing Macchiata.

Where was the bitch? Surely she knew better than to wander off ratting now, in the middle of their escape. And it was costing him energy to keep her invisible.

He hesitated to call out for her, because invisible was not the same as inaudible. Painfully, Damiano squinted up the stairs into the darkness of the house.

There came a scream, followed shortly by a curse, and then the guard at the door fell flat on the stucco landing, bellowing. Macchiata's squat form scuttled down the stairs and past Damiano. He had to run to keep up.

"I bit them both, Master!" she panted, exultant. "I bit both soldiers and old Marco, too! Three in one day." Suddenly she came to a stop, turned, and threw herself, slobbering, upon her winded master.

"Oh, Master, I have never been so happy. This war is wonderful."

Damiano could not spare breath to disagree.

CHAPTER 3

The moon rose just before sunset. It hung as invisible behind the slate clouds as Damiano had been to old Marco at the well. But Damiano knew where it was, out of a knowledge so accustomed he didn't know whether it was his father's blood in him or his father's training. He always knew where the moon was; he could have pointed to it. The five planets came harder, but he had a feeling for them, also. Even with peripatetic Mercury he was usually right.

Though Damiano's eyes were faulty in daylight, he had a compensating ability to make use of moonlight, even moonlight behind clouds. For most of the month he could read without candlelight and could perceive things in the dark that most people could never see at all (nor did they want to). The full of the moon also tended to sharpen his other senses and put his feelings into a roil.

Guillermo Delstrego had liked to say that male witches were like women, with their monthly cycles. It was a joke Damiano had found in the worst taste.

Tonight the moon was at her third quarter, waning. Damiano felt as dull and heavy as a water-soaked log. For the past three nights he had tended the batch of tonic, sitting on a hard-backed chair so that he could not doze off for more than an hour at a time. The mixture had been ready this morning, and Damiano had bathed and gone immediately back to the workroom for his lesson with Raphael. He would not be able to walk the night through.

Besides, to the vetch field it was two and a half days' march. How did the citizens do it, with old women and babies, and Alfonso Berceuse with his one leg?

The road into the hills was also the road to Aosta—good and wide, open almost all the year. Why hadn't he heard? Why hadn't someone told him? It was sad that they would all go off and not think of Damiano, alone without family or servants, sitting up and brewing medicine for their sakes.

Damiano was swept with self-pity. He hated to be forgotten. And he couldn't bear the thought they had left him behind on purpose. And now three toes on his right foot had no feeling at all.

But Father Antonio would not have left him behind on purpose. Since Delstrego's death Father Antonio had been very kind to Damiano and had spent long evening hours with him in the parlor of the rectory—the good father felt constrained to avoid the Delstrego tower, though he knew Damiano worked no impieties there—drinking spiced wine and talking about sanctity and Holy Mother Church. It was a subject about which Father Antonio seemed to know much more than anyone else Damiano had met. More than did Raphael, for instance. Father Antonio was the sort who never forgot anyone—not the least of his parishioners, in their good fortune or bad. If he had left without Damiano, it was because he had believed Damiano to be gone already.

And why not? Damiano hadn't set foot outside for three

days, not let a candle shine, nor lit any fire save that under the caldron. There was no need for him to feel neglected.

Still, forgotten or no, he had to sleep. Damiano lifted his eyes to the rounded hills on either side of the road. Immaculate, white, they seemed to give off their own faint light. Damiano knew this landscape with a child's minute memory. He remembered that the hill with a lump on the side of it, three back from the road, concealed a long, skinny cave, dry for most its length. He remembered also that from the top of that hill one could see Partestrada down in the cup of the valley, where the Evançon ran under this road. He had stood there in summer twilight and watched the lamps twinkle through the soft air.

Plunging into the snow-sprinkled gorse at the side of the road, he looked at his footsteps behind him. There was no need to concern himself with covering them over. The wind was doing that. The tiny toe-dimples of Macchiata's progress were half obscured already.

A good thing, too. Damiano wasn't sure he had the strength left to work a wind spell. "How are your feet, Macchiata?" he asked the dog, his words coming slurred through frozen lips. She replied that she couldn't remember, which was probably meant as a joke, although with Macchiata one never knew for sure. He heard her behind him, bulling her way through the low shrubbery.

At the top of the hill he stood and looked down, gripping his staff as tightly as his clumsy hands allowed. There was a light in the valley: one smoky firelight where there should have been dozens. The wind billowed his mantle out before him, and the ermine lining glimmered brighter than snow. There was no sound but the wind and the crackle of his breath, along with the heavier, warmer sound of the dog's breathing.

Already he felt removed from Partestrada, both in distance and in time. His removal had been surgically quick, but as he considered now, quite thorough. All the strings that bound him to his home had been cut: Carla was gone ahead, and both Macchiata and the lute were portable. Damiano felt an unwarranted lump in his throat—unwarranted because, after all, he was not leaving Partestrada forever, but just for so long as it took him to find his people, and to do something about this General Pardo. Perhaps two weeks, he estimated.

He clambered down from the crest of the hill, poking amid the dry growth with the heel of his staff, looking for the mouth of the cave he remembered.

It was still there. Crouching down he crawled into it, his hands smarting against frozen earth.

Inside there was no wind, and the rivulet that had created the cave was frozen on the floor of it like a broken silver chain. He inched over it. Macchiata slid behind.

There, as he remembered it, was the hole in the wall: an egg-shaped chamber that had been the perfect size for a boy alone to play in. It was tighter for the grown Damiano and his lute, and tighter still when Macchiata squirmed in, curling between his nose and knees. The staff would not fit in at all, but he laid it along the lip of the chamber with its silver head hanging in. He touched this, mumbling three words in Hebrew, and it gave off enough light for him to arrange the furry mantle between his body and the stone.

"This is not too bad," he whispered to the red spot on Macchiata's withers. She grunted in reply.

He let the light go out. "Tell me, little lady, did you see anyone come near the house while I was tending the kettle? Did anybody perhaps stop and look for a light in the windows, and then pass by?"

Macchiata squirmed sleepily. "I saw many people go by, and horses and carriages, too. All the dogs of the city, I think. They wanted me to come with them; they said it would be fun. —But of course I didn't.

"Also somebody knocked on the door one day. Not today. I don't remember when."

"Ahh!" Damiano lifted his head. "Father Antonio?"

Macchiata yawned. "No. That Carla with the blond hair."

Damiano's skull struck the stone roof of the chamber, but that didn't distract him from his joy. "Carla Denezzi, at my door? Why didn't she come in?"

"Because I didn't let her in," explained the dog. "You said you were not to be disturbed. I offered to take a message, like always, but she just stared and ran off. She's timid as a cat, that one."

Damiano's happiness was such that he had to hug someone. Macchiata gave a piglike grunt. "Timid? Ah, no, little lady, she had courage, or she would not have come at all. If that lout Denezzi knew she had come alone to the

house of Delstrego, he would . . . well, I don't exactly
know what he would do, but he would be very angry. And
she must have had endless matters to attend to: sorting
and packing and settling with all the tradesmen. Oh, don't
say she is timid, Macchiata."

The dog stuffed her nose down among her folded paws
in meaningful fashion and said nothing at all.

When Damiano awoke, the cave walls were chalky with
diffuse sunlight. He was warm, but very hungry. Macchiata
was gone, but he heard her at the entrance to the cave,
snuffling among the shrubbery. Rolling onto his back, he
dug into his sheepskin bag and found the waxed wrappings of a cheese, which emitted a tiny crackling.

Along the path of the rivulet he heard a frantic scrabble,
and Macchiata slammed her broad head smartly against
the end wall.

"Mother of God, what is it?" demanded Damiano,
blinking down the length of the tunnel.

"Breakfast. Maybe?" she answered, wagging everything up to her shoulders.

Damiano laughed. "Maybe," he admitted.

He divided the cheese expertly in half, as was his
custom, knowing that although she was much smaller than
he was, he had never had an enthusiasm for eating that
could equal Macchiata's. (It was for this reason that
Damiano was thin while his dog was fat.)

He washed down his bread and mozzarella with wine.
Macchiata lapped snow. Gathering his gear and cradling
the lute against his stomach, Damiano crawled out of the
cave.

It was a beautiful morning. The sun beat gloriously over
snow a foot deep, and the occasional pine trees wore
blankets and hats. Not a print marked the road, which ran
smooth as a plaster wall upward toward the north. In the
distance, beyond the foothills and even beyond the black
band of forest, a jagged rim broke the horizon.

The Alps, clean and sharp as puppy teeth. Even
Damiano's eyes could distinguish them.

"By John the Baptist and by John the Evangelist and by
John the Best Beloved!—if they are indeed three different
Johns—this is magnificent!" He clambered down the slope,
showering snow. "A good night's sleep, a full stomach, and
the road spreading before us like a Turkey carpet! Were it

not for the plight of the citizens of Partestrada, I would have nothing else to desire."

Macchiata peered up at Damiano, her brown eyes puzzled, a lump of snow on her muzzle. "But you could have slept in the cave anytime, Master. You didn't need to be thrown out of your house to do it."

Damiano grinned from ear to ear and sprang over the little valley where the stream ran down from the hill. "You're right, little dear. And you know what? I think you are very wise."

Macchiata's ears pricked up. It was not a compliment she had known before.

"We live our lives bound by our little tasks and possessions and never know how free we could be unless God sees fit to pry us away from them. You know who knew true happiness? I'll tell you—Giovanni di Bernardone, whom our Holy Father has sanctified under the name of Francis. He had nothing in the world, and the world had nothing in him, and he used to walk barefoot in the snow, singing."

Damiano himself began to sing, though he was not barefoot but instead wore soft leather boots with woolen linings. He found it difficult to sing and climb at the same time.

"You have a lovely voice, Master," said Macchiata, feeling that one good compliment deserved another.

"Eh? Thank you, Macchiata, but it is nothing special.

"Say, you know what I think I'll do?—after finding Carla, of course. If the soldiers have robbed her, I'll give her my money, and for those who catch the flux . . .

"Anyway, I think I'll cross over the Rhone to France, and maybe after that to Germany, for there is the heart and soul of alchemy, you know. Why not? I am young and strong."

And he did feel strong—strong enough to bend down a young bull by the horns, as the burly peasants did to show off during the harvest fair.

"I have an intellect, too, and have studied hard." Suddenly Damiano remembered that Carla Denezzi would not be in Germany but at home in Partestrada. "And then," he concluded more soberly, "when I have a name and my words mean something to men of birth and

education, I will use my power for Partestrada. I will
return."

Macchiata had been listening with some concern.
"What about me, Master?" she whimpered.

Damiano glanced down in surprise. "Why you will be
beside me, little dear. While we both live on this earth, we
will not be parted!"

After this promise they walked some while in silence.
Macchiata's robust little heart was filled with happiness
and touched by the importance of her commitment of
Damiano. He, at the same time, was busy with thoughts
and plans. He would lead the people of Partestrada into
the Valle d'Aosta, for Aosta was many times larger than
Partestrada and also much closer to Chambéry and so to
the Green Count of Savoy. There Pardo would not dare
follow.

Then Damiano would go on to France, where he would
write a poem about the Piedmont and Partestrada. It would
be called "The Sorrows of Exile," and it would burn men's
souls. He could feel it within him now, stirring like a chick
in the egg. It shouldn't be a poem only, but a work of
music, like the ballades sung by the old trouvères, and
Damiano would play his lute as Raphael had taught him—
France was far more musically liberal than Italy—till hearts
bled for Partestrada as Dante had made them do for
Florence, with its confusing lot of Guelphs and Ghibel-
lines. Was not art, after all, the greatest weapon of man?

Damiano considered, as his boot soles crunched down
on snow. It was great, yes, but tardy, and Dante had never
returned to Florence. Damiano sighed and shook his head,
for the first energy of the morning was gone and so was the
warmth of the wine. The snow was deepening as the road
climbed; Macchiata cut into it with her breastbone as she
trotted beside him, holding her head up like a nervous
horse. The risen sun glinted in the corner of Damiano's
right eye.

Perhaps Germany was a better goal. In Germany there
was at least one emperor, and emperors can afford to be
generous. But Damiano was not a fool; he knew what it
meant to allow the ass's nose within the tent or to ask help
of a foreigner in settling a local grievance. It would be no
great sort of fame to be known as the man who invited the
northern wolf over the Alps.

In Nuremberg there were said to be many scrolls written by Mary the Jewess, and students of the great Hermes Trismegistus himself, and in Nuremberg now dwelt the sage Nicolas, who was called the prophet. Though Damiano did not know what help the art of alchemy had to offer defeated Partestrada, he would like very much to visit Nuremberg.

"Master," began Macchiata, as she leaned her shoulder against his calf.

"Uh. What? Macchiata, little dear, am I going too fast for you?"

"No," she replied, with a dog's inability to recognize weariness until it had throttled her. "But I was thinking . . . If I am your little dear, and we'll never be parted until somebody dies, then why do you send me away all the time?"

"I don't!" cried Damiano, stung.

"Yes you do. Every spring and every fall, for two weeks."

"Oh." Damiano's eyebrows lifted and his tangled black hair fell over his eyes. "That is necessary. It is not something I want to do, but you are a . . . female dog, and such have their times when they must be alone."

"But I don't want to be alone. Ever," she said simply. "Nothing is different then, except that I feel . . . friendly, and then I hate most to be in a pen."

Damiano stared stolidly up the road. The wind blew over his uncovered ears, which had gone very red. "It is the things you say," he admitted. "During those times you are not yourself."

Beside him Macchiata gave a whuffle and a bound to keep up. "What do I say? I don't remember a thing about it."

"I know. God be praised for that!" He marched on in a businesslike manner and would discuss the subject no further.

Forest grew up around them. By midday they were in a dark hush of pines. Here the air was still and smelled somehow ecclesiastical. They had seen no one and passed no one.

This was not surprising, since even in times of peace, travel between Aosta and the south slowed to a trickle after snowfall. There was another road ahead, which creased the base of the high hills from west to east, and which would intersect the North Road some ten miles ahead. Less than a mile along the right-hand path of that road stood a village of a dozen huts. It was called Sous Pont Saint Martin, which was a French name and longer than the village itself. Damiano assumed that it was as deserted as Partestrada. But it would shelter him at least as well as a cave, and there might be food. If the sky was clear, however, he would walk through the night.

Contemplating an all-night journey made the young man's muscles ache with weariness. It was now as near midday as no matter. And weary legs on numb feet made the army of General Pardo seem a more serious problem than it had after breakfast. Certainly he couldn't trot off to Nuremberg or Avignon while Pardo ravaged the hills. Damiano gave a large, round sigh.

He had outdistanced all his solitary childhood rambles an hour ago and stood in a brilliant, wild landscape unknown to him. Damiano noticed a rock standing ten feet from the road, sparkling in the sunshine with mica or ice. He squatted against it, wondering how many travelers it had sheltered since the six days of creation. Its cracked face was the color of honey, and Damiano leaned his cheek against it, half-expecting it to be warm. The snow swam before his eyes, as though moles or tunneling rabbits were disturbing its surface. He rummaged for the wine bottle.

"I hope you de-tuned your lute," said Raphael. Damiano realized that what he had taken for snow were the outstretched wings of the angel, who was sitting motionless on a rock not four feet away. Raphael's robe was whiter than the white ground and without ornament. His hair shone as colorless as sunlight.

Damiano's grin spread slowly, because the skin at the corners of his mouth was cracked. "Seraph! O spirit of fire! How do you like the snow?"

Macchiata ploughed over from whatever private business she had been on. "Raphael! You found us!"

"Yes! Yes, I found you!" replied Raphael, in tones of enthusiasm that he reserved for the dog alone. He rubbed the sides of her head till her ears snapped like leather whips. Damiano felt a slight pang of jealousy.

Raphael turned back to him. "I like the snow very

much, and the mountains. I think they have a beautiful voice."

Damiano gazed at Raphael until his eyes smarted. He was so glad to see him he could think of nothing to say, and his mind filled with inconsequentials.

Had Raphael skin beneath that lustrous garment, or was he no more than face and wings—an illusion worn so that Damiano would understand him? And why, since angels were immaterial and sexless, did Raphael seem to Damiano entirely male? All the painters gave their angels the faces of women.

Had Raphael seemed a woman, Damiano, easily swayed by such things, would not have been able to bear it. He would have made a fool of himself, for certain, and perhaps sinned in his heart. Perhaps, Damiano reflected, that was why Raphael did *not* appear so, since the good God did not offer a man temptations he could not possibly resist.

The chiseled face tilted sideways, almost like that of a curious bird, and the wings swept snow into the air: snow that broke the light like a thousand prisms. "Why are you looking at me like that?" asked Raphael.

Damiano swallowed; he realized his hand still clutched the neck of the wine bottle. "I had forgotten how amazing you are, Raphael. Seeing you under the sky, like this . . . is very beautiful."

The angel's face remained unchanged, as though the compliment had gone through him. "The blue sky is very beautiful," he agreed, tilting his head upwards. "But then so it is in the rain, and the snow."

Damiano's cold and nervous hands fumbled under the folds of the mantle and found the pear-shape of the lute. He brought it out. "You see, Seraph. I loosened all the strings, knowing the cold might have snapped the neck."

Raphael knelt in the snow and took the instrument in both his hands. One by one, he adjusted the eight strings.

"This is as loose as they need to be," he remarked. "Unless you are going to the top of a mountain."

Damiano sighed, thinking how much there was to explain. "Only as high as the summer pastures, where the people of Partestrada have fled. Then . . . I don't know, Raphael. Perhaps France, or Germany, but not until . . . tell me, what should I do for my city?"

Raphael gazed at Damiano until the young man felt he were standing alone beneath hosts of stars. Had he known how, he would have laid open his soul to the angel, with the history of his every thought, and let Raphael judge him and decide his path. No matter the pain, weariness, or worldly shame, Damiano believed, he would have done Raphael's bidding.

But he did not know how to bare his soul, and he was certain that Raphael was not about to tell him what to do with his life, so instead Damiano dropped his eyes to the cork and the green glass of the wine bottle. Consequently Raphael's words caught him by surprise.

"Pray, Damiano! Pray for the people of Partestrada, and pray for yourself; for guidance. It may be you will need it." The angel spoke with a clear intensity, and Damiano flushed at his own omission.

"Of course, Seraph. Since yesterday . . . all has been topsy-turvy, and I have forgotten. But aren't you my guidance?"

Raphael laughed and Damiano, too. It always worked that way. "No, Dami, I'm not here as a messenger of the Highest. It was your will that first called me and my own will that chose to come. I am not your guide but your friend."

Damiano bowed his head to follow the angel's advice, but immediately he raised his eyes again and saw Raphael sitting before him, wings folded back. Macchiata lay curled on the angel's lap like a white piglet, slightly soiled. "Don't go," begged Damiano. "I'm afraid when I look up again, you'll be gone, and you just got here."

Raphael took Damiano's hand and held it.

The mortals ate while Raphael looked on. They didn't speak of Pardo or Partestrada or the horsemen who even now must be combing the uplands for the city's unfortunate people. In fact, later, when trudging the road that afternoon, Damiano looked back upon their conversation, and it seemed they had talked about nothing at all. Raphael had turned down Macchiata's invitation to walk along with them, saying he was not much of a walker.

The afternoon clouded up, and the snow that the sun had softened began to freeze. Black walls of evergreens

now were not such an inspiring sight, for the travelers had
seen nothing else since morning. The climb continued.

By the time the shadows covered the road it had
become slick, and Damiano began to fear for his lute. If he
fell on the little instrument, which was only the size of a
toddler's potbelly, that would be the end of it.

He did fall, injuring his right hand but not the lute. As
he was a witch, and therefore left-handed, he thanked God
for small favors, but the fall let him know he could not go
on through the night.

The sun had failed when Damiano saw a wink of yellow
light at the top of the slope to the right of the road. In his
state of weariness he stared dumbly at it. "What could that
be?" he mumbled to the world in general.

"It's sausage," answered Macchiata promptly. "And
three people. Men. With an oil lamp. And wine."

Damiano gaped in amazement. "You learned all that by
smelling?"

Macchiata wagged her tail, but her nose pointed like a
lodestone toward the glimmer of light. "My nose gets
better when I'm hungry.

"Can we go say hello, Master?"

Damiano chuckled at her greedy eagerness, but he
didn't feel so different himself. It was the thought of fire,
however, that drew him. He found himself shivering under
his wool and fur. "They may be Pardo's soldiers," he said
uncertainly, but he stepped toward the light as he spoke.

"No. Not soldiers," answered Macchiata with authority.
"They don't smell like soldiers."

Damiano didn't question her statement. He followed
the dog up the slope, climbing with his toes and one
bruised hand, while his left hand dug the staff in behind
him.

He came close enough to recognize the stone hut that
marked the meeting of the North Road and the west, and
which had held a guard in his great-grandfather's day,
before the house of Savoy had made the land safe. Then it
had become a traveler's shelter. Now, perhaps the new
ruler of the Piedmont would open the guardhouse again, at
least until Amadeus VI drove him away.

Damiano stepped closer, brushing snow from his trousers as quietly as he could.

There were two windows overlooking the North Road.

One was dark, being stuffed against the cold with rags and scraps of firewood, along with a single, soleless leather boot. The other window was smaller and had panes of cow's horn. It was through this window that light was pouring.

In the amber glow Damiano stood, gripping his staff in both hands. "Mirabile! Videāmus," he whispered. "Let us see."

And he saw three men, as Macchiata had said. All of them were his age, or thereabouts. They were not soldiers; they wore clothes of fashion, though these were time-stained and not of the best. From their belts hung the jeweled, effete daggers of the young bravo, yet all three had taken the clerical tonsure. Damiano smiled, hearing French laced with Latin: the speech of students. Damiano spoke a passable French.

The staff throbbed in his hand—a reminder from his instincts to himself to be careful. These were not three Poverelli of Francesco, to be sure, whatever their clerical bent. Since the Holy Father had moved to Avignon, it seemed all of Provence had adopted the styles of the Church, saints and sinners alike. And these fellows had been drinking.

But still, they were students, and what else was Damiano? The brotherhood of students was as close as that which existed in any cloister, and more entertaining besides. Damiano knocked his damaged knuckles against the wooden door, while Macchiata whined in her most placatory manner.

What had been boisterous conversation became silence. "Qui?" called a voice, and then in broken Italian, "Who there?"

"Naught but a traveling student," answered Damiano in Latin. "And his dog."

More silence followed, and then a scraping. The door opened, revealing the scene Damiano's craft had shown him before. Three men, a smoky hearth, and a tin lamp set on a table strewn with food. Damiano blinked against the beauty of the sight.

"Enter then and be welcome," said the fellow who had opened the door. He was moonfaced, plump, and balding, despite his youth. The two others regarded Damiano from their places at table. One was dark and square, the other towheaded with a long face. This last mentioned student held a greasy spiced sausage in his lap in a manner most proprietary.

"My name is Damiano Delstrego," Damiano said, bowing. "This lady is my dog Macchiata. We thank you for your courtesy on this icy evening."

The dark youth rose, smiling slightly. The bow of the fellow at the door was a marvel involving three separate movements of the foot. "Signor Dottore Delstrego. Let me present our small company. This one standing, with the shoulders of Hercules—he is Paul Breton, and he is a poet. The blond without manners is called Till Eulenspiegel. We are golliards, the impossible children of Pierre Abélard himself."

"Till Eulenspiegel!" Damiano burst out, involuntarily.

Slyly the blond looked up. "What's wrong with that?" He spoke an egregious Italian.

The first student stepped between them. "You see, Dottore, we believe that a name chosen oneself or by those who know one is more meaningful than the one chosen at birth. It is the custom of golliards to forego allegiance to country, town, and family for the highest fidelity to learning itself. Therefore Jan Karl is Till Eulenspiegel, and world watch out.

"I myself," he concluded, "have the honor to carry the name of Pierre Paris, because that is the place I like best."

A chair was sought for Damiano, to no avail. He who called himself Pierre Paris offered his own, but Damiano chose to sit on the table. From his pack he took the remainder of his bread and cheese, pulled off portions of both for Macchiata, and put the rest on the table. The dog wolfed what she was given and retired to the space beneath Eulenspiegel's chair, where she lay consuming the aroma of sausage.

"Delstrego," drawled the Dutchman. "Doesn't that mean 'of the witch'?"

"Yes it does," admitted Damiano. He had become impatient waiting for someone to invite him to eat and so had begun unasked.

"Is it also"—the blond ran out of Italian and switched to French—"a title self-chosen?"

Damiano shook his head forcefully. "Definitely not. It was my father's name and his father's before him for I don't know how long." He continued in Latin, for he was quite at home in it, having the advantage of being Italian. "If I took a name for myself it would be Damiano Alchemicus."

"Not Damiano Musicus?" asked Pierre Paris, as with lightning speed he whipped the long sausage from Eulenspiegel's grasp and cut a section for their guest. The blade of his dagger he wiped on the hem of his black overshirt. "I was hoping we would hear that lute you have cradled so carefully in the corner."

Damiano followed his glance to where the lute rested, wrapped in the white fur of his mantle. "Perhaps later, Signor Clericale, once it's warm. But I'm not very good." Half the thick slice of sausage disappeared into a wet mouth waiting under the table. The other half Damiano held between his fingers, nibbling.

"Good students," he said, "for such I see you are— though I had thought that war and pestilence had ended the golliard's jolly times—I am a student also, both of science and spirit. Why do you travel weaponless through a land devastated by war?"

Paris stared owlishly at Breton, who in turn looked toward Eulenspiegel, who kept his eyes fixed on Damiano. "Who would devastate the barren mountains, and how would one be able to tell they had been devastated?" inquired Paris, who in all matters seemed to be the spokesman of the three.

Damiano felt a variety of envy for them, whose lives had not yet been touched by the present troubles. He assumed that because his troubles were not theirs, they had no troubles. This supposition on his part was a human error, certainly, but it could have been dyed a much deeper hue had Damiano felt contempt and alienation from the three because of their fortune.

Instead he wanted to help keep them safe and carefree, and to that end he said, "Believe me, Signor Clericale: we are little more than a day's travel from what was a thriving city and is now abandoned to General Pardo's soldiery."

"Pardo?" spoke up Eulenspiegel, who seemed to have a quick ear, though a slow tongue. "The condottiere in the service of the pope? He was at Avignon a few years ago."

Damiano peered stricken at the blond at the other side of the table. He was just at the limit of Damiano's close sight, and Damiano could not be sure Eulenspiegel was joking. "You mean . . . It could not be that the Holy Father is sacking the towns of the Piedmont?"

Paris broke in smoothly. "It could be, but I think it isn't. The condottieri serve contracts, not men, and I remember hearing when I was at the papal court last that Pardo's time was lapsed, and either he or the Holy Father did not renew.

"And, my dear brothers, what is a condottiere without lands or employer, but a brigand?"

"They're all robbers, anyway," sneered Eulenspiegel, glaring dourly into the distance. Damiano reconsidered his conception of this man; there was doubtless sorrow in his past.

"Nonetheless, I beg you to beware, Signori. Do not follow the road down from the hills or you may find you have walked into trouble. And if you hear the sounds of many horses on the road, then leave it quickly and hide where you may."

"Would in any case," growled Eulenspiegel, while the poet just sighed.

"Ah! I thank you, friend Delstrego," said Paris, placing both the basket-covered wine jug and a husk of bread in front of Damiano. "I drink to your health, for you have cared for ours." He picked up Damiano's green bottle and did as he had promised. "Now you must drink too, or the toast will be invalid."

Smiling sheepishly, Damiano drank their wine. To his surprise, it was as good as his own. He complimented them upon it.

"Should be good," said Eulenspiegel, showing his teeth.

Paris cleared his throat. "I appreciate your advice, Signor Dottore Delstrego, and believe we are all grateful. Yet our path was decided for us before we left France, and to veer from it would destroy the meaning of our journey.

"Let me tell you, friend in the wilderness, that we three are retracing the steps of the great Petrarch from Avignon to Milan, seeing every inch of the countryside about which he wrote."

"Ah, the verse!" cried out Breton, the poet. "Immortal verses, wild as the god Pan!"

Damiano started. It was as though a dog had talked—another dog, not Macchiata.

"I saw him, in Milan," ventured Damiano. "He was very gracious, and let me copy four of his poems into a book. I dared not ask for more, for I was sitting in his office where the window looked out onto il Duomo, and he sat across from me, asking which parts I liked. It was a great moment for me. Yet I don't believe Petrarch rode from Avignon in the beginning of winter, did he?"

The poet opened his brown eyes very round. "He has spoken with you? The laureate himself. You sat in his house?"

Damiano shrugged in a self-deprecating manner. "Only for an hour. I doubt he would remember my name."

"Delstrego would be hard to forget," remarked the blond. "I've been looking at that," he added, pointing at the staff, which rested like a baby in the crook of Damiano's left arm. "You use it just to walk?"

Under the combined stares of four pairs of eyes the black wood hummed. Damiano stroked it, embarrassed, as he was at any mention of his witchhood.

"No, although it is very useful and sturdy in that way. I use it as a focus for my concentration, because otherwise the—power—roams free in the body and clouds the mind."

"You're a witch?" breathed Paris, and the room froze.

"A wizard," contradicted Damiano, immediately wondering why on earth he had said that. The three students huddled like birds before the eyes of a snake, and Damiano blushed harder.

"*Domine Deus*, my friends, there is no need to be afraid of me for that! I am a scholar and a Christian!" But still they sat, and they sat very still. In a moment Damiano was sure someone would say "but the devil can quote Scripture," a proverb that always made him wince. He groaned deeply and rose from his chair, placing his staff by the wrapped lute in the far corner of the room from the fire.

"There, Signor Clericale. My power is there and I am here. I cannot hurt you now even if I would. Is that enough?"

Till Eulenspiegel relaxed, wiping the sweat from his pale forehead. The poet sighed once more, and Pierre Paris reached for the green wine bottle, a conciliatory smile on his round face.

The staff boomed a warning, alone and helpless in the corner, as Paris lifted the bottle and brought it down with force on Damiano's head.

CHAPTER 4

Damiano awoke to cold and pain and a feeling of being
stifled. This last was due to Macchiata, who was lying on
top of him, her nose anxiously denting his face. "Master,
Master. Get up and move!" she crooned. "Or you'll die and
freeze and leave me alone always!

"Please!" she cried, her voice like the neighing of a
horse, in his ear. His arms moved to placate her, to ward
her off.

"Can't breathe," Damiano gasped, and the effort of this
sent waves of nausea through his body. His eyes closed
again.

"Master!"

Damiano turned, bringing his hands under him. He
remembered the golliards and the bottle against his skull.
His head rose and his poor eyes peered through the little
hut, at the table, with its remains of bread and cheese, the
hearth, where the fire still blazed (thanks be to God), the
shape in the corner that must be his lute. That glint of silver
along the floor meant his staff was intact; had any of them
tried to touch it, woe unto them. His mantle lay upon him
where Macchiata had dragged it, off-center and with the
lining upwards.

"Where are they?" he asked the dog, his voice as shaky
as that of an old man. He sat up and wrapped the mantle
about him. Her response was a growl as preternaturally
ominous as the sound of an avalanche in the distance.
Damiano turned his head with difficulty and looked at
Macchiata, who stood stiff as wood and spiney all over. All
her teeth showed, as yellow as the tushes of a boar, and in
her eyes was a rage he had never seen before. He began to
shiver.

"They are far away, Master. So far I can't hear them or
smell them. They will never hurt you again."

Through his haze of misery he tried to understand.
"Did you . . . kill them, Macchiata? All three?"

"They were not dead when they ran down the hill and

down the road. But there was only one of them without a hole in him." The ugly dog softened. She lifted one paw up to Damiano's shoulder and licked his eyes, one after the other.

"Go sit by the fire, Master. It will make you feel better."

Pulling his garment tighter, Damiano obeyed her, but first he fished across the floor for the length of his staff. With this in hand, he sank gratefully down on the ashy stones of the hearth. In passing he noted that the firewood that the three "students" had been burning was composed of a splintered chair and a heavy oak footstool, as well as half a shutter. He sighed: their behavior was all of a piece. But why had he not noticed this last night? Macchiata clambered onto his lap.

"Master no more, dear one," he sighed. "Say rather I'm little Dami, your foolish pet. Imagine what my father would have said, if he had seen me put my staff aside in a room full of strangers." The grown witch had tried to make his son careful. In Damiano's mind came the vision of his father snatching the black wood from the dozing boy's hands and simultaneously giving him a cuff on the ear, while he laughed, laughed, laughed . . . The memory gave him the added warmth of shame, but it made his head ache more.

Macchiata snorted, piglike. "Of course you are my Master. Only you are too trusting for your own good."

Damiano's brows drew together, which brought lancing pain along his scalp. The fire, however, was helping him.

"It was Pierre Paris's fear that caused him to strike me. Had he not known I was a witch, it would not have happened."

"You are wrong, Master," said Macchiata, quickly but diffidently, for she was not used to contradicting Damiano. "I'm sorry, but it's true. The one with the pale hair tried to stop that one. He said he'd be sorry for it. Then the one with no hair on his head asked what was the difference: a knife in the back at night or a wine bottle at dinner?"

"They were robbers? They meant to kill me in my sleep?" asked Damiano, incredulous. "What else did they say?"

Macchiata's skinny tail slapped his leg: once, twice, then rapidly. "They didn't have time to say much. I was asleep, but the sound woke me up."

"The sound," repeated Damiano. "The echo of the blow resounding in my braincase. That's what woke you up."

She licked his hand. "But I cursed them for it, and I bit them. I bit the black one on the thick part of the leg, but on the blond my hold slipped, so I made a big rip in his shirt, and bloodied where he would sit."

"So the one you missed altogether was the one who hit me with the wine bottle," remarked Damiano, not meaning to denigrate her victory.

"Yes, because he tried to beat me off with your staff. It bit him."

Damiano felt the blackwood beneath his fingers. "Signor Paris may never have use of that hand again," he said.

"Both hands. But it was my curses that chased them out the door without their packs. I got the words from your father." Macchiata wrapped her tongue around her muzzle, then smiled till her bristly muzzle resembled a cat's face.

Leaning on his staff, Damiano rose to his feet. "Packs?" he murmured, and shuffled off to see. "And curses? I only hope, Macchiata, that you didn't compromise your soul with evil wishes. They are very deadly."

"Have I a soul, Master?" She asked in a tone of casual interest. "I never heard that before."

There were two bundles under the table, besides his own sheepskin bag. A third huddled against the hearthstones. "Of course you have a soul, Macchiata," he answered, and although he knew himself to be on shaky theological ground, still he believed that anyone who liked Raphael as much as the dog did, and who was so liked in return, had to have a soul. "And a great spirit, besides. . . .

"Now let's see what the three scholars have left us."

Within the packs was an assortment of trash, along with a few objects of peculiar meaning and value. The first sack dumped on the table offered a lady's hairpin in gold and pearls, along with three silver florins in a needlepoint pouch. The second bag held a double handful of walnuts, together with a bundle of faded letters written in a script that was not quite German. Out of the final bag dropped a squarish parcel wrapped in linen and tied with twine. Damiano undid the tiny knot with a tiny loosing spell.

"*Domine Deus!*" he breathed, as a book in vellum,

bound in both wood and leather, flapped onto the table. "So they weren't totally false!"

It was a volume of the poetry of Petrarch, copied in painful, schoolboy script. The premier letter of each verse was illuminated in the old manner, with awkward care and much gold paint.

These items were heavy, and he did not really want to be reminded of their former possessors. Yet books were like children; they could not be abandoned to the snow. And he did appreciate Petrarch.

In the end Damiano decided to take all but the clothing as spoils of war.

Their fire, too, was his by right. And their food. He felt almost well enough to care about that. His eyes scanned the table.

"What became of the sausage, little dear? Did our friend the German carry it with him out into the snow?"

Macchiata's tail and ears stood up. She dashed to the corner and nuzzled under Damiano's lute, backing out with something black and dirt-covered in her mouth.

"No, he dropped it," she mumbled, placing an irregularly shaped piece of greasy meat in his hand. "I saved half for you."

In the first light Damiano woke once more and spent a few minutes playing his lute. He had a headache and a spot of numbness on his scalp. Further, his eyes refused to focus on the strings. Raphael did not appear, but then the angel would scarcely have fit in the hut, and besides, Damiano had no time to spare. He took a swig of the wine in the basket-jug, and for luck, another of his father's tonic. Then he stepped into the cold.

After a half-mile's march the headache had grown to fill the world, and the light of the new sun on the snow pierced his eyes. Tears ran along his cheeks, and even the dog had nothing cheerful to say. Damiano was not too far from wishing he were dead, but the alternative of every person in the winter wilderness—curling up in the snow and sleeping—had no attraction.

"We shall be there today, and early," he muttered. "Except for the weather, we might have reached the pastures by yesterday nightfall." He watched for the cluster of huts that housed the shepherds of the mountains and a small number of hunters whose livelihoods kept them in the heights all winter. The nearest real village was Pont Saint Martin, on the North Road two miles from the spot where Damiano had turned, which was the reason this poor assembly was known as Sous Pont Saint Martin. Damiano had been there only once, in July, when his father had been called to treat the sheep for a bad flux.

The road had been swept by wind and the abrasive, frozen snow of the night before. In rare spots the wind had come again and shaved the earth bare, leaving only the strange, reversed prints of men and horses, made of pressed snow and glistening white against the black earth. Who knew how old these were?

The slopes dropped away on either side of the road, and the travelers came to a river: the Lys. It ran wide and violent, though ice crusted each bank like sheets of shattered glass. Across the river a stone bridge led. It was wide and smooth, with waist-high guardwalls on either side. It was the sort of craftsmanship the country people dismissed as Roman work, heavy, useful, built to last. There was no evidence it was old Roman, except in the fact that no Piedmontese was likely to take such trouble on a mountain bridge. Roman work was like the hills themselves: whether or not men could make such things today, they were there for free and so not to be admired too much.

As he crossed over the span the wind hit him and turned his head to the left, from whence the river flowed.

His left foot trod on his right, and then Damiano stopped stock still. "Mother of God! Can it be?" he cried and sank down on his knees in the wet snow.

There stood peaks ranked against the sky: an awesome white phalanx, blinding bright from the teeth of their summits to the green cloaks that wrapped their feet, which were banded with silver rock. They were so tall they crowded the sky, and they grew taller as they seemed to rush at the kneeling youth. In their silence were all the voices of an infinite, inhuman choir.

Two presences dominated. To the left sat the highest peak in the Valle d'Aosta: Mont Emilius, whom the peasants called Grandfather. Rugged and glistening, it had roots reaching almost to the road. To the right, far away and behind a palisade of mountains, out of a shimmer of light rose a single white fang, sharp as the tooth of a dog, and crooked at the tip, like a dog's tooth, but unearthly clean. Damiano did not know it was Mont Cervin: the peak called the Matterhorn.

As he stared, kneeling, he wept, knowing the beauty he saw must be like that of Raphael, if the archangel were to fling aside his little human cloak and appear as a flame of divine love. This the angel would never do, of course, out of a concern for the limits of man. The mountains, however, were less merciful. Damiano's ecstasy bid fair to do him damage.

"Master! Get up! Please, your knees are getting soaked. Master! Damiano. What is the pain?" Macchiata danced a circle around him, nuzzling his hands with her warm tongue and her cold nose.

"Little dear, I see a beauty fit to kill a man! Can't you see the . . . thrones of the ages?"

"Thrones of who?" She prodded him to his feet.

"Of the . . . the mountains. Mont Emilius and another. Doesn't their loveliness pierce you?"

She snorted. "I see nothing. The wall is too high. But if piercing is what loveliness does to you, I want no part of it!

"Come, Damiano. You can't stop here, in the wind, and now wet besides."

Docile, made meek by so much splendor, he allowed her to lead him forward. In a few minutes the village of Sous Pont Saint Martin peeped out between two hills. Damiano passed between them into a natural rock shelter, where the wind swirled aimlessly, carrying snow spray in a high spiral into the air.

The west side of each square hut was braced with a flying buttress of white. The patch of ground blocked from the wind by each building was scattered with bootprints, along with the prints of shod hooves. Many riders had been here recently.

But were not here now. The village was desolate. Silence rumbled in Damiano's ears. Or was that Macchiata, growling?

Damiano glanced down at the dog in surprise. Her hackles were up, her squat legs braced. Nervously, her eyes met his. "Let's go back to the road," she suggested.

"Why, Macchiata? Here is shelter, and my feet are frozen. What's wrong, little dear? Do you smell soldiers?"

"Yes. No. No soldiers now. Just blood. Frozen blood."

Damiano took a wary step forward. Macchiata scrabbled in front of him and stood barring his way. "No, Master. You are too sensitive; looking at mountains hurts you. This will hurt you worse!

"Let's go back to the road. Our people aren't here."

Damiano's easy color rose to his cheeks, and he gazed resentfully down at her. "Love of beauty is not the same thing as cowardice, Macchiata.

"Wasn't it I who found my father perishing in torment? And have I not grown up hearing Father Antonio remind us that all flesh is the food of worms—flesh of both dogs and men, little one? Dead men hold no terror for me."

The dog dropped her head and Damiano swept by.

In the circle formed by the huts was a little meadow, which in the summer was browsed by chickens and the occasional hobbled goat. Now it was swept by wind and ice and snow, with the gray stubble of grass exposed where the wind had scraped most deep. In this field lay the broken bodies of three men and an old woman, frozen clean and uncorrupt. The edges of their many wounds were fresh and sharp: the color of good pork.

At Damiano's feet lay the severed head of one of the men: a young peasant with a reddish beard. The skin was blue and white and waxlike. The neck was chopped neat. With the hollow windpipe arched through it and the spine running through the back, the neck looked like a slice cut through a fish. Ice crystals had grown from the edges of the empty veins. The head wore an expression of slack bewilderment as it stared at the sky over Damiano's shoulder. One eye was open wider than the other.

Damiano thought he was doing very well until he tried to move. The horrid field reeled, and only his staff held him to his feet.

He shuffled from one body to another, mouthing an incoherent prayer for the dead that was also a plea for Christ to sustain him through this nausea. He dared not look at Macchiata.

The head was the most horrible, but the old woman was the saddest, for she had been trampled and her fusty black skirt torn off. Around each of the forms the snow was tinted a faded ruby, much like the color of the stone at the tip of Damiano's staff.

He raised his eyes to the sound of rhythmic lapping. A

dog was licking at the bloody snow by the severed head. For a terrible moment he thought it was Macchiata.

It was not, of course. It was a shaggy herd dog, doubtless belonging to some man of the village. Perhaps the beast's master lay dead here before him. Whatever, it could do these poor figures no hurt.

Macchiata noticed the cur at the same moment. With a bull bellow she flung herself upon the stranger, who offered no fight, but tucked tail and fled.

"Come back, Macchiata," called Damiano, as the red spot that was all he could see of her bobbed into the distance behind a row of huts. "There may be more of them. Come back!"

A human voice answered his with a cry shrill and weak. Damiano's hair prickled. He stared around him.

There was nothing to be seen: an ox wagon, its tongue buried in drifts; a stack of brushwood for burning; a pitchfork, wooden tines protruding from the snow like bird claws; the imperturbable gray stones of the huts. No more. But the cry came again, from across the expanse of wind. Damiano sprang toward it, plunging knee deep. He leaped over a dimple in the snow, not knowing it was the village well and twenty feet deep. The row of buildings greeted him with silence.

"Hello!" he cried. "Who's there?"

"In here!" came the answer from behind a door. He put his shoulder to it.

The door sagged in, hanging by one hinge.

The darkness within took his sight, and he gagged at the smell. "Speak!" Damiano commanded, swaying in the doorway. "If there is a Christian soul within . . ."

"Here," she replied, and he saw her: the pale spot of a face in the corner by the door. She was covered in blankets and the skin of a cow. One hand held the wraps under her chin. That and her face was all he could see. He knelt beside her.

Damiano's eyes saw her young face waver as though seen through the steam of a boiling pot. She was taut with agony. She stared at him. He pried the covers from the grip of her hand, and he dared to pull them back.

She was naked. With her other hand she was holding—like a woman with an apron full of peas—Mother of God, it was her guts she was holding, spilled out of the rent in her belly and sticking to the coarse wool of the blanket.

"Lord have mercy," whispered Damiano, letting her pull up the blankets once more. "Forgive me, Signora." Somewhere a dog was howling.

"We're all dead here," she said quite calmly. "Ernesto. Sofia and her brother. Me. My little 'Lonso. Renaud. We are only six and said nothing, and the soldiers killed us all. I am the last, but I'm dead nonetheless. Give me water."

"Ahh?" Damiano felt about reflexively and realized he was still carrying his sheepskin bag. His cold hands dug into it. "I have only wine," he told her, and heard his own voice trembling. He held the bottle to her lips.

She drank greedily, and Damiano tried not to think of the red wine trickling out of her belly below. "Thank you," she gasped when the bottle was empty. "It will do me no good, but thank you anyway.

"Renaud threw a pitchfork at the first soldier to stick his head between the guard hills. They cut his head off and killed us all, and I don't even know who they were or from where. It does not matter from where. I curse them. I curse the women who bore them and the man who sent them here. I curse the place they came from and the place they will go to.

"I curse . . ." And she stopped for breath. Damiano could feel the curses hanging in the air, like thunder on a still day. They stole the mutilated woman's strength, and she flickered before his eyes. As his father had flickered: a dying fire on the tiles of the workroom. The dog howled. Was it Macchiata?

"No more, Signora," he whispered, stroking her black hair back from her face. "Pray instead. For peace. For forgiveness."

The woman cried out in sudden pain and rocked back and forth on the straw bed. "Forgiveness? I have done nothing, not even to throw a pitchfork at the pig who tore me open! And I forgive no one. Least of all God, who let this happen."

Damiano knew something of healing, but he also knew that for death there was no remedy. He tasted in his mouth the salt of his own tears and could think of no way to help.

Except for a little charm, not a witch's charm but a child's, to steal the pain of boils and bruised fingers. He took the dying woman's right hand in his right hand and hugged the black staff with the left side of his body.

* * *

"Charm, charm
Cure the harm.
Tell the pain
Be gone again."

This he repeated over and over, with great concentration, till he felt himself no more than a black hollowness, like the length of a flute, through which the invisible passed. He played the charm like a tiny song along the length of his mind's body, opening certain passages to the power and stopping others. With what small part of his mind was not involved in the spell casting he prayed that this little charm might grow into one large enough to shroud the pain of a deadly wound. Meanwhile, the moaning of the dog went on and on.

Her hand softened its grip on his. Damiano opened his eyes.

The woman gazed steadily up at him. Her breathing was easy. "The pain is gone," she said, and sighed. "But you . . . have a palsy. Your hand shakes."

He shook his head. Exhaustion nearly toppled him onto the blood-soaked pallet. The woman patted his hand.

"I see, you are a witch," she said. "Like the man who came when the sheep were sickening. He shook like that and then slept an hour in my brother's bed."

"My father . . ." began Damiano, but she wasn't listening.

"If I were a witch, I would not be lying here with my bowels torn. If I were a witch, I would have justice."

Struggling, she raised up on one elbow. "What right have you to live?" she asked him, her voice rising shrill again. Her image wavered like sun on water. "Give me justice."

Damiano caught her as she fell back. Her slight weight almost overbalanced him. He found himself shouting "Raphael! Raphael! I can't help her. Help me, Seraph! Help me!"

And white wings filled the squalid hut.

Damiano took the archangel's perfect fair hand and laid it upon the woman's. Raphael glanced down, a distant pity in his eyes, then looked again at Damiano.

The woman's gaze had not moved. "Witch, give me

justice, or have my curse too." Her words came faintly
through dying lips.

"Raphael?" The angel merely shook his golden head.
"Raphael, comfort her, give her peace. I cannot!"

"Peace? I forgive no one, least of all God," she stated.
Her light flared and was gone.

Damiano covered his face with one hand. He turned
away from the angel and barged into the light.

"I'm sorry, Damiano. She could not see me."

Raphael also wavered in Damiano's sight, through a
haze of tears. "Couldn't you have spoken to her—told her
something of God's goodness—if not to stop the pain at
least to sweeten her bitter heart? She has gone to judgment
with a weight of curses on her back."

". . . neither see me nor hear me. Dami! I could not
touch her. And if I could have, what would I dare say?"

Puzzled by the angel's words, Damiano blinked his eyes
clear. Vaguely he noticed that Raphael stood on the dimple
in the snow that he had leaped over in his dash for the hut.
The angel left no mark in the snow. Damiano walked
around him.

"Damiano, my dear friend. I am spirit and cannot die.
Likewise I cannot understand death. What comfort do I
have to give a mortal, who is in love with what seems to me
a trial and a bondage? You are earth itself that has been
given the nature of the Father: God in his most infinite
humility.

"I am . . . only a musician. Even less, I am only
music. Your pain is so far beyond me . . ."

I should have closed her eyes, Damiano thought.

"I don't understand what you are saying, Seraph. I'm
too tired. I'll think later on your words."

"But do not forgive me later, Damiano. I know I have
failed you. Give me your hand."

Raphael shone like ice in the sun as he extended his
hand. Dull from too much crying, Damiano squeezed it.
Then he turned again to face the crazy-doored hut. "If
there is failure here, it is mine, no doubt. I'm going to bury
them now."

The bodies in the meadow were frozen stiff as wood.
He dragged them over to the body of the young woman,
not forgetting the grisly head of Renaud, who threw a
pitchfork at a soldier and so destroyed six lives.

Six? He had only four. There were two more to find. He raised his head and listened to the dog's moaning. Was it Macchiata? He called her name.

The howl cut off abruptly. "Master!" came the yip from the slope behind the village. "Here! It's here."

He forced his feet to move.

Macchiata lay curled at the foot of a dead man. The thin howling escaped her as though she had no will in the matter. "It won't get warm. They threw it in the snow and it won't get warm."

"He's dead, Macchiata," said Damiano, wondering at her. "Like all of them, killed by the soldiers."

"This one too?" The dog uncoiled and stepped back, exposing the stiff, blue body of an infant. "It isn't bloody or anything, and it's so little! Can't it be alive?"

Damiano stared and blinked. "No," he answered, feeling nothing through weariness. "No it can't." He picked up the tiny corpse and dragged the man by one rag-wrapped foot.

When all the bodies lay in the fetid darkness, Damiano braced his staff on the hard earth outside. Using his horror and the last of his strength as tools, he shivered the stone walls from top to bottom. The hut fell into rubble, burying the dead beyond the reach of weasels and starving dogs.

Raphael was gone. Damiano had not seen him depart. He had more to say to the archangel, but it would have to wait. He turned back to the road.

CHAPTER 5

The road remained empty and the countryside bare, but this need not have been due to war or the passage of soldiers. Only fifteen years previously the pestilence had swept up from the south, and within the space of a year the population of these hills had been cut in half, and many towns and villages disappeared entirely.

Partestrada had escaped the Death entirely, some said through the influence of Guillermo Delstrego, while others claimed it was because they had locked the gates of the town and posted archers to slay any who tried to get in.

Damiano, who had been six years old, did not remember much about it except that it had been a hungry time. But he had grown up knowing that the world had been better, once, and that men died easily.

Now he plodded through an empty landscape, and hummed a sad trouvère's tune.

At last he found footprints, on the path that snaked down from the West Road to the mountain meadows. Here, where time or some cataclysm had shattered a rock wall so that it looked like brickwork, was a small lap of ground protected from the wind. The snow lay only inches deep, old and crusted. Were these the prints of the refugees from Partestrada, or were these marks left by the pursuing soldiers? Certain of the imprints were soft edged, either weeks old and sun softened or left by the rag-wrapped feet of the peasantry.

Damiano bent on one knee. Inches from the face of the wall was a soft print that seemed to overlie the clean print of a leather boot. That was a good sign; infantrymen did not wrap their feet in rags.

"What does your nose tell you, little dear?" Damiano asked of the dog, who sat beside him, her thin-furred belly steaming in the noon sun.

"It tells me that men have been by this way, and that the black man is near." She spoke without dropping her muzzle to the ground.

"The black man?" For a moment he wondered whether she meant the Devil himself. Absently, his fingers traced the metalwork on the staff, which had not left his hand since his waking that morning. It, too, spoke of a visitor, but not a supernatural one. His lips tingled, along with the fine hairs inside his nostrils. Damiano rose and strode forward along the path.

Where the rock wall ended, a white glare filled the path. Damiano stopped still, for in the middle of the light stood a figure black as night and obscured by the brilliance. Something sparkled: a sword.

"Who hides in the shadows?" spoke a voice Damiano recognized.

"Denezzi? Paolo Denezzi? It's I, Dami Delstrego. I've been looking for you for two days. Is Carla . . ." Damiano

stepped into the sun, expecting Denezzi to give way for
him, but the heavy figure stood like the rock wall behind.

"Delstrego," echoed Denezzi, in tones of contempt. "I
should have known." The sword slid into its sheath.

Damiano had not expected such a greeting, but though
his feelings were wounded, he was in no mood for an
argument. Damiano stepped around Denezzi. "For two
days I have followed after . . . Why didn't you stop and
tell me you were evacuating the city?"

Paolo Denezzi was a bull-faced man with a full beard
and as dark as his sister was fair. He snorted, looking more
bull-like than ever. "I had thought it was fairly plain, to
anyone who looked out his window in the last week."

Reluctantly he met Damiano's look of reproach. "We
didn't leave you behind on purpose, Owl-Eyes. It seemed
that you left before us."

Damiano flushed at the hated childhood nickname and
at all implied by Denezzi's words. It was on the tip of his
tongue to tell Denezzi that Carla, at least, had known
where he was, but discretion curbed him.

"Where is . . . everybody, Paolo, and how did you
evade the soldiers?" Only a narrow path marred the white:
a path such as a single walker might make, breaking the
thigh-deep snow. But greasy smoke hung in the sky ahead.

"What soldiers?" Denezzi glared as Macchiata, huffing
and panting, squeezed between his legs and trotted off.
"Pardo's men? They don't know where we are. I made sure
of that."

"He does. They do. They left the day I did, but earlier."

Suspicion and confusion played a dangerous game on
Denezzi's face. "What do you know of this, witch?"

"Pardo told me, and he told me he had sent a party of
soldiers after the citizens. Not to slay, but to rob. He wants
money to finance an attack on Milan." Damiano saw
Denezzi's hand move and heard the terrible slick sound of
steel. He stood motionless, holding his staff in both hands.

"It was not I who betrayed you. I've come to help."

Silently he added, "Through cold and peril, you obdurate black donkey."

Denezzi drew his sword, but let its tip drop into the
snow between them. "What were you doing, sharing
words with the general himself, eh? And who betrayed us,
if indeed we have been betrayed?"

Damiano paused for only a moment. Marco's deed could not be hidden, not after the gift of the vineyards. "It was old Marco who told. He has been given the Anuzzi property. I spoke to Pardo to discover his intention toward the city."

Denezzi's small eyes were lost in wrinkles of doubt. Fur of black martin rustled as he shrugged his huge shoulders. "If I could believe you, Delstrego, I would be sure you are a fool. But as it is, no soldiers have bothered us." He turned on his heel. "You had better go back the way you came." As Denezzi walked he sliced with his sword into the snow on either side.

Damiano took one step after the man, when he heard Macchiata lumbering back along the path toward them.

"Master, I have found them," she called. "All the men, Master."

In a fury of irritation, Denezzi raised his sword above the dog, who gaped upward in stunned surprise.

"No, Paolo. You will not touch her!" The lean form sprang forward. Paolo Denezzi felt himself in the middle of a cloud like a promise of thunder, which stole the warmth from his heart and the air from his lungs. His hand slipped on the leather sword-hilt. His anger grew as his strength lessened.

"What will you do, Owl-Eyes? Squinting in the sun, you can hardly see me."

Damiano was indeed almost blind. His brown eyes were sore from glare and from weeping, and at distance they had always failed him. Yet he knew where Denezzi stood and how the sword hung in the air, as though that figure were mapped within his brain, and he saw Macchiata inching backwards down the path, though a wall of snow lay between dog and master.

"Whether I see you or not, Paolo, if you strike Macchiata you're a dead man," he stated. In pure fury, he was willing to commit the violence that Pardo's threats could not force from him.

Slowly the dark man lowered his sword, eyes fixed on Damiano. The dog was long since gone. "This is a silly quarrel," he grunted, turning back along his footsteps. "But may God curse you if you've betrayed us, witch."

Damiano followed without speaking.

It was a shelter thrown together out of brushwood and

brambles and waxed cloth, piled between a cliff rise and an old, dry rock wall. Smoke runnelled upwards through the twigs and dead leaves, and the feet of men and horses had trampled the snow of the pasture.

Macchiata nosed between Damiano's legs, her belly to the ground like a cat's. Her tail thumped hopefully, but she kept her nose on Paolo Denezzi.

Damiano approached the rude shelter, aware he was the focus of dozens of eyes. Covertly, he kicked the dog away. "Now would be the time for me to fall flat on my face, you idiot," he hissed. She whined an abject apology and leaned harder against his leg.

The men of Partestrada huddled like rooks on a tower. Over a hundred men shared the ghost of warmth between the cliff face and the ancient wall. They had strewn the snow with pine boughs and dead bracken, which they now fed bit by bit to damp, unwilling fires. Even in the open air, the smell of hot wool was overpowering.

Macchiata had been exactly right. They were all men. Every face that met his grew, or was capable of growing, a beard. The response to his greeting was a spiritless mumble, more wary than hostile.

Belloc, the blacksmith, and two pot-bellied burghers edged aside for him, and Damiano sank down beside the most flourishing of the fires. His staff rested in the crook of his elbow, but the lute he wrapped in his mantle and set behind him. Heat beat against his face, potent as the grace of God.

"You really shouldn't keep the fires going in the daytime," he remarked, watching the gray smoke sail out into the air, roiling, bending east. "You are visible from a distance."

Belloc raised one shaggy eyebrow. "Not all of us are as well clothed as you are, young Signor." He stared pointedly at the ermine.

Damiano flushed. He had always liked the blacksmith, who once had sealed his father's caldron so that the elder Delstrego had never known that Dami had allowed it to break. With guilty haste he pulled the instrument from its wrapping.

"I don't need it." Belloc half smiled, looking away from the offering. "But there's some that might."

Damiano flung the mantle onto the piled branches. He didn't look to see what hand plucked it up.

"Besides," continued the blacksmith, and he sighed, "no one is looking for us."

"According to him, there are soldiers on our trail," said Denèzzi, from behind a pile of embers that seemed to be his alone. All faces turned to the new arrival amid a sudden silence.

"Where are the women?" demanded Damiano. "And the old men and children? Surely there is no cave, or concealment nearby, that . . ."

"The women are in Aosta," answered Belloc, with a dour satisfaction. "Along with the children, the lame, and those men born under a lucky star. Also in Aosta are the money, the carriages, most of the clothes and food . . .

"We sent them straight on, while we came to this forsaken rock covered with frozen sheep dung and hungry sheep lice."

"Why?" Damiano looked from one uncomfortable face to another. "Why didn't you follow them to Aosta?"

Denezzi broke the silence. "If we abandon our homes, Owl-Eyes, we will return to find them occupied." Other men grunted assent, but Belloc spoke again.

"That was your reasoning, Signor Denezzi. But I left little I can't do without. My tools and my anvil have gone up the hills in an oxcart. Still, it is important we hang together, if we're ever to be a town again." His sighs were deep, as befitted the size of his ribcage.

Damiano was at first heartened by the news that the most delicate part of the city, at least, was safe. But then his mind began to turn over Belloc's words.

"Signor Belloc," he began, sliding his hands absent-mindedly in and out of the flame. "Your news troubles me."

The blacksmith stared fixedly as orange flames licked Damiano's fingers. "I could use hands like that," he muttered. "I wouldn't need the tongs."

Shyly the youth pulled back. "It will burn me too," he admitted, "if I leave them there."

"The Devil takes care of his own."

Damiano swiveled at Denezzi's remark, but the black beard was cut by a toothy smile. "I am not serious,

Delstrego. All the world knows you're the first in line at the communion rail."

"Listen to me, Belloc, Denezzi, all of you. I know there are soldiers after you, for your money. The whole town is to be squeezed dry. You especially, Paolo . . ."

Denezzi scowled. "Why me?"

"Because Marco told Pardo you were very wealthy."

The big man's cry was pitiful. "Aaii! No! Why did he say that! It's a lie!"

Belloc chuckled.

"Because he doesn't like you, Paolo. I can't think why not." The laughter that greeted Damiano's sally raised the effective temperature inside the shelter.

Damiano continued. "If you haven't seen them by now, it means they either passed along the West Road unnoticed . . ."

"We've kept a sentry at the road," interjected Belloc.

"That's how I found you," added Denezzi.

"Worse and worse." Damiano rubbed his face with palms hot from the flames. "Then Pardo's men must have turned back and headed north, either by mistake or intent, and come upon the carriages of the women."

The shelter erupted in noise and movement. Half the men cursed, while the other half rose to their feet, knocking snow-damped wood into the fires.

"Impossible," roared Denezzi, then added in calmer tones, "When would they have passed the fork in the road?"

"On horseback? Two days, perhaps. I know they stopped at Sous Pont Saint Martin."

Cries, sobs, and gasps followed one another down the huddled line, as Damiano's news was relayed.

"God . . . help us. They may have caught them," whispered Belloc, and Denezzi stared dumbly into the fire. "Perhaps they will only take the money."

"Will they resist?"

The blacksmith did not understand.

"Signor Belloc, this very morning I buried those who dwelt at Sous Pont Saint Martin. A peasant threw a pitchfork at a soldier, you see . . ."

Muscles tautened in the blacksmith's massive jaws. "Jesu! Boy, do you come to kill our hope?"

"I've come to help, if I can," said Damiano.

Denezzi stood, and all eyes looked at him. Damiano felt a hot pang of envy toward this man, whose strength and brute temper had won him more respect among his fellows than had Damiano's selfless dedication. "We'll have to take the chance he's right. I will lead a party of horsemen back to the North Road.

"But tomorrow. There's little light left today." He glanced down at Damiano. "For men's eyes, anyway."

"In the meantime, if you want to help us, then find us food. Else we will have to draw lots to see whose horse is butchered."

Damiano glanced sharply at him. "What do you expect of me: loaves and fishes? I have a jug of tonic in my bag; it's the reason I missed the evacuation, you know. I was minding the pot."

Despite the worry in his face, Belloc grinned. "Ah, yes, that pot."

"What did you expect to eat," continued Damiano. "Coming out here with little more than the clothes on your backs."

Denezzi growled, throwing tinder into the flames. "We expected to go home!—when Pardo had passed through: perhaps a week's time. And I expected the shepherds to drive the flocks home as soon as they heard of the advancing army.

"But they never showed, though I held up the march a day and a half to wait. Probably they are long since in Turin, and have sold the sheep as their own."

"Give them the benefit of the doubt," grunted Belloc. "They may have been overrun, and all our mutton sitting in the bellies of the southerners." Denezzi was not comforted.

"You gave the order to march?" mused Damiano, idly fingering the slack strings of his lute. "Yourself, not the mayor, or the council?"

Denezzi gestured as though to brush away flies. "I'm on the city council. My opinions are heard. Besides, most of the councilmen are not of military age; the mayor himself went to Aosta with the women."

Damiano peered through the lacework of the ivory rose that ornamented the lute's soundhole. Was there dampness within? "I have neither meat nor bread, Paolo. Nor can witchcraft create them. You'll have to kill a horse, I'm afraid."

"That will be a sore burden on some poor fellow," replied Denezzi. "And unnecessary. I think you can help us, Damiano."

"How?"

"You can call us meat from out of the hills."

The young witch's head snapped up in startlement, but Denezzi continued, "I have seen you do it, when we were both boys, calling rabbits from the fields and dogs from their masters' kennels. And my horse: I remember how he threw me and ran to you, pushing his black nose into your hand. Oh, yes, I won't forget that."

"I didn't ask him to throw you, Paolo. That was his own idea." Damiano had his own memories of the episode, foremost of which was the bloody lip Denezzi had given him in consequence of the fall. This had occurred when Damiano had been nine and Denezzi thirteen.

The young witch furrowed his brow, trying to explain a thing that was not easily put in words. "You see, Paolo, I can . . . tempt the beasts to come to me, for bread or a pat on the nose. But I can't force them. And if I call them saying, 'Come to me and be slaughtered,' well I think I'll be calling a long time."

"Just say come," suggested Denezzi. "I know how little you like the sight of blood, Owl-Eyes, so you just pat the goat or whatever on the head, and we'll do the rest."

Damiano dropped his head again. "That's betrayal." He heard a man snicker on the other side of the fire.

The witch ground his teeth together. "It's very hard to lie, Paolo, without using words."

Denezzi rustled beneath his black pelts. "It's very hard to go hungry. It's either a wild beast or a horse, Owl-Eyes. You can at least try."

He could have pleaded weariness as an excuse; in truth he was swimming with fatigue. But he felt eyes on him, and he had offered to help. What was more, Damiano knew most every horse in Partestrada by its simple, unspoken name. He rose from the fire.

He passed through a gap in the brush pile, and a chill hit him. "I'll need my mantle back," he mumbled sullenly. There was no response until he turned his black eyes into the crowd. Then the fur-lined wrap was handed out.

"If I bring in a goat," he said to Denezzi, "you must give me time to get out of it." The big man turned his face away.

Damiano trudged through crackling slush to the middle of the pasture. Shadows were growing, striping the field with blue. Tucking his mantle under him, he sat down on a hummocky stone. The shoe of his staff was braced between his boots; he leaned his face against the staff's lowest silver band.

For half a minute his mind floated free. Then he spoke a silent "Come," and unbidden to his mind sprang the image of a sword. He heard it snick free of the scabbard. By willpower he burst the image, only to see it reform in the shape of a pitchfork, tines protruding through the snow.

He was very tired. He tried again, and his call carried the odor of an abattoir, of a hut filled with dying. Mother of God! He didn't want to do this. He wanted to sleep, here in the sun, if no better place offered.

In the emptiness of his mind he saw how lovely it would be to rest. He remembered the honey-colored rock where he had eaten and talked with Raphael—only yesterday. He felt the heat of the hearth, where a chair was burning. How wasteful, but how warm.

His mind was flooded with the memory of this very pasture in the green of summer, when his father would treat the sheep with tar poultices and incantation. Grass up to his half-grown knees, except where the flocks had cropped it. It had been cool then, in the mountains, but pleasant. Sheep's milk. Napping at midday, surrounded by curious, odorous, half-grown lambs.

All the while Damiano dreamed, his call continued, rising into the air, growing, following the wind like smoke.

He remembered waking up with nothing to do all day, a condition he had experienced as recently as a week ago. He remembered the warm flood of sound Raphael pulled out of the lute. He remembered Carla, sewing as he read to her from the gilt-edged volume of Aquinas. (Her little brass needle caught the sun. She made only the gentlest fun of Damiano's squint as he read the fine script.) He remembered how quickly and quietly the days had passed before this war.

A shadow fell across the sunlight, and his drowsy eyes opened. A face stared down at him: Sfengia, the cheese-maker. The man's eyes were wet with longing. He was not alone, for Damiano sat at the center of a circle of silent figures that was even now increasing. They came for the sunshine, for the summer, for the memories of August and the dusty roads that caked a boy's bare feet and legs. They came at Damiano's call.

He felt their minds around him, open to his. There was Sfengia, afraid for his three daughters, and Belloc, heavy and mild. Behind them all, drawn but unwilling, Damiano sensed the brittle presence of Denezzi.

Th witch smiled wistfully. He had never compelled such rapt attention. It was very pleasant to sway men's minds. Let Paolo equal this.

Suddenly Damiano knew how to fulfill his task. It was all very easy. He imagined himself an animal, a hoofed beast: a sheep or a cow or maybe a goat. He allowed his dreams to shift in consonance with his animal being, though the call continued.

Green grass. That was good. Tall dry grass, with grain spilling out of the head. Free water running. Sun.

No halter. No wire twitch against the tender lip. Damiano touched the mind he had been seeking, the warm, wordless brute mind. It was tame to him and unafraid. It answered from very near. Unsuspicious, it opened to him and let him in. His meadow visions it made its own, improving them in the process. Salt. A warm back to rest one's head upon. Sage in the wind.

The old stable, out of the wind, and the smell of mash in the pail.

Once more the sun stroked Damiano's face; this pastoral rhapsody was losing him his human audience. But he scarcely noticed, for he was sharing the eyes of the cow that passed down into the dell along the lee of a cliff face, seeking summer just ahead. It was no wild beast, but lonely, lost. Its udder was shrunken, and its dappled sides gaunt. It stopped and looked around. Damiano saw the meadow and himself in the middle of it, motionless on the rock like a dark tree stump.

Summer was calling. His mind shouted it. Grass, crackling hay. The cow trotted forward.

She smelled man and stopped—curious, innocently wary.

When the first watcher beheld the spotted cow ambling down the hill toward them, he hissed a warning. All the

townsmen froze. Those who had swords put their hands to
the hilt. Belloc hefted his blunt hammer.

The cow stopped, her conviction failing as Damiano's
did. Her ears revolved, and she peered over her shoulder
at strange movement. One dainty foot was raised.

"Take her," shouted someone, and a half-dozen swords
caught the light. Belloc raised his hammer.

Damiano saw the blow descending. "No!" he cried, or
tried to. "No! Let me . . ."

The cow fell to its knees, and Paolo Denezzi opened its
brown and white spotted throat. It died in the snow
without a sound and was butchered where it lay, steaming
in the air like a kettle of soup.

Carlo Belloc plunged his bloody hands into the snow
and turned away from the carcass. He was most surprised
to see young Damiano face down in the snow; a splash of
gold and scarlet. Denezzi was looking down at him.

The blacksmith hurried over. "What did you do to
him?" he snapped at Denezzi.

"Do to him?" Denezzi shook his head. "I did nothing.
I'd pick him up, but that bitch of his . . ."

Macchiata's bent legs straddled her limp master. Her
mouth was a rictus of hate, dripping slaver. Belloc regarded
her earnestly, from under beetling brows.

"You can talk, can't you dog? Tell us what's wrong with
your master?"

She licked her lips, and her fury was extinguished. "I
don't know. He fell down when you hit the cow." Her nose
burrowed through the hair at the back of Damiano's neck,
to assure herself he was still alive. "He's very sensitive,"
she added.

Denezzi bit off his laugh at Belloc's warning glower.

"Allow us to pick him up and carry him to the fire,
puppy," said Belloc. "If he has taken hurt, we will help
him. We're his friends."

The blacksmith lifted Damiano easily and set him over
one huge shoulder. The staff lay where it had fallen until
Macchiata, seeing her master laid gently before the fire,
returned. Taking the brass foot in her mouth, she dragged
the stick to Damiano's side.

The men she passed got out of her way.

* * *

Time was a trickle of chilling blood. Red went brown. Brown went black. Memory fell apart. Sense fell apart. He saw nothing, heard nothing, felt nothing, and knew nothing except that he saw nothing, heard nothing, and felt nothing.

Hope fell apart.

Damiano's eyes were open, staring blindly at the fire. When Belloc spoke to him, he made no answer. He neither stirred nor spake the night through, nor did the smell of roasting beef rouse him. Macchiata lay by him, equally quiet. She, however, ate her fill.

At dawn the light of the rising sun stole his gaze from the fire. He propped himself on his elbows, and Macchiata uttered a whinny of glad relief. She smothered with kisses his dull and unprotesting face.

"Eh, boy? Are you with us again?" murmured Belloc, who had watched half through the night and finally pitched his blankets next to the tranced form.

Damiano slowly turned his face to Belloc. "How long?" he whispered.

"Have you lain there mazed? All yesterday evening and night. It's dawn already, Dami Delstrego. Where have you been?"

The answer was halting. "I have lain trapped in the body of a dead beast. Dead. Knowing myself dead.

"Was it only one night? I thought it was decades. I thought my time had passed. I thought there would be no escape until the last day, and judgment." His eyes were still very wide, brown and soft like a cow's, and his face expressed nothing.

The blacksmith sighed. "If you were trapped within the cow yesterday, then you spent the night in a hundred stomachs. I think you're still not well, Damiano," said Belloc. "Stay here for today, while a party rides to Aosta. There's plenty of firewood left, and I saved you some meat."

Damiano had started to rise, but at Belloc's last words his stomach rebelled. He gagged but was empty as a dry bucket. "No," he panted. "I'm riding with you. You will need me, should you find what you are looking for. And I—I am beginning to see what must be done. I'm riding with you."

CHAPTER 6

The procession wound down and east, past the abandoned village, where the ruins of one hut were already softened with a cloak of blown snow, back over the river Lys, and toward the crossing of the roads. They were a somber line of men, and they pushed their horses, but they were not soldiers.

Damiano rode one of Paolo Denezzi's geldings, with a leather strap for a bridle and no saddle at all. It was a black horse; all of Denezzi's four horses were black. The witch reflected on what Denezzi had said the previous afternoon—how hard it would be on some poor man to lose his mount to the knife. And here was the rich man with one to ride, two for pack, and an extra. Damiano smiled grimly.

The horse was nervous bearing him. Well it might be, for Damiano's mind was filled with cold and weeping blood. The call that he had begun the day before could not be utterly silenced.

Bored with the slow pace, he turned his horse's head once more to the straggling tail of the company, where men rode on cart horses and hinnies. There was even one fellow, Aloisio by name, who sat astraddle an ass, his bootless feet dragging in the dust. He was a tanner by trade and carried neither sword nor spear. But he had a long hide-splitter, razor sharp, and a young wife in the train to Aosta.

"Aloisio, can't it move any faster?" asked Damiano, looming over the man from his seat on Denezzi's lean horse. He had intended his words to sound warmer.

The tanner raised his head, wary but unafraid. "No, Signor Delstrego, it cannot. Not unless I get behind and push."

Damiano nodded in resignation and tried to smile. Dryly his lips slid back from his teeth. He fell in place beside Aloisio, at the tail of the line, where he could make sure no one became lost.

The tall peaks, crystalline now in the easterly sun, stood

in the distance at the right of the road. Damiano squinted and wondered what he had seen in them, only the day before. They were unscalable stone, as they had always been, and they harbored neither food nor beauty.

Thinking about the peaks and his previous intoxication led him to think about Macchiata. He felt again her wet, impertinent nose against the palm of his hand and heard again her fluttering worry, like that of a hen as she prodded him from his knees in the slush. In the universe of ash in which he found himself, the little dog could spark a tiny flame of gladness.

She scrambled at the proud horse's feet, pottering into every mark and blister of the snow at the side of the road, panting very hard. A few days like this and she would not be so ridiculously fat.

Damiano placed his hand on the horse's knotty head and without words suggested that it trot back to the head of the line, to Denezzi's side. The animal started and plunged at the contact, almost costing Damiano his seat.

Very soon the crossroads came into view. Damiano led his mount to the snowbank where his own trail from the guardhouse broke onto the road. He gave the reins into the hands of his nearest neighbor and leaped down. His lean legs disappeared into the trail, stepping high and storklike. The procession slowed to a disorderly stop.

He emerged from the shelter bearing three soft bags. "Clothing," he said. "Not very good. Not clean. But for any man who needs it. And for any man who needs a hair pin." He held up the jeweled ornament. Two dozen eyes stared uncomprehending, before he slipped the pin back into his belt pouch. As he climbed onto the horse's back Damiano rustled like dry leaves or paper, and a flat weight hung forward inside his woolen tunic.

The North Road was a steady climb, slick as wellstone. Some of the heavy steeds at the rear of the line, especially those without shoes, had trouble. Damiano noticed with dull amusement that Aloisio's ass was doing very well under the new conditions and was climbing toward the front of the company.

Damiano turned to Belloc, who had ridden silently on his gray gelding since breaking camp. "I learned to play the lute from an angel," he said. "An archangel, to be exact.

No one can see him but me—and Macchiata." Belloc turned on him a slow, suspicious eye.

"Doesn't that sound silly, Signor Belloc? Until yesterday, it seemed quite natural to me. My lessons were, perhaps, the most important things in the world. As important as the quest of alchemy. Now . . ."

He turned his head in a circle, peering around with eyes that could not fathom distance or endure the sun. Belloc stared at him with a sort of stolid, masculine pity. "Now it seems very irrelevant. Both the angel and the lute. And alchemy as well.

"It was spending the night in the dead body of a cow. That puts a different perspective on things. It makes one see life as it really is, in all its misery. Or possibly it only makes one sick."

"Sickness plays tricks on the mind," rumbled Belloc in reply, not sure whether by sickness Damiano meant seeing angels or not caring to see them. "I told you you should have stayed back at the pasture."

"Eh? Why? We're not going back there, you know. If we find no one on the road all the way to Aosta, there'll be nothing to do but stay in the city. Most of us, anyway. If we catch up with Pardo's soldiers, then either they will kill us, or we will kill them, or we will all kill each other. If it is we who survive, then we'd better keep going—for Pardo's men have many friends, and Partestrada has none. Unless the Green Count comes to avenge us. In the spring, of course."

Damiano's eyes shone dry like polished stone. His skin was white. Belloc shook his head. "When did you eat last, boy?"

Damiano shrugged without interest.

Paolo Denezzi, who was riding a few feet in front of the two, as though he were a commander and the others his lieutenants, peered back over his shoulder. After a weighty silence, he spoke. "We will go to Aosta," he conceded. "Those with friends or family there may stay. Or those with money to buy. The rest I will lead to Donnaz, where we will prepare our own vengeance."

Damiano felt a challenge rise up in him. When had these plans been adopted? When he had shown up at the camp no such idea had existed in the men's minds, and he'd heard no talk since. . . .

But then for many hours he had not been listening. And

could he provide any better destination? Denezzi at least
had the good of the city in mind.

Besides, Damiano did not believe events would pass so
smoothly. A troop of hardened cavalry did not disappear
into the hills forever.

Belloc cleared his throat. "You have property in the
town of Donnaz, Signor Denezzi?"

Denezzi nodded, distrustful. "What of it?"

"I was wondering where you would put our homeless
neighbors."

"They will pay me back," stated Denezzi. His thin
mouth was dour, and his moustache bristled.

Suddenly Damiano could stand it no more: the intermi-
nable, straggling march, the presence of Denezzi, even
Belloc's taciturn kindness. He called Macchiata, ordering
her to stay by the blacksmith until he returned, then he
kicked his mount forward.

"Where are you going, Delstrego?" demanded Denezzi,
rising in his saddle.

"Ahead," answered the witch.

The dark man opened his mouth as though to forbid
him. He remained that way for a moment, uncharacteristi-
cally indecisive. Finally he said, "If you break my horse's
leg, boy, I will break your head."

Damiano smiled thinly. "You're not even four years
older than I am, Paolo. And as for breaking my head . . ."
He swiveled front again, and the black horse sprang
forward as though whipped.

Alone was much better. His head was clear, with that
peculiar ringing lightness that comes with fasting. The
horse climbed energetically, in a dumb effort to leave its
rider behind. Damiano felt some pity for the beast, but not
much. Pity was deserved all around and could be spread
much too thin.

His tall staff passed under his belt and lay against the
horse's flank like a sword. Damiano secured it with his
right hand, so it would not slap with every ironshod step.

In a short time he left the clatter and creak of the
citizens behind. Up here the road wound the shoulders of a
peak like epaulets and crossed two great chasms, one on a
bridge of rough wood, and the other on a splendid stone
arch twelve hundred years old.

The North Road was deceptive, folding back upon itself, taking whatever path or purchase it could, so that Damiano once found himself staring across a sheer drop no wider than a snowball's throw, at a length of snowy road he was not to touch for half-an-hour's climb.

Sound was deceptive too, for now he heard the speech of men again, together with the blow and whinny of horses. He looked below, but could see no sign of the ascending company. He turned a corner and looked ahead.

It was the troops of General Pardo, displayed against the smeared white cliffs like chessmen. They rode in order, two abreast. There were fifty of them, and behind them lumbered five ungainly wagons. Damiano stared wide-eyed at the wagons.

Four were heavy laden, covered in waxed linen, pulled by four oxen apiece. The last wagon was open, and packed with . . . women. Damiano blinked and clutched at his staff. He was sure they were women, wrapped in shawls and blankets, mostly black. But these were not all the women of Partestrada, by no means. There could not be more than twenty in that sad, paintless farm cart. What was this? Was Carla among these? He did not know whether to hope she was or to pray she was not.

Damiano heard a stentorian cry. As he watched, so he was being watched.

Though he sat in hailing distance of Pardo's cavalry, a large loop of road lay between them. A single soldier broke from the head of the line and drove his mount back against the direction of their march, between the third wide wagon and the empty edge of the road. The beast was frightened; its legs splayed stiffly against the slick road, and it backed against the wood of the wagon, its brown eyes rolling at the sheer drop.

The horseman peered over at a figure gorgeously dressed in scarlet and gold, its hair in wild black curls that obscured half its face. It rode a fine horse as a herd boy will ride a cow: bareback, sitting the withers, legs bent and feet gripping the beast's ribs. Unaccountably, the soldier's neck prickled.

Damiano perceived less about the soldier because he could not see as well.

"You!" shouted the soldier. "You are to come here!"

Damiano barked a laugh. "Why?" he replied in more normal tones. "Very soon you will all be over here."

The horseman scowled. "What? I don't hear you. Don't you hear me, man? Come here!"

Damiano didn't want to shout. He didn't want to talk to the fellow at all. He turned his horse's head and started back down the road, not daring to canter him on the bend.

Another cry split the air, sharp and shrill: a woman's cry. Damiano twisted from the waist to peer behind him, and at that moment something hit him on the breastbone, with a blow no harder than that of a hard snowball, well thrown.

His shock sent the black gelding skidding into a gallop that quickly put a wall of granite between Damiano and Pardo's men. Damiano let the horse run while he blinked down at the shaft of the arrow protruding from his clothing. Then with one hand he reined in the horse, while the other very calmly worried the arrowhead from the wood and leather cover of the works of Petrarch. Further examination found that the arrow had penetrated quite half of the vellum pages and left a clean incision through an entire packet of letters written in an unknown, Germanic tongue.

"If I live," he murmured to the wind on his face, "this will be something to talk about."

When Paolo Denezzi spied his black horse hurtling down the North Road toward him, bearing its light burden clinging about its neck, he cursed foully. But before he could gather his breath to release his roar of anger, Damiano had slid from the horse's back.

"Off your mounts," he cried to the company. "Every man on his own two feet and forward with me."

"No such thing!" bellowed Denezzi. Men paused, one foot in the stirrup, as authority flew confused. Denezzi, however, sprang down to confront the witch.

"What is this, Owl-Eyes?" Without thinking he grabbed for the chain of Damiano's mantle. The silver head of the staff flashed across his knuckles, and he drew back a bleeding hand. "Don't touch that," snapped Damiano. "If they'll obey you, then help me save their lives. Get the horses away from them."

Denezzi's face was wine purple. He sucked his damaged fingers. "Why? What's coming—the soldiers you prophesied?"

"Yes, and either they will kill us all or terror will. Off your horses to save your lives," he repeated, shouting at the top of his lungs.

"Asses too?" drawled the tanner Aloisio, but as he spoke he lifted his weight on his toes and allowed his little beast to walk out from under him. Ten men laughed, but fifty dismounted. Belloc got down from his gray.

"They are not twenty minutes behind me," announced Damiano. "They can't move fast, because they are leading wagons—ox wagons, Belloc, and one of them was once yours."

"Catarina?" gasped the blacksmith, but Damiano raised his hand. "There are a few citizens with them, but I couldn't pick them out at the distance.

"Listen, my friends. I am going up there . . ." and he pointed along the sloppy road whence he'd come. "To conceal myself, if I can. When the soldiers ride by, I will . . . surprise them. Be ready to take back our wagons. And be ready to run." He turned and in half a minute had vanished from sight.

"Do we do as he says?" asked Aloisio, standing behind Denezzi with the halter of his ass in his hand. "I'm afraid young Signor Delstrego is a little bit . . . disturbed."

"I will, anyway," responded Belloc. "I can't speak for any other man."

Denezzi suffered no such limitation. "We will. If these ghostly soldiers of his really exist . . . well, he seems to have a plan. If not, I swear I will bury that foppish simpleton by the side of the road." He strode forward, dropping the reins of his horse, trusting someone would mind the beast. Aloisio wordlessly did so.

Damiano huddled behind a hummock made from the roots of a tree and the few hundred years' worth of soil it had collected. He waited to hear the jingle of the cavalry harness. Behind him the ground dropped abruptly away, farther than he could focus on.

He felt Macchiata beside him, worming her way into the scant cover. "Macchiata, no!" he hissed. "Get out of here. Don't be near me!"

"Don't be near you?" she repeated in accents tragic. "Don't be *near* you, Master? How can you say that? I have already been parted from you for hours today, and we were never to be parted while we both live; you said so . . ."

Damiano was unmoved. He crouched close to the earth, his eyes fixed on the upper road. "Yes, little dear, and if you don't get out of here and down the road very fast, one of us will not live much longer. GO!"

Macchiata went.

The men of Partestrada were assembled a few hundred feet to Damiano's left, in a spot visible from behind the trunk of the pine, but concealed from the upper slope of the road. They milled about, swords and cleavers dragging. They did not resemble soldiers, but at least their horses were nowhere in sight.

Damiano saw the head of the column, with his swart uniform and dull brass, at the same time he heard the ring of shod hooves on ice. The captain was the same who had spied Damiano and ordered him to stop. Damiano peered behind him, to see which of the men carried bows.

The captain passed before Damiano's earthy concealment. He led fifty men: twenty swordsmen, twenty spear, five archers, and five more to mind the booty. They passed so near Damiano he might have swung his staff and brained one.

Instead he stood up, filled with grave excitement and a thrill of dread. The nearest soldier leaped back in superstitious fear, to see Damiano appear as though he'd floated up the sheer cliff.

Damiano took his staff in both hands. Its ebony length filled his mind, and he allowed his dark, invisible power to flow into the wood. With perverse satisfaction he let free the deadly refrain that had stifled in him since the cow went down.

"Come!" The terrible call rang against rock, out of hearing, impossible to ignore. "Come! Come and be slaughtered!" it shrieked.

Every horse pitched in blind hysteria, and every man clapped his hands to his ears.

The screams of the beasts were one with his, as Damiano made them believe in death. Men, who already believed, fell from their saddles and lay in the mire.

In front of the women's wagon the oxen were thrashing, kicking the air uselessly. One of the bullocks gored his yoke-mate's face, and the bellows of the wounded animal punctuated the cacophony. The women themselves were screaming. Damiano opened his eyes in time to see a horse leap blindly over the edge.

It was all wreckage. No rider controlled his horse; few sat mounted. As he watched, the oxen of the front goods wagon broke the wooden brake lever and plunged from behind the company, careening forward, trampling men and horses alike. Tall, brightly painted wheels left tracks shining red.

The men of Partestrada stood plastered to the inner cliff wall; Damiano could scarcely see them. The ox wagon swung wide at the bend. The outside wheel spun in emptiness, then the wagon tipped. Frenzied bellows rose into shrieks that grew thin and keen, as though the beasts were singing on their way to the ground.

Damiano contemplated the destruction. Men crawled on hands and knees, like horses, their swords abandoned. A chestnut gelding lay flat on the ground before him, crying like a man. A few soldiers had risen and stood propped against the face of the rock. One held a bow. With clumsy, clattering movements the archer raised it, pointing it at Damiano.

Without haste, indeed without enthusiasm, Damiano propped his staff between the archer and himself. It drew the arrow, as Damiano had meant it should. The limber feathered shaft broke in pieces.

But the archer had not acted alone. A man staggered forward, leaning, his head lowered, as though he breasted the wind. It was the troops' captain once more. His belt still carried a sword, and as he approached the heart of his terror he unsheathed it and stood upright.

"So," thought Damiano, looking into the face of the man before him, seeing the gray metal unveiled.

He knew nothing of fighting, with swords or without. Even had he the strength to run, there was nowhere to go except to follow the oxen. And as it was his strength was used up, along with all his caring.

"So," said Damiano to himself, and he waited for what would happen.

What happened was that the captain swung his sword back over one shoulder, aiming for a decapitating blow, and then Belloc's great hammer came down on the man's head. Beneath the helmet of leather and iron, the captain's skull splintered. Damiano looked away, to encounter Belloc's square head and ashen face. The blacksmith's lips were gray with horror, but he was not looking at the bloody ruin he had created. He was staring at Damiano. Then Damiano watched the death of Pardo's captain with his strange sight. Light flickered green and golden over the still form, like rags soaked in oil and burnt.

Then the fire departed and the man was gone.

Gone. Escaped. Not here in this ruined shape at all. Damiano blinked at this; it was death and yet not what he had thought he knew. It was cold and terrifying, like a night of no stars, but it was not the mindful death he had known, despair in rotting flesh. It was not what set him screaming. Damiano's hideous call was cut off sharp.

Belloc took a deep, shuddering breath. "Boy," he gasped, "are you Satan himself? Or how is it you have not burst, doing this?"

Damiano heard the voice, but not the words. His ears were ringing with silence. His gaze slid wearily from Belloc's face to his black, brain-spattered hammer.

"Ah! The hammer. Yes, Belloc. That was very fitting." He smiled at Belloc, or he tried to.

The citizens of Partestrada scrambled heavily up the road, their rude weapons in their red-fingered hands. They fell upon the dazed soldiers like men threshing wheat. Damiano walked toward the two remaining ox wagons, where one beast hung dead in the traces. He did not look back at the carnage.

The women were still in the middle wagon: they had been tied there. Damiano looked at faces he knew.

Old Signora Anuzzi was there, stuffed in a corner like a black sack. And Lidie Polsetti, and Vera Polsetti, and little Françoise. And Signora Mellio, the widow who looked after Father Antonio. And Bernice Roberto. They were all crying at once, faces striped with tears and noses slimy. Damiano could hardly blame them; he had worked this misery himself, and though he was not tied, he felt much the same as they. Still, he could get no sense of them.

He hauled himself up and into the wagon, groaning with effort. As he lay on the wooden boards, his eyes closed, he heard the only voice that could have pleased him.

"Dami! Damiano, are you wounded? Were you hit by the arrow up above? Dami, speak to me?" He looked up into Carla Denezzi's frozen, wind-chapped and fear-whitened face.

"O Bella! Bellissima!" he whispered, and he smiled at her as though the two were alone.

Wonderingly, the blond girl extended her bound wrists. She touched his breast awkwardly, where the arrow had left its neat cut: a slice no longer than the last joint of a finger. He took her hand in his, grimacing at the ropes. An instant later, every binding in the wagon took life, and like snakes, wriggled free. The wagon tongue dropped to the road and a dozen women shrieked at sudden freedom and missing laces.

"Damiano!" hissed Carla, who either wore no lacings or did not care about them. "I prayed I would see you again, but I had little hope. How did you get through? I think the Devil himself has flown over us. Could you feel him?"

"Eh?" Damiano turned his face away. Though a bare two minutes ago he had stood between life and death, indifferent, Carla's presence had revealed his own face to him again. The Devil himself? He was ashamed, not knowing quite why.

Meanwhile, murder was running like a flame all over the snowy mountain road. Damiano didn't want to look upon that, either, so he regarded the rough wooden boards.

"The children," he stuttered. "All the rest of the women and the old men. What happened to them? Father Antonio . . . Did they . . ."

"Everyone of them is in Aosta," spat Signora Aluzzi, who had always felt herself to be a class above any mere artisans like the Delstregos. "They went under a guard of soldiers, all very proper. As though the poor scum were royalty! Only those of us who are worth something have been tied up like pigs to market!"

"The soldiers . . . offered no violence?" Damiano blinked stupidly from one face to another.

Signora Aluzzi snorted. "We haven't been raped, if that's what you mean, you young gutter rat!"

He scratched his head in simple puzzlement. "But . . ." He glanced again at Carla Denezzi. "They're all being killed," he said, and then fell silent as though awaiting confirmation of his words. She regarded him soberly and silently, her hand resting lightly upon his.

"The soldiers are all being killed, for revenge of their crimes against you. And it is I who have made that possible," he concluded.

"God be praised!" grunted the old signora of the vineyards.

Carla felt Damiano start. She caught his stricken glance and held it. It was only her perfect understanding at this moment that kept Damiano from being swept away, blown into tears or madness.

The wagon tilted. Paolo Denezzi was climbing aboard. "It is done," he announced, and he saw Damiano and Carla.

"You don't touch my sister!" he roared, throwing half the women back into quaking hysteria. "She is a pure dove. And you . . . you, Delstrego, are a monster!"

"Paolo!" shouted Carla, in anger and indignation. But Damiano very slowly drew his hand back. He said nothing and slunk out of the wagon. He picked his way amid the graceless figures on the road, which lay so still they might never have known life at all.

CHAPTER 7

Aosta was a larger and more prosperous town than Partestrada, since it lay at the most pleasant dip in the only road entering the Piedmont from the north. Damiano had often thought this an unfair advantage for a city that did not have much else to recommend it. It shared with Partestrada a rushing river, which was named in the mountains the Evançon, though at the feet of the hills it changed its name along with its tempestuous personality and was called the Dora Baltea.

Much of the gold Damiano had brought out of the Delstrego tower had gone to buy shelter for the poorer refugees, and even so these would have to find work quickly or move on. Had the burghers of Aosta known that this ill-timed influx of business had left fifty soldiers and eight horses buried in the snow of the passes, their welcome would have been short indeed. The Valle d'Aosta, feeling some protection from its mountains but not much, had no desire to involve itself in battles that ought to have been fought by Amadeus himself.

As it was, there was no need for the Aostans to know. General Pardo himself would be slow in finding out, for not a man would return to him.

Still, find out he would. Now that the matter of the citizens had been cleared up (or at least Damiano felt no further responsibility for them), he had time to reflect.

It was strange to realize that he had no more virtue than Pardo, no more than the soldiers who put a tiny hamlet to the sword because one peasant showed fight. Damiano had killed fifty—he did not allow the knives and hammers of Partestrada credit for the blood—in revenge for that six. Or perhaps it was a revenge for the soldiers' crimes against the women of Partestrada—a meaningless revenge for crimes that had never been committed.

Whatever—Damiano had not felt wicked in action. He doubted General Pardo did, either. "Man is born in sin, and his nature is evil." Father Antonio had announced that from the pulpit, though it was not a subject upon which the good priest had dwelt in his leisure time. Never till now had Damiano thought about it.

Were the peasant woman's curses now satisfied? Would she rest peacefully, now that her murderers were all dead?

And while he was asking questions, where was Father Antonio, anyway? Damiano needed direction (the sort of direction Raphael would never consent to give). And he needed it immediately.

The dank common room of the inn where Damiano sat, though warm and crowded with his companions, was sullen and quiet. Damiano rose from the crude table of wooden slats, leaving behind him crumbs of bread, the wax rind of a cheese, and an untouched length of sausage. A whine beneath the table prompted him to throw the meat to Macchiata.

Carla was unreachable, in the house of friends and guarded by her villainous brother, but Damiano could at least go looking for his friend the priest.

The basilica of San Sebastiano at Aosta was really just a small round church. Damiano stood at the door, certain he would find the priest nearby, but feeling a stiff, unreason-

ing reluctance to enter. As he stood undecided, Carla
Denezzi stepped out.

"Damiano!" she gasped, and caught him by the hand.
"Step in here, quick." He let himself be dragged into
shadows smelling of wood smoke and incense.

Left of the door was a baptismal, separated from the
vestibule by a lacework of wood. As though this offered
concealment, she sat him down.

She was wearing a cream-colored shawl. Her face was
clean and rosy, and the sight of it brought the past once
more to life for him: warm, filtered sun threading through
the pales of the loggia, and bright threads lying on a
basket, neatly sorted, and ideas neatly sorted, and laughter. Damiano wanted to tell her how glad he was to see her,
and how he had missed her, and sought her, and thought
of her as he lay curled in a black cave in the hills under
snow, but the very cleanness and rosiness of her face
stopped him. It made Damiano shy.

"I shouldn't have my staff here," he murmured. "It isn't
right."

She had reached out her small hand, meaning to lay the
stick aside, when she remembered and drew back. "Ah! I
forgot one mustn't touch it."

Smiling with an odd sadness, Damiano took her hand
and touched it to the ebony wood. "Signorina," he
whispered, "nothing of mine will ever hurt you. I promise
that. You could put your hand on my beating heart, and it
would do you no harm."

She chuckled at this fervid gallantry, wondering how
such a deed could hurt anyone but Damiano himself, but
with a reawakened memory her hand went to the breast of
his tunic—to the hole. "Your beating heart," she echoed.
"How is it—by what miracle, Damiano . . ."

"The miracle of a book." He laughed in return and
slipped out the volume to show her. "The miracle of
Petrarch's poetry."

With a small cry of wonder, Carla took the book. She
gave his hand a tiny squeeze. "Oh, Damiano, I thank God
for that. When I saw the man raise his bow I screamed
aloud, for I knew by your colors it was you across the gap. I
prayed that he had not hit you, but I feared every moment
we would pass your body in the snow."

"It must be that I owe my life to your prayers," he said sincerely. There was a moment's happy silence.

Then Carla sighed. "Your soul and mine comprehend one another, dear Damiano. I wish you were my brother instead of Paolo."

This, although it denoted affection, was not the sentiment Damiano wished to hear from Carla. He caught his tongue for a moment, rehearsing words. Of course he would tell her how he loved her, but how and to what end?

Should he say, "Carla, beloved, I am going to Provence where my music in your honor will make you famous. Wait for me"? Or was it to be, "Carla, best beloved, I am going to Nuremberg, where my alchemies in your honor will bring you glory. Wait for me"? It was certain he could not say, "Carla, little dear, friend of my childhood, come with me to Provence or Germany and starve."

But it was Carla who spoke. "My brother is not pleased with me, old friend. You alone in the world, Damiano, have the soul to understand why I have applied to the convent La Dolerosa at Bard."

Damiano gazed blankly at the pink marble christening bowl, lily-shaped and smoother than flower petals in the faded light. "Why you what? Say again."

Carla leaned forward. Her hands folded together on her lap. "I have applied—and been accepted—at the cloister of Our Sorrowful Mother at Bard. I will enter on my birthday, next month. Paolo would stop me if he could, having plans to marry me to a cousin in Donnaz, but by law he cannot stand between me and the vows."

His ears rang. The font, the lectern, the marble leaping fish, all stood out in impossible relief. "Carla? You are going into the cloister? You will become a nun?"

She nodded, slowly and fervently. "I will become one of the sisters of Saint Clare. I will dedicate my works and prayers to the poor and the suffering." Something in Damiano's expression daunted her. "You . . . aren't happy for me, Dami?"

"I will never see you again!" cried the youth, his voice rising to a wail. Carla put one finger very near his mouth, darting a glance left and right.

"Hush, Damiano! My brother rarely sets foot in a church, but . . . If he found us, he would come at you like a bear—he is so furious."

Unable to restrain himself, he took her hand and kissed it. "Carla, *cara,* my dear, my Beatrice. Don't leave me and hide yourself behind stone walls forever, or I will die!"

Her little chin dropped in surprise. "What are you saying, Damiano? Am I going mad?"

"Please!" he implored. "When the soldiers marched into the city, all I thought about was you, and when I knew that you were gone, I feared for you. I marched through the cold and snow and was assaulted by thieves. I spent a night of death alive in the torn carcass of a dead cow, and then I sinned, killing men to save you . . .

"Mother of God, Carla, don't leave me! Let me serve you instead. All I have. All I am. All the days of my life. . . . I will not touch you, if it is your will that I do not. Though I hope fervently that is *not* your will! Please, it must be the will of God that I want you, for I could never want anything so much by myself!" His words broke off in a sob.

Carla sat still. Damiano, suddenly abashed, released her hand. Slowly she began to shake her head.

"Damiano. Where did this speech come from? In all the time I have known you, our conversation has been of God and of the sciences. You introduced me to the philosophers of the Church, whom I might never have known. You read to me interminably—I mean at length—from blessed Hermes, whose name I could never find on the list of saints, and taught me the elementals and how they combine, and the orders of the angels. . . .

"But you never spoke to me of love—worldly love. I had thought you would scorn such a feeling!" Her eyes wandered hidden in the darkness.

"Eh? God. Study. Love. Is there a difference among them?" he blurted. Damiano no longer knew quite what he was saying. He shrugged spasmodically. "I love you, Carla. I swear to God that I love you."

"I didn't know that," she said simply, shifting on the stone seat.

"Perhaps because I didn't either. Please, Carla, believe it now. Pretend you have always believed. Let it make a difference to your decision. Can't you?

"Can't you?" He stroked the air above her knee, not daring to touch her.

Her slow denial was inevitable and crushing. "No, my dear Damiano. I can't."

"This is a world of much bitterness; you have seen that as I have. Life is wracked with pain and cut short by war and pestilence. The weak suffer under the strong, and the strong, like my poor, fearsome Paolo, suffer under their own passions. Seeking after happiness itself leads to sin and greater suffering. We were not put here to be happy."

"That's good then," Damiano said, putting his elbows on his knees and his head in his hands. ". . . because I certainly am not . . . happy."

Reluctantly, knowing she shouldn't, Carla stroked Damiano's black hair. "We who are allowed to see this, my brother, my dear brother, brother of my soul . . . we are not given the choice of whom to love—for we must act love toward all, even the most repellent—nor whom first to serve. It is God himself whom we must serve. But for the rest, it is as you say—it must be with all we possess, and with all we are.

"And I am called by Him to prayer." Her smooth brow frowned momentarily. "I believed that you were, also, Damiano. It is from you I have learned my lessons, and I brought with me to Aosta the big book of Thomas Aquinas you gave me, and also the poems of Brother Francis that we read aloud together and were so beautiful. Can't you also feel your vocation?"

He lifted his head with a brief, choking laugh. "Me? A bastard, you know, cannot become a priest, but even a bastard is more welcome than I. A witch is barred from religious life: even from lay orders. They think we are not quite right, you know. Some say we are even damned."

Damiano's shoulders twitched, but he immediately straightened and wiped his tunic sleeve on his face. "Forgive me, Signorina. I am weary and . . . not pleased with myself. I will offer you nothing more to sour your resolution. I do understand it, though it . . ."

He took a deep breath and started again. "Believe me, Carla, if you wish to be a sister to me, I will be a brother to you. If you disappear behind the stone walls of La Dolerosa, and I never see you again, then I will still love you and be glad to love you, for it is better to love than not."

She stood beside Damiano, her blond hair escaping the confines of her shawl. He turned stiffly, lest motion should make him cry once more (which would be too many times in too few days). He strode out of the baptismal and through the vestibule. At the arched doorway Damiano winced and turned his face from the cold light of the sun.

Night fell early in the valley now, at the end of November. Aosta sat in shadow, in the cupped hands of the hills. The air was filled with wood smoke.

Damiano had paid a townsman to take him in that night—him and Macchiata. If he went within now, there would be a fire and hot soup, no doubt. (To stretch one's dinner to feed a stranger, one always made soup.) But instead Damiano sat on a log in the meadow, where the banks of a frozen stream hid him from the wind. He had wound his ermine mantle close around him, and his booted feet were buried beneath the mass of a warm dog.

The sky had faded, like violets pressed in the pages of a book. The ice of the stream was gray.

"With all we possess. With all we are." She had thrown his words back at him, and they scalded. What Damiano had, money and property, had been quickly dispersed. What he was, seemed nothing worth the gift.

He shivered, and Macchiata shifted on his boots.

Still, anything could be turned to use some way. A chair that could not be sat on could be thrown on the fire. A man whom no one needed, whose actions turned to harm, could serve a similar purpose. Damiano had a sudden, dreadful idea that fit his mood. He rose and started back toward the street.

An hour had passed. Macchiata had been put to bed at the landlord's hearth. She had not objected. "Raphael," he called, sinking once more onto the lonely log.

"Raphael. Seraph. If you can spare a minute . . ."

The archangel sat himself gracefully on the frozen water.

"I can spare eternity," said Raphael. His smile was filled with that potent sweetness that man can appreciate only from far away. It gave Damiano unexpected pain, that smile, though he had seen it so often before.

"I would like . . ." He stopped, not knowing what to say. "Raphael, sit with me awhile, because I may never see you again."

The angel fluffed his feathers, and his eyebrows rose in a gesture as simple and dignified as that of an owl.

"Don't say 'never' to me, Dami!" Then Raphael's smile returned. "It's a word I cannot understand." Reflectively the angel added, "—though I understand 'forever' quite well. The two words are very different in quality, I think."

Damiano did not reply but clutched his knees to his chest. Slowly Raphael reached out a hand, and then a wing, taking the young man into his circle of light.

"Shall I play for you, Damiano?" he asked, as minutes passed.

"The lute is in the cabinetmaker's house, with Macchiata." Damiano's voice was phlegmy. He cleared his throat.

"I have my own instrument," said the angel, diffidently.

Damiano's eyes flickered briefly with curiosity, but that brightness failed.

"Thank you, Seraph, but I can't afford the peace such music would bring to me. There's something I have to do, and I must remain strong for it.

"Please sit beside me, Raphael, and don't ask me to talk."

To huddle in the compass of the angel's wings was like sitting on the disk of the full moon, except that the moon was both more gaudy and more tarnished. Damiano was no longer cold. "You must continue to believe, Raphael, even if it becomes difficult . . . you must believe that I love you."

Raphael's black-blue gaze was beyond surprise or judgment.

Young Carla Denezzi walked the dark streets from the basilica to the inn, chaperoned by the Signora Anuzzi. They had passed the evening praying for the souls of the dead. The old signora's prayers had been specifically for her nephew Georgio Anuzzi, the owner of the vineyards, who had refused to abandon his holdings before the influx of soldiers and was now presumably among the departed. Any spiritual benefit that overshot this target would presumably go toward the souls of the two Partestradan men slain in the battle of the road.

Carla's prayers had been less exclusive. She had prayed for the souls of all who lay dead in the mountain snow. In fact, she had disbursed her prayers among some who were not dead at all, but only unhappy.

The sky was starless, and the women picked their way with worried care, fearing a fall on the frozen mud of the street. Signora Anuzzi muttered hard words to the air. At last they stood at the iron-bound inn door. Carla looked along the street to its ending, and she spied an angel in the fields beyond.

It was white and beautiful and unmistakably an angel, with huge wings folded forward and down—wings like a girl's white woolen shawl. It sat motionless on the earth, praying. It must be praying, for what else would an angel be doing alone at night, when many men were new dead?

"Signora, look!" she whispered, pointing into the darkness. "Do you see?"

"See? Child, I can scarcely see your finger, on a night like this," the old woman snorted. Abruptly she turned away and went through the door.

Carla Denezzi bent down on her knees in the cold. With the angel for company, she uttered a silent prayer that all men and women, live or dead, should know peace.

CHAPTER 8

The night was black with no clipping of moon. Damiano stood alone in cold that made his ears ring, and his breath crackled against his face like a tiny fall of snow.

And he was afraid, though not of the cold. His staff stood braced before him, unfelt by frozen hands, and he whispered words he did not remember learning—unless he had heard them in sleep, from his father. With a prickle and thrill the young man intuited that his father had spoken these words at least once.

"*Sator arepo tenet operá rotas. Ades, Satan!*" he pronounced, but at the concluding word "*Dominus*" he choked and the word went unsaid.

The omission was meaningless, for a sheet of blackness disassociated itself from the night and flung Damiano into the air—or into the ground. The young man could not tell the difference, for both air and earth had gone suddenly impervious and malevolent. His limbs were stiff in an uncleanly paralysis, and Damiano had no breath to scream. He sailed through winds that were eddies of pain.

This was hell, he thought, and he had not needed an interview with the Devil to find it. He mouthed the words "O God!" not knowing what he said.

The darkness broke under an assault of noonday light. Damiano put his hand to his face and in wonder noticed that he was still on his feet, that his blind, sweeping passage had not disarranged the folds of his mantle.

Under his feet was rock, round and hollowed like a riverbed but colored carnelian. Around him curled huge tines of the stuff, taller than his head. In the distance rose a cliff wall, taller than the Grandfather itself, and within it an enormous arched opening, like a window. Beyond that . . .

With simple, terrible understanding, Damiano realized that the arch *was* a window and the cliff wall *was* a wall, and the rounded, fleshy rock he stood upon, miles above the ground, was an open hand. He swiveled so quickly he fell down, on a palm that was easily as hard as river rock.

The face of Raphael leaned down over him, beautiful, pure and clean-chiseled. It was the angel's face, but it was hot and ruddy, mountainous in size. "Mother of God!" yelped Damiano in terror.

The face instantly retreated. "Would Father Antonio appreciate such language?" it asked. "Common politeness itself forbids . . ."

The voice that spoke these words, though naturally enormous, was civilized in expression and modulated in tone. But still, there was something about it of the dry, abrasive sound of a shovel cutting through ashes, and it was not Raphael's voice at all.

Nor was the face quite as much like that of the archangel as Damiano had first supposed. The lean cheekbones arched out below the eyes in more aggressive fashion, perhaps more barbaric and perhaps also more interesting. Raphael's hair, though fair enough, was reduced to a childish flaxen next to the gold that curled fastidiously over this enormous head. It was a gold that deserved to be minted in coin.

Then Damiano remembered that Lucifer, too, had

begun as an archangel, and Damiano knew he was in the presence he had summoned. The witch sat on the Devil's palm, his staff across his thighs, toes pointed to the unimaginable ceiling, and he continued to stare.

The terrible eyes narrowed, as a man's eyes will narrow when he tries to focus on the form of an insect he has captured. "Well. What is the problem, my friend? Did you not expect that little voyage? Did you think I would come to you, when it is so much easier, and more fitting as well, to bring you to me?"

Damiano's ears were buzzing, and his head was filled with woolly numbness. He dared not open his mouth, for he had no idea what sounds would come out of it. Yet he spared a glance around him.

The view was endless, and the young man's vision was not, but he saw enough to convince him that he was in a room of some sort. Four flat walls, chalky white, supported hangings indistinguishably embroidered in red. There was an enormous expanse of polished, tile floor on which stood a table the size of a cathedral, supporting a bowl filled with tawny grapes. Four windows looked out in four directions, displaying respective cloudy vistas of blue sea, green fields, ice-bound rock, and featureless sand. Though these views were incompatible, and for the most part uninhabitable to man, as Damiano peered from one window to another he felt a keen longing to be in any of them, flying through the sweet, free air (flying? Why flying? Damiano had never in his life flown anywhere). In freedom, true freedom, under sunlight or shadow, answerable to no one, not even to . . .

"It is my audience chamber. A pleasant place, is it not? Merely to sit in it and breathe the air calls forth the best qualities in a man. And it is convenient to all places and times. I too have spent many hours gazing out at my dominions."

Damiano nodded absently, thinking that the attraction was more out the windows than in the room itself, where the air smelled flat, like a dead fire. He wondered if perhaps that was how Satan himself felt, and whether that was not the reason he spent hours staring out at the places where he was not. Also, if these vistas were like others the youth had seen, then they were a cheat, for once one had labored toward them, one invariably found one was still standing on soil that was similar in looks and feel to that of

home, breathing and rebreathing the cloud of one's own
breath. Damiano could understand if Satan felt that frustration when he gazed out his windows, for the great demon's
breath was particularly stale. In fact, for one brief instant
he felt he understood the Devil very well, but then that
moment passed.

Satan cleared his throat. "I think you requested an
audience, Dami?"

Hearing his name spoken, Damiano shivered uncontrollably. Delstrego would not have been so bad to hear,
though any evidence that the Devil knew one was unpleasant to the ears. To have Satan call him by his Christian
name would have been understandable, since most everyone in Partestrada called him Damiano, having known him
since a child. But to be called Dami, as Carla and as
Raphael called him Dami, by these lips that were only too
massive to be Raphael's, and in that scraped-ashen voice
. . . that was worse than having the Devil reprimand him
in Father Antonio's name.

Yet he planted his staff and climbed to his feet again.
"I did," he answered, his voice sounding unexpectedly
steady. "If you are Satan, that is."

The fair brow shot up in a gesture distractingly familiar.
"I am," whispered the gray voice, "Lucifer, the ruler of the
earth and of mankind. I heard you, and since I try to be
open and accessible to all my subjects, I have helped you
hither to me."

Damiano's gaze of confusion continued, and at last the
huge face flushed. The effect was like sunset on the
mountains. "You speak of audacity! You act as though you
don't believe I am who I say!" Fingers curled around the
young man, threatening to shut out the light.

Damiano recalled how Father Antonio had once said
that no man is as offended at doubt as is the habitual liar
who has for once told the truth. Though he stood in a
dread so thick as to be indistinguishable from despair, this
small observation comforted him. "I believe you, spirit. I
believe you because you look so much like the archangel
Raphael, whose face I have seen and whom I know to be
related to you. But still that paradox astounds me, that you
should look so much like an angel."

The once-highest of the archangels went redder than
beets, until his face had the look of flayed flesh. His fingers

curled around the tiny figure of gold and scarlet until it seemed he would crush it.

But Damiano stood braced, and the huge embrace halted, with a perfectly manicured thumbnail resting against the young man's throat. "There was," admitted Satan, "a litter of creatures spawned, with a superficial resemblance to me. Imitation, no doubt. But I am by far the greatest."

Damiano nodded, feeling the cold horny nail against his adam's apple. "I was told you were greater than they," he replied. "I only brought it up to explain why I was staring." He coughed, backed away from the thumbnail and felt the end of a hard finger between his shoulder blades.

Satan smiled, thereby destroying the last resemblance with Raphael. "Who," he crooned, "gave you such good information? One of my lieutenants on the earth, I presume. A murderer, or the pope at Avignon?"

Damiano glanced up sharply, "Raphael told me. He said you were always the greatest of the angels."

Rude laughter barked and boomed, till Damiano swayed on the palm of the Devil's hand, his own hands over his ears and eyes. "Humility!" roared the red face. "I love it!" Then, with whip-crack speed, it was sober. "And I am gratified to find a man without an exaggerated respect for that twittering crew."

Damiano stiffened and set his jaw. He had not come to get into an argument with the Devil, like the one he had been dragged into by General Pardo, but he was an Italian born and could not hear his friend so demeaned. Not by any man or devil. "Power is not everything, Great Lucifer," he stated. "I don't think it means anything, to Raphael. Not like music does. And though he may be less powerful than you are, he is still far above me."

Satan set his eyes on Damiano as a wolf might have set its teeth in his neck. He could neither move nor look away.

"He *is* far above you, boy, because he has made you believe it. Be aware that spirits are very subtle and they say nothing by chance.

"I have a certain reputation in that direction myself, Damiano, but I swear to you that I am forthrightness itself, compared with the spirits who bow to the Beginning."

"The Beginning?" echoed Damiano.

Satan sighed and his face knit into lines of pure philosophy. "All things, and spirits, came out of the Beginning. Exploded from It, you might say. It had no choice in the matter and would certainly have maintained us all as part of Itself, if It could have.

"But It could not, for freedom is as old as the Beginning, if not older. Ever since all of us, spirits and creatures alike, escaped and became ourselves, It has been trying to cozen us into returning, so It can consume us again. With that in mind It spread the tale that It transubstantiates into bread, to be consumed by man, so that man will feel less objection to the truth that It consumes man, like bread.

"To be dissolved into another! That is the antithesis of freedom."

It was God he was talking about, Damiano realized.

"In fact, Damiano, though I am the lord of the earth I am also the one apostle of freedom upon the earth, and those who serve me know the gifts of liberty, for there is nothing I will deny a man. I will not even deny him the intellectual pleasure derived from bowing at the alter of the Beginning, if that is his desire, though that Other does not extend such courtesy to me.

"In fact I have many who worship me in such part-time fashion, some of them worthy men in cardinal red. I . . ."

Damiano had lost the thread of Satan's conversation, for he was still trying to understand how freedom could be both natural and a gift. Perhaps his lack of attention was written in his face, for the Devil stopped in midsentence.

"But here now. You didn't come all this way to discuss histories, or to tell me that that fluttering limpid brother of mine knows his place. What do you want of me, Damiano Delstrego? What is your desire, my dear brother witch?"

Damiano filled his lungs with dry air, more deadly than fumes of sulfur. "A bargain," he announced.

"Of course. A bargain," echoed the red angel, and his smile held a languorous ennui. "Everyone wants a bargain from me. You'd think I were a tradesman, instead of only the inventor of trade." He dandled Damiano gently between his fingers, knocking him to his knees.

"All men lust after my bargains, little friend, though some pursue them harder. It seems to run in families, for you are not the first Delstrego with whom I have spoken . . ."

Damiano made no reply, though the blood in his heart congealed. Still he knew better than to trust the Devil concerning his father. Raphael had said to have hope, so he cast his eyes down at the immaculate ruddy palm.

"Bargains . . ." Satan ruminated, and he sat back in his gilded throne, which was the only chair in the room. "I am sempiternally bored with striking bargains with mortals. They never have anything interesting to ask, or anything worthwhile to give." He sighed like a gale in a cave.

"I think you want what I have to give," began Damiano, grimacing as he spoke, but the Devil cut him off.

"That comes second, little witch. First is the matter of what *you* want."

This was simple to say and not frightening. "I want peace," stated Damiano.

After a moment's pause, Satan grunted. "There are many avenues toward that goal, Damiano. I could build you a castle in a green valley where no man has ever set foot. Obedient demons would do your will and never say no to you. Succubi, too. Unrest is a product of your interaction with other mortals, believe me. With no human company, you would be sure to have peace.

"Alternately, I could provide you with one hundred years on the oil of the eastern poppy, with never a bad dream. That is peace, and poetry, too. I recommend it over my first proposal.

"Then I could make you my vassal over all Europe, of course. That is a popular request, since many men have come to the realization that power is freedom and freedom is happiness." Cold gray eyes regarded Damiano, eyes much larger than platters. "And what is happiness, but peace in action?

"You would make a comical emperor, Damiano Delstrego. You have a kind heart."

Damiano frowned and sat back on his heels. He struck the shoe of his staff against the devil's palm. "No. No, Satanas, I want peace, not for me, but for all the Piedmont. One hundred years without war."

Satan peered closely at the tiny thing in his hand. "With you as duke, of course?" he drawled.

Damiano shook his head. "I can't . . . I mean I thank you for your confidence in me, but my talents don't lie in that direction. Only once have I been able to unite and fire men's minds, and that time I . . . No, I don't want to pay that again. I am a man of the arts; an alchemist, a musician, maybe a poet, too, though I have not much experience in that, as yet."

At a thought his tongue thickened and he grew visibly paler. "Or at least these were the things I had planned to be." Then he flipped his sleeves and hair back and began afresh.

"With any suitable man as a duke. Or without a duke, as one grand republic with Partestrada as capital. Or eight little, quiet republics, with Partestrada as the largest."

"That is imp . . ." The Devil cleared his throat, and Damiano seemed to see a cloud of ash spread from his well-molded lips into the room. "Your love for your city does you credit, Damiano, but let's talk concretely. I can give you General Pardo's head on a pike."

Damiano had expected this offer. "That's no good. Pardo alone isn't the problem, for there will always be another wolf to raven the fold. I want a respite from wolves. I want peace and prosperity for the Piedmont."

"Before you said only peace, Damiano. That was bad enough, but now you've added prosperity."

Damiano squinted at the looming face. "I mean peace, but not the peace of devastation and pestilence, when all the people are dead. I mean a thriving peace."

"The head of Pardo plus the head of Paolo Denezzi." Damiano swallowed, abashed at how intimately the Devil had read his worst desires.

"No," he replied weakly.

". . . And I will burn down the convent of La Dolerosa at Bard before the month is out," concluded Satan. "That will change many things, my eager young lover, and you may return to your own tower with a beautiful bride."

Damiano's eyes stung, and his cheeks flushed, though nowhere so red as those on the elegant face of the Devil. "No." He was scarcely audible. "Do nothing to touch her."

The angry trembling of the great hand ran through Damiano and made his teeth vibrate.

"I find your bargaining to be rather of the take-it-or-leave-it variety, little witch," Satan rasped, and he laid his hand down on the table. Damiano stared, fascinated, at the pond-sized shallow bowl that he had thought to be filled with grapes. "You ask more from me than any man in a handful of centuries," snapped the beautiful red mouth. "What on earth or in hell do you have to give in return?"

Damiano blinked three times and then was certain that the objects in the bowl were fresh human heads. This knowledge, rather than frightening him, gave him a certain hopeless courage. "Myself," he said. "My life. My soul. You can have it now without waiting."

The next instant found him tumbling across the polished wood surface of the table, his staff tangling with his legs.

"Your soul? Damiano, why don't you try selling me this throne, or my own left hand?" As Satan leaned over the table Damiano felt the wood creak complaint and the air grow very hot. "Boy, don't you know what it means to be born a witch?"

Damiano lay flat on his back with his eyes closed. Panic brushed his face. "I know no man is born damned," he hissed. "Father Antonio has said it, and my heart tells me it is true!"

The deadly ire subsided into irony. "To be what they call damned is only to be free and to declare you are free, shaking your fist at brute authority. I will give a lot to free a man, Damiano, but you're right; I can't do it alone. Each man chooses his own 'damnation.' And you"—the fiery face turned away—"chose the black path to my door."

Damiano waited for flames to take him, but after ten seconds passed uneventfully, he opened his eyes.

He lay under the rim of the pottery bowl, which was the color of dried blood. One of the heads brimming over the edge stared down at him. The slack features were those of the captain of cavalry whom he had seen brained by the butcher's hammer not one day ago. That spotted thing behind it: was that a cow's head? Damiano closed his eyes again. He became aware the Devil was speaking.

"You are a fool, and you have wasted my time, boy. But as you are a witch and a freethinker and so have some call on me, I will be very generous. I propose a bargain that will almost exactly suit your needs.

"I will arrange what you call peace for Partestrada. Not the entire Piedmont, mind you, and not for one hundred years, but just for the lives of the present inhabitants. You will be the mayor—simply because you are the only man who will be able to understand your perverse motivations in this matter. Partestrada will happen to lie outside every path of conquest from Italy, France, and the north. Harvests will be adequate. Not ample, perhaps, but adequate. No plague will touch the city. Is that not a good approximation of peace?"

Damiano gazed up fixedly, as though engaged in colloquy with the head of the dead captain. "Possibly. What do you want for it, if my soul is of no value?"

Satan chewed his lower lip and peered out his southern window at endless sand. "I?" He spoke slowly, dreaming. "I, like you, am an altruist. I ask nothing for myself. But the situation imposes its own restraints.

"You are right, little witch, in supposing that the town of Partestrada contains the seeds of greatness. Its location on the Dora Baltea, three quarters of the way between Turin and Aosta . . . its salubrious climate, nurturing grapes yet in the shadows of the Alps . . .

"But I tell you that fifty years of unexceptional peace will kill Partestrada. She will fade and mummify, and her young men depart for Milan and Turin, violent cities of more promise."

Damiano sat up. "That isn't the way it has to be."

The Devil raised one eyebrow in the familiar gesture of Raphael. "Let me finish, please. Not only will Partestrada fade and be forgotten, Damiano, but you yourself. All you have done and dreamed. The alchemical discoveries you are destined to make, the music that even now your unfulfilled love is awakening in your bosom, all your wisdom, your easy gift of friendship, your very name and your family name and your house and the place where your house once stood and your face . . .

"All will be lost and forgotten. In a century you will be a man who might never have existed from a city with a forgotten name."

Damiano put his head between his knees. "No!" he said, and repeated it stubbornly, his voice shaking in his throat. "No. That's not the only way to get peace for my city."

The Devil seemed to shrug. "It's what I offer," he replied. "I can see no other way. Greatness, in man or nation, is incompatible with that emptiness that you call peace."

Damiano rose slowly to his feet, using the edge of the
bowl of heads for support. "You can *see* no other way?
Raphael can't see into the future. He says no created being
can . . ."

Harsh laughter boomed out, along with the odor of a
wet fire. "Raphael? My little brother has a long history of
confusing dare not with cannot!

"Believe me or doubt me, boy, but you came here to
bargain. This is my offer, and if you were the . . . the
saint you seem to be, you would snap it up. Even Raphael
couldn't fault such a bargain; it reeks of yielding resignation. *And* humility. What do you say, little witch? Will
you take it?"

"No," answered Damiano. "The more I talk to you the
more I believe in Partestrada. Decay is not the only way to
peace!"

The Devil snorted in jovial contempt. "Fine words! But
you are a hypocrite, after all," he said. He smiled as though
he had just won a hand at cards. "Or a coward. Either way,
you're no better than I thought!"

Then the bitter wind took Damiano again and flung him
at the wall.

CHAPTER 9

Damiano spent the next morning lying motionless on a
pallet on the floor of the cabinetmaker's house, Macchiata
curled beside him. When he woke, his interview with the
Devil might have been a dream, except that his knees were
bruised from falling on that stony red hand and his nostrils
were caked with ash.

At intervals during the morning, the dog left Damiano,
only to return and find her master as dull as before. At last
she inserted her damp nose between Damiano's stubbly
chin and his neck.

"Master," she began, her voice muffled by the contact,
"Master, are you sick?"

"No, little dear," he answered slowly. "I just want to
stop the sun for a while." Then, remembering Macchiata's

literal mind, he amended his statement. "I needed time to think."

The dog sat placidly beside him, her brown eyes a few inches from his. As he watched, a flea crawled out from behind her ear and disappeared among the white hairs of Macchiata's muzzle. "And did you think?" she asked. "I mean, are you done thinking? What *did* you think?"

Wrestling with the heavy felt blanket, Damiano turned onto his back. "I think . . . there's got to be another way. For both my city and myself."

"I'm sure there is," said Macchiata staunchly, "if you think so." And she scratched the side of her face with the stubby nails of her back foot.

It didn't bother Damiano that the dog should express her agreement with him without knowing the subject matter of that agreement; he was as used to Macchiata's loyal ignorance as he was to Raphael's smile.

"I need help," he continued, thoughtfully glowering at the black beams of the ceiling. "I need advice."

"Certainly." She sat, ears pricked, and waited.

Damiano bent his head toward her, and a snort of laughter escaped him. "I meant—and I hope you will not be offended, Macchiata—from someone wiser than I."

The dog grinned lazily, and her tongue slid out the side. "Not at all, Master. I know I am only four years old, whereas you are one and twenty. But where are you to find one greater than you are—that I don't know."

Damiano's grin matched hers. The dog's ludicrous flattery never failed to amuse him, because he knew it was sincere. He sat up, throwing the weight of covers aside. Beneath the blankets he was wearing his ermine mantle and nothing else at all. Limberly he twisted right and left over the floorboards, fishing for his tunic and trousers among the tangles of cloth.

"Unless it's Raphael, Master. He must be very wise, because he never gets upset. Perhaps he is even wiser than you."

"Perhaps," Damiano agreed, and his grin grew rueful. "But I know his advice in any case; it is not of the world, as he is not, and unfortunately, our difficulty is very worldly. I can't sit back and pray.

"Besides, if the archangel discovered what I did last night, likely he would never speak to me again."

"Last night when I was asleep, Master? What did you do?"

"I had a chat with the Devil, little dear. And he threw me out."

Macchiata thought. "Is the Devil wiser than you? Did you go to him for advice?"

Damiano pulled his trousers up, wondering how many of Macchiata's fleas were hiding in them, and how many of his own. "I guess I did—go to him for advice. But that doesn't mean I have to take it."

He knelt to fold the blanket. His knees were very sore. "You know, little dear, it feels good to be thrown out by the Devil. Not as good, perhaps, as being welcomed in by the Father himself, but then, after the latter experience one is not usually walking the green earth. I think I know what I shall do next."

"What *we* shall do next, you mean," replied Macchiata, standing unconcernedly in the middle of the blanket her master was attempting to fold.

"What we shall do, then. We are going to take a trip. A very pleasant trip into a beautiful land. Just the two of us."

Macchiata cocked her head to one side, and the tip of her tail began to wag. Slowly the wag gained both speed and mass, until her body was still only from the shoulders forward.

"To Provence, Master, as you said last week?"

Damiano threw the blanket into the corner and stood. He thrust his head out the single small window the room possessed and took a chestful of clean air. "No. Last week I was dreaming childish dreams. I was dreaming of my own happiness. But still, where we are going is more beautiful than Provence. We are going to Lombardy, little dear. To find the witch my father said was the most powerful in all the Italies: Saara the Fenwoman, whose dominion . . ." and then his tongue clove to the roof of his mouth, as he remembered where last he had heard the word "dominion." "Whose power is over both snow and sunlight. She *must* help us.

"—For I don't know anyone else to ask."

The parting with Carla Denezzi was hard. It seemed to Damiano he had never known how he loved her until she was lost to him. If he had been more forward . . . but then he had not suspected there would be a limit to their time together, and feelings, like fruit, ripen slowly in the high air.

Damiano bought the black gelding from Paolo Denezzi, who was more than willing to help Damiano on his way. The last of his coin was spent on food and warmer bedding than even his closet at home had provided. Was General Pardo now storing *his* garb in the Delstrego wardrobe? It was quite possible, since the tower was nearly the best house in Partestrada, and certainly the most defendable.

Now that Damiano stopped to think about it, the general would be running quite a risk if he did plant himself in Damiano's house. A man could come to harm, nosing about in the Delstrego tower, even though Damiano had quenched the fires in the workroom before leaving. There were still the chemicals, and the elementals . . . Damiano entertained the possibilities. A problem or two would be solved if Pardo exploded along with a sealed retort. But it was an idle notion: there was nothing the witch could do at this distance to encourage an explosion, and besides, he did not know for sure that Pardo was staying in his house.

Damiano rode back along the road south out of Aosta. He rode bareback because that was most easy for him. Guillermo Delstrego had never kept a horse; animals hadn't liked him, and he had returned the feeling.

Or perhaps it had happened the other way around. In either case, Damiano had not learned to ride along with the other boys of family in Partestrada. He had not learned most things along with the other boys, but he had learned quite a few things by himself, and among them was bareback riding.

And the horse liked him much better, now that Damiano's madness had burned itself out. The gelding stepped easily down the packed surface of the road, where a warm day had thawed the brown ice and hollowed it, making sheets brittle and thin like isinglass. Shod hooves ground the stuff into slush.

Macchiata pattered about, behind, before, and beneath, interfering in a hundred ways with the patient steed's walking. Occasionally the horse put its head to the ground or thrust its lippy muzzle into a crack of the rock wall, in the forlorn hope of grass. Damiano did not correct it because he had no rein on the animal, and also because he had not the heart.

They passed the spot where Damiano had first been hailed by Pardo's captain and then the bend in the road where Damiano had destroyed the soldiers with his memories of a butchered cow. Finally they passed beside the small crevasse where fifty-two men were buried beneath snow and branches. For Damiano this journey was another form of the stations of the cross. He said nothing, nor did Macchiata, though her nose had a long memory of its own.

The horse, who had memory but no words, rolled its eyes, and the hide over its withers twitched.

A mile south of this point, as Damiano stopped to take a pull of wine from the bag at his left side he heard a quick clatter of hooves. With his heel he prodded the horse to the side of the road and called Macchiata to stand beneath. Then he pulled his staff out from his bedroll and spoke the spell; it came easily, for he was both rested and in practice.

When the goatherd passed with his tiny flock, he did not notice the prints of shod hooves that led onto the smooth snow of the shoulder of the road and then stopped abruptly. The goats were more observant. They stared with their crazy yellow eyes, pupils rectangular as money boxes, and the witch didn't know whether they could see him or whether they knew he was there by other means.

When almost all had passed, one weatherworn buck halted before the horse, examined them sagaciously and urinated into his own beard. Macchiata growled at the insult. The goat presented its horns.

"Don't get involved," hissed Damiano helplessly from above. At that moment the goatherd stalked over, and with his supple leather whip, sent his charge bawling up the road.

"Well," said Damiano, when they were alone again. "It might have been soldiers."

By midafternoon Damiano had passed the fork in the road where the stone hut stood abandoned and empty, passed by the shoulder hills that concealed the dead village of Sous Pont Saint Martin, and left behind the footpath where the bones and raw hide of a cow had been tossed to rot in the first thaw. Thus all the tragic histories of this past week were behind him.

The sky was streaked with fairy clouds of ice that scattered the sunlight. He felt warm under his furs, warm and sleepy. "Let's start again, little dear," he murmured to Macchiata. "No more of the Devil. I went wrong somewhere—I don't know where, exactly, and I have no one to ask, but it doesn't matter. Maybe Saara can tell me, eh? She's been round awhile and must have seen much of life, traveling from the Fenland down to Italy."

He waited for an answer, because Macchiata always replied to his questions, even the rhetorical ones. After a few seconds of silence, he looked around, then leaned over to peer under the horse's belly.

"Macchiata?"

When was the last time he had heard from the dog? Sighing, Damiano slid to the ground.

To the left of the road rose hills, more rounded than the peaks visible from the crossroads, pocketed with green-black growths of pine. To his right the land hollowed out, and standing water had turned to sheets of ice. He squinted at the bright white road behind him.

A tiny speck of russet was bobbling in the distance. It became recognizable, and Damiano relaxed, leaning one arm over the black horse's back. As Macchiata galloped she rolled like a small but heavy-laden ship, and her tongue lolled in desperate manner.

"Why didn't you tell me you couldn't keep up?" asked Damiano. Macchiata looked up at him, pulled in her tongue, and then all four of her bandy legs gave at once. As she hit the packed snow of the road her jaws clashed resoundingly. Her inadequate little tail lay flat out behind.

She was hot as a bed warmer when Damiano scooped her up. "That's terrible, Macchiata. Your pride might have gotten you lost! Now lie there a minute and don't move." As he spoke he deposited her across the withers of the horse, where she lay as limply as the goatskin of wine. Damiano leaped up next to her.

"This poor horse," he began, as he clucked the gelding to a walk. "Two riders, two bags, a bedroll, a wineskin, my staff, and the lute besides. It's lucky for him neither of us weighs too much!"

The dog only groaned.

"Do you wonder," asked Damiano, when a few minutes had passed, "why I should care about Partestrada so much? To go running hither and thither, fighting battles in the snow?"

"No," answered Macchiata, and she clambered precariously to her feet on the horse's back, her blunt nails digging in for grip. Damiano had barely time to grab her middle before the twitch of the black hide sent her slipping. He sat her on her tail before him, one arm holding her around the middle. Her back legs lolled in the air.

"No, Master. Partestrada is our home."

"But some might question whether she is worth it. After all, Partestrada isn't the largest city in the area, and she hasn't produced any great poets or philosophers—yet."

"Partestrada is our home," repeated the dog, as though there was nothing more to be said.

But Damiano was not listening. "I think . . . it may be the fruit vendors that make it so special. The way they push their vans down the alleys bawling, 'rubies, rubies, red rubies' when all the world knows they have only apples for sale. Or it may be the way the sun seems to roll along the crest of the mountains at mid-winter, and the dawn and twilight colors last half the day.

"Of course, it could be our wool, because the sheep get to stay cool both winter and summer and yet get enough to eat. We all get enough to eat, as a matter of fact, unlike cities like Florence, where bread might as well be wrapped in gold leaf, for what it costs, and I'm told a man may have a house of marble and yet eat bread laced with sawdust and bran.

"Or it may be the fact that we make our own wine, though frankly, Macchiata, it isn't good wine—not made from the grapes they use in the south." He slapped the gurgling sack smartly.

"And then again, little dear, though they make fun of us Piedmontese because we are so mixed up between France and the Italies, I think this mixedness makes us flexible. No one is as proud as an illiterate Tuscan peasant, though he has naught to be proud of except a field of sunbaked clay! A man with a Lombard father and a Rhenish mother-in-law must develop a sense of humor—to survive.

"But all in all, I think it is the vendors."

"I'm mixed," introjected Macchiata. "My mother is a ratter and my father . . . I don't know, exactly."

"Certainly! And see how fortunate you are in that? Strong, enduring, and, though you are not the largest dog in the Piedmont, fierce enough to put three highwaymen to flight." He squeezed Macchiata till her breath squeaked out her nose.

Then Damiano's dark eyes grew somber and earnest. "Though I know that the highest love asks nothing, still I would like . . . little dear, I would like Partestrada to know me before I die. To know how I have cared."

"We know." Macchiata squirmed around to lick her master's bony hand. "All your friends know."

Damiano flinched, for he had just been reflecting that, although he was very friendly, he had not many friends.

By the early dusk they had reached a region of upland hills similar to those of home. Grass and wild corn stood exposed in sodden patches, and the steady north wind had bent the stalks of the corn until they trailed the ground like willow. Here the road widened. Damiano spied a shape trudging through the distant, soggy fields, bent almost double beneath a load of faggots. Whether this was man or woman or child he could not tell, and he did not hail the creature, for it was enough to know there were people in the world who had nothing to do with war.

"The road tends south," he remarked to the dog, who sat awkwardly and stiffly before him. "We've climbed almost out of the snow."

Macchiata snuffed. "There are too many mountains, Master. And they are too high."

Damiano laughed. "We barely touched them, little dear. The Alps continue northward, far beyond the most distant peaks we could see, where burghers perch their houses in valleys higher than the tops of our hills, and they speak not only French and Italian, but German as well. In the west the mountains continue into France, while in the east . . ."

"I'm tired," said Macchiata.

He hugged her in quick contrition. "I'm sorry, Macchiata. Both you and the horse deserve a rest. But I wanted to leave memories behind.

"And we've done so, for I don't know where we are at all. Let's find some brush out of the wind and make a real camp; it'll be our first!"

Damiano snarled pine boughs into the living branches of a berry bush, and over this he flung a length of smelly oilcloth. He wove more of the slender, resinous evergreen as a mat over the half-frozen earth. He gathered a tinder of dry oats and sparked it between his cupped hands. The fire he nurtured was more suitable for a harvest bonfire than for the night's camp of a single traveler, but Macchiata appreciated it, and even the black horse sidled in toward the warmth.

He picked through his sizable store of cheese, bread, dried meat, fruit, and fish. He could afford to be choosy. He picked out an apple, pink and withered like an old woman's cheek, a hard Romano, and a strip of salted pork. He shredded a bite of the pork and found himself controlling his stomach with effort.

"Gah! I can't eat flesh! I shouldn't even try." He flung the entire strip to Macchiata, who looked quite sorry for him as she gulped it.

"Monks survive without it," mumbled Damiano. "Or they are supposed to. And after all, how is my life different from a monk's? I have no money, no home, no family . . . and no mistress."

"You have me." The dog's tail punctuated her statement.

Her master blinked. "True, Macchiata, and that's quite a bit. Remind me again if I forget." He divided the cheese in two.

After dinner, Damiano took out his lute and examined it by firelight. The finish had gone milky over the inlay of the back, but that always happened in the dampness. A good dry day would cure it. All the strings were sound. He plucked a sad melody he had made up himself a year since.

He was out of practice and his fingers stumbled.

"This won't do," he said to the basking dog. "It is a musician's duty to find time daily for his instrument."

"You've been busy." Macchiata yawned, already half asleep.

"I'm always busy," answered Damiano. "That's no excuse." And he practiced the modes till his own yawns screwed his eyes shut.

The weather in and around the Alps is unpredictable, and it tends toward small pockets of virulence. In the middle of the night the sky assaulted the travelers with hail that spat in the fire and drove the gelding whinnying out of sleep.

"Dominus Deus!" grumbled the witch. "One thing after another!" He hadn't the heart to resist as the horse bent its legs and hunkered into the lean-to, though neither horse nor shelter had been constructed with such an end in mind.

Soon the hail turned to sleet, and the fire died of the insult. The framework of branches and cloth lost its mooring and fell on the horse's back, which Damiano didn't mind as long as the beast didn't move, but the corner of Damiano's mantle was soaked.

"After last night we must be very good friends, eh, Festilligambe?" Damiano said to the horse, fixing it with soft brown eyes much like its own. (*Festilligambe* means *sticklegs* in Italian.) "I think I felt every one of those big feet of yours against my back. And with the grass you've been grabbing by the road, your digestion is none too good! So you get us to the vales of Lombardy the quickest way you know." The gelding nodded as though it were about to speak.

And given enough time alone with Damiano, it might have. But Lombardy could not be far away, for the travelers were entering more populous country, leaving the realm of white winter behind.

That swath of broken soil to the left, for instance, lying on the slope of a hill like a tossed blanket. It had known recent tillage. And unless Damiano's eyes were failing him (a distinct possibility), ahead of them, at a hump of the winding road, was a house.

It was a house, but it was the merest hovel, with a thatched roof rotted black in places and walls built of mud as much as stone. Two toddling children peeped out the door at the passage of the magnificent stranger and his dog. They were scantily clad for the weather, and one was barefoot. Damiano brought Festilligambe to a halt and regarded them with the attention he reserved for small wild things. There was a stir in the darkness of the hut, and a girl appeared behind the children. Tawny-haired and plump she was, with a face as round and innocent as a dirty flower. Her dress was patched gray wool, and it was pulled off one shoulder. In her arms she held an infant that she was nursing from one bare, ample breast.

Though women had to nurse their children and did it how and as they might, still Damiano sat abashed before so much revealed femininity. This girl had hair like Carla's. And these blue eyes that stared shyly into his were the eyes of a May bunny: the eyes of a child. She was much younger than he.

Before the silence had time to become unbearable, Damiano heard Macchiata growl. Startled, he glanced around to see a lean figure running full tilt across the bare field toward him. The girl noticed at the same time and took a single step back into the hut. The children scampered right and left and were gone.

The peasant was only as tall as Damiano but much wider. He wore nothing but his long woolen shirt and the rags on his feet. He, too, was very young, but he wore at his belt a knife with a blade as long as a man's forearm. He placed himself between the black horse and the door and, still panting from exertion, looked Damiano up and down.

"The Monsignore desires?" he asked, in a patois so thick even Damiano had trouble understanding.

"Eh? Well," replied the witch from horseback, "we request of the other Monsignore to tell us if we will find a town up ahead."

"We are not an hour from San Gabriele," answered the peasant reluctantly. Then, as Damiano moved to go, he added, "The Monsignore does not wear a sword?"

Damiano turned and glowered at the man. "No. I have no need for one. My pure heart protects me." He clucked the horse to a canter, thinking with some satisfaction that his virginity must not be perceptible to the casual observer.

San Gabriele. That was a good sign. Though Gabriel was not Raphael, he was still an angel.

"I didn't know that," said Macchiata, huffing along at his left side, "—that you don't need a sword because your pure heart protects you. I thought you didn't carry one because it got in the way of your staff."

The rider sighed. "That was a joke, Macchiata. The real reason I don't wear a sword is that if I wore one, I would eventually have to use it. That is the way with weapons. Besides, my big flute, here," he said, patting the stick of black wood, "is a hundred times more useful."

The surly peasant hadn't lied; they were approaching habitation. More sheds and hovels sprang up among the rough and borderless fields. On their left they passed the rickety structure of an irrigation pump, an affair of spokes and buckets abandoned for the winter. Next they overtook a goat cart, drawn by a rotund nanny and filled with baskets of squawking geese. Damiano gave the gawky lad who led the boat a pleasant salute.

Macchiata snorted and snuffled in pleasant anticipation, and soon Damiano's nose, which was more acute than that of an ordinary man (though not of canine quality), picked up the odors of dung and garlic.

The town of San Gabriele had been built in a dry scoop in the hills, forty feet above the highway. The rutted road that led into town was littered with wains, carts, and barrows; the oxen that had pulled the wains wandered hobbled in the ploughed fields at either side of the road, still keeping to their pairs. With an outsize thrill Damiano realized that it was market day in San Gabriele. He dismounted and led Festilligambe up the incline, one hand holding to the gelding's glossy mane.

The village boasted two strong gateposts of stone, but these supported no gates, nor were they flanked by walls of any sort. Indeed, to the left of the left-hand post grew an oak of enormous width and therefore age. This seemed to indicate that the walls of San Gabriele had fallen centuries before, if they had ever been built. Damiano passed beneath the bare, gnarled arms of the tree.

Here was life again. Stalls flanked the street far beyond the confines of the town proper, displaying woolens and wickerwork and brilliant dried peppers. The first man he saw wore homespun, and the second a robe of otter. Seven bleating ewes were driven down the main street, dodging past a man in motley who balanced a wine bottle on his nose.

Damiano hadn't known that he was starving for the sight of bright-dyed bolts of cloth and piled winter marrows, for the chatter of well-to-do peasants and the howls of the beggars. Macchiata, too, whined with an indefinable longing and thumped her tail against her master's leg.

"Wait a bit, little dear," whispered the young man, and he led the horse off the path and over the stubble of the field. "I know the air is intoxicating, but we can't have noble Festilligambe here eating the apples off some fellow's cart."

The hoed field was bordered with a paling of poplar trees. Damiano marched toward them, the horse stepping carefully behind. Beside the gray trunks he stopped and delved into his pack.

"Here," he said, dropping his still-folded oilcloth to the ground. On the square he spilled a quantity of oats. "Can I trust you to stay here and not get into trouble until I return?"

The eyes, ears, nose, and tail of the beast replied in unison that he could not. Damiano sighed.

"Then, as I have nothing for a tether, it's a binding spell," he announced. "And that will probably frighten you into hysterics. As well as tiring me unnecessarily."

The tall horse conceded. It lipped Damiano's hair. "Good then. Trust is best. And, Macchiata—will you guard this gear until I return from the fair?"

Macchiata stared at him, stricken. Her head sank and her wormy tail crawled between her legs. "Oh, well," Damiano said. "All right, then. I'll carry it."

Piece by piece he flung over his back the saddlebags, the wineskin, the sack of food, and the lute. Under each arm he stuffed a roll of blankets, out from one of which poked the silver head of his staff. Thus encumbered, Damiano staggered back across the field and into the town of San Gabriele.

A market is no fun for a penniless man. Damiano discovered this with surprise, for he was unused to being penniless.

There was blown glassware, both clear and in colors, some of it flawless and rounded perfect for alchemical use. Damiano was considering buying a lovely open tube, long as one's arm and thin as a soap bubble, when he realized he could not pay for it, could not transport it, and had no home in which to keep it. And there was a hat of golden marten that nearly matched the Delstrego colors. As Damiano hadn't a hat, he felt he rather deserved this one.

But worst of all were the pastries, dyed gold with saffron, blue with heliotrope, purple with amaranth, or green with parsley. There were little ones in the shapes of fish, and large ones square like castles. Some were filled with honey and some with quails. The odor of butter bubbling through wheat nearly drove Damiano to his bruised knees. Macchiata, whom he had controlled by prisoning her between his legs, whimpered with an agonized longing. He shooed her away.

"I'm sorry, little dear, but we have no money."

She licked her hairy lips. "Maybe the man will give us some anyway, because we're hungry."

Damiano snorted. "Not likely. Besides, we're not really hungry. We ate not four hours ago—cheese and bread. We just want what smells good." The dog whimpered agreement.

They passed a juggler, who had a chair teetering upon his cap of bells, and six zucchinis describing a complex orbit between the poles of his hands. Damiano regarded the man with respect, especially when he noticed the wooden bowl in front of the performer, half-filled with copper.

Damiano leaned against the white, warm wall of a stable. "We don't belong here," he whispered to the dog. "We can't eat, drink, or sleep at the inn, presuming there is one in this little place. We should just be on our way."

"Oh, no, Master," Macchiata crooned. "I'm tired, and Festilligambe is tired, and in all this crowd someone will surely drop something.

"I'll share it all with you, no matter how big or little," she concluded. Smiling ruefully, Damiano slung off his burdens and rested them against the wall.

"And Damiano's tired, too," he admitted. "Though he shouldn't be, with a long journey yet to go." He slid down the white stucco, squatting on his heels. "Still, I'd be willing to scrabble with you for the tail of one of those little wheaten fishes, even if it had dropped on the ground."

A shadow fell upon Damiano, and he found himself peering up at an urchin of indeterminate age and with the fair coloring of most of Northern Italy, topped by fox-colored hair. Damiano greeted him with a friendly flash of teeth.

The boy hesitated in response. Possibly he was deciding whether to use the familiar or the polite on this well-dressed stranger who was hunkering against the wall.

"Did that dog talk?" the boy inquired suspiciously.

Damiano nodded. "But she rarely talks to strangers." The child was wearing a grown man's woolen shirt, which hung so long over his legs he was covered as closely as a woman. He sat down two feet from Macchiata and subjected her to scrutiny. The ugly white dog returned the favor, and her neck hairs bristled.

"'T'sokay, dog," said the boy, scowling fiercely. "I like you."

Macchiata's anger subsided into confusion. She licked her already-wet nose.

"What'r you doing here, mister? You don't live in San Gabriele, and you aren't selling or buying anything."

Damiano regarded the ragged boy more closely. "How do you know I'm not selling or buying?"

The youngster produced a true Italian shrug: one that used the eyebrows as much as the shoulders. "I been watching you. I know you don't buy anything, and you don't have anything anybody'd want to buy. So I guess you're just sitting there wishing you had two sous to scrape together."

His amusement at the boy's perception sparked both Damiano's smile and his confidence. "You are quite right, my young observer. Actually, I am of a sanguine temperament, so I was trying to think of a scheme by which I could make two sous to scrape together, or more exactly, to buy a buttered wheaten fish."

The child thumped his wiry buttocks on the ground next to Damiano. "I've been there," he said, nodding sagely. "I've been there. Why not have the dog talk? She don't have to quote Dante, or anything. Just to have her answer would bring in real silver."

Macchiata wilted visibly. She hid her nose behind her master's heel. He stroked her side.

"Macchiata is many things," he stated. "She is a ratter, an alchemist's assistant, a great traveler, and the friend of angels. You might not believe it to look at her, but she saved my life not a week ago, vanquishing three brigands who were bent on murder! But whatever she is, she is not a public performer."

The boy listened to this paean with his head cocked, as though to say whether he believed or not was his own business. "But you, mister, are a man of quality, by your clothes and also by the way you talk. Surely you have something the people want—if not a golden ring, then at least a rare skill or two."

Damiano's glance slid from the soiled small face to the road. "I have no gold rings, unfortunately. But I do have certain abilities. I can assay gold—with the proper equipment. And I can treat illness in men and animals—but again, not without medicines. I can clear the evil from bad wells and open locks that are stuck and find lost jewelry and cows"—Damiano's voice caught unexpectedly— "and cows."

"I can do many things, little friend. But I am used to having clients come to my house and request me to do them. I have never learned to . . . promote myself."

He watched the scorn on the boy's face turn to outright disbelief. "I speak the truth, philosopher. Watch—I can make myself disappear." Damiano nudged his left hand into the bedroll until his fingers touched the shoe of his staff. In a moment, he was not there.

In another moment, he was. "Stop! My friend and adviser! Don't go; I promise I won't do it again." The boy froze two steps into his flight. "You *can* disappear! You're a witch!"

Mildly, Damiano admitted to it. "Yes, I am a witch, among other things. But I'm not a street-corner sorcerer. I lived in Partestrada in a decent tower my grandfather built. There was occupation there, and it kept me comfortable. But Partestrada—or perhaps you have heard?"

The boy nodded and spat into the street. "Has changed hands. Thank Gabriele that his town is too small and too high in the hills to interest Pardo and his free company."

Damiano peered bleakly down the street, with its babble and smell. "You can never be certain of that. But as I was saying, I don't brew love-charms, and I don't engage in cursing. What effects I can produce tend to terrify people, rather than amuse them. Yet this little lady and myself have a strong desire for hot pastries. What shall I do?"

Then Damiano's eyes narrowed. "Perhaps, with effort, I could float six zucchinis in the air and pretend to be juggling them, but that smacks of . . ."

"What's this?" the youngster interrupted casually, knocking one knuckle against the glossy rounded back of the lute. "Can you play it?"

"The lute," said Damiano, stunned by the obvious.

"Yes. I can play it. But I've never played for money. I don't know if I can."

The boy shrugged again. "The people here aren't very critical. But then, neither are they very generous. You can only try."

Damiano took the instrument onto his lap and tuned it. "Music for money," he murmured. "If you knew my teacher, philosopher . . ."

The little *liuto* was true-toned and clear. The boy leaned forward at the first notes. "Maybe I do. I know all the musicians who come through. And the acrobats, too. What's his name?"

"Raphael," answered Damiano shortly, for he was engaged in salting the melody with counterpoint, and he was not used to talking and playing together.

"Nope. Don't know him."

CHAPTER 10

The fingerboard was cold and slick beneath his fingers as his hand spidered its way through the melodies. He was not so out of practice as he had thought, and the familiar patterns came to him like old friends greeted in a strange place.

The pale winter sun seemed warm to a man who had spent the last week trudging through snow. He stretched his legs in front of him, in the hope that his boots might dry. Marketers passed by, their feet smacking through patches of mud. A matron of middle years stepped over Damiano's legs; her skirts dragged against his knees.

"Pinch that thing!" cried the redhead of San Gabriele, with the authority of a musical expert. "Let the whole town hear it!"

Damiano was no performer, or he had not thought he was, but he was well taught. He pinched the little lute, and at least a reasonable portion of the town could hear. All the old tunes—the simple, conservative airs and dances that would not have offended even dirty Marco—he played them all and he played them again.

"Louder!" cried his single listener. Damiano smiled thinly.

"This is a lute, not a bagpipe," he grumbled, but he obeyed. When he glanced up, the ragamuffin child was dancing a gavotte. No one had ever danced to his music before—not even Macchiata. His own booted toes were tapping together.

"Where's your hat?" A tall young woman loomed over him.

Red hair, a color not too rare in the more northern Italies, seemed to run in San Gabriele, for this one had hair like copper wire that hung in spiral curls down her back. Her green dress stretched tautly over her bosom, and the curve of her hips was emphasized by a belt of amber, ending in a tiny crucifix that swayed back and forth in front of Damiano's eyes. "How do you expect to make money without putting a hat out in front of you?"

Damiano stared at the crucifix, enthralled by its terribly inappropriate motions. "If I put out a hat, Signorina," he said haltingly, "will you drop a coin in it?"

She giggled as though he had said something witty. "I'm a poor woman, Signore. By your appearance, you ought to be dropping your coins into my bowl instead!"

Damiano's face flushed, and even the palms of his hands turned pink. But though his fingers stumbled, he did not lose the beat. "Fortune is fickle, beautiful lady, and yesterday's velvet purse hangs empty. Fortune is also jealous of beauty, and she uses time as her claw." He came down hard on the last downbeat of the dance and damped all the strings. His dark eyes flashed as he glanced up at the wanton. "Take care, Signorina." She stepped back, swaying, for real wit was an article she was not used to, especially on so serious a subject. Yet she lifted her chin disdainfully.

"Seminarians do not usually play the lute on street corners, black eyes."

Damiano shrugged. "I'm no more a seminarian than you are a nun, bold lady with eyes of green." Those green eyes dragged a smile from him, almost against his will.

She smirked at the wall over his head. "Then you're very little of the seminarian indeed," she said airily.

The urchin, who had stood unnoticed, following this conversation, now strode forward. "Enough! Enough,

Evienne—you get in the way of paying customers. This man has a living to make, and he's not your sort of fellow at all. Go your way . . ." And he put one grubby hand unceremoniously against the small of her back and attempted to propel her along the street. With a scowl she slapped his hand away. "You touch me, Gaspare, and you will be floating in a well before morning!"

The youngster showed his teeth to her belligerence. "Yes? You'll stab me with your hairpin while I sleep, maybe? But that would do you no good, nor me either. And this gentleman would still not be your sort of fellow at all!"

Then he continued in more civilized tones. "Be reasonable, Evienne. Would you like me to get in between you and your work? To walk beside you when you are so beautifully displaying your wares, as though I were a jealous lover . . ."

"You, Gaspare? Everyone in this stinking village knows better than that!" With a toss of her head and a final wild swing of the crucifix, Evienne stalked away. Damiano watched her progress along the street and then stared with no great gratitude at the dirty face of his deliverer.

The boy made a flat, emphatic gesture of the hand. "That one's no good," he stated. "No good at all. You'll get nothing from her."

"I didn't want anything from her," Damiano answered quietly, hoping it was the truth.

Gaspare's eyes narrowed. "I mean, she won't even sleep with you; she's that mercenary. She goes from town to town on market days, because San Gabriele's too small to support a full-time whore."

Damiano's ears were prickling like sunburn. "Still, she was correct in what she said." He leaned sideways and shoved one hand into a leather pack, where he rummaged blindly. "We need a hat. Or this . . ." and he pulled out the wooden soup bowl that was both plate and cup for his travels. As he set it before him he stared down at his boots, for he was proud and had never before had to ask for money.

He played the old pieces through one more time, listening to young Gaspare spin and cavort before him, in the steps of the bransle and the lascivious saraband. Damiano's right hand was becoming looser minute by minute. The movement felt sure and practiced, and the sun above was yellow. Damiano swept into the French music—the music of contrasting lines.

The thump and patter of feet was stilled, but the musician didn't raise his head. He was lost in the intricacies of the many-parted music, and the rhythms were leading him as they never had before. As he played he mumbled and hissed to himself, wordless encouragement. But he was beyond the need for encouragement now, and if Gaspare called out to him, Damiano did not hear.

Raphael—Raphael should hear this one day, for it was the fruit of all his teaching. But no—placed before his angelic teacher, Damiano knew he would stammer and halt once more, whispering the strings as timidly as a young girl. The difference was that here no one knew him as Damiano, the good boy who was learning to play the lute. Nor as Delstrego, the witch who killed fifty men with terror. Here he was—he was whatever he showed the people he was.

Redheaded, dirty Gaspare was kneeling in front of him, slack jawed. "By Gabriele himself!" the boy exclaimed. "What game were you pulling on me, asking how you're to earn your bread? The new music!"

"Ah? You have heard contrapuntal music up here in San Grbriele? It doesn't offend men's ears?"

Gaspare flung over the market a look of ripe scorn. "Here? I haven't spent my whole life *here*, my friend. But how can ears that hear nothing sweeter than the bleating of goats be offended by what comes out of the lute? Play on!"

Damiano raised his hand to obey, when a gleam against the black wood of the bowl caught his eye. "Where did these come from," he asked stupidly, nudging the two split pennies with his forefinger. "Did you put them in, Gaspare?"

The boy's green eye was coldly tolerant. "If I had money, would I be dancing my hams off on the street? That came during your last song. Leave it sit; maybe it will breed."

The afternoon floated on rivers of tune. Intoxicated by his own success as a lutenist, Damiano began to sing. He had never before sung in public, or even for his teacher, yet Macchiata had been right in saying he had a good voice.

The bottom of the entertainer's bowl turned brick red,

lined with coppers tarnished by long residence in sweaty,
peasant hands. The glances he spared toward it were filled
with an astonished pride, as though the poor handful was
the price of a kingdom. Damiano discovered that he
garnered more money by his singing than by his lute
playing, though singing was by far the easier of the two.
He sang till he was hoarse.

His throat burned. He broke a treble string. The sun
was westerly, and Damiano rubbed his face in his hands.

"Enough," he croaked.

"More than enough," sighed Gaspare, and he leaned
against the warm wall, elbowing Macchiata aside. The
boy's face had been washed by sweat. "The market is done
for the day. Let's divide up the wealth!"

With a sly grin Damiano picked out of the bowl four
ruddy coins. "This should be enough," he mumbled, and
stood on legs stiff from disuse. "I'll be right back," he said,
and darted away.

To the young man's immense and endless disappointment, the pastry stall on the next corner, which had filled
the surrounding air with temptation, was gone. Nothing
remained but postholes and the prints of the town dogs
that had scoured away the last crumbs.

"The baker quits early," said Gaspare, coming up
behind Damiano, "because he has to get up every morning
in the middle of the night."

"You knew that?" asked Damiano wearily. "But I told
you I was trying to get money for . . ."

Gaspare slapped Damiano's shoulder in comradely
fashion, a gesture that required him to stand on tiptoe. "I
forgot. You get carried away, dancing. But never mind that,
my friend. What we have here"—he jingled a worn but
serviceable leather pouch—"will buy us both dinner at any
house in the town."

San Gabriele appeared tired and empty as the bright
stalls were folded away and tied into bundles, and the
unsold produce packed again to ride the ox wains home.
Damiano led his new colleague back to the stable wall
where Macchiata was guarding his gear. "I always marvel,"
he commented, "at how quickly a market can disappear
and become just an ordinary town again." He lowered
himself onto the imprint in the dust, shaped like an upside-
down heart, that showed where he had spent the after-

noon. The sun crawled sideways along the side street, so low that buildings blocked it. Soon the saw-blade of the mountains would cut it through. Damiano pulled free his mantle, intending to wear it, but he noticed Gaspare shivering in his sweat. He threw the fur over the boy's bony frame.

"Here," grunted Damiano, offhand. "Save your money. I'll show you something that will surprise you." He dug into his store of food and came up with half a romano, a loaf, a piece of salt-pork, and a leathery withered trout. The cheese he divided into three pieces and the pork into two. The hard bread he used as trenchers.

"We're not poor," he admitted, waving to include the dog. "Merely penniless. And we wanted hot pastry, Macchiata and I. Well, so what? Here's to a full stomach, a full pocket, and a wonderful afternoon!" Damiano filled his mouth with rough red wine, after which he deposited the sloshing bag on Gaspare's lap, where it sat and wiggled like a puppy.

Gaspare asked no questions; he drank. And he ate Damiano's simple food with appetite. But when he was finished, or at least had slowed down, he spilled the coins in the dust of the street and divided the pile in two. He had a practiced eye for the value of liras, broken florins, francs, pfennigs, and weights of lead, and his division was eminently fair. "You owe me two," he said when he was done. "You took four coppers out of the bowl for cakes and you still have them."

Damiano blushed. "Those four coins are all I want," he insisted. "For memory's sake."

Gaspare shot him a glance of disgust and spat on the wall. "Do you really want to insult me that bad? Or are you merely an innocent from birth?

"Besides—if you leave the pile with me, I'll have to share with Evienne, unless she has had better luck. Which I doubt."

"With E-Evienne? The whore?" Damiano stuttered. "Do you mean . . ." and his voice trailed off, for he could think of no delicate way to phrase his question. The boy seemed hardly old enough to employ her services, and far too hungry to spend his little bit of money in that manner.

"I mean she is my sister, and the only family I have, may Gabriele pray for me!" As the boy spoke he was dropping his harvest into the leather bag.

"But you said she was worthless."

Gaspare peered at Damiano from under a ragged red brow. "She is," he stated. "She can't make a decent whore no matter how long she's at it. You saw her today, wasting time with a musician while the town is full of fat peasants with full pockets. Evienne is like me in that way—we are too civilized for our own good."

The boy obviously enjoyed Damiano's discomfiture. "I think maybe you are one of God's innocents, my friend. What's your name, eh? When you are famous, I want to be able to say I danced with you."

Damiano chuckled, opened his mouth, and then closed it again. "If I tell you my name, Gaspare, I may never be able to play the lute for you again."

Gaspare's breath hissed in. "I thought so. You play by magic!"

"No. Not magic. Just human nature. You see, I don't usually play the lute so . . . spiritedly. But today I forgot myself. If I tell you my name, it will remind me."

The boy burst out laughing, and the scarlet cloak slipped to the ground. Damiano felt a silly smile stretching over his face. He dropped his eyes to his knees, which were propped in front of him. "Just call me Festilligambe," he mumbled.

"Festilligambe! Is that your nickname, musician? It's hardly elegant."

Damiano shook his head. "That's my horse's nickname. And he's really a rather elegant horse; I gave him that name after a storm, when he tried to crawl into bed with me and it felt like sleeping on a pile of sticks.

"And speaking of Festilligambe—*Dominus Deus!* I left him in the field with the oxen, all this time ago. I'd better go." Damiano rose and began the task of piling his gear once more on his back. Gaspare helped him. "I'm not used to having a horse," Damiano added. "I never should have left him alone so long."

"No. You'll be lucky if he's still there," the boy agreed. "I hope you at least tied him well."

Damiano shook his head abstractedly, while he peered about him to see what he had forgotten. "No. I don't own a rope, and anyway I'm better at untying things . . ."

He turned then and stared full at Gaspare, as though he were trying to memorize the freckled, peaked face. "Gesu be with you," he said. "Gesù and the Virgin. I hope we meet again."

Gaspare glared, as though parting itself were an insult. "Where are you going, musician? Don't you need a dancer, maybe, and a man to pass the hat?"

Damiano blinked, startled, and almost overbalanced beneath his heavy burdens. "I'm going to the lakes of Lombardy, Gaspare," he said, "where the witch Saara dwells. I won't have time to play the lute on my journey, except around the fire at night, and there'll be no one to hear me at all."

The urchin's scowl grew more fierce. "Why? You could make a name for yourself with that lute, and it wouldn't be Festilligambe."

Damiano shrugged, and his gear rattled in sympathy. He took a step backward, away from Gaspare's disappointment. "I'm doing it to save my city," he explained in a whisper. "If I could do that by playing the lute, things would be much better, but . . ." He shrugged again, noisily, and turned away from the boy and the street corner in San Gabriele.

At his feet Macchiata spoke, breaking a silence that had lasted all the afternoon. "He gets upset very easily," she remarked. "I thought maybe he was going to hit you. Then, of course, I would have bitten him." She sighed and trotted on.

"You must understand, little dear, that he is poor. And being poor is one continuous disappointment.

"But even if he is poor, Macchiata, our Gaspare is never mean. He is generous and fair, and a lover of the arts, besides—which is a quality that runs in his family."

At the top of the path sloping south from the village, Damiano stopped to drink in the sight of the quiet, tended fields, where the colors were already growing dim. As a man of his time, he found a greater beauty in tilled soil than in wild grass, and he favored orchards over forests. But then, in his travels he had seen far more wild than tended land, and he knew how hard it was to break the earth with a hoe.

Perhaps he would set his camp where he had left the gelding: by the paling of live poplars to the right of the road. The weather promised to be fair—though Alpine weather was notoriously faithless regarding its promises. It

only remained now to see whether Festilligambe had also
proved faithless.

Damiano peered ahead as he clambered over the
roughly broken soil. He touched his staff to sharpen his
vision and could see what might be the dark outline of the
horse against the trees, silhouetted against the setting sun.
But if it was the horse, it possessed light spots that were
bouncing about in most unhorselike fashion.

Then the witch's vision cleared (the moon was waxing),
and at the same moment Macchiata started a growl in her
belly that threatened to shake the earth. Damiano stared,
and understood, and finally broke out laughing. He
stepped steadily forward toward the poplar fence. "Don't
get upset, Macchiata. This is really quite funny," he said.

The black outline was indeed Festilligambe, while the
white shape bouncing upon it was not part of the horse at
all, but a frustrated human rider, in shirtsleeves, who had
tied a crude rope bridle upon the animal and was now
bounding in his seat while his heels kicked, his bony hands
slapped, and in other ways he tried to encourage the horse
to move.

The black gelding, however, stood with its legs braced
against the earth as though it planned never to move again.
Its little ears were laid back as flat as a cat's, and its liquid
eyes were rimmed with white.

"Did I doubt you, noble steed?" whispered Damiano,
as with one hand he held Macchiata by the scruff, lest she
interfere with the comedy. He crouched to the earth and let
his packs slide off his back. At that moment the man on the
horse raised his head a fraction.

Damiano choked on his own breath, and his eyes
widened as though he had seen a ghost (or more correctly,
as though an ordinary man had seen a ghost). For in that
fair and somewhat sullen set of features he recognized a
man he had thought never to see again: the uncommunicative golliard, Jan Karl. And the thief had not seen him.

This was too wonderful. Quietly Damiano bent and
took his staff in his hands, whispering the words of the
spell that was almost his favorite, becoming invisible to
prolong the wonder of the moment. Then he stepped
confidently forward.

Jan Karl—or Till Eulenspiegel, as he seemed to call
himself—was no danger to a wary man, let alone one with

the powers of Damiano. His thin, soiled student's shirt hung on his starved shoulders as on a hanger of wood. His lank fair hair was brown with dirt and lay plastered against his face, which had been touched by that shade of gray-purple that indicated too much exposure to the cold. A rag wrapped two fingers of the thief's left hand; Damiano suspected frostbite. He remembered the golliard's frantic flight into the night, sans coat or mantle.

He remembered the bundle of letters he still carried in his pack, arrow-pierced and written in a strange tongue. And Damiano had not forgotten what Macchiata had said: this thief, at least, had not wanted to kill him. As he stood in thought beside the tableau of obdurate horse and ineffectual rider, the horse became aware of him. Festilligambe's cavernous nostrils twitched and his ears revolved like mill wheels. Macchiata, who leaned invisibly against her invisible master's calf, gave an answering whuff. With an audible snap, Damiano broke the spell.

The horse bucked in shock, and Jan Karl toppled from its bare back to the ground. A totally impossible figure loomed over the golliard, outlined black as Satan against the light of the setting sun. It growled like a dog, or somewhere a dog was growling, and the young blond's misadventures had made him very sensitive to that sound. "*Lieber Gott!* Spare me!" he wailed in a mixture of German and French, covering his face with his discolored hands. "It is all too much!" he added in bastard Italian.

Damiano peered down at his fallen enemy from under a corrugated brow. He sighed, feeling an inappropriate stab of pity for the fellow and feeling ridiculous besides. Even the less forgiving dog forgot to growl, running her tongue over her bristly lips and plopping her backside onto the broken soil. Damiano cleared his throat. "You didn't do as much," he said, in tones that were meant to sound menacing and came out more querulous, "to spare an innocent stranger who thought to be your friend."

At the sound of Damiano's voice the northerner raised up on his elbows, his purple visage paling to one of white terror. "No. You're dead! *Donner und Pfannkuchen!* Do me no harm—it wasn't I who killed you. It was that damned Frenchman, and I only met him in Chamonix . . ." The blond began to cry, in great, hysterical sobs.

Damiano shifted from foot to foot. "I know," he began

lamely, but his words went unheard. He started again, louder.

"I know it wasn't you who killed . . . I mean *tried* to kill me. I'm not dead, you know," he added. "Ghosts don't generally look like this. But that's no thanks to you."

Karl's face went blank, then wary. "Not dead? Then why are you haunting me?"

Damiano snorted. "I'm not haunting you. That's my horse you're trying to steal."

With a groan and a thump, Jan Karl fell back against the earth. "*Donner und* . . . Blast me now. Get it over with."

Seeing the scarecrow figure lying there, limp and theatrical before him, Damiano couldn't hold back his grin. But he turned his attention to Festilligambe the honor of whose word had created this situation. "You're a good fellow, Festilligambe," he whispered into the tiny black ear. "No need to stay planted any longer. Go shake your heels in the fields a bit, and then we'll eat."

The gelding made a stiff bound into the air, as though the strings that had held him had snapped. As he descended his teeth clicked playfully into the corona of Damiano's hair, and then he was off, barreling across the empty field, sending sprays of dirt behind him.

"Eh! Watch you don't catch a leg in a hole!" Damiano shouted after him, then he turned back to his captive, whom he half expected to find gone—whom he half *hoped* to find gone.

The golliard lay as he had before, passive and shivering on the ground: the very picture of oppression. Macchiata lay next to him, her tail wagging in quiet satisfaction. "Wh . . . what are you going to do with me?" Karl blurted. Damiano regarded the man irritably.

"Well, since you won't run away. Or can't," he amended, sparing a glance at the dog, "I guess we'll have to do something. Let me see your hand."

Karl did not oblige. "Are you going to cut it off?"

"That may not be necessary." Damiano pulled the bandaged member from the blond's side; Karl had little strength to resist him. "At least not all of it." As he unwound the rag, the prisoner stiffened and cried out. The inner layers of cloth were blackened with dry blood.

The little finger was dead, the ring finger gone to the second knuckle. The hand itself was swollen and veined

with red and black like a small map. Damiano swallowed,
swept through once more by his ungovernable pity. He
took a deep breath and spoke as harshly as he could. "This
was going to kill you, man. Didn't you know?"

Karl's water-blue eyes widened. "But it doesn't hurt
much, like it used to. With all the miserable things that
have happened in the past ten days, I haven't had time
to . . ."

"Eh?" Damiano interrupted, staring gently into the
distance, at nothing. "It's been a hard week for you, has it?
Well, things run in cycles, like the moon. And the moon is
increasing. Wait here and don't move," he commanded,
rising to his feet, "while I set up camp. This place is as good
as any, as long as the husbandman doesn't show up
brandishing a pitchfork." Damiano picked his long-legged
way over the hummocks of soil to his pile of gear. He
returned burdened and threw a blanket down.

"Here," he said. "Wrap yourself in this and stop
shaking." When the wondering Karl had done so, Damiano plunked the wineskin on top of him. "Start drinking
now, you skinny Swissman. You're going to need it later."

Picking up the leather sack with his right hand, Karl
obeyed, asking no questions. After two or three good
swigs he stopped to gasp air, his nose prickling with the
fumes of alcohol. "I'm Dutch," he announced. "Not Swiss.
And I'm a long way from home."

Damiano paused in the process of driving a stake of
poplar into the ground. He leaned his hammer-rock against
the butt of the stake and cocked an interested eye at Karl.
"That's true," he admitted. "I know very little about that
country, except that it is wet. But with two rotting fingers
you would never have returned to the Low Countries. Nor
would you have ever read another letter from your dear old
mother."

"My mother died when I was born," said Karl, and he
took another drink, or series of drinks.

Damiano shrugged as he pounded. "Sweetheart, then.
Whosoever letters you keep in a bundle in your pack."
Seeing the dawning of slow understanding on Karl's face,
Damiano chuckled and dove into his saddlebag, from
which he pulled the faded, pierced bundle of letters. He
tossed them onto the blond's lap.

"They've shared my dangers with me, Herr Eulenspiegel. That's an arrow hole through the middle, which ought also to have pierced my chest."

"This saved you?" murmured Karl, examining his little bundle with an intensity that was already half drunken.

"No, not exactly. It was a volume of Petrarch that saved me, for it was bound in wood. I owe that, too, to our convivial first meeting, for I found it in the sack of one of your friends when I woke the next morning. It was a bad morning, that. . . ." Damiano finished the stake with an extra-hard thump of the stone.

"For me too," admitted Karl, whom wine was making more garrulous. "I lost my fingers when the sun came up, because I lay down in the snow. They say you should never do that, no matter how tired you are."

Damiano nodded. "Look on the bright side, Jan. At least we're still alive. Both of us. What about the other two?"

Karl's brow furrowed stupidly. "You know, I never saw them again. All I know is that I turned right at the crossroads." He swigged once more. The wineskin, though very large, was beginning to appear flabby. Damiano looked with approval. With the night's work that was in store for him, he hoped the blond would pass out.

"They might have continued up to Aosta," reflected Damiano. "But when I came there a day later, I didn't see them. And Macchiata's nose is good. . . ."

"They probably went back west, the way we'd come," suggested Karl. "To Provence. That makes most sense. This is a terrible country!"

While Damiano made a comfortable camp, Karl talked. He talked a lot. The volume of his monologue more than made up for his taciturnity on the night of their first aquaintance. He related to Damiano the story of his youth on the fishing boats at Amsterdam: he had been a poor boy but brimming with scholastic promise. He told how he had at length journeyed to Avignon, to study Church history where the pope sat. But knowledge did not come for free, nor did bread or the necessary roof. The Dutch lad had borne three years of privation and had reached no other heights than to be elected king of the pre-Lenten fete, when all went topsy-turvy for a week and the clerks ruled the roost. It was after that that he realized he had neither the right nationality nor the right friends to gain advancement in Innocent's church.

"Nor the right temperament," Damiano added silently, looking critically at the figure wrapped in the rough blanket.

Karl didn't notice his host's sharp glance, as he explained how, in great bitterness and with very little money, he had set out east to try his fortunes in old Rome itself. In the pass he had met the youth Pierre Paris, whom he had known slightly at the university, and the Breton who claimed to love Petrarch. Paris had devised the story that the three of them were retracing the poet's journey to Milan, though it was a silly tale, and the reality was that both of the others were thieves.

Damiano's hands were full of tinder. He chuckled as he sparked the evening's fire. "Both of the others?" he echoed, and turned his head to Karl.

The blond Dutchman nodded solemnly, closed his eyes and fell into a peaceful, childlike sleep.

Leaving the dog to guard both camp and patient, Damiano returned to San Gabriele, where without meeting either Gaspare or Evienne, he filled the empty wine bag at the village well. As he trudged back down the hill he could feel the chill of the deeply shadowed earth rising up through his boots, and his little campfire winked at him like the eye of a friend.

He was glad he had eaten before this necessity arose; he would not want to eat later. As he approached the light he smelled the alarming odor of burning hair. He dashed the last few yards into camp, the wine bag leaping in his arms like a live thing, only to find a picture of unbroken peace.

Macchiata lay spread-eagled over the remaining bedroll, two paws on either side, as though she were riding a log. Her dreamy gaze was fixed on her charge, Karl. The gelding quietly stood close by the fire, leaning into the warmth.

"Festilligambe," cried Damiano indignantly. "Get away from there! You're burning your tail!" He dropped the bag on the ground by Macchiata and darted around the campfire to where the big animal was now examining its disfigured tail with calm wonder.

Damiano grabbed a handful of mane and pulled the black head around. Fixing an ear in each hand, he glared at it.

"You," he pronounced, "are a most unhorselike horse."
The gelding swished a tail that was reduced to half its
former splendor.

"If you catch on fire, what am I to do? There isn't
enough water in the entire well to put out a horse!" In
response—perhaps in apology—Festilligambe raised his
muzzle and lipped Damiano on the nose. It wasn't pleasant
to see the yellow, boxlike teeth so near to one's face;
Damiano turned away.

He had brought nothing resembling a medicinal dressing in his pack, and early winter was not the season to
gather herbs. Nonetheless, Karl's fingers would have to
come off, and Damiano's father had been known to resort
to hot packs and lye soap when nothing else was available.
The young witch filled his only pot with water and set it
into the fire. Into the water went one of his two linen
undershirts, torn into strips. He pulled a bundle of folded
cloth out from the bottom of his pack and carefully
unwrapped a little knife.

It was not terribly strong or sharp, because it was
intended more for witchcraft than surgery, and its blade
was silver. The handle was crystal, and was cut with all the
phases of the moon, the full moon sitting at the top, like a
tiny sword's pommel.

For a few moments he did no more than to kneel on the
blanket by Karl, the knife resting in his palm, while his
mind settled. He had never done such an operation
without an effective sleeping draught for the patient,
without compresses, clean linen, and a few men to hold
the sufferer still should the narcotic fail. He would have to
be very sure.

With his right hand—the hand that never touched the
knife—he reached out and yanked a tuft of dry grasses.
These he sprinkled over Karl's emaciated limbs, while he
whispered a spell of binding. The gray strands clung like so
many fine ropes, but as they did so his vision blurred a bit
and his feet fell asleep beneath him.

Binding was a very expensive spell.

Next he consecrated both the knife and his hands to the
coming task. The silver blade briefly grew too hot to touch.
He twisted the knife in his fingers till it had cooled.

He lifted Karl's gangrenous hand and secured it between his knees. The sleeper didn't move. With the bright

blade, no longer than a beech leaf, Damiano pierced the living skin beneath the suppuration that had been Karl's little finger. He cut around the knuckle point.

A little spell to staunch the bleeding. Another to stir the breeze (this job didn't smell too good). Pray God this poor sinner didn't wake. The tendon and cartilage broke with small popping sounds, like sticks crackling in a fire. The blade was speckled with crimson, and thick, unhealthy blood ran down the white arm and onto Damiano's knees. The finger bone pulled free and gleaming out of its socket.

The ring finger he took off at the big joint, but after a glance at the flesh exposed, Damiano shook his head and cut again, removing the whole of that finger as well.

When he was done, he regarded the raw wound gratefully. It was simple and clean and would be easy to wrap. He had left a fold of skin hanging on both the top and bottom of the hand, to wrap over the exposed bone and flesh. Later that skin would probably fall away, to be replaced by knotted scar tissue, but for now it would close the wound.

But before he closed it Damiano held Karl's hand out from the blanket and freed the blood to flow. The oozing became a fountain that spurted with Karl's heartbeat. He heard Macchiata whine from her perch on the bedroll; the smell of human blood upset her.

After allowing the hand to bleed for half a minute, Damiano pinched the wrist tightly and reapplied the spell.

The water by now was bubbling and hissing. With the blade of the knife Damiano fished into the pot and skewered a length of linen. When he offered the cloth to the night air, a phantom of white steam coiled up from it. "That's not what ghosts look like, either," muttered the witch, and while the cloth was still hot enough to redden skin, he slapped it over Jan's bloody hand.

Then Damiano looked away from his surgery, away from the steaming rag and the three blackened stumps on the ground with the shaft of white bone protruding. He let his eyes rest on the fire for a moment, then raised them to the early stars.

The sky was a field of radiant indigo. The breeze, growing colder minute by minute, seemed to sweep directly down from that eternal, unchanging expanse. In actuality the air flowed down from the Alps, of course, but that was much the same. He let the night close his eyes.

"I would really rather not be involved in this," he whispered aloud. "He may still die.

"And there are others I would rather share my campfire with than this sullen, craven Dutchman." He longed suddenly for the presence of Raphael, so much like the night sky himself. It was on his lips to call out to the angel, to beg him not for a lesson but for a few minutes inconsequential chat by the fire. But he remembered the dying woman in Sous Pont Saint Martin. Raphael was not permitted to play a part in a mortal's trial or death, and here was poor, sly Jan Karl, his torn hand scalding under hot rags. He could wake at any moment, and it would be awkward, for he would wake screaming.

Besides, there was still the matter of his interview with the Devil. Could the archangel know what had passed between Damiano and Raphael's own, wicked brother? If so, he had not come by to ask for an explanation.

At least half the reason Damiano did not call Raphael was that he feared discovering the archangel would no longer come.

It was a weary night, for Damiano had to keep changing the hot packs. And it was a cold one, for Karl began to shiver uncontrollably and had to have both blankets. Before it got too late, Damiano rose, went into town and pounded on doors until he found a householder who would sell him more wine, at a terribly inflated price. He drank none of it himself, for he had to stay awake, but when, toward morning, Karl awoke (not screaming but weeping without pause), he forced it down the man's throat.

With sunrise, Karl became quiet. Damiano induced him to eat a piece of wine-soaked bread, and then another. He watched his patient with red and grainy eyes, thinking that it was odd to save a man's life and still not like him. "I can't stay with you, Jan," he said dully. "I'm on an errand that's very urgent to me."

Karl's face registered all the surprise his weakness allowed. "I didn't think you were going to. Why should you?"

Damiano sighed. He knew all the reasons he should remain: the wound was fresh, certain to bleed and apt to go sour, Karl was hungry and unable to work, even should any peasant take him on, and he, Damiano, had begun the job . . . But he set his jaw and peered over at the houses of the village, which were white and black with sunrise.

"I don't even know why you did this," added the Dutchman, as he stared fascinated at wet pinkish cloth that had taken the place of two fingers on his hand.

"It was necessary," said Damiano shortly, without looking around. "It's not the sort of thing I do for fun."

"Necessary for me, maybe," answered Karl with a sick little laugh. "But not for you. You didn't have to tend me, feed me, cover me . . ."

Damiano pulled up his knees, covered them with his folded arms and rested his chin on top. He was a long time answering.

"It's difficult—to learn to do a thing that not many people can do, like amputating fingers, and then to see a need for it and not to do it. You see? And then it is difficult to spend the time and effort on a man and then let him die for want of something simple.

"But I can't afford any more—time, that is. The world is full of distractions, and I must get to Lombardy before the snows creep any lower. I'll leave you one of those blankets and some coppers I made in San Gabriele. Also the pot; if you neglect that wound, you'll certainly die after all." Damiano's brow furrowed fiercely as an idea occurred to him. An idea he distrusted. "Something more, Jan. There is a boy in San Gabriele named Gaspare. He has red hair, and he comes about to my shoulder. He's just a street urchin, but he has a genius for making the best of things. He may be able to figure out something you can do to earn your bread while you recover and to help you on your way to Rome. He has a sister, though, that . . ."

Damiano glanced over at Karl's wary eyes and starved torso. He chuckled to himself. "Never mind the sister. But, my dear cleric, I promise you that if you mistreat this boy, or betray him in any way, you will know what a curse is."

Karl was silent while Damiano rose and began to break camp. His watery blue eyes followed Damiano reflectively. Finally he spoke. "You're a very good man," he said. "Like the Samaritan, in Luke."

Damiano spun around with a face full of anger and hurt. "Don't say such a thing. I am nothing like a good man. I'm only . . . a mozzarella!"

Karl blinked in confusion. A short laugh burst out of his throat. "A mozzarella? That's a cheese?"

"That's an Italian expression. It means . . ." Damiano waved his hands in a gesture that explained nothing. "A good man follows the commandments. I, on the other hand, am merely softhearted. I cannot bear to eat cows and pigs.

"—But I killed fifty men with witchcraft," he added, and he slipped his packs over Festilligambe's elegant back.

Karl made no answer.

CHAPTER 11

The road slipped east; it rolled up and down. Damiano rode through a silence of trees. In a birch-covered valley the sky above him was filigreed with bare branches. Dead leaves, sodden after the autumn's rains, padded the horse's hooves like cloth wrappings. The sun and the trees wove a pattern of warm lace over Damiano's head. He nodded sleepily with every step, as did Festilligambe. Macchiata had nothing to say; she spent the day in her nose.

The road tilted upward an hour before sunset. In the distance Damiano could make out the crown of the hill, with another, steeper rise behind it, black with pine. He decided it was better to rest now and take the climb fresh in the morning.

He brushed the dried sweat from the horse's flanks with a boar-bristle brush that was also Macchiata's brush and his own. The gelding's mane was tangled and its tail a sorry sight. Before sunset Damiano gathered wood and made a small fire, though without a pot he had no way to cook on it. When he wrapped himself for the night in blanket and mantle, the day's silence was still unbroken.

Who was Saara, that he should be seeking her across two Italies in early winter? Damiano knew very little about her, but that little was more than most Piedmontese knew, or most Lombards, for that matter. He knew what his father had told him, long ago.

She had come out of the far north country, the Fenland, in his father's youth, flying from war into exile. Of the war,

Damiano knew nothing. The exact place of her exile he also did not know, though Guillermo Delstrego had described it as a green hill, round as an egg, set among the lakes of Lombardy. It was also Delstrago who had told his son that Saara the Fenwoman was the most powerful witch in all the Italies, perhaps in all Europe. That was not an admission he would have made easily.

In fact, Saara the Fenwoman (or Finn) was just about the only other practicing witch whose name Guillermo Delstrego let pass his lips: probably because she dwelt too far away to be competition. He had painted his son quite a colorful sketch of Saara, with her braids and sing-song magic, and the birds all doing her bidding. Being sentimental as he was, Damiano had added his own pigments to the picture, believing the Fenwoman to be beautiful as well as wise, and merry and virtuous besides—or sometimes only merry.

Damiano let the gelding amble on while he sat on its broad back and idly plucked his lute. For a week they had traveled east: the young man in his ermine and tangled hair, the elegant black horse, the ugly white dog. Work and time had hardened the muscles of the horse's back, but they had equally hardened the rider.

Damiano had always been lean, though, and lean and lazy or lean and tough, he looked much the same. On Macchiata the difference was striking. She looked every inch the fighter now, or the ratter at least, and the bunched muscles of her thighs rippled beneath her short hair. The fat she had lost made her triangular head appear larger and heavier than ever. She spoke less, following her master's lead, but she was in trim to follow the horse all day.

Damiano's fingers spattered notes up the lute's neck. The treble string squealed like a pig. The little daisy-petal ears of the horse reversed, and it shook its head.

"Eh, Festilligambe: You've become the critic?" mumbled Damiano. "Well, let me tell you, horse. You are no authority on music; you can't keep time. And if I could warm my hands up well, you would really hear something."

He raised his head and looked about him with a sigh. It was cold here, even south of the mountains. The forest of ash and oak was bare. But it was not drear to him, for he had the eyes of his father, and the moon was near the full. In the corner of his eye, beside the road, he saw a stir of the earth that meant a mouse was burrowing, and a gray gleam marked the winter nest of a rock dove. That splash of orange beneath a fallen log was neither leaves nor lichens but a fox. Damiano did not tell Macchiata.

The trees were sleeping, and their limbs creaked like the snoring of old men. Damiano imitated the sound, drumming his bass course with two fingers of his left hand, on the neck.

"If I had my way," he mused, "I'd travel like this from town to town on market days—to perdition with the higher knowledge. I'd rather make music than be wise."

Macchiata snorted, and a powder of dry leaves shot into the air. "I'd rather chase rabbits than be wise," she said.

"But you never catch them," countered her master. "Doesn't that frustrate you, little dear?"

Macchiata whuffled, sat down, and scratched the matter over. "Because I don't catch *this* rabbit," she said, "or *that* rabbit, doesn't mean I will never catch *any* rabbit."

Damiano had no answer for this. He returned to his own subject. "I really would like to find another market. Porto was a disappointment: all day playing for only a tankard of beer. And our supplies are getting lighter. I notice that every time I pick up the saddlebags. We must find Saara soon."

The dog turned to Damiano with a glance full of anxiety. "Supplies, Master? You mean food?" Damiano nodded.

"How soon, Master? How many days is soon?"

Damiano frowned. "Just . . . soon," he replied.

Ludica was not holding a market, but it seemed to be a much larger town than Porto or San Gabriele. Perhaps it was larger than Partestrada. Leading Festilligambe down a cobbled street between buildings of stone, Damiano was impressed.

Ludica supported not one but two inns and a stable. Damiano left the gelding there, to enjoy for one night its fill of grain and mash. If he could not pay the keep by morning, he could surely redeem his horse with a linen undershirt.

The first inn was dim and empty. An old woman in the

doorway regarded him with no great welcome. Damiano did not go in.

The second inn was called The Jolly Pilgrim. Its common room smelled like the cork of a wine bottle. The innkeeper was fat, and his black brows were the only hair on his head. He spoke staccato, with a sharp lilt, and by this Damiano knew he was in Lombardy at last. Damiano offered to play and sing in exchange for dinner and a bed, but after two minutes of bargaining he found he had promised also to cut wood for the fire and instead of a bed would get only the left side of the hearth.

Still, it was good to sit in a room, for a change, and to be warm, front and back. When the room filled up—with drinkers, travelers, and smoke—it felt even better to play the bransle and the saraband so that the men stamped their feet. Had he drunk all the wine that was bought for him, he would not have been able to see the strings, let alone pluck them, and one jolly pilgrim, a wool merchant who loved the vintage so much his cheeks had turned purple, gave Damiano a broken silver florin.

Best of all was to eat someone else's cooking—cabbage and carrots and fresh pork in gravy, over a slice of black bread as thick as a man's wrist. And though Damiano couldn't eat the pork Macchiata was willing, and there was plenty of food for both.

The wool merchant called him Frenchie and laughed at the way Damiano slurred his words. Since the best of the new music was French, Damiano did not take offense or correct the man. Besides, it was not good sense for a Piedmontese to strut himself in Lombardy, where they who cannot swim are as proud of their lakes as the man of Turin is proud of the mountains he cannot even see.

In the morning he sought out the landlord and asked what that worthy knew of a woman named Saara.

The black eyebrows in the pink face gave the man's skepticism an eloquent frame. He stared and he sighed and he beckoned Damiano to follow him.

The yard of The Jolly Pilgrim was dusted with snow, and dry flakes like talc wavered through the air. Winter had followed Damiano into Lombardy. The bald landlord threw the hood of his tunic over his head. The steam of his breath obscured his features as he pointed up and beyond the town to where six hills stood clustered together, as if for warmth.

"See the Sisters?" asked the Lombard. His voice was sharp and harsh in Damiano's ears. "Which of them is different?"

Damiano squinted and peered, leaning on his staff. "Two of them are taller," he said. "Almost mountains. One of them is round topped and has no snow on the south side. What difference do you mean?"

The landlord stuck his hands up his sleeves. "Doesn't it seem the least bit strange to you, boy, that one hill among many, has no snow on it? And it never does. That's the hill of Saara, and she's a witch. The man is ill-advised who makes that climb."

Damiano didn't take his eyes from the high hills, where many hawks were flying circles in the gray air. He smiled at his fortune. For here he was in Lombardy, not knowing when he had left the Piedmont, and chance or aid had dropped his desire into his lap. "I don't know if that's the result of witchcraft, benefactor. Notice that the green hill is protected from the north wind by both the taller hills. It would be the warmest, and the last to collect snow."

The fat Lombard took one step away from Damiano. He rumbled his throat and spat into the white powder. "Believe what you want, young Frenchman, but we who live here know what's what in our own backyards. Witchcraft is real under the sun or moon, no matter what you write in Latin in your books."

Damiano's eyes widened, for the man's misunderstanding of him was so complete he didn't know where to begin to correct it. But the landlord wasn't done.

"There was another fellow like you who stopped here and asked for Saara, lutenist. He was a southerner with a sharp tongue and a sharp sword, and he disappeared into the witch's garden—that's what we call that slope of the hill—and was never seen again."

Damiano blinked and regarded that far patch of greenery with intense interest. "I have no sword," he murmured, as much to himself as to the landlord. "And, as for my tongue, I hope it is more honeyed than sharp, because I have to convince that lady to help me."

The Lombard laughed, and coughed, and spat. He left the one who he thought was a young French dandy, leaning on his prettified walking stick, his face a study in concentration, his curled black hair turning white with snow.

Damiano left the horse and the florin in the care of the stable keeper, and he and Macchiata started around the small lake that stood in between Ludica and the Sisters. It had been a while since he had done any amount of walking; his knees ached.

"I am still bruised," he said ruefully to the dog. "Purple-and-black a week later. I wonder if that is Satan's little joke, to remind me that I went down on my knees before him. Though it was not my idea to do so."

This was not the sort of conversation to interest Macchiata. She trotted ahead along the path by the water, her ears a-prick, her twiggy tail wagging stiffly behind her. Damiano trudged behind, burdened with packs, staff, and the lute, which he ought to have left back at the inn. The snowfall was halfhearted and soon died completely. By noon the sky was sudsy with white clouds, and the travelers had come to the feet of the hills.

On two of them the bare bones of rock were exposed; these were the tall ones. Most of the rest were weathered grassy domes, pale now with snow. The middle hill, however, was clothed in timber, and the south slope of it shone green. Through the gorse and heather, a little path— no more than a goat track—led toward it.

"This isn't difficult," Damiano mumbled, pushing his way forward against the clinging brush. "There must be somebody who visits here and keeps the way passable."

Macchiata disappeared into the undergrowth; not even her tail was visible. But Damiano could follow her snuffling progress with his ears. "You know . . . little . . . dear," he panted, as he fought through a waist-high bramble. "If Saara is in truth an exile from her home, our task may be easy. How could she not sympathize with Partestrada?"

A black nose appeared, and then a white muzzle hanging with burrs. "An exile is someone who was chased out of home, Master? If this one got chased away from her home, then how can she chase the soldiers out of yours? I mean, she may not be fierce enough."

Damiano stopped dead, his bags swaying at his sides. "That's a thought, Macchiata. But we don't really know the

truth about Saara's home, only that my father said she was
the most powerful witch in the Italies. And besides, here
there will be two of us, she and I. And though I am not the
most powerful witch in the Italies—and may not even be
among the most powerful (how am I to know?)—I do know
a few things."

"Of course you do, Master," attested the dog. She
waggled over and placed one dirty white foot against
Damiano's knee. He played with her ears while he examined the path ahead. It vanished under an arch of pines,
dark as the door of a tomb. Damiano straightened and
peered, then leaned on his staff and stared intently.

"There. Ahead is the gate to Saara's garden. Not
welcoming, is it?"

"But I smell magic," Damiano added, and strode
forward.

Though it was dark within, it was also warmer, and
Damiano could see well enough in the dim. The air was
thick with the evergreen frankincense; like a church, it
almost made one sneeze. The path wound steeply upward.
Perhaps it was a goat path after all and had never been trod
by man. But if it was a goat path, then there was something
ahead besides pine forest, because a goat does not subsist
on pine needles alone.

"It's a good thing we left Festilligambe behind," whispered Damiano. "He wouldn't do well on this road." The
dog growled her own opinion.

There was light ahead, atop a rocky outcrop that
reduced Damiano to climbing on hands and knees, with
his staff wedged into his armpit. He winced each time the
lute slapped down against his back, not for the pain of it,
but for the instrument's sake. When he reached the crest,
sunlight blinded him a moment. Then he saw his hands,
scratched red and coated with a honey-dust of crushed
sandstone. He sat up and allowed the dog to lick his hands
clean.

"Look, Macchiata," he cried. "The witch's garden. I
wish it were my own!"

As a garden, it was very wild, for the grass grew knee-
high and bobbed its wheaty tails in the breeze, and black
logs and branches choked the little stream that wandered
left and right over the meadow, cutting it into room-sized

islands. Wind-carved rocks lay scattered about, not by chance, but as though tossed by a carefully artless hand. Above rose a stand of birch, still holding its yellow leaves, which rattled together like flags of paper.

But as a wilderness, it was sweet and comfortable, for the sun shone softly over grass that still held a touch of green, and flowers dotted the meadow: late asters and early crocuses, bronze and white. The standing stones themselves looked inviting. They were colored a deep bricklike red and pitted and hollowed all over, so that they carried an assortment of tiny gardens on their backs, each harboring three stalks of grass, perhaps, or a cornflower.

Damiano felt the sun touch his lips. It made him yawn. "We'll stop here," he said to Macchiata. "Maybe all day. We can eat lunch on the south side of that biggest rock."

Macchiata agreed to the proposal, and the two of them walked through the sea of soft grass toward the further-most standing stone, which looked like a seat with a huge, scallop-shell back and velvety moss over the cushions.

At the foot of the red stone grew a thicket of rosemary, dotted now with blue flowers and droning with bees. "It's Dami, golden people," announced the witch as he climbed. "Out of the way so I don't crush you and so you don't sting me." Obediently the insects circled wide of him.

This was a chair for a giant. Damiano could lie full length on the cushions of moss and still have room for his baggage and a restless dog. They ate stale bread and cheese and a carrot Damiano had stolen from the inn kitchen. Then he filled his wooden bowl from a child-sized pond where a rubble of rocks had dammed the stream. Tiny silver fish darted around his hands, each not much bigger than a fingernail. He hoped none had gotten into his drinking water.

A few inches from his eyes, as he knelt there, was a patch of blooming crocuses. He broke off three blossoms and carried them back to the rock, where he lay down on his stomach on the moss and peered down the flowers' throats.

They were shining white but veined with purple at the bottom of the petals. Within each little cup proudly stood the stamen covered with saffron, which left a film of gold on the young man's finger.

At this distance, too, the moss was radiant with color:

gold, green, russet, sooty black. Damiano laid the crocuses on the moss and closed his eyes. Macchiata lay down beside him. "I wish . . ." she said, and then was silent.

"You wish what, little dear?" murmured Damiano. There was silence. He turned to the little dog, who licked her lips nervously.

"I . . . it would be fun to play with Raphael now," she blurted at last. "It's been a long time since you called him."

Damiano's eyes closed again. "Yes, it has. But I don't imagine he's drumming his fingers, waiting. He is a blessed angel, Macchiata, and we are . . . creatures of the earth. He has all eternity, while we have the hours between lunch and dinner, as it were.

"And he cannot understand the affairs of men." Damiano yawned again, and since his chin was resting on the mossy stone, the effort raised his whole head. Then he frowned.

"Actually, little dear, I don't understand the affairs of men either. I appreciate the affairs of . . . bees, let's say . . . much better. But I am a man, so it is up to me to act the part."

Damiano squirmed onto his back and placed the white cup of a crocus over each of his eyes. "I can see the sun through them," he commented. "Tinted white and pink and purple." When he took the flowers away, his lashes were dusted with gold. "These crocuses look sort of like Raphael to me: all white and gold and radiant. Though the white is his robe, of course."

Damiano yawned once more, screwed his eyes shut, and rubbed the gold all over his face. "Then again, since what we are seeing when we see Raphael is only an image for our mortality's sake, perhaps he *is* the robe, and there is nothing under it. What man would dare lift it to see?"

"I know what Raphael looks like under the robe. I looked," said Macchiata. Damiano opened his eyes very suddenly.

"You what?"

"I looked. I stuck my head under and looked, Master. A long time ago. I was curious."

Now it was Damiano's turn to lick his lips. He tasted saffron. "And what . . . No, little dear. Never mind. I don't think it's for me to know." He sighed, turned his face to the sun, and composed himself for a nap.

He did miss the angel. In the three years since he had first had the temerity to speak the summoning words (that was after his father died, when many things in Damiano's life got easier), he had never gone as long as a week without a lesson. Indeed, the lute, though important, was only a bridge by which to reach Raphael, who was Damiano's closest friend.

Second closest friend, he amended to himself, feeling a slimy nose against his palm. That made two friends in all, unless he could count Carla, whom he would never see again.

Lying there on the moss in the sun, the young witch thought of the Devil's words and did not feel in the slightest bit damned. But for the plight of his city, now so far away, he would be the happiest fellow on earth. And the sleepiest.

What instrument *did* Raphael play, by choice? The lute had been Damiano's idea, since he happened to have a lute, and the angel had never demurred. He played the lute masterfully, but it was hardly likely it was his only instrument.

Gabriele (whom Damiano had never met) played the trumpet. Of course. But there was no reason for all archangels to be alike. If they played together, it would be more reasonable to have both winds and strings. That is, if the winds could be taught not to overpower the sound of the string players. Among angels, there would surely be more consideration than among Italians.

Paintings often showed angels playing harps, but that was because harps were so common; when your imagination fails, you could always paint a musician with a harp. They were easy to paint, too, having three angles and only two curves.

But Raphael showed such a delight in shuffling between modes, and in flatting his seventh . . . Damiano could more easily see him at a lute or chitarre. Or perhaps a large vielle—a hurdy-gurdy—with chromatic keys.

Then it occurred to Damiano that since Raphael was a spirit, he had no need for a material instrument; the trees could make his music, or the bones of the earth. So what did the archangel mean when he said, "I have my own instrument?" Next time Damiano saw him, he would ask straight out, "Raphael, what do you play?"

With this decision off his mind, Damiano fell asleep.

* * *

The bees were crawling over him: thick, droning, coating him with gold. They had a thousand voices, warm and nasal like the vielle itself. They were the voices of friends. Damiano strained to hear them, to pull out one voice and recognize it. To know a single name. "Solitary," they whispered, all together. "Solitary boy."

The weight of the bees was on him, soft and heavy. He could feel it on his arms, his body, his lips. The golden drone echoed in his chest. Damiano struggled upward from sleep and knew he was under a spell.

A hand was upon him, invisible, gentle—as the hand of a girl might cover a baby rabbit. It was at once caressing and imprisoning. He heard Macchiata whine. He heard a song.

> *"Boy, boy, solitary boy.*
> *I see you in the garden,*
> *Alone in the garden,*
> *Sleeping in the sun.*

It was a woman's voice, throaty and deep, rich as a multitude of bees. "Boy," it chanted. "Solitary boy."

Damiano turned his head toward it, pushing slowly against the invisible hand. He cracked his eyes open and peered out from under the concealment of his thick lashes.

Her hair was sunny brown and wound in peasant braids. Her cheeks were blushed rose and dimpled, for she was smiling. Her eyes were green and brown and golden, all together, in a pattern that swam and made his head swim. She wore a blue dress embroidered with stars of red and yellow and Damiano found her utterly charming.

It was not a strong spell that held him; he could have broken it with a word. But it was the most intimate touch he had known from any woman, so Damiano lay still and did not speak.

> *"Young one, I can see you,*
> *I can peel you like an onion,*
> *I see backward, through your days.*
> *I unfold you like the petals of a rose.*
> *Book-friend, rabbit-friend, your playmates*
> *   are the beasts in the stall.*
> *What do you study, boy, that makes you so alone?"*

* * *

Her touch into his mind was like a feather under the chin. It tickled and made him smile. Then the feather withdrew in surprise.

"Dark boy, do you know who you are?
There is power in you, young one, like floods under stone."

The hazel eyes widened, and she drew back. The spell shattered, tinkling, as Damiano heaved up on one shoulder. He opened his eyes. "Don't go," he whispered. "And I'm not as young as all that."

The woman stopped where she stood, eyes wide and wary. Neither did Damiano move, and though she did not try to enter his mind once more (he would not have obstructed her, having nothing to hide), slowly her smile grew again.

"You're a witch," she said, amusement and surprise in her words. Even when not singing, her voice had a lilt to it that was nothing like the Italian of Lombardy. "You're most certainly a witch, and you know it, too. But those black eyes are worse than witchcraft, boy. Don't turn them on me like that."

Damiano blushed to the roots of his hair. "You're making fun of me," he said. "What have I done to deserve it?" But the truth was he liked her teasing and was liking everything about the woman more and more. This was Saara. It had to be.

She had the round face of a country girl of seventeen and the knowing air of a *belle dame* of Provence and the lightness of movement of one of the wood sprites, whom even Damiano could only see out of the corner of his eye. Best of all, she was not a country girl or a great lady or a pagan sprite but one of his own kind, a human witch.

She didn't answer his question. Instead she put her hands on her hips. Damiano sat up, noticing she neither carried a staff nor seemed to need one. "Who are you, boy?" she asked. "For boy you are, to me. I am much older than I look, I warn you. And you are in my garden."

Suddenly Damiano remembered the southerner the landlord at Ludica had described to him: the man with the sharp sword and sharp tongue who had vanished in Saara's garden. But looking at Saara herself, he was not afraid.

"My name is Dami," he said, "Damiano. We have traveled here from the Piedmont, my dog and I, to talk to you."

Saara spared a glance at Macchiata, who still lay under the spell, flattened like a white pill-bug on the cushions of moss. With a giggle and a wave of the hand she released the dog, who scuttled (like a white pill-bug) out of sight behind the rock.

"I would like to talk to you too, Dami. It is rare to find another in Lombardy who is tuned to the powers. Rarer still to find one who is friendly. But if I allow you to come much closer to me, you will make an enemy you don't want to have. He might remove your curly head from your shoulders!" She sat down cross-legged on the green and silver grass, too far away for Damiano's close vision.

Damiano dismissed this possibility with a shrug and a wave, and he slid down from the rock into the rosemary bush. Saara sang a line in a tongue that seemed to be composed mostly of *k* sounds and long vowels, and which was to Damiano no more than birdsong. Instantly limber fingers of rosemary whipped out and hugged his knees and calves, bruising themselves with the strength of their grip and filling the air with herby sweetness.

"All right," said Damiano, and he sat down obediently in the thorny patch. Casually, with one hand, he reached up behind him and found his staff, which he laid carefully across his lap.

Saara sat straight as an abbess, her feet crossed over her knees. She pointed at the ebony stick. "Those," she said. "I have seen you southern witches use them. You lock yourselves into them, like men who trade their legs for crutches. Why? Any leg at all is better than the most beautiful crutch."

Damiano frowned uncertainly. "The staff is a focus, lady—like a lens. Do you know what a lens is? It's like a drop of water, which makes sunlight into a bright point. The staff is the focus through which my craft touches the world. It makes my spells more . . . the same, from day to day. I have used this staff for years; all my powers are tuned to it, and without it I'd have nothing."

"That's dangerous, boy. It makes you too vulnerable, needing an outside object like that. My . . . lens . . . or drop of bright sunlight, is my song. My song cannot be taken from me."

Damiano lifted his eyebrows. "Music? Lovely lady.
What a pretty thought. I play music too, but not for magic.
To do that seems, somehow, to sully the tune."

Saara's little pink nostrils flared, and woody rosemary
crawled over Damiano's hands. "Sully the tune? No! For
both magic and music are sacred!"

"Sacred?" Damiano sighed. "Music, yes, but witchcraft
. . . I don't know, lady. I have seen too much done with
witchcraft that had nothing to do with God's will. I release
my own powers into the staff because running free through
me they can . . . make me drunk. Then who knows what
deed I might do."

He raised his eyes to the pretty woman in her bright,
childish dress. "Because I am, after all, a man, lady. And
men at times are slaves to their passions."

Saara made as though to laugh at him but changed her
mind. "You must learn to know the powers," she said
seriously. "The good from the wicked. The pure from the
twisted. When you are possessed by a spirit of wisdom,
you can do nothing bad."

Damiano shook his head, dissatisfied.

"Perhaps for you, lady, that is true, but for me . . . I
don't trust so much. If I allow a spirit to command my
actions and then kill a child or burn down a house, who
will it be who comes before the throne of the Almighty for
judgment: the nameless spirit or Damiano?"

He shuffled amid the ·fragrant, prickling branches,
trying to win some comfort. "Besides, even if the spirit is
pure, I am not. At this moment, my lady Saara, I look at
you and am filled with a sweet longing that is not pure at
all." Immediately he lowered his eyes to the grass, overcome by his own gallantry.

The witch Saara put one braid-end to her mouth and
giggled like a little girl. "We have different ideas of purity,
Dami-yano. But I tell you, as long as you keep your power
as a thing apart from yourself, you will not come to your
full strength."

He shrugged, as though to say 'so what?' but his smile
apologized for the gesture even as he made it. "It is your
power that has led me all this way in the snow, Saara. I
need your help."

She let the braid drop. Her greenish eyes went wary.
"You mean you didn't climb here just to speak words of

hopeless love to me?" Her words were lighter than her guarded expression.

Before answering, Damiano paused, running his fingers lightly over the jewels of his staff. "Beautiful lady, I think I could speak words of love to you—and more than speak—forever. If they are hopeless, then I am desolate, but since I have only just met you this hour, I may recover.

"But I have lived in Partestrada all my life, and she is in great trouble. It is for that reason I have disturbed your peace: because I am told you are the most powerful witch in the Italies." He glanced up to see whether his words had offended Saara. She looked merely concerned.

"Who told you that I was the most powerful witch in the Italies, boy? No one in the Italies knows me." But rather than waiting for his answer, she continued, "Great trouble, Dami. That would mean—plague?"

Both his eyebrows shot up. "Mother of God! No! Not that! Not again. I meant war. And tyranny."

"Ah." The syllable expressed dying interest. She turned her head away from Damiano and toward the fluttering, yellow birch leaves. "War. Well, there's nothing I can do about that."

"No?" For one moment he faced the possibility that his search had been useless, that there was no hope for Partestrada or for any small, industrious, unarmed peoples. Perhaps neither logic nor magic could hold the gates, for plague and Pardo were Fate and God's will. Just for a moment he stared at this possibility, and then he turned firmly away from it.

At a single word from Damiano, the tendrils of rosemary sprang away and hung as coils in the air around him. "I don't believe you. You say there's nothing you can do, but I read in your face that it's just not worth the bother." He stood, and Saara stood. The air spat tiny sparks that smelled like hot metal. "Well it *is* worth one person's bother, and much more, and in the service of my city I have been beaten and frozen, gone hungry and sleepless and done deeds . . . that I shouldn't have done," he concluded less forcefully. "In fact, I've done what no man should do. I've tried to strike a bargain with the Father of Lies, to deliver my city from bloodshed and poverty. Even he refused me. You are my last hope, Saara. I cannot believe the greatest witch in all Europe doesn't know of a way to free a town from the power of one Roman brigand.

"I'll do whatever need be done, lady. I'll fight Pardo's men alone on foot, if need be. I'll swell the Evançon to wash them from the streets. I'll go to any amount of work, and through any peril.

"I only need you to tell me how." The faith in his eyes was an unreasonable as a child's, and his jaw clenched again and again.

Saara tried to break the link that locked her green, slightly tilted eyes to Damiano's. She failed, for the power that held her was as old as sorcery and far stronger. "I'm not the greatest witch in Europe, Dami-yano. In my home we are all witches, and there are some much stronger than I, and wilder. That is why . . .

"But, boy, you are free of that place, and of General Pardo. The world is yours—although not this hill, I must remind you. General Pardo cannot follow you everywhere."

Damiano squinted painfully and shook his head. "He has my city, lady. My home. There is a great difference between a traveler and an exile. Ask Dante. Ask Petrarch."

Saara cocked her head at the unfamiliar names, and then she laughed. "I need no one else's opinion. A city is a collection of stone walls. My people need no cities; they follow the reindeer and are free."

"Reindeer?"

Saara grinned at his puzzlement. "Shaggy deer with great antlers and big feet that can stand on the snow. We ride them and milk them and also eat them, though not the same ones we ride."

Looking at the impish set of Saara's smile, Damiano was not sure he was supposed to believe her. He decided, sighing deeply, that he should let the matter pass.

"We Piedmontese—all Italians—do need cities. We invest our hearts into them. A city is like a mother, lovely lady. She gives us our food and our friends and our amusements. She sets an indelible stamp upon us. Yet a city—she can't defend herself. Who will take care of her if not her children, eh?"

The Fenwoman's elfin face softened with something like pity, yet she shook her head. "That is a pretty thing to say,

Dami. But a city is not a person. Nor has it life like a tree. It's a thing like the staff—it's your choice to put care into it or to be free. I would sooner help you be free."

Hesitantly, Damiano stepped forward, trying to smile. When he was close enough to see her well, he was also close enough to touch. He put out his left hand and stroked her arm and shoulder. So roughened by the strings were his fingertips they scraped against the thin felt of her embroidered dress.

"Saara. My lady. If it is your wish that I don't live in my city anymore, so be it. I will live in a black forest. Or in a boat on the ocean—I don't care, so long as it is by your will. But first I must help Partestrada, don't you see?"

She watched his hand carefully but did not withdraw. He continued "I am told . . . by whom it doesn't matter, that a city can only prosper with blood and war, and that I could save Partestrada at the expense of her own future glory. I came to you to find another way."

Damiano spoke in a whisper, and as he spoke his fingers traced a small wheedling circle on her shoulder. So intent was Saara on this motion that she seemed not to be listening. But she answered "I know nothing about glory, unless you mean the lights in the winter sky. I won't go to war with you, Dami-yano."

"Then show me how to succeed without war," he whispered, and as she raised an ironical eye to his insistence, he kissed her softly on the side of her mouth.

Saara caught her breath and closed her eyes and stepped back from him. "This is no good," she said weakly. "Neither what you say nor what you do. Dami-yano, I have a man who would kill you for that."

She rubbed her face with both hands. Damiano's smile, as he watched her, was slow and sad. "Maybe," he admitted. "And maybe it was worth it, Saara."

"No maybes about it," she said sternly, then realizing what she had said, she added, "—about his killing you, I mean. He is just like you, too: lean and dark and unpredictable. His name is Ruggiero, and he comes from Rome."

"From Rome!" cried Damiano, stung. "Then he can be nothing like me at all. I am Piedmontese."

Her mutable eyes danced. "No difference that I can

see—save that you are much younger and do not wear a sword.

"Take warning by that, Dami-yano and go back to Ludica. There is a world of charming girls out there. You need not a mother or a city or . . . a wicked old woman like me." With those words Saara vanished, and a pale gray dove flashed upwards into the heavens.

Damiano followed the flight with his eyes, till the sun blinded him. He had never seen anyone turn into a bird before; such magic was impossible to one who worked through a staff.

There was a snuffle and grunt by his feet. He glanced down to see Macchiata, obscured by a dancing, round afterimage of the sun. The dog looked earnestly into his face.

"You licked her—kissed her, I mean," said Macchiata.

"Yes," responded her master. "I . . . like her."

Still the dog stared. "I've never seen you kiss anyone before, Master. Not anyone but me."

Damiano's lips twitched, but he controlled the smile. "That's true, little dear, but does that mean that I can't kiss anyone else?"

Macchiata thought about it. "You never kissed Carla Denezzi," she commented sagely.

Damiano's reply was short. "No. But I should have." He turned back to the rock, where the bees still droned and the moss lay like a cushion in petit point: green, gold, russet, black.

"I should have." He picked up the lute by the neck and began to finger it, indecisively.

Macchiata heaved herself up beside him. "But she doesn't like you, Master. This one. She told you to go away."

The treble trilled wanly. "That's because she doesn't want me to get in a fight with her . . . her Roman friend. One must like a person somewhat to want him not to get his head lopped off. Of course, there is really no danger of that. Saara underestimates me. She thinks I'm younger than I am." He came down on the bass course so forcefully that the strings buzzed against the bridge.

"She will come around," Damiano stated. "We'll camp

on her hillside until she does." Macchiata's ears flattened
with doubt.

"But you said, Master . . . that we would soon be out
of food. Remember?"

"We don't need to eat," said Damiano, and he set his
jaw. The dog stared for a long time without a word.

The camp he set up at the edge of the birch wood that
evening was small, since he hadn't been able to carry much
by foot from Ludica, and neat, since he felt in a way that
the meadow was the lady Saara's parlor. And although he
hadn't exactly been welcomed by that lady, he hoped to
make himself a pleasant guest.

He and the dog ate bread and raisins while nightingales
ornamented the wind in the leaves and a single late
sparrow went "peep, peep, peep." After dinner Macchiata
lay before the fire and sighed.

Damiano was in a better mood. "You know, little dear,
what is the best thing about Saara?" he asked as he peered
down the neck of the *liuto*, checking it for wood warp. He
didn't wait for an answer. "It's that she's wise as a great
lady and yet free as a child."

"Those are two things," Macchiata commented, but her
master was not listening.

"She was barefoot; did you notice, Macchiata? Her little
white feet seemed scarce to bend the grass."

The dog emitted a slow groan that ended in a grunt. "I
noticed that she had a very heavy hand, when she pushed
me down on the rock."

Damiano shot her a glance in surprise. "Heavy? No,
that was not heavy, Macchiata. Didn't I feel it myself? For a
heavy hand, you must remember my father. Now *he* had a
heavy hand."

The lute was sound, but its finish had undeniably
suffered in the climb. Hoping the bass course was true,
Damiano tuned the rest of the strings by it. (Among his
gifts was not that of absolute pitch, which Raphael said
was more of an ordeal than a blessing to the musician
possessing it.)

"Yet, Saara the Fenwoman is greater than my father
was. I'm sure I could learn much from her, and the learning
would be more pleasant."

Macchiata raised her head. "But you don't want to be a witch, Master. You want to play the lute and go from place to place. You said so."

Damiano cocked an eyebrow in irritation, and at that moment a mid string snapped. The small explosion echoed through the little gold wood and the birds all went quiet together.

He stared down dumbly for a moment, then began to pull off the remnants of the string. "Both ways of life," he stated, "have their advantages. And disadvantages.

"It may be I'm tuning too high," he concluded, and started the tuning again.

"But Saara has the best of both worlds, for her music is her magic. And vice versa. Her way, I think, is more suited to a woman than a man, for we are by our nature more forceful and less gentle. If my feelings ruled my craft . . . well, we'd have a lot more storms in the sky, Macchiata."

This time the tuning was completed without incident, though the empty space on the fingerboard was as bad as a missing tooth. "It must be that the lady's pure heart is her strength. That and her green eyes. Green and golden eyes. And smooth, dimpled skin . . ."

"Master," broke in Macchiata. Her own eyes, earnest and brown, were concerned. "Master, do human men ever have to go to the stable?"

He peered across the fire at her, blinking, his chain of thought—if it was thought—broken. "What, Macchiata? Do human men ever what?"

"Ever have to stay in the stable. For two weeks. Alone."

Damiano's glance slid away, and his complexion went many shades darker. He cleared his throat. "No, Macchiata," he said with authority. "No, never."

In the dark, in the rustling quiet of the birch trees, under the round white moon, Damiano began to play. His music was French, but it was not the new music at all. He played songs that were two hundred years old: the chansons of Bernart de Ventadour, whose love of his patron's lady was so unwavering that he was banished for it, and who then chose to love Eleanor of Aquitaine.

And Damiano sang to the lute in old Provençal, a language he could barely understand. The mode was Ionian, but the tune was very sad.

> *"Amors, e que'us es vejaire?*
> *Trobatz mais fol mas can me?"*
> (Love, what is your opinion?
> Can you ever find a greater fool than I?)

He heard in his own voice greater depth and feeling than he had imagined it to possess, for there is that about any foreign language: speaking it one becomes a different person, capable of new and astonishing things. His voice carried him away, till there were tears in his eyes with pity for the song and for himself.

> *" . . . Farai o,c c'aissi's cove;*
> *Mas vos non estai ges be*
> *Quem fassatz tostems mal traire."*

Little wings fluttered in the tree nearest the fire: neither the wings of the lark nor the sparrow. Damiano did not look up as Saara swooped to the earth beside Macchiata and sat there, feet folded under her blue felt skirt. But he sang the last part of the verse again, in Italian.

> *"I'll do what I must.*
> *But it does not become you*
> *To keep me suffering this woe."*

Saara whispered "Ah," and Macchiata slunk away from the fire. The greatest witch in the Italies twisted her brown braid around and around one pink finger. "Very pretty, Dami-yano. Your music is like you: warm and dark and lonely. Only very young men are lonely in that way."

There was silence while Damiano regarded her from across the campfire. Though her face was a blur at that distance, under the full moon he saw things with his witch's eyes and was abashed.

"I've come to tell you something, Dami—I'll call you that; it's easier. I've come to tell you why I won't help you fight a war."

"I don't want . . ." he began, but she cut him off with a sharp gesture.

"In my home, which is Lappland in the far north, we were all sorcerers among the Haavala tribe: all Lapps are sorcerers—witches. We have power over the herds and the wild beasts and, most important of all, the weather. We keep the weather just bad enough to keep other peoples out."

"Weather? You mean raising the wind and calling clouds or dispersing them? I can do that a little."

She smiled. "I mean making a downpour in a drought, or a garden without winter."

Damiano shrugged humbly and shook his head. "I cannot even imagine that much strength."

Saara chuckled. "To control the elements, Dami, you must be willing to become one with them. That you refuse to do.

"But I want to tell you about me, and why I'm here.

"I was young, Dami. As young as you. I had a husband—Jekkinan—and two little girls with black hair, like their father's.

"Jekkinan was the head of our tribe. He was a strong man, and could cage a wolf with a song of three words. He was also proud and haughty, though he tempered his words with me.

"In the autumn was the gathering of the herds, when the men go out alone. There was a fight over the division, and a man was killed. I am told Jekkinan killed him, though I cannot believe . . .

"Whether or no, he came home and said nothing to me about a fight, but the next day I went out alone, and when I came home, Jekkinan was dead, and the—and the chil—children. Dead on the floor, pierced by spears. The open wounds were mouths that spoke the killer's name."

An involuntary cry escaped Damiano. "Ah! Lady, I'm so sorry." He leaned forward till his face was almost in the fire.

Saara glanced upward with dry, locked eyes. "That isn't why I won't help you, Dami-yano. The same night that I found my children dead I came to the house of the man who killed them.

"And I killed him with a song—him and his wife. His children were grown, or I might have killed them too. Then the tribe came together and decided—for shame—not to be a tribe anymore, and the herd was divided and they went apart, taking the names and the manners and the stitch-work of other tribes. I am the only one left wearing the two stars of the Haavala.

"That is why I won't help you, Dami. I have done what hate made me to do. For all my life."

Damiano stepped through the fire and sat beside her. "We are more alike than you know, Saara," he whispered. His sun-darkened hand rested on her own.

"Oh, I do know, Dami-yano," she replied, her hand motionless but unyielding beneath his. "When I felt you in the breezes of the meadow, I knew you, both by your delight in my garden and by the pain that brought you to it. You drew me to you like a lodestone draws a nail, and even now I cannot help but . . ."

With these words she edged away from him and turned her face to the dark. Damiano did not release her hand.

"If you know me, lady, you know that I don't want vengeance, but peace for my people."

Saara's rose pink lips tightened. "Let them find other towns to live in, as my people found other tribes."

He sighed. "It's not the same, lady. A man without property—with only a wife and hungry children—he's not especially welcome anywhere. Exiles are so many beggars.

"A city is like a garden. Everything grows together, and the roses shade the violets. A man belongs in his own city. Can't you help me, Saara? If you have the power to cage a wolf, can't you cage a brigand, or at least scare him away?"

"Can't *you?*" she replied. "Men who have no power are easily cowed by it."

Damiano smiled ruefully and scratched his head. His hand disappeared amid the tangle of black curls. "I can't think how," he admitted. "The only ways I know to frighten an army are ways Pardo suggested to me himself, and so I doubt they'd work on him.

"But with rain and lightning, lady! I'll speak the spell myself, so if it is risky or demands heavy payment, it will come back on me . . ."

Saara shook her head emphatically. "You can't, black eyes. Not bound to this staff as you are, and even if you let it go, you would have to learn again like a child.

"I would have to do this thing for you, and I won't." Her face was set. "In the morning you go back to Ludica."

Damiano flinched. He squeezed her hand placatingly. "Please. I'd like to stay here a few days, in case you change your mind."

Saara glared at Damiano. She pulled on one of her

braids in frustration. "I told you you can't, boy. Ruggerio will go into a rage, once he knows you're here."

Damiano picked up a pebble and threw it into the fire. His own quick fire was wakened. "Well then, he must be very easily enraged, Saara. For if the truth be known, I myself am as much a virgin as a day-old chick. If I tried to do you violence, lady, you would probably have to show me how!" And with his admission he turned away from her, rested one hand on his knee and his head on his other fist and stared unseeing across the meadow.

Saara smothered her laughter with both hands. "Oh, my dear, my sweet boy. I know. I knew that from the beginning. But Ruggerio—will either not believe or not care. He is proud and quick to anger. Like Jekkinan, I guess. And it's his boast that he keeps men out of the garden."

"Proud and angry and not even a witch. What do you want with him, Saara?" growled Damiano, still with his back to the fire.

He missed the lift of her shoulders and her dimpled smile. "He's very faithful," Saara offered.

"So's Macchiata—my dog," he grunted in turn. He turned again to see the lady scratching her bare toes thoughtfully.

"Understand, Dami. When I came to this country I was very unhappy. Filled with grief and regret. When the southerners discovered who I was—a foreigner and a—a witch—they would not speak to me. The children ran away.

"A man came to me, then: a southman, but a man of our kind—the first witch I ever saw who bound himself to a stick. (How that puzzled me!) He told me he had felt my presence in the wind of his own chimney, far off, and could not stay away.

"He was young, like you, and dark. I thought I loved him. I *did* love him; he was like Jekkinan, with both his power and his storms. One night he . . . he did something very bad; he crept into my mind. He moved to steal my strength from me, and so I discovered that he had never loved me at all but had desired my power.

"It was horrible to find I had been so wrong—to find I had lived as wife with a man and it had all been planned as a trick! He had the skill of lying with the heart itself—never had I heard of such a thing.

"But he had exposed himself too soon. I fought back, and I was the stronger. He went fleeing down the hill, and I've never seen or heard of him again.

"But I remember; I remember how I saw through a man, or thought I did, and was a fool. And I will not trust another like him! So I allow no one on the hill and rarely step out of my garden. And that was why I was surprised to find that people in the far Piedmont know my name.

"Ruggerio has no power," she continued, in calmer tones. "And his temper is a trouble to me, Dami. But he loves me, and because he is only simple I know he is not hiding . . ." She stopped in midsentence, staring at Damiano's face, where anguish and shame and a dread certainty were growing. "What is it, boy? What have I said?"

He swallowed and croaked, "The witch who betrayed you. His name. What was it?"

Her brow drew forward painfully. "I . . . don't repeat it. What does it matter to you, Dami-yano?"

His hands clenched each other as Damiano uncomfortably glanced everywhere but at Saara. "It . . . it couldn't have been Delstrego, could it? Guillermo Delstrego? Because if it is, I really am sorry."

Saara's breath hissed out. She took Damiano's head between her hands and looked into his eyes, reading the truth she had missed before.

"I *am* sorry," he said, thick voiced. "I wouldn't . . ."

"No!" she cried out. "I've done it again! Again! Great Winds, will I never be free?" And Saara vanished upward into the trees.

Damiano huddled against a blast of frozen air. "Dear Jesu," he whispered, as the fire guttered out. A few minutes later he added, "Papa, you have so much to answer for."

Macchiata crawled out of the night and sat beside him.

CHAPTER 12

The cold faded soon, and Damiano was too depressed to restart the fire. He wrapped himself in his single blanket and hugged Macchiata close, both for warmth and comfort. Sleep came nowhere near.

Damiano almost called upon Raphael for comfort, since the angel, at least, knew he was not party to the wrong-doings of Delstrego, Senior. Yet that business of the interview with Lucifer stopped his mouth. Even if Raphael had no knowledge of what had passed, Damiano did, and he knew his face would proclaim his deed.

And what of Raphael's face? Now that Damiano had looked into the eyes of the Devil and recognized the angel, what would he see in the eyes of the Devil's brother? Not sin, certainly, but . . .

And on the other hand, how could he communicate to his spiritual friend his feelings for the lovely Saara, with such depths in her eye, and such sweet impudence in her mouth? Even the dog doubted the purity of his intent. Silently Damiano cursed the purity of his intent.

No, he did not want to see Raphael right now. He turned back to the comforter of whom he was sure.

"How can I be to blame, little dear? She looked into my soul so far as to see me as a child, in the days before you were born, playing with rabbits. If I was like my father, surely she would have seen it then."

Macchiata laid her long nose on the blanket by her master's head. Her tongue flicked out in consolatory gesture, touching the tip of Damiano's nose. Licking faces was a thing Macchiata was not usually allowed to do, but tonight her master didn't chide her for it. "I think I know what it is with Saara, Master," said the dog.

"Unph!" He rose up on one elbow. His dark hair snared the stars in its tangles. "What is it, Macchiata?"

The dog rolled over, presenting her unlovely belly to his scratching fingers. "It's like that with a cat. Something—anything—gets a cat upset and then there's no sense in her.

No use to talk; you just have to go away and lick your nose."

"Lick your nose?"

"The scratches. Saara is upset at your father, so she claws you instead."

Damiano smiled at the image of Saara as a cat. With her little face and tilted eyes, she'd make a good cat. His sigh melded with a laugh and came out his throat and nose as a horse's whinny.

Doubtless Saara could become a cat in an instant, if she wanted to. A big cat. Damiano regarded the susurrous meadow grass with new caution. But no. Had the lady wanted to destroy him, she could have done it before, in the midst of his surprise and shame.

"Even a cat calms down, eventually, Macchiata," he murmured, reclining again. "Calms down and curls by the fire, so one can pet her. In the morning I'll find Saara again and tell her she can look into my head all she wants, till she is sure I am true. Perhaps if I put down my staff, she'll believe me."

Macchiata whined a protest and wiggled free from the blankets. "No, Master! Remember: you did that before and got hit on the head!"

Damiano grabbed at one of her feet. She evaded his hand. "Those were ordinary men, Macchiata. They were afraid of me."

"So is Saara," the dog reminded him.

Morning came, with strings of mist curling up from the waters. Damiano's blanket was damp; so was he. Breakfast was cold water and the last of the bread. Macchiata ate a dead frog and then wandered off in search of more.

Damiano had the lute in his hands, wondering where under heaven he'd be able to find a replacement for the broken string, when he became aware of a man in the pine wood. It was neither vision nor sound that informed him, but the instinct he had inherited from his father.

It was a slight pressure, like the light touch of a finger on the face, an irritation hardly noticed. Indeed, in the streets of Partestrada, Damiano suppressed this sense, as a distraction and hindrance. But here in solitude with the moon at its full, Damiano could feel the stranger's size and shape, and even, to some measure, his intent.

He put off his mantle and laid it on the rock seat. He smoothed his clothes and ran his fingers through his hair. Since he had no sword to don, he slung his lute across his back instead. Then, with unconscious dignity, he proceeded to the edge of the meadow, where the pines cast a barrier of shadow. When the man stepped out Damiano bowed to him in a manner neither proud nor servile, and he wished him good day.

The stranger was tall, and where Damiano was slim, this fellow was lean like a starved hound. His face was long and his eyes glinted black in the early sun. His nose was so high-bridged his face would have appeared arrogant asleep. As he stood there, peering down at Damiano, the expression upon that face was an insult.

Silence stretched long. The stranger shifted his weight onto his left hip with mincing grace. His left thumb was thrust negligently between the hilt and the scabbard of a sword that was neither new nor ornamental. The worn nap on his velvet tunic proclaimed the fact that this gentleman wore the sword at least as often as he wore the tunic.

His eyes went from Damiano's dirty boots to his rude, mountain trousers and thence to his woolen shirt, where the white linen peeped out at neck and wristline. The black glance wrote a silent satire on each article it lighted upon, and when it reached Damiano's face, its narrative was so amusing the man broke out in laughter.

"The wolf has a very small puppy," he announced, speaking to an invisible audience. "Perhaps this is only a bitch-whelp, after all."

Damiano leaned upon his staff, allowing the flush to pass from his face. "By all signs you are Ruggerio," he said. "I don't want to trade insults with you, Signor. But I do want to talk to you."

Ruggerio stepped forward in an airy toe-dance about which there was nothing feminine. He circled around Damiano to get the sun out of his eyes.

And into Damiano's. "But only one of us has anything to say, whelp. Take you from my lady's hill."

Damiano sighed deeply and scratched his head. "You have a sword, Signor, and I do not. That is a strong argument in your favor. But much as I would like to avoid trouble with you, I cannot leave without seeing the lady Saara again."

Ruggerio paused, a black shape against the sun. "I see, fellow. And that in itself is an argument almost as strong as a sword, for my lady is more beautiful than the new rose, and her speech is like water to a man in the desert. If I prevent men from Saara, it is because otherwise her garden would become a litter of broken hearts.

"But, little wolf, with you the matter is different. It is not I but Saara herself who has ordered you gone from here. Isn't that enough, fellow? You have seen my lady's face; how can you not now bend to her wish?" Damiano heard the practiced, smooth draw of the sword from its scabbard.

He stepped back behind his staff, as though it could conceal him. "I would indeed bend to her wish, Signor. Every wish but this one. If she told you who I am, she must have also told you why I am here."

The sword reflected light like water. The long grass stood away from the base of Damiano's staff as though blown by wind. "Like your dog of a father, fellow, you covet my lady's powers," said Ruggerio.

"I don't want her powers, Signore, but her help. I need her to save my city from destruction," replied the witch, and he raised his staff off the ground. As the Franciscan in his homespun robes may raise the cross before some Muslim caliph, so Damiano raised his black staff before Ruggerio. And Ruggerio laughed.

"You have a pretty name for ambition, churl. I'll admit that.

"But enough, now. Go." The sword made an abortive feint toward Damiano's midsection. "Or I'll prick you with tiny holes, like bedbug bites, that will get bigger and bigger as I lose my temper. You see?" The steel flickered in motion and was deflected by Damiano's staff. A sweet tinging like that of a bell cut the air. Ruggerio circled his wrist, and the sword lunged again.

Sparks flew as steel hit silver, and again the strike went wild. Ruggerio grunted in his throat.

Damiano's eyes (never very useful to him) went soft and vague as he turned his inner attention to Ruggerio. He swayed to the right out of the path of the swordsman's attack.

"I'm not about to let you stick me with that pin, Signor

Ruggerio," Damiano said aggrievedly. "Not even a prick like a bedbug bite."

It was not agility alone that preserved the young witch, for with each sword thrust his staff called out to his opponent's blade and took the force of the blow upon its own wood and metal. Three more times Damiano evaded the taunting feints, till the tall southerner stepped back with a hiss of breath.

"You will drive me to kill you, fellow," Ruggerio spat.

Cautiously Damiano stepped sideways, until he could discern the features of his enemy's face. "Is that what the lady said, Signore? That you were to kill me if I did not run away?"

The Roman snorted. "She didn't stipulate. Being a delicate creature, my lady leaves such necessities to me. I am very willing to . . ."

Ruggerio's sentence ended in a scream of rage, which turned to one of pain as ivory dog-fangs clashed against the bone of his ankle. He kicked, and Macchiata flew through the air above the meadow grass. Seeing the tip of the sword touch against the ground, Damiano stepped down upon it, but Ruggerio withdrew his weapon, slicing halfway through the wood and leather of Damiano's boot heel. "Leave us, Macchiata," called Damiano. "I can handle him; you'll only get yourself killed."

Ruggerio's cry was wordless. The edged blade flashed in a scintillating arc toward Damiano's head.

"Mother of God, help me!" whispered the witch, as he threw his staff into the path of destruction. The blade sparked and recoiled, while the wood itself sang like the reed of a cathedral organ. "Don't do that, Signore," Damiano warned.

Ruggerio switched his sword to his left and stuck a numbed right hand into his belt. "Ah? So it's the stick you need, puppy. I forgot my lady said something to that effect. Then I'll cut it out of your hands or cut your hands off with it; that's the fitting punishment for a thief."

The knowledge that Saara had given away his weakness hit Damiano like a slap. For an instant he heard the forest ring in its own silence and felt a weakness in his chest. Ruggerio swung again, scraping his blade along the surface of the staff. Damiano spun the ebony length just

fast enough to escape with his hands. The knuckles of his
left hand oozed blood.

But it was Ruggerio who cursed aloud at the pain that
shot up his wrist and arm. "Let the staff be, Ruggerio,"
shouted Damiano, drawing back a step. "Striking it is
deadly."

The tall swordsman stood motionless a moment, eyes
intent, face expressionless. He swayed lightly, as though to
music. "Is it, fellow? To me or to you, I wonder? Where will
you be, if I cut off that pretty silver head with the yellow
stones? Will your own head roll in the dust? Let's see." And
Ruggerio's blade whirled above his own head.

Damiano yanked sideways on the staff, and the sword
flew clean. He started to step away. "No, Signore. You will
only get . . ." And in that instant his torn heel caught in
the grass and Damiano went down, falling flat on the body
of the lute. He heard the snap of wood, Ruggerio stood
above him, and the blade was falling.

"Mother of . . ." Damiano whispered, expecting to
end the phrase in heaven or in hell. But the blade came
down with terrible force not on flesh but on the silver head
of the staff, where five topaz made a ring, almost directly
on top of the single, small ruby.

The sword itself made a noise like a broken string that
echoed through earth and air. Ruggerio dropped the
weapon, shuddered, and put both hands to his heart. On
his greyhound features was a look of embarrassed surprise. He dropped beside Damiano, who still lay with one
foot trapped in the long grass. The witch saw the man's
spirit, like light, like water, like wings, shake itself free of
the body and be gone.

The wind made mumbling sounds in the grass. In the
birch wood a single sparrow repeated "peep peep peep."
Damiano knelt before the body of the swordsman. He
began to shake his head, though he himself didn't know
why he was doing so. He closed the man's eyes and
arranged the sprawled limbs, then he leaned back on his
heels and folded his hands on his lap. He began a
Paternoster, for want of anything else to do.

The wind grew louder, its wailing growing moment by
moment until the wind became a white bird, which became
Saara the Fenwoman. She took the body of her lover in her
arms and cried out in a strange and bitter tongue. Her face

was white and unbelieving. Her eyes stared, and she, too, shook her head at the sight of death.

Damiano shuffled back and rose to his feet. His jaw seemed to be locked; there was nothing he could say. He staggered, dragging one wooden heel held only by a strip of leather. Macchiata whined and thrust her head between his knees.

Saara looked up slowly. Her face was ashen and blank. Her eyes were dry. It was a long time before she saw Damiano standing there before her.

The single sparrow went "peep peep peep." The wind sorted through the grass. Damiano noticed his left hand was red with blood. Blood from his knuckles had slicked the black staff, but the wound itself had no feeling.

Then Saara opened her mouth and began to keen.

Cold struck Damiano like so many blows to the face. His nose stung, and the roots of his teeth. Frozen air scraped at his lungs as he raised his hand to his face. In another instant the wind had knocked him from his feet, and he rolled on grass that snapped like ice beneath his weight. He closed his eyes to the cold and cried out.

His ears felt Saara's song as a deadly pain. Damiano screamed as his right eardrum burst. He clambered to his feet and ran toward the pine forest, horribly dizzy, stumbling as he went.

Saara's song reached before him, and the gentle air froze, leaving each green needle clothed in ice. There was a crackling like a fire, as branches too suddenly stressed broke and fell to the ground. Snow came out of nowhere and stole Damiano's breath. He fell again and gobbets of snow and frozen stream water pelted him from behind, beating him, seeking to bury him alive. From nearby Macchiata howled "Master!" He freed his face of the drift. He called to her.

Then the rough black tree trunk at his right hand cracked like a twig underfoot, and forty feet of pine loomed over Damiano and came crashing down.

He couldn't move, trapped under the weight of snow. But by instinct he twisted, and he raised his staff to the falling monster as he had done against Ruggerio's sword.

"No!" he shouted, with his foolish little protection waving above him.

The air crackled with a smell of burning metal. Damiano's hair stood away from his head, and the black wind whistled through his ebony staff.

The tree stopped falling.

Its mammoth bulk lay suspended in the air for three seconds, then it caught fire. Rude orange flames lit the shadow, and the sound of burning was like an enormous, damned choir. Damiano lay half-buried and helpless as the heat of flame warred with winter, and feathery ash fell upon his face. It began to rain in the covert.

And then the tree was gone.

He rose slowly, unhindered, and stared down at his bloody hand. He mouthed the words *"Dominus Deus!* Did I do that?" Wondering, he shook his head again.

Yet, even now, Damiano wasn't weary. Destroying the tree had been easily done. It was as though he had all the fires of hell to draw upon. The very idea of that made him shiver.

He peered all around himself at the blasted wilderness that had been a garden only minutes before. The red rocks glistened beneath jackets of ice, and the flowers in their tiny rock-bound plots lay frost-white and broken. The bed of the wandering stream gaped empty, while snow bent the grass double. Nowhere was there body or bird that could be Saara.

And it was quiet. Even the sparrow had ceased its din, either frozen or frightened away. Damiano stepped into the meadow again.

There was the body of Ruggerio the Roman, lying upon grass untouched by frost. And there, very near to it, was the little lute, broken like an egg. Damiano sighed and came closer.

As Damiano stepped his toe thudded into a lump in the snow. He caught his balance with difficulty and glanced down.

The snow was white and the lump was white, but there was a red spot like a bloodstain upon it. Damiano went down upon one knee and touched not blood but ruddy short fur and the hard, cold ugly bulk that had been Macchiata.

"Macchiata?" he said stupidly, and he turned the dog over. "Little dear?"

The body was stiff as wood, with three legs folded

under and one held out, little toes spread like the fingers of a warding hand. The lips were pulled in a perpetual smile of terror, and the eyes—the eyes were dull chestnuts, no more.

The obvious truth hit Damiano slowly. He took the frozen dog on his lap, hugging her to him. Then he grunted, dumbly, and for the third time he shook his head. His staff clattered to the ground, and Damiano wept like a child.

Saara came toward her enemy, stepping through the snow barefoot. Her face was colorless; her eyes round. Beneath the gay felt dress her small shoulders were hunched stiff, as though she expected blows.

One hand she raised, finger pointing, then she dropped it. She stood motionless and unseen before Damiano's grief.

"Ah, Macchiata," he crooned to no one but himself, and he stroked the white head. It was like petting a piece of wood; even her little petal-like ear was stiff. "Little dear. So small a thing to be dead. Why does it have to be?"

And his unthinking question awoke in him the memory of Macchiata's own words as she mourned the murdered infant in Sous Pont Saint Martin: "It's so little. Can't it be alive?"

"No, Macchiata. It can't," he had said. And with that memory his grief grew harder.

He looked up and saw Saara standing barefoot in the snow, hands at her sides. The simple, girlish figure wavered in his vision as though he were looking through water. He rose. The staff was again in his hand.

"He was my man," she said. "He loved me. He thought I was beautiful. I'm not young, Dami. I'm old. Where will I find another like him?"

Damiano did not reply. Perhaps he did not even hear her. He heard the sound of fire in his ears, and he knew the flames were near, to be drawn through his staff like air through a flute. He tilted his head to hear what the fire was saying.

Saara looked at his face and turned to flee.

The white bird rose, but fire seared the sky like the lick of a whip. She dropped and dove, and a beast like a shaggy deer sprang away. It carried backswept antlers, and its hooves were wide like the pads of a camel.

It was true, Damiano thought distantly. She was not lying; there is such a deer.

A tongue of flame raced toward the pine wood; where it touched the snow, the air went white with steam. It reached the edge of the meadow before the leaping animal and flashed sideways, turning the reindeer, prisoning both it and its captor with a wall of deadly heat. Grass sizzled. The fire burned wood, earth, snow. It needed nothing but itself to burn.

I have only begun, thought Damiano without emotion. Hell is vast; I could char all this hill. All of Lombardy.

Saara turned at bay, and as she cast off her animal form, she was hidden by the thickening mists. It didn't matter. Damiano could feel her presence on his closed eyelids. He advanced toward her.

Suddenly the air dazzled and snapped with thunder. Above both witches the heavens convulsed, and a drenching rain smote down.

The ring of flame guttered, and for a moment Damiano saw Saara plainly: a small and slender figure kneeling on the flattened grass, streams of rain running along her long braids and down her breast. Her hands were raised to the sky. She was singing.

She was as fair as a dryad, as a child. Her beauty hurt him, and with his pain he built the fire higher. Saara screamed at the touch of boiling steam. Damiano felt nothing.

The clouds lifted, but there was no woman on the grass, merely a flock of doves, watching him. He closed his eyes and stepped toward Saara.

A white bear rose above his head, black mouthed, ten feet tall. It swung a paw at him that was thicker than Damiano's waist. He dodged and thrust a staff of fire at the creature's eyes. It turned and faded.

Lightning smashed down upon him, and the mad staff drank it, singing as though with joy. He threw the bolt at the woman before him, and she fell.

Damiano leaned over her. Water ran from the snakelike curls on his head to spatter in her face. He put his boot upon her stomach; the broken heel snagged and tore the red and yellow stars. The silver head of his staff he pressed against her throat. "No more singing," he said.

Then he raised his head. The ring of fire, unattended,

had flickered out, but Saara's rain continued, cold, dull, and gray. Damiano ground his teeth and stared without seeing.

In another moment he would kill her. Or walk away. He desired . . . what he wanted he did not know. He flexed his damaged knuckles on the staff.

The staff knew what *it* desired. It told him, speaking the same language as the fire had used. It desired increase— power. It vibrated in his hand.

Saara cried shrilly and gasped for air. Damiano glanced down in surprise, all hate forgotten between one moment and the next. He lifted his foot.

And then he was struck by a blow of greater power than that of the lightning. It came through the wood of the staff itself and ascended his arm, striking into his heart and his head.

It was cold rain and distance and falling. It was sunlight and unrecognized tunes and a wealth of meaningless words. Damiano floated in stunned silence. He would have flung the staff away, had he known how. But he was not now master. The staff had been created by Damiano's father, and in this moment, it reverted to type. It was strong, and it was thirsty. It dragged the young man into its own magic.

But it was the only weapon he had or knew how to use, so he fought the chaos with that length of black wood, until it was subdued to it.

Time and time and time passed away.

Saara was still screaming. Rain pelted him in the face. Damiano climbed swaying to his feet. He stopped the rain.

She stared up at him in horrified wonder. "You have it all," she whispered, and huddled in a ball on the mired grass. "What your father wanted."

He looked down at the woman's full hair, gray at the temples, and her eyes, which were seamed by sun and hard weather. On the backs of her clenched hands the tendons stood out clearly, and veins made a faint, blue lacework. Her face was burned by steam.

But nothing he saw was a surprise to him now, for he knew Saara very well—in her body, in her song, and in her power, which had become his.

"You are still beautiful, *pikku* Saara," he said, not

knowing he spoke the far Northern language. "And you are not very old."

Saara turned her head to him, and what she saw hurt her eyes. She started to shiver.

Damiano limped away from her. In the middle of the waste that had been a garden he stopped and tapped his staff upon the soil. Grass roots ripped, and stones. A black hole gaped before him. Within it he placed the corpse of a dog. He made again the small journey to the dead man's side, and he picked up, not Ruggerio's body, but the pieces of the broken lute, which went into the grave beside Macchiata. In another moment the earth shut its mouth.

Leaving the grave unmarked, Damiano turned away from the meadow, where a winter wind blew across the sullied earth. He did not look back at Saara.

CHAPTER 13

When he was well into the privacy of the pines, Damiano sat down on a log. He stuck a bit of moss into his painful ear, to keep out the cold, and with this his dizziness grew less. With a bread knife he pried off the heel from his intact boot, making his steps level.

His new powers whispered in his right ear, like a friend standing too near for comfort. That broken ear could hear nothing save the memory of chants sung long ago, in a language repetitive and strange, yet to Damiano understandable.

Fly, the words repeated. Find the sky. Leave vestment and body behind. He clung doggedly to his clomping staff.

"It isn't what I wanted, lady," Damiano said aloud, his voice echoing oddly through his left ear only. "I am not my father."

Suddenly it occurred to him that even he did not believe himself. He stopped in his tracks, chewing his lower lip. He began to review his actions, step by step, since leaving home, both through the eyes of his memory and through this strange new vision that had become his. He sat down.

Before Damiano moved again, the endless evergreen

twilight had deepened. An owl stretched its downy wings in the crotch of a split fir, and cold spread down from the high meadow into the wood.

Only the silver on his staff was visible as Damiano hauled himself again to his feet, using a sapling for support. He cleared his throat and glanced about him, marking each mouse-stir and badger's yawn: the living rustle of the forest.

This time the invocation should be easier. He had merely to follow his own fire to its source, and he would locate the spirit he sought. Closing his eyes Damiano descended within himself until he touched, far down and glimmering, the trace of the fire.

This he followed, through blackness and void, and it grew stronger and brighter as he approached its source. At the shore of a molten ocean he stopped, daunted not by heat but by terror.

I was born for this, he thought, and with that understanding he might have wept, except that he had used up all his tears. He did not kneel, but stood with his knees locked, braced by his staff. "Satan!" he called. "I am here."

There was no response. Damiano opened his eyes.

He was in the black forest, in full night. His journey had gone nowhere. Puzzlement knit his brow. "If those are the fires of hell," he mumbled to himself, "then this Lombard hillside must be hell itself. And I've been many places worse."

Frowning, he dismissed the matter and began his conjurement in the traditional manner, with staff and palindrome. At the word Satanas, he again felt the pull that would wrench him from the damp pine needles to the Devil's palm. Every weary bone in Damiano rebelled at the thought of that wild flight.

"No," he stated, and rooted himself to the earth. The spell tightened like a rope around him, but it neither shook him nor did it tear. The jeweled head of his staff sparked, then glimmered like an oil lamp, and Damiano found himself staring at the fine ruddy features and elegant poise of Satan, who shook the dead needles from his shoes and bowed.

The Devil was just his size.

"So you are no longer the sympathetic little dove who had words with me a week ago," he said to Damiano.

The witch shrugged. "You don't have wings," he remarked, pointing. "I didn't notice before, when you were so big. You don't have wings anymore."

The red face twitched with scorn. "I am what size it pleases me to be. And as for wings, young mortal, I don't need them to fly."

Damiano blinked and scratched his chin. "Perhaps, Signore, but I don't need my eyebrows either, and yet I don't pluck them out."

Scarlet deepened to crimson, but the Devil's urbanity remained otherwise intact. "Did you bring me here to throw insults at me, Delstrego? If so, I warn you, you are not yet that powerful . . ."

"No, Signore." Damiano ran one hand through his hair in a businesslike manner. "I . . . asked you here because I want to take the bargain you offered me last week."

Satan's smile was slow and grudging. Under the flickering staff-light it looked a bit . . . satanic. "But you were sure there was a better way, little witch."

Damiano nodded, lips pursed. "Yes. I'm still sure of it. But not for me. Everything I have done has led to blood."

Very quietly the Devil said, "You are one of mine." Damiano stared down at his boots and nodded.

"The bargain," he repeated.

Satan sank indolently down upon a chair that hadn't been there before: a chair that looked very much like the one Damiano had seen burnt in the guard shack at the crossroads below Aosta. He fixed Damiano with a knowing eye.

"Why that?" he began diffidently. "Now that you know the truth, I can give you freedom itself."

"The bargain. I will trade the future of my city, and my own, for peace."

"Renounce the shackles of the Beginning, and you can have whatever you want."

Damiano snorted and sat also, not on a magical chair, but on the ground. "Why would I renounce my Maker, Signore. He has done nothing ill."

Satan's eyes widened in shock. "He has covered the earth with pain and despair, Damiano. His cruelties are so enormous that even his ministers curse him in private. You have seen his work well these past few weeks. Open your poor, nearsighted eyes."

Damiano took a deep breath, and still regarding Satan, he scratched his forehead on the wood of the staff. "I have seen cruel and angry men and men who are mistaken. I have seen my own misbegotten nature. And I have seen a lot of bad weather.

"But the world He made, Signor Satan, does not despair. It is beautiful. No, I admit that I am wicked, and that my destiny is hell. But that does not mean I must love hell, or all that is wicked, and I do not.

"I love the green earth, Signore, and the Creator who made it. I also love your gentle brother Raphael, and the city of Partestrada in the Piedmont. What of the bargain you offered?"

The Devil's eyes flickered. "Don't be a fool, Dami. You can do better than that."

"That's what I thought, once. The bargain."

Satan folded his florid and shapely hands in his lap. Damiano noticed beneath his chair a settled pall of smoke, and the tang of burning cut the incense of the pines.

"The situation has changed," announced Satan. "You yourself have changed it, youth, by your . . . adventures. It will have to be approached differently."

"Explain," replied Damiano, drumming his fingers on his staff.

"You have become larger, Damiano. Much larger. And you are a disturbing influence, with your ultra-modern ideas and your quaint mortality. Men such as yourself exist only to make trouble." The Devil grinned tightly.

"And you will make trouble—for your village, for the Piedmont, for the Green Count himself, in years to come—for you will inevitably come to disagree with Amadeus, whatever the man does.

"If you want what you wanted last week for your village—pardon me, your city—peace and stagnation, you will have to pay a higher price."

Damiano's black eyebrows came together in a V between his eyes. "You said the city would fade and be forgotten. And I myself. Have you found something worse to offer, Satanas?"

Satan's smile was pained. "I? Damiano, I'm trying to help you construct the future. You have created the possible choices, not I.

"And this one . . . isn't good. In order for Partestrada

to squat in comfort for the next half-century (before decaying into the soil), it is necessary that you be out of the picture."

Damiano shrugged and watched the smoke crawl like so many snakes over the forest floor. "So I can't go home?"

The Devil sat immobile. "That's not enough, as it was not enough to exile Dante from Florence. You must die," Satan said calmly.

Damiano's eyes shot to the red, expressionless face. "Die?"

"Yes. Die. And soon. So you see, Dami, it's not much of a bargain after all, is it?"

The young man's mouth opened. His black eyes stared unseeing. "How soon?" he whispered, repeating Macchiata's words once again. "How soon is soon?"

A slow smile pulled at the perfect lips as Satan watched the mortal man shiver. "Soon. I can't say, exactly. Perhaps a year or two. Perhaps tonight. It is certain, if you strike this fool's bargain, that you will not live to become wise." And he observed Damiano's misery with trained appreciation.

But his enjoyment was short. Damiano raised his head, met the Devil's gaze, and nodded.

"Done," he said.

Satan scowled, and his huge anger cracked through the carnelian mask. "What game do you think you're playing? You can gain nothing by theatrics, boy! The Beginning has cast you off already, and mankind will never know!"

Damiano placed both hands on top of his head and rubbed his face against his knees. "Eh? Yes, but I will know, Signor Satan, and that is something."

The Devil stood up and flung the spindly chair into nothingness. He spat on the forest floor in front of Damiano, leaving a spot of smoking ash. "You will know, boy? When you are in my hand you will know what I permit you to know, no more. You will remember only the idiocy of your actions, forever!"

Damiano rose slowly. "Then I know it now, and that will have to be enough. Come, Signor Satan. It was your bargain to begin with; hold to it. Shall I sign in blood?"

Ruddy nostrils twitched, and Satan glared at the man with barely disguised rage. "Unnecessary, Damiano. I will have blood enough at the end.

"So be it, fool. I give you your bargain." The Devil

sighed, and his pale eyes narrowed. "Go back the way you came. What you see on the road will make your path obvious.

"As for what you are to do, do what seems best to you. Employ what tools you are given."

Pulling on composure like a cloak, Satan bowed and was gone.

The young man drew his hands into his mantle and leaned against the rough trunk of a tree. "I'm cold," he said aloud, with no expression in his voice. "And very tired."

But the full moon and his unfamiliar and exotic powers pulled upon him. The staff in which they were caged was warm in his hand. He scrambled down the steep incline toward the lake.

A patch of moonlight stopped Damiano. He focused on the knobbed head of his staff; something was different.

Indeed. The silver had gone black—black as soot. And the jewels at the top were six small chips of jet. What was more, his clothing had turned an equally inky color; ermine shone like sable.

"So he has put his stamp on me, for all to see," whispered Damiano, speaking aloud because he was not used to being alone. Horror chilled the blood in his fingers. His shoulders drew up to his ears.

"Mother of God, keep me from hurting anyone else!"

He reached Ludica in the gray-violet light of dawn. The streets were empty, and Damiano went directly to the stable. Festilligambe whickered at his smell.

From a pile of hay and blankets came a phlegmy snoring. Damiano nudged it with his staff. "I have come for my horse," he said.

The stableboy crawled out of his nest and stood upright before the shadowed figure. Then, with a cry of terror, he fell to his knees, hiding his face, praying and babbling together.

The witch stood puzzled, then his back slumped wearily as he turned toward the horses. "It seems he has most certainly put his mark on me," he said.

The ride west from Ludica was quiet, very quiet save for the tumult in Damiano's injured ear, where foreign speech, foreign desire, and homeless memory mixed together in a murmurous yearning. But either the eardrum was healing

rapidly or he was getting used to the voices, for they no
longer bothered him.

During Damiano's few days in Lombardy, November
had given way to December. Damiano reflected that his
birthday had passed unnoticed. He was now twenty-two
years old. Twice that age would be younger than he felt
himself to be.

But he would not live to be forty-four, he reminded
himself. He would not live to be twenty-five. It was quite
possible he would not live past the night. With consuming
fire at the end of it all, it didn't make a pleasant subject for
thought.

Snow was falling and had been all morning. Damiano
was sincerely tired of it, as well as tired of the wind, the
frozen ruts, and the bare trees. His only comfort was that
he was also too tired to question both what he had done
and what he was about to do.

He huddled in his furs and began to sing a sad ballad of
Walther von der Vogelweide. It sounded odd in his own
head, as though the singer were actually someone standing
near him on the left, but the familiar tune comforted him.

Was he still able to pray? he wondered. Well why not?
He'd said his little Paternoster by the swordsman's body,
and the only difference then had been that he had not
known he was damned at the time.

"Sweet Creator," he began, in Latin as was proper for
all prayers, "of this green world . . . I thank you for it,
though it is not to be mine for very long. And though I am
wicked in nature, I hope you will not take it amiss if I ask
you to take care of certain people. . . ."

Damiano broke off suddenly, blinked, and stared at the
road ahead of him. As he saw the delicate glory of white
wings rising upward in twin interrogative curls his face
stretched into a welcoming, gently relieved smile.

But the expression was stillborn. With the sight of
Raphael, Damiano's plodding numbness broke in pieces,
and he remembered. Shame froze his heart and heated his
face, which went dusky. His hands twisted into the horse's
mane. His eyes slid down to the road. "Seraph," he said
thickly. "I didn't mean to call you. It was only a prayer."

"I know." The archangel Raphael did not try to smile.
He gazed intently at Damiano on his horse, and the wind
riffled his yellow hair.

The angel raised one ivory hand, and Festilligambe loped forward, lipping the air and nickering. The heavy, swart head pressed against Raphael's bosom.

"I know, Damiano," Raphael said again, scratching the beast forcefully behind the right ear. "But I wanted to see you." And the angel's gaze was simple and open, yet so searching that Damiano felt himself go red from head to foot.

That's why Satan looks red, he thought to himself. Bold as he is, his spiritual body is ashamed of itself. As I am ashamed. And now I understand why he hates his brother.

Damiano's jaw clenched. "You do see me, Raphael," he snapped, more sharply than he had intended, and he stared over Raphael's shoulder, where black trees gave way to fields of dead grass, crusted in snow. "And now that you have seen me, what is there to do but go away again?"

The young man waited. Out of the corner of his eye he could see the easy slow drift of a wing, like the twitch of a cat's tail. He dared not look at Raphael's face, to see why the angel stood there, not speaking, for Damiano feared that either the beauty of that face or the compassion written upon it would knock him to the ground.

"Go back to heaven, Raphael. My lute is smashed. My dog, too."

"I am sorry for you, Damiano." It was said coolly, as a statement of fact. "But you must not grieve for Macchiata."

Damiano's answer was flat. "I have not been. I haven't had the time. Or perhaps the feeling.

"It's my life that is smashed, Raphael. I have no more use for a teacher." Then his need to know how the angel was reacting outweighed both fear and shame, and Damiano's eyes turned to Raphael.

Slowly the angel smiled. "I love you, Dami," he said.

Damiano's head sank forward onto the gelding's neck. His face hid in the long mane, rough and black as his own hair. He shuddered until the horse's black back twitched beneath him. "Oh, no," he cried softly. "*Dominus Deus!* No. Don't say that. Not to me."

Raphael stepped to Damiano's side. "Why, Damiano? What is this distance? Do you no longer love me? You said that you did, not a month ago, and you said I was not to doubt it. I *will* not doubt it.

"—I can be very stubborn."

The witch flinched at the gentle touch on his knee. He screwed shut his eyes and ground his teeth together. "Of course I love you, Raphael. And that is turning me on a spit!

"Go away now. Begone! Fly! You can do it fast enough when you want to." And Damiano made blind, ineffectual bird-shooing gestures.

The touch of the hand grew heavier for a moment. "I go," said Raphael. "But we will meet again, Damiano. I am sure of it. At least once more. And then we will talk this over."

Suddenly the horse snorted and turned his head left and right. He stamped an iron-shod foot in disappointment, and his breath blew a cloud of steam. His whinny rang among the iron-gray trees. Damiano opened his eyes, knowing the angel was gone.

CHAPTER 14

The weather continued inclement, with the sky a dark nimbus and the earth cold and wet. Damiano made slow progress westward, waiting for a sign.

He encountered a girl with a shoulder yoke and two baskets of hens. After one look at him she fled screaming, abandoning her squawking wares. Damiano righted the baskets and continued on his way, wondering what it was she had seen in him. When he placed one hand on each side of his nose, he felt the same face beneath them.

That same day a man on horseback approached from a side road. His antipathy was as pronounced as the peasant girl's had been, and what was worse, his champing horse seemed to share the terror.

"This is good," mumbled Damiano sullenly. "No one here to bend my ear with unwanted company and bad jokes. I can have some peace for a bit." And he sighed.

He had been riding for almost a week along the empty road when his witch sense felt the presence of people ahead, thick and hot like the smoke of a wood fire. He took a deep breath, closed his eyes and listened with his mismatched ears.

There were many men ahead—more men than women. Soldiers, in fact, if his powers were any judge. The part of him that had been Saara grew very wary, feeling this.

But at least there was no sound of fighting. Damiano urged the gelding forward.

Half the walls of San Gabriele had gone to make rubble for the barricades. Behind these makeshifts, the black leather and brass of the army of General Pardo filled the town. Because the men were Romans, mostly, they cursed the wind and the constant cold. Because they were soldiers, they glanced dourly over the barricades and the ploughed fields to another camp, where blue tents flapped in the wind and the flag of Savoy was pitched, and spoke of other things.

Ogier, illegitimate son of Aymon of Savoy, sat in his quivering tent and also cursed the wind. He wanted to mop up this little pope's man—this upstart—and go back to Chambéry.

But Amadeus had given him only three hundred troops for the task, while Pardo had at least five. True, Ogier had been able to gather together a few score of the peasants uprooted by Pardo's passage, men with a grudge who would fight for almost nothing, but these were not soldiers, merely angry queenless bees.

He rose from his leather-seated campstool, stretched to his full six feet in height, and scratched the scalp beneath his yellow hair. As soon as he started to release the tent flap, the wind caught it and snapped it out of his hands.

Spread before him was the three-day-old camp of his little regiment. The loose earth was dotted with man-sized shallow holes, which some of the men had dug as a protection from the wind. These made a depressing sight, resembling graves as they did. The air smelled of smoke, human feces (the men were not used to the water in this place), and burnt mutton. No one was doing much; till Ogier gave the order to attack, there was nothing to do.

But his men were not fools or chattel. He could not send them blindly into a bloodbath, hoping in the process to somehow dispatch the Roman. They would not obey such an order. Nor would Ogier have given it, for he was a civilized man; he respected his soldiers, and he knew that giving orders that will not be obeyed only serves to break an officer's authority.

He wondered, not for the first time, whether his half-brother had assigned him this task in order to shame him. Certainly that would be unlike the Green Count, whose obsession with honor and chivalry had caused him to storm off under the banner of Jean le Bon, fighting Edward in Brittany merely because he had sworn to do so.

The gesture had made Savoy appear weak in the eyes of jackals like Pardo, and sending a force of three hundred men after the Roman had merely reinforced that impression.

Which was false. Savoy was not weak; it was merely led by a ruler whose moralities were passé. Ogier scratched the yellow stubble on his cheek.

No, Amadeus had not sent him after the brigand to shame him. The count was not subtle enough for such maneuvering, and besides, Ogier had to admit that he himself was not strong enough to be a threat to Amadeus. Still, by plan or no, this encounter could shame him.

He needed a stratagem to get past the relative weakness of his regiment. But what was strategy without cities or rivers to work around, and when two small forces can see one another clearly? Twice he had sent mounted patrols into the surrounding hills, attempting to circle San Gabriele, and each time enemy trumpets sang out the Savoyard position. Men on hillsides could not hide very well.

He fished for the rope closure of the tent flap, secured it again, and sat down heavily on the campstool. He absently fingered the tip of his long lace collar. It found its way into his mouth, where he bit down upon the already draggled fabric.

He had been gone from his estates six weeks now. He wondered if his wife had yet taken a lover.

At the hour of sunset, as Ogier took supper in his tent, alone and thinking, he heard a single scream, and then the hubbub of raised voices. He cursed himself for delaying too long, and he cursed Pardo for a treacherous Roman bastard. Snatching his sword from the tent floor, he leaped through the open tent flap and landed, rolling, on the stamped earth outside.

There was no battle, he decided in one swift glimpse. The men sat by their cook fires, necks craned to the east road. Or they stood, their hands at their sides or their fingers pointing at a thing that approached through the fading light of day.

Ogier, too, stood motionless and staring as the creature approached, riding a horse of white bones.

The rider was black, save for a bone-white face, and it wore the shape of a man. Two eyes like spear wounds, black and ragged, peered over the blue-clad assemblage. Ogier froze with the sudden belief that those deadly eyes were looking at him.

The worst of it was that the apparition was burning— burning like a doll of pitch, like a witch's toy made for a curse. Its murky red-orange light lit the trees from underneath and shone through the gaping eye sockets of the horse's skull. It advanced.

"Let us shoot it, Commander," urged Martin, his second. "Before it does us harm. Look, it steals men's courage by its very presence!"

The second's teeth were actually chattering as he spoke. This observation broke Ogier's paralysis. "Not . . . yet, Martin," he replied. "It is hideous enough, surely, but it's done us no damage. And what if our weapons can't touch it? Then we will be sorry. Wait," he concluded, adding, "and pray to Saint Michel the archangel, whose duty it is to rein in the hosts of Satan." And Ogier strode forward into the apparition's path.

With one will, the men drew back from this encounter. The burning figure stopped before Ogier; its mount's grisly head turned left and right.

At close range it was the same, or worse. "At least there is no stink of burning flesh," said Ogier aloud, in order to be saying something.

The dead face peered down. "Mutton is what I smell," it said in tones unexpectedly mild, and with a strong Italian accent to its French. Its voice gratified Ogier, who had always suspected the Devil was Italian.

It slid down from its seat of bare ribs, and for a moment the Savoyard's vision wavered, and he thought he saw an ordinary fellow (though rather small) standing next to an ordinary horse. But that glimpse was gone in a wink, and Ogier could not be sure he had ever seen it.

"You are the commander of these men?" the apparition inquired casually.

"Ogier de Savoy," he found himself saying, and he executed a precise, ceremonious bow. Somewhere in the crowd of soldiers one man cried out and clapped his hands. Ogier smiled tightly to himself, thinking this interchange would do his reputation no harm, assuming he lived through it.

When the apparition returned the bow, flames hissed like a flung torch. "Well met, Marquis. I know well the House of Savoy."

Ogier raised one eyebrow and tilted his head. He was not a marquis, but it did not seem necessary to correct the thing. "So? I hadn't thought my family had lived so ill. But no matter, Monsieur Fiend, I stand here at your service. For what have you come so far?"

The creature sighed and patted his skeletal horse. "I would like to talk to you in private, Marquis. It is to both our benefit."

Ogier's other eyebrow joined the first. "The only private place in the camp is my tent," he said. "And I greatly fear you'll burn it down."

The cadaverous head jerked around. "Burn . . . ? Marquis, I promise wholeheartedly I will not burn your tent down. Why did you think . . . Am I glowing red in your eyes, or something like that?"

A smile twitched over Ogier's long face. "Something like that," he admitted, and he led the apparition through the hushed camp to where his blue tent flapped and fluttered in the wind.

"Leave the horse alone," said the creature unnecessarily, but as it stepped away from the structure of bone, that monstrous steed wavered, and in its place stood a black gelding of good breeding, wearing no trappings of any kind. "Stay," the apparition commanded, as though the horse were a dog.

Ogier and the fiend disappeared into the tent of blue silk, which shone then like a lantern in the gathering dark.

"You have men from Partestrada in your army, my lord Marquis," Damiano noted. As there was only one seat in the tent (the folding leather campstool), he settled himself upon the dirt.

Ogier also sat, his face expressionless, his eyes watchful. "I have men from all over the Piedmont in my retinue, good Devil, but only the ones I brought over Mont Cenis are soldiers."

The witch nodded appreciatively. To Ogier the effect was like that of paper shivering in the blast of a flame. The Savoyard sat bolt upright and suppressed a shudder.

After a meditative pause, Damiano spoke again. "Am I correct in assuming you are pursuing the condottiere Pardo and have him cornered in San Gabriele?"

Ogier sucked his cheek before answering. "Aside from the fact there are no corners left in the village you speak of, the situation is as you say. May I inquire, Monsieur Demon, how it is you involve yourself in this matter?"

Ogier found himself confronted by two earnestly gaping eye sockets, filled with night. "I, too, am hunting General Pardo. I think you and I can save each other both time and bloodshed.

"In fact, my lord Marquis, I was promised I would find a tool to my purpose, and I believe your army is the very thing."

Promised? Ogier's mind raced, and the hair on the back of his fair neck stood on end. He repeated to himself "Jesus, Marie, et Joseph," three times. "I regret, Monsieur, that I am not empowered by the count to make treaties, neither with man nor with man's Enemy. I do not wish to offend a being of your evident grandeur, but . . ."

Two arms rose, leprous white and burning, burning . . . Damiano slicked his hair back from his face. "I do not ask you to make a bargain with the Devil, Marquis. Nor with me, if there's any difference there.

"I am merely explaining to you that I need your men, or at least a goodly portion of them. I am going into the village tonight, and once I have captured the general, I will need troops to keep his own men from causing trouble."

Ogier started, snorted, and then thought better of it. "You are going to kill General Pardo, spirit? Tonight?" As if by chance, the blond shuffled his left foot forward until it almost touched the flickering figure: *no heat*.

Damiano frowned. "If need be. I had hoped to deliver him to you, though that would be hypocrisy on my part, eh? Since you would, in turn, slay him."

There was a moment's silence, broken by Ogier. "Why do you seek the Roman's life? What could he have done . . ."

"I was born in Partestrada, Marquis," answered Damiano.

Ogier leaned forward on the stool, his revulsion tempered by sudden interest. The lace of his limp collar hung in the air before his coat of sky blue. "So you were mortal once, Monsieur Demon?"

Damiano blinked in surprise. Feeling a chill, he drew his soot-colored mantle closer. "Yes, Marquis. But it was a very short life and painful at the end.

"Enough. It's dark already, and there's no reason to delay. Assemble your men now, and the battle will be done by midnight." He rose to his feet, using his black staff for support.

Ogier remained seated, staring at the ground. After some moments he shook his head. "I'm sorry, Monseigneur Demon, but I may not do that. You see, although I am a soldier, I am still a Christian."

"Then I will," said Damiano easily. "But they would be happier led by you, I think." As he turned away, the witch heard the now familiar sound of a blade pulling free. He swiveled and pointed his staff.

With a cry Ogier dropped the weapon and cradled one badly singed hand in the other.

Damiano bent and stepped through the tent door.

The night was windy but clear. None of the Savoyard soldiery seemed to have moved during their commander's interview with the Devil. Some shadowed figures were standing, weapons in hand, while others squatted by the meager cooking fires. All faced toward the hellishly radiant tent, and when the burning corpse appeared again, they backed slowly away.

Damiano felt the fear and hostility in the air he breathed. He glanced up at the uncaring stars, as if borrowing their indifference. He raised his staff just as an arrow shot out of the night toward him. Its bright yellow length splintered against the tarnished silver midband, and the goose-feathers sizzled and stank.

"None of that," said the witch quietly, staring past three fires into the crowd, directly at the archer who had loosed the arrow. "The next man who tries to harm me will flame like that arrow.

"And he will die for nothing, because I cannot be hurt as easily as that."

Damiano glanced around him, and his nostrils flared. The skin of his face sorted the men around him. He strode forward at last, and men squirmed out of his path like the Red Sea parting.

He stopped before a cluster of fires a little apart from the others. "Belloc," he said. "Aloisio. I am glad to see you still alive and healthy.

"Tell me, old friend and benefactor. Where is Paolo Denezzi? Is he not among you?"

The square blacksmith gasped. "God's wounds! It's young Delstrego!" Then a form stepped between them.

"I'm here, monster," growled the bass voice Damiano knew and disliked so well. Though his full beard hid most of the expression on Denezzi's face, the small, ursine eyes held more challenge than fear. Damiano met his gaze and said nothing.

"My sister," Denezzi announced, "is locked in the convent at Bard. She is of no use to anyone, that way, but at least she's safe from you."

Damiano nodded. "Good. To be locked away is by far the best kind of life." Then he turned his attention to the men huddled by the fire.

"I am going to take Pardo tonight, men of Partestrada. I thought you might like to ride behind me."

"Behind you?" repeated Denezzi, in tones evenly divided between hate and scorn. "We will take Pardo, all right, Devil's spawn, but not behind you."

Damiano shrugged. "As you like." He turned away. Over his shoulder he called, "We will all be going to San Gabriele soon, however."

He returned to the middle of the camp, in front of the gay tent, which night had reduced to a lumpish shape like a couchant cow. Ogier stood there, weaponless, saying nothing, his face taut and sharp. Damiano ignored the man, for he was preparing himself for his work.

He gazed left and right into the distance, examining his canvas. The half-moon beat down on the low hills as though its light and nothing else had flattened them. The grassland before San Gabriele and the half-forested hills

behind the village lay open and empty of man. The sky was
clear and translucent, not yet black. The Savoyard camp
was a small blot of shadows on the soil. The ruined village
was another.

Wind blew Damiano's mantle back from his shoulders,
and its silver chain pressed against his throat. With his
right hand he pulled against the chain. His left hand held
his staff—held it so tight he felt it pulse and knew that
pulse for his own.

"You are perhaps planning to slip through Pardo's
sentries in secret, Monseigneur Demon?" Ogier's dry
words broke the witch's concentration. "Or should I call
you Monseigneur Lost Soul? Either way, your peculiar
. . . ornamentation will make it difficult."

Damiano was aware the men were slipping away into
the darkness. He could feel the terrified feet stumbling over
the barren fields like ants on his skin. He took the staff in
both hands. "Why so, my lord Marquis. What is it I look
like, anyway?"

Ogier smiled with an odd satisfaction. "You are
aflame," he said.

The dead white face split in a dead laugh. "Appropriate,
Marquis," it whispered, "for you are about to see quite a lot
of flames." As he spoke a serpent of fire hissed and spat
from the swart head of the staff. It wriggled after the fleeing
men, who screamed at the orange light. Some fell to the
earth, while others huddled where they stood, praying and
cursing together.

But the gaudy snake passed them, burning nothing but
the ground and the night air. Damiano slid his hands to the
foot of his staff and swung it over his head.

The serpent of fire became a ring, a wall, a prison for the
Savoyard soldiery. When the witch set the foot of his staff
back upon the earth, the ring of fire remained, taller than a
man and booming thunder. Ogier put his hands to his ears.
The cries of men faded and were lost in the wail of the fire.

"But as you see, Marquis, I am not planning a secret
approach." Damiano shouted above the noise. "Such
would be a mistake, I think. My weapon is terror.

"Using terror, I will save men's lives," he added.

With an effort, Ogier dropped his hands to his belt.
"Save men's lives?" he repeated. "You are the tool of the
Father of Lies himself. May Saint Michel the archangel fling

you to the bottom of the deepest hell if you destroy my good and true men!"

Damiano stopped, a word on his tongue concerning another archangel, but he turned his face to the sky again, and the word went unsaid. "Weave me a storm," he whispered to the foreign powers trapped within his staff.

The stick throbbed and went warm in his hands, warmer than it had been belching flame. A wind whistled somewhere far away, from the north.

Dusky clouds snarled and tumbled over the distant Alps, moving with impossible speed. Out of the west, where the land was flat, blew skeins of mare's tail. The gleaming hills emitted white fog like breath. Minutes passed while Damiano watched this tumult in the sky.

Fire shrieked a protest, and two cloud-soaked winds smashed together above the circlet of fire that held the Savoyard forces. The sky was ripped by lightning, again, again, and again, and thunder drove men to their knees.

A spatter of rain caught Damiano across the face. "Enough," he muttered absently. "We don't need to put out the fire." He fingered the staff. "Wind, little instrument. Not wet."

The wind raged, and the circle of fire bent like the black shadows of the trees. East it went, then south. The silk tent took sparks and blazed suddenly. The men crawled to the middle of the circle, hugging the bare earth. All the air smelled of pitch and metal.

Like a flute, the black staff sang, and Damiano fingered it gingerly. It was not meant to channel such power, let alone to imprison it. The silver bands burnt his hands when he touched them.

He took a deep breath of the clamorous air and let it sigh out again. "This will do," he announced. "Now we ride."

"Ride what?" shouted Ogier, terrified and angry. "The horses are all on the other side of that . . . that . . ."

Damiano glanced around and noted the truth of the statement. "Eh? Well, I ride. Everyone else walks. After all, the village is very close." And he whistled for his horse.

The black gelding cantered over, eyes rolling and ears flat. In another instant it had become the grinning mount of Death.

"Forward!" he cried to the despairing company. "Fol-

low me, soldiers of Savoy, men of the Piedmont. Follow
me, and you need not fear the fire, for it will be your
friend." He added in a lower tone, "And with that as your
friend, I doubt you will find many enemies to fight."

As he nudged the horse forward a hulking man's figure
appeared in the way, blocking him. "Give me a horse,
Delstrego," rumbled Paolo Denezzi, "and I'll ride beside
you. Not behind."

Damiano peered down. With the staff whining in his
hand, he had not much mind to spare for this. But as he
glanced up past Denezzi at the ring of fire, a dark gap in the
brilliance appeared, and a confused chestnut mare trotted
through, dragging her tether rope. The beast was blind to
the fire and heard nothing except Damiano's undeniable
call. "There's your mount, Paolo," the witch snapped.
"Don't ask for a saddle to go with it."

Awkwardly Denezzi hefted his bulk onto the chestnut's
back, and the two men started forward.

The fire parted before them and ran, twin trellises,
toward the hill and the village. Behind them it herded the
Savoyard soldiers like sheep.

The air was seared with the unending lightning. All
sight was confusion. Damiano's left ear was stunned with
the bellow of the elements, and in his right ear was a
passionate, seductive keening. He had the staff in his
hands, it whispered and moaned. He could suck all the
power from it and be free. He could fly over the village,
alone, bodiless. He could pluck Pardo from hiding and
carry the Roman high, up past the storm to the lucent air
where the stars sang. The heavens themselves, then,
would kill the fleshly man. Or he could drop him.

Or better, far better, sang the voices in his right ear, he
could simply forget this onerous task and fly away.

He raised the black wand before him. After tonight, he
said to the voices, you will be free. After tonight.

A white-hot bolt smacked down ahead of them, at the
top of the hill of San Gabriele. It spun over the earth and hit
the dusty oak by the broken village gate. The old tree
flamed.

San Gabriele itself was coming apart: dark fragments
rolling and scuttling down the hill in all directions.
"Pardo's men are deserting," commented Damiano quietly.

Denezzi glanced at Damiano. The man's heavy face

might have been made of wood. "Where?" he asked. "I can
see nothing but blackness and the fire."

"And you call me Owl-Eyes," was the witch's answer.

They were at the base of the hill. There the repellent
corpse-thing stopped and descended from the horse of
bones.

The wall of flame split again, and a black gelding trotted
through, followed by the pretty chestnut.

Damiano and Denezzi climbed the rutted market road
to San Gabriele. Ogier followed, with his empty scabbard,
and then the Savoyard troops, all slave to the constricting
fire.

Pardo was not one of those who fled; Damiano was sure
of that, as he had been sure of the general's presence since
first riding out of the woods and beholding San Gabriele.
Pardo was unforgettable, like a blister on one's palate. But
the general was not in the open, at the barricades of rubble
by the gateposts. At that moment, to be exact, there was no
one manning the barricades. Damiano smiled and passed
under the blasted oak. Almost three hundred men followed him, their faces gleaming with the heat.

Then the fire trellis parted, and two raging streams of
orange raced each other over the heaps of rubble Pardo's
men had built. They met behind the ruined village with a
smack like canvas against water. San Gabriele was enclosed, as were both the panicked Romans and their
terrified conquerors. Now there was only finding the
general himself.

But Damiano glanced around uneasily. Pardo was not
the only person in town whose feel he could recognize.
Other presences licked his skin, tiny as the tongues of
mice. He felt, obscurely, that these presences were not
things he should ignore.

"Wait here," he called over his shoulder, but seeing
Ogier's expression of open, though impotent, insolence, he
stopped in his tracks.

The Savoyard troops were huddled in sullen unity just
inside the gates. The displaced men of the Piedmont made
another group. Ogier's blue gaze was hard steel directed
toward the witch. And Denezzi—well, Denezzi stood by
Damiano's left hand, hating him.

These were not horses or dogs, or even human friends,
who would stay at a word. These men had wills and plans

of their own. If the Savoyards engaged with Pardo while
Damiano was following his own curious nose, there would
be unnecessary death. And it was to avoid that that
Damiano had devised this bizarre attack.

With a gesture he drew a fiery chord through the circle
of fire, separating the forces of Savoy from those of Pardo.
Two rams in a pasture, he thought with some amusement
as he turned away.

He strode down a street made unrecognizable by the
ruin and by the multiplicity of dancing lights and shadows.
Halfway along its length, on the right-hand side, stood a
shed of dry stone, its stucco facade crumbled. This edifice
seemingly had been too solid for the soldiers to destroy.
Perhaps it was old Roman work. Damiano's smile flickered
wider. He stopped at the door of brass and wood.

"Gaspare," he called. "You are in there, aren't you?
And . . . is that your sister? Or no . . . that's my old
friend Till Eulenspiegel, no?"

There was a buzzing of speech, and then the heavy
door rattled. Damiano flattened himself against the wall.

"Don't come out! Don't look at me. Just talk through the
door."

But a pale, freckled face, topped by greasy red hair,
peered around the doorjamb. "Festilligambe!" shouted the
boy. "Why not? You're alone on the street. Is the village
burning? How could that be? There's no wood or thatch left
in it. What a time for you to return, you old . . .

"Eh, Jan, did I ever tell you about this one? He can
make lute strings cry for Mama. . . ." Gaspare reached
out and took Damiano's wrist in his scrawny, strong grip.
He pulled him in.

Within the stone shed, the air smelled of old wood and
wine. Light filtered between the naked stones, and Damiano's eyes discovered rows of barrels. One of these had
been rolled into the middle of the shed and turned on end,
and on it lay a huge sheep cheese, broken and gouged at
random all over its surface.

Jan Karl slouched next to this makeshift table, seated on
the rounded surface of another barrel. His bandaged hand
rested on the greenish, mold-cased surface of the cheese
wheel in proprietary fashion. Beside him, very close, sat
the beautiful Evienne in her dress of green.

Damiano took a slow breath and felt his shoulders

relax. "What do you see when you look at me?" he demanded of the company.

Methodically, Karl reached out and clawed a morsel out of the cheese. Methodically, he chewed it. Evienne giggled. "What should we see?" asked Gaspare. "It's pretty dim in here. You look tired, I think. That's understandable, considering the political situation."

Damiano closed his eyes in simple thanks. "I am under a curse," he tried to explain, as he sank down onto the barrel across from the redheaded woman. "Or perhaps it's not a curse but a premonition. People tell me I appear to be burning alive. They run. They cover their faces." He sighed and leaned on his staff.

"It's been very useful to me."

Jan Karl swallowed. His narrow blue eyes regarded Damiano doubtfully. "Maybe you are the butt of a joke, Delstrego. You don't look different to me."

"Nor to me," added Evienne. She looked like she might have added more to that but for the restraining presence of the Dutchman next to her.

Damiano shook his head. He realized there was too much to explain, and he could only devote a part of his attention to the amiable scene before him while his fire imprisoned both the village and the Savoyard forces.

"Where's your lute? And your dog?" asked Gaspare, standing near the open door. He didn't wait for answers. "Have some cheese and put your mouth to the bunghole of the barrel under it. You spill a lot that way, but we've got a lot.

"I really do think the village is burning."

"Broken," replied Damiano distantly. "And dead. No, thank you. I don't feel like cheese, tonight. Nor wine."

Gaspare stepped over and looked his friend in the face. "I'm sorry, Festilligambe, if your dog died. I liked her. I like dogs. And your lute, well . . ." The boy shrugged. "These are terrible times to live in."

Both Jan Karl and Evienne grunted in unison. "Midwinter, and they rear all the buildings down," continued the boy. "Then they make campfires of the thatch and furniture. Was that sensible, I ask you? Everyone with anywhere to go gets out.

"Me, I stay to watch over Evienne, but it's no good for her, either. Lots of business, yes . . ."

"If you can call it that," introjected the prostitute, glaring vengefully at the wheel of cheese.

"But they don't pay," added her brother. "And Jan Karl here . . . Where's he going to go with a hand like that, too tender to touch anything yet and not a sou to his name? Where is San Gabriele when we need him?"

Damiano shook his head to all these questions. "Well, my friend. It's over, now, for Pardo. The army of Savoy is in the town." He rose to his feet.

"As a matter of fact, I must get back to them, now," he said, and turned to the door.

"The Green Count?" Gaspare gasped, and he danced from one foot to the other. "You are with the Savoyard army?"

"They are with me," corrected the witch. "And they don't like it much." He stepped out.

"Gesu and all the saints guard you," Damiano added, quietly, and with a certain formality. The door creaked shut.

The flames flapped and roared, and he passed through them. The Savoyard company turned to him as one man. "I know where Pardo is hiding," he announced briefly, and the fire that bisected the village stuttered and died.

Ogier snapped a word, and the men, for the first time that night, made ranks. Damiano led the way along the central street of the village.

He found Paolo Denezzi at his side. The man's bearish aspect was much reduced, for the hair of his face and head was singed to the root and his naked skin gleamed a taut and ugly pink.

"You attempted my barrier," remarked Damiano. "That was a mistake. The fire is not an illusion." Denezzi made only an animal noise.

Damiano turned to the commander. "My lord Marquis," he began. "Do I still look as I did before? Burning?"

Ogier concealed his amusement behind a mock civility. "You must forgive me, Monsieur Demon, if you have been engaged in *la toilette*, and I did not notice. To me you appear much the same."

Damiano merely nodded, and they passed through the smoke and wind to the center of San Gabriele, where a few stone buildings stood undamaged.

"He's here," said the witch. He stood with his eyes closed before a squat square tower. His head moved right, then left, as though he were rubbing his face into a pillow. "He's in the cellar, with a few men. Follow me, please."

Before Ogier, or troublesome Paolo Denezzi, could object, Damiano raised his staff before him and leaped onto the outside staircase. He bounded up.

At the door to the interior he was met by a sentry with a sword. The man cried out and dropped the glowing weapon. Damiano passed in.

It was like home, this place: the well-built tower of a family with means. The floor of the entranceway was tiled in red and blue, and the walls were soot free, washed fresh white. None of these carved oaken chairs or velvet divans had been burned for campfires, and woolen tapestries added their warmth to the rooms.

Damiano passed down the long stairs; no man dared to face him. Behind him was a cry and the sound of massed footsteps. Damiano ground his teeth against the knowledge that someone had slain the weaponless sentry.

The cellar had not been meant to be lived in. It was a warren of boxes and barrels and furniture stored on end. Though he could see reasonably well in this darkness, certainly better than any ordinary man, Damiano sent light into his staff.

General Pardo, neatly built, clothed in black leather, lounged amid the clutter on a chair upholstered in cloth of gold. His sword lay on his lap. Before him stood three swordsmen wearing his colors, each with sword and round shield. These men wore hauberks of link-mail. Pardo did not. All four faced the apparition without flinching, and the three guardsmen advanced upon Damiano.

At the moment Damiano saw Pardo his attention snapped away from the fire, and all around the village it fluttered and died.

"No, Carlo," called Pardo in moderate tones. "Roberto, Gilberto, no. I fear your techniques will be . . . worthless here."

Pardo stood and bowed. "I take it, Signore, that the Devil has allied himself with the cause of Savoy?"

Damiano was struck by the literal accuracy of that statement. "Yes," he admitted. "You may say that."

Pardo looked about him and rested the tip of his sword

blade upon the earth. "Well then. By all rights I ought to have made an alliance with the Almighty against that possibility, but . . . unfortunately . . . I neglected my strategies there."

"Your men have all run away." Damiano stared at Pardo. The lithe dark figure was fascinating in that it was only that of a man.

"Run away?" echoed Pardo, raising his head with a glimmer of hope. "They were not all burnt to death, then, or swept into hell alive?"

"There is only one man dead, that I know of," said Damiano, and Pardo's eyes narrowed.

"Do I know that voice?" he asked aloud. "Yes! Are you not the young patriot from the town below—the one who claimed he could not use witchcraft for the purposes of war?".

"I am," Damiano admitted, and he heard men on the stair behind him. He did not turn to greet Ogier and his men. Paolo Denezzi advanced to the witch's side, growling like a beast at Pardo.

"I am, General, but you yourself convinced me otherwise."

"What about the price, witch, that you said was too high for a man to pay?" Pardo's eyes shifted from face to face. Recognizing Ogier, he bowed insouciantly.

"Ogier de Savoy, I believe. I think we met at Avignon last spring, at the salon of our Holy Father."

Damiano could not see whether Ogier acknowledged the salute. "The price?" he said. "Look at me, General, and you will see the price."

With a theatrical sigh, Pardo let his sword drop to the dry dust floor. "It is too bad, then. You could just as well have damned yourself for me as against me. I admit I was a bit precipitous at your first refusal, but . . ."

"You could not rape Partestrada and expect me to join with you, General."

Pardo shrugged. "Why not?"

Damiano took a deep breath and adjusted the flaming stick in his hand. As he glanced behind him he saw only a wall of hate, directed at the Roman general and directed at him. "Because a man's city is like his mother."

With a snort and a sigh of weariness, Pardo sat back

down on the glittering cushion. "That again." He looked up at Damiano with his dark eyes steady and fearless.

"It is idiocy that has damned you, Delstrego, and ideas wildly mistaken. A city is not a woman, and its affections are purely . . . commercial."

There was a titter from behind Damiano, probably from one of the Piedmontese, since the Savoyard soldiers generally spoke French. "It is true," admitted Damiano, thoughtfully, "that Partestrada never really loved me, but she was a kind enough mother for all that, and it is for her sake I have worked toward your fall."

Pardo glanced meaningfully from the apparition to the blue coat of Savoy. "And this one," he said. "Will he be any better?"

Ogier put his hand on the pommel of the plain infantry sword he was now wearing. He smiled dryly. "That should be of no interest to you, pope's man," he said.

"I have it on authority that he will be," said Damiano. "He or his brother, or his brother's son. For the next fifty years at least." Ogier's eyes widened.

"Kill him!" bellowed Denezzi in Damiano's ear. The witch jumped at the sound, for he had begun to think of the big man as a mere brute. "You've talked enough. Kill the southerner already and be done!"

There was a murmur of support for this idea and Denezzi stalked forward. Pardo, in his chair, froze, his fingers clutching the carving of the arms.

Damiano felt a sudden sweat break out on his face. This was not what should happen, though he was not at all sure what the alternatives were. But not Denezzi—it should not be the brute Denezzi.

The witch waited for Ogier to say something, to call the man back. But the Savoyard stood there, his blond hair gleaming in the torchlight, and he said nothing.

There was a sound of clashing swords as the three Roman guardsmen sprang out of hiding and made for their chief. Paolo Denezzi paused, uncertainly, his head lifted toward the sound.

Pardo struck so fast only Damiano saw him move, and he could only blink and watch as Denezzi was tripped and grabbed from behind. Then Pardo had the big man bent backward and a dainty dagger prodding at Denezzi's short, trunklike neck.

The three guards making for their master's side were met by a dozen swords of Savoy.

Denezzi shouted in rage, and he kicked, helpless as a bull locked in the shackles. Damiano raised his staff.

"I can kill him very quickly, Signor Delstrego," shouted Pardo in warning. "See the position of the knife? It's at the big vein; I can feel the pulse up through the blade. Though you strike me into a toad or sear me to ash, this one'll be dead with me. He's your townsman, isn't he? Perhaps you would have reason to miss him."

And it seemed to Damiano that he had stepped out of the path of time, and this cellar in San Gabriele was as flat as the tapestry on a wall: a picture of men locked in combat and men lying dead and men watching. In the wild torchlight the picture wavered, like a tapestry in the wind.

And he, in the center of the composition, had all the time in the world to make a decision.

Reason to miss Denezzi? How ironic. Of all the people in the world Damiano could do without, Paolo Denezzi . . . He looked again at the big man with singed chin and eyes rolling like an angry bull's. But for Denezzi, he might have had Carla.

Better he didn't, seeing what he now knew about himself. But Denezzi was everything the young witch disliked: boorish, bullying, crude, self-important . . . He had made life difficult for Damiano in every way he could, for years beyond remembering.

And Pardo was dangerous; Damiano had not suspected how dangerous until that lightning grab for Denezzi's throat. With his men alive, though scattered, Pardo was deadly. He had to be eliminated, for the sake of peace in the Piedmont.

As all these reasons lined up in Damiano's mind he knew absolutely he could not allow Denezzi to die. He let the heel of his staff thump in the dirt. Pardo smiled.

But other parties had made decisions as well. "*Coupe sa tête!*" drawled Ogier in a bored voice. A hundred men surged forth.

Denezzi bellowed like a bull, like a cow in the shambles, as Pardo's little knife opened his throat. His frantic, unavailing kicks scratched the dirt. Martin, Ogier's second, scrambled past Damiano and raised his blade over Pardo's head.

"No!" cried Damiano with almost no voice, and then again, "No!" His staff slipped in his sweating palm, and at that moment Denezzi's dying spasms kicked the object out of the witch's grasp.

Pardo's head bounced and rolled on the ground unheeded, for almost every eye in the company was locked in fascination on the slim, motionless figure with tangled black curls and black eyes that peered back at theirs, uncertainly.

Ogier leaped forward and kicked the staff out of Damiano's reach. It rolled over the hard floor like the stick of wood it was, and it disappeared into the shadows.

"Take him," said the Savoyard commander, and a dozen soldiers bore Damiano to the ground. It was a deed quickly done, for Damiano hadn't the slightest idea how a man ought to fight.

Ogier paused and examined the field. He rubbed the fair stubble on his jaw. "An excellent engagement," he remarked to Martin. "I don't think we lost a man, except this poor lout here. And we will give thanks for it by sending this creature back to his rightful home.

"Tomorrow, though. Not during the darkness it has made hideous. If the oak at the village gate is still standing, hang a rope from it."

CHAPTER 15

Half the night passed over the village of San Gabriele, while dead fires and crawling fog wove a net of tangles in the air. The last of Pardo's soldiers slunk out of the cellars in which they were hiding and vanished over the stubbly fields. Before the week was out many of these would be recruited by the polyglot Savoyard army, but tonight memories were too green, so they departed quietly.

Most of the natives of San Gabriele were gone as well, save for those who, having nothing, had lost nothing. These roamed like dogs around the broken houses, avoiding Ogier's soldiers and sorting hopefully through the rubble of the streets.

Damiano lay in the cold on the wine-soaked floor of the very stone shed where he had found Gaspare, Jan, and Evienne. His wrists were bound behind him.

Where his three disreputable friends had fled to, and whether they were still free, still alive at all, he had no way of knowing, for without his staff Damiano was like a man struck blind and deaf. Nor had he much time to care, for the stars heaved slowly to the west, pulling the sun behind them, and with the first light he would die.

They had thrown his mantle over him, lest he freeze during the night and cheat them of their revenge. Soldiers outside guarded the corners of the shed; their slow passage blocked the moonlight that seeped in between the stones. Their presence and the dry, choking fear that filled his throat kept Damiano from weeping.

Instead he shook uncontrollably, until his shivers caused the fur mantle to slip off, and between the pain of his wrenched shoulders and swollen hands, he could not crawl back under it.

The earthen floor smelled strongly of wine and mice, and as he twisted to free his nose of the caking dust, the wad of moss in his ear fell out and cold lanced in. No voices, just cold.

Why would the marquis do this to him? Couldn't the man see that Damiano had given him better than any commander could hope for? Victory with no loss, all in an evening. And if a man was damned, then that was his misfortune, and nowhere was it written that he should be murdered on top of it. To kill a damned man must be a crime worse than to kill a saint, for a damned man had no good except that found in this life—forever.

Damiano's eyes stung in self-pity, which he forced back, lest he lose control and begin to howl. He had only a few hours, and then, according to Satan's promise, he would remember nothing good, nothing of beauty, nothing he had loved.

Yet he didn't regret his bargain with the Devil, for it was not his bargain that was sending him to hell. The bargain was only to die, and all men must die sooner or later. "Later!" cried a voice within him—not a voice of power, but a small, insistent voice like that of Macchiata, like that of Dami the boy. Later would be better. Much better!

What had he answered Satan, when the Enemy had

told him he would not remember, nothing except what Satan desired? "I know it now," he had said. "That will have to be enough."

So. He was still alive, these few hours. He would remember: what was good and beautiful, what he . . .

Damiano swallowed the pungent odor of mice. He curled his knees to his chest and closed his eyes. Then he heard another small voice, not in his head, but from outside.

"*Hein!* Festilligambe," it hissed. "Or Delstrego—whatever you call yourself. Are you awake?"

Damiano's eyes sprang open. "Gaspare!" he hissed. "What are you doing there?" There was a vague dark blotch behind the fieldstones. It shifted and the boy replied.

"One of the soldiers went to take a leak. Only a moment. What can I do? To . . . Wait . . ." Starlight appeared where the blotch had been.

Damiano waited as still as a man carved of stone, his eyes wide in the darkness. Then the shape of the sentry passed by again and despair crept back. There was a lock of iron on the door anyway, and Ogier de Savoy had the key.

Gaspare was a good fellow. That was something to remember, as long as it did not make him weep. It *was* making him weep. Ah well, he could do that quietly.

"Hsst!" came the voice again, from the front wall this time. Damiano lurched over, and when his weight fell on his pinioned arms, he whimpered in pain. "I'm here now. Evienne is . . . distracting the guards. What can we do for you?"

He swallowed twice before he could reply. "Nothing, Gaspare. You can't help me, except that you have, a bit, by . . . Run off, now, for if they catch you, they'll hang you too."

Gaspare's inaudible reply was probably a curse. Then he hissed, "Become invisible, Festilligambe. I'll say I saw you run down the street, and they'll open the shed to see."

Damiano had to smile at the plan. "I can't," he replied. "They took my staff. I can't become invisible. I can't do anything.

"Go away, Gaspare. This is something that was decided before. I can't escape it, and I'm not Christ, that a couple of thieves should hang beside me. Go away."

He had to repeat it three more times before the shadow faded off.

What day was it, anyway, or *would* it be with the first morning's light? One ought to know what day of the week one was dying on. He figured in his head, counting the days since the full moon. It was coming Sunday, the twelfth of December.

O Christ! It was a terrible thing to die cold.

Suddenly Damiano's weary, strained body stopped shivering. His mind was flooded with the pictures of a spring he would never see, and he smelled not mouse droppings but the breathing earth and the scent of lilacs. He grunted and sagged down against the floor, regardless of the pain.

To see the spring again, and to lie in the grass. To be investigated by silly lambs, newborn, all knees and nose, with their placid mothers bleating. To see silk dresses on the street again, when the girls' faces and necks were pink with the sharp morning air, and they were determined to wear their dresses anyway, for the calendar said spring. To go out into the fields and search for blooming herbs, arrowroot, angelica. Spending all the day and having little to show for it, because the fields were bouncing with new rabbits, like the children's little leather-sewn balls.

To endure the last fasting week of Lent, while every oven in town was baking for Easter, and then the great gold and white mass on Easter Sunday morning, and all the townsfolk singing together in their terrible, wonderful, untutored Latin "Alleluia, Alleluia, He is risen, He is not here."

Last year, on the day before Easter, he had spent all day in the hills and come home with two armfuls of flowers and a burnt nose. The best of these: the pink early rose and the lily of the marsh, he had put in vases and left them for Carla to find, stealing onto her balcony at night while Macchiata had kept watch. (He had never told Carla.) The rest of them—the yellow lily and bright mustard, and the tiny nodding snowdrops on their stems—he had put into a bag and had dumped the lot on Raphael, like a shower bath. Though Damiano couldn't remember the expression on the angel's face, he remembered one fluffy brush of gold mustard dangling at the end of a fluttering wing, and the white robe gilded with pollen.

The act had been neither very respectful, nor very manly, but no matter. Raphael had taken it well. And now . . . now Damiano sank into memory. His mouth softened.

To die in the spring would be easier, for one would die drunk.

The winter was beautiful, too, or had been beautiful when he was warm, climbing up the road to Aosta. And of course, the gleaming high Alps were lovely, despite what Macchiata had said.

Macchiata had been beautiful, too, the most beautiful thing of all, in some ways. But her he could not bear to think about.

"*Dominus Deus*," he whispered, his lips brushing the dirt, "you made a pretty world." It was not meant to be a prayer.

Cold air on his injured ear was making him dizzy again, for he could not feel the ground, and the room was swimming with lights of pearl, lights of sunstruck clouds. Damiano's head was gently lifted. He looked up into the eyes of Raphael.

Great wings curled in, hiding the walls of stone. The archangel took Damiano onto his lap, and the young man felt no cold at all.

"That's right," whispered Damiano. "You said we should meet once more."

Raphael did not smile. He stroked the young man's hair back from his face. "I said *at least* once more, Dami. And I said we would talk."

Damiano raised his head for a moment and let his eyes rest on the figure of quiet beauty. Then he let it fall back. "Once is all I have time for, Seraph. And there's not a lot to say. They're going to hang me at dawn."

Raphael looked down at his friend like a man staring into a well. He said nothing.

"Did you know that already?" asked Damiano, looking back.

The angel nodded and touched Damiano's face lightly with the backs of his fingers. "That's why I'm here, my friend."

"This will be it, for you and I—for our friendship—my

dear teacher. For I am damned and am going to hell, where I doubt very much you will come visiting."

Both wings exploded outwards, slapping the little shed walls. "Damned, Damiano? Damned? What are you saying?" For a few moments the angel was speechless. "Where did you get this idea? I never heard you speak such . . . such . . ."

Damiano had not believed the perfect face could assume such a blank, startled, almost silly expression. Nor had he imagined that the celestial wings could rutch so like a sparrow's.

". . . such miserable folly!" Raphael concluded with effort.

Through his crushing misery Damiano almost laughed, but his face sobered with the effort of explanation.

"It was Satan himself who first told me . . ." he began.

The complex play of feeling on Raphael's face was replaced by simple anger. "He? He is the Father . . ."

". . . of Lies. I know. I've heard that many times, especially recently, Raphael. But forget that. Not all he says is a lie, and I have my own evidence in the matter. I have touched the unquenchable fire, Seraph. I have traced it back to its source, and I know now that its source is within me."

One wing went up, and the other went down, and Raphael's head tilted in balance to the wings. "Dami. If you are trying to tell me you have fire in you, save your breath, for I've known it long since.

"You are as warm as a hearth, young one, and like a hearth fire, open and giving. Till this moment, I would have said as . . . as confident as a hearth fire, too, for I have seen you go through pain and horror, and glow the brighter for them. Do you think it is out of a sense of duty that I love you, Dami? Or that it is your witchcraft that has compelled me to teach you music these three years?

"I have no duty toward mankind. None. I was created not for duty but to make music. Nor can the actions of mortals force me into time's stringent bondage.

"But you are such a silly one, Damiano Delstrego. Your hands are too big for you. Also your eyes. And your opinions. You try so hard, in a world whose pain I cannot bear to comprehend. And within you, you know what is best and love it despite all error. That's why I cannot

understand how you could be so cozened as to believe . . .

"Ah, Dami, Dami!" And Raphael held the young man
to him and rocked from side to side. "Do you know what it
is to be damned? It has nothing to do with fire. To be
damned is only not to love."

"Not to love God, you mean, Raphael," murmured
Damiano, who lay with eyes closed, feeling his pain ebb
away. "I've heard something like that from Father Antonio."

Raphael paused, and his fair brow frowned in concentration. "All created things," he said at last, "are the mirror
of their creator. Can one love anything, with whole heart,
and not love its source?

"Maybe a man can—men are a mystery to me—but I
cannot. And, Damiano, look at me.

"You are a sudden flash of light, child. A tune rising
from nowhere. I am not flesh, and I cannot understand
you, but I love you, and I know you are not damned!"

Damiano blinked up at the angel. Raphael's face blurred
in his vision, and he blinked harder. "Is that so?" he asked.
"Is that *really* so? Then I'm very glad to hear it," he added,
"because I didn't want to go to hell."

Then he wept without shame against the spotless white
robe.

Minutes passed, and then Damiano lifted his head.
"You know what, Raphael?" he asked. "I'm sorry to say
this, after all you have done for me, but . . . but . . . I
find I still don't want to die, either. Isn't that petty of me,
after all I've done to get myself in trouble?"

And then the angel pursed his beautiful lips and rocked
Damiano back and forth. "We all get into trouble sometimes," he whispered, "doing what we shouldn't. Sometimes we *should* do what we shouldn't. Don't worry about
it, Dami."

This statement was difficult. It was also dubious morality. But Damiano was past trying to make good sense out of
Raphael, or good morality, either. Perhaps angels were not
expected to be moral, but just to be angels. Were they even
Christians, these pure spirits?

No matter. It was better just to listen and to trust
Raphael. And it was wonderful, being rocked by him. It
was music and it was rest. It was falling, falling weightless-

ly like snow, his face against the spotless white garment,
falling through a room filled with the lights of pearl.

Pain was forgotten, and fear. And if tomorrow—today
almost, for it was near dawn—if tomorrow the rope
worked properly, and he did not strangle, then perhaps
death would be no more than this.

He was not damned.

Damiano almost slept, curled on the angel's lap, his
hands bound behind him. He would have slept, except for
the irritating, familiar poke against his hands and the
awkward voice calling "Master, Master, Master," incessant-
ly and too early in the morning.

Damiano opened his eyes. "Macchiata," he whispered,
and the heavy triangular head thrust before his face, and
she licked his wet eyes. She was as solid as life, and almost
as ugly as she had ever been.

"Oh, poor Master, poor Master," she crooned. "All tied
up. It's terrible to be tied up. I remember."

Damiano slid to the floor and sat upright. "Little dear,"
he said. "It's so good to see you. I . . . I . . . don't know
what to say, except maybe we can be together again
tomorrow."

But she left him and struggled onto Raphael's lap.
"We're together right now," she said, and then turned her
attention to the angel. "I got it," she announced. "I
dragged it all the way up and down the stairs of the big
house and nobody saw me. But I can't get it through the
door. Help me; I can't get Master's stick through the door."

Raphael petted her from ear to tail with easy familiarity.
Damiano had to smile.

"Don't ask him that," Damiano chided the dog.
"Raphael can't arrange a man's life. Or death. He can't
interfere, being not of this world, Macchiata. I've told you
that a dozen times."

But the little white ghost with a single red spot ignored
him. She trotted to the door on her bandy legs, then back
to Raphael. "Open the door," she insisted. "I can't do it,
and it's late. Open it."

The angel looked over at Damiano, until the young man
hung his head. "Stop, Macchiata," he whispered. "He
can't do it."

Then Raphael, still sitting, leaned over and opened the
door of the shed. Starlight flooded in, and the iron padlock,
still intact, swung back and forth against the wood.

Macchiata scuttled out and then in again, dragging the
ornate length of ebony wood. She maneuvered it, with
much thudding and thumping, till it touched the fingers of
Damiano's bound hands.

He cried out as power flooded into him. "Raphael!
What have you done? You have . . . have interfered!"

Raphael's smile was contained and inward-turning.
"Yes, I have, Dami," he said, and he laced fair fingers over
one white samite knee. "It feels very interesting," the angel
added. "I wonder . . ."

Damiano could wait no longer. He spoke three words.

The massive door was flung back against the shed wall
with such force the stones shook, and the one iron hinge
burst in fragments. All through the ruins of San Gabriele
rang the echoes of similar doors swinging open and
parchment windows ripping open. The sword belts of the
sentries writhed unbuckled and fell.

The laces of jerkins and tunics sprang free of their
eyelets, and Damiano's bonds escaped him like frightened
snakes, and at the gateless gateposts of the village, a noose
of rope, prepared for the morning, spiraled free of the tree
and lay limp as a worm on the trodden road.

Damiano crawled to his feet. With one numb, purple
hand he scooped up the small ghost of a dog. He embraced
Raphael and kissed him enthusiastically on both cheeks.
Then he stepped out into the street, where night and
morning were touching and the east was gray.

The sentries saw him emerge, splendid in his tunic of
gold and his robe of scarlet, lined with stainless ermine. He
was young and unwearied and fearless. He grinned at
them as he passed, thumping his tall staff in time. And if
they saw the archangel, or even the spectral dog, they gave
no sign of it but stood frozen, holding their clothes up with
both hands.

Before the square tower Damiano stopped and called
out until a blue form appeared on the balcony. "Marquis?
"There is no need to hang me after all. I'm not damned;
it was all a big misunderstanding."

Ogier made no answer, so after a moment Damiano
added, "I'm Monsieur Demon—remember? But maybe I'm
not so hideous after all, in the morning light."

"I see you," said Ogier, and the marquis looked left and
right along the streets. "You look much more comely this
morning. Am I to understand that none of my men are

willing to take arms against you? Yes, well, I quite understand their reservations." For five seconds the marquis stared fixedly at Damiano, and Damiano beamed up at him.

"What are you going to do, Monsieur who is not a demon?" he asked finally. "Seeing we cannot prevent you, that is."

Damiano shrugged loosely. "I'm going to leave, of course.

"But I thank you for your assistance last night. It saved much bloodshed."

"Overjoyed to have been of service," responded Ogier, with chilly, ironical politeness.

There was a drum of hooves, and the black gelding racketed into the village, passing between the gateposts and spurning the fallen rope. Damiano turned to the horse, which snorted delicately and bit its master's curly hair.

He pulled himself up. Raphael stood before him on the road, wings outspread and glorious. The little dog sat beside him, scratching impossible fleas. "Seraph," he said, leaning left around the black gelding's neck, "I have one more debt to pay, and it's one that should not wait."

"I know," answered the angel quite calmly. "We'll come along, if we may." The little dog chimed in, "Of course we'll come with you, Master. We haven't been here any time at all!"

He left San Gabriele with his scarlet cloak flying like a banner in the early light. Bright wings soared in the air above the galloping horse, for any to see who had eyes to see, and a small dog ran at his left hand, trotting easily over the ground and never falling behind.

CHAPTER 16

It was a ride like all rides through the Piedmont during this bleak season of the Nativity. Mud spattered the horse's cannons, and ice crusted its shaggy face, till it scraped its muzzle with its hooves like a dog. But the mud was rich, and the ice was glorious, and the snow that whipped

Damiano's cheeks and caught in his hair—that was so much eiderdown. He rode singing, sometimes sweetly, sometimes voice-cracked and hoarse, sometimes in strange harmony to tunes whose burden no one heard but him.

And he laughed at nothing, wiggling on the patient gelding's back. At night Damiano nursed great bonfires and squatted by them, talking like a crazy man. Talking, talking, talking to the air.

Beside a cairn of rocks couched Saara the Fenwoman, wrapped against the cold in a rough woolen blanket. Still she was cold, always cold. Being cold didn't interest her.

She brought a few rocks every day, and though sometimes wolves or dogs came and dug a few of them away, Ruggerio's grave was becoming more secure.

One dull brown braid flapped in the wind. She tucked it back into her blanket. She should go down to Ludica, she knew. This high hill was no place for her, alone and in the winter. The steam-burns on her arms and under her chin pulled in the cold and ached. She would go down to Ludica; when hardly mattered.

She could sweep floors. A woman could always sweep floors.

The wind sang over the flat, marshy field. It had done so day after day, singing a bleak, mindless, winter song. Though her ear was trained to the sounds of wind and water, she was rapidly learning not to hear this song of despair.

But now she had no choice but to hear, for the tone of the wind was changing. She cocked her small head to one side, and her tilted green eyes narrowed.

This was a south wind, and a very familiar one. As any weaver can recognize her cloth, even when it is cut out of shape and sewn, so Saara recognized her own soft south wind, woven to cover her garden.

She stood, and she saw Damiano step out from the pines, swinging his black staff and striding toward her. His raiment shone under the winter sun, and his hair was black and free as a horse's mane. His eyes were filled with the beauty of youth and with purpose, and in his face shone power.

Saara turned from him, anger warrring with shame. She thought to run into the birch wood where all the leaves rattled. But anger won and she stayed, standing between the witch and the grave of the man he had slain.

Damiano looked down at the stones. "Lady, please let me by," he said.

"Why?" she asked in turn, and her voice shook like paper, like a dead birch leaf. "What more harm would you do to him?"

His nostrils flared. "None. He is beyond harm, and I intend none." Then his face softened. "Please, Saara. Let me by and you shall see why I'm here."

His pleading was more painful to her than his presence, and she stiffened under it. "See what? Can you bring Ruggerio to life again, after weeks in the earth?"

"No," replied Damiano, and with his staff he forced her aside. "All I can do is this." And holding the staff by its heel, he raised it high over his head.

"Leave the grave be!" she shouted in rage, but the staff whistled through the air and smashed down.

There was a snap and a screech of wood and metal. The staff cracked. It split up the middle and broke into two pieces.

There was no flash of light, nor booming of thunder. The air did not smell burned. Yet Saara staggered as all that was her own came back to her, and more, and more. She shook her head against memories she had never known before: books unread, unfamiliar flowers and faces.

A girl's face, with yellow hair. The face of an air spirit, awesome and mild. The face of a dog.

Then she saw the face of Guillermo Delstrego through other eyes.

Daily lessons in the great stone workroom with the wood fire hissing. Daily dinners, crude but filling, cooked on the same enormous hearth. Whippings—both the deserved and the undeserved. A gift of apples. The gift of a staff.

And finally the screams from above, and, oh, pray for my father, he is dead, my father is dead. Saara cried in anger but could not resist, violated to the depths by the pity she was compelled to feel for Guillermo Delstrego.

After minutes or hours she sighed, putting the images away.

The young man—the boy—stood unmoving, staring stupidly down at the piled stones and the shards of wood and silver. The heel of the staff dangled limply from his hands. His mouth was open. Finally he dropped the stick and rubbed his face in both hands. He cleared his throat.

"It's what he wanted, Saara. Ruggerio, I mean. He had a chance to kill me, but he chose instead to try to break the staff. Well, no one but I myself could do that, while I am alive." He turned to her, squinting as though the light was too bright.

"My lady Saara, you are so beautiful! A beautiful witch and a beautiful woman. It's not just the witch power. When I came up the meadow, you were beautiful then, too, but you didn't give me a chance to mention it."

Saara took a deep breath, sorting the chaos within her. "I don't want all this," she said to him. "Only what was mine. Take back what is yours."

He shrugged and dropped his eyes. "I can't. Besides, I don't want it anymore. Your song, my lady, was never meant to be bound in wood—it wasn't happy with me— and as for mine, well I give it freely, so it won't make any fuss. Please accept it; it's like a homeless dog. It can't survive alone."

Saara stepped forward, letting the blanket slip from her shoulders. Her embroidered dress shone gaily under a sun that was growing warmer. Rags fell, leaving her feet pink and bare. She touched Damiano.

"This is too much to understand," she said, and he nodded.

"I find it so myself. But, lady, I trust you with power more than I trust myself. I told you so once before.

"Besides—what is all power but fire? And I have had too much of fire, lately." He stepped away, then glanced again at her, one hand scratching the side of his head.

"Please forgive me," he said, "for all I've done to you. It was never the way I wanted it." And he walked away.

"Wait," Saara called. She opened her mouth to sing his feet still, but shame stopped her. Instead she ran after Damiano, her bare feet splashing over the wet ground. "Where are you going, like this?" she demanded. "You're helpless as a baby." He turned to her in surprise.

"I'm going west," he said. "I thought to Provence, or as far as I get. And, my lady, don't worry. I'm no more helpless than any other man."

"Go home instead, if you can," she countered. "Or if that general will not let you, then stay in Ludica."

"You'll learn what it is to be alone, now, Dami. Cold and alone. Believe me: a witch without power . . ."

He scratched his tangled head again, and he grinned at her. "Don't worry, I said. I know what cold is like already. I've had a lot of practice.

"And alone? Saara, *pikku* Saara! Our closest friends are sometimes those we cannot see."

He leaped one coil of the broad, choked stream that cut the meadow into islands. Landing, he slipped and fell on one knee, then stood again, laughing at himself. He met the Fenwoman's gaze, he squinting with the distance between them. "What a body this is; nothing seems to work right." Then his grin softened. "Look at me, Saara. I'm happy. Haven't you eyes to see?"

Then he turned on his heel and darted across the meadow. Saara watched him until, slapping a low branch with his hand, he faded into the dark trees. When he had vanished, she lifted her head to the high, singing brilliance that went with Damiano, shining above the pine wood.

She had the eyes to see.

DAMIANO'S
LUTE

Has he tempered the viol's wood
To enforce   both the grave   and the acute?
Has he curved us the bowl of the lute?
                                EZRA POUND
                            "Pisan Cantos"

            To my mother

PRELUDE

Saara's song could make a garden out of a barren mountainside, or cover a hill of flowers with snow. When she sang, it was with a power that killed men as well as healed them. She could sing the winter and the summer, weeping and dancing and sleep. She could sing the clouds in their traces and the water in the bog.

She sang (this particular morning) a mighty song, replete with clouds and boglands, barren hills and lush, summer and winter, weeping, dancing and every other sort of earthly event. She sang from dim matins to high prime. At the end of this singing her voice was ragged; she was blue in the face and she saw spots before her eyes. But Saara's power of song had for once failed her, for she had not been able to sing one doe goat into a good mood.

And this was unfortunate, for Saara neither wanted to kill nor heal, and she desired neither carpets of snow nor flowers, but only the trust of this one ungainly creature, as companion in her loneliness.

Of all creatures (except perhaps for the cat) the goat is the hardest to sing-spell, having more than its fair share of natural witchery. Further, of all the changes one can work upon a goat, contentment is the most difficult state to obtain. To make things even more trying for Saara, this particular doe was encumbered by a dead winter coat she was too out of condition to shed, and was uncomfortably pregnant besides. Her gaunt sides resembled a hide-covered boat matted with brown algae. She wanted nothing to do with company, and had to be chased from the pineslope to the hill-dome crowned with birches before allowing herself to be befriended.

Yet this obdurate goat was all the company springtime had delivered to Saara amid the Alpine crocus and the purple hyacinth. Saara was not about to let the beast starve herself through obstinacy, not while Saara herself so needed some kind of voice in her ears besides her own.

But this was not strictly true—that she heard no other voice but hers. There was one other: the one that echoed in her head like her own thoughts, and yet was foreign to her, a voice soft and deep in slurred Italian. A voice which asked her questions.

"Where is he gone?" it asked her and, "Is it time to go home? Can I go home now?"

Never had Saara any answers for it.

This bodiless voice had been couched within her own head for over a year, serving only to make Saara feel as discontented as it was and more howlingly alone.

To distract her from these unanswerable questions she had tried work, until now her garden was blooming as never before and all her herb-pots were full. Then she had played with the weather, making the nearby villagers miserable. Following the visit of a brave delegate from Ludica, she curtailed experimentation and attempted to lose herself in her own woods, in bird shape. But that effort was least effective of all, for what reply has a wood dove to questions a Lappish witch cannot answer?

Now, as springtime took hold of the earth, Saara found nothing in all her wild refuge to interest her but this one strayed goat.

And the goat was disappointing. After spending all morning trying to entice her, Saara could approach just close enough to feed the doe a few willow withies and some fiddleheads of the new ferns. Most of these treats the animal spat out (as though to say she was no common nanny, to eat anything that happened to be green and given).

So Saara sang the goat a new song: a song of the first day in June, with a romping kid on the hilltop (instead of kicking in the belly), crisp sun in the sky and dry feet in the grass.

Saara sang in the strange tongue of the Lapps, which was her own. It made as much sense to the doe as any other tongue. The animal stared dourly at Saara with amber eyes the size of little apples, each eye with a mysterious black box in the center.

After receiving enough song-spelling to turn all the wolves in Lappland into milk puppies, the doe condescended to recline herself in the litter of spring bloom.

Saara was already lying down, flat on her stomach, head propped on hands, mother-naked. She had braided her hair into tails when she had her morning bath. It subsequently dried that way, so now, when she freed it from its little pieces of yarn, it gave her a mass of rippling curls which shaded from red to black to gold in a cascade down her petal-pink back.

She might have been a tall peasant girl of sixteen. Her body was slim and salamander-smooth, her face was dimpled and her green eyes set slantwise. With one foot pointed casually into the pale blue sky, Saara looked as charming and ephemeral as a clear day in March.

She had looked that way for at least forty years.

"Goat," she announced, aiming at the animal a green disk of yarrow, "you should eat more. For the baby."

But the goat was still chewing a sliver of green bark she had deigned to take ten minutes before. She flopped her heavy ears and pretended she didn't understand Lappish.

"Haven't you ever been a mother before?" continued Saara. "I have. A mother has to be more careful than other people. A mother has to think ahead."

The goat made the rudest of noises, and with one cloven hind hoof she scraped off a wad of musty belly hair, along with some skin. Then she bleated again and rolled over, exposing that unkempt abdomen to the sun.

"I could sing you a song that would make you eat every leaf off every tree in the garden—or at least as high as you could reach," the woman murmured, yawning. "But then you'd explode, and that, too, would be bad for the baby." Saara, like the goat, was made lazy by the sun. She turned over and watched her blue felt dress, freshly washed and dripping, swinging from the branch of a flowering hops tree. The wind played through the hair of her head, and through her private hair as well. She chewed a blade of grass and considered.

The goat bored her, though there was a certain satisfaction in helping the beast produce a sound kid. But Saara came from a herding people, and did not regard livestock with sentimentality.

No, it was not Saara, but the child-voiced presence within her that wanted to talk to the goat. She could isolate this presence from herself-proper and feel its warm edges. It was a bundle of visions, memories, instincts and . . . and fire. It was a shadow with dark eyes and skin: a guest in her soul. It was young, eager, a bit temperamental. . . .

And undeniably full to bursting with sentiment. It liked to talk to goats.

Its name was Damiano Delstrego—or at least the presence belonged by rights to this Damiano, who had left it with her, like some foundling at a church door, and not part of his own being.

It was wearisome that he should do this, wearisome in the extreme. Sprawled flat on the sunny lawn, Saara let her song die away. Then, for an instant, she had the urge to rush at the sad, partial spirit she harbored, dispossessing it and recovering the unity of her own soul. But if she did that, she knew that Delstrego himself, wherever the fool had wandered (west, he had said), would be half dead, instead of only divided in two.

Despite the passage of seasons and the bitterness with which Saara and the Italian had fought on this very hill one day, killing two loves together (or maybe three), Saara remembered Damiano as he had knelt in the snow before her, weeping over the body of a little dog, and so she refrained.

Besides, the dark immaterial eyes with their sad questions trusted her and depended upon her, and Saara had been a mother.

And the most important reason that Saara did not evict her strange tenant was the same reason for which she courted the attentions of this unmannerly goat. She was lonely. For the first time in twenty years and more Saara was lonely.

She flipped onto her belly again and used her hands to thrust herself off the earth, snapping her feet up under her. The goat also sprang up with a startled bleat, flailing her broomstick legs in all directions. Sunlight kissed the top of Saara's nose—already slightly burned with such kisses—and polished her shoulders.

Once upright she stood still, panting. Suddenly she

flinched, though nothing but sun and soft wind had touched her. At the peak of her irritation with the voice in her head, a realization had come to her. It was Damiano himself who was making her so unaccountably lonely. It was he whom she wanted to see: this son of a bad lineage, who had ripped her soul apart, and who afterward had spared no more than ten minutes out of his affairs to come and repair the damage he had done.

Leaving her with a burden it was his own business to bear: a voice inaudible and dark eyes unseen. It was Saara's immaterial baby, and would never grow up. After a year and more its longing for Damiano had become her own.

She ought to find him, she thought, and make him take it back. Whether he would take it or not, still she would be able to see the fellow again, and to discover what he was doing. For a moment she was quite intrigued, imagining where the dark boy ("boy" she called him always in her thoughts, to remind herself that she was no girl) might have gone to, and what strange languages he might be speaking, to what strange men. And women.

She had every right to seek him out, for he was a witch born, and so one of her kind.

For a few minutes Saara played with the idea of finding Damiano, but then uncertainty rose in her mind. It whispered to her that if Damiano had a matching desire to see her, this would have been plain in the regard of those dark eyes that looked at her through the darkest hours of night. If he thought of her as often as she thought of him, then surely she would know it, holding his soul as she did. But the eyes stared without seeming to know what they saw, and the voice which accompanied the eyes never spoke her name. It seemed to Saara that all the caring in this strange bond was on her side.

And even if Damiano would welcome her . . . even if time had changed his unpredictable Italian mind . . . to search him out through all the plains and ranges of the West would be an arduous task. It could be done, certainly, by a witch as experienced and learned as she was. But though Saara was powerful, she was a woman of the northern emptiness. She was disturbed by throngs of people, and the close dirt of cities disgusted her. And at bottom she was afraid of such a journey: most of all afraid of another meeting with Guillermo Delstrego's son.

Why should she want to visit Damiano anyway—a witch born with command in his voice and a mind that might learn wisdom, who had maimed himself, throwing away wisdom and birthright together? That denial was inexplicable: an act of perversion. So what if Damiano played the lute and sang a pretty song or two? Any Lappish witch could sing, and Damiano's southern songs had no power in them (save over the heart, perhaps. Save over the heart).

He was nothing but a moonchild, twin to the hopeless presence he had left Saara to tend. There were no signs he would grow into a full man. Without a single soul, he could not.

All this Saara repeated to herself, letting the long-sought doe goat wander off among the birches. If she reasoned long enough, surely she could talk herself out of a long journey that must only have disappointment at the end of it.

But as she reflected, her criticism became something else entirely. It became a certainty as strong as presage: a certainty that Damiano as she had last seen him (a creature neither boy nor grown man, splashing carelessly over the marshy fields) was all the Damiano there was destined to be. She shuddered in the sun. Whether foresight or merely foreboding, this certainty caused her surprising pain.

Saara sat wretchedly in the grass, undecided about her journey and about her own feelings, but reflecting in how many ways men disorder the lives of women.

CHAPTER 1

The grass showed two colors, like a riffled deck of cards. All the early marguerites bobbed in waves, up and down the hills. Each hill had an oak or two, while the wealthier elevations also possessed orchards of apple or plum—bare-branched, but with twigs swollen purple, pregnant with Easter's bloom. Brambles crawled over the fields and on to the single trodden road. Even these brambles wore a charming infant green, and their withy limbs sprawled thornless. The sky was a cool washed blue, spittled with inconsequent clouds.

This landscape was Provence in high morning during the third month of the year. Nothing ill could be said about it, except that mornings had been warmer in spring, and mornings had been a bit drier. But this springtime would doubtless produce warmer and drier mornings in its own time.

So much was of nature. As for the man-made element which completes a landscape, there was available nothing but three roofless huts by the road (each with blue light shining out through the windows, clean as an empty mind) and a trundling green wagon with two young men on the seat, pulled by a black horse.

There was one other presence in the landscape, one which was neither quite artifactual nor quite a part of nature. That was a bundle that lay hidden in the long reeds spawned of a rivulet running between two hills. The bundle consisted of four human bodies, tied together with rope and lying damply dead. They had been there for two weeks, and the thrusting horsetails had grown around them closely, forcing themselves into the linen shirtsleeve, between the wooden button and the hand-darned hole, and along the mutely gaping lips. The bodies were blackish, but since it was only March, there were few flies buzzing.

These blindly ambitious reeds stood to the west of the road, and since the wind was blowing from the east, not even the nodding horse was aware he had passed a green charnel.

This was an impressive horse: not a destrier or battle charger (that close cousin to a plow horse) but a lean, light horse built for speed and cities, built for races down graded boulevards with the vendors all up and down the course selling ypocras and squares of marchpane. It had movement, this horse, as was evident by the way it lifted up its front feet just one razor cut before its back feet overstrode them. It had elegance, as it proclaimed in its clean, glistening throatlatch, its ironic black eye and supple crest. By its lean dished head and serpentine neck-set, one could see the horse carried Arab blood. By its size of bone, and the untrustworthy set of its eye, it was part Barb. It was a tall animal, deep-chested and long of shoulder. It was a horse to produce wagers.

And it seemed not only to be bred for races, but to be in training for them, for it was thin as a twist of black iron, and its head snaked left and right with energy, snapping its poor harness of rope.

But it was not, of course, training for any such thing, for racehorses do not train by pulling wagons.

This wagon, like the knotted-together harness, did not fit the quality of the animal that pulled it. The harness was made up from bits and pieces: some of leather, some twine, some of velvet ribbon. The wagon (theoretically green) had a number of side-slats which had never been painted and were different in length and cut from one another, as well as from the green boards. Along with these went places on the vehicle's high sides and back which offered excellent visibility into the interior. The wagon was nearly empty and made a great deal of noise as its wooden wheels rolled over the earth.

The driver of this rolling drum was as black of hair and eye as his horse, and his skin was burned dark, as though the man had been in the elements all winter. This impression was furthered by his woolen tunic, which was colored too delicate a rose to be a product of the dyer's art. In fact, this color had been produced in the same manner as the wearer's tan. This young man was as thin as his horse, and he, too, possessed some degree of elegance and movement (though not of the sort to cause men to wager money). Like his horse, he was tall but not wide, and like his horse he nodded. But where the animal nodded to his own hooves' rhythm, the driver appeared to nod asleep.

"You know he shouldn't oughta *do* that." The still younger fellow beside the driver spoke in coarse North Italian. This one's hair was red, knife-trimmed and carefully finger-curled. He wore a dagged jerkin of too many colors to list. He was, if such a thing is possible, thinner than either the horse or the driver beside him. He infused his few words with a degree of rancor impossible for the casual listener to understand, unless the listener first knows that these two travelers were really close friends, who had spent too much time in close company with one another.

The driver of the wagon sat blinking for a moment, as

though he were translating his companion's words from a foreign language. His eyes were fixed glassily on the gelding's swishing croup. He was thinking in a passive and random fashion about goats.

At last he answered. "It doesn't matter, Gaspare. The worst he will do is unravel the ribbons, and then I can tie them up again." The black horse chose this moment to give a particularly doglike shake, which freed the single-tree end of a length of rope and sent it snapping over his back. At this sudden attack he bolted forward, and his passengers skidded into the hard back of the hard wagon seat. Hard.

"Poor Festilligambe," muttered Damiano. "He was never meant to pull a load. And he has little enough to please him these days, lean as he is." The dark young man was suddenly stricken with a desire to gather leaves and twigs for the gelding, although he knew quite well that horses don't eat leaves and twigs.

When one's companion smarts under a weight of self-pity, it is not a good idea to send one's condolence in other directions. It does not promote the peace.

"Poor Festilligambe!" hiccoughed Gaspare. "Festilligambe? He alone among us . . ." Emotion choked the boy, and his face grew as red as his hair. "If I could live on the grass by the road, I'd have no more complaints."

Gaspare's face was singular in its parts. His nose had an aquiline height of bridge and narrowness along its length which any man of birth might have been proud to call his own. His eyes were large and soulful and his complexion was milk and (more usually) roses. His mouth was mobile.

Yet in all these features there was no harmony, but rather constant war, for the nose was too long and sharp for the shape of his face and the eyes were too big for anyone's face, and his mouth—well, since it was never without a word, a twitch or a grimace, it was very hard to say anything about Gaspare's mouth.

He was just fourteen, and he hadn't had a good dinner in far too long.

"Nebuchadnezzar did," replied the dark youth, referring to the possibility of living on grass. His voice was distant, his less ambitious but more proportionate features almost slack. "Or it is said that he did. But I don't recall that he was happy eating grass."

Gaspare swelled. "I'm not happy, eating nothing!" Out of sulks he yanked a lock of hair that tumbled over his right ear. The spit curl went limp. His finger coiled it again, tighter. The boy's head looked heavy, as will a round child-face that has grown too thin over its bones. Both his leanness and the dandified clothing he affected made Gaspare appear older than he was. Consequently his tempers seemed more scandalous.

Damiano lifted one eyebrow. His form was also drawn out by fortune. In fact, he looked almost consumptive, with his face reduced to dark eyes he could hardly hold open and a red mouth that yawned. "*Hein?* My friend, I'm sorry. I would like to eat, too. But don't begrudge the horse his horseness; if he had to eat bread we'd have been carrying our goods on our backs all the way from the Piedmont."

Gaspare could say nothing to this, and so was made even unhappier.

Even in March, the warmth of noonday made wool itchy. Young Gaspare scraped his bottom against the seat, first right, then left. He was an unusually sensitive boy, both in spirit and in skin, and since he was also an unusually poor one, his sensitivities were an affliction to him.

"Surely in such lovely countryside, we'll find a town soon," said Damiano, though the forced heartiness of his reply betrayed a lack of skill at lying. "Or perhaps an abbey, where we may be fed without having to put on a show."

"Or a rich penitent on pilgrimage," Gaspare continued for him. ". . . strewing gold coins. Or a road leading up to heaven, white as milk, with angels beside it ranked like poplar trees—angels playing flageolets and cornemuse, but the angels will be made of cake, of course, and the pipes all of breadsticks, and at the top of the road will be a piazza paved with bricks of sweet cakes, and a gate of crystallized honey.

"By the gate will stand Saint Pietro, dressed like a serving man, with a napkin over one arm and a wine cup in each hand, bowing and smiling. He will not stop us, but will thrust a cup lovingly into our hands. Then the sky will be all around us, floating with white-clothed banquet tables like so many clouds, and piled on each of them olives, puddings, pies, sweet and peppered frumenties . . ."

"I despise frumenties," murmured the driver, rousing a bit. The black gelding had maneuvered the wagon so far to the left of the road that his hooves scythed the bright and turgid grasses, and now he reached down for them in full rebellion. Damiano's eyes stayed open long enough for him to pull the reins right.

They were strange, those eyes of Damiano. They were dark and soft and heavily feathered, and in all ways what one desired and expected in a Latin eye. They were the sort of eye which is obviously created to house mysteries, and yet their only mystery was that they seemed to hide no mysteries at all, no more than the dark, soft eyes of a cow at graze. When Gaspare looked deeply into Damiano's eyes (as happened most frequently when Gaspare was angry) he sometimes had the fantasy that he was looking straight through the man and at an empty sky behind. At those times the little hairs stood up on Gaspare's arms.

Gaspare's own pale green eyes flashed. "Well, do not be alarmed, musician, for I don't think you're about to be offered frumenty. Nor olives, nor breads, nor roast pork, nor wine, nor . . ."

"Do be quiet," sighed the other, his loose shoulders slumping in exaggerated, Italian fashion. "This kind of talk doesn't help. If you could think of something constructive to do about it . . ."

Gaspare set his jaw, watching the last of the three ruined huts pass behind the wagon and be gone. "I have thought of something constructive. I told you, we should eat what God has put in our path."

The weary black eyes lit with amusement. "God sent that wether on to our road? Might He not also have sent the shepherd to follow? In which case our skins might have been stretched over a door alongside the sheepskin."

"We saw no shepherd," spat Gaspare.

Damiano nodded. "Ah, true. But then we killed no sheep!" He spoke with a certain finality, as though his words had proven a point, but there was something in his words which said also that he did not care.

Gaspare's expressive eyes rolled. (He, too, was Italian.) "I wasn't even talking about the sheep, musician. Nothing to get us in trouble with the peasants. I meant hares and rabbits. Birds. The wild boar . . ."

Damiano peered sidelong. "Have you ever seen a wild boar, Gaspare?"

The redhead responded with an equivocal gesture.
"Not . . . close up. You?"

Damiano shook his head, sending his own black mane
flying. His hair was so long and disordered it was almost
too heavy to curl. "I don't think so. Though I'm not sure
how it would differ from a domestic boar." With one hand
he swept the hair back from his face, in a gesture that also
had the purpose (vestigial, by this time) of throwing back
the huge sleeves of a gown of fashion.

"But, my friend, how have I ever stopped you from
availing yourself of these foods? Have I hidden your knife,
perhaps, or prevented you from setting a snare? Have I by
word or deed attempted to discourage you . . . ?"

Gaspare broke in. "I can't do it . . . when you won't."
Nothing about his colleague bothered him half so much as
Damiano's educated vocabulary and poetical syntax. These
mannerisms struck Gaspare like so many arrows, and he
never doubted that Damiano used them that way to keep
Gaspare (guttersnipe that he was) in his place. Gaspare
would certainly have used such words in that fashion, if
he'd known them. Yet at the same time the boy was as
proud of Damiano's learning as if it had been his own.

Gaspare's unspoken respect for his partner bordered on
religious reverence, and he lived under a fear that someday
Damiano would discover that. This thought was insupportable to the haughty urchin.

Damiano, of course, had known Gaspare's real feelings
since the beginning of their partnership. But that knowledge didn't make the boy any easier to take. The musician
looked away, resting his gaze upon the purple horizon. He
didn't like quarrels. He didn't have Gaspare's energy to
spend on them. "I don't know how to set a snare,
Gaspare," he mumbled, and let the breezes of Provence
wind through his vacant mind.

The boy snorted. "But would you set one if I showed
you how? Would you pluck a lark, or clean a rabbit, or even
eat one if I cooked it for you?" He forestalled his friend's
slow headshake. "No, of course you wouldn't. Well, that's
why I can't, either—or I'll be a bloodstained shambles-man
in my own eyes. And so we'll both starve to death."

Damiano gently corrected the horse. He yawned, partly
because of the sun through a woolen shirt, and partly
because discussions like this exhausted him. He wished

there were some way he could communicate to Gaspare how like a blind man felt, or perhaps like one who could not remember his own name. Not that Damiano was blind (only nearsighted), and not that he had forgotten anything. But he had been a witch and now was one no longer, and that was more than enough. Surely if the boy understood . . .

But all he could bring himself to say was: "Please, Gaspare. I get so tired."

His lack of response brought the flush stronger into Gaspare's face. "We will starve, and it will be *all your fault!*" he shouted, in an effort to be as unfair as possible.

Damiano did not look at him.

Gaspare's color went from red to white with sheer rage. That he should have to follow this lifeless stick from place to place like a dog, dependent upon him for music (which was both Gaspare's living and his life), for companionship, and even for language (for Gaspare spoke nothing but Italian) . . . it was crushing, insupportable. Tears leaked out of Gaspare's eyes.

But tears were not Gaspare's most natural mode of expression. Convulsively he grabbed Damiano's arm and drew it to him. With a canine growl he sank his teeth into it.

Damiano stood up in the seat howling. Gaspare tasted blood but he did not let go, no more than any furious terrier, not until the wooden handle of the horsewhip came crashing down on his head and shoulders.

Damiano then threw himself down from the seat of the moving wagon, clutching his bleeding arm and dancing over the shoulder of the road. The gelding pattered to a halt and turned its elegant, snakelike head.

Above, on the high wooden seat, young Gaspare sat, red as a boiled crab, and puffing like a bellows.

Damiano stared, slack-jawed, at him. "You *bit* me!" He repeated it twice, wonderingly. "Why?"

Suddenly Gaspare was all composure, and he knew the answer to that question as he spoke it. "I wanted to see if you were still alive at all. You don't act like it, you know, except when you play the lute. I thought maybe you died last winter, during the battle of San Gabriel, and had not yet noticed.

"A man gets tired," Gaspare concluded, "of talking with the dead."

Still gaping, Damiano pulled his woolen sleeve up. "Mother of God," he whispered, staring at the neat oval of broken skin, where stripes of crimson were welling over the bronze. "You have bitten me like you were a dog! Worse, for no dog has ever bitten me." His head went from side to side in shocked, old-womanish gestures, and his eyes on the wound were very large.

Gaspare sat very tall on the wagon seat. The yellow and green of his dagged jerkin outlined the ribs over his emotion-puffed chest. "Best work I've done in weeks," he stated. "Should have seen yourself hop."

Then he settled in the seat, like a bird shifting its weight from wings to perch. "You've been unbearable, lutenist. Absolutely unbearable for weeks. No man with a spirit could endure your company."

Receiving this additional shock, Damiano let his wounded arm drop. "Unbearable? Gaspare! I haven't even raised my voice to you. *You're* the one who has been howling and complaining since we hit the French side of the pass. . . ."

"Exactly!" The boy thrust out one knobbed finger. "Even though it is to meet *my* sister we are traveling across France and Provence in cold, dry Lent. It is me who complains, because I am a man. And you bear with me with a saintly, condescending patience which undermines my manhood." Now Gaspare stood, declaiming from the footboard (which wobbled) of the high seat.

"To err is human. Yes! I am a human and proud of it! To forgive . . . and forgive, and forgive . . . that is diabolic."

Suddenly the older fellow's dark face darkened, and he kicked a wheel as he muttered, "Did you have to say that—exactly that, Gaspare? Diabolic? A man can also get tired of being called a devil."

Gaspare snorted and wiped his nose on his long, tight sleeve. "No fear. You possess no such dignity. You are the unwitting—and I do mean *unwitting*—tool of wickedness, designed to lead me to damned temptation! By Saint Gabriele, Damiano, I believe you lost your head with that cursed Roman General Pardo in the town hall cellar, for you've been nothing but a ghost of a man since."

Damiano stared at Gaspare, and then stared through him. Five seconds later, for no perceivable reason, he flinched. His uninjured arm gestured about his head, dispersing unseen flies. Without a word he stepped to the side of the wagon and climbed into it through one of its large holes. A moment later he was out again, carrying a bundle with a strap and another bundle wrapped in flannel. The first he slid over his back (it made a tinkling noise) and the second he cradled with motherly care. Then he strode off and disappeared to Gaspare's eyes, hidden by the bulk of the wagon.

Gaspare heard the receding footsteps. He stood and hopped from one foot to the other. Failing to see Damiano appear around the wagon, he sprang gracefully to the dirt.

It was true. The lutenist was leaving, plodding back up the road toward Lyons, Chamonix and the Alps. Without another word, he was leaving. By conscious effort, the boy turned his sensation of cold desolation into his more accustomed red anger. He caught up with Damiano in ten athletic bounds.

"Hah!" he spat. "So you think to stick me with that unmanageable swine of a horse? Well, it won't work. The crows can pick his ribs for all I care!" And he executed a perfect, single-point swivel, flung up his right arm in a graceful, dynamic and very obscene gesture, and marched back down the road west and south. His small, peaked face was flaming.

Damiano, in his outrage, had forgotten Festilligambe, and he now felt a bit foolish. His less acrobatic steps slowed to a shuffling halt, while he heard Gaspare rummaging through the wagon. At last, when the noise had faded, Damiano came back.

The horse, while still standing between the traces, stared curiously over his shoulder at Damiano. He had a marvelous flexibility in that neck, did Festilligambe. Damiano tossed his gear back into the wagon and carefully deposited the lute into the niche in one corner which he had built for it. (This corner had no holes.)

Slowly and spiritlessly Damiano walked over to the horse. He examined the knotted, makeshift harness and the places where it had worn at the beast's coat. Festilligambe lipped his master's hair hopefully, tearing out those strands which became caught between his big box teeth. Damiano didn't appear to notice.

"I shouldn't be doing this to you, fellow," he whispered, stroking the black back free from dust. "You are no cart horse. It's clean straw and grain for which you were born. And fast running, with victory wine from silver cups." Thick horse lips smacked against the young man's face, telling him what the gelding thought about silver cups. His near hind foot suggested they start moving again.

Having no ideas of his own, Damiano was open to such suggestion. He boosted himself up to the driver's seat and reached for the whip he had dropped after drubbing Gaspare. Carefully he pulled up his sleeve, bunching it above the elbow to allow the sun free access to the neatly punched bite on his forearm.

The horse did not wait for a signal to start.

What a misery that boy was. Squatting passively on the plank of wood, Damiano let Gaspare's offenses parade by, one by one.

There had been that housewife in Porto. She had had no business to call the boy such names, certainly, but you cannot drive through a town cracking strange women on the head and expect to get away with it. Not even when they are bigger than you. Especially not then. She had almost broken the lute over Damiano's shoulders (though he was by rights not involved in the exchange of insults, only easier to catch than Gaspare).

And in Aosta they had come near to fame, or at least a comfortable living, playing before the Marchioness d'Orvil, until Gaspare ruined things and nearly got them sent to prison with that sarabande he insisted on dancing. In front of the marquese, besides. Damiano blushed even now, wondering how he could have missed seeing all winter that the dance was obscene. Gaspare had no delicacy.

But he was touchy as a *condottiere*, where slights to his small self were concerned. And jealous. Though he never let Damiano forget the young man's inexperience with women, Gaspare's attitude was as possessive as it was mocking, and his green eyes watched Damiano's every move. Let the lute player offer one gallant word to a female of any description, whether it be a girl with the figure of a poker or a mother with a dozen children, and Gaspare purely trembled with agitation.

You'd think he was a girl himself.

And hey! Gaspare was even jealous of the horse. That was what lay behind his silly resentment of the animal. He was jealous.

Heat laid a dry hand against Damiano's face. The clouds had dissolved in the sky. The black gelding trotted now easily, ears a-prick, long head bowing left and right to an invisible audience. It was as though this trip to Provence were Festilligambe's idea, not Damiano's. Or rather not Gaspare's, Damiano corrected himself. Damiano had no pressing desire to meet Evienne and her thieving clerk of a lover in Avignon on Palm Sunday. It was Gaspare who had arranged the rendezvous and set the time. (And what a time! How they had gotten through the snows of the pass at that season was a story in itself, and not a pleasant one. It had almost done for the lute, not to mention the three living members of the party.)

Gaspare babbled endlessly about his sister, calling her harlot, slut and whore with every breath and always in tones of great pride. He had badgered Damiano into crossing the Alps two months too early, just to keep faith with this sister with whom he was sure to squabble again in the first hour.

There was nothing wrong with Evienne, really. She had a warm, ripe body dusted with freckles, a wealth of copper hair and a strong desire to please.

But when Damiano compared her to another woman of his acquaintance—a lady whose tint was not so rare or figure quite so generous—all Evienne's color and charm faded into insignificance.

Next to Saara of the Saami, all of female humanity came out second best, Damiano reflected ruefully.

And when Gaspare met Evienne again, along with her lover and pimp, Jan Karl, the boy was sure to learn more pickpocket's tricks. He was certain to wind up hanged as a thief, if he didn't die brawling.

Damiano shut off this silent arraignment of his musical partner, without even touching on Gaspare's salient vices of gluttony and greed. It was an arraignment too easy to draw up, and rather more pathetic than damning. The upset of spirits it was causing in the lutenist was making his arm throb harder.

So what if Gaspare was nothing but trash, and daily becoming worse. Who had ever said otherwise—Gaspare himself?

No. Especially not Gaspare.

And there was the truth that disarmed Damiano's argument. Gaspare expected nothing but failure from himself—failure, acrimony, wounded pride. He *knew* he was difficult to get along with, and he accepted that Damiano was not. Therefore he considered it Damiano's responsibility to get along with him, as it is the responsibility of a hale man to support a lame companion, or a sighted man to see for a blind.

And this last tirade, in which the boy had accused Damiano of exactly nothing, had been built on a bizarre foundation of humility. For by letting the lutenist know how disappointed in him Gaspare was, he also let him know how much he had expected of him.

Damiano's head drooped. Grass-broken road swept by below the cracked footboard. His fine anger dissolved with the shreds of clouds, leaving a puddle of shame.

The truth was he didn't really like Gaspare. Not wholeheartedly, except when the music gave them a half-hour's unity, or during the rare moments when they were both rested and fed. Gaspare was simply not very likable.

But the problem was Damiano didn't like anyone else wholeheartedly either, except of course one glorious angel of God. And that took no effort.

Gaspare had been right, Damiano admitted to himself. He had failed the boy. He had given him very little, on a human level, since the beginning of winter. Aside from his music, Damiano had felt he had nothing to give.

And wasn't the lute enough? Damiano rubbed his face with both hands. God knew it was work to study and play as hard as he had done for the past year. It required concentration, which was the hardest of works, as well as the best.

But no. Damiano might be a madman about his instrument, but he was not so deluded as all that. One could not pass off a *bourrée* as an act of friendship, any more than one could disguise as human warmth what was mere good manners and a dislike of conflict.

And what had he taken from Gaspare in exchange for that counterfeit friendship? Rough loyalty, praise, energy, enthusiasm. . . .

Once Damiano had had his own enthusiasm. Enthusiasm and a dog. The dog died, and then the enthusiasm, and he had had only Gaspare.

Eyes gone blind to the spirit, ears gone deaf to the natural world: it seemed to Damiano he had given as much as a man ought to be asked to give, for the sake of right. He ought to be allowed some peace now, for as long as he had left.

But how could he say that to Gaspare, who had never possessed what Damiano had now lost?

Suddenly it occurred to him to wonder which way the boy had gone. Surely he would continue to Avignon, to Evienne. Damiano raised his eyes.

A minute later and Gaspare would have been out of sight, or at least out of the lutenist's poor sight. But he was visible in the far distance ahead, a bobbing splotch of motley, jogging along faster than the horse's amble. Frowning, Damiano tossed his hair from his face. Gaspare's physical endurance inspired awe. Doubtless he would make it to the city alone, and probably he would go quicker and plumper than he would have in the lutenist's company.

Then truth stung Damiano's black eyes. Beloved or no, Gaspare was necessary to him. In a manner totally removed from the question of like or dislike, Damiano Delstrego needed Gaspare because the boy believed in him—as a lutenist, as a composer.

As a man of possibilities.

Damiano did not believe he was the best lutenist in the Italies, any more than he had believed himself to have been the most powerful witch in the Italies—when he had been a witch. After all, he had only been playing (obsessively) for a handful of years. But Gaspare did believe that, and more. Gaspare was the first and only person in Damiano's life who was convinced of Damiano's greatness.

It had been at first embarrassing, and then intoxicating, to have someone so convinced.

It had become necessary.

The world was filled with strangers. Gaspare, with all his prickliness and his ignorance (ignorant as a dog. Unreliable as a dog in heat.), had become necessary to the musician.

Damiano asked the horse for more speed, snapping the whip against the singletree. Festilligambe bounded forward, honking more like a goose than a horse. Harness snapped. The wagon boomed alarmingly.

This was no good. Two miles of this speed and the mismatched wheels would come off.

·Damiano cursed the wagon. He'd rather be riding. But
if he was to travel with Gaspare again, he'd need the
ramshackle vehicle. Perhaps he ought to catch Gaspare on
horseback, and then return to the wagon.

But what had become of the boy? Damiano rose up in
the seat, bracing one large-boned hand against the back-
board and one ragged boot against the footrest. He
jounced, clothes flapping on his starved torso like sheets
on a line. His black screws of hair bounced in time with the
wheels' squeal, except for one patch in the back which
sleeping on branches had left matted with pinesap. He
squinted in great concentration.

The road opened straight before him, swooping south
and west, losing elevation as it went. Grass gave way to
ill-tended fruit trees and bare stands of alder, and the
wet ground was hummocked with briar and swamp maple,
which twined like ivy. Less inviting countryside, was this,
certainly. The clouds had returned and were multiplying,
or at least swelling. In the distance appeared what might
have been a village. (Or it might have been rock scree.
Damiano was always tentative about things seen in the
distance.)

But nowhere could he spy a lean shape of yellow and
red and green, neither floating over the grass nor angrily
trampling the briars. No Gaspare on the road or among the
swamp maple. Not even a suspiciously bright bird shape
amid the alder groves.

Damiano's curse began quite healthily, but trailed off
into a sort of ineffectual misery. For seeking people missing
or lost he was even less equipped than the average man.
He had always before known where people were, known it
literally with his eyes closed—been able to feel a distant
presence like a breath against his face. But he didn't know
how to *look* for a boy, using patience and reason, going up
one country wagon rut and down the next. He felt that at
twenty-three he was too old to learn.

As a matter of fact he felt too old for many activities,
and the best life had to offer was most certainly sleep. As
his mind spun in gripless circles around the problem of
Gaspare, his lower lids crawled upward and his upper lids
sank downward until his rebellious eyes closed themselves. His hands, too, had snuck up one another's sleeve
and hidden in the warmth.

So little was pleasant in this life, and most of what there was turned out to be a mistake. Magic was self-delusion and war just a patch of bloody snow. Even one's daily meat was the product of violent death, while love . . .

The gray stone walls, burying a nun. A gray stone grave on a hillside. A small grave in a garden without a stone.

Only music was uncorruptible, for it meant everything and nothing. In the past year Damiano had done little but play on the lute.

His present lute was his second, successor to the little instrument smashed in Lombardy and buried beside the bones of an ugly bitch dog. This lute boasted five courses and its sound carried much farther than that of his first pretty little toy. But it was shoddily made and did not ring true high on the neck, no matter how Damiano adjusted the gut fretting. In only fifteen months' play he had worn smooth valleys along the soft-wood fretboard.

But now he didn't want to play. There was no one to hear but the horse, who was tone deaf and appreciated no rhythms save his own. Besides—Damiano's hands would not come out of their hiding.

The sun winked in and out of clouds; he felt it against his face, like a memory of his missing witch-sense. His head filled with the mumbling voice which was always present if he allowed himself to listen.

Sometimes it broke into his dreams, waking him. More often, like now, it droned him to sleep. Either way, he never understood it.

And there came odd images, and thoughts. Naked women (a radiant, young naked woman: Damiano knew her name) he could understand, but why should his head be filled with concern for goats?

He let such concerns fade with the sunlight.

The horse did not know his driver was asleep. He needed neither whip nor rein to urge him to do what he liked most to do, which was to keep going. He lifted his feet, not with the exaggeration of fashion, but with racing efficiency. He nodded right and left to his invisible audience. His high, Arabic tail swept the air.

He thought about oats, and never wondered why he should do so.

Suddenly Festilligambe recognized something much better than oats. Philosophical amazement caused him to stumble, and his trot became a shuffle. A halt. He craned his long neck and regarded the crude seat of the wagon, his whinny pealing like bells.

Damiano woke up smiling, in the presence of light. His hands leaped free of his shirt and he hid his poor, inadequate eyes behind them. "Raphael," he cried. "I'm so glad to see you—or almost to see you."

Between the mortal's shut fingers leaked an uncomfortable radiance. Damiano turned his head away, but as if in effort to counteract this seeming rejection, he scooted closer to the angel on the seat. Meanwhile, the horse was doing his level best to turn around in his traces.

"I'm sorry, Dami," said the Archangel Raphael, settling in all his immateriality next to Damiano. "I don't know what to do about that."

Damiano gave a sweeping wave of his hand, accompanied by one scornful eyebrow. "Don't think about it, Seraph. It is my little problem. At least I can hear you perfectly, and that is more than most people can. Besides, I remember well what you look like." He opened his eyes, staring straight ahead.

And he sighed with relief. It was pleasant to talk to the angel again. Very pleasant, especially now when he was feeling so completely friendless. But conversation was one thing, and study another. Today Damiano was not in the mood for a lesson.

Yet Raphael was his teacher, and so Damiano felt some effort was incumbent upon him. "I've been saving a question for you, Raphael. About that *joli bransle* we were toying with last week."

"The *bransle?*" A hint of surprise rested in the angelic voice. "You want to talk about the *bransle* right now?"

"I was wondering if I ought to play those three fourth intervals in a row. Or not, you know? It's not like they were fifths, which would be too old-fashioned and dull, but still, I feel the measure would go more if I descended in the bass."

There was a moment's silence, along with a rustle like that of a featherbed. Then the corona of radiance said, "Dami, what are you going to do about Gaspare?"

Involuntarily, Damiano glanced over. Silver filled his eyes, cool as starlight, chillingly cool, set off by seas of deep blue. Damiano was falling, fearlessly falling, out into depths of time.

There was a curtain of silence. He tore it.

And the brilliance then was white-hot and immense. It was not infinite, but full within limits set perfect for it, shining round and glad, and it would have been meaningless to suggest this brilliance might want to be larger or smaller than it was, for it was glowingly content. And it was a brilliance of sound as much as of light: wild sound, like trumpets in harmony, yet subtle as the open chords of a harp. It drowned Damiano. His problems dissolved.

"Dami," came the soft, cool, ordinary voice. "Dami. Damiano! Close your eyes or I'll have to knock you off the wagon."

Eventually the young man obeyed, dropping his head, clutching the seatback as though fighting a formidable wind. "I . . . I . . . ooof! Forgive me, Raphael. It leaves me a little sick."

The angel emitted a very melodic sort of whine. "That's terrible, Dami. What is the matter with me that I affect you so badly?"

Through his undeniable nausea, Damiano had to laugh. "The matter with you, old friend? Don't worry about it. It's what I get for being neither witch nor truly simple. And the sickness I feel happens only as I come back to myself."

He sat upright once more, and reached out at random to slap an immaterial shoulder. "It's good for my music, Seraph. You have no idea how much I learn each time I get sick looking at you."

Raphael's sigh was quite human. He plucked at Damiano's head. "You have sap in your hair," he observed.

Damiano wiggled his fingers into the snarl. "I know. Gaspare wanted to cut it out. That seemed a very radical solution to the problem, so I . . ."

"Gaspare," echoed the angel. "What are you going to do about Gaspare?"

Damiano bristled his brow. "How can I tell you? He just ran off not an hour ago. Maybe he'll come back. And how did you know about that anyway, Raphael? You were listening?"

Wings ruffled again. "Yes, I was." After a few seconds' silence on the human's part, Raphael added, "Shouldn't I listen?"

Damiano shrugged. "It makes me feel I have to be always on my best behavior, that's all."

This time it was the angel's turn to pause. "Best behavior? Is that like your best clothes? I'm flattered that you would want to wear it for me, Dami, but you needn't. And if you wish, I will stop listening.

"In fact"—and the angel's voice grew even softer, (softer, slower and indefinably droll)—"I ought to send you a note beforehand, each time I visit, so that you can be wearing your best behavior. And your best clothes."

Damiano snorted, smiling wryly. "I *am* wearing my best clothes. They have become indistinguishable from my worst. Like my behavior." There was something harsh in the laugh with which he followed this.

"I'm going to follow Gaspare down the road, Raphael. All the way to Avignon, if need be." His smile grew tighter as he added, "And I'll even apologize to the little weasel, when I find him.

"*That* is what I'm going to do about Gaspare. Does it make you happy, my teacher?"

Before Raphael could reply that that *did* make him happy, the conversation was interrupted by a huge crack and snap of wood, followed by a pained whinny, as the frustrated horse finally succeeded in turning around in place. The sting of the trace breaking at his right sent Festilligambe into a series of stiff-legged jumps which destroyed the last of the makeshift harness. Then, as Damiano bit his fingers in consternation, the gelding laid its long head on the footrest of the wagon and gazed up at the angel, moaning like a forge.

"There goes the wagon," cried Damiano. "So much firewood!"

"I'm sorry," said the angel (for the second time that day).

Damiano's gesture was magnanimous and very Italian. "Forget it! He's my horse. Besides—how can you be sorry about anything when you're a perfect spirit?" He swung down from the seat and marched forth to release the horse from its tangles.

"I'm not perfect," replied the angel, almost hurt in tone. "That's very bad theology. Only the Father is perfect. I am only sinless. And it is because of me this lovely fellow has broken all his straps. Let me fix it."

Damiano stopped with two handfuls of rope. The horse's gently swishing tail was flogging his kneecap. "Fix . . . the harness? But you are not to become involved in human affairs, remember?"

Raphael glided over the horse's head and hung in the air for a moment before alighting. Damiano looked down.

"True," came the angel's voice from above, "but that is a complex matter, my friend. If I caused the accident, then am I not becoming more deeply involved if I neglect to repair the damage?" The angel's voice now issued from beside Damiano, who flinched his face away.

After a moment he asked, "Is it done yet, Raphael?"

Wings clapped together in what might have been consternation. "Done, Dami? I have scarcely begun. There are a lot of knots here, you know."

The young man dared a peek at one of the broken lines, to find that the whole thing had been retied: the flax joined to the hemp rope with a neat series of square knots, while the leather (which had to slide) had been linked in with a bowline.

Damiano had to laugh. "I thought you were going to use magic."

There was a pause before Raphael answered. "I'm not a witch, Damiano. I don't really possess much magic, but my . . . my fingers are clever enough."

Damiano took this statement for what he thought it was worth and, grinning, he raised his hand to scratch his head.

"Ouch. Are they clever enough to get this mat out of my hair, Seraph?"

Smooth fingers felt around the elf-lock. "Well, I can certainly make some improvement, Dami. Have you got a knife?"

The last remnants of a former vanity caused Damiano to cringe. "You mean you'll have to cut after all?"

The angel chuckled. "Yes. The harness was one thing, but this kind of neglect is another. But I think I can do it without leaving too much of a hole."

Damiano sat perched on the wagon seat, being barbered with his shaving razor. He kept his eyes closed. Raphael did not stop when he had removed the matted patch in the back, but took this opportunity to shape the whole head according to his personal taste.

"Phew," spat the mortal. "Hair in my mouth. Gaspare won't know me, when I do find him. I haven't had my hair cut since last autumn."

"Why not?" asked the angel, as black hairs floated through his stainless radiance.

"No money," replied Damiano, but even as he spoke he knew it wasn't the truth. Gaspare badgered him weekly to let him cut his hair in the style in which he arranged his own orange locks. Damiano, who could not imagine himself looking like Gaspare, had steered clear.

"Or rather, Raphael, I am beyond caring what I look like."

"Why so?" The angel's voice seemed preoccupied.

Damiano hesitated before answering. It was not a subject that made easy conversation. "Because, Seraph, I have been told not . . . to expect . . ." His head was gently pressed forward while attention was paid to the nape of his neck. ". . . to expect to live much longer."

With absolutely no change of tone Raphael murmured, "One is told a great number of things by a great number of people. I'd be careful whom I believed."

The razor swished near Damiano's left ear. "Besides, Dami. Even if your appearance doesn't matter to you, it matters to the girls. The pretty girls: they care what you look like."

Damiano jerked around and almost looked at the angel. "What kind of thing is that for *you* to say? You—an angel of God!"

"Is there something wrong with girls, Dami? Why should you not want to please them, when I know they try so hard to look pleasing to you?"

Damiano shook a great dark cloud into the air. "Have you no . . . no regard for chastity, Archangel?"

The razor was placed carefully back in Damiano's left hand. "Chastity, yes. Ugliness, no."

Damiano growled, "Saints are often quite ugly, and filthy besides, yet I am told that God holds them in high regard." He began to pick hair from his tunic.

"I know that to be true," replied the angel equably. "But I am not the Father. And you, Damiano . . ."

"I know. I know." The razor was wrapped in rags and

slipped into the back of the wagon. "I am no saint. But I do my best, Raphael."

The wagon was moving again. Raphael said nothing for a while, and Damiano dared not look around, but he knew the angel to be there on the seat beside him. Finally Raphael said, "God be with you along this road, Damiano." It sounded so like a farewell that Damiano replied with an *"Et cum spiritu tuo."*

But the angel remained: unseen but almost palpably present. A mile passed, then another. Dullness took Damiano, along with a drowse that the company of his bright friend made pleasant.

The gray shape on the far hill was indeed a village, and growing closer. It had a wall. Smoke fingered the sky. There was something in the road before the village: something brown and slowly moving, like a yoke of oxen.

Perhaps it was market day, and the road was deserted only because everybody was already in town. Damiano was peering ahead for any sign of Gaspare when the angel spoke in his ear. "Keep trying," he said, and then he *was* gone.

Keep trying for what? To find Gaspare? To look at Raphael? To stay well groomed? Damiano could think of nothing else Raphael might have meant—except, of course, keep trying to stay awake.

The road was filled with fresh ruts, but no vehicles either passed or had been left beside the village's mudplaster walls. In the distance someone was singing in an aggressive and undisciplined bass. Those were men in the road in front of the village gate; it was their coarse brown robes that caused them to resemble oxen. Over all hung a faint odor of the shambles.

The singing grew louder.

Surely this was market day, and in a good-sized village, besides. Damiano's hands twitched on the reins, as he began to pick out his program for the afternoon.

This place would welcome nothing delicate or too subtle, certainly, and besides, much fingerwork wouldn't be heard over the noise. Country dances were the thing, and part-songs the drunks could sing along to. Too bad he hadn't a longer background in the local music; the Provençal and French music he had learned in Italy was High Art stuff and wouldn't do at all.

Damn Gaspare for running off just when his capers would come in handy.

Now the gates were clearly visible: logs of split maple hung by great square nails. They hung open. Damiano sat up in surprise to discover that the robed men in the road were engaged in whipping three other fellows who knelt in stocks set right in the open gateway.

His first reaction was typical of his time and culture. He snickered aloud, wondering how much bran these bakers had put in their bread. Then the metal tips of the cats glittered in sunlight, and he saw the blood running.

Poor sinners, he said under his breath, while the frightened and excited horse first snorted and then jammed backward, jarring the wagon and causing it to yaw. Damiano slipped down from his seat and took the reins in one hand, beneath Festilligambe's head.

The floggers wore robes, but they were not tonsured. After each blow they paused to utter a penitential prayer. The victims were nearly naked, and they did not make a sound. The monk in the middle, whose long scourge cracked like a horsewhip with every stroke, was a huge fellow, full-faced yet grim, with odd pale-blue eyes. A froth of blood spattered with each stroke. His brown-haired victim might have been dead, for he lay in the stocks with no movement.

These were felons, not cheeseparing merchants, Damiano decided. Someday Gaspare would surely come to this, if he continued on his path. The lutenist hoped his errant dancer had encountered this sight, or was perhaps watching this minute from within the town. It would do him good.

Buy why had it fallen to the Third Order of Saint Francis to execute the punishment of miscreants? Dominicans, who were called the Hounds of Christ, would be quite at home in such a role, and Jesuits even more so. But both orders were relatively dapper, and most certainly tonsured. Franciscans were the only ones who sometimes went shabby. Damiano had always felt a strong affinity for Giovanni di Bernardone (called Francesco, or Francis), who had been a musician as well as a saint. He was very disappointed to find that the Franciscans whipped people.

Even more upsetting was the fact that this display effectively blocked his entry into the village. With difficulty he maneuvered the spooky horse off the road and on to the trampled green at the foot of the wall. He yanked his bag of clothes and cookpots through a hole in the wagon wall and dropped it on the ground. Carefully he lifted out his lute and set it atop them. He slipped the gelding's black head into a halter and untied its harness. The hulk of wagon he left behind, half hoping it would be stolen.

Leading the horse, he would be able to pass between the stocks and the village wall. He hoped his passage would not offend the clerics but, really, one must be able to get in and out of a town, especially on market day.

Here the coarse singing was very loud, and shared by more than one voice. Drunken, most likely. But the sound of a silver bell, rung by the middle monk, cut through all, and as Damiano passed directly behind the burly flagellator, the man leaned forward, threw open the stocks, and tenderly lifted out his victim. The others did likewise, and the poor sufferers staggered to their feet.

Then, with a booming cry, the huge man tore off his rude and filthy robe and flung himself into the stocks, which framework shook with the impact of his weight. The other flagellators, like shadows, followed. Despite their bloody and battered condition, the former victims each picked up an iron-tipped cat and set to work with a will. Even the middle one, whom Damiano had thought half dead.

Damiano had heard of the order of flagellants (if indeed there was any "order" about it), but this was his first sight of them, and it left him feeling queasy. Surely there was bravery in their actions, and they undoubtedly canceled out a great number of sins, but still it seemed to Damiano there was more to be gained from a well-sung mass. As he passed beneath the village gate, crude and heavy as a deadfall, he met the pale eyes of the former executer, now victim. They were bright, round and electric with pain. At first the man's face held his gaze by its power to raise pity. But that power faded as the musician saw in those eyes nothing pitiful, but rather a horrible sort of ecstasy, which lit the gray face from within like living coals under a bed of ash.

And then, between one moment and the next, the penitent's face underwent a subtle alteration without seeming to change at all. Damiano stared down through the man's flesh at another face that glowed from within: a face with perfect, elegant features which were molded out of malice and fire, and which stared burning malice up at him.

It was a face Damiano had known before—a face strangely like that of Raphael, were the angel seen in a wicked dream.

It made his heart shiver and jump within him, and his knees buckled. But for his hand on the horse's lead rope he would have fallen, and it was only the strength of the gelding (who only saw the Devil when leaves blew over the road) which led Damiano by.

This was not the first time that Damiano had seen Satan face to face, but it was the first time in a year and more, and never before had Satan appeared to him unsummoned. Fear coursed like cold water through his body.

Inside, he turned the horse and looked back, only to find a perfectly normal-looking fanatic being scourged by another of the same variety. He stood confused, listening to his heart regain its proper rhythm.

The streets and stoops were littered with people, yes. But despite that, this was no market, for there were no barrows to be seen. Also, the shops were closed, unswept, some of them boarded. Drunks and singing implied a festival, yet this looked like no festival Damiano had ever seen, unless it were the third hour of night after a long day's carouse.

Along the foul street lounged men in gay velvets, sitting in the dirt next to men in rags. Women, too, mixed with them in the gutters on terms of easy familiarity. One fat woman seemed to be wearing every bit of white linen she possessed, in onion-layers over a purple woolen gown. She squatted on the stoop of a decayed shop, while above her a cart-wheel-sized wooden olive swung on chains in the wind. The door of the shop was staved in, and a pungent litter of broken olives lay scattered about the street. Her apron, too, was filled with olives.

Beside her, not touching, removed as if by time and distance, sat the undisciplined bass, singing "gaudeamus" as he juggled olives in his oily hands. He was not smiling, this reveler, nor was the well-(or at least much-) dressed woman. Nor was anyone on the street or in the square beyond. The dry smell of wine warred with that of olives, while above both rose a reek of excrement.

And this whole assemblage of unsmiling maniacs gazed directly at Damiano. Festilligambe froze, shaking all over.

And though he had no longer any witch's staff to warn him, and would not have been able to use it if he had, Damiano sensed wrongness before him as strongly as a blind man may sense the noonday sun. He thought to back out the way he came, but the white-eyed horse stood rooted, while behind him rose the terrifying soft prayers and sharp strokes of the flagellants.

The bass voice was climbing to his feet. He approached Damiano. Indeed, the whole somber riot of them was drawing near, staring with puzzled intensity at one dark-skinned, thinnish traveler with a horse.

The singer bowed from the waist. "Welcome. Welcome to Petit Comtois, my brave one. Forgive our deshabille: we were not expecting visitors. And yet we are delighted to see you." At the end of this announcement, the fellow forgot to close his mouth.

Damiano dropped his bag of clothes and pots. His head was swimming unpleasantly, and he didn't know whether the scene before him was as bizarre as it appeared, or whether it only seemed so to eyes which had just endured the sight of the Devil. He cleared his throat. Once, twice, three times he tried to answer. The fat woman hove up beside the first villager. She stared at the horse, and then at Damiano. She touched the mane of each.

"Hasn't he nice hair," she observed to the world in general. Her mouth was a rosebud and her eyes were glazed like candy. Damiano stuttered harder as her fingers played through his new-trimmed locks.

At last he was able to say, "My name is Delstrego, good villagers. I am a musician, and I have come seeking after a friend."

The bass singer nodded sagely. "Good Monsieur Delstrego, welcome again. No one could please us more than a musician seeking after a friend. In Pe'Comtois you will find many friends. In Pe'Comtois we are all friends. Friends unto death." And he smiled a wise, lunatic smile.

Damiano backed away, and the horse backed with him, trampling the bag of pots. He felt a stiff, foolish smile stamp itself upon his face. He could not tear it off. Then the silver bell of the flagellants tinkled once more and Festilligambe bolted forward, dragging his master beside him.

But the heavy villager grabbed the gelding's cheekstraps, and the beast went rigid with terror.

Behind them, wooden gates swung shut. The horse moaned helplessly.

At this Damiano's courage awoke. "I'll take the horse," he snapped. "He doesn't like strangers." And he pulled the villager's fingers, one by one, from the rope halter. Then he turned foursquare and confronted the town.

"What is wrong, here?" he challenged. "I can't tell whether you are all in mourning or on holiday. You are all dressed up and yet it looks like the village has been looted. Is there war? Sickness?"

He pointed over the first row of houses to where black smoke still increased. "What is burning?"

The fat woman turned to the odd-dozen villagers behind her. "He asks whether there is war," she announced. "He asks whether there is sickness. He asks what is burning in Pe'Comtois." She giggled. "He has such a sweet Italian accent."

Damiano, being only human, reacted to this with a certain amount of cold hauteur. But the male villager put up a restraining hand. "Peace, Monsieur Italian. I will show you what you want to know. I will show you what is burning. I will show you the very soul of Pe'Comtois. Follow me."

Damiano followed, between two dry stone buildings and across another desolate street. The bizarre audience faded behind, lacking either energy or interest. At the next narrow intersection Festilligambe balked, and rather than suffer the villager's unsettling aid, Damiano left the lead rope hanging over a post, knowing no one could walk off with the animal. The truth about Festilligambe was that although he would not always obey Damiano, he would never, under any circumstances, obey anyone else.

Here the smell of dung was stronger, but it was overwhelmed by burning wood. It was houses that were burning, the white stone walls containing flame like cupped hands, while fire-tongues licked through the windows. Around the perimeter of the blazing area stood men with pails and pokers, watching the flames with proprietary interest.

"It is . . . on purpose?" asked Damiano, shifting his lute from hand to hand. "You are burning your houses on purpose?"

"In Pe'Comtois," stated the villager, "we are very rich. When we are tired of a house, then—*pfft!* Up she goes. There are always plenty to go around.

"Enough houses, gowns, linens, foodstuffs, wines— no, not enough wines, forgive me. But enough of everything else." He led the other across a court, where stood an enormous church, high-spired, windowed with glass. It was a church far too big for the village that contained it. It was a Provençal church. Together they passed in.

"And how are you so lucky, in Petit Comtois?" mumbled Damiano, his words echoing in dim stone.

With every step he grew more distrustful. Sacred ground or no, this place stank. And his ears told him it was not empty. The nave door swung open.

There, under high tiered windows of scarlet and gold, upon carved pews of oak, were strewn bodies: the dead and dying, piled neatly head to toe.

"Because there is no one left to eat, to wear clothes, to live in houses . . ." announced the singing villager, sweeping the chamber with a gesture.

"We are all dead, you see. Plague."

CHAPTER 2

From the right came sounds: the weak rebellion of the dying, and their terrible, whistling breath. From the left came only the echoes of the sounds, for all who reclined on the pews on that side of the church were already dead. Even as Damiano's eyes adjusted to the dim jeweled light from the stained windows, two cowled men lifted one of the passive shapes and promoted it to the left side of the aisle. No word was spoken.

"This cannot be," Damiano whispered tentatively. Then hearing his own words in his ears, he fell silent.

Festilligambe stood in the beneficent spring sun, shifting from one pair of legs to the other. It seemed to him that if he wasn't going, he ought to be eating. Or at least rolling. He tested the length of his rope. Not quite long enough.

Too bad. Of course he could always pull the rope away; it was not attached to the thin wooden post in any way. But that he was not supposed to do.

For a few minutes he amused himself scratching against the painted stone wall, leaving mats of black winter coat caught on every roughness. Then he scraped his halter methodically against the windowsill. He bit off a chunk of painted plaster, and then spat it out with disgust. Festilligambe didn't know he was elegantly lean, but he knew he was hungry.

Someone was coming. The gelding pricked his fox-tiny ears and snorted. He wasn't very fond of people, except of course for Damiano. Not that anyone had ever done him any real hurt, but he was a Barb, and there it was.

It was a horse approaching. A big horse. The gelding's ears went back, because he really wasn't very fond of other horses, either. He especially disliked bigger horses, who might tend to think too much of themselves.

As it turned out, this horse wasn't really too big. He was shorter than Festilligambe although far heavier built. He had a human with him. That was good; it meant there would probably be no fight, and fights were not amusing unless the other horse was much smaller. One look in the gray stallion's placid ram-face and Festilligambe knew this horse would offer no difficulty. He crested his black neck and hissed at the draft horse, for though Festilligambe was a gelding, he knew what pride was.

Now the human was lifting his halter rope from the post where Damiano had left it. Wouldn't he be surprised to find that Festilligambe could not move from the place he had been told to stay?

He never had moved, not since he had made that agreement with Damiano in San Gabriele over a year ago, when Damiano had promised never to spellbind him if the horse would stay where put. He never had moved, and he never would. Never, never, never. The elegant black set his every muscle for the balk.

The human, however, did not try to pull. Instead he tied the halter rope into the gray horse's harness straps. Holding the gray's cheekstrap loosely in one hand, he clucked to the massive animal.

The rope tightened. Festilligambe dug in with his hooves. In two seconds he found himself flipped in the air and landing on his left shoulder and hindquarters, his legs still straight out before him. As he was dragged gently along the dry road, his face was a mask of equine bewilderment.

Plague. There must be some mistake. The plague had vanished sixteen years ago, after destroying almost half of Europe. Surely it was like Noah's flood, and God would not send it again. This must be some other pestilence; typhus or cholera. Something that would do its little damage (great enough to the people who died of it, and to the families of those who died of it) and fade away. Man was heir to so many diseases.

Slowly Damiano began to pace along the great central aisle, cradling his lute high against his chest, his breath half choked by the stench. He peered only down the rows to his right.

This man was a farrier; Damiano could tell because he still wore his divided leather skirt. Touching his head were the bare feet of a tall woman in black lace. Her handsome face, not young, had gone green. (At first he thought it was the window light, but no, there was no green glass in any window. She was green.) Her breath whistled two notes at once. She stared stupidly at Damiano's lute, and her lips moved.

What could he do but shrug his shoulders, apologizing for his healthy presence: a lute-carrying mountebank at death's grim door? In reply she spoke one word, which he could not hear.

There was a man at Damiano's elbow. One of the religious who had ported the body from the right side to the left. A brother of Saint Francis, the musician noted.

"It was kind of you, my son, but I doubt many of them would notice."

It took Damiano a little time to understand. Then he shifted the lute from hand to hand. "Oh. Forgive me, Brother. I don't mean to disturb."

He found himself repeating his words from the village gates. "I am a musician, and have come off the road seeking after a friend."

The Franciscan nodded. He lowered his eyes and replied, "Look, then. But for your own sake, do not touch."

This misunderstanding shocked Damiano. But as he opened his mouth to tell the friar that Gaspare could not possibly lie here among the dying, having preceded Damiano down the road by only an hour, it occurred to him there was no use in it. Gaspare (if he had entered Petit Comtois at all) was subject to real danger.

And so was Damiano. Between one moment and the next he remembered Satan's words. *"Soon. Perhaps a year or two. Perhaps tonight."* And once more he touched the black bedrock of his existence, which was the fact that Satan had told him he was going to die.

His hand trembled on the neck of the lute and he chided himself, asking himself why he should be frightened now at the sight and thought of death, when he had spent the last year and more preparing himself for that inevitability. After all, was that not the reason he had avoided involvement with women? And was it not at least part of the reason he had fallen into sleeping so much, sleep being death's close kin?

But no preparation could suffice; he was not at all ready to die. There were matters unsettled—matters such as Gaspare, who was angry with him. Such as that vision of green eyes and brown braids, and the singsong voice in his head which he could not quite understand.

Saara. He wished he had said more to her.

It came to Damiano all at once that his life was not a rounded whole; it had no progression or shape. As an artist, he couldn't call complete a work which possessed neither structure nor moral—or, at least, no structure or moral evident to human eyes.

And he felt a great dissatisfaction with this method of death, perishing in hopeless and frightful stink. A man wanted to die heroically, with someone standing by to take down his final words. To sicken and die of plague, in company of a hundred others, nameless and forgotten . . .

"In a century you will be a man who might never have existed from a city with a forgotten name."

But it was Satan who had said that. The Father of Lies, and his one purpose had been to hurt. "I'd be careful whom I believed," Raphael had said. Damiano did not believe this prophecy because Satan had given it, but rather because he himself had accepted it. As a bargain. Yet at the same time he did not believe it at all because the archangel had also advised Damiano that no created being—including Raphael's brother Lucifer—knew the future of men. At any rate, believing or not believing, Damiano was not ready today to die.

All this passed behind his black eyes in a moment. He found himself speaking to the Franciscan. "It is the plague, Brother? Not typhus, or . . ."

The friar lifted his eyebrows so forcefully his scalp wrinkled above his tonsure. "Didn't you know? My poor, innocent traveler. You have come along a very bad road."

"God be with you along this road." Cursed angel. He could cut hair. He could fix harness, but he couldn't say one little word about the plague lying ahead.

Immediately Damiano reprimanded himself. He could not blame the archangel for keeping to the limits assigned him. Especially since he had broken those limits once already for Damiano, saving him from the hangman in the village of San Gabriele. Raphael was definitely not supposed to involve himself that way.

(Yet the angel still called himself sinless. Not perfect but sinless.)

Turning to go from that deadly church, Damiano thought of one more question. "Brother. Those monks I saw at the village gates. The flagellants. Are they Franciscan also?"

The friar's frown was lit crimson, blue and gold. It was formidable. "They are not monks of any sort. They are not true Christians. Pay them no attention, my brother. Fear and despair may drive men mad, and Satan enjoys our misery."

"Satan?" echoed Damiano, and he wished he knew a way to tell the friar what he had seen in the face of the flagellant at the gate. But no, the Franciscan would only think him mad. He turned to the white light of day that came through the entrance door. But he heard a call. "Lute player. Lute player."

It was the green woman in the black lace. "Play," she said. "Play for me."

The Franciscan was not around.

Damiano did not want to play, nor to remain in that house of plague for any reason, but he lowered himself gingerly onto the arm of the pew, by the feet of the unconscious farrier. Quickly he tuned.

"What do you want to hear?" he whispered to her in conspiratorial fashion.

"Play sweetly," the sick woman replied. "Quietly. I don't want to dance just now."

He played a sad Palistinelied by Walther, and then one of his own, written in midwinter, that he had called "The Horse's Lullaby." When he was done, she said no more, and only by her rough and bubbling breath did he know she was not dead.

As Damiano paced toward the vestibule a man passed him: elderly, upright, dressed like a burgher. This composed old fellow proceeded slowly up the aisle, peering down every right-hand pew. Looking for someone, Damiano decided. But then the old man paused, discovering the opening left by the body recently carried off, and he sat down, crossed himself, and lay back.

Damiano flung himself toward the light.

The air of the street was pleasant, being sullied only by smoke. "Dami Delstrego, you must stop crying," he growled to himself, blinking and blundering across the court. "You mozzarella! Someone will see you in a moment."

Was it fear or pity that clutched his windpipe? He could not tell. He had not felt so shaken since leaving the Piedmont. Since before that. Since . . .

He remembered the crack of his staff breaking and the terrible sense of falling, falling. He remembered Saara's glorious face, and all the rest of the world going gray.

Damiano resolved to get out of this fearsome town, if he had to inch up the stuccoed wall.

And speaking of getting out, where had he left Festilligambe?

Though Petit Comtois lay not far from the High Pass, and was in construction similar to the stone towns of Piedmont that bore Damiano, it was French enough to be confusing to him. The streets were narrow, very narrow, and they wound like ivy. The buildings were not as high as the square towers of Italy, but they tended to spread out sideways, sometimes blocking the road. And though he could read langue d'oc passably, there were no signs to be seen.

There had been an alley with a flight of stairs, where he had to leave the horse. Was this it? It was dark enough, and the burning houses were to his right, as they should be. He danced down three worn blocks of granite and on to something soft.

Staggering back, Damiano almost dropped his lute. But it was not a dead man. It was a dead rat. He went more cautiously down to the next street.

There—down at the far end of the street—that was a horse. Damiano sprinted under sunlit skies, and over a pale, packed-earth street. The beast came around the corner. It was attached to a wagon. That lumbering, round thing was not Festilligambe. It was gray, and its neck, thick as the Barbish gelding's loin, arced in a half-circle. It regarded the panting human with kindly unsurprise.

"Hah! Welcome again, Monsieur Delstrego," said an unpleasantly familiar voice from atop the wagon. The villager, who was not now singing, held the slack reins in one hand. "Do you like my stallion? He is no racehorse, certainly, but he is of the ancient Comtois line. He will pull weight all day, and when he is done with his life's work, there is no better eating!"

Damiano flinched as though the man had suggested eating his own children. "My horse! What have you done with him? You haven't . . ."

The villager's laughter was merry and unperturbed. He wiped his nose against his sleeve. "Oh, you Italians are excitable! Don't worry, monsieur. There is no hunger in Pe'Comtois, that we should slaughter your little pony. He is well, probably better than he has been in a while, since he is eating oats and barley. We have fodder to spare."

At this news Damiano felt more alarm than gratitude. "Oats and barley! He hasn't had anything like that since January. You will colic him. Take me to him at once!"

The wagoner only snorted. "All in good time, monsieur. I have my little duties first. I must take a little drive outside the wall, and . . ."

"The gate will open for you?"

The answering grin was a shade contemptuous. "Oh, they will open for me all right. Come along, musician, and entertain me on my way."

Damiano was torn between his desire to flee the stricken town and his concern for the gelding, which if permitted would certainly eat itself to disaster. But the townsman knew where Festilligambe was, and Damiano did not. He waited for no second invitation.

The wagon was so heavy it scarcely shifted under his weight. Damiano sat his lute on his lap and looked over his shoulder.

A large oilcloth covered a load of many bumps and prominences, some of which were long, and some round as a ball. One lump was quite unmistakably an elbow.

"I take my little trip from the church to the end of the common lands every day," the driver was saying. "It frees the pews, and keeps things sort of fresh, you know? Lately, though, it's been twice a day, which is unfair, since I'm paid only by the day, not by amount of work."

Damiano said nothing. The driver inhaled deeply. "Wonderful day, today. Good clean breeze. Give us a little tune, monsieur." The townsman prodded his passenger. "It will help pass the time."

Damiano stared down at his hands, which seemed to have no feeling in them.

Gaspare prowled outside the town wall as wary as a cat. His situation boded more unhappiness than Damiano's, because, while a musician may play without a dancer to dance, people expect a dancer to have music. And he only had a word or two of this silly, spineless language. So he approached covertly, in case something useful (or unlocked) might come his way.

He heard chanting, and saw that within the gate a small troupe of religious were setting up stocks. Not liking the looks of this, he slunk off.

Attached to the plastered wall itself, on the far side of the town from the wooden gates, was another of those roofless, useless stone huts. He entered, stepping delicately over fresh ashes. He dusted a stone with his rag of handkerchief, sat on it and mulled things over.

By his strenuous trot through the fields toward the village he had put off feeling sorry over biting the lutenist. Now he could put it off no longer, and regret seeped through him.

Gaspare thought of Damiano, and he began to wiggle all over. Whenever the boy tried to think, he wiggled, because he was a dancer. As Evienne always said, his brain was in his feet.

And he could not think of Damiano Delstrego without wiggling very strenuously, for in his cynical way Gaspare stood in awe of Damiano. From the first time he had heard the fellow play, sitting on the corner of San Gabriele on market day, he had known.

Here was a new music. A music of unearthly complexity. A music that could shake kingdoms, and played all on a tiny *liuto* of four courses.

And wonder of wonders, the man who created it let Gaspare himself come along, to be part of the source and the nourishment of that art. Gaspare had never really believed his luck. How could it be that no other cunning fellow had heard Damiano before Gaspare, and taken him in tow? He was such easy prey, full of fancy ideas and nearly blind as a bat. Soft, too, and agreeable. Easily bullied. It was as though all the musician's passion was stored within the lute.

The story the fellow had told—of learning to play his instrument from the Archangel Michael, or some such—that Gaspare had taken for artistic metaphor. Damiano also claimed to be a witch, and on that first day he had accomplished a good imitation of disappearing. Gaspare could never remember if that had taken place before or after they drank the skin of wine. He rather thought it was after.

But of course Damiano never really did anything magical—except play the lute that way, of course. Gaspare had been with him now for a year, and if there were anything in the least bit sorcerous in Damiano's makeup, the boy would know.

Gaspare had been forced to realize that Damiano was a bit mad. Not dangerous, mind you—he was as gentle as a lamb, come what may—but just unbalanced.

Or maybe not mad, but just sheep-simple, for God knew he needed watching like a guileless ewe lamb. He looked like one, too: a black lamb, with all that curly hair and soft black eyes. Girl-faced, yes, but the girls themselves didn't seem to mind that. The lutenist wouldn't look half bad, if he'd trouble to take care of himself.

Gaspare had made it his business to take care of Damiano—at least to keep him from starving. Let the

fellow believe it was his quick hand on the strings, and not
Gaspare's in the passing pocket, that put pennies into the
bowl.

When he had gotten them to Avignon, Gaspare intended to unveil his musician in the courts of the Pope,
saying, "See what I have brought from the wilderness. I,
only I have recognized greatness in its infancy."

But it was hard to travel with a madman. Him and his
angel, when he spoke wide-eyed to the air. Also him and
his Devil: he claimed to have spoken with Satan as well as
Gabriele (or whoever), and hinted sometimes at dark
dealings that made Gaspare nervous about the real source
of his proficiency upon the lute. (Gaspare, like most
people, found it much easier to believe in the Devil than in
angels.)

The most irritating thing about the musician was his
silly preoccupation with chastity. Gaspare had directed one
kind and easygoing girl after another at Damiano Delstrego, and carefully watched the results. Each time the
player smiled, turned color and went into retreat. Chastity!

Who cared?

Delstrego should have been born a girl.

And now it was all for nothing. Gaspare had taken a
chunk out of the fellow's arm, and no man could forgive
that.

No man with sense. A madman could, maybe. A simpleton, perhaps. A man as soft-natured as Damiano. . . .

Gaspare sighed, burying his sharp-nosed face in his
hands. Why did he have to have such a temper? Evienne
said it came with the red hair. He wished he could tell all of
this to his sister, though she would only yell at him.

With a single, fluid motion, Gaspare was out of the hut
and balanced on the wall. He sneaked into Petit Comtois
and beheld the plague.

"You are a cat with one kitten, monsieur," expostulated
the Comtoisian. "Your little horse will come to no harm; I
promise you. I will take you to him later, when my
passengers are taken care of—you see?"

This was said as the dead wagon approached the gates
of the town. Damiano was more certain every moment that
Gaspare had had more sense than to enter a plague town.
The boy was not really sensible, but he was very cunning.

But if Damiano left now he would have to steel himself to go through the wooden gate again, because Festilligambe must be found.

Preferably before grain colic killed him.

Damiano slipped to the packed earth of the random, almost circular town square, where the crowd lounged in their unaccustomed leisure, wearing the clothes and eating the food of the dead.

There were fewer now. Damiano counted only fourteen, as the cloddish hoof-falls faded away in the distance, along the eastern road. That was not because of plague, certainly, but the midday rest. (Even leisure must have its breaks.) Yes, there in the broken doorway of a goldsmith's (the shop was picked dry) curled a plump young mother with her infant on her lap, both asleep. The little one's mouth was open like a red rosebud. Its mother snored.

They should go home, he thought to himself, but then there occurred to him possible reasons why they did not. Damiano shrugged.

His scuffed, shapeless kit-sack lay on the earth, undisturbed. Why would anyone want to steal a wooden bowl and two raggy tunics, after all? Although his silver knife was fine, with its crystal and its phases of the moon. It was useless to him, now, as a tool of witchcraft, but still it was a fine knife. Damiano rummaged it out and stuck it into a slit in his leather belt. The rest of his gear he kicked carelessly into a corner.

He would quarter the town, calling. Festilligambe would answer, if he were not too stuffed with oats.

In truth, Damiano was a little disappointed that a mere bribe of food would tempt his horse away. He had struck a bargain with Festilligambe, once, back when his powers had given him something with which to bargain. But why should Festilligambe give him more than other horses gave their masters, when lately he'd been getting much less from Damiano? Much less food, that is.

He took a stride forward and opened his mouth to call. The next instant saw him leap stiff-legged off the ground, swallowing his words, for two plump pink arms had embraced him from behind, while a thick voice in his ear wheeled, "Aww, Monsieur Trouvere! Give us a little song."

"Madam!" he croaked, or rather squeaked, swelling his shoulders to release himself and spinning in place.

"Madam. I think, perhaps, with the troubles this town is suffering . . ." Here he paused to breathe, to gather his wits and to step away from the woman of many layers. "I think perhaps it is not the time for song."

She giggled and made a little moue. "Not if one has the plague, of course. But we are the ones the plague has passed over, and for us entertainment is very necessary."

She really was not bad to look at. Her eyes were bright blue, and tilted in a manner which reminded Damiano of someone or other. Her hair, escaping from the underside of her wimple, was barley-fair. And Damiano had nothing at all against plumpness.

Yet he found this woman appalling. "Is it over, then?" he mumbled, looking around at the sunny square. "Is the plague at an end?" Under this blue heaven he could be easily convinced the plague was over, purified by spring weather alone.

She shrugged, and the many layers of linen (the top layer was real lace) puffed with air before settling once more around her. It occurred to Damiano that these Provençal people did not shrug like Italians, forthrightly. They had sly shrugs. "It has killed most all those it is going to kill," she replied, as the baby in the doorway gave a tiny, sleeping cough.

He looked into her face, and then Damiano smelled olives. His long-nursed, familiar hunger awoke like a lion, nearly driving him to his knees, while at the same instant he felt he would much rather die than eat anything he found in Petit Comtois.

"Must go," he mumbled, and he took two smart strides down the main street. Then the woman had a grasp on his left leg, and was dragging him to his knees.

"Music," she cried out. "We must have music."

An instant later a half-dozen villagers, mostly female, had added their soft, unyielding pressure to hers. Damiano sat down on the street, cursing, holding his lute away from their curious, bejeweled fingers.

Yet he was not entirely proof against this rough sort of flattery, and when someone dropped a great gold pendant with a red stone around his neck, he was not proof against that, either. With a broad, forthright and very Italian gesture, he yielded.

It was too bad Gaspare wasn't here. These mad souls

would have loved Gaspare. (Like calls to like.) Yet he wouldn't wish this place on the redhead, nor on anyone. He took the pendant off and stuffed it in his belt-pouch lest it scratch the finish of the instrument, and began to play.

These people didn't need a professional dancer after all. The way that fat woman was capering was an education to watch. And the butcher jigging on one foot next to her. For a moment Damiano thought the man in the bloodstained apron was the same he had seen in the church, lying still and awaiting promotion to the left-hand side. But no. The sentence of the plague was never commuted; the only similarity between the two men was in the leather apron.

He gave them the rondel and the crude estampie, and when they were warmed up—indeed, hot was the more accurate word—he played that sarabande of Gaspare's which he had so much reason to dislike. In his single year of playing for bread, Damiano had learned to judge an audience correctly, so he wasted none of the difficult polyphonics, and nothing Raphael had taught him at all.

And if his fingers pinched the strings with a hint of contempt, and if he damped a bit harshly, well, that was all to the better, considering that Damiano's natural touch was too delicate for everyday tastes.

He lifted his eyes to see a huddle of drab brown at the edge of this graceless circle. Even the flagellants were drawn to the sound of festival, it seemed. In a moment they would be dancing.

"Mother of God," whispered Damiano to himself. "Is one fury interchangeable for another?"

Then the sound of bone against flesh broke through the music. A year ago this would have caused the young man to stop, or at least to drop a beat. But now his fingers continued their course while he glanced up to see the man in the apron laid low by the biggest of the flagellants. With a noise of childish outrage the woman of layers bounded across the dust of the square and kicked the flagellant in the middle of his horsehair and ashes.

This was not the first time Damiano had played for a dance which became a melee. His policy was to continue playing, while backing away from the ring of trouble. In this situation he found it most advisable to scrape along the row of ruined shops on the left of the main street. Following this course, he would eventually put the flagellants between him and the merry madmen (who were certain they were not going to get the plague) and seek Festilligambe in peace.

He was fingering a spirited *bransle* (what else do you play when the audience is brawling?) when a round, soft, little noise behind him caused him to turn his head.

This was the doorway of mother and baby, but mother was presently out in the sunshine, engaged in pulling someone's hair. Baby lay alone in the darkened goldsmith's shop, dressed in white christening robes, coated hands and feet with a precious, glittering dust, and coughing.

"Mother of God," groaned Damiano once again, and for a single instant he entertained the idea of taking the child with him. But in his twenty-three years Damiano had never so much as held an infant in his arms, and all he knew about their care was that he was fairly certain they could not eat grass.

Avoiding the tiny mite, he set his instrument within the shop, in the safety of a dark corner, and then he went back out to find his horse.

"Festilligambe," he called, trying to be melodious as well as penetrating. There was no answer.

His next cry was less modulated, but still he heard no reply, except from the brawl in the square. A silver tankard rolled, clanking, past his feet. He ignored it.

All these houses marched down to the street, and of those which had stables below, all were open and empty. The packed earth would hold no imprint. "Festilligambe!" bellowed Damiano. There was a scuffle of feet behind him.

It took Damiano a good two seconds to understand that the flagellants were chasing him. For one more second he stood his ground, belligerently resentful that they would try to get him involved in an argument between two breeds of lunatic. Then he sprinted.

Had he been less outraged, or had he understood the situation a bit quicker, he might have escaped, for his opponents were weakened by their mutual abuse. But four pairs of hands gripped his tunic and his feet were kicked out from under him.

"Damn the lot of you," roared the furious musician, suspended by his shirt three feet off the ground. His fist connected twice, on what felt like hard pieces of anatomy. "I've had just enough idiocy!"

Then his head was lifted from behind, by the hair. The expressionless features of the chief flagellant looked down upon him. "Corruption," the man stated. "Human flesh is corruption, and the worm is its end. You are a sinner and partake of the nature of the beast. You must be freed from your corruption." There was a tinkle as of tiny bells, as the tips of a cat jingled together.

Then Damiano was no longer furious, but frightened.

With sweat prickling all over, Gaspare backed away from the dead man he had come so close to touching. There was no doubt in his mind what had killed this fellow: those horrible round lumps like oak galls on the neck, the pus-y, discolored face and the general attitude of being left to lie where it fell . . .

He did not need the row of yawning doors and the desolation of the quarter to confirm his opinion. Gaspare had no trust in the world to delay his acceptance of sad reality. This was plague, just like that which had slain half the world a generation ago, and Gaspare was going back over the wall quickest.

Sinking back into the ashes of the hut where he had earlier sat in unhurried thought, Gaspare shivered all over. What an ass he was, not to have guessed why they burned the place down! He minced out through the gaping door, shaking clean one foot, then the other.

Distrustfully—hungrier than ever despite the crawling horror—he examined the road west. Rumor had it that plague, like mankind, followed the roads. And it hadn't come from above, to the east in Franche-Comté or the Chamonix Pass. Perhaps Provence already suffered the worst. Perhaps Avignon was dead, as it had been only sixteen years before. Perhaps . . .

Evienne.

Gaspare's heart banged his fragile chest wall like a prisoned enemy. He felt each mile that lay between his sister and himself as an unendurable deprivation: a personal insult against him and his.

An affront to pride. He flared his pinched nostrils against it.

It did not occur to him that being with Evienne would not prevent her (or him) from contracting plague. Avoiding the plague was not the issue for Gaspare. Getting through the plague to Evienne was.

Why had he let her run off with that miserable, horse-faced Dutchman, anyway? Bad enough she should be a prostitute at home in San Gabriel (among family, as it were), let alone spreading her scandal into foreign countries.

Leaving him nursemaid to a lute player who saw angels.

Damiano! Gaspare's head jerked up, and he moved away from the wall where he had been leaning. Where was that soft-eyed simpleton: lumbering the old cart back up toward the pass? Or would he have continued west? Gaspare cursed himself for not stopping to make sure. His feet led him over the cleared land which surrounded the wall of the town and into the head-high brush.

Why would Damiano go back, after all? It was he who originally wanted to see Provence, whence came the music. The lutenist had only wanted to wait until May before attempting the Alpine passes.

Well, they were over the passes. Easier to go on than back. And that meant Damiano would trot that spoiled, sullen-tempered horse straight into trouble.

Gaspare could close his eyes and see it happening: a scene complete, with Damiano yawning, the horse snapping harness right and left, the rickety wagon trundling its oblivious way past rows of grinning corpses and burned shops. His soft-shod feet gathered speed.

Looking up the road past the gate, Gaspare saw nothing. He breathed with relief. Then he noticed the familiar, derelict wagon squatting at the edge of the cleared land, its shafts angling out like the long curved tushes of a boar.

Damnation and buggery. What could be *done* with the fellow? Gaspare washed his hands in the air. It was a gesture that relieved his feelings but did not change the fact that he'd have to go in and drag Damiano out.

He went over the wall with the speed of practice, and padded nonchalantly down an empty street. Why should he skulk, when he'd broken no laws (so far) and besides, could outrun anyone he'd ever met?

The first street was without interest. So was the second. Along the third, he heard a noise: a regular and

workmanlike thumping, as of a hammer against wood.
Exercising greater caution (because although he had broken no laws so far, there was no assurance he might not
want to break some soon), he decreased the distance
between himself and the source of the disturbance.

It was coming from a half-door set into the first floor of a
square stone building no different from any of its neighbors, except that it smelled a trifle more rank.

Gaspare peeped obliquely in, to discover a horse, which
was eating with its front end and kicking with its back end.
It performed these actions in sequence, first chewing a bite
of oats, then swallowing, then heaving up and delivering a
massive blow to the oaken panels of the door. Gaspare
found he could count to six during each iteration of the
cycle.

The horse was Festilligambe.

Gaspare leaned negligently against the stones of the
stable wall, considering what he saw.

As a picture, he liked it. Damiano would, no doubt,
be quite concerned that the horse would injure himself
kicking the door. The owner of the stable might legiti-
mately be concerned as well. Gaspare, however, liked both
the animal's rebelliousness and his realistic attitude. It
wasn't Gaspare's door, after all. Nor his horse.

But how had the horse gotten here? Damiano hadn't a
sou to pay for oats. And he wasn't likely to have sold the
brute. Christ, no! The lute player would sooner part with
his bollucks. And why did Festilligambe have such a
grudge against dry straw and good grain? He was a
perverse horse, but not that perverse.

Gaspare had a strong hunch something was wrong. He
leaped lightly to the top of the door, timing his move for
the moment the horse took a mouthful from the manger,
and then landed lightly on the blond straw on the far side
of the box from the gelding.

"Hey! Festilligambe. Idiot-face," hissed the dancer. The
startled animal shrieked and spewed oats into the air.

"Shut up," rapped Gaspare, and he pointed in peremptory fashion. "So. You came into a fortune, eh, old friend?
Well, one friend's fortune is another friend's." And reaching into the black and bitten wood manger, he filled both
his jerkin pockets (which were bigger than such pockets
had any right to be) with golden grain. Then he filled his
purse.

With enough oats, one could make frumenty. Or flatbread. But it wasn't with the clear idea of cookery that Gaspare loaded himself with the grain. It was only that it was there for the taking.

When sufficiently laden, Gaspare took the gelding's dangling halter rope and wound it securely around his wrist. Then he led the now-docile horse to the door. "We're going out now, nag-butt," he whispered up at the black ear, a foot above his head. "We're going out to look for old sheep-face Damiano. Can you find Damiano for me, boy?"

The horse blinked down at him mildly. Gaspare untied the leathern thong that held the door. He was nervous. If the truth be told, Gaspare was afraid of horses. A crack of light appeared as the oak door began to open.

Festilligambe hit it, chest on, roaring, and with a display of Barbish speed and temperament, flung himself along the empty street. They were halfway to the next corner before Gaspare's pitiful scream hit the air.

His arm was caught in the rope. His feet never hit the ground. There was nothing for the boy to do but grab a handful of mane with his left hand and hang on.

Except for Delstrego Senior, no man had ever laid punishing hands on Damiano. Or, more accurately, no man had gotten away with it. Damiano was less prepared than most men for the touch of the whip, and the first lick of the tipped cat stiffened him from bucking and thrashing into mute astonishment. The second stroke knocked him to his elbows. On the third he cried out, or tried to.

With the fourth multifingered assault upon his back, he gathered himself together and fled—fled in a manner he himself did not understand—through the ragged, empty socket in the middle of his mind.

It was dark here, and green with the background of fir trees. The grass was dotted with crocus and snowdrops, and with gold brushes of flowering mustard. Over the flat meadow wound a stream which expressed neither decision nor ambition, weaving its course as random as a snailtrack.

Over and through the branchlets of the stream splashed a doe goat, bleating unhappily, tied with a garland of grape hyacinth. It was a brown goat, cow-hocked and very gravid, still wearing great patches of its winter coat.

The weaver of the garland was a more delicate creature. She rubbed one bare toe against the other leg, while she tickled the underside of her own nose with a yellow-brown braid.

"Behave like a lady," she said to the goat, speaking with firmness, and pointing to the fragile band of blue flowers. "If you tear that off, I'll stuff it down your throat."

The goat stopped still, but not out of docility. It chewed an uneasy cud, and rolled its square-pupiled eyes at what it saw.

Saara turned also, and her own green, tilted eyes widened. She dropped her braid.

"You!" she whispered, half to herself. "Dark boy. Damiano!" One hand, small, pink and slender, made a circling gesture.

And the lute player knew her as well: Saara of the Saami, barefoot girl who was the greatest witch in the Italies.

Damiano knew Saara's powers well, having both suffered them and then stolen them. And now all the strength was hers and he had none at all.

Damiano felt himself step closer to the witch (though he himself did not know how he did it, not having a body with which to step). The placid water passed beneath his substanceless flesh without disturbance.

"You cannot be dead! I would know it if you were dead," she stated, yet by her voice Saara had her doubts. Her hand reached out toward him, as though to wipe haze from a glass, and quietly she began to sing.

Once again Damiano was aware of having feet, and hands. They tingled. He brushed back the coarse hair from his face. "I don't think I am dead," he heard himself saying. "For though I can imagine nothing more like heaven than your garden, my lady, I have been led to expect there will be a matter of judgment to endure before I reach such a paradise. Assuming I am found worthy of it."

How odd his voice sounded in his own ears: a bit thin, perhaps, but quite composed and calm. And how confidently he stepped through air that had more substance than he did. Now Saara was almost close enough to touch. In three steps, she would touch. She chanted sunlight into the young man's eyes. He blinked. His feet sank into marshy ground.

Then Damiano remembered. "I'm not supposed to be here!" he announced, stepping back and into deeper water. "This is Lombardy, and I'm in Provence. I shouldn't have come at all!"

Saara paused, her feet resting on the tussocky grass. Her small face tilted like that of a wary bird. "But I knew you would come, at last, Dami. Part of your soul is waiting here. You have only come after it—there is nothing wrong in that." She stepped into water, and Saara, greatest witch in the Italies, sank ankle-deep in the mud.

Floundering backward, Damiano shook his head. "No, signora. I followed my lost powers, surely, but I did so in my effort to escape the lash, not to mention the plague. And in this I have done myself more harm than good."

Saara stopped in midcurrent. Her blue felt dress darkened as it absorbed water. Her chant first slowed, and then stopped. From behind her, the doe goat bleated loudly.

"Plague, Damiano?" she asked quietly. "The lash? Where are you? Where have you left your body?"

He stared down at hands like clear amber, glowing with their own light. His breath came out soundlessly, and he looked up at the witch again.

"Somewhere between Lyons and Avignon. In Provence, where the music is born. And I must go back, before I . . . I forget how."

He turned away from her, then, as though he were about to walk down the hill, and he stared confusedly around him.

"Saara, it's you that is holding me, isn't it? Let me go back." His voice rose with a tinny, faraway urgency.

Her hand rested on the goat's ridged horn, while the scruffy, decorated beast nuzzled Saara's hip. "Don't worry, Dami. I won't hurt you. Don't I have half your soul in my care, and by *your* wish, not my own? But before I let you go you must tell me . . ."

"Won't hurt me! You will kill me, I think! Let me go before it is too late." Damiano blundered forward into the same streamlet where Saara stood. Water plashed against his legs and hands, feeling more real by the moment.

And the slim shape in peasant embroidery, too, was very real. As Saara stood beside him, frowning doubtfully, disarmingly, Damiano felt that it was too late already, and that the cord which tied him to this body was frayed beyond repair. That Provence and life together were done with him and he would be nothing more than a captive elemental: a domestic spirit in the garden of the lady Saara.

And he was glad of it.

For life was cruel and Provence dying, while Saara was beautiful. And she, like him, had been born a witch, with his own strange senses and stranger arts. Damiano knew suddenly that he loved Saara, and that he had loved her since their first meeting on this very hillside, amid the drone of bees and the sharp fragrance of rosemary.

And as once before he had risked a rival's blade for a chaste and unpracticed kiss in the witch's garden, so now he stood calf-deep in the spring thaw of the mountains, and he reached out one doomed, immaterial hand.

"Saara," he whispered. "Pikku Saara. You should not be so beautiful!"

Saara laughed, hearing the Fennish word in the Italian mouth. She looked into Damiano's black eyes. Then her little nostrils twitched, and the laughter was cut off. She examined his amber visage with a cold, scientific thoroughness. She raised a hand, but did not touch.

"You were right!" she stated. "You should not be here. It is very bad for you."

Then Saara clapped her hands, or she made as though to clap her hands. But Damiano heard no sound, for his whole world went out like a candle.

Where the hell the beast was going Gaspare had no idea. The boy forced his eyes open, lest the spiteful horse scrape him off the wall. If it tried that, Gaspare promised himself, then he would make his hands let go. Right now he could not quite manage the feat, for his fingers were welded into the black mane and the halter rope, which he should never, never have wound around his arm.

Festilligambe swung around a corner and Gaspare's heel plowed dust. Fear itself drove him to mount to the horse's back.

"I swear, you pig-head, you pig-heart, pig-collops, pig . . . pig of a pig! I swear I'll wear your hide someday soon, and if you dump me it will be today, I swear by Saint Gabriele and by Maria, the Mother of Christ, I'll eat your eyes and tongue roasted on a skewer and sell your bladder for a fool's toy. I swear . . ."

With a constant stream of such encouragements in his flattened ear, Festilligambe bolted past the basilica, where the odor of death was only a bit less terrifying than that of the burning houses on the street beyond. Each of his yellowing teeth was exposed to the wind. His nostrils were round as drainpipes, and gorged purple. His eyes were ringed, not with white, but red. He ran with his belly to the ground, carving the dry, packed road with his hooves. He went rough. He cornered viciously. He went from sun into darkness, leaping a flight of alley stairs and landing in sun again on the next street.

He made straight for the square of Petit Comtois where the wooden gates stood solidly shut. Gaspare's scream was soundless but heartfelt.

There in the road lay a woman's shirt of linen, and beyond it another of lace, stained olive green. Gaspare flashed by them too quickly for curiosity. Still farther toward the gate he passed a plump and fair-haired woman dragging along a monk by his long, untonsured hair. Both were bellowing; it all seemed perfectly natural to the panicked Gaspare.

The wooden gate loomed, solid, oak-barred and five feet tall. The horse had no sense—he would brain himself against the palings, and Gaspare as well. It was time to let go.

Gaspare told his fingers it was time to let go. He tried again. He shrieked at them, but from fingers they had become gnarled tree roots wound in the black earth of the gelding's mane.

A circle of brown-robed friars stood before the gate. Evidently Festilligambe intended to smash into them on his way to oblivion. Gaspare held to the selfish and forlorn hope they would cushion the impact.

But neither the collision with the religious nor that with the maple palings happened, first because the brown robes scattered like so many dun doves of the wood, and second because Festilligambe ceased his mad pounding between one step and the next, and Gaspare's convulsive grip dissolved. He went over the horse's head and landed rolling. Twice he rolled free, escaping harm with the elasticity of youth and training, but on the third roll he came up against flesh. His warding hand slipped against

skin slick with blood, on the lean, whip-scored back of a
man whose head and arms were tied up in a shirt.

All the bumps and knobs of that back were vaguely
familiar, and in the leather belt that circled it was stuck a
tiny, intricately-worked knife which was very familiar.

"Pig's head of an ass!" ejaculated Gaspare, as he
plucked free the knife and cut the shirt apart.

Damiano's eyes were wide and staring. "Gaspare?" he
asked, his usually rather deep voice cracking. "Gaspare—is
this still Franche-Comté? Or . . . Lombardy, or . . . ?"

Fury warred with a strange ache in Gaspare's heart. He
took the shaggy black head (no, not shaggy any longer, but
trimmed somehow) in the hands that had so lately been
locked in the gelding's mane, and he shook Damiano's
head roughly back and forth. "You damned, swiving
sheep-faced lunatic," he shrilled, and then he bent the
unresisting head down and, still more roughly, kissed the
top of it.

Damiano, meanwhile, was staring nearsightedly
through the four black pillars that arched above him, at a
huddle of wary, pointing townsmen, both of the robed and
the bejeweled variety. He squinted, but they were too far
for him to make out the expressions on their faces. He
brought his own, soiled left hand up to his face and flexed
it, looking puzzled.

Gaspare also looked at the whip-wielders, and his
excellent vision gave him cause for alarm. "Get up,
Damiano, before they regroup and come back to you. And
once we're five miles from this foul-stinking bed of misery
you can explain to me just what . . ." and as he tried to
rise Gaspare's head hit something. He ducked once more,
swiveled his head, and discovered why the townspeople
were pointing.

Gaspare collapsed once more on top of Damiano, the air
whistling out of his throat. For above them stood a half-ton
of rigid outrage, iron-legged, hissing, with a tail stiff as a
terrier's. The gelding's head coiled left and right as though
the beast were a dragon, and it dripped white froth onto
Gaspare's upturned face.

"Call him off!" shrieked the sufferer. "Dear Jesu, call
him off and I will sin no more!"

Damiano, too, looked up, but either trust or poor vision
saved him from Gaspare's terror. "Festilligambe!" Awk-

wardly, like an old man, he climbed to his feet. Dirt grayed
his hair and caked to the ooze on his naked back. He
leaned one arm over the sweaty, trembling withers. "Hey. I
went looking for you. But you found me instead!"

The gelding nickered, but its defiance did not weaken.
It stamped one hind foot. Gaspare moaned.

The lute player peered down at Gaspare (squirming full
length on the ground between the black hooves) as though
he could not remember how the boy had gotten there. He
reached down one hand and yanked him up. "Stand up.
You shouldn't play games with an animal this size," he
chided.

Then he added, "We've got to get out of this town,
Gaspare. They're all mad here. You can never tell what
they're going to do next."

"Mad?" Gaspare rolled his gooseberry eyes. "Oh,
certainly, yes. I've noticed it myself. Well then, we should
certainly get out of here, shouldn't we, Damiano? In fact,"
and the boy pointed surreptitiously to the wall by the gate,
"why don't we just run over there and slip over that wall?
I'll help you up and you pull me up behind, heh?"

Damiano frowned hugely and touched his still-bleeding
shoulder blades. "Don't be silly, Gaspare. We can't take a
horse over the wall. Nor a lute.

"I'll go get my lute now," he finished, and Damiano
calmly stepped across the square toward the yawning black
doorway of a shop. Gaspare watched him go, and he
watched the tall shape, black as vengeance, stalk behind
him, black tail slashing like a blade that would love to cut.
The gelding's muzzle hung just above Damiano's shoulder,
unnoticed. Damiano seemed to be quietly talking to
himself.

It was very lonely, standing in the middle of the square,
without even a vicious horse for protection. Gaspare
shifted from one foot to the other and raised his chin
high into the air. No one came near, for all eyes followed
the wounded musician and his strange protector as he
vanished into the dark shop and reappeared, bearing his
sheepskin-wrapped instrument.

Damiano was frowning. "There was a baby in there
before," he said to Gaspare, "but it's gone, now. I certainly
hope it was its mother that came back for it. So much
despair around, you know." Then he raised his left

eyebrow very high, and regarded Gaspare with more rationality than he had yet shown, saying, "It is the plague that has hit here. You knew that, didn't you?"

Gaspare sighed hugely. "Yes, musician. I was aware of that, and that is another very good reason for . . . for hastening our departure, maybe?"

Damiano swung onto the horse's back. His mouth gaped with the pain of his flayed back. He leaned down and reached a hand toward Gaspare. "Get up in front," he commanded the boy.

Gaspare backed. "No, thank you. I have already ridden that horse once today."

"Get up," said Damiano with some temper, and he snagged Gaspare's unwilling hand. "I don't want to lose you again, before I even have a chance to tell you about the strange thing that happened, or a chance to apologize, as I promised Raphael I would."

"Apologize?" Gaspare was so astounded he allowed himself to be pulled up in front of his friend on the steaming black back. "You, apologize, after I bit you?"

Damiano was not listening. "I think if we just ride confidently up to the gate, that huge fellow in the robe—he's not a real monk, you know—may just open up for us. Or at least not interfere with *our* opening it.

"What is important," he added, sententiously, "is always to appear to know what you are about, and most especially when others are uncertain. That is a fourth part of magic and the half of all medicine. It is most important of all in military matters, such as . . ." And Damiano gave a gentle kick (a nudge, really) to the gelding's sides.

The beast reared, turned on its haunches, and spurted along the street directly away from the gate. Then it spun again, nearly toppling both its riders, scrabbled its hindquarters under it, and flew directly for the wooden fence.

A woman screamed. So did Gaspare. Damiano looked merely irritated as he clutched the mane, the lute, and a hysterical passenger. "He's going to kill me after all!" wailed Gaspare. Once more the townspeople fled.

But Festilligambe did not hit the gate. Instead, eight feet from the oak-bound, maple palings, he gathered himself under and leaped.

The ground fell away. Weight fell away. Festilligambe nicked one black hoof against the top of the gate and he grunted an equine profanity. When his forefoot touched down, his rider was ready—ready enough to have Gaspare secured against falling, and to soften the thump of his own descent on the horse's back with his knees. Together Damiano and Gaspare lurched against the gelding's neck as it came up, pitching them back into position.

The horse came down galloping, and galloping they disappeared along the Alpine highway.

It was dark before they dared sneak back for the wagon.

CHAPTER 3

The countryside south and west of Petit Comtois was even gentler and more temperate than that which they had left behind them. What was more heartening, there were scattered almond orchards and fields of green lavender.

But the almonds were in bloom, not fruit, and what use to a hungry man was lavender, sweet-smelling though it was?

After Gaspare stole the clutch of some peasant's goose, nearly having his finger broken and finding in the end the eggs were useless, being ready to hatch, well, it seemed the least said between them, soonest mended. Along the road they met no one, save the occasional meandering and always dry cow.

It was unusually warm for the month of March, or at least it seemed so to Damiano. But then neither he nor Gaspare had ever experienced any but the Alpine spring. The present temperature was a saving grace to him, on this, the third day since his whipping in Petit Comtois, for he could bear no touch upon his scabbing back. He lay upon his stomach in the booming belly of the wagon, his woolen shirt folded under him and swaddled around his sides.

He was husking oats, by hand, one by one. Boiled oats had been their diet ever since leaving the town. They had discovered that oats took a long time to boil. This little double handful was the last from Gaspare's purse.

Damiano's face bore a look of pained concentration.

Each ovoid seedlet went into the bowl of his lute for safekeeping, since no simple cup would maintain them through the roll and pitch of the wagon.

The husks went all over. Many pale flakes had found their way into his hair and eyebrows.

"I feel so guilty, doing this," he mumbled, his voice coming strained because of the angle of his neck.

Gaspare was driving, which is to say he sat in the driver's seat, his hands clenched doggedly upon the tattered reins. But the lines hung from hand to surcingle, and from surcingle to bit in great, looping swags which swung left and right with the horse's steps. Festilligambe was trotting decorously down the road solely because that was what he felt like doing.

"Guilty?" echoed the boy. "You feel guilty husking oats? By the Virgin and every saint, Damiano, do the little grains cry out as you break them?"

Damiano sighed and rested his chin on the boards for a moment. The muscles of his back hurt. He was also lightheaded from lack of nourishment, and his temper was on edge. He therefore collected himself before answering, "No, of course not, Gaspare. I meant I feel that Festilligambe is expecting us to give the stuff to him."

Gaspare's florid face grew pinker and his mouth worked. But he bit off whatever he'd first intended to say, and said only, "The creature would be better off with wealthier owners."

Damiano did not reply, though it was on his tongue to remind the boy that Festilligambe did not have owners but *an* owner.

Emboldened by this silence, Gaspare spoke the corollary to his statement, which was that the owners would be a lot wealthier if they sold the horse.

Damiano rested his face on the backs of his hands and resisted a temptation to escape from this unpleasantness into the familiar vacancies of his mind.

"Gaspare," he began, "please try to understand. That horse likes me."

"Likes you, maybe, but doesn't listen to you a pig's fart. And he doesn't like nobody else in this world. Especially me."

Damiano glanced up, for he heard a tone of real hurt in his companion's voice. "Oh, he likes you all right, Gaspare. He likes you better than he likes anyone else except me.

"And in the beginning . . ." and Damiano's thoughts went back over a year in time, to the sheep pastures above Partestrada, where he had first seen the black gelding in the string of Carla Denezzi's brother. The horse had been flourishing then.

So had Damiano. He had worn soft boots, white linen and a full cloak of weasel skins.

Painful and distant came the memory to Damiano that he had once been respectable. He had sat at a table with the parish priest. Once, he had spoken with Petrarch.

He had had a house. And a city.

Now that was over, and he was that pitiful creature—an Italian in exile. According to his bargain with the Devil, he must not return home. According to the Devil's bargain with him, he was now living the tag ends of his days.

For a moment's intense, ashen melancholy, brought on perhaps by starvation, Damiano was sorry the plague had spared him. But then that moment passed, and he remembered what he had.

He had an angel. An archangel, who had shared with him as much as mortal may share with spirit—which is to say, music. And he had a horse—a temperamental horse, but a fine one—and a still more temperamental distinguished colleague.

He watched a roadside row of plums pass by the wagon, just entering into their pale bloom. The tended landscape was sweeter than anything he had ever seen in Italy, and the soft air was gauzy. The sight and the smell and the warmth together sank Damiano into a diffuse and pleasurable stupor in which he could almost forget the stiffening lacerations that crisscrossed his back.

An angel and a horse and a friend (of sorts). And of course a lute, too. That was important, even though it wasn't much of a lute. Together, Gaspare, angel, horse and lute made a total for which it was worth losing a bit of respectability.

Especially while the weather remained so fine. Respectability was much less important in good weather.

Oddly enough, thought the sleepy musician, in some ways Raphael was the least respectable of his companions. It was talking to the angel, after all, that caused people to edge away from him. Were it not for Raphael, Gaspare would have no cause to think Damiano a madman.

All these reflections took the time of one long sigh and a

shift of weight from left elbow to right. Damiano continued his interrupted sentence. "And in the beginning, the horse liked me least of all men.

"But, Gaspare, I want you to listen to the strange thing that happened to me when I was being whipped in Petit Comtois."

Gaspare's laugh was not kindly. "I can think of many possible strange things. . . ."

The half-naked man ignored this interruption. "I sort of blacked out. But not really, for I found myself standing somewhere else. In Lombardy, I was, in a place I have been once before, though I never talked about it to you. A beautiful garden."

The ironic light died behind the boy's eyes. "That happens," he admitted. "When a man is in pain, or sick. When I was five and had the spots I had such a fever Evienne says I thought she was Saint Lucia, though why Saint Lucia, I have no idea. . . ."

Damiano raised his chin again and frowned fiercely at Gaspare. "I spoke, not with Saint Lucia, but with a woman I know. A very beautiful woman. . . ."

"A beautiful one? Sounds less and less real all the time."

"And she was surprised to see me standing next to her. I was like a spirit, for my body was left in Petit Comtois. We both agreed I should not have come there, and she sent me back."

One rusty eyebrow shot up. "She sent you back? Isn't that the way with beautiful women? But you should learn persistence, musician. Otherwise there will never be any little black-haired, sheep-eyed babies running around."

Damiano pushed himself off the floor of the wagon. It seemed the heat of his own irritation was lifting him.

"This woman I speak of is a great lady, Gaspare. The most powerful witch in the Italies, if not in all of Europe. You must learn to think before you speak of people, or you will never grow *old* enough for there to be any little red-haired, pointy-nosed babies running around.

"And surely by now you know me enough to take seriously what . . ."

Gaspare's small brow beetled enormously. The reins dropped from his hands and lay on the footboard of the seat. "Do you think I'm not old enough already, lute player? I'll have you know that I may only be fourteen, but some fourteen-year-olds are men already, while some twenty-three-year-olds . . ."

Damiano would not be sidetracked. Not even by this subject. Especially not by this subject. ". . . to take seriously what I say on the subject of powers unseen. I was trained from birth to feel and manipulate these powers, by a father who was no mean witch himself. . . ."

Gaspare's eyes dropped with queasy self-consciousness. He plucked up the reins.

"And on top of his training, and my natural predisposition to magic, I have added a thorough course of study in the works of the great Hermes Trismagistus, along with the additions and commentaries of Mary the Jewess. If I, out of all mankind, tell you I have visited Lombardy in immaterial form, then me you can believe!"

Gaspare set his long jaw. Rough-mannered as he was, he had always avoided this particular confrontation with Damiano. Now it seemed inevitable. He pulled on the reins with a long, exaggerated "Hoa." Festilligambe stopped out of sheer surprise.

"Damiano. My dear, close friend," he sighed. "You have no magical powers."

Damiano blinked. "Of course not. Not since last year. I gave them all away."

Gaspare's regard was steady and pitying. The horse shook his glistening, sweaty mane under the sun and opened his nostrils hugely.

"You gave them away."

Damiano blundered stiffly onto the seat beside him. "Yes. But I still had them when I first met you in San Gabriel. Don't you remember? I disappeared in front of you and scared you half to death."

Gaspare was affronted. "I don't remember being scared half to death by you. You had a trick or two, I grant. You could make it seem your bitch-dog talked. That was fine, and I'm really sorry you lost that dog. I like dogs. Much better than horses."

Damiano pulled his hair in consternation, while he bit down on his large lower lip. "Gaspare! What are you saying? I'm always talking about how I was a witch, and how my staff worked, and about Raphael, whom I summoned—or rather requested audience of—and so learned to play the lute. I know you don't believe everything I say, but if you don't believe that I was a witch, then you must think I should be locked away in a cellar!"

Gaspare glanced up and away again. He brushed a stray fly from his colleague's back. "Not at all, Damiano. But I think that it is important to you to feel special."

"Eh?" The dark, curly head jerked up, and the black eyes opened round.

"It is important to every man to feel special," continued Gaspare moderately. "But what you don't realize is that you *are* special. You are singular. You are the finest lute player—oh, God's bollucks, the finest *musician*—we have seen in all our travels. I doubt there is another here or back in Italy as original and progressive as yourself. Being a magus or a wizard fades to nothing next to that. You need not wish to be a sorcerer. You need not ever think about it again."

"I was not a magus, or wizard, or sorcerer. Just a witch." And he stared and stared at Gaspare. "But what you are saying is simply that you do not believe me."

"I do not believe you," replied Gaspare quietly.

Damiano snorted. He folded his large hands together and his eyes wandered over the gentle Provençal horizon, where stood small cots and ricks, and ponds of water floating with ducks. Five seconds of silence grew into ten. Into twenty.

"I feel very strange right now," Damiano announced.

Gaspare shot him one wary, concerned glance. "Perhaps that is how it feels to come to your senses," he suggested, trying to say it as inoffensively as possible.

But Damiano spared only one distracted glance. He stood up on the footboard, and then climbed on the seat itself, holding to the wagon eave for support. Both Gaspare and Festilligambe looked up at him standing above them.

"No, Gaspare. I mean I feel magic. Even now. There is power in the air above us." He waved hugely at the empty sky.

"Oh, Christ!" groaned Gaspare. "I have done it!" He hid his face in his hands. "He is beyond recovery."

And now Damiano was pointing. "Look! Look, Gaspare. It is coming. Can't you see?"

The boy peeked. "I see a little bird," he said in a flat

voice. "A little bird bobbing and flapping, like little birds
do."

"She is looking for us," the other insisted. "She is
looking for me, I think." Now he gesticulated with both
hands, nearly overbalancing on the flimsy seat.

The horse snorted. Unobtrusively Gaspare sidled to the
edge of the seat. The little bird (it was a dun-gray dove,
with a ring around its neck) passed overhead, banked in
the air and circled the wagon.

Gaspare glared from the dove to Damiano. The action
was too perfect. He suspected this whole scene was a trick
arranged especially for him, but for the life of him, he
couldn't think how it had been done. As the bird circled
again, Gaspare began to feel silly. He watched the dove
descend to the dust of the road, where the horse sniffed it
and uttered a very wise, deep nicker.

And then, while Damiano clambered down from the
wagon seat, capering with what enthusiasm his striped
back would permit, and as Gaspare's vision swam, the dun
dove turned into a very beautiful—not lady, certainly, not
with that blue felt dress which showed feet and ankles and
more besides—a most exquisitely beautiful brown-braided,
barefoot peasant maiden.

She put one hand upon the horse's shoulder, perhaps
with the apprehension that her sudden appearance might
have upset the beast. But Festilligambe might have been
accustomed to transforming people since foalhood. His left
ear twisted around but his right ear did not feel it was
worth the effort. His head neither inclined nor flinched
away. He inched away from her touch with only his usual
diffidence.

She looked at the horse and the wagon and she looked
at Gaspare (and at that moment the boy knew that this one
was a great lady after all, even barefoot and in felt, so he
swallowed firmly and bit down upon his unruly tongue)
and then she looked through him and finally she allowed
herself to look upon the young man standing in front of
her.

"Where is this plague?" she said, speaking Italian with
a strange, broad, bouncing accent. "Neither of you has
such sickness in you." Her small face showed concern,
along with a certain shade of accusation, but as she
frowned at Damiano, the tiny hairs that escaped her braids

caught the sun. "Your only trouble is that you don't eat right."

Damiano was looking at the gleaming bronze hairs instead of at the frown, while he himself was smiling so that he thought perhaps he would not be able to talk. "You—you came all the way from Lombardy, Saara. To see me? Because of my strange visit to you? Gaspare here was just telling me that you were a fever dream, like the time he had the spots and saw his sister as Saint Lucia."

Then, before his bubbling triviality might have time to irritate Saara, he added, "Yes, my lady, there is plague behind us, and if we have escaped it I am only too glad. And the flogging I mentioned, which caused me to flee to you—that was real, too, though nowhere so terrible as the plague. But I did not think you would trouble yourself so. . . ."

Saara the Fenwoman put her hand on Damiano's bare arm, intending to turn him around. As they touched she saw some shade of feeling in the movement of his eye and she said, "Don't worry, Dami." Her frown dissolved. "Now that we are both present in body, it is no longer dangerous for me to touch you."

Damiano's eyes opened wide. He scratched his own bare shoulder, and from his confusion he rescued some element of gallantry. "No longer dangerous? My sweet lady, it is because of our bodies that danger enters into it." But as he spoke, pride turned his mangled back away from her.

"It is nothing worth looking at," he declared. "No more than bramble scratches. Forget I ever spoke of it. I took off my shirt because the day was warm."

Damiano met Saara's eyes slowly, for he was not a good liar, and he found in them a swirling, green-brown angry fire at this silliness of his.

As around Saara (and around the power of Saara) all things had unexpected color and focus, so even her anger took on brightness. Though once Damiano might have met, or at least understood this light of anger, now he could not even look at her. For she was the greatest and most assuredly the most beautiful witch in the Italies, while he had not even the fire with which he had been born.

So he was silenced and his eyes slid away. And as Saara

saw this, her anger faded into something like pity, or like hurt, and upon that emotion yet another sort of anger fed.

"You fool! What under all the winds have you been doing to yourself? Don't you know that plague is death, and not all the magic that is in the earth can overcome it? And this . . ." as she spun him about and pointed to the scabbing weals, "how did you let *this* happen? Do you forget who you are? You! You who were once strong enough to carry half of my soul away with you, and then wise enough to bring it back!

"I know you, witch, for I carry around a dark child you have abandoned, and all it does is whisper your name! You cannot lose your self-respect without bringing shame to me. And if you should die, witch—Damiano—if you should die of plague in a far country, then what am I to do with that little shadow?"

Self-possession returned to Damiano between one moment and the next. His head snapped up and he rested his own large hand upon hers. "When I die, Saara, then you must release anything of mine that you hold. A dead man should be dead."

Saara blinked: catlike, green, but uncertain. "Not 'when,' but 'if,' Dami. You are not sick, remember, but only underfed." And in a whisper she added, "And I am much older than you."

In that instant their positions were reversed, for the young man stood with quiet assurance, while Saara stepped back a pace, slipping her hand from his.

"And I ask again . . ." She raised both her arms in a world-embracing gesture. "Damiano, in a land filled with food, why have you starved yourself?"

During the prior conversation, Gaspare had sat on the wagon seat as motionless as the whipstock, while magic and talk of magic turned his head around, and while talk of dark children turned his ideas of Damiano on their heads.

But at this last question Damiano himself turned from Saara to Gaspare, and what he saw in that pinched, ruddy face caused him to break out laughing.

The boy took this as a sort of permission, and his own strong need pulled him from the wagon seat to the presence of the terrible, angry, beautiful barefoot lady, where he knelt and clasped his hands about her knees.

"Oh, signorina bellissima! He will never admit it, being

too stiff-necked and mad besides, but he is starving to
death in truth, and I am also. And if you are as great a
lady as your appearance declares you, you will have pity
on us and give us a little something. If you have no silver,
then bread will do. Enchanted bread is very good, I have
heard. Or enchanted roast pork, or even enchanted boiled
greens. . . ."

Saara had been aware of Gaspare on the wagon seat,
just as she had been aware of Festilligambe between the
traces, but when the boy fell at her feet, and clasped her
embroidered dress she gaped from his red face to Damiano's dark one.

"Who?" she asked.

Gaspare's gesture began at Damiano and ended theatrically, slapping his own breast. "I'm his dancer," he
announced. "And if he has lost a little of his looks, signora,
do not exclude him from your graces. Some of his decay is
age, of course, as he is all of three and twenty, but most of it
is only hardship, curable with a little kindness."

His gooseberry green eyes stared wildly into her green
ones as he stage-whispered, "I beg you only to remember
the dark child!" Then, seeing in the elven face no perceptible sign of softening (indeed, Saara's expression was
frozen by complete incomprehension), Gaspare added,
"But if after all these entreaties, it still seems the fellow is
beyond saving, it is perhaps worth noting that I am only
fourteen at present, so my best years are certainly before
me."

Saara shifted within Gaspare's unslackening knee-
clasp. She looked up once more at Damiano, who was so
trapped between anger at Gaspare, sympathy with the boy
and a general desire to laugh at the picture he made, that
his face had gone nearly as red as the redhead's.

"Why do you need a dancer?" Saara inquired of him.

He cleared his throat. "Gaspare. Let the lady go now,"
he commanded.

Obediently Gaspare released. Then in a reaction toward
dignity the boy stood upright, brushing himself off.

Damiano brushed one hand through his hair as he
continued, "I need a dancer, Saara, because I am a
musician. I play. He dances. People pay us—when they
feel like it.

"That is also why we are starving." He laughed at his

own words, not because they were very funny, but because he found it easy to laugh around Saara.

"I don't mean because we're bad, so no one wants to hear or see us. I don't think we're bad, either of us."

"We're certainly not," interjected Gaspare with a great deal of confidence.

"But no one in Franche-Comté knows us yet, and we don't even know where and when the markets are, so . . . it is not easy."

Saara continued to stare, and though Damiano believed, or wanted to believe, that he knew the woman well, he could not read her expression. From somewhere within him a spark of defiance rose. "So why should I apologize?" He shrugged. "Being hungry isn't a sin."

The woman started, in abrupt, birdlike fashion. "Ruggerio would talk like that; he would say, 'If I want to sleep till midday, so what? It isn't a sin.' Or in the summer he would say, 'When you walk around without your clothes like that, Saara, you are sin waiting to happen.'

"Someday I must learn what a sin is," she concluded.

Gaspare's guffaw at the mention of walking around without clothes was rather overdone. But then he thought that line expected a guffaw, and was rather annoyed that Damiano had missed his cue.

Because he did not like to be reminded of the Roman he had killed, Damiano remained sober. "I myself am never certain, my lady. But I have found that harm done to another person is usually a sin, while harm done to myself usually is not."

Saara took her left braid in her right hand, and her right braid in her left, and she yanked on them both. Thoughtfully she regarded the sweet hills of grass and trees.

Behind them rose a height of vines, their leaves just breaking, waxy green against the chalky soil. Down ahead the road looped around water, and the rough calls of ducks rose in the air. Set back from both pond and highway was a house: a rural mansion, limed white and possessing at least four rooms. To the right of the road spread pastureland, dotted with sheep. As though apprehending her notice, a sheepdog began to bark.

The witch stood motionless, her lips twitching slightly. Gaspare opened his mouth to speak, but Damiano elbowed him neatly, for he knew what Saara was doing. "There."

She pointed. "Three people are in that house. There is a whole new lamb hanging over a smoke-fire. Also a barrel half filled with sleeping roots: turnips, maybe. And in the oven, pot pies are baking now; I think even the simple nose could smell them."

Gaspare emitted a strengthless whine and leaned against Damiano, who could scarcely support him. Saara, with the forced patience of a mother with very slow children, spoke slowly and distinctly.

"You go down there and clap at their door, and tell them that you are hungry and have nothing to eat."

A dozen expressions chased themselves across Gaspare's features.

He whispered, "And you will enchant them into feeding us, O great and beautiful lady?"

Saara's smile was scornful. "Of course not. I will do nothing. They will give you food because it is what they ought to do, and they will be glad to do it."

The boy deflated, and even Damiano looked a trifle wan. "I'm sorry, Saara," he said. "But they will not. These are the civilized peasants of France, and they will give away nothing for free."

She looked at him sidelong, but the honesty of his regard was convincing. "But how do they expect to live themselves, when their sleds are empty, if they do nót feed the unfortunate now?"

"They rely on providence and their own management to prevent that from ever happening," he replied, and Gaspare chimed in with, "They are hard, the people of France. Very hard!"

Saara sought advice from the black, disinterested eyes of the horse, and failing there, from her naked toes. She nibbled delicately at the end of one braid. Finally she raised her chin and nodded.

Her face was stern. "I believe what you tell me, Damiano, though I cannot see how a land can work so. Things are more just in the land of the Lapps. . . ." Her words fell away, as though her memories had changed in midsentence. "Well, no mind. If they will not feed you, you must take what you need. It is only fair."

Gaspare jumped up and down in place. "Hah. That's what I've been telling him since November last!"

Damiano did not respond to the boy. "Saara," he said

instead, "if we are caught stealing we could be hanged, or could have our hands chopped off. Without a hand I will not be able to play the lute."

Saara sputtered, and her pink feet danced over the road. "Is that all it would matter to you? That you would not be able to play the lute? Well, Damiano, I will try to see you do not get caught. What more can I say?"

Pain added an extra glitter to Damiano's eyes, for he had donned his woolen shirt. The three thieves strolled casually along the dry and empty road, with Saara's witch-sense keeping watch. Damiano walked stiffly, and the Fenwoman kept to his side, so that left Gaspare to lead the foraging party.

As was only appropriate.

Stepping her sun-browned feet in the dust next to Damiano, Saara was touched with meaning, with an importance of line, of color, of gesture that was almost deadly to him. It was nothing she did, for she did nothing but patter along childlike on his right side. It was not the beauty of her face or form, for though her skin was infant-fine, her green eyes were tilted like those of a fox, and were foxlike sly, and of her figure, though Damiano felt that he knew quite a lot about it, still all he had ever seen was the shapeless, felt dress.

But the sun became glory, when it burnished her hair. And the road of dirt became adventure, because reaching out Damiano could touch her. And this hot March afternoon marked the clear end of something, and the beginning of something else.

Yet under the heat of his face and behind the smiling mouth Damiano was not happy, for his feelings knew too much of yearning and not enough of rest. If this was love, it was not the same passion he would have said he felt for Carla Denezzi, now behind convent walls at Bard.

This was no blessed or consoling feeling. He thought perhaps he wanted to strike Saara, to hit her across her petal-pink lips and knock her down. But of course he would not be able to strike her; if he lifted his fist she would turn and look at him and he would be the one to fall.

Or perhaps he wanted only to shout at her, to tear her heavy dress off, to shock her in any way possible.

Why? Was it because he wanted her, and desire made him feel like a fool?

Then Saara turned her glance from the gray ducks of the pond to Damiano. In an instant he felt his mind had been read, and flinched with guilt, but what Saara said was, "Why 'sheep-face,' Dami? Why did he call you sheep-face?"

Relief was exquisite, and the silly question settled his mind as little else could have done. "Because he thinks I look like a sheep," he answered her, and then he yielded to the temptation of adding, "Can you see a resemblance?"

Saara's eye went dry and analytical. Damiano swallowed.

"I see what he means. It is the nose, mostly. It is broad down the middle and almost turns under. And the eyes, also."

"I see," said Damiano, as stoutly as he could.

"I myself have been told I look like a fox about the face," she added, but Damiano interrupted with an angry hiss.

"Not at all!" he cried, with all the more heat because he had been thinking exactly that—that Saara looked like a fox. "There is no resemblance! Your face is as fine as ivory and roses, and you move like a bird in the air. Fox indeed!"

She skittered two feet away, amusement written all over her fox-face. "So. Is that the way I was supposed to answer you? 'There is no resemblance!' Well, I can look like roses and a fox, too, I imagine, and you, Damiano Delstrego, are a vain young man, just like . . ."

"Don't say 'like Ruggerio,'" he pleaded. "I am not a duelist like him, and he was a Roman besides."

"I was not going to say that," she replied, subdued suddenly. "But never mind. I think you are a handsome boy, Damiano. Handsome and more besides. And you can be all that and still look a little like a sheep." The part in her hair (straight, but slightly off-center) came just under Damiano's eye level. As he looked down upon it suddenly his roiled emotions clarified and he did what he wanted to do, which was to kiss that warm, bronze-brown head.

"I love you, Saara," he whispered, regardless of Gaspare, trotting on ahead. "I know all men have to love you, so that is nothing special to you, and I know further that I am last of all who should speak to you of love, but I do love you.

"I hear you in my mind a thousand miles away, and

your image floats to me through pain and darkness, like a golden lamp. I have nothing to give—not even time—but still I love you."

Saara stepped back and her gaze was not soft but shrewd. "You don't love me, Damiano, though I might wish you did. You hear your other part; your broken self is calling to be whole."

Damiano heard her. He answered nothing, though his mouth formed words. He shivered. By the pure Mother of God, he whispered to himself alone, she's right, or at least partly right.

Of course Saara was important, her every gesture imbued with meaning. *Her* every gesture was flavored by *his* every gesture, and her eyes gave back his own familiar fire. How could he not have seen? He had become simple indeed to stand next to his own spirit and not feel it.

He was ashamed.

He was ashamed, but he raised his head. "You know what I do not, Saara. Probably you know me better than I know myself, anymore. But still I love you."

They had stopped together, just beyond the duckpond. Together they stood under the sun, amid the buzzing of the season's first dragonflies. And Saara's smile was most maliciously sly. "All right, my pretty, sheep-face Damiano. So if you do love me what do we do about it?"

But if they had forgotten the purpose and urgency of their mission, Gaspare had not. He danced back, his feet impatient and demanding. "First you dawdle," he hissed. "And then you stop entirely. I'd like to know how you expect to win your bread that way. Are you still bothered that our purpose is not holy enough, Damiano?"

The older fellow glared, but he was really glad of the interruption. A greater interruption followed, as the sound of unhurried footsteps scuffed up the road toward them, their maker hidden by the last hillock between the pond and the house.

With instinctive smoothness Gaspare's face became casual and innocent—far more respectable than its usual habit. He bent down and snatched up one of his cloth-booted feet, and examined the many rents in the material with proprietary interest. He also pointed to his foot, looking up at Damiano so that the approaching house-holder would see a tableau that raised no suspicious questions.

But to the ruin of his plans, Damiano's barefoot lady
began to sing. Perfectly loudly she caroled, and tunefully,
too. But her eyes were closed, and the words were quite
mad.

> "Damiano, Gaspare, me.
> There is nothing here to see.
> Damiano, Gaspare, me.
> There is nothing here to see."

The fine hairs on Gaspare's arms prickled. He stared
wildly at Damiano, but his friend's dark face wore a
peculiar expression of listening, colored by satisfaction. His
face shifted from Saara to the person approaching as that
one rounded the hillock.

It was a girl of perhaps sixteen years, her smooth hair
hanging loosely over her shoulders. Her dress was pale
homespun. She swung a flat basket, looking as bored as a
sixteen-year-old girl may look, when out to gather eggs.

> "Nothing but sky above your head,
> Nothing but dirt on which you tread,
> Damiano, Gaspare, me.
> There is nothing here to see."

The girl passed them by and she did not look toward
them at all.

Damiano was grinning broadly. "It has been a long
time," he whispered in his throat, and then to Gaspare, "I
don't know how she finds the rhyme so quick."

But Saara paid him no mind. Still singing, she jerked on
Gaspare's sleeve and signaled them both to follow. Feet of
pinkish-brown leaped from the dust of the road to the
grass bank, and hopped tussock to tussock into the wet.
Gaspare and Damiano imitated her steps, Damiano with
less agility, for despite adventure and an epiphany of the
heart, his back still hurt.

> "Damiano, Gaspare, me
> There is nothing here to see.
> Hear no sound of splashing legs,
> Nor ducks' squeal as we steal their eggs.
> Nothing but sky above your head

And slimy ooze through which you tread.
Damiano, Gaspare, me . . ."

"It is getting longer," said Damiano for Gaspare's ear only. "And she changes it a little as she goes. It's a wonder she can remember!"

Gaspare leaped over a freshet and helped his friend after. His spare face was transfigured, and his prominent eyes stood out. "Is this magic?" he hissed back. "Real magic? The goosegirl cannot see us?"

Damiano nodded. "But that is not to say she cannot hear us talk." But even he could not resist adding, "Well, what do you think of magic—real magic?"

The boy made an owl face. "It is silly! And in terrible taste. But if it works, it's wonderful, of course."

"Of course. All wonderful things are silly, and most are in abysmal taste."

Saara, with unerring instinct, took four eggs from three squalling, sitting ducks, and then would search no more. Instead she slipped the eggs down the neckline of her embroidered dress, causing Damiano and Gaspare to wonder what held them there. Saara left the goosegirl rummaging through the nests, cursing the nips on her ankles, and she led her small parade over the grass and to the house.

"There is nothing here to see,
Nothing moves but wind in tree."

They entered the farmyard, which was marked out by being slightly boggier and more laden with manure than the surrounding grass. A shortish, stocky horse of the Comtois breed stood grazing not fifty feet from the white house wall. The calloused scars of the ox-yoke covered his shoulders.

Damiano spared a moment's disapproval. "A horse shouldn't plow in a yoke. There are perfectly decent horse harnesses. Or better yet, they should get an ox for plowing."

Both Gaspare and Saara shot him glances of irritation. She took him by the wrist and put a finger to her mouth, all the while singing her simple, repetitive song.

> *"Damiano, Gaspare, me,*
> *There is no one here to see.*
> *Nothing stirs upon the planking,*
> *Form is missing, voice is lacking."*

"Ouch!" whispered Damiano, and Gaspare (who in all matters of art was sensitive) cringed his shoulders. Saara spared one offended sniff and then pulled them in behind her. Into the house.

It was dim within, and the stones were damp. Yet in this, the largest room of the house, two cook-fires gave their smoky warmth, and the odor of lamb and pastry was overpowering.

In the middle of the room, where the black rafters rose highest, a long table had been set, with benches at either side. On one side sat a man: burly, bearded, short, liberally daubed with mud. He reclined on one elbow, while he played with the last corner of the hard piece of flatbread that had been his dinner trencher. On the far side of the table sat a mug, surrounded by crumbs: remnants of the goosegirl's meal. A tall woman, thinner than either husband or daughter, was tending the fire beneath the iron oven-pot, which was raised on fieldstone to the height of her waist.

"It don' draw none," she declared in a patois of langue d'oc and langue d'oil even Damiano could scarcely follow. "It needs you to build it again."

The man turned to his wife with the slowness of seasons revolving. "You want I should build something, the time to say that is winter, not when the ground is open."

"In winter you say you can't work stone because the ground is froze," she replied, but without rancor. Indeed, this entire interchange had been conducted with a boredom on both sides equal to that shown by the girl at the duckpond.

Saara took Gaspare by the shoulders and set him down on the far end of the bench from the householder. Damiano she motioned to the bench on the far side of the table. Both young men sat in a paralysis of fear, to find themselves in such close and protracted contact with the people they were robbing. Gaspare's pale green eyes glowed almost white.

Now Saara's song changed, fading into the back of her throat, and the odd words Damiano could pick up were not Italian. She moved with practiced efficiency through the smoky kitchen, carving a quarter of lamb and cutting black bread with a knife as long as a boar spear and thin from much sharpening. Both the meat and the bread she wrapped in a scrap of dirty linen which lay by the pot-stove. This bag she dropped on the table in front of Gaspare, but as the boy goggled at it between terror and fascination, his mouth wet and working, she shoved it across the boards to Damiano, thinking perhaps that he would be the more trustworthy keeper. Then she went from the kitchen into a darker room behind it. Damiano heard her digging in sand.

The goosegirl returned, her wood-shod feet making a great racket on the floor. Gaspare started in panic, but Damiano leaned painfully across the table and put his restraining hand upon the boy's bony shoulder.

"I can't believe," the girl announced, setting her basket between the intruders. "Only two eggs."

Her father grunted heavily. "Not right, this season. There should be a half-dozen, at least, with all the ducks we kept over the winter. It must be the foxes again. I'll set the dog on them."

This last suggestion infused Damiano with a warm glow—a ridiculous warm glow, as though he had been personally praised. A fox it had been in truth: a lovely, sly, green-eyed fox, and he heard her now in the pantry, stuffing things into a sack.

Magic or simple, whole or sundered, let no man say he did not love Saara the witch. And for a moment, in the middle of peril, with one hand on the racing pulse of Gaspare and his nose full of the smell of food, Damiano convinced himself that this was his own house he sat in, at his own kitchen table, with his own Saara singing from happiness in the next room.

Of course if it were his, the house would be light and dry, the walls fresh-limed, and the floor painted tile. If it were his, there would be rows of books, and one would be able to look out the window and see the clean mountains. And the beasts in the stable would be full-fed and glossy, with never a scar.

And this vision of bucolic contentment raised in him

such a dizzying desire tht he choked on it, and Gaspare looked up, his own fear turned to concern. Damiano frowned hugely, to show he was all right.

The peasant rose then, moving ponderously for his moderate size, and the goosegirl took his place by the table, staring. No word passed between her and her mother.

One year ago, or fifteen months, perhaps, Damiano reflected, he had lusted after immortal greatness. He had wanted the name of Delstrego to be linked with that of Hermes, the alchemist, and with Dante, the patriot. His only quandary had been whether to achieve his greatness through literature, music or natural philosophy.

And he had accomplished something.

For one night he had led an army (much against its will). On one winter's day he had bested the greatest witch in the Italies in single combat (and there she was in the pantry, singing). He had won a peace for the city to which he had bargained away his rights, forever.

And now, in the spring of his twenty-fourth year, Damiano could imagine no greater happiness than to live an unexceptional life within four rooms by a duckpond, in the company of a woman—a rose-faced, fox-faced woman—who went barefoot through the cold.

Viciously he informed himself that he could not have that form of happiness, nor any other that came upon the earth, for along with his rights to Partestrada, he had bargained away all his rights to the future.

Damiano was standing by the table when Saara came singing from the pantry.

Sunlight hit them like a blow; even Saara blinked against it. Damiano gave Gaspare the bag and took from Saara the rough sack she she had slung over one shoulder. The witch trotted them up the road the goosegirl had taken.

Without warning, a dog—the forgotten sheepdog, the dog that was to be set on foxes—exploded from a ditch at their feet. It was a heavy creature, almost the size of one of its own wooly charges, headed like a mastiff and bobtailed. Gaspare shrieked but clutched his parcel to him.

Damiano leaped forth. He stood between the animal

and Gaspare, raised one arm and shouted, "Go! Go home!" in his most commanding bass.

The beast slavered, crouched down and sprang for Damiano's throat.

It was a sharp stone the size of a man's fist, and it caught the dog exactly over its left eye. Its charge went crooked and it landed on its outsized jaw. It peered at Saara—author of the stone—with a single working eye which was the size of that of a pig. With its little tail tucked down against its rump, the sheepdog backed sullenly away.

Damiano was full of admiration. "Not a beat!" he exclaimed, hefting his sack once more. "You missed not a beat while you jumped sideways, bent down, found the stone and tossed it!"

Saara returned his glance without enthusiasm. Her face was slick with sweat. Yet still the sure line of melody passed her lips, endless as a Breton ballad. She led them back to the wagon.

Out of green brush and long grasses Damiano hacked a nest for Saara. He bathed her face with water from Gaspare's leather drinking bottle, and dried it on his single change of shirt.

"You must keep watch," she said weakly. "I won't know if someone comes near. I'm too tired."

"I know," replied Damiano, as he sat beside her, his head resting on one propped knee, his hand smoothing her braid. "Who should know better than I, how weary song-spelling becomes? In fact, when the girl came in, I half expected the spell would fray."

Eyes closed, Saara shook her head. "No. But if I had been singing in Italian it might have. What inspired me to try that, I don't know. I do not much speak the tongue, let alone sing in it!"

She looked up at him. "I guess that was for you, Dami. So you could know how it is I work."

"I know already." Damiano smiled. "You sang all the snows of winter upon me, along with a very large pine tree."

Then Saara looked away again. "Is Gaspare keeping watch?"

"He is keeping watch and eating," came the reply from above her head. The redhead sat cross-legged upon a spit of rock, with a trencher of black bread on his lap, piled with lamb. "He is very alert, and can do both at once," the boy added.

Saara's face shifted from Gaspare to Damiano. "You," she said. "You should be eating, too."

He shrugged. "I'll wait for you."

Saara pulled a soft pouch on a string from around her neck, and from it came four perfect, white eggs. She caught Damiano's eye. "I bet you were wondering," she whispered slyly.

She divided the remaining bread and lamb into two piles, giving the greater share to Damiano. He, in turn, piled the meat back onto her trencher. "I can't eat it," he admitted, shamefaced. "Not since I was a cow once."

Saara stared. "I have been a cow before. I have been a lamb, for that matter, and yet I have no trouble."

Damiano looked past her, and past the clearing off the road where the horse was tethered, to the light of the westering sun. "Ah, but were you ever a cow that someone butchered, my lady?"

She shook her head forcefully. "No, my dear, I was not." And she scooped the shredded lamb on her fingers. "How about eggs, Damiano?" And then she giggled. "Unless you have been an egg that someone has cracked. . . ."

Damiano's heavy eyebrows rose. "You are sounding more and more like Gaspare, Saara. No. I can eat eggs, as long as they do not have slimy unborn ducklings inside."

"Oh, no," replied Saara. She held up an egg, pierced it with an experienced fingernail, and drained it raw. "These are fresh this morning."

"Nobody can eat old eggs," vouched Gaspare, rattling down from the spur of rock. "But even old sheep-face can eat fresh ones." He took an egg, snipped it against the edge of one ragged tooth, and followed Saara's example.

Glowing green eyes looked into his pale ones. "Don't call him sheep-face too much," she said to Gaspare.

CHAPTER 4

The sun was sinking and the travelers' fire lit the hummocked rock walls of their tiny dell. As always, Festilligambe's ardor for fire had to be restrained, lest the gelding burn off his mane and tail. Gaspare was almost as bad; having no warming fat upon his body, he huddled so close to the flames he would occasionally singe his nose and knees.

It had been surprisingly easy to fill up their bellies. Strange that a hunger built for months at a time should disappear within two meals. Damiano sat cross-legged, practicing left-hand changes upon his lute and wishing he could lean back against something. Satiation demanded rest, but he refused to lie flat on his stomach like an infant with Saara watching.

At night it was bad enough—in the wagon with her gentle breathing on one side and Gaspare's adenoidal rasp on the other. And Gaspare so pointedly turned his head away. (Gaspare had explained that his instinct was to withdraw into the wood and leave Damiano alone with the lady with whom he seemed to share such a disturbing past, but that there were not sufficient blankets to spare, and on cold ground he would never last till morning. And Damiano had replied, of course, that it didn't matter at all where Gaspare slept.)

"Whose fief is this through which we're driving?" he asked casually, just to be saying something.

Gaspare grunted. "Dunno. There's nothing important between Lyons and Avignon. It may be the riots have swept the area already, and no one greater than a monsignore has a head on his shoulders. . . ."

Damiano shook his head. "The riots were in the north, in France, and their year is ended, anyway. Gaspare, you are just trying to frighten the lady."

"What is a riot?" asked Saara, sounding not at all frightened.

"It doesn't matter. They are all in the north of France," replied Damiano, a touch too sharply.

And he chastised himself for it. It was bad enough to move like an old man in winter, and to know one looked like a beggar (save for the hair), but now he was becoming surly as well.

"Is it like the plague?" she pressed them.

Gaspare, making some connection in his brain evident only to himself, gave a nasty laugh. "Not at all," replied Damiano.

But the witch wasn't ready to let the subject drop. "About the plague. You must be very careful, for if you should catch it, I cannot help you."

Damiano glanced at her sidelong and sighed. "I know, my lady. My father read to me at least a dozen collected cures for the plague, and at the end of each one he said 'That is very fine, except that it doesn't work.' I grew up knowing that there is no cure in grammerie for the pest."

Saara reacted to this mention of Delstrego Senior by staring at the fire. "Yet a strong witch," she qualified, "will not catch the plague."

Heavy black eyebrows lifted. "That I didn't know. So you, Saara, are in no danger?"

"Neither would you be," she added casually, "if you were undivided."

Damiano dropped his eyes to the lute.

Those green eyes rose a vanity in him, and more than vanity, a desire to impress. He switched from exercises to a newly learned piece in the sharp, Spanish mode, only to find his fingers unexpectedly clumsy.

Resting the instrument on his lap, he flexed both hands together. "I'm tight all over," he mumbled to the world at large. "I need a lesson."

Saara was lying flat on her back, at a four-foot remove from the fire. She needed far less heat than the two Italians, and in the wagon at night used no more than a corner of Damiano's woolen blanket. As he spoke she was playing with a feather, a white down feather, which she was sailing right and left with puffs of air. Languorously she turned onto one hip.

"A lesson?"

"From his angel," came a voice from the crackle of the fire, and Gaspare withdrew a red face beaded with sweat.

"Damiano takes lute lessons from an angel whom one cannot see or hear."

"One—meaning Gaspare of San Gabriele—cannot," answered Damiano mildly. "And I will not inflict upon Gaspare Raphael's invisible presence." Scissoring his legs, he rose in place, and with the lute in one hand, walked to the edge of the circle.

"My lady Saara," he began, suddenly formal. Suddenly uncertain. "If you have any desire to meet my teacher . . . he is a wonderful person. An archangel he is, with great spreading wings—but very easy company."

Saara's interest was quick. Amusement made her eyes slant further. She popped to her feet, stroking her chin with a bronze braid. She accompanied him out of the circle of light.

There was a lot of moon showing tonight. Perhaps it was full. Once, Damiano would have known the hour and minute of the moon's fullness. Once, it would have affected him. Perhaps it still affected him, but he was no longer aware of it.

He was thinking he should not have invited Saara. Introducing Raphael had never been a great success, since other people could not see him. (Or since nobody else could see him except Macchiata, who had been a dog and therefore did not count. And now the horse, who counted even less, being without speech.) Saara was a fine witch, certainly, but Damiano wasn't quite sure that being a witch was enough. And if she was able to see the angel, Damiano knew that he himself would wind up showing off in his lesson instead of working.

Here—on this bright dome of stone, with its glitter of glass in the granite rock. This would make a good setting for an angel, if the wind were not too high. Being in all things an artist, Damiano liked to set Raphael like a jewel against his surroundings.

He sat himself down, noting that moonlight hadn't warmed the rocks. Saara folded herself a few feet away from him. He cleared his throat.

"Seraph?" he called into the shining night. He spoke as another student might call "Professor?" down rows of musty bookshelves. "If you have the time . . ."

This was meaningless, as he knew. Raphael always had the time, if he chose to come. In fact, he probably had an assortment of times to choose from. But Damiano had never been able to reconcile angelic dimensionality with human courtesy, and he was, after all, human. So he called, "If you have the time . . ."

And Raphael appeared above them, descending light as milkweed. Damiano felt him and looked away.

He gazed instead at Saara, who had no difficulty with the angel's form. She stared at Raphael brightly and bird-wisely, but without reverence. Without, in fact, a great deal of courtesy. In an instant Damiano was regretting the introduction of two powers, neither of which he could control.

"Good evening," he began politely, letting the angel's radiance leak into his closed eyes.

"Yes, isn't it?" replied Raphael, and his voice held such a rich and living equanimity that the mortal relaxed a bit. Surely the Archangel Raphael was too great to be offended at a certain lack of respect out of Saara. He had never demanded respect out of Macchiata, and in some ways a pagan was much like a dog.

"Very good. Air and earth are singing together," continued the angel. "And if you are quiet you can hear them."

Saara was smiling with that secret, superior amusement of hers.

"I was rather hoping for a lute lesson," he replied to Raphael, wishing he could see whether *he* was watching Saara.

"That needn't break the peace," was the answer, and then, unexpectedly, Raphael added, "God's blessing on you, Saara Saami."

She showed the composure of a small, grinning pagan idol as she replied, "So you are what these Italians call an angel, Chief of Eagles. How curious."

The dark musician glanced wonderingly at Saara. "You know him already?"

"Every Lappish child knows the eagle-spirits of the high air. There are four of them."

"Once there were five," added the archangel.

Damiano, in his confusion, made the mistake of glancing at Raphael directly.

When the dizziness passed, Saara was speaking, an edge of sharpness in her voice. "So why don't you take care of him, then?"

Raphael's answer was slow in coming. "I don't know how to do that, Saara. Do you?"

Damiano focused with effort on the witch's face, which was a little too faraway for his eye's comfort, especially when he was already woozy. What he saw gave no comfort, for Saara's fox-face was to the fore. Not only was she lacking reverence, she did not appear even friendly toward Raphael. "I have a certain earthly wit," she was saying. "Mother wit. I know, for instance, that he cannot continue in the way he is."

"Mortals by their nature cannot continue in the way they are. What matters, I am told, is the direction in which they change." Raphael's words were slow and reflective; Damiano could barely hear them.

But they gained clarity as the angel added, "Be careful, Saara."

To Damiano's pained astonishment, the witch laughed outright. "That advice I will take," she crowed. "I will be very careful." She leaped to her feet, shook dust from her heavy dress and padded off the moonlit dome.

Damiano did not know what to say—whether he should apologize for Saara, explain her background or merely ask what had transpired while he had been hors de combat.

But Raphael spoke first, and he spoke very calmly. "On what did you want to work tonight, Damiano?"

The young man took a moment to collect himself. His fingers drummed on the thin wood belly of the lute. "I'm all tight again, Seraph."

Raphael waited the perfect moment before he replied, "Yes. I can imagine."

Gaspare was still haunting the fire. When he saw Saara approach alone he settled back and squinted at her cannily, as though there were a sly understanding between green-eyed people. "Is there an angel?" he inquired.

With a lift of her chin she repelled this familiarity. "Yes, there is an angel," she replied. "A great spirit of the air. Did you think Damiano was lying to you?"

Gaspare shrugged. "No, lady. I just thought he was mad." He snickered ruefully. "You have to admit, when a fellow talks about being a magician and then never *does* anything magical, it's easy to doubt."

Then Gaspare's interest drifted in a different direction. He poked the fire with a stick. "This angel, Lady Saara. Does he play the lute like old sheep—like Damiano? I mean, is that where he got that style of his?"

Saara stood above the blossom of flame, and to Gaspare's amazement, she thoughtfully began to braid the fire, as she would her brown hair. "I . . . don't know, Gaspare. I didn't stay to listen."

When Damiano awoke, the wind was blowing against (and through) the wagon side. Already the sun was well risen. Saara sat at the open foot of the vehicle, combing her hair with her fingers. Her feet swung in the tree-dappled light.

Damiano's back was taut and stiff, as it always was upon waking, and his neck muscles were sore from the lack of variety in his sleeping position, but he could tell he would feel much better today.

He was wearing his rough mountain trousers. He did not usually wear them to sleep, but with a woman so close . . . His first touch of the morning air caused him to reach for his shirt.

He blundered about, probing and peering, until he had covered most of the wagon. The lute protested hollowly as he banged it with one knee.

Saara observed him idly. Finally she scooted back into the depths of the wagon. "Gaspare has it," she announced. "He was feeling very cold this morning. He has no blood."

"Then what is it that makes his face so red?" mumbled Damiano, and he sat back on his haunches, wrapping the wretched blanket around him and over his head. His face he rubbed between his knees, grunting.

"He's got my shirt? Well, what about me; is my flesh less sensitive, or am I any bloodier? And where is he, anyway?"

Saara regarded him with the superiority the quick riser feels for the poor brute who wakes up slowly. "He is out setting rabbit snares. He said he would rather do it while you were sleeping. And since the grass is so good here, we thought we'd rest the day. So you can stay in the blanket."

"Deprived of all dignity," muttered Damiano, and he slid to the ground and stalked away, robed and cowled like a monk, to perform his morning offices in privacy.

Breakfast was mashed turnips, and a cup of the goat's milk that Saara had acquired without fuss or explanation. Damiano was not really in a bad mood, but he did not know how to behave around Saara, having grown up without mother or sisters.

One could not remain gallant and lyrical for three days unbroken.

"Speaking of dignity, my lady," he began, and then reconsidered his angle of approach. "Or rather, I am curious to know why you did not . . . like . . . Raphael very much."

Saara's eyes grew almost round with surprise. "Not like him? But I do like him, Dami. As much as I have liked any spirit I don't know very well. Why do you think I don't like him?"

Damiano folded his large hands around his knees. "You did not seem trustful, Saara. And then you walked away from him."

Her child-soft mouth tightened. "Should I stay to chat with him, like two women at a well? Him? It is the custom in the North that spirits keep to spirits and people keep to people. And as for trust: you, Damiano, are much too trustful."

Damiano's hands clenched over his knees. He made a rude noise. "If there is one sort of . . . of person, spirit or flesh, whom you can trust, it is an angel of God! And speaking of that, why did you call him Chief of Eagles? Raphael is his name."

Very carefully, Saara crossed her feet on her lap. Her face showed no expression, yet the air in the old wagon was charged.

"I know his name as he knows mine. I call him Chief of Eagles because that is what we call him. After all, he is a white eagle in form, isn't he?"

"No," replied Damiano, nonplussed. "Of course not. I used to see him quite clearly, and he is a man—a beautiful man with wings."

"An eagle," she contradicted. "With human face and hands."

Damiano recoiled from the idea. "Monstrous! Why would he look like that when the angel form is higher and more beautiful, and he himself is by nature high and beautiful?"

She snickered. "Evidently you think the body of a man

is more beautiful than that of an eagle. There are two ways of thinking about that. And as for being higher, well, you cannot dispute that an eagle is much higher than a man. Most of the time."

His forehead creased with puzzlement as Saara continued. "And I say again you trust too easy, Damiano. Even if this Chief—this Raphael—is all you say, as true as the Creator (and with the way you defend this spirit, young one, it is too bad you cannot marry him), still you place your trust in other strange places."

"In Gaspare? It is not so much I trust him as . . ."

She shook her head till the braids flew. "No, Dami. In me. Why should you trust Saara, after all? I hate—hated your father. You killed my lover. I killed your little dog. We have torn at each other worse than wolves. Yet you place your soul in my hands and go off, like leaving a baby at grandmother's."

Damiano hung his head. "But there is no more to it than that, Saara. Also, we know each other as well as any brother and sister, for I have walked in your mind, and you in mine. You know I never hated you, and . . . I would like to think you have forgiven me.

"When I broke my staff and gave you my power, I thought it would be a useful servant to you."

"It is a charge," she amended. "A burden."

"It has not made you stronger? When I held your power I was terribly strong, I felt, and could do almost anything I could think of."

Then Saara stared out the open back of the wagon, and her face was cold, distant and unreadable. "Oh, I am strong now, all right. Damiano—remember how your father told you I was the greatest witch in all the Italies? Well now, holding your fire with my own, I am without doubt the greatest witch in all of Europe.

"And if I wanted, I could go home." She made a small noise in her throat. "I could go home to the North, where all are witches, and make a tribe around me. My power would stand as a wall of protection against winter and all the lesser enemies. I would be great, and the men of the fens would fight each other for my notice. They would pile skins at my feet: milk-colored skins of the reindeer, soft as butter. They would chant a new kalevala to me."

Her glance shifted back to Damiano. "The thought makes me sick."

Damiano was so sun-darkened that when pity drew his face darker, he seemed to fade into the shadows. "I understand. Last year, my own strength made me so sick I had to be rid of it."

Saara drew closer. "But it is not last year now, Dami. It is this year. Will you take it back, your power? Your broken soul?"

"No."

His answer was abrupt, almost involuntary. Saara snapped her head back, and bit down on one knuckle in frustration.

"Let me explain, Saara. It is partly the lute, you see."

"The lute?"

"Yes. When I was a witch, then being *that* came first. It had to. A witch must be true to his senses first, before anything else.

"But an artist—a musician especially—he must be *that* first, and there is not much left over." Damiano spoke very earnestly, fearing it was impossible to communicate what he meant. "And music is far more important than magic.

"That, at least, is what I believe."

"You are muddled, Damiano," Saara answered him, but not with anger. "They are not two things, music and magic. Unless you want to say my small songs are not magical. Or not musical." And she smiled at this last.

"Neither one, little nightingale." And with these words the prickle and tension between them dissolved and was gone. In the dim and fusty warmth of the wagon they heard one another breathing. On impulse, Damiano took her hand.

She let her fingers rest on his. "So," she whispered, "there is an old question unanswered. If you love me, Damiano, what are you going to do about it?"

It was not a large gap between them: two feet at most. Damiano reached across and placed both hands on either side of her waist. He pulled her to him, so that she sat between his knees, both of them facing the green world at the foot of the wagon. The blanket, which had fallen back as he stretched forward, he arranged once more, wrapping them both in.

He laid his chin on her shoulder. "Saara. I also said I had nothing to give."

"Not even time, you said. Does that mean your practicing the lute leaves you no . . ."

"No." He chuckled and softly kissed her at the nape of the neck. "I'm not such a madman. But I have struck a bargain with the Devil. Do your people know the Devil—the most evil spirit?"

She nodded, and her hair tickled his nose. Saara was very warm to hold, and Damiano grinned to think that had he been a little bolder, he might have given his blanket to Gaspare.

"Yes. We know many wicked ones, like the bringer of famine, and the ice-devil, and others whose tricks do harm. But the worst of the devils is the one called the Liar. Any man who deals with him we call a fool."

Damiano's grin went hard-edged. "It is the same all over. Father of Lies. Yet I struck a bargain with him, and I am no liar and—usually—no fool."

Saara twisted in an effort to see his face, but Damiano held her tightly. It was easier to say certain things while staring out at the grazing horse. "It was after we fought, you and I, and I felt full of ashes. I traded him my future for the sake of my city. It is to have peace for fifty years, and I may not return to it.

"And I am to die," he said. "Very soon, now, for he said the situation could not permit my living more than two years more, and that was over a year ago."

And now he could not hold the woman, who writhed snakelike around and fixed him a look of astonished accusation. "What? Are you about to walk up to his door and say, 'Throw me in your caldrons of mud and sulfur?'"

He, in turn, stared at her shoulder. "No, certainly not. He said it was not he who was going to . . . to kill me at all, but circumstance."

"And you agreed to this?"

"Yes, of course. Saara—that was the smallest of my concerns. He also said Partestrada itself would shrivel and die unless fed on the blood of violence, as is Milan. I am an Italian, my lady, and my city means to me what a mother would mean to another man. That was why I came to you, rather than accept the evil one's judgment."

"And I said to you 'go away.' I sent a man to whip you away." Beneath his hands, her shoulders hardened like steel.

"No matter, Saara. He did not succeed. Anyway, all my efforts turned bad; neither my city nor I am meant for greatness. We will be forgotten," he said, but without bitterness, and he rested his head against hers. "But we will not be murderers: neither Partestrada nor myself anymore."

Now he turned her face to his by force. "Saara, don't start crying. I was not trying to make you unhappy."

But the witch was not precisely crying. She was tight and trembling under his hands, but full of rebellion, rather than sorrow. "What is it?" she asked herself aloud. "That every man I touch . . . even as much as touch . . ." Her gaze was wet and angry.

"Why couldn't I have met you thirty years ago?" Saara took Damiano in a hug that squeezed the wind out of him. "Thirty years ago, when I was as foolish as you are."

"Thirty years ago I wasn't yet born," he replied, hugging back. "And I'm heartily sorry for being so tardy. Hey, dry up now. Don't be a mozzarella, like me, crying for every little thing," he chided, rubbing a large, square finger over her reddening eyes.

And Saara's leaking tears did cease, between one moment and the next. "You're a fool to give up, Damiano. The Liar does not keep faith with men, and does not expect any better in return."

"I still want the bargain, Saara. It is a good bargain." He scratched his head furiously, as his eyebrows beetled over a scowl. "It is just—just that this year and a half has been a very long coda for a very short song."

The Fenwoman's face was stern, but filled with an odd fire, neither cold nor hot, but wild like the green lights of the north. "Damiano—witch—I say to you you are a fool, but you are not as easily killed as you think. Take yourself back to yourself. The Liar cannot hurt you."

Damiano closed his eyes, bathing in her fierce radiance. "He cannot hurt *you*, my lady. That I'll grant!" His hands held her closer, and his knees pressed against her.

There was a moment's silence, and Saara leaned back her head. Their mouths were very close. "What if I were to say," she whispered, "that all I want of you is to couple together, and let the future go hang?"

His reaction was something between a snort and a chuckle. "I would say, Saara Fenwoman, that you should learn a more elegant vocabulary. But if you thought I intended to let you go now . . ."

He was wearing only one piece of clothing. So was she. Soon the blanket covered them both.

"You feel so warm to me," murmured Damiano in her ear. "That must mean I feel cold to you."

"No, Damiano. Don't worry." Her reply was even softer.

And then he giggled. "What if Gaspare returns now?"

Playfully she pinched his ear. "You sound like a young girl behind the shed!"

He ran his hands down the length of the woman's body. His mouth was dry, and his throat full of pounding. With her hot flesh against his, he seemed to be embracing the summer earth itself, lying prone upon it, dissolving into it.

And it seemed he was touching himself as well, for there was a familiar fire, the floating strength he remembered as a birthright. He heard the mole scrabbling in the earth beneath the wagon. All the planets, too, reached out and spoke to him, with the voice of a long, black flute.

And of course he *was* touching himself—touching that part of him he had exiled, and exiled with reason. Fire sprang through his hands into his head and heart, flame as blinding as the punishments of hell.

He snatched himself away. "Saara!" he screamed, still half-choked with passion. "What are you doing to me? You . . . you . . ."

Saara lay wide-eyed and panting on the blanket. Naked, she shone like a sword in the black cavern. No words came out of her, but only a grunt of animal surprise.

Damiano shrank from her to the wall of the wagon. He was shaking. He shook his head as though flies were buzzing, and his eyes were staring mad. "You knew what would happen. You tricked me."

He hugged himself tightly until the shivering slowed. "It's gone again," he whispered at last. "I have only just escaped."

Saara was grabbing her dress. "So have I. Only just. Goodbye, Damiano."

Gaspare came whistling back at noon. He found Damiano still in the wagon, blanket-wrapped. "Eh! Why didn't you put on the white shirt?"

"There is no warmth in it," replied Damiano, and indeed, he seemed to need more than the warmth of wool, for he was shivering and blue. His eyes wandered hungrily in the dark.

"Where's Saara?" asked the boy, plumping himself down on the boards beside his friend. His jerkin pockets were hugely distended.

"Gone," said Damiano shortly. "Flown away." His eyes, seeking somewhere to rest, fixed on Gaspare's pocket, from which protruded a brown, dead hare's foot, its black claws spread like spokes of iron.

CHAPTER 5

It was the blackest time of the night, and it was raining. Gaspare lay huddled under every blanket of their mutual possession, listening to Damiano practice the lute. First the fellow spent a half-hour practicing every scale in common usage, taking it through various times and rhythms.

These ought to have been simple exercises, boring to the player and listener, but Damiano's playing tonight held such a brooding intensity that Gaspare listened in a sort of tranced horror, as though to a madman who whispered to himself while the rest of the world slept. Just as the boy began to fear for the lutenist's mind, ornament appeared in these repetitive exercises, as though squeezed by effort out of the structure. Finally, after almost two hours had passed and gray light was beginning to leak in through the cracks of the poor wagon wall, he exploded into melody.

Gaspare said nothing. Who was he to criticize the pursuit of excellence, especially in one whom he considered rather his own creation? So what if the sounds were not restful? Gaspare, too, was an artist and he understood.

Besides, he was a little afraid to talk to Damiano anymore. Especially when the musician had the lute in his lap.

He let the covers slip from his head, only to discover that the air outside was not cold. The lute player saw the movement. He stared at Gaspare with wide black eyes.

"Good morning," the boy was emboldened to say.

A moment's silence followed, and Damiano sighed heavily. It seemed by his face and by the strain of his breathing that he was approaching Gaspare from a distance, laboring to get close enough to exchange words. Finally he said, "Today I want to try that castle we saw off to the east. They may be interested in entertainment, even though it is Lent. There is certain to be a village with inns nearby."

Gaspare squirmed uneasily, exposing one shrimp-pink foot and a portion of his rib cage to the air. "I . . . would like to get to Avignon as quickly as possible. There are only two weeks—I think—until Easter."

The dark, drugged gaze didn't waver. "Three, by my count. We are very close to the Rhone, I think. In the village we can find out whether we are on the right road. And I thought you had objections to being hungry."

Gaspare wanted to shout that Damiano's argument was a cheat, that they both knew full well that the musician wanted to play because he wanted to play, not because he was worried about his own hunger or Gaspare's. There was little Damiano did anymore besides play the lute, in a music which grew more fluid and yet more passionate every day. When he spoke, it was usually either to himself or to his angel; Gaspare rarely knew which for sure, and never asked.

All the strings of the battered lute were fraying.

"I'm up," said the boy apologetically, as though it had been a case of his lateness instead of Damiano's inability to sleep. He slipped out into the rain to void his bladder.

Damiano did not like to see the daylight well up, for it intruded upon a world he had created for himself alone, and which he had filled with order. When he played the lute he was not a witch grown blind, deaf and witless. When he played the lute he was not a man who had thrown away life and love. When he played the lute he was all the musician he could be, and let the rest of the world burn. Now that the sun was rising, he would have to go back to being maimed.

His fingers hit the lute neck harder and plucked with more force. The lute whined and a wild overtone sang out of the treble. As if in answer, the horse called out to him.

* * *

Indeed rioting peasants had not swept the local land-holders (nor any other fief of Provence). The Comte de Plessis sat in his fortress as had three hundred years of his ancestors, bestowing law and breaking it. Requiring entertainment, one hoped.

Damiano did not know how Gaspare arranged for him to play before the comte. Damiano himself, were he a seneschal of some great nobleman, would find it difficult to take seriously a ragamuffin like Gaspare.

But Damiano did not appreciate how Gaspare changed when acting on Damiano's behalf: how the honor and responsibility of the position of artist's agent turned the disreputable boy into a man of character. Or in other words, how confident Gaspare was as a salesman that his goods were the best. Damiano only knew that Gaspare had a gift for getting jobs.

The ancient wagon creaked up through the village that the castle had spawned and into the nobleman's demesne. It was a few hours before sunset and the two companions held ready expectations of being offered a cooked dinner before playing their part in the comte's grander meal. And there was always the chance that Festilligambe might take some share in the oats of the fortress destriers.

Gaspare, who never had to be shown the way more than once, led Damiano through a field of adhesive mud, along a wall of pearl-gray buttresses and into the kitchen quarters, where the seneschal had his offices.

He was a sandy man of no great size, taut of skin and sharp-faced, as Gaspare himself might be in twenty years. He glanced at the boy with recognition but no great welcome, and when he saw Damiano his ragged eyebrows shot up.

"This is the lute player?" The man's voice was as tense as his appearance. "He can't go before people like that."

Gaspare bristled. Damiano merely stared.

"He looks like a lout."

Gaspare's right arm went up in an Italian gesture of devastating scorn which was quite wasted on the Proven-çal. "This is the finest musician you have ever had in your establishment, and the finest you will ever have!"

"Certainly the shabbiest," added the seneschal in an undertone, but Damiano's opaque black eyes had locked on his own, and the tawny official fell silent.

Damiano took a step forward. His square, spatulate hand rested on the tabletop. When he spoke it was in good langue d'oc, and very quiet: "Shabby clothing makes an outfit with an empty purse. Employment can alter both together. We have traveled all the way from the borders of the Italian Alps in a bad season, and our appearance only reflects that. My friend Gaspare's purse has a few oats sticking to the lining, so he is less shabby than I, for my purse is completely . . ."

And he slapped the small leather bag on his belt, only to discover that his words were false; there was something in the bag after all. Something hard-edged and tiny.

Between two words, regardless of the others in the room, Damiano sat himself on the carved oak table. He pulled the pouch from his belt and upended it onto his open palm. A small twinkle of gold slipped out of the leather, dotted with bright blood.

"Ah, yes," he murmured to himself. "I had forgotten this, which was given to me in Petit Comtois—to induce me to play."

Gaspare, standing behind, could not see what Damiano was holding. But it was understood between them that their visit to that town of the pest was not to be mentioned in public, lest the reputation of the place had spread to discolor their own. So he cleared his throat, and when he saw the face of the seneschal fall open like a book of blank pages, he feared his lunatic charge had ruined their hopes.

Then "That . . . is a ruby?" asked the tawny man.

Damiano shrugged. "I believe it is. Once I could have told you with more certainty, for the ruby and the topaz are the stones my family is accustomed to wear on their person. But of late my . . . eyes are not what they were, and this could be some other stone of similar coloring but other virtue. For all stones have their virtue, you know, and the most precious is not always the most useful."

The seneschal took this lecture meekly enough, his eyes resting in a kindly manner upon the jewel which dangled by its golden chain from Damiano's fingers. Then, gazing at the dark man with new appraisal, he cleared his throat.

"I think, monsieur," he said at last, "that you are not too different in size from myself, and I may be able to find an outfit to suit."

* * *

"You forgot?" whispered Gaspare once more, as Damiano slipped the shirt of black brocade over his linen. "You simply forgot you had been given a ruby?"

His colleague regarded him as if from a great distance. "It was a day crowded with events, Gaspare," he replied, and Gaspare shivered at something in the sound of Damiano's words. The musician adjusted his somber velvet sash. Lace shone at his collar and cuffs, white as teeth against his sun-darkened skin. "Besides, I can't wear it or I'll scratch the top of the lute."

"I wasn't thinking of your wearing . . ." began the boy, and then fell unaccustomedly silent.

He *was* afraid of Damiano, now. This was no more the gentle simpleton he had shepherded from San Gabriele to Provence, whose greatest fault had been absence of mind (along with an unreasonable concern for the proprieties). This fellow had a face like Damiano's but it was a face carved in stone.

It occurred to Gaspare that he had traveled with this man for exactly a twelvemonth, and had never known him at all.

Damiano now was staring out the arrow-slit window, drumming finger-patterns on the stone: three beats with the left hand, five with the right. He carried the rich brocades as though he'd worn nothing else in his life. That was encouraging, but could this black presence be trusted to play tonight before important people? Gaspare bit his lip.

He might break out in tears—the old Damiano had been known to do that (always for reasons that made no sense to Gaspare, like seeing that kid with a worm in his eye in Chamonix, or finding in ruins a church he had read about once in a book).

But no, this Damiano was dry as sand. He wouldn't cry.

He might kill someone, however. Squinting critically at the lean figure (hard as an English mercenary, the phrase went), Gaspare imagined him with those big square hands around some pasty throat. He might easily kill someone and get them both hanged, the boy reflected, but this Damiano wouldn't cry.

It was all that witch's fault: the silly peasant girl with her dirty feet and her terrible, magical rhyme. Clearly she'd been infatuated with Damiano, and something she'd said or done had caused this alteration in the lute player. Strange—for she had seemed easy enough. Not the sort of woman to keep her lover on the other side of a door.

And Gaspare had thought that, for once, old sheep-face wouldn't refuse an honest offer. In fact, Gaspare would have laid florins on his chances of coming back that last sunny day to find them both under one blanket.

What had gone wrong, to make her depart in a puff of whatever?

Suddenly he found a new perspective on the problem. He asked a question.

Damiano raised his distracted head. "Physical problem? What kind of problem, Gaspare? I don't understand."

This was going to be more difficult than Gaspare had thought. "A . . . lack of compatibility, perhaps? A difference in size, or in expectation?"

Damiano frowned tightly, and one of his hands ceased its drumming. "I don't know what you're talking about. Start again."

Gaspare took a deep breath and leaned back into the leather chair so kindly provided by de Plessis. "You . . . seemed to be getting along very well with the pretty little witch, and then . . . and then you weren't."

"She is the Lady Saara," replied Damiano, with hooded eyes and obvious restraint, as though correcting a stranger. "And no. There was no physical problem."

All this while Damiano's right hand had continued beating its rapid five-beat rhythm. Now his left hand rejoined it, tapping in threes, sharp as a fast horse running. "There is no problem," he repeated. "Except that I have to practice now."

"Practice what?" asked Gaspare, for the lute lay swaddled on a table in the corner.

"This," came the laconic reply.

Gaspare listened, trying to imagine how one would dance to such a rhythm. "What is it?"

"I don't know," said Damiano. "Yet."

There were fourteen people sitting at the high table with the Comte de Plessis and thirty-five at the long table just below the dais. They began with a soup of dried mullet and onions, followed by various roast birds decked in feathers that had never been theirs in life. The sweetbread

was saffron, and the wine was amaranth purple. A tall
honey cake, studded with raisins, had been built into the
exact image of the Fortress Plessis; the diners demolished it
without superstitious. scruple.

More souls than sat under torchlight broke their trenchers in the shadow, on crude slatted benches at the far
end of the hall. These did not eat of saffron or amaranth,
nor did they pick raisins out of their honey cake, for they
had no cake. But they did eat.

Gaspare sat in the shelter of an arras, one leg propped
before him and one leg folded. He was neither hiding nor
was he precisely there to be seen. His eye was on Damiano,
who tuned his lute on a stool behind the main table, and
whose garment shone like black damask under the light of
torches.

The musician spoke no word, and his face wore the
expression of inviolability it always assumed when playing
the lute.

Gaspare had given up expecting the player to make
amusing patter. Damiano almost never spoke when playing, and when he did it was in a whisper that could not be
heard five feet away. But it was better that he should be
quiet than to speak at the wrong time.

Before this fearsome Comte de Plessis, for example. The
landholder's right arm was the size of Gaspare's thigh, and
his blue eyes were leaden. A puckered scar pierced the
man's mouth, giving him a perpetual snarl, and he ate with
great concentration. Better be discreet before a man of this
kidney. Discreet and conservative.

The process of tuning took a bit longer than necessary,
Gaspare thought. But then Damiano never would hurry his
tuning or apologize for it, and the lute's rather brittle
wooden tuning pegs were crotchety. Laughter was heard to
rise at the high table, but it did not issue from the comte,
whose mouth was full. A rather beefy-faced bald man in
soiled white was gesturing at a dark woman in yellow. He
pointed with a bird's leg, scaly foot still attached. He
chewed with his mouth open.

The dark woman was young, demure, clean-faced,
quick-eyed. She divided her attention between the coarse
gentleman and the figure in black behind the dais.

The musician's fingers brushed the open strings with
harplike effect, while his left hand twitched over the

tuners. After a while the left hand hovered, not touching, while the right hand began to dance. Tuning became music imperceptibly.

Damiano did not use a plectrum on the lute, because in the beginning he had not known he was supposed to use one, and later because he did not see the use of the quill. He struck the strings with his nails, playing as many lines as he had fingers, all together. "Devil's music" had said old Marco of Partestrada, and in that opinon he had not been alone. But Damiano's teacher had been the Archangel Raphael.

Now the lutenist was playing in earnest, his left hand spread spiderlike over the wide black neck, his curled right seeming not to move at all over the strings. Gaspare recognized it, and was relieved. This was an ancient piece, just right for Provence, and if Gaspare could remember correctly, by Ventadorn. Damiano played a great deal of Ventadorn; it was popular.

But then the musician inclined forward, rounding over the instrument until his wiry black hair fell over the lute face. He rested his cheek against the wooden neck and swayed from side to side with the beat of the music.

This was not so good. Better not to call attention to oneself in that way. Gaspare watched, wondering if anyone besides himself thought Damiano was looking a trifle mad. The simple Provençal tune, too, was changing. It took on a strange new form under Damiano's fingers, salted with sweet, knotted ornamentation in Hibernian style. Out of nowhere was added a bass line from Moorish Spain.

Gaspare looked into Damiano's black eyes then, and he knew that this night would not be safe: not safe at all.

Where was the troubador's tune? Had the fellow slid into a new piece without stopping? No, for there was the melody again, or a piece of it. But, great Saint Gabriele, what time was this? Three-time? Five?

It was five over three, and it went on and on, under the melody and over it, changing the love song of Bernard de Ventadorn into something lunging and bizarre. For a moment—one cowardly moment only—Gaspare considered sneaking out alone.

But the ancient tune did not die under this treatment; it lived and grew, thrown from treble to mid to bass as a juggler throws a ball.

The player's mouth was open, but no sound could be
heard. His head nodded left and right with his music, and
he baby-rocked the lute.

He has forgotten we are here, thought Gaspare. He has
forgotten the comte.

He has forgotten me.

He is finally unmanageable, decided the boy. Mad
beyond concealment. He looked around to see whether by
unlucky circumstance any of these doltish noblemen were
paying attention to the music.

No. Only the woman in yellow, who watched calm-
faced, with eyes Gaspare did not trust.

And then between one moment and the next Gaspare
did not care whether Damiano was mad beyond concealment. For the rhythm caught up with his fears and
outpaced them, and one particular turn upon the melody
took him by the throat.

He was standing; he didn't know how that had come to
pass. He was standing between two folds of musty
tapestry, gold-chased. He saw Damiano's head nod with
the driving beat, moving up and down like that of a horse
in the traces. The musician's lips were pulled back from his
teeth.

What was he playing now? This was not Ventadorn, or
anything Provençal. And it was not Italian, not with that
bass, and the great arcing sixths of the melody. Christ! Had
he ever complained that Delstrego did not have enough
bass?

But what was it? Gaspare had never heard this piece,
though tiny licks of melody (tiny, delicate, curled like cats'
tongues) were familiar.

And then the boy realized he had heard the piece
without knowing it, incomplete and embryonic, through
the booming of rain in the darkness. It was Damiano's own
music.

The redhead smiled a smile that made him seem old.
"This," hissed Gaspare to himself, "this is my reward for
sitting up all the night while he makes noise. For keeping
food in his belly, and keeping his pennies safe in his
pocket.

"He was created to make this music," continued
Gaspare, speaking quite audibly to no one at all. "He was

made to play, but it is I, I myself who nursed him to it. It is I who made this moment possible."

And wind pulled the arras into billows and splashed the red torchlight over the floor. It turned Damiano's black brocade into embers, deep burning, and struck stars from his black hair. It blew a thick river of music over the dais of the high table and through the cold, dark hall where the bread was also dark. The servants lifted their heads to listen.

And even at the comte's table, conversation had died. The warrior in soiled white still leaned toward the woman in yellow, but his head was craned back and his flat gray eyes stared at the table.

And she stared at the musician directly now, as light played games with her yellow-brown eyes. Her small nostrils flared and two spots of color stood on her cheeks.

"So," whispered Gaspare at her from twenty feet away, his motley making him invisible among the brilliant threads of the hanging, "so you think you understand, do you? You think perhaps this music is for you, pretty lady with red cheeks?"

Then he snorted. "Well, it is not for you. Nor for you, Plessis, who has finally condescended to stop chewing and listen. You have not the brain nor the training to understand Delstrego. Nor have you suffered enough to pay for the music you hear.

"No, nobles of Provence, or of Italy or China, for that matter. His music and this moment are mine."

And silently Gaspare stepped out of the folds of the arras and stood beside Damiano, quiet as a young tree, and as straight from pride.

Damiano raged within his music, but could not escape. Sweet Mother of God, that the planets should arc above him and he not see them. That the mouse should squeak in the stone and he not hear. That a horse who served him should speak and be not understood. And that men—and women—should walk by and leave him as numb to them as a dead man.

He *had* died last year in Lombardy, breaking his staff on the stones of a grave. He had died and felt not the pain of it until now.

If only Saara had let him be, dead or alive, but free from pain.

I feel my blindness, he sang, using no words. I am deaf, I am numb. There is nothing in my life left.

Nothing but this, replied the lute.

The Comte de Plessis had a brow that might have been dug with a plow. His right hand was full of cake. Raisins dropped through his fingers. He brooded at Damiano. An ancient in gray doeskin addressed him; he shrugged the man away like a fly.

A peg had slipped. Damiano was tuning. The comte extended an arm as wide and hairy as the haunch of one of his own hounds. "You," grunted the comte. "Where are you from? Where did you learn all that?"

Gaspare's stomach tightened like dry leather. Genius was a very fragile fire, as compared with feudal arrogance. Genius can be guttered by a stupid man's blow.

Damiano stood respectfully enough, despite his drunken eyes. "I am from the Piedmont, my lord," he replied, with a three-point bow. "And the music . . . is from no one place."

De Plessis settled back on his ebonpoint stool, which creaked beneath his weight. He cast his eyes over the assembly at the high table, which waited in silence for what he might say.

"Good," is what finally came out of that misshapen mouth. "Good enough for Avignon. He ought to go to Avignon."

"That is the tack we must take," repeated Gaspare, bouncing ahead, his shoe heels not touching the ground. "No more playing for loutish dances. It is not the size of your audience but its quality that will make you famous."

Damiano was leading Festilligambe by a handful of mane. The horse's ears were back; he had been very nervous for the last few days—since Saara left, to be exact. The lutenist leaned against the brute's black shoulder, for he was tired. "Ah," he replied. "Is that so, Gaspare? Well, I have always thought it more pleasant to play before wealthy people than poor, and before the educated rather than the ignorant. But the problem has always been that there are so many of the poor and ignorant and so few of the educated and wealthy."

The redhead dismissed this observation with a headshake, as together they passed through the jaws of the portcullis. The echo of hoof-falls rang in the dry ravine beneath the castle bridge. "Yes, but now we have the ruby. We can afford to wait."

Behind Damiano's weary eyes a curtain was almost drawn away. Almost, but not quite. They flickered, and he put his hand to his leather pocket as he replied, "If it is a ruby."

"It is genuine; the seneschal recognized that right away. It is your good luck—or, no, your rightful reward after what I heard tonight. We must sell it in Avignon and buy more suitable clothes."

"Clothes?" Once again Damiano was clothed in his tunic of inappropriate blush pink. "A better lute is what I need. I have to keep hopping over those terrible frets in the middle."

The boy raised an admonishing finger, which shone like a white worm as they passed a cottage window lit with oil light. "A lute will come, Damiano, but right now respectable clothes are more important. Listen to your manager."

Amusement lightened the black eyes for a moment. "My manager? I thought you were my dancer."

Gaspare snorted. "The music you are playing now can't be danced to, sheep-face."

"Enough of that." Damiano's whisper was metallic. The horse shied suddenly, almost pulling its mane from Damiano's clutching fingers. "My name is Damiano."

The boy came to a shivering halt. It flashed upon him like lightning that having gotten the musician to Avignon, to the feet of power and acclaim, it might be felt he was no longer necessary. In fact, to one who silenced the high table of the castle of Plessis, and who sparked the massive Comte de Plessis himself to say "Good enough for Avignon" (much too good, if the hulk really knew it . . .) and who had in his pocket a gold-set ruby, what use was Gaspare at all?

The black tail of the horse swished ahead of him. Damiano's pale pink shirt was melting into the darkness. Gaspare folded his arms in front of him, hugging himself. They felt like steel bands around his ribs.

Damiano slowed the horse. He turned, his white teeth visible under starlight. "What are you waiting for . . . manager?" he inquired.

* * *

"I have it in writing. I asked him to give it to me in writing." Gaspare tapped his bony breast. "It is here."

Damiano sat at the back of the wagon, cleaning his teeth with a bit of chewed stick. Sometimes he didn't shave, or comb his hair for days on end, but about his teeth he was fastidious. "Who—the comte? You were crazy enough to ask the Comte de Plessis for a recommendation. In writing?"

Gaspare sprang from the earth onto the floor of the wagon, landing in a front roll. "I was. I did. Why not, after all, if he liked you? And he did."

Damiano spat out flecks of wood. "I am rather surprised the man can write."

Gaspare pulled a rather furtive smile. "He can't. He got his daughter to do it. Do you remember her? She wore daffdowndilly yellow."

Damiano nodded. "I thought perhaps she understood a little of what I was doing. At least she paid attention."

Gaspare peered studiously out into the night, where the only sound was that of equine jaws grinding. "She . . . has an interest. I was told to tell you she will probably be hawking tomorrow, with her ladies."

Damiano stared. "Why should I know that? Do you mean she wants . . ." The question dissolved in a noise of contempt.

"We are going into Avignon tomorrow," he said finally. "Easter is coming very fast. We don't have time for play."

Gaspare delivered an oddly formal punch on the arm. "Delstrego," he said. "Delstrego, you are going to be receiving a lot of attention: this kind and other kinds. Isn't that what you've wanted? Isn't it the game for which you've come to Provence?"

Somewhere out among the invisible leaves an owl hooted. Damiano cringed from the sound, and bit down savagely on the knuckle of his left thumb. "I want a game that is worth the price I've paid," he muttered, but only to himself.

CHAPTER 6

They came within sight of the Rhone River, which had in times past carved out the sweet and fruitful valley through which they had driven half the length of Provence. Now the road bent toward the river, kissed it, and followed it into the white city of Avignon. Gaspare and Damiano passed beneath rusty gates and into a checkerboard of limed shops and limestone cobbled streets.

Under the vernal sun Avignon wore a smiling face.

Gaspare trotted tiptoe ahead. Festilligambe stepped heavily behind. Damiano walked in the middle, one hand upon a shoulder of each. Gaspare was more difficult to manage.

"Perhaps we'll find her right away," yodeled the boy, skirting a public well and three men carrying an alabaster urn. "Just sitting on a corner, talking to some new gossip. Or cadging sweets; Evienne has no shame where sweets are concerned."

Frantically Damiano prodded the black gelding out of the stonemasters' way. "I didn't know she had shame of any kind," he mumbled, and then added in a louder voice, "Well, it's more likely we'll meet her on the streets than in the Papal Palace. But if I know Jan Karl at all, he will see us before we see him. He likes so much to be on top of things."

Gaspare didn't hear him, for the boy's nervous feet had carried on ahead along the row of close-set stucco buildings.

The street was very narrow. Very narrow. A stream of pedestrians flowed about him and threatened constantly to clot about the horse. Avignon made a Piedmontese feel smothered.

And Damiano could not make the confused gelding hurry.

He could not see Gaspare anymore; he gave up trying. With a sigh, he put his weight against the high chalked wall of an enclosed garden. Festilligambe, in turn, tried to put his weight upon Damiano.

"Don't do that." muttered Damiano, jabbing the beast with a thumbnail.

And then he said "Hush!" and raised his head.

Festilligambe, who had been making no noise at all, pricked his ears also.

They heard music, not loud but close enough to ring clear: a flow as complex as water broken on rocks. It shimmered from many strings together, like an entire concert of lutes—if lutes had been strung in metal.

For half a minute longer Damiano listened, motionless with the rigidity of a pointing dog. Finally, with a word to the gelding to stay, he leaped upward and boosted himself onto the wall.

It was a small garden, planted with tubs of rosemary and fennel. Three anemic olive trees fluttered their silver, sword-shaped leaves, while the cool smell of thyme warred with Avignon's odor of almonds and human feces.

In the far corner of the garden, under a vine-woven trellis, sat a man playing on a harp strung with brass. It was from him the broad splashing music had come. But even as Damiano spied him, the player paused to examine his left hand, which was clawed like the talon of a bird. With a fragment of pumice stone he buffed his middle finger, muttering.

"Hello," called Damiano, letting himself slide onto a walkway of stones. The harper glanced up and his handsome fair face expressed his disturbance at finding a stranger where no stranger should be.

Damiano noticed, and he grimaced an apology. But though Damiano had manners better than the average, certain things were more important to him than manners. "I'm sorry, monsieur, but I had to come right over. It is because of your bass line."

"Because of my what?" The harper was about fifty years old. His flaxen hair had been made frizzy by lime, and a line of stubble made clear that his high forehead had known the assistance of a razor. His eyebrows were black (whether by nature or art) and his eyes blue. He was impeccably groomed and clean shaven, and dressed in a house robe of full Provençal cut. But his gentlemanly appearance made his talonlike nails even more noticeable.

"Forgive my langue d'oc. It is awkward, I know," said Damiano with no sincerity. "I said because of your bass line, monsieur. That which you do with your right hand, at the bottom of the instrument. I could not help but notice that you pull your hand off smoothly, so that the notes come off almost together. They sound together, in fact."

The older man listened without apparent comprehension. Damiano tried again. "Perhaps you think of it as ornament—what you are doing. But I hear it as polyphony. A polyphony of many lines."

Still the harper's heavy-browed, snub-nosed face remained blank. What am I doing here? Why do I care? thought Damiano, and answered himself: There is something to be learned here.

He added, "And polyphony is what I am doing on the lute, you see. It is a technique I have had to invent myself, for I have never heard anyone (save for my teacher) try to put so many lines on one instrument."

The harper took a deliberate breath. "And this is why you climbed the wall into my garden, breaking the law, and getting yourself covered with chalk?" He regarded his visitor with less wariness and more humor. "Because of my right hand?

"Well, lad," the older man said didactically, "that is neither called polyphony nor ornamentation. It is merely the style of the clàrseach: ascending and descending strikes of the right hand, using fourths and fifths. It has always been the style of the clàrseach. It is not the style of the lute."

Damiano shrugged. "Never yet," he said. "But my teacher . . ."

"Why not let the lute be the lute, and if you want to sound like a harp, play one?" The sharp talons curved, and the harper flurried up and down his strings.

Damiano smiled, crouching down before the harper with his chin resting on his knee. He had not come hundreds of miles through snow and sun to hear somebody tell him "it's done that way because it's always been done that way." Nor was he impressed by pyrotechnics: he possessed a number of impressive effects himself. But the sound was pleasant and the man made a striking picture. When it was quiet again Damiano sought to say something appreciative. "You make me understand why it is common to paint angels with a harp."

But the fellow was either tired of this particular compliment or didn't take it as a compliment at all. " 'Tisn't angels who play the clàrseach, young man. It's Irishmen."

"Oh?" Damiano lifted his head. "You are an Irishman?"

The man had mobile nostrils and a wide mouth. The first flared, while the second tightened.

He curled his barbed hands before him and squared his broad shoulders. With a round gesture he pointed from the heavy harp with its ranks of gleaming strings to himself.

"What—do I look or sound Provençal to you?"

Damiano showed his teeth politely. "I cannot say, since I myself have just arrived in Provence. And never have I met . . ."

Unwillingly he let himself be interrupted by a grunt and a scuffle from the other side of the wall. He sprang up. "Forgive me, monsieur. I have left both my horse and my lute."

He attacked the wall once more, growing twice as chalky as before. There below him was Festilligambe, as Damiano knew he would be, still bearing his lumpy pack of belongings, the neck of the lute protruding behind. The horse wore also a crude rope halter, however: wore it with very poor grace, and against the fat man pulling and the fatter man with the switch behind, he had set his obstinate will.

Since the ground seemed fully occupied, Damiano slid down onto the horse's withers, first giving the beast a warning whistle. Both fat men gaped.

"This is my horse, messieurs," announced Damiano, and since the two were both too loud and too clumsy to be thieves, he smiled at them. "Is it that he is where he should not be?"

The fat man in front (he was wearing a dirty apron) had difficulty with this sentence; perhaps Damiano's langue d'oc did have its faults. Finally he replied, "But the animal wears no restraint, monsieur. It was our idea he had run away."

Damiano slipped to the cobbled road. He removed the contrivance from Festilligambe's head. "No, not at all. It is only that he does not like ropes, so I don't use any."

The man in the back had hitherto stood silent, brushing the ground with his weed-switch as though it were a broom. Now he said, "Monsieur. You were visiting the Master MacFhiodhbhuidhe?"

Damiano tried to fit this collection of sounds into his mouth. "MacFhiod . . . the harper. Yes, I guess I was."

The fellow (this one was dressed in serge d'Nîmes. He did not wear an apron) pointed with his switch at the head of the lute. "You are perhaps also a musician by trade? An Italian musician, if my ears do not deceive me?"

Damiano began to brush himself off. It was a fruitless effort, which was just as well, for a coating of chalk concealed much of his clothing's decay. "I am a musician, certainly, monsieur. And that I am Italian cannot be concealed. Why do you ask? Have you need of an Italian musician?" he asked, and he laughed at this conceit.

"Yes, I have," replied the fatter fat man, astounding Damiano completely.

"I thought I would never find you," stormed Gaspare, throwing himself on to the far end of the bench where Damiano sat. The musician had a green glass cup of wine sitting before him and he wore a tunic of wine-red, chased with gold. He was in the best humor he had been in for weeks. He brushed white bread crumbs from his front.

"Find me, Gaspare? I am not a hundred feet from where you left me, running off as you did, like some goat in the mountains. Indeed, it was you who were lost, and I feared Avignon had eaten you."

The boy stared from Damiano's face to the street before the very pleasant inn-yard where they sat. He did not seem to know or care where he was.

"You did not find her," stated his friend.

"No." Gaspare was hot—flushed. Possibly he had been crying.

Damiano's shrug communicated a certain sympathy. "Did you really expect to? This is a city of many thousands of people, and our appointment is not yet for a week or more. According to the innkeeper here, my account is correct and next Sunday is Palm Sunday."

Then Gaspare's green eyes drew out like the stalked eyes of snails. "Innkeeper? Damiano! What are you wearing? And eating? What *is* all this?"

On impulse Damiano reached out and ruffled Gaspare's carefully managed hair. "This, my dear manager, is human comfort. I have been to see a jeweler—also a harper, but that is a less relevant story. The jeweler and I had an interesting conversation about the hybrid nature of electrum, as well as a mild disagreement as to whether amethyst or adamantine is the stone more pure. He gave me thieves' prices for the ruby, I think, but where could I have gotten better?"

Gaspare blinked about him, then, and Damiano placed the green glass cup in the boy's unresisting hand. Gaspare downed it and stared again at his friend. There was something pinched, thwarted and ancient in the boy's face that stung Damiano's own eyes and tightened his middle.

"You shouldn't have shopped without me," Gaspare declared, growing a bit belligerent from confusion. "I would have advised you to buy black. You look more impressive in black."

Damiano pulled a lopsided smile and reached across the table to deposit the last heel of the loaf in Gaspare's lap. "I'm black enough in other ways, my friend," he murmured. "But whether the name be for fame or shame, I am still Delstrego—the only Delstrego left—and our colors are crimson and gold."

Gaspare felt his role as manager slipping away from him. He bolted the bread and more wine. "But you should not have spent this kind of money before even trying to find work."

"I have found work," answered Damiano gently.

Two years ago Damiano might have scorned an inn room like this one: slate-floored, poorly lit, smelling of piss. His father, with whom Damiano first went to Torino and Milano, would not have stayed a minute, and it would have been bad for the innkeeper who had shown him such quarters.

But two years can make a difference. In two years a baby can talk. In two years a dead man can turn to earth.

Damiano sat by one of the long slit windows, tuning the lute.

The sun was up, slapping long bars of yellow light against the ground between buildings. The air was changing so fast it was hardly worth the bother to tune, but then Damiano was hardly aware he was doing it.

The other six inhabitants of the room had vacated for the day, including Gaspare. Certainly there was no reason to lie huddled on straw upon stone and within walls of the same: not when it was actually warmer out-of-doors. But Damiano had slept poorly and was without ambition for the moment.

It had been an owl. Somewhere in Avignon an owl had hunted, calling half the night, and for some reason Damiano could not hear an owl without remembering all he had lost. And this morning it was still there for him: a distant knowledge that the heavens were circling in their complex rhythms without his consent or understanding. That wolves conversed and ghosts walked, but not for him.

And locked into this grief—to his greater misery—was a memory of his lips against skin in the cold of night, and the smell of clean flesh under blankets.

Out the window he could see a vertical slice of the city, where the white stucco housefronts stood identical, shoulder to shoulder. On the ground floor of this inn—Heather Inn, it was called—Festilligambe had been stabled, in a large, square box with two goats and a Sicilian donkey. Damiano hoped the horse was enjoying himself. Perhaps he was sleeping late.

Without warning Damiano's melancholy became unendurable. He rose from the upended box he was sitting on, as though he would fling himself out the door, down the stairs and into the crowded street below. His heart pounded. Mastering himself, he sat down again to think.

Perhaps he should visit the horse—make sure he had food and water. But the groom would think he was crazy, for he had seen the buckets filled already this morning. Neither would Festilligambe understand such a visit, for although he liked his master he was not a sentimental horse.

Where was Gaspare anyway? Out looking for his sister, certainly, though he had not said as much to Damiano. Gaspare's need to find Evienne had grown into a pitiful thing, and Damiano was a little afraid of what would happen if she failed to show up at their long-planned appointment.

This last worry was too much. The musician needed someone to talk to. Someone reliable.

He put the scuffed bottom end of his lute down upon the tops of his boots and laced his fingers together around the neck. With his eyes closed and his forehead resting against the tuning box he cleared his throat and spoke to the empty air.

"Raphael . . . Seraph. If you have the time . . ."

By the sound and by a faint flutter of shadows behind his eyelids Damiano could have sworn that Raphael had come in through the far window. It was an illusion that made the man chuckle, for he had the sophistication to know that heaven was not in the sky above Avignon, or any other worldly place.

"Good morning, Dami," said Raphael, in a voice like the sweet after-ring of a bell. "How do you like Avignon?"

"So far it has been very generous with me," answered Damiano, in an effort to be just. "But still, I am not in a very good mood today."

"You are lonely," replied Raphael without pause.

Damiano squirmed, trying to keep his eyes fixed on the stripes along the back of the lute. It was unsettling and a bit demeaning to be read so easily. "How did you know?"

There was a shrug of wings: a noise like heavy-falling snow. "Because there is no one here. And you have just come to a city that is strange to you. From what I have learned about men . . ."

An idea came to Damiano. "Do you know Avignon well, Seraph?"

"No."

The man had not expected this answer. He lifted his eyes from the lute. "You do not? But it is the Papal city."

Raphael's wings were bowed forward in the confines of the room. The first pinions touched together on the floor almost at Damiano's feet. "I don't know the Pope, either. I have never been to Avignon before," the angel said.

"Not even with messages?"

Again that feathery shrug. "I am not a messenger by calling."

Still, Damiano's idea must be spoken. "I . . . had wondered if perhaps you knew where Gaspare's sister, Evienne, was staying. We are supposed to meet her, you see, and the boy is very nervous."

Raphael's pale hair was heavy as the mane of a horse, and like a horse's mane it fell where it would. His midnight eyes gazed out from a frame of light. "I know where Evienne is," he admitted.

Damiano straightened with the news. "You do? Well, where is she?"

It was the angel who dropped his eyes. "I would rather

you didn't ask me, Dami. I think there are other ways you could find out."

The mortal sat again. "Of course, Raphael. Of course. I am embarrassed. I . . . asked without thought, forgetting that you are not supposed to involve yourself . . ."

And then this small understanding was lost within a larger. "Raphael!" cried Damiano. "Raphael, Seraph, Teacher! I am seeing you—really seeing you. And I am not sick!"

The angel's grand, opalescent wings rose up like flowers opening, till their tips lodged in the corners of the room. His look of joy was as full as Damiano's. But it was mixed with something less definable.

"I am glad, Damiano," he said. "It was never my desire to make you sick."

Placing the instrument hurriedly down to one side (for he treated the lute with the care necessary to something upon which his living depended, and not the care deserved by a tool one loves), Damiano crouched down at Raphael's feet. He squeezed one alabaster hand. He slapped a samite knee. He fished a bright wingtip from the air and held it between his hands, as though to restrain Raphael from flying untimely away. "Hah! Raphael, my dear master . . ."

"Not master," said the angel, and Damiano nearly lost the wing.

"Teacher, then. You are a vision to rest my eyes. And it has been so long. . . . I thought my sight would not be so rewarded on this side of death's door." Behind his grin Damiano's quick mind raced.

"You know, Raphael, I think I know how it is I can see you again. It is because of Saara, and the trick she played on me."

"Ah? So it seems to you that it's you who have changed?" asked Raphael, and there was a shade of diffidence in his question.

"What else?" Damiano pushed closer to the angel, until he was almost sitting in Raphael's lap. I am clumsy as a dog, next to him, he thought. Like Macchiata, I wag my tail so hard I knock things over. But I don't care.

Aloud he said, "Of course the change is in me. You are an immortal spirit—how can you alter?"

The fair, chiseled face grew serious for a moment. "Not

alter? Dami, even if that were true for me, standing out of
time and place, once I had set foot upon the earth of
Provence or the Piedmont, and spoken with you, who alter
so dramatically every moment of your life, and touched
you, too . . . how can I not change?"

Now Damiano let the great pinion slide through his
fingers. "I don't want you to change, Raphael. And for
me—me to be changing you? That doesn't sound good."
Again he cleared his throat and scooted a few inches across
the stone floor, away from the simple, gleaming robe. "I
don't want to be a bad influence on you, Seraph."

Raphael laughed. His laughter was never like bells, or
sunshine, or running water. Raphael laughed like anyone
else. "Don't worry about it, Dami." His lapis eye glanced
down at the lute in the corner.

"Did you want to play something for me?"

Without taking his eyes from the angel, Damiano
scooped up his instrument. "I have a dozen things I could
play for you." His voice took on a note of warning as he
added, "They are not like your pieces. . . ."

"I wouldn't want to listen if they were," answered
Raphael dryly.

Of course, contact with the stone flagging had put the
crotchety lute out of tune again. As he worked it back,
Damiano had a sudden idea, brought on by the splendor of
the moment. "Hey, Raphael. Do you think we could . . .
I mean, would you be willing to play with me? I mean, not
as a lesson, but for fun?

"It has been a long time that I've wanted to do that," he
added plaintively. "And I think my playing has improved
lately."

Raphael's left eyebrow rose. His right wing twitched
like the tail of a thoughtful cat. "I did not bring my
instrument," he demurred, but his fingers drummed his
knee as though hungry for work.

"Your lute? Or harp, viella, viol, recorder? My dear
teacher, what is it you play when you are not giving lute
lessons?" demanded Damiano, and in asking that question
(which had bothered him the better part of two years), the
young man felt he had crossed a sort of Rubicon.

Raphael opened his mouth to answer, but then his
flaxen brow drew down and he turned his head, listening.
There were trotting steps in the passage. Raphael extended

his hand and shook Damiano gently by the shoulder. "Later," he whispered. "We have all the time in the world to play. Right now the boy is unhappy."

White wings and white gown flashed upward, fading into the rising light of day.

Gaspare burst the crude door open. His face was red and white in blotches. "She isn't anywhere," he growled. He kicked his bedroll and cursed. "Not in the taverns and not in the churches. She's not washing, nor praying nor eating nor drinking nor whoring. Not anywhere."

An Italian musician, the innkeeper had said. How ironic that seemed to Domiano, whose journey to Provence was largely a pilgrimage for the sake of its music. After a bit of questioning, Damiano became certain that it was not any essential Italianate quality that the man desired in an entertainer, but only that he be an exotic, like the Irishman. Damiano was confident he could give the fellow something he hadn't heard before.

This was no poor establishment, the inn across the street from Monsieur MacFhiodhbhuidhe's house. Had it possessed sleeping rooms, Damiano and Gaspare would never have been able to afford the use of them. But it was only called an inn for lack of any better word to call it, being a place where wine was served by the glass and little tarts on salvers of pewter. Originally, before the Papacy moved from Rome, it had been the house of the Bishop of Avignon, and still, of an evening, functionaries of the court of Innocent VI filtered through the guarded gates of the Papal Palace and lounged about in the great top-floor assembly room, eating, drinking, gossiping and ignoring the music. The Bishop's Inn maintained a pastry kitchen and offered a large selection of wines, both local and imported. In fact, it was almost a café, in a country in which coffee had not yet been discovered.

Damiano considered this perhaps the most civilized establishment he had ever seen, and he was glad to be employed in it. He was also nervous. He was—barring the pink-cheeked serving girls—the youngest person in the music room, too. That made him even more nervous.

He sat in the shadow of the pillared colonnade at one side of the room. Above his head a small window let in the twilight and the rooftop breezes of the city. Vine tendrils sharpened one another not far from his ear. He toyed with a spice bun he had been allowed to buy for half-price.

These old men, and churchmen, too. If ever there was an audience before which he ought to play conservatively, this was it. Could he? Touching the top of his lute (damned instrument: poorly made, badly fretted. No hope for it), he knew he could not.

For he was the tool of his music. As once his will had passed like braided winds through the length of his black staff, so now the music which sounded on his lute seemed to come through him from another source. If he tried to play for prudence—if he tried to play as he had played a year and a half ago, he would only play badly.

Gaspare sidled in. Now Damiano was not the youngest man in the room. "Almost ready, the fat man says," hissed the redhead. His drooping finger curls were oiled glossily. He wore a bright green velvet mantle which pulled his shoulders back and pressed against his neck. Having just bought the garment today, Gaspare was immensely vain about it and would not take it off, even though torchlight and the heat of many bodies had made the chamber stuffy.

"Don't call Monsieur Coutelan that to his face," chided Damiano, and he fished in his pocket for the piece of soft leather which would keep the bowl of the lute from slipping on his lap.

Gaspare ignored him. "You know, Delstrego, there is a guild in Avignon. A guild of musicians."

The dark man grunted, lost in tuning. "A guild is a good thing. We should join it."

Gaspare danced a nervous step. "I told Coutelan you were a member already."

"Then we will certainly have to join," said Damiano, and he walked toward the torchlight.

He did what he could, in the beginning. He played the dances of home, which bored him, and he emphasized the treble at the expense of the bass. He played no piece that the average man of Provence might be expected to feel he had desecrated. He did not sing.

Yet, for all that, it was not anyone's usual music, not even in Avignon, where the New Music had been born, for Damiano's polyphony went from two lines to three to four, and sometimes dissolved into a splash of tone in which no separate lines could be discerned at all. He pulled his strings with his left hand till they whined like the viol. And he brushed his strings with his right hand till they rang like a harp.

And after ten minutes, when he realized that none of this plump, balding, oily-eyed crowd was listening, he gave up trying to please them. Instead he did as he had done very often in the past year, when the audience was drunk, argumentative or merely absent. He played for Gaspare.

In a way, this was fortunate. In a way, this made him happy, for with Gaspare there was nothing he could not do without being understood; the boy knew his idiom as no one else could, and could not be satisfied by anything other than the best Damiano could do. Damiano played for Gaspare as one old friend might converse with another: fluently and without theatrics. In his self-satisfaction he began to sing a nonsense descant above the melody, adding sweeping arpeggios to the accompaniment.

"Let the lute be the lute"? Why, this *was* the lute, and anything it did well belonged to it by right. Damiano smiled to himself. He liked what he was doing and how he was doing it. It didn't matter if the audience was not listening.

But it had grown very quiet out there. Perhaps they *were* listening, now. Even the comte had started to listen, after Damiano had quite given up on him. Damiano glanced up without breaking rhythm.

He could see five ornate little tables, each with a small group of men—only men, of course—seated around it. Beyond that distance his eyes couldn't focus.

And these small groups were silent, and their attention fixed not on Damiano, but on a half-dozen well-dressed fellows who stood between the musician and the audience, leaning on brutal-looking wooden clubs.

Damiano blinked at six faces set like stone into bad intention. It took him another few seconds to realize that their hostility was focused on him. Then he was aware that Gaspare was standing behind him.

All his confused brain could do was to repeat to itself, "At least it was never much of a lute. At least it is no great loss." He was just finishing the refrain of a Hobokentanz.

He began it again, and he spoke to the men who he knew were about to attack him.

"If you are all planning to hit me together, I don't think there is much I can do about it, messieurs. However, I would like you to know that I have no idea what I have done to offend you." And then he kept playing.

One man, a tall, narrow-chested fellow wearing a dagged jerkin of red, hefted his thorn stick. The others followed. "Mother of God," whispered Damiano, "this is terrible." He felt Gaspare behind him, shaking like an angry dog.

Then a blond head swam out of the red torchlight into Damiano's shortsighted vision. It belonged to the harper of the impossible name whom Damiano had accosted the day before. The Irishman put out a hand on each side and the ruffians froze.

And so Damiano played on. He played thinking that this might be the end for him—that he might never play another song—and so he played to please himself. He freed the base line. He feathered the strings (let the harper glare). He sang to his lute like a mother with a sleepless baby.

And he finished the piece without being knocked on the head.

There was silence. The ruffians had gone; the harper stood alone. Damiano rested his lute on his boots as the harper approached, stepping with great dignity in his Provençal robe.

"So that is what you meant," he began, with his odd, shushing, boneless Irish accent, "by all that babble about bass lines and polyphony and my right hand."

The younger man nodded, half smiling. "Yes. That is what I meant. Does it seem . . . terrible to you? An offense against the nature of the lute, perhaps?"

The blond man pulled up a chair. "No. It does not. But then I am not particularly sensitive to offenses against the nature of the lute, especially when they seem to flatter the harp." He shot Damiano a sharply pointed magnificent glare. "Oh, my philosophy is unchanged, young man. It is always better to treat an instrument as what it is. But I cannot criticize your music. Because it works. It obviously works. And when music works, philosophies cannot touch it.

"Now I am going to get a honey and walnut roll from these people, along with a glass of something, and then I shall come back to listen once more."

Damiano was so caught between confusion and gratitude that his face grew hot. But as MacFhiodhbhuidhe rose again, the harper paused to say, "Oh, by the way, monsieur, you cannot play the lute in Avignon without belonging to the guild."

"Eh? Is that why the . . . gentlemen were upset with me? Well, I didn't know it was an obligation, and now I most certainly shall join."

Two black eyebrows arched up and the harper's smile was wry. "It isn't so easy. Men have waited ten years to be accepted into the Guild of Avignon. And unless you have a sponsor, it is very expensive."

Damiano heard a cry and a stamp of disappointment from Gaspare behind him. He himself stared down at the parquet floor, wondering, "What next? What next?"

"But I wouldn't worry about it tonight," continued MacFhiodhbhuidhe, as his eyes roved the hall, seeking the attention of a maid. "I myself happen to be the Mayor of the Guild of Musicians at Avignon."

One more surprise would leave him numb, thought Damiano. "And . . . you . . . would consider sponsoring me, Monsieur MacFhoid . . . MacFhioda . . ."

With a contemptuous wave of his taloned hand the harper swept away both Damiano's incipient gratitude and the problem of his name. "I said don't think about it tonight." The maid appeared then, with a wooden tray upon which were piled seven varieties of heart's delight.

As Damiano tuned, preparatory to playing again, the harper downed the last of his honey walnut roll in a long draft of wine infused with violets. He wiped his mouth with the back of his hand. (Like a cat, the harper kept his hand soft and round, the claws hidden within.) "You know, Monsieur Delstrego," he said conversationally, "it is part of the duties of the Mayor of the Guild to lead the disciplinary companies."

It took a moment for Damiano to digest this. "You mean . . ."

"Yes. To beat the pulp out of any intruder who dares to play an instrument for money within the limits of Avignon." And MacFhiodhbhuidhe chuckled mildly to himself, took out his block of pumice, and began to file his nails.

Damiano and Gaspare grinned uncomfortably at each other.

CHAPTER 7

Last summer, during the excited farewells spoken by Gaspare and Evienne and the more composed ones of Damiano and Jan Karl, Gaspare had arranged to meet his sister again at the door to the Papal Palace in Avignon on Palm Sunday. Jan had said there was such an edifice as the Pope's Door, and the rest had believed. From that ten months' distance it had seemed that to slice through time with an accuracy of one day was feat enough.

Now Damiano wished heartily that they had stipulated the meeting more exactly, both in time and space. The Pope's Door probably meant the main door into the Papal enclosure, but one could not be sure.

Gaspare and his friend had set down stools, courtesy of their employer, near the station of the right-hand pikeman at the gate. This pikeman was a tow-headed northerner, very tall and quite amiable. He was glad for their company because Damiano had brought his lute.

Of course they had come at dawn, because dawn was part of Palm Sunday. Damiano had left this station of waiting long enough to attend mass, but otherwise the two of them sat like toads on a log, as hour followed hour.

It was not hard on Damiano, for this day was mild, and coincided with one of his periodic spells of lethargy, brought on perhaps by daily performance and practice. And it was quite gratifying to find how many out of the Sunday crowd already knew or recognized him, stopping for conversation and compliments.

"Already you're making a name for yourself," whispered his youthful manager. "Not seven days into Avignon and people of the better sort recognize you."

Damiano grunted sheepishly as the most recent well-wisher departed: a fellow whose embroidered tabard signified that he served a cardinal. "I was born with a name, just like everybody else. And by what criteria do you judge that these are people of the better sort, other than by the fact that they recognize me?"

Gaspare did not answer. His repartee was not at its best, today. He was not happy: torn between an expectation too strong for comfort and a fear that fed upon that expectation. His face was sweaty and his hair (despite much attention) lank. He could not sit still—not for a moment—but neither would he let himself stir from his post of waiting. The result was an itching agony.

Damiano did not wonder at the boy's distress. If he had had family of any sort (he thought) he would cling to them like glue. Had Damiano a sister, he would have used any means, whether force of persuasion or force of arms, to prevent her fluttering off to a foreign country with a scapegrace conniver like Jan Karl.

Had Damiano a sister, of course, she would never have had to start selling herself on street corners. His fingers ceased to move on the strings as he became lost in reverie on the subject of his nonexistent sister.

Life would have been different, certainly. This sister (without doubt she would have been younger than he. He could not imagine an older sister, bullying him and calling him a dirty boy . . .) would have been the natural playmate of Carla Denezzi. Damiano would have then had far more occasions to meet with the lovely Carla, for whom he still had a sweet and somewhat painful regard. Perhaps he would have proposed marriage to Carla in better times. Perhaps she would have accepted.

How strange that would have been! He would by now be a different person entirely. Certainly a man with a wife could not have left the Piedmont for Lombardy, seeking the greatest witch in the Italies, nor subsequently wandered down into Avignon and sat in the sun by the Pope's Door, to pass the time of day politely with a cardinal's functionary.

Would he have ever met Raphael, had he had a sister?

Damiano was beginning to regret the existence of this imaginary sibling. She would be a girl of problems. If she had proven a witch, as was likely, she would have had a difficult time finding suitors. No simple man wanted to marry a witch, and even the sighted were just as happy with a simple wife. (And it was not too much easier for the male witches, for no father wanted to give his daughter to a man who might, in fit of irritation, turn her into a snake. Guillermo Delstrego had had to search all the way to France to find a suitable helpmate. Of course Delstrego Senior had had problems of visage and temperament as well as livelihood. Damiano was always grateful that he had taken after his mother in all ways but one.)

By the crowded calendar of saints, what if Damiano's sister had looked like her father? Oh, it was much, much better that the girl had never been born.

Reverie and sunlight together filled his head with sweet, amber adhesive honey. He could not think anymore. There was no need to think anymore. His right hand nestled into the strings over the soundhole. His left hand fell away from the lute's neck.

Damiano had no idea how long he had been asleep when either the shadow on his face or the rough voice woke him up. He opened his eyes and started in terror, for it was the tall, narrow-chested guildsman who had come so near to assaulting him ("beating the pulp out" of him, to quote) on his first day at work.

This time the fellow had no club, but he looked angrier than ever. His langue d'oc was far too rapid for Damiano to follow, so the Italian made the universal I-do-not-understand-you gesture with both hands. The response to this was a grimace of disgust, and then the fellow began again, more slowly.

"It is bad enough that you crash into the city of Avignon, and I am forced to watch you receive what better men than you have waited years to have. This is shameful, and if we had a Provençal for the Mayor of our Guild, as we should, this would not happen.

"But you are not content with one of the most honorable and lucrative positions in the city; you must also ruin the livelihoods of poor men by playing them off the street. I must assume, monsieur—and your misshappen nose confirms me—that you are some Jew whose lust is for money, and who strides through Avignon with the idea that the protection of the King, the Pope and the Mayor is everything . . ."

Since it is not pleasant to have someone yelling abuse six inches from one's face, Damiano squirmed in his seat, and turned his head to the side. There were so many recriminations in the man's tirade that he could not keep track of them, let alone answer.

And this last, accusing him of being Jewish, was only confusing. In Partestrada there had been no Jews dwelling, but only old Jacob benJacob, who was Swiss as well as Jewish, and who came through once every three-month, selling, among other things, thread. It was from him that Damiano had purchased his first little lute. No one had suggested to him that Jacob was rich.

In Torino there was a Jewish quarter, certainly, and it was also from a Jew that he had purchased the gold-embossed volume of Aquinas which he had given to Carla. This had struck him as odd at the time, since if the man was Jewish he by definition could not be a Christian, and so what was he doing with a book of theology?

But for the most part, Damiano had never thought about the Jews for good or evil.

But his nose, now. He *had* thought about his nose, having at least the average share of vanity. And he had just been congratulating himself at having escaped the physiognomy of Guillermo Delstrego. This was disheartening.

Gazing resolutely across the avenue which was never for a moment empty, and where the Sunday garb of the strollers gave only the slightest nod toward Lenten repentance, he spoke. "Monsieur Guildsmember, you do me wrong. I am not trying to steal the brass sous of the street musicians (although I must say I would not regret them, being not as well paid as you think). I am only practicing, for I must play this evening. You notice no bowl?"

The fellow did not look down, except to spit. "Worse. Who is going to pay for music, if you give it to them for free?"

Damiano's fingers drummed on the spruce face of the lute. He was losing his patience. And where was Gaspare, anyway? Wasn't it a manager's job to keep him from this kind of disturbance?

He searched the street as he replied in his slow, careful langue d'oc, "Monsieur, I do believe it is you who are the mercenary one, for I was sitting here quite content to play for myself, in quiet practice to which no one, as far as I can tell, was listening. And in further answer to you, no, I am not Jewish, though it was necessary for me to learn to read Hebrew as a child, along with a small nibbling of Greek.

But in fact, I have just come from mass, and with the communion in mind I hesitate to trade insults on . . .''

The words froze on Damiano's tongue and his tongue itself clove to the roof of his mouth. For as he stared across the busy street where butchers and bishops came and went, one passerby stopped to stare back at him with the face and hair of Raphael.

Damiano's expression flashed through stages of confusion, welcome and again confusion. The pedestrian stood stock-still. He was dressed in an elegance of gray and scarlet. If only he were closer.

Damiano stood, squinting, and shoved past the belligerent musician. "I . . . I . . . I mean, that is . . .''

And the ruddy, arrogant face came into focus. Satan smiled at Damiano, flourished and bowed, and then disappeared behind a wicker cage on poles filled with chickens and carried by two boys. This utensil swayed by as ponderously as the sedan chair of some dowager, and when the squawking affair had passed, so had the apparition.

Damiano swallowed. "That was . . . someone I know," he whispered, feeling both frightened and foolish. The guildsman then grabbed Damiano by the arm and spun him around. The lute banged alarmingly against the wall.

"You will not ignore me, you black-faced peasant!" the fellow bellowed, and swung his bony fist at Damiano's face.

He ducked, but even before the fist passed above his head the gleaming length of a sharpened halberd sliced the air between them. The guildsman blinked at it, his arm still cocked for the blow. Damiano followed the wood and iron length back to its wielder, the gate guard both musicians had forgotten was there.

"Enough," growled the guard. "No fighting around the Papal Palace. Haven't you any respect for the Holy Father?"

The guildsman evidently did have respect, either for the Holy Father or for the instruments of war, for he backed off, cringing and snarling together, like a dog.

"Hah!" grunted the guard, once he and Damiano were alone. "That was one of the few amusing moments of my day." His weathered blue eyes twinkled down at Damiano, who had sunk strengthless back onto his stool. "That and your pretty playing, of course. Don't mind that fellow. I know him: he's usually here, with a hurdy-gurdy out of tune, playing the same five songs. He's got at least a dozen children, and his wife leaves them with him while she takes in laundry. Quite a racket, they make."

Damiano smiled his gratitude, as he reflected to himself—they protect me. The strangest people protect me: guardsmen, Irishmen, horses. Dogs. Why? And then he thought, The Devil. He is in Avignon. What does that portend?

Gaspare returned in late afternoon, looking worse than ever. Damiano put down the lute. "Where did you go?" he asked, offering the boy some of the bread and dates he had paid a child to buy for him.

Gaspare wanted nothing. "Around. To every other gate into the enclosure. And then to each of the outer gates."

"All around the city?"

The boy threw himself upon the ground against the stucco wall, regardless of his exquisite new mantle. "I thought . . . I thought perhaps we had the place wrong. I wanted to see if they were waiting elsewhere. They weren't."

Damiano said nothing, for there was nothing he could say, except that he had seen Satan on the streets of Avignon. And that was not something Gaspare would want to hear right now. So he spent another hour improvising quietly on the treble strings, and when it could no longer be avoided, he said, "I'll have to go now. I have to work."

Gaspare glanced up at the setting sun and flinched as though he had just received a blow. His arms, nothing but skin, bones and twisted tendon, were wrapped around his knees and he buried his head between them.

Damiano bit down on his lip. Poor child: his sleeves did not come within three inches of his wrists, so fast he had grown in the past winter. Damiano for a moment had the feelings of a father. He put the lute behind his stool and considered what he might say or do to help.

But Gaspare was beyond easy consolation. He rocked stiffly back and forth, his dusty boots soiling the velvet of the cloak. "Perhaps she never reached Avignon," he said in a strangled voice. "Perhaps she has been dead the greater part of a year!"

Damiano grunted. "We have no reason to . . ."

"She is dead! I feel it. I have felt it for a long time!" Now Gaspare raised his head, and, yes, as Damiano suspected, the boy was weeping, reddening his protuberant gooseberry eyes. His nose was as pinched as an old man's, and indeed, Gaspare looked very aged right now, aged and in despair. "She was all I had. All I had. No father, no mother, no name of our own, and she was only a dirty slut, but she was all I had! And now she is dead and I have nothing!"

It was on the tip of Damiano's tongue to say that Gaspare still had him, but that seemed such a conceited thing to say.

Evidently the guard had some Italian, for bending at the waist and pushing his steel helmet back from his forehead, he whispered in Damiano's ear, "What a shame. How did she die?"

"We don't know that she *did* die," hissed the lutenist back. "She simply did not show up for an appointment."

Raphael knew where Evienne was. Damiano was tempted to tell Gaspare as much, to allay his fears. But how could he reveal that, without being therefore obliged to ask the angel for more specific information, which the musician did not want to do. Besides—was Raphael's knowledge a comforting thought after all? The fact that Raphael knew where the girl was did not mean necessarily that she was alive. For all Damiano knew, angels were on close terms with the dead. He remembered the little ghost of Macchiata, half hidden by Raphael's robe, and he decided not to mention Raphael's words to Gaspare.

Damiano crouched down in front of the boy and with both hands forced Gaspare to look at him. "You are being very unreasonable, Gaspare. Think whom we are dealing with. Evienne has no more sense than a kitten—I doubt she even knows how to read a calendar, and Jan . . . well, Jan Karl would not get out of bed to save his mother's life. Not if the bed were comfortable.

"Evienne is not dead; we have merely been stood up."

Sadly Gaspare shook his head, but there were no more hysterics. Damiano left him to keep faith during the last daylight, under the small blue eyes of the interested guard. He ran the whole way back to the Bishop's Inn.

Damiano knew that Coutelan, the innkeeper, did not know what he was saying when he said Damiano had a genius; probably the man didn't know the difference between a genius of the lute and a genie in a lamp. Coutelan only repeated and magnified anything the Irishman said. Mac Whatever, who lived next door and had invested a certain amount of money in the operation of the inn, was his authority.

Which was why Damiano had gotten this job in the first place. It was because he had been seen by the innkeeper exiting the harper's garden in that unorthodox manner. And because he had an accent.

But though Damiano repeated these things to himself, he was still human, and praise could make him drunk. Especially after a long winter and hungry spring. And tonight he had gotten a good dose of it, for MacFhiodhbhuidhe had walked in leading a good ten other men, all musicians, and he had called Damiano his "glorious exception to the rules." The young man had also been bought three glasses of violet wine, which was the harper's favorite but not Damiano's and consequently he now had a fire in his middle and a bad taste in his mouth.

In spite of this, as he wrapped the lute in its baby blanket and strode out into the street toward his poor accommodations, Damiano was singing to himself.

That owl on the wall there, making noise every night. Bothersome as a tomcat: it was a wonder somebody didn't kill the creature with a brick. And what did it find to eat in the stone and stucco city of Avignon?

Damiano, who was not the man to flip a brick at any animal, snapped his fingers and clucked to the bird as he went by. It followed his motion with a head that turned ridiculously far around. Its eyes were two orange full moons, mirroring the one in the sky. He went through the quiet, leather-hinged door.

And then Damiano remembered Gaspare and the sister who hadn't shown up. Queasy pity hit him, making his stomach worse. At least, he hoped, the boy had been able to sleep. Reaching the Heather Inn, he tiptoed down the hall and into the room they shared with four other men. One of them was snoring.

On Gaspare's pallet the clean straw glistened under the

spear of moonlight admitted by the street-facing window. His blankets were lumped beside. There was no Gaspare.

Damiano cursed under his breath. By his own pallet he left the lute, still swaddled, and his lean legs took him out of the room and out of the inn in five strides.

Guilt that has been stored gathers interest, and Damiano was feeling very guilty at leaving Gaspare to wait. He loped the moon-washed, empty streets, stepping silently through long training—his father's training. He imagined Gaspare squatting there by the Papal Palace all evening, as the sun went down and the friendly guard was relieved by another, and the shops closed and the hawkers shut up and slowly all the avenue became still.

While Damiano, who did not really care if Evienne missed the appointment, save for Gaspare's sake, and who did not care for Jan Karl at all, had been playing to a room full of gentlemen, receiving heady praise and sweet wine. Shades of hell, that was a sorry thing, and most especially since Damiano's genius had always been Gaspare's faith, much more than Damiano's, and so the confirmation and the praise rightly belonged to Gaspare.

Above his head Damiano saw the silver white body of the owl float by on noiseless wings. He watched it swoop down upon a roof. Just before it struck it emitted a sharp, predatory cry. It did not reappear.

But then Damiano thought of another explanation for Gaspare's tardiness. Perhaps Evienne *had* come after all, and taken the boy with her to wherever she lived (preferably apart from the Dutchman). That made sense. And of course they would come back for Damiano, sooner or later, after the first flush of reunion was past.

With this conviction, Damiano's feet slowed to a more comfortable pace. He sighed deeply, feeling some great crisis had been only just averted. He strolled as far as the Pope's Door, to see whether they'd left any message.

There was the high, Gothic-arched gate, with a glistening sentry at either side, behind an avenue that the full moon made look decently clean. And there, like a bundle of rags beside the right-hand pikeman, was the huddled shape Damiano had decided would not be there. And because he had decided this halfway between the inn and the Pope's Door, Damiano was not prepared for the sight.

"Mother of God!" he whispered to the moonlight. "He

is there. What on earth am I to do about this?" And he came to a stop, still a hundred feet away from the pathetic thing in the green velvet mantle. "What on earth *can* I do?"

And worldly fame turned to ashes in Damiano's soul. He turned on his heel and ran away, down the first, random crooked street he came to, fleeing because he could not meet the boy he had no way to help.

But had he no way? Raphael had said he knew where Evienne was, and would tell him at need. But he had also said there were other ways he could find out. There were, of course. If he were a witch he could find the girl, just as a hound could find her, given time enough.

If he were a witch.

Well, for God's sake, why not?

Because of his music? Hell and damn. What did it matter if he was the smoothest and most intellectual lutenist in all Provence and Italy? Was it important that ten men with reputations came to judge him as though he were a prize cow, while they ate pastries and talked musical philosophy? (While inside he nursed a slight contempt, knowing he was better than they.) Someday, then, he could be five and forty years old, and sit judging the young whose reputation is still to be made, secretly afraid that they might be better than he. Afraid they might be nursing a slight contempt.

Damiano then remembered the little tunes Raphael delighted to play: children's pieces without ornament or heterophony, and how the angel's head bent over Damiano's instrument, lost in simple melody, far beyond self.

Tears stung his eyes, and his stomach hurt like sin.

For what reason, besides devotion to the lute, had he refused his powers, when pressed by Saara? He had told her he was afraid his magic would hurt people.

It *had* hurt people. He'd killed at least fifty men with a force of terror one winter's day in the Alps. Perhaps he also saved that many, or five times that many, by circumventing a battle between Savoy and the *condottiere* General Pardo. But one was never sure about saving men, while killing them was incontrovertible.

And Gaspare was hurting already: hurting in a way that only magic could help. And of all the people in the world, Gaspare had most claim on him.

So all his reasons, musical and magical, were empty. In

fact, what did it matter whether it was wise or foolish, saintly or sinful, for him to deny his witchhood?

What did Damiano matter at all? He had mattered too much to himself in the past year. Gaspare—loyal and uneducated, without philosophy, lost in the sea of his own sorrow—mattered. He had to be helped.

His feet raced on for another half-block, almost of their own accord. He passed a man who was casually pissing out of a ground-floor window. The white owl circled overhead, silent as any of the planets. When he finally stopped he realized that this decision carried him no closer toward a solution to Gaspare's problem.

For Saara held Damiano's witch-soul within her own, and Saara had said goodbye to him. Not *arrivederci*, or *au revoir*, or any other of the thousand ways to say she would see him later. She had been angry and had said goodbye. By now she was in Lombardy.

She could not be expected to come to him again.

The weariness of the long day descended on Damiano then, and he leaned upon the nearest wall for support. It was a dirty wall, stucco and timber like all the rest in Avignon. There was a bestial roar and a thud. The wall itself trembled and Damiano snatched back his hand.

Bandog. Mastiff. He backed away and for the first time looked about him at the sagging, dilapidated rowhouses, and the cobbles mired with human filth. He had not previously seen this side of life in the Papal city. He found himself standing in the exact middle of the street, scanning the shadows for movement. He feared thieves.

What a difference in fortune a week can make, he thought. I might have been lurking in the shadows myself. Slowly he turned on his heel and departed the way he had come, accompanied by the barking of the mastiff and the silent white owl.

He must try. Though Saara might refuse him, though she would certainly laugh at the way he was denying all his carefully thought-out reasons for remaining simple, still he must make the effort.

If he could remember how.

There—that silver strip against the hill with the river beyond—that was the wall of the enclosure. There stood the pikemen. There sat Gaspare, beneath his weight of fear. It was try now or never.

Damiano came to an ancient grapevine trained into an espalier. The wood was heavy, the burgeoning leaves few. The dirt of the city had half killed it and age was completing the rest of the task, but it was yet alive, and its leaves rustled as he laid his face against its trellised surface. He took comfort from the strength of wood as he tried to remember.

It was difficult—difficult and painful as well, for he no longer trusted the torn vacancies of his mind where he had slept away a year. He clung in fear to the smell of furry grape leaves, to the rough brush of bark, to the sound of the hooting owl. He could not let go.

Damiano began to sweat with effort. It seemed he had lost the art of withdrawing which had protected him since losing his powers, and which had once taken him to Lombardy, to the garden of the witch.

Would he need someone with a cat-o'-nine-tails, to whip him into remembering? "Saara," he whispered, and he closed his eyes. "Saara."

But in his mind's eye he saw not the winterless, stream-broken garden. Not the goat with flowers around her rusty neck. Not the fairy shape in a blue dress embroidered with stars. He saw the human woman's form: naked, hot against him.

"Yes," she whispered to him. "Yes, Damiano. I am here."

He heard clearly but he saw nothing except the red darkness behind his closed eyes. He opened them to find Saara standing before him on the cobbled street of Avignon.

He felt as he had sometimes in the past when riding—when Festilligambe came to a sudden stop and he almost did not. The world lurched, and he put out his hand to brace himself. But there was nothing to hold on to except Saara, so he took her firmly by the wrist.

Her eyes narrowed at his astonishment. "What is wrong, Dami? You called me, didn't you? You are still calling me; I can hear it."

As he straightened he dropped her wrist. "You are here. You are not in Lombardy."

And as she said nothing in reply, he added, "Why?"

There was no expression in the witch's face as she answered, "I don't know if I could have gone far, Damiano.

Not after . . . last week. My strength is half yours—more than half yours, I think—and it wars against me. But anyway I did not want to go, for I was afraid for you."

"For me?" he echoed. "You feared I might do myself harm?"

She shrugged an Italian shrug. (Had she learned it from Ruggerio the Roman? From Damiano's father?) "I have pain, young one. Like I was having a baby and the head would not come out. For you it cannot be any better."

He said nothing.

"Why did you do it, Damiano?" she continued. "To throw me away like that. In my long life I have never been treated so."

Damiano's eyebrows disappeared underneath his hair. "I—why did I . . . ? Saara, it was a dirty trick you played me, leading me to think you wanted . . ." He took a deep breath. "I don't think I want to talk about it," he said.

The Fenwoman had taken a step backward, and her stomach tightened with a miserable understanding. "You thought I wanted you only to be rid of the burden I am carrying? That is dreadful. It is not true. I will carry it until I die rather than have you believe that."

"No," answered Damiano in a voice that sounded foreign to himself. "No. I need it back now." And as Saara stared, openmouthed, he added, "I need to be a witch again. Tonight."

The moonlight (and only the moonlight) streaked Saara's hair with gray. She stood in an oddly formal pose, her hands cupping her elbows and her bare feet gripping the cobbles.

"You do? Tonight?"

He nodded. "It is not my need but Gaspare's. His sister is missing, and I need full sight to find her for him."

One of the woman's hands crawled toward a hanging braid. White fingers clawed into the hair, tangling it. Saara glanced from the foul street to the eaves of the crowding buildings. She did not look at Damiano. From far away, the bark of the bandog could still be heard. "It would be easier if I found the girl," she suggested.

Damiano shook his head and, leaning against the ancient grapevine, he slid down till he sat on his heels. "I thought of that, Saara," he admitted. "I also asked Raphael's help, when I first knew there was going to be a

problem. But he told me to look elsewhere before asking
him to do what he should not do—and since then I have
had to think about what I am asking of everyone."

Saara squatted beside him, her toes splayed out before
her like those of a frog. "More thinking, Dami? You think
too much, I think."

Though her words were friendly, he ignored them. "I
need witchcraft, or at least 'sight,' to find Evienne before
Gaspare throws himself in the Rhone, or sickens with grief.
If I use your skills just because I don't want the responsibility, then I have done the deed and yet tried to evade the
price, don't you see? And we both know that does not
work, in witchcraft or in life."

Still she did not meet his eyes.

"Saara. What is it? Don't you want me to take back
that . . . that illegitimate baby that confused Gaspare so
much?"

This pulled a smile from her, and a quick green glance
that made it hard for Damiano to swallow. "No," she
replied. "Now that the moment comes, I do not. A person
gets used to being the way she is."

Then she reached toward him, a flame of concentration
on her face. "Here, Damiano. Take my hand. Quickly."

He obeyed, but his black eyes darted up and down the
cobblestones. "Here? In the middle of the street?"

Saara giggled. She seemed herself again. "All *that* is not
necessary, Dami. Nice, but not necessary." She squeezed
his hand roughly and leaned forward, placing her other
palm against the young man's forehead. "Only remember,"
she whispered.

Saara's touch was warm; that itself was easily remembered. And with that warmth came other memories from
beneath the blankets in the old wagon: the mouse in the
woodwork, the mole beneath the grass, the planets circling
(each with its name, each with its song), the lake of fire
which somehow came not out of hell. The corona that lit
each living thing from within, and arcing green flame of its
extinction. The touch of human presence, like a feather
against his face.

Hermes Trismegistus, Albertus Magnus, the broken
black staff, taller than his body, banded with silver,
crowned with red and gold, through which once (as
though it were a great flute) he'd played the wind of his
will.

Once, only two years ago, he'd played that music better than he played the lute.

Damiano remembered, completely and without violence to body or mind, all he was born to be.

His blood was singing like a chorus. He felt the hard, rounded stones beneath him, and recognized that they had been pulled from the Rhone. He heard the bandog, and a hundred other hounds crying, droning, quarreling or snoring through the city of Avignon. He heard that segment of the human population which was awake at this hour; they sounded much like the dogs.

As a man orients himself in time by glass or sundial, he felt (with his tongue against the roof of his mouth) for the hour by the position of the heavens.

And in the next street he heard the sorrow-clogged breathing of Gaspare, who had fallen asleep against the Holy Father's wall.

Damiano opened his eyes and was forced to squint against the glare of the moonlight off white walls. Saara's face, too, appeared bleached and colorless. The fingers of her left hand, which had held his, hung limply.

"You are weary," he whispered, and helped her to her feet.

"Of course I am. Not you?" Saara disengaged herself from his arms. She inspected Damiano minutely and impersonally: head, hands and booted feet. "You are not tired, nor sick?" With a proprietary shove she turned him completely around.

He submitted to these attentions with the docility of a child. "I feel," he announced, "as though I will never be weary again. Nor sick."

Saara smiled wanly. One of her braids was completely undone and hung in waves, like falling water. She looked pale and thin and, despite her height, frail. Damiano could see a pulse pounding in the hollow at the base of her neck. "Good. Then it has been worth all the mice and rats."

"All the what?"

Saara seemed to feed off Damiano's confusion. The sly smile returned to her mouth, and color to her cheeks. "Mice and rats. I had to eat something in Avignon, you know. Since, as you say, these people will not feed a stranger."

Damiano felt obscurely guilty, as well as revolted. "Mice and rats? Surely, Saara, if you had let me know . . ."

Saara giggled then, lifted one leg cranelike, and (since her braid was pulled apart) nibbled on one twisted lock of hair. "It is not so bad, if you are an owl."

"An owl? You are the bird that has been ruining my sleep since I have been in Avignon?" Her grin spread to Damiano's face. He snatched Saara off her feet, knocking the breath out of her as he spun her around. "Not a fox and an owl, too? Saara. You should be nothing but my little dove!" Her bare heel knocked against the gnarled trunk of the vine. With an apology Damiano put her down.

Forcefully she pulled away. "It is good you feel so strong, fellow. But you must be careful; you don't know what you are doing, now. You are like a baby."

"A baby?" Even moonlight could not steal the warmth from Damiano's olive countenance. As Saara spoke he closed the gap she had made between them and embraced her again. He kissed her on the cheek, the chin, the side of her neck. Her skin tingled his lips and tasted like wine. "How a baby? I have been a witch all my life, minus only one year and a little bit, and the whole time has been spent in study. I studied," he declared fervently, "until my brains began to curdle."

Then Saara sighed, and the irritation in that single sound chastened Damiano completely. He took a step backward and let her continue. "You were a witch whose magic was locked within a stick. You lost both magic and stick. Now you have had the magic back for two minutes, and already you have both bruised my foot and made me angry."

"I'm sorry," he said, and through the glow of his exaltation remorse did seem to be working. "I was just a little drunk with . . . being able to see and hear. I will be a gentleman from now on."

Saara muttered something he was not meant to hear. It might have been "Too bad." Then she spoke aloud.

"You will be all right, Damiano. Come with me and I will teach you to sing-spell. You will be very good at it, I am sure, having made so much music of the simple kind."

He broke out in surprised laughter. "Simple? My music—simple? Well, each to his own opinion, my lady." But his antic mood softened again. "Saara, Saara, I will most willingly come under your tutelage. (There is at least one lesson between us still incomplete.) But till Good

Friday my time belongs to Bernard Coutelan and the Bishop's Inn. I must remain a baby that long."

"Then until Friday I must eat mice and rats," interjected the Fenwoman, and for a moment her eyes went round, bright, orange and moonlike. Damiano sputtered with laughter.

"No, my lady. Return to the Heather Inn with me and eat like a burgher, if not a queen."

Saara made a prim little grimace. "That place? I have sat in their courtyard every night, watching men and women make their beds in straw a reindeer would not touch. The fleas, mice and bedbugs have an easier life than the people."

Damiano shrugged. "That is an inn. I have been in much worse."

Saara wound her fingers in Damiano's coarse hair. She drew him to her for one more slow, thoughtful kiss. "I would rather eat rats than have them run over me.

"Friday," she added. Then with an odd, almost angry look upon her face, Saara shrank into a white pillow of feathers, orange-eyed. This flew onto Damiano's shoulder where the outsized talons pricked his skin. Then she hooted maliciously into his ear and rose into the sky on soft, shrouded wings.

CHAPTER 8

When Gaspare was awakened, his first thought was that the deep, commanding voice belonged to the Holy Father's pikeman, or some troublesome soldier whose job it was to keep poor souls from cluttering the streets of Avignon. But the hand that reached down to take his was lean, calloused and very familiar, and when Gaspare raised his head . . .

"By Saint Gabriele, Damiano," the redhead hissed, "the moon in your eyes made me half frightened of you!" Then as the boy locked his knees in the upright position and freed his hand from the lutenist's grip, he remembered why he had fallen asleep at the Pope's Door.

"Oh, Christ, sheep-face. She never came. I will never see my whore of a sister again."

Damiano let the nickname pass. His wide drunken eyes stared from Gaspare to the swarthy face of the night gate guard, and across the wide avenue to where hundreds of black holes in pale walls revealed the sounds and smells of human sleep. His left hand was twitching like a small animal. Once more he snagged Gaspare.

"If Evienne and Jan are in Avignon, we will find them tonight," said Damiano with sweeping confidence. "Come, little dear," he added. "Start walking."

Gaspare's offense at being addressed as "little dear" was drowned completely in his amazement at the rest of Damiano's behavior. He found himself dragged along the wide street, his eyes still grainy from sleep, his long mantle flapping behind.

If the Damiano of the past year had been unaccountable . . . if the Damiano of the past few weeks had been enough to make Gaspare tread warily . . . this new Damiano was an Act of God. He strode through the empty streets like the conqueror Alexander, his black eyes flashing, his rather large nose turned arrogant by the force of authority in the shaggy head. Though the night was chill, and Gaspare suffered despite his velvet cloak, the hand that held his was warm—warm like beach sand in the sun.

At the first corner, an abrupt change of direction nearly popped the boy's arm from its socket. "What are we doing?" he yelled in protest. Half a dozen dogs were set off by the noise. "How are we going to find her this way? I have been up and down these streets every day for a week; she's not to be found."

Damiano looked back over his shoulder. "If she's not here, Gaspare, then we won't find her. Otherwise we will."

"How?" demanded the boy, pulling free with great effort.

Damiano smiled mildly enough, though his eyes were still dangerous. "I will feel her presence. I am a witch again, Gaspare. I will know."

Gaspare felt a sinking in his heart, though he would have thought it impossible for him to get any lower. "Oh, no, Damiano. Not that again."

The dark eyes flickered with irritation and Damiano

raised his hand. For a moment Gaspare believed he was going to hit him, but then from Damiano's outspread fingers five points of flame sprang up.

Gaspare staggered back.

"Not a Hand of Glory," whispered Damiano. "But my own." He laughed at the boy's goggle eyes and general air of amazement, but as he did so the tame, domestic fire in his hand leaped upward like the flame of a torch dipped in oil. He shook it out.

"Needs practice," he muttered, slightly shamefaced, and then cleared his throat. "So you see, Gaspare . . ."

"Don't hurt me," the redhead blurted, stepping still farther back.

As the flame had gone out from Damiano's hand, so now it went out from his face. With almost a look of suffering, the witch replied, "Hurt you, Gaspare? No. All of this is particularly to avoid your hurt. And I am only the same fellow you befriended in the market of San Gabriele, who knew how to disappear, but not how to make a broken florin. But enough time for talk after we find Evienne." Without putting his hand upon the plainly frightened boy, he turned again and strode off down a side street, his lips parted, his face to the wind like that of a hound.

The city of Avignon existed because of the Rhone. Both the secular city and the city which was the Papal Palace crowded the water's edge. But while the stone and stucco of the ecclesiastical center sat on a prominence from which garbage was piped into a river that was not even seen, the burghers built their jumbled houses in intimate contact with the mud. Damiano saw parts of the city that night which he might never have seen otherwise: not though he had lived in Avignon for years. And had he been a simple man, he could not have seen what he saw at all.

The houses of Avignon were not jammed with residents, despite the way they crowded together on the occluded streets. Some of them had no more than a single sleeper breathing within. Yet it was not a city of the rich, to be sure. Poverty had its own odor, and it was stronger and less mistakable than any expensive perfume. Damiano smelled poverty and rotting fish on the mud flats of the city.

"There are three men sleeping under that boat," he observed to Gaspare as they hurried by a small neighborhood wharf.

"Men?" repeated Gaspare. "Not Evienne." He stopped to stare.

Damiano frowned. "Not Evienne. I just thought it worth mentioning. There are also people sleeping beneath the stilts of these waterside houses. What they do when the river runs high I don't know."

Damiano tilted his face to the sky and stood silent for a moment, as though he were reading something. Then he looked behind him, to where Gaspare still wandered on the dried mud by the boat dock. The boy had his arms out stiffly before him. "Gaspare," he called quietly, "what are you doing?"

Gaspare was startled, hearing his guide so far away. "Heh! Damiano. I can't find you. I can't find anything."

The witch covered the ground between them in three strides. "What's the matter, Gaspare? The moon is full. Are you night-blind?"

The boy caught his arm and stared with goblin eyes. "Night-blind? I don't know. What does it matter? Lately I have taken to sleeping at night, you know." The arm beneath his pulled him away from the river once more.

"Damiano, where are you taking us?"

"Everywhere."

"It will be easier for me to find Jan Karl," murmured Damiano, talking for Gaspare's sake. "I have this little knife in my belt, with which I cut off two of his fingers. Did he ever tell you about that?"

"Yes" was the short reply. Gaspare was stumbling and out of patience. Then he remembered more.

"He told a weird story. He said you got him drunk and then cut his fingers off in some kind of magic rite."

"They were infected," replied Damiano with some reproach in his words. "Gangrenous. Did he not tell you that?"

"No."

Damiano sighed. "He was grateful at the time. I would not have done it for fun, I assure you, and especially would not have sacrificed all my supply of wine to play an ugly trick on a Dutchman. Didn't he ever mention his night in the snow?"

"Certainly. He was benighted in the Alps in November and nearly froze."

Damiano smiled grimly. It was on his tongue to explain to Gaspare how Jan Karl's two roving companions had tried to kill Damiano, and but for the fierce (and loquacious) bitch Macchiata would have succeeded. It was Damiano's dog that had driven the thieves out into the Alpine winter and thereby frozen Jan's fingers.

It was a wonder the Dutchman hadn't found some way to turn that story on its head and present it to Gaspare as an example of Damiano's perfidy and his own innocence. Damiano was liking him less and less as time went on.

And for that reason he did not speak. Why impress upon the distracted boy that his sister was off with a lout of such repulsive character, now that it was too late for Gaspare to do anything but worry?

They ran on together: Gaspare through empty streets, Damiano buffeted by the presence of thousands. Fifty thousand had Avignon before the great pest. At least half had died. Now the city had begun to swell toward its former size.

Damiano fingered his little knife as he jogged along. He sang wordlessly under his breath, both his own tunes and those he was picking up daily from MacFhiodhbhuidhe. Meanwhile, through his mind was running a different sort of melody: a tune which, like the music of Raphael, could find no expression in the hands or voice of man. Just now he was not trying to express the music in his mind; it was expressing him.

Never grow weary. Nor sick. He felt like a scrap of paper in the draft of a chimney, flaming and floating, weightless.

But Gaspare was wheezing like a wind-broken horse. The boy had started at a disadvantage, under a debility of sorrow. Now, as they watched a lone man in white—a baker—trudge toward his work with lantern in hand, Gaspare was near spent.

He pulled down on his friend's arm. He sat in the street, miring his mantle further, and without words he shook his head.

Damiano put one hand on the boy's head, which was sweaty. He did not attempt persuasion. Instead he said, "You'll cool down fast. Take my overshirt."

Gaspare peered up incredulously as Damiano yanked the red-and-gold tunic over his head. "You didn't like it when I took your shirt before," he panted. "And why should I have both overshirt and mantle and leave you in your linen?" Yet he took the tunic from Damiano, who paced in circles, toying with the sliver of silver and crystal in his hand.

"Because you are going to be cold and I am not," the witch replied. "Not tonight." Damiano whined—again like a hound. "I keep thinking about that no-good. I feel we are close."

"Don't call my sister a no-good," growled Gaspare sullenly. He was not offended enough to get up.

Damiano smiled with all his teeth. "Why not? You call her much worse. But I was not referring to little Evienne, of course, but to Jan Karl. It is as though I can hear him talking in my mind. Or snoring, maybe."

Gaspare peered around him. "Well, my dear old sheep—uh, Damiano, I don't know what you see or hear, and I myself can hardly see my hand before my face, but I have a funny feeling we're back where we started, having covered Avignon with a layer of shoe leather."

Damiano glanced at the open mouth of the Pope's Door without surprise. "That's exactly what we have done, though to be sure we haven't covered but half the city. We've been by this spot four times, and do you know it is always here that I begin to simmer inside about the Dutchman. I think we'll find him on the other side of that wall."

Gaspare glowered from Damiano to the gate and back again. Exhaustion gave birth to scorn. "Maybe Jan's been elected Pope, eh?"

Damiano was too intent to rise to the bait. "He started out as a cleric, Gaspare, right here in Avignon. Do not forget that. Though he may be a thief and a procurer in other lands, behind those walls he will be remembered as student and lector of the church." Damiano sighed. "I've wasted time. We should have started looking in the Papal Palace."

The boy scooted around on his behind until he also was peering through the darkness toward the looming white hill of the Pope. "Great," he grunted. "We'll just walk up to the pikeman there and announce that we must enter in order to search for a prostitute and a pimp." Then he turned on Damiano a glare that was hard with disappointment. "Shall I go first or would you like that honor?"

Damiano was chewing on his lip. "That method might have had a chance while the big blond was at the gate, although even then . . . Now, I think, we shall have to resort to skill."

"Over the wall?" suggested Gaspare with a glimmer of professional interest.

Damiano chuckled in his throat, and there was behind that laugh a feral arrogance that Gaspare did not associate with the lutenist. "No, Gaspare. A different sort of skill."

He crouched down next to the boy. "Don't you remember the ducks' eggs and the peasant's house south of Lyons? How Saara took us in and out unnoticed?"

"Saara isn't here," said Gaspare unnecessarily.

Damiano pulled him to his feet. "We don't need the lady. Invisibility used to be a specialty of my own, remember, and I don't feel that I've lost any of my ability. Watch."

And Damiano sorted himself out for the effort. Within his head, behind closed eyes, he allowed the world of stone and night air to penetrate, so that his body would be no obstruction: not to air, sound or moonlight. It was a pleasant discipline while in process, and only tended to weary him afterward.

Out of habit he reached for something—for his staff, which was a focus for his power and his intent. His hands touched only Gaspare.

He jerked back. God knows what would happen, either to the boy or to the spell, if he tried to use a human being like the wooden length of a staff. He had no staff and would simply have to do without.

The spell was familiar, and he certainly hadn't lost any of his ability. He felt the scattered moonlight, heavy as mist, penetrate the borders of his body. Shape fell away. And thought.

Very pleasant.

There was commotion and someone flailing about in the street. Gaspare was shouting his name in a whisper. "Damiano! Damiano! Where have you gone?"

The boy crashed right into him and took him by the shoulders. "You stupid sheep-face! Where by the sufferings of hell have you been for a quarter-hour?"

Damiano cleared his throat. He could not rouse an anger to match Gaspare's. "Ho. Nowhere, I guess." he scratched his head with both hands.

"You know, Gaspare, not to be—I mean, to be *not*, you know, is not bad at all. I don't mean not to be born, of course, but rather . . . Never mind." Damiano shook his head forcefully to clear out the moonlight, and returned to the work at hand.

"Well. I'll have to make some changes in the way I do things, I see. I need a tool. If I can't use a staff, like a respectable magician, I'll do like Saara."

Gaspare frowned dubiously. "Are you going to make up bad verse now?"

Damiano turned his head and struck a belligerent attitude toward the gleaming hill of the Pope. "I am," he declared.

> "We pass beneath the arched gate.
> Unperceived. No blade will strike . . ."

They were right under the door, with the black iron portcullis raised above their heads. Damiano stopped to stare and his concentration faltered. (Strike. What rhymes with strike? Dike, like, pike . . .)

> "And leaning is the sentry's pike
> Against the wall. The hour is late."

If they were challenged, thought Gaspare, they would simply plead innocence. For there they were parading openly through an open gate, with guards at either hand. It was not like being caught climbing a wall. If they were challenged . . .

They were not challenged.

> "So quiet are the cobbled streets
> Where the Holy Father sleeps,
> Or his prayer vigil keeps
> That . . ."

Streets. What rhymes with streets? Sheets (terrible). Sweets. (Worse. Oh, God!) Beats?

"That one can hear his slow heartbeats."

The doorway loomed deep in shadow. Damiano
plunged in, dragging Gaspare behind him. Once concealed, he began to blow like a winded horse. "That," he
wheezed, "was awful. Hideous."

Gaspare's hand made an equivocal gesture, unseen
even by the witch in the dark of the overhang. "Oh, I don't
know. I think it was much better than Saara's. The ABBA
rhyme has more subtlety than . . ."

Damiano snorted. "I'm not working in a foreign language. But it was terrible, nonetheless. I thought I would
be found standing there under the portcullis, mouth open,
knees knocking, and all for lack of a rhyme. There's got to
be another way to work it."

This was what people meant all over Europe, when
they spoke the word "Avignon." It was a single building
and an entire city as well: the Holy Father's city. Damiano
and Gaspare passed sedately down its passages, expecting
to be impressed.

First glance was a little disappointing, for the nearest
hall was a rather musty library of no great size.

"I've seen better," murmured Gaspare. Being illiterate,
he wasted no time staring at the books.

"Oh? Where?" replied his friend absently. "In San
Gabriele?" But even his interest faded when he discovered
that the library specialized in canonical law.

The chambers beyond were plain but serviceable.
Damiano fingered his little knife as he went. Jan Karl was
not too near.

"I don't think, after all, that we entered by the main
gate," he remarked to Gaspare after a minute. "For these
seem to be little-used offices. Perhaps it was we who
missed the rendezvous."

"Nope. I ran circles around the building," grunted
Gaspare. "She wasn't anywhere."

Turning a corner, they came upon a region where the
passages were broader and admitted more moonlight.
"How straight the walls are," murmured Damiano. "Look
at them. It is hard to believe this whole enclosure is only
one enormous building."

"That doesn't give me any trouble," replied Gaspare,

whose ignorance of engineering principles made him blasé. "But what gets me is that there's no smell of shit anywhere."

"I've read that there are tubes in the rooms and one can piss into them and it travels all the way down to the Rhone," commented the lutenist. "Very civilized."

"Oh, I dunno. Must make the river stink. Is that any better?"

Damiano could not answer this question. He did not try, actually, for he had found a door with light behind it, and very carefully he was opening it.

Here was a courtyard, larger than many large houses, and soon the pair of intruders stood beside a massive pile of stone carved with bulge-headed dolphins, spouting thin streams of water into the velvet night. Damiano's hand rested on his little knife and his lips moved soundlessly.

Gaspare put his hand on his friend's arm, for the moon was setting and the dolphins' faces bore a monstrous cast. "What is it, Damiano?"

"I . . . I am annoyed. Really annoyed," was the reply. "Though I can't think why. And therefore I think Jan Karl is near." He pointed toward a high, brass-doored entryway on the far side of the court. "Through there, in fact."

Gaspare followed the dim finger. He trembled appreciably. "There? That is where the Holy Father lives, I am told."

"Ah?" Damiano lifted his eyes to the bulk of the building. The palace appeared heavy, squat, ungainly from within. He felt the presence of humanity beating against his face like the heat of a hearth. Which of these sleeping souls was the Holy Father himself? No way to tell. "Well, it could very well be," he assented. "Good for Heer Karl. I always knew he had it in him. Of course it may be he is merely robbing the rooms of his superiors. Let's go find him."

Closing his eyes, he prepared the beginning of his song.

"Through the palace now we tread . . ."

And then he stopped. "No," announced Damiano to the darkened dolphin court. "No more of that."

He began to improvise a lullaby: wordless, full of

ornament and with a tune that wandered. He sang high in
his nose, almost at a whisper, like a mother with a baby
who was already asleep. Gaspare strained his ears to hear.

Damiano took Gaspare by the hand. He touched the
brass door and found it unlocked. Together they entered.

Here the windows were shuttered against the night air.
Into unbroken blackness Damiano introduced fire: a tame
blaze which he held in his hands and stroked. The walls
danced and then revealed themselves to the intruder's
eyes.

Perhaps this was the Holy Father's wing of the palace,
but evidently he didn't reside on the ground floor, for there
were no hangings or rugs, though the hall was of marble.
Thoughtfully Damiano latched the door behind them. "No
use inviting thieves," he whispered, and then gestured up
the large staircase which stood before them. "He's up
there."

"You are so sure?" hissed Gaspare, clinging very closely
to the taller man.

"I am," replied Damiano lightly, and led him up the
steps.

The palace made no sense to Gaspare, but then he was
at a disadvantage, being largely in the dark and quite
terrified besides. He followed Damiano from one cold
length of passage to the next, his normally quick feet made
clumsy by the hour. He watched the tiny tendrils of flame
wrap themselves around his friend's fingers; Damiano's
face was lit satanically from below.

But it did not look satanic. That was Gaspare's sole
comfort. His good friend looked both cheerful and interested, and darted from passage to passage with the
confidence of a man who has finished a long strange
journey and reached neighborhoods he knows very well.

And Damiano sang as they went: sang, hummed and
even whistled a snatch of his tune which bounced from
wall to wall of the huge, frescoed chamber they were
passing through. Gaspare yawned, though whether it was
Damiano's lullaby or his own long sad day making him
sleepy he could not tell.

"I would like very much to see the Pope," said the
musician to Gaspare, standing beneath a dome of blue and
gold. He extended his arms, allowing the flame to crawl up

both to the elbow, the better to examine the architecture. "Wouldn't you?"

"Not under these c-c-circumstances," replied Gaspare, whose teeth chattered despite the wool and velvet. "Can't we hurry, please?"

Lowering his eyes from the painted grandeur, Damiano obediently strode on.

The black wood doors were plain along this wall: like what one imagined of the rooms of vowed religious. But still by their spacing the doors said that these were not poor quarters inside, and the wall itself was inset with parquetry. Damiano stopped and leaned against the stone, sighing.

"We're lost?" quavered Gaspare, drawing his cloak around him.

"No," whispered the witch. "We're not lost. He's found. Jan Karl. He's within."

His was an unfortunate head for a tonsure, being pointed slightly off-center. That head and the drawn, ascetic face below it were all that was visible of Karl, poking out of a roll of soft blankets on a bed with sheets.

"Nice situation," mouthed Gaspare to Damiano, who was singing and therefore could not reply. The witch fed his pet flame to a candle, then shook his hand out. He knelt tenderly down beside the sleeper.

Oddly enough, it was when Damiano stopped his singing that Jan Karl awoke, to see figures standing over him by the light of his own devotional candle. Before he could open his mouth Damiano had clamped a hand on it.

"Early for matins, I know," he whispered cheerily into the man's ear. "But after all, it *is* Holy Week."

Jan gurgled, and when Damiano brought the candle close to his own dark face (the flame touched the skin) and to Gaspare's (he was more careful) the Dutchman seemed in no way reassured. His deep-set blue eyes shifted warily and his swaddled form thrashed about.

"No fear, Jan," crooned Damiano. He removed his hand. "It was only that I did not want you to wake your saintly neighbors in your surprise at seeing us."

Gaspare was standing behind Damiano. He pushed forward. "Where's my sister?" he demanded. "Why weren't you at the Pope's Door, like you said you would be?"

Karl sat up, dragging his blankets with him against the night chill of the stone walls. "Gaspare," he began in his wretched Italian. "And Delstrego, of course. I did not forget our appointment. No, not at all. But there is a story behind that . . ."

"Evienne!" spat the boy. "Tell me now. Is she alive or dead?"

Karl raised his hands to his head in a gesture of horror which turned into an admonition for Gaspare to be quiet. "She is alive, of course, and may Christ preserve her in health."

"Where? Where is she?" pressed the boy with unabated volume. Jan Karl turned to Damiano as the more sensible member of the pair. "We cannot talk here," he said. "Let us meet someplace later."

Damiano smiled beatifically. "I'm afraid later may lead to another story, Jan. Let us go someplace else and talk now."

The blond head (bald in the middle) shook from side to side. "No. Impossible. I'd never get out of this building unnoticed."

The dark musician rolled a little ball of blue fire between his hands. He squatted convivially next to Karl and showed the trick to him. "Oh, yes, you will," he whispered. "You'll be surprised at how easy it is."

And again he began to sing.

They sat like three rocks on the stone step of the dolphin fountain, under cover of the plash of water. Jan Karl was in the middle, with Gaspare and Damiano crowding him close on each side. Both Gaspare and Karl, wrapped in wool, shivered in the predawn chill. Damiano, who shone like a ghost in his white linen undershirt, felt not the cold at all.

"You have to understand," repeated the Dutchman for the third time, "it has been a year. Things change in a year."

"Things change in a day—in a minute," replied Damiano. "Gaspare cannot forget it has been a year since you left with his sister."

"Where is she?" One of Gaspare's bony hands flexed painfully on Karl's thigh, causing the cleric to wince. "In a single word, you can say it."

Karl stared peevishly at the boy. "At Cardinal Rocault's great house. There. I've given you five words. Are you any the wiser?"

"Explain," suggested Damiano, and he dealt Karl a comradely blow upon the shoulder, using a hand from which fire only lightly flickered.

Jan turned on him between fear and anger. "Delstrego, you have it in you to be a real bully, do you know that?"

Damiano only smiled.

"This child's poor sinful sister has had the spiritual elevation of finding a place in the household of a very important man, in the cardinal. I rejoice in her good fortune."

Though Jan was speaking Italian, not French, it took Gaspare a few seconds to translate. "In the household of a cardinal? What is she doing for this cardinal—scrubbing pots?"

The Dutchman tried vainly to hide his smile. "I think her position is more delicate than that." He smirked.

Damiano blinked at Karl as earnestly as a dog. "Cardinals are all very old men, are they not, Jan?"

The grin on the Dutchman's wide mouth grew and grew, but it didn't change his blue stone eyes. "Some are, some are not. Cardinal Rocault, for instance . . ."

"Yes. It is about him I ask."

"He is not an old man at all. But very learned." The Dutchman's smile went out. "And powerful."

Gaspare took some time digesting this information. "My sister," he began at last, "has attained to high position?"

"High position?" Jan considered. "You could say so. A position under the cardinal, anyway."

Once more, he cringed away from the witch's licking flames.

"I have some authority," he stated, his face expressionless, though his eyes sought back and forth to see what effect his words had. "I translate when necessary from the Dutch and German. I manage the Holy Father's ordinary dinners occasionally. I have been able to find work for . . . friends."

"My sister's work," grumbled Gaspare, feeling that the conversation was departing from its proper channels. "Did you find that for her?"

The Dutchman opened his cold-sea eyes very wide and innocent. "I did, though I did not know the trouble it would cause."

Damiano broke in. "You mean, you did not know that the cardinal would become enamored of Evienne?"

Jan's long face grew wry. "I didn't know that the cardinal would become enamored of the Papacy. That is the problem between Evienne and myself. And—that is why I had to miss our appointment today.

"Yesterday, rather," he corrected himself, gazing with obvious forbearance at the black heavens.

There was puzzled silence from his two listeners. Jan pulled the foot of Gaspare's mantle over his knees and elaborated further. "Cardinal Rocault, you ought to know, expects the Holy Father to die at any time. He is an old man, and not very sound, and Rocault helped elect him, judging that Innocent would live just long enough for his own campaign to come to fruition.

"Well, how long has it been? Six years? Six years of Innocent VI, and the old fellow is in better health than when he started. All the world knows that Rocault is getting impatient."

Damiano's eyes were more earnestly doglike than before. "Are you saying, Jan, that Cardinal Rocault has designs upon the life of the Holy Father?"

Karl recoiled against a stone dolphin. "I did not say that, did I?"

"But it seemed to be your meaning."

"Seeming and meaning are free, Delstregó," pronounced the Dutchman. "Saying can cost you your head. If you are to live in Avignon, you must remember that.

"But to return to the subject. When first I returned to Avignon, the party of Rocault had not come into open confrontation with Innocent, and I used my position on the household staff to introduce Gaspare's sister . . ."

"Your lover . . ." interjected Damiano, just to keep things clear.

"Evienne of San Gabriele," countered the Dutchman, "to the cardinal's steward. It was a happy circumstance, at least for a few months. But now there is a great deal of tension between the cardinal's staff and those of us already here in the palace.

"I am watched," Jan Karl announced. "Always watched."

Damiano was not impressed. "So what does it matter, then, if you are seen with us? I, for one, am not of any Papal party. I am not even a thief."

Because of his wide mouth and the length of his jaw, Jan Karl's grin seemed to cut his face in half. "It is true, Delstrego, that your language does not give a bad impression, and your manner is haughty enough. But you and Gaspare are both so raw to Avignon that you may compromise me any time you open your mouths."

The open earnestness died from Damiano's face. "It is true," he whispered. "I can think of very little truthfully to say which would not compromise you, Jan."

Jan stood. "I can have you thrust out of here on the point of a pikestaff, Delstrego."

"I can send you to hell at the point of a pitchfork," answered the witch, as fire of three colors bloomed in his outstretched hand.

"Please," hissed the boy Gaspare, whom both the others seemed to have forgotten. "Please do not argue with him, Damiano. He has yet to tell us how to find Evienne."

But this exchange of unpleasantries had the contrary effect of cheering Jan Karl considerably. His lean shoulders wiggled under the wrap of bedding and he chuckled at the dark and glowering Italian. "I will tell you how to find her, Gaspare. The rest is your problem.

"But Damiano—I just remembered. Do you still play the lute a little, like you did last winter? If so, maybe I have a job for you. Private dinner, on Easter Saturday. For the Pope and the terrible cardinal together."

Damiano felt the blood drain from his face. "To play? For the Holy Father?"

"And Cardinal Rocault. It is to be quite an occasion. Keep your eyes and ears open and you might learn something. Which you must relate to me, of course."

Damiano said nothing. He was breathing hard.

"Are you afraid, Delstrego?"

Gaspare spoke up. "Of course he is not! He is merely planning what he should play."

CHAPTER 9

Damiano woke because the lute was gouging his skin. He wormed his hand in between the neck of the instrument and his cheek to feel a rectangular gridmark of strings and frets. He felt alert and ready for the day, though he had slept only a few hours.

Last night (this morning really) he had known ten minutes' panic that his change of state had destroyed his ability to play. But that had been only nerves, as well as a confusion of sensations to which his past year as a simple man had left him unaccustomed. And since the other occupants of the inn-chamber were already waking for the day, he had been able to practice until sleep took him.

Gaspare was still asleep. Of course—yesterday had been harder on him than on Damiano. Deliciously, Damiano stretched his feet out over the yellow straw and yawned, feeling more at home within himself than he had for long months. He could not think why he had allowed himself to remain immersed in melancholy all that time, when life was really quite enjoyable.

Tomorrow he was going to play before the Holy Father. That was enough to make one nervous. But it would quickly be over, and why should he think Innocent would be listening anyway, with Cardinal Rocault across the table from him?

More important to Damiano's practical concerns, he had five days more at the Bishop's Inn. Five days of playing in the corner of the high gallery, being alternately praised and ignored, while smiling respectfully at both Coutelan and MacFhiodhbhuidhe (who spent more time in the inn than the innkeeper). And on the last day maybe he would say to them, "Messieurs, your interests are very limited. I myself am going off into the countryside, to make my music with a lovely white dove."

No. He would say nothing of the kind, for he would want to come back. Besides, he should be nice to the

Irishman, for he intended to ask him to take over at the inn for him tomorrow.

And also, such proud words could prove false, for Saara might not come in the shape of a dove at all. She might be retaining the form of an owl.

Or she might be a woman. Most likely she would be a woman.

Suddenly Damiano was very nervous: more nervous about Saara than about the Pope. He threw back the blanket. It was quite warm out.

Had he crawled off among the vines with a wine-stained Alusto grape crusher at the age of fourteen, like other boys, his heart would not now be assaulting his lungs in this manner. Had he not panicked under the covers with Saara herself, a few days ago, he would have no more reason to be nervous.

Damiano pulled on his clothes, all the while telling himself that a man ought either to fornicate like a dog as soon as he was able or keep his chastity for life.

Half-measures just made a body awkward.

Yet he felt unshakably committed to the impending effort at sin, and even his attack of nerves could do no more than spice his expectation. He trotted down the corridor and stepped into the sun.

Along the white cobbled street strolled Damiano, accompanied by the Archangel Raphael. Early afternoon sunshine liquefied the air around them, and the cries of hawkers (for Avignon was a huge market that never closed) echoed against the limed stucco, meaningless and ornamental as birdsong.

The mortal felt very privileged that Raphael had decided to come along, for as once before the angel had said, he was no great walker. He could no more walk without moving his wings than a Latin—Damiano, for instance—could talk without moving his hands. The great shimmering sails arced up and out, or down, or rolled together behind or in front, or pointed like great fingers to the sky. And it seemed an effort of concentration for the angel to put his foot to earth and keep it there.

Yet his progress was not clumsy but terpsichoric, and Damiano regarded the seeming fragility of his companion with great fondness. Whenever there was no one else within hearing, he spoke. "Seraph, your feet are not really touching the ground, are they? I mean—you are barefoot, and these cobblestones are dirty."

In a very human gesture, Raphael brought his right foot up along his left shin and held up the sole for inspection. It was dirty. At Damiano's air of apology his eyes flickered with amusement.

"Would you apologize for the entire world, Damiano? Did you create it, that you should feel responsible?" Raphael walked on.

There was something infinitely touching about the appearance of Raphael today, reflected Damiano. Of course this was the first time in a year and more he'd been able to see—to really *see* the angel. Perhaps memory had made him more intimidating than he really was.

But look now: save for his galleon-sail wings, he was no taller than a man. No taller than Damiano. And he seemed to be made of spider-silk, so delicate were his face and hands. Damiano felt obliged to step between the angel and a passing merchant sailor whose entertainments had known no Lent.

"You know, Raphael," whispered Damiano, ducking under his left wing, "four years ago, when I was young, you frightened me a little. It seemed you were like a . . . great cloud in the sky, which could produce lightnings if I wasn't careful."

The tip of that wing curled over Damiano's head like a great question mark. "And now I don't seem that way?"

Damiano shrugged and smiled. "No. I don't mean to offend you, but no, you do not seem so dangerous."

Both wings touched together along their forward edges, from just above Raphael's head to their tips many feet in the air. (They barely cleared an overhanging third floor.) For a moment Raphael made a picture of formal symmetry, like one of the row of angels behind the altar of Saint Catherine's Church in Partestrada, far away.

"You certainly do not offend, Dami. I have never desired to frighten anyone. If I do no longer, then that alone has made it all worth it."

Damiano stood stock-still, even after a woman with babe in arms slammed into him from behind, cursing.

"That alone has made it worth it." It had been said in the same tone in which Saara had said, "Then it has been

worth all the rats and mice." Damiano felt uneasy. He
cleared his throat.

"But, Seraph, this change has been in me, not in you."

Raphael shook his head—a gesture Damiano had never
seen from his teacher before. He replied, "No, Dami. I
know it becomes hard to tell, when people, like boats
moving across the water, have no reference point. But I
know I am not what I was."

"Then what are you?" blurted Damiano, regardless of
the press of people on both sides of him, who were
carefully not touching the madman. "Is it something I have
done?"

For the sake of other pedestrians, Raphael nudged
Damiano forward. For a minute he did not speak.

The angel's midnight-blue eyes roved from face to face
with a probing interest, but he found none who looked
back at him. He maneuvered his charge onto a less
crowded street.

"What I am, my friend, is one of the Father's musicians.
Or perhaps one of his pieces of music: it is not an easy
distinction. And like any music—put into time—I go
through change. It is not against my will."

Damiano stood between disreputable housefronts,
where wooden shutters still sealed the windows on this
balmy and seductively breezy day. Before him an ancient
grape twisted out of a hole in the cobbles. He was only a
few feet from the spot where he had met Saara the owl.

But his thoughts were on Raphael, and he considered
the angel's last statement. "Then, outside of time . . . you
would not appear to change?"

The fine-etched golden brow drew down. "Damiano,
you are not making sense," the angel said, and raising both
wings behind him he continued his careful parade.

Damiano did not feel like making sense today, but he
did feel like talking. After the passage of a laundress, a red-
tabarded member of the Guild of Sign Painters and two
louts of undiscernible occupation, he began again.

"You were right, Seraph. I was not meant to be a saint."

The angel turned in a baroque curl of feather. "I was
right? I, Damiano? Did I ever say you were not meant to be
a saint?"

The mortal thought back. "Well, almost. When I said

that God loved dirty, sloppy-looking saints, you answered that you were not God and . . ."

Now the great wings pulled down and back, like those of a teased hawk, and Raphael's perfect nose grew a trifle sharp. "That I was not the Father. And that was all I said. I certainly didn't mean to put a limit upon your aspirations, Damiano."

"Oh." Damiano found himself staring at a misshapen alley corner which was decorated with plush blue mildew and yellow mold. He scratched the day's worth of beard on his chin. "Oh. Well, I don't even aspire to being a saint, Raphael. You see I plan . . . to . . ."

The wings lifted slowly, as though raised by ropes. "Yes. Yes. You plan to . . . what?"

"To . . . uh . . . marry Saara the Fenwoman."

In truth, the word marriage had never occurred to Damiano until this moment. But what else could he tell an archangel: that he planned to copulate like a dog?

Besides, why shouldn't he marry Saara? She was lovely and amusing, and had talents which could do his own career no harm at all.

Because she had been his father's lover, replied a whisper within his own head. Wasn't that enough reason?

But Raphael was speaking. "That is a very important decision, Dami," said the angel slowly. "But what has it to do with becoming a saint? Or with not becoming a saint?" As he spoke he very carefully preened his flight primaries with both hands.

Damiano watched the process. Surely Raphael's were not real, physical wings for their feathers to become disarranged. It must be that he needed something to do with his hands. The angel seemed to be nervous, in fact, for he shifted from foot to foot and his dark-sky eyes were wandering.

"Marriage," Damiano began, "is the mediocre way, not the path of perfection. Very few saints have been married, I believe, although many were wicked and licentious until God showed them their error."

It must have been that Raphael was not really listening, or else he would not have replied, "Well, why not begin by being wicked and licentious, then, Dami?"

The mortal grunted in disbelief which changed to

confusion as Raphael turned as though oblivious of him and passed into the alleyway of mold and mildew.

Damiano followed, out of the sunshine and into damp, odorous shadow, and as the chill patted his face, there came a cough out of the alley: a cough rich, phlegmy and spineless.

Never before had he understood the expression "his blood ran cold," but now the witch had to retreat for a last breath of sunny air before following the glimmer of samite into the murk.

The coughing continued, horrid as that of the dying farrier in the church of Petit Comtois, and Raphael was leaving him behind. Damiano bounded forward, fixing his eyes on the clean form once more before it rounded a corner.

Here was sun again, for they had come out on another street. The taint of decay vanished, to be replaced by an odor of wet ashes, as though some nearby housewife had scrubbed an entire winter's dirt out of the kitchen hearth.

Raphael stood talking to someone; his wings were spread sideways and Damiano could not see through them.

Wonderment, spiked with jealousy, bent Damiano around the cloudy wing. Who could the angel be talking to, when no one except Damiano (and Saara, of course, and assorted domestic beasts) could see him?

He was talking to his own image, which sat at a small round table, dressed in gray and scarlet, toying with a bowlful of grapes.

It took no time at all for Damiano to recognize Satan. The witch's first impulse was to duck back behind Raphael's sheltering wing. But that panic faded in a moment and a more belligerent reaction took its place. Damiano stood upright. He strode forward out of the shelter of the angel's wingspan and stood between Raphael and his brother.

And was ignored by both.

Satan had plucked a purplish orb from his bowl of dainties, and was rolling it from hand to hand. (Somehow Damiano's stomach was bothered to realize that the grape-like things in the bowl really were grapes.) He was saying:

". . . really don't look very well, my dear brother. I might almost think your decisions had gone awry, except of course, for knowing that you do not *make* decisions, but rather float on the Divine Will." The Devil's voice was urbane and well modulated, expressing just the right shade of sympathy touched by the diffidence due before an estranged member of one's family.

"I am rather pleased by the way I look," answered Raphael, and Damiano felt a fierce pride in the fact that the angel's voice (though not overly subtle in modulation at the moment) was more beautiful than Satan's. "It was just today I heard pleasant things about my appearance."

Satan let his deep-set blue eyes slide from Raphael to the young man at his side. Looking at Damiano, Satan very deliberately coughed. "If one travels widely enough," observed the Devil, "one will eventually find someone to verify one's prejudices.

"But then, Raphael, you have always had an antic taste in companions." Satan leaned back and peeled a grape with his thumbnail. "How is the fat bitch-dog? Have you tired of shepherding about that meaningless little shade?"

A lump grew in Damiano's throat, and nothing except the hand of Raphael on his shoulder kept him from assaulting the Devil barehanded. "She is well, Morning Star. Happier than you are."

Satan's guarded face did not change expression, but Damiano heard the faint sound of ashes falling, light as snow. Then the Devil glanced toward Damiano. He shifted on his three-legged stool and propped one elegant boot insouciantly against the table. Satan had a small foot—almost too small—and the toe of his black suede boot curled up as though there were nothing within it.

"But you, Signor Delstrego. It has been a good long time since I have spoken with you."

"A year and three months," said the witch from behind clenched teeth.

"Ah? You keep a close record. But then, you are a careful worker in all things. I suppose then . . ." Satan let the worried pulp of the grape slide from his fingers to the dust beneath the table, "that you have kept your affairs in order. No debts outstanding, no good works undone, nothing to make your . . . passing an inconvenience to the people around you?"

A swarm of flies was circling Damiano. He heard them.

And Satan and his repulsive bowl of grapes seemed to be retreating from him, down the length of a black tunnel.

How had I forgotten, he railed at himself. Here I am talking about marriage, when I am only going to die.

Were it not for Raphael behind him, surely he would fall on his face now. Perhaps he would be dead already.

And Satan was coughing again.

"Begone, miserable sufferer, and come not near this man!" It was Raphael's golden voice that Damiano heard. But gold, like any other metal, may be sharpened to an edge.

The angel had stepped forward, his pinions stretched taut in a great circle that brushed the wall of stucco. His face was lit from within by a white fire of anger. Yet he was only as tall as a man, and his wings were made of feathers, not fire. As Satan slouched to his feet, laughing, Damiano became painfully aware of these facts.

"Come not near him?" the Devil mimicked, his scraped-ashen voice no longer bothering to be subtle. "But my dear nest-mate, it is my right and privilege to come near him. You, on the other hand, are overstepping badly. One look at you and it becomes obvious."

Damiano also looked at Raphael, and his empty heart filled again, this time with a protective fury. He crowded between Satan and the angel, and with a single, unsubtle, inelegant kick, he upended the little round table. Grapes bounced over the strangely empty street. "Worm!" he bellowed. "Twisted snake!" he roared. "I am finished with your lies. Finished for good!"

He spat dryly, like a cat, in Satan's direction. "If you have the power to kill me, then do it. Otherwise, get out of here. You smell bad!"

The Devil stood, letting the three-cornered stool fall behind him, and as he faced Damiano he swelled and quivered like the snake he had been named. His face turned wine-red and his eyes went white. "Piece of mud!" he hissed, with a mouth full of teeth like needles. "Ordure! Worm, you called me? Well, you are food for worms, you walking bladder of blood and scum: bizarre travesty of spirit, created for the amusement of a jaded God . . ."

All resemblance to Raphael was gone now, for hate had given Lucifer a goat's face. Damiano glanced from one to the other and was glad.

Though it was getting quite hot in this corner of Avignon. Satan had dropped his human form entirely for one red and boneless and loathsome. The leather of the little stool smoldered. The table burst into flame. The smell of ashes was overpowering, and joining it now came the reek of sulfur, like an alchemical experiment gone out of control.

He can do no more than kill me, whispered Damiano to himself. He cannot hurt me more than that. He can do no more than kill me.

And as the Devil threatened and Damiano defied, Raphael withdrew a step and stood motionless and intent, like a man watching the play of actors in a drama.

The witch sheathed himself in a close coat of blue flame as he spoke aloud. "I have fire of my own, Satanas. Not as hot as yours perhaps, but less offensive to the nose."

The red flames licked out, touching the blue, spreading against it, attempting to envelop it. Where the fires touched, they created a purple glow which reflected in lights of pearl from Raphael's peacefully furled wings. And though the red was the larger and the noisier flame, where it touched Damiano's aura it grew quieter, and its color changed.

Damiano himself stood with eyes closed and hands over his face. He only looked up when the snap of withdrawing energy told him the contest—if it had been such—was over.

Satan had regained his composure in a marvelous fashion, and neither his tight jerkin nor his odd-shaped boots were soiled. "Delstrego," he said conversationally, "are you aware you carried the plague in your pocket from the north?"

Damiano stared. "I did not. We were all clean. Saara said so."

"Saara? And who is that?"

"Someone you don't know," was Damiano's growled answer.

Satan let this pass. "In your pocket." Satan smiled sweetly. "You had it in your leather pocket all those miles."

And then he was gone.

Raphael's wings slowly settled. He turned toward Damiano and his eyes were as mild as they had ever been. "Once," he began, his voice distant, "there were four of us:

Michael, Gabriel, Uriel and myself, who stood together against him and his followers. We were the instruments of his downfall, as he does not forget."

The angel shuddered then, not out of fear, but as a bird will shudder its plumage into place. "Also the instruments of his own desire, since to be cast off from peace was what he most wanted."

Damiano felt himself returning from that silent fury to his human nature again. It was like climbing out of a hole. He bent and touched the charred table which lay on its side in the road. Its flames went out. "Yet you called him 'miserable sufferer,' Seraph. Why? Do you pity him?"

One angelic eyebrow shot up while the other pulled down. "Pity Lucifer? No—should I? Remember, Damiano, he is not locked into being what he is. It is a matter of his own choosing, always."

The stool he treated like the table. The leather seat had burned clean through. Together the two pieces of furniture made a sorry little picture beside the fire-discolored wall. "His own choosing? Of course. Yet one can be locked into his own choosing. As a mortal man, I understand that. When I act my worst, I know I am sinning, and that thought makes me wickeder than ever. I can pity the Devil."

The mortal blinked nearsightedly from the wreckage to the street beyond. Now, with Satan removed from the scene, he recognized it as one of the shabby streets which led down to the mud of the Rhone. "Though if I had the power I would smash him flatter than a cutlet."

The Archangel Raphael gazed deeply at the unaware Damiano, then clapped the mortal from behind with an enthusiastic wing. "Dami, Dami! You have a power of philosophy beyond the merely angelic. Perhaps you have hit on the reason for man being what he is."

Damiano was tired. He remembered he had to play for the Holy Father, and that he had not yet asked Mac-Fhiodhbhuidhe to substitute for him. "Reason? I did not know we *had* a reason for being, Seraph. To understand the Devil?"

"To forgive him. It is more than I can do."

Slowly the man found the ability to think again, and he thought about what had just happened. "What . . . what he said, Raphael. About me. Was any of that true, do you know?"

"About your dying? I do not know the future, Damiano, and I don't think he can know any more than I. At any rate, he certainly backed off . . ."

Damiano shook his head till the black curls flew. "No. With that concern I am through. Whether I live or die is no one's business—and least of all my own. I meant about the plague."

"Why should that be straight, when all else he says is twisted?" Raphael put his hand once more on his friend's shoulder and drew him in.

"Well, you see, by coincidence I *did* carry something in my pocket from Petit Comtois to Avignon. It was a ruby pendant that some madwoman gave me."

The angel reflected. "Is it rubies, then, that carry the pest through the world?"

Damiano shrugged. "Who knows? It comes without warning and leaves when it is ready to leave. But I saw, or thought I saw, Satan's face on a man in the plague town."

"Ah! Then he would be expected to know that you had a pendant. Dami . . . he is a very clever fool, my brother Lucifer. He would make you believe your own nose was your enemy, if he could. Besides. Is there plague in Avignon?"

Damiano gazed up and down. There were people on the street: a good dozen. Masons, laborers, clerics, mothers, gentlefolk. Where had they been before? He sighed in confusion. "Not to my knowledge."

Damiano brushed nonexistent dust from his clothes. "Raphael, I am supposed to play before the Holy Father tonight."

"Good for you," replied the angel. "Give him something he has not heard before."

"I am suddenly terrified of it. Please come with me."

Raphael laughed. "I will. I would be interested to see the man."

CHAPTER 10

This was just more of the same, said Damiano to himself. Placed here in the corner in insufficient light, playing to a drone of conversation, he might as well be back at the Bishop's Inn. At least in that high gallery, he wasn't half hidden from his audience by an armoire.

Audience? He knew better than that, too. The Cardinal Rocault had not looked his way once, and as for Innocent himself, though he was facing the musician directly, and though he occasionally let his eyes rest upon Damiano's quick-moving hands, it was obvious that his attention was taken by his demanding dinner guest.

Yet Damiano did have listeners. The table servants flashed him quite human glances, and Gaspare (who was in no good mood, having spent all the previous day and part of this afternoon haunting the house of this same ambitious cardinal, hoping for a sight of his sister) was offering his support. The boy, who was wholly hidden from the view of the diners along a passage at the other side of the chamber, stared at him with an intensity designed (by sheer effort of will) to prevent Damiano from making a mistake.

And Raphael had come, too. The angel sat within touching distance of Damiano, curled sideways around a heavy-backed chair. He listened as though he had never heard his protégé play before.

To Damiano's slight disappointment, it seemed the Holy Father was as oblivious of an angel's presence as was the great mass of humanity. Of course the Pope was not a witch, but surely some preternatural authority ought to have been vested with his office along with the spiritual. Enough, at least, to recognize an angel when one plumped himself down in your dining room.

At least the acoustics were better here than in the Bishop's Inn. The voice of the lute neither echoed nor faded within the intimate, muraled chamber, for there were just enough hangings to keep the sound clean. It was as though the room had been built with his art in mind.

"Give him something he has not heard before," Raphael had said, so that is what Damiano did. Scorning the ballades of Provence and the boring (to Damiano) folksongs of his native Alps, Damiano played what he had composed himself: music so new it was hardly born yet, wild in both time and harmony, colored slightly (almost against Damiano's will) with the ornate ornamentation he was picking up from MacFhiodhbhuidhe.

He had no intention of listening to the dialogue of the Pope and the cardinal, though Jan Karl had arranged his concert with that end in mind. He had no desire to get mixed in with politics he could not be expected to understand, and besides, if he were playing at his best, he would have no attention free.

But the conversation impinged upon his attention, because of its subject.

"They tell me three hundred, in Lyons. Mostly children, of course," the cardinal was saying. He was a big man, black-eyed, brown-haired, who looked good in the color red. Damiano had a long stare at the back of his head.

"Of course," echoed Innocent, who appeared much older, but not appreciably frail. The Pope's nose was raptorial, his eyes fine. "These days the plague prefers youth. I have it on good authority that is because those who were subject to it of my generation died in '50.

"But it comes back every year, or every other year, somewhere in Europe. Last year it was Spain and Poland. This year it is France. Next year Italy, perhaps."

Damiano's fingers kept playing while his mind reeled. Plague again. He could not escape it. He had a fervent, irrational desire that people would shut up about plague in front of him, for he had been through too much lately.

"All very well to take the long view, Your Holiness," interrupted Rocault smoothly. "But people expect you to do something about it."

Innocent's elderly-eagle eyes flickered from the cardinal to the lute on the other side of the room. The old man seemed to have no problem seeing at a distance. "Ah? Well, I am, my son. I am praying daily, and offering the mass.

"Or did you—forgive me, did the people—have in mind something different? Something more like a bull?"

"That is what I had in mind," replied Rocault dryly. He followed Innocent's eyes and regarded the musician with no very friendly stare. For a moment he said no more.

What was Damiano to do? He had been told to play for the Holy Father, and he would continue until that one told him to stop. Surely Cardinal Rocault was not distracted by the sound of a single lute in the corner.

Perhaps he merely did not appreciate the New Music.

"A bull, certainly, Your Holiness, would let the people of France know they are in your prayers. And the best sort would be a bull rescinding your predecessor's protection of the local Jews."

Jews again. Jews and the plague. Damiano wished momentarily that he were back in the north of Italy, in Partestrada, sans plague and with only one Jew to speak of.

Innocent chuckled, and tapped his silver knife on his golden plate. "Hah, Rocault, my old friend. Here we have gotten half through our dinner without your mentioning this *bête noire* of yours: protection of the Jews. I had even begun to hope you had left it behind.

"You know I think it is silly; Clement's very reasonable exposition of why the Jews cannot have caused the plague did not prevent the burning of the ghettos, nor the murder or exile of thousands. If I should publish a statement turning Clement's logic on its head, would that make the behavior of the populace any different?"

Damiano snarled a finger and returned his attention perforce to his playing.

There was a sound of thunder above their heads; the good weather was at an end. Raphael leaned—no, slouched—against the chair back, one elbow propped on the finial of cherubs carved from oak. With his calm, interested visage and generally passive attitude, he might have been any intelligent listener at the Bishop's Inn, with a seed cake and a cup of violet wine on the table before him.

There was a piece Damiano had written only the previous week, which reminded him of Raphael. (It fell short, the lutenist thought, but then of course it would.) Though it was not part of his professional repertoire, he played it now for the angel.

"There is everyday truth, and then there is a metatruth, Your Holiness. And while in actual fact the plague may not be due to the Jews poisoning the water supplies, the higher truth is that all our misery upon the earth is due to the wickedness that murdered our Saviour . . ."

"I thought," murmured Innocent, seemingly inattentive to the cardinal's words, "that our misery was due to the sin of Adam, expressed anew in every man, and that the sufferings of our Lord were our happy redemption." The Pope cleared his throat, laid down his knife and gestured for his chair to be moved to the other side of the table, closer to the music.

"After all, Rocault, it *is* Eastertide, you know, and we generally try to adopt an attitude of thankfulness."

When the old man finally spoke to him, Damiano had gone so far from attention to the conversation that a lackey had to nudge him on the shoulder.

"Lutenist." Innocent stood immediately in front of him. Damiano rose hurriedly.

But the Pope sat, knowing a chair would appear to receive him, and he gestured the same for Damiano. "You sound like an entire consort of lutes, here in your corner. Along with a harp or two, and at least one tambour."

Damiano mumbled his thanks, and then, to his astonishment, Innocent VI reached out, asking if he might see the lute.

The Holy Father played a few quiet scales. He smiled. Back by the dinner table, Cardinal Rocault was not smiling.

"It sounds very different when I try to play," observed the old man.

"I did not know, Your Holiness," began Damiano (and his voice humiliated him by cracking on the word "Holiness"), "that you played the lute."

"A little. When I have time. I play enough to wonder why you, who get such a variety of sounds out of your instrument, don't play more at the far end of the neck."

"The lute is not true up there," replied Damiano.

Innocent chuckled to himself. "Not true. Nor metatrue?" And his glance at the young man sharpened and held a covert amusement. "Are you Jewish, young man? You could be, by the look of you. Sitting here and listening to all this talk, it would be very frightening for you if you were Jewish. You would not easily forget, nor keep secret what you heard, if you were Jewish."

"I am not," said Damiano in turn. "I am Piedmontese, and this nose I got from my Italian father. It is very frightening to hear anyway, but I don't understand enough to repeat it. Nor do I know many people in Avignon to whom I could repeat anything."

The Pope smiled sweetly at him and smothered a yawn. "No matter, my son. I am not about to issue proclamations this season, and the whole world is permitted to know that." His Holiness stood, and his chair was toted back to the table.

As the old man turned to follow it, Raphael rose from his place and stood beside him. His fair face was only inches from the Pope's ear. "Claude," called Raphael softly. "Claude Rabier!" And then he whispered in the Pope's ear.

Innocent grimaced and blinked, rubbing one age-stained hand over his eyes, but he did not pause.

The angel watched him go. White wings drooped down to the carpet.

"He couldn't hear you?" whispered Damiano.

"I don't know if he heard me or not," replied the angel. ". . . you forget the usuric taxes, Rocault. Your cardinal's vestments were purchased out of Jewish . . ."

Damiano felt easier at heart. Not that he was about to confuse the astute Innocent with Saint Francesco, but now he had a certain faith in the man as well as the office. The old Pope was not about to be ground under heel by Cardinal Rocault.

Damiano was more and more certain that he did not like Rocault, who was making life more difficult for everybody, from the Holy Father to Gaspare.

And therefore for Damiano.

The food was cleared away. Was the music supposed to be cleared away as well? Damiano looked about for some sort of signal from one of the lackeys. Discovering none, he continued playing.

Rocault had a plan which he insisted on describing to His Holiness. It involved the disestablishment of all lending institutions except those beneficiary associations belonging to the guilds and (of course) the church itself.

Innocent listened with what appeared to be little attention, occasionally murmuring phrases on the order of "killing the goose which lays the golden eggs."

From strain and general weariness, Damiano had created a small headache. When the lackey who had handled the Pope's chair returned with a bundle in his arms, his eyes could not at first make out what the thing was. When by its shape it proved to be a lute, he was filled with mixed feelings.

Did the Holy Father want to play for him? Or with him? That could be interesting. Or dangerous for Damiano, since it was a direct insult to the cardinal, who plainly wanted to talk. It could also prove embarrassing, since the Pope was the successor to Saint Pietro, but music was still music, and about it Damiano could not lie.

He kept his head down toward his strings but out of the corner of his eye Damiano watched Innocent open a case of gilded leather and pull out an instrument.

Mother of God, what an instrument. As Innocent carried it from the dining table over to Damiano's corner, the lutenist could no longer pretend to be uninterested.

The lute was larger than Damiano's, but by the way the old man hefted it, very light. Its back was of many woods and its soundboard bleached white. The neck of it was black ebony, inlaid with gold wire, and the pierced cover of the soundhole was a parchment lace as fine as cheesecloth. The tuning head of the lute bent sharply back from the neck, the better for the musician to play in ensemble.

Damiano was stricken with base jealousy: that a man who played "when he found the time" should have such an instrument, when Damiano, who ate and breathed the lute, was forced to carry a box poorly joined and false at the top of the neck . . .

But he shoved himself roughly back into line. How could he object to the most important man on earth owning a pretty lute? Besides, it was probably made for show and possessed a voice like a crow's.

Innocent sat himself down between Damiano and the angel, who was also regarding the lute with interest. Perhaps the lutenist's conflict of feeling had not passed entirely unnoticed, for the first thing the Pope said was "People give me things." And he shrugged.

"Lutes, among the rest." With a touch of a quill to each string, the Holy Father checked his tuning. He seemed to know what he was doing. Then he took Damiano's lute by the neck and made an exchange.

"I want to hear that piece with the bass like a harp again. On this."

Damiano said nothing. When he touched the top course with his fingernail, the lute thrilled weightlessly on his lap. He played an aeolian scale, to get used to the spacing, and then a myxlodean. He found he was holding his breath.

The instrument had a soul. Before five measures of the song had passed Damiano had forgiven it its excessive prettiness, and with the final sprinkle of notes he forgave it for not being his. He extended it to its owner.

Innocent VI shook his head. "I like this one better," he stated. "It is such a poor lute, and when I look at it I can remember to what heights you took an instrument which showed so little promise. When I consider my own soul, I would like to remember that. And besides, I, who am a halting musician, can play this instrument without feeling unworthy of it."

"But neither am I worthy of this," blurted Damiano. And he believed it, without for a moment discounting his own abilities. For it seemed to him that the only sort of musician who ought to have such a lute was an old man who had played all his life, on the good instruments and the bad, and who had surmounted his obstacles and learned all that life was going to teach him.

Damiano saw himself, on the other hand, as a beginner. A beginner who was already better at his art than most masters, but a beginner nonetheless. He tried to give the lute back.

Innocent would not take it, and neither did the old man smile as he said, "That's not for you to say, lad. But it wouldn't matter anyway. An instrument like this—one cares for it a while and then passes it on. As I do, to you. I was not its first owner, and perhaps you will not be its last. Something told me it was time to pass it on." Innocent shrugged. "If you meet a man who is more worthy, or who has the greater need . . ."

The old man fixed Damiano with a fierce hazel eye. "Is it a trade, musician?"

"You . . . Your Holiness," stuttered Damiano, and he tipped his chair over as he rose to bow.

"Gabriele!" exploded Gaspare, as soon as they were out of the private quarters. "What a present! And from the Pope himself! You should have gotten him to sign it."

Damiano glanced up from the case of gilded leather. "Sign it? Don't be an ass, Gaspare. Sign it where? The signature of God himself is on this lute; it is perfect."

He looked over his shoulder. "What do you think of it, Raphael? Isn't it perfect?"

Gaspare giggled at the sight of Damiano conversing with empty air.

Raphael was smiling. He marched with wings straight out behind him, for the passageway was low and narrow. Because of this posture, he resembled a man fighting gale winds. "It's a lovely lute, and as soon as you let me play it I'll tell you more," he answered. "But I doubt I'll have much to criticize.

"I'm glad he thought to give it to you," added the angel, with more than a hint of complacency.

They descended to the clean cobbled streets and the guard watched them walk away. Damiano sang in the rain all the way back to the inn.

"Do I look so old to you that I can't carry my clàrseach by myself?" bristled MacFhiodhbhuidhe, stooping to place one hand beneath the base of the soundbox, while the other hand rested on the serpent-curve of the string arm. Grunting, he hefted the weight of black wood.

The harper's instrument was garnished with a great deal of silver and crystal. It was splendid, certainly, but to Damiano's Italian eye it lacked grace. It looked heavy—not like MacFhiodhbhuidhe's music, which was almost frivolously light.

"It's lighter than you would think," the harper said, almost as though he had read Damiano's thoughts. "It's carved out of willow. The box is hollowed from a single piece of wood: like an old log boat!" MacFhiodhbhuidhe chuckled.

"But here, boy. You can carry my stool," he added grandly, handing the item to Gaspare, who had not been the one to volunteer his help.

The big Irishman, like Damiano himself, was in a glorious mood. "I haven't enjoyed myself this much in years. And it has been years since I played like this, in public, for whoever wanted to stop and listen. For the most part, I have my patrons."

He stood at the door of the inn, peering out on to the

wet pavement, scowling against the chance it might still be sprinkling. Finally he decided to chance it, and strode out to the street. Damiano and Gaspare tagged behind.

"Your patrons, Monsieur Harper?" piped Gaspare (when he should have kept his mouth shut). "Is the Holy Father one of your patrons? Have *you* played for the Pope, like Damiano?"

Nothing in Damiano's witchcraft had ever taught him how to drop through solid stone, or else he might have vanished from view then and there, out of sheer embarrassment. He gave the boy a shake and a barely suppressed hiss. But MacFhiodhbhuidhe only stopped in the middle of the road and peered down at Gaspare. A chase of cloud and moon flashed his image larger than life, and his long, carefully frizzed yellow hair bushed out like a halo. "Many times, child, have I played for His Holiness. Every good musician in Avignon has been heard by the Pope, whose interest in music is active.

"Of course," continued the harper, "not every good musician has been given an instrument by the Pope. Your friend has a right to be proud."

"I'm not proud," mumbled Damiano, following MacFhiodhbhuidhe through the gate of his pretty little garden and into his pretty little house. "I'm only astounded. And besides, he said he did it because of a song that sounded like a harp."

The Irishman's elderly serving woman came with a candle in each hand, and lit them in.

In the middle of the harper's front room stood a cabinet, lined with woolens, floored with absorbent sand. In this cabinet the clàrseach lived. As MacFhiodhbhuidhe placed it upright in its sand, he sighed. "Everyone is attracted to novelty. But I'm sure His Holiness had more reason than that.

"But the clàrseach, you know: it is different from all the other instruments." The burly man gave a tolerant glance over his shoulder, knowing he would not be understood. "Looking at that great, weighty thing of wood and brass and silver, would you believe that there is nothing holding it together but its strings?

"That is the case, however. A clàrseach is three pieces of wood, fitted with pegs and holes. The box is female, the bow male, and the arm, half and half." His bushy black brows drew together in good humor.

"We Irish are very fond of threes. We pretend to have invented the Trinity."

Damiano, though he enjoyed the occasional intellectual exposition, was more interested in the instrument than the philosophy behind it. He bent around the wider man, examining the harp's joints. "Do you ever take it apart?"

MacFhiodhbhuidhe sat back and allowed him to touch. "On the long trip from Galway to Quimper and through Brittany and the valley and south . . . there it traveled wrapped like a bundle of fagots. That was an odd trip, my friends, and a fortunate one for me, because I took it in the year of the Death."

Damiano flinched unnoticed.

"Yes, I left Ireland before the plague struck, and entered Provence when its fury was spent here, consequently I never encountered the disease at all. Spared by grace, I have always said.

"But to return to the clàrseach: it is better for an instrument, as it is better for a man, to remain taut—fit for work." He thumped his round and sizable chest.

"As long as I live, these three pieces will remain in one."

"Why did you want to hang around talking to *him?*" whined Gaspare, querulously dancing from one foot to the other.

Damiano, who paced the shining streets with his thumbs in his belt, turned on him. "Why did I . . . ? Why did *you* have to be so unforgivably rude? Asking him if he, who has been my greatest benefactor in Avignon, had ever had good fortune to equal mine . . ."

Gaspare lowered his head like a spindly goat. "What does he matter, lutenist? His music is of the past, and so is he. You have a better ear and better hands than he; he is privileged to help you."

Damiano hunched his shoulders. "God preserve me from friends like you," he growled. But within him was some part, not wholly submergible, which agreed with Gaspare's analysis, and was buoyed up by the redhead's cruel words. He recognized this in himself, and it made him more angry than ever.

Gaspare hung back, silent for a moment, while both of them paced determinedly down the main north-south avenue toward the Rhone.

Finally he spoke again, lugubriously. "What do you expect out of me, Damiano? I'm not your angel, you know. I am only a man, and I must say what I feel. Besides, it's not three hours ago that some churl of Rocault's assaulted me, merely because I asked him whether my sister was being kept within.

"This business is wearing upon me. I can't count when I last slept a night through, what with worrying about Evienne."

Damiano recognized the truth of this. Though it was not a complete truth, since Gaspare spent his nights very quietly, for a person who wasn't sleeping. "Well, we're doing something about that right now, aren't we?"

Gaspare trotted up beside Damiano. He nodded. "Yes, musician, we are. We are going to get ourselves killed, to be exact, and have our heads stuck on pikes over the cardinal's wall."

Damiano grimaced. "Why do you talk like that, Gaspare? This was your idea, remember? And we are attempting nothing we did not do easily within the Papal Palace itself."

"Certainly. But bad-talking is good luck. It is an old thieves' custom."

"I am not a thief," insisted Damiano once again: obdurately, but with less conviction than he would have shown a few weeks previously.

The night before last the moon had been full, but tonight's fast-scudding clouds stole its brilliance. And it was late; soon the night orb would set, leaving darkness even Damiano would find thick.

Yet he couldn't ask Gaspare to wait longer, and he himself was eager to try his abilities on the task for which he had reclaimed them.

"Quite a wind," mumbled the boy, who in the interest of stealth had worn neither his richest nor warmest clothing.

Damiano agreed, feeling his feet skid on muddy stones. "I hope the cardinal's roof doesn't leak," he added. "A wet reunion would be a pity."

He glanced ahead, along the low riverfront road. His vision, imperfect in daylight, was sharp enough now to catch the pattern of light on the ruffled surface of the

Rhone, and the movement of restless gulls that clustered under the house eaves. There was the outline of a bridge half spanning the river. Broken, or incomplete. Vaguely Damiano wondered who had built it, who had broken it and why it wasn't repaired. "I see the house, I think. At least I see a building larger than all else by the wharves."

"That's it," replied Gaspare. "It has peach trees flattened against the west wall—they are in bloom—and vines covering the south."

"I see the espalier. It looks like it is shielding the house from the wind with a fence of flowers."

Avignon was no city of gardens, but with the immense thrift of Gallic peoples everywhere, foodstuffs were grown there wherever a square foot of soil stood undisturbed, against any white wall that caught the sun. The mansion of Cardinal Rocault rose high and proudly enough, but pots of kitchen herbs dangled out the first-story windows, and from the small enclosure came a sleepy quarrel of chickens. Damiano also smelled rabbits through the sweetness of the blooming trees.

"It's no Papal Palace," pronounced Gaspare, with the easy criticism of the man who has nothing. "I can see why the good cardinal is envious of the Pope."

Damiano crept up to the wall which fronted the river road. Seven little peach trees, no taller than the second-story windows, had been pruned and trained into shapes as flat as heraldry. The sight and smell of them made him drunk; he rubbed his face against pink-white blossoms. "I myself," he whispered, "have a certain envy of Cardinal Rocault, for I would sooner own this pretty house than inhabit the Pope's warrens."

But a snort and sniff from within silenced him. Damiano held up a warning hand to Gaspare and began one of his oldest magics: one learned neither from Saara nor Guillermo Delstrego, but particular to Damiano himself. With images of hearthrugs and bowls of hot porridge he seduced the cardinal's bandog. With a bodiless scratch in places no dog could reach, he turned the creature from its duty.

Even Gaspare, who was watching his friend curiously, not understanding, heard the scrape of heavy dog claws at the other side of the wall. He hissed and bounced back into the road. "It's the watchdog, Damiano."

Damiano had begun to sing. "Shut up, Gaspare," he crooned melodiously, "or I'll throw you to him."

The studded gate was locked by a mechanism more complex than any the intruders had seen before, but it opened itself at the witch's cheery adjuration.

They entered, and Damiano was almost knocked flat by a gigantic course-hound which dropped its front feet onto the witch's shoulders and demanded the promised caress. Standing head to head with Damiano, the beast was only halfway upright.

Gaspare cursed weakly as Damiano produced the tickles and scratches. "What *is* it?"

"A war-dog," caroled Damiano, catching his balance and placing the huge feet on the ground. "From the islands. Scotian or Caledonian. Described by Cambrensis. I have seen pictures of such as this."

Gaspare understood none of this, not knowing that Scotia was Ireland or Caledonia, Scotland. And never having read Giraldus Cambrensis, being unable to read. But he saw his old friend take liberty after liberty with the gray and shaggy pony-sized creature.

"Not much of a warrior, for a war-dog, is it?" said the boy critically, as the dog bowed its forequarters till its muzzle touched earth, then set off in a lolloping gallop around them.

"We won't get into that," replied Damiano, and he led Gaspare (and the affectionate dog) past the coops and the hutches, through the truck garden and into the back door. "He probably has another face to show to strangers."

Damiano was enjoying himself again. One of the unhappiest aspects of being a simple man had been his loss of special understanding with the animals around him, dogs especially. The memory of the sheepdog's attack at the farm south of Petit Comtois rankled no end, for he had been used to believing that the beasts saw in him something wonderful: something the narrow eyes of men could not. That day he had to come to grips with the truth that it was no moral excellence that gentled the predatory canine, but mere witchly trickery.

Now, once more he could forget that humbling verity, and others of like nature.

Never be weary or sick . . .

Inside the back door a fat man was sleeping, for all the

world like another watchdog. Damiano had to croon with great concentration to wedge the door open without awakening the sleeper. The witch and his two companions then crept by, the great hound wagging furiously at finding himself in the house.

"Watch his tail," whispered Damiano, too late, for Gaspare winced and grabbed at his stinging thigh. They found themselves in a looming, sooty kitchen, lit by the orange embers of a fire so large that no single night of inattention could kill it. It smelled still of the evening's roast veal.

Gaspare grimaced, still rubbing his smarting leg. The hound's tail had the lash of a bullwhip. It occurred to Gaspare as he hopped by the fireside, that between the Holy Father and Evienne, Damiano's dinner (and his own) had been forgotten.

Damiano, meanwhile, had scooted himself onto the great plank table which filled the center of the kitchen. There he sat, his hands laced around one knee, casually humming to himself. His eyes were closed.

Gaspare prodded his musician with a gentle finger, but pulled back in alarm when the war hound put back its rough ears and growled.

"Uh, Damiano. No time for daydreaming. Don't fall asleep."

Black eyes flashed open, filled with firelight. The lullaby was cut off. "I am not likely to fall asleep in the middle of events, Gaspare. The Damiano who did that sort of thing is gone, and I don't think he'll return. But I am having difficulty finding Evienne."

"Oh, no! She is taken. She is dead." The great dog lifted his head from an intensive search for scraps on the floor, and Damiano darted a glance out the hallway, where the round-bellied sculleryman slept.

"No fear, Gaspare. It is only that there are many sleepers within here, and it has been a long time since I have seen your sister. I never knew her very well."

"You alone out of all the world," grumbled Gaspare. Then he whispered, "She is taller than me, being five years older. She is bigger in the hips than in the bosom, though plenty big in both. She has a lot of temper, and of course, red hair like mine."

The witch's face lit. "Red hair! Now there is something real on which to focus. Gaspare, come here."

Gaspare approached, strangely unwilling. "Why? What is it you . . ."

Damiano grabbed the boy's carefully curled hairdo in both hands. Gaspare smothered a squeal of protest, and the bandog put its long head between them to see what was going on.

"Aha." Damiano chuckled. "No more difficulty." Releasing Gaspare's rumpled head, he swung his legs off the table. "Follow your general, troops."

Evienne of San Gabriele put her small nose to the linen sachet and whuffled. The trouble with all sachets and pomanders was that after a while you didn't smell them anymore, and then you didn't know whether the fragrance was gone, or whether your nose simply had grown used to it. Then you added some rose oil or orris root, and someone would come in—someone like Herbert, in a bad temper—and shout that the sweetness was making him gag.

But that was his own fault, for if she were allowed a promenade every day, or even to do her own shopping, then she would be able to tell when the room smelled too sweet.

Better than smelling like a pisspot, anyway.

Evienne turned on her back (it was more comfortable for her to sleep on her back) and sighed. Herbert was so difficult: not letting her wear red, even if it matched her hair, and keeping her indoors nine days out of ten, without even a girl companion.

What good were baubles and silk, if you didn't have another girl to show them off to?

And he made her the butt of jokes—funny dry jokes in private, when there was no one to laugh. Just because she was not educated, not a real lady. In that way he was like Jan, but of course with Jan you always knew where you were. Jan needed her. (Had needed her? No. Still.) The cardinal was a different matter.

She wrapped her arms around her body, over her ample and growing abdomen. *This* might give her a certain hold on Herbert. Maybe.

Of course men could be so cruel. And what if the baby had yellow hair? No one of the cardinal's family (she had ascertained) had yellow hair.

But because Evienne had a naturally sanguine temperament as well as blood-colored hair, this worry could not depress her for long. She still had three months during which the cardinal would surely not boot her out.

But Jan—if she started thinking about Jan, then she'd be crying all night. For Jan had not come to see her in two months, and the last time was only to steal away certain of the jewelry she'd been given by Herbert. He was going to copy it in glass, in case Herbert wanted it back someday. He'd never even come back with the copies.

Had he been torn apart by Couchicou, the dog? The hound had almost gotten him once before, he'd said. But surely she would have heard about that. Had he taken ill, then? There was no one she could ask.

Or was that stinking tomcat already back in Italy, accompanied by another, younger, less pregnant woman?

Evienne's fists balled into the pillow. Her jagged nail caught a thread. Herbert was telling her all the time to stop biting her nails.

She sobbed. Why was she doing this—caged in a chamber of goosedown and brocade, if not for Jan's sake?

Evienne thought she heard singing. Because the sound was more pleasant than her thoughts, she listened. It was a lullaby, soft and sweetly sung. Not a woman's voice.

Who in the cardinal's house could be singing a lullaby in black night? The closer she listened, holding her breath, the more she thought she could recognize the voice. Now it was a trifle louder.

Without warning, Evienne fell asleep.

At the very top of the winding stair Damiano stopped. His lips were parted and he sniffed the air pensively, adding a staccato character to his melody. He turned right down a low-ceilinged narrow hall, dragging the night-blind Gaspare behind him. "Close," he murmured.

Suddenly the witch stiffened. His song died in his throat and he seemed to convulse under Gaspare's grip. "My God, Damiano," the boy whispered almost without sound. "What . . . ?"

"I . . . I . . ." Damiano said no more, but grabbed a double handful of his shirt and buried his face in it. Three times he sneezed, each time more convulsively than the last, until Gaspare felt the sweat break out on his friend's forearm.

Then Damiano lifted his head, taking a slow, deep breath. "Orris rood," he pronounced phlegmily. "Terribly stong. It has cofused my sedses."

Gaspare himself sniffed, and then nodded. "Evienne. My sister all the way. Now *you* follow *me*."

The young thief led Damiano along the black and dismal hall, his less sensitive nose working stertorously. Damiano wiped his eyes (and nose) on the hem of his overshirt.

The source of the floral bouquet was a small wooden door with a simple lock on it. Damiano did not need his nose to encourage the mechanism to work itself.

He shoved behind Gaspare into a room in which sweet smells had taken on a fetid aspect.

It was small, hardly wider than the height of an average man, and scarcely longer than it was wide. Its single window was inadequate and firmly shuttered. A rug carpeted the floor, while other hangings of similar nature lined the walls till it was all as furry and as stiflingly close as a cocoon. Save for a closet of white oak huddled in one corner between folds of heavy wool, the place was occupied solely by bed: a soft and formless bag of white linen stuffed with feathers (Damiano's nose was tingling again) lying on the floor like a very fat dog.

And on that bed, half unblanketed, with her left shoulder and left breast wholly exposed to the night air, lay Evienne of San Gabriele, Gaspare's sister.

Gaspare had not moved. After a moment Damiano remembered that his friend was simple and could not see in the night. The witch lit a dim blue fire-pet in his right hand and stroked it with his left.

"Evienne!" hissed Gaspare, and he stalked closer. The boy's first action, motivated either by shame or by a strange sort of fraternal caring, was to adjust Evienne's blanket under her chin.

Damiano stepped backward and sideways as far as he was able, which is to say, two steps. He felt woolly fibers against the back of his neck and had to stifle a sneeze, crushing his domestic flame in the process. He lit another and watched the scene before him.

He had forgotten how pretty a girl Evienne was, with her heavy auburn hair, pink cheeks and infant-round limbs. Had she always possessed such a delicate complexion, and such amplitude? Damiano regarded Evienne intently while Gaspare did the same at close range.

The young woman had stirred after the moment of Damiano's sneeze, but as he began his song again (this time almost without sound, like a man who hums while adding a column of figures) her slumbers grew quiet once more.

"Shall I let her wake, Gaspare?"

The boy nodded. "Her, but not everybody else in the house, hey?"

"You ask a lot," replied the witch tunefully, but stepping over to the bed he placed his nonfiery hand upon Evienne's.

Gaspare had his hand ready to muffle his sister if she should wake up screaming, but it was not necessary. Evienne was not the sort of girl to react in that way to the presence of a man in her bedchamber.

"Herb . . . ?" she moaned, then opened her eyes and looked blearily at Damiano, who seemed to be cupping a votive candle in his hands, and so possessed the only spot of light in the room. "Who?"

Damiano simply pointed at Gaspare.

Recognition came slowly, but the subsequent embrace was bone-cracking. The boy escaped his sister's arms long enough to deliver a savage tweak to her pretty pink cheek.

"Hah!" he growled, with what seemed perfectly unmixed fury. "Here you are, wrapped in perfume thick as a cloud of summer dust, lolling on goosedown, speckled—positively speckled—with priceless gems, with no thought of your poor brother, walking every street in Avignon, thinking you were dead."

Evienne opened her eyes very wide and sat up straighter, thoughtless of the effect this action had upon her modesty. "That isn't fair, Gaspare! For one thing, I'm not wearing a single gem, and for another . . ."

Her angrily suppressed voice trailed off then, and Evienne's green eyes wandered from Gaspare to the linen sachet on the pillow by her head. She inhaled in a great, unladylike snort. "Does it really smell strong in here?"

"Nearly choked him," attested Gaspare, pointing with his thumb in the direction of Damiano.

Evienne saw a dark young man, looking impossibly tall

and slim in the light of the strange bright candle in his hands. His hair cast black river-shadows against the ceiling. Damiano looked back at the half-naked woman, hoping his expression displayed a suitable insouciance.

Evienne thought he looked a bit cruel. "Who . . . who is he?" she mumbled to her brother.

Gaspare glanced from one to the other in surprise. "That's Damiano, my lutenist, Evienne. You remember him." Once more he tended her blanket.

It was hopeless, for Evienne sat completely forward, peering closely at Damiano. "Oh, yes. I do remember. Funny you two should still be together. Jan always said he didn't see why."

Damiano had tried hard to keep his eyes on Evienne's face, but with her last comment he relaxed the effort.

She was a very pretty girl, only a trifle big in the belly. Just a trifle.

"There are a lot of things," he whispered, still keeping the tune of his lullaby, "that Dutchman cannot see, I think."

Her loyalty to Jan Karl did not extend to the point of defending him against slights of so vague a character. Especially now, when she was feeling his absence as a slight against her.

At the sound of Damiano's voice she lifted her head and remembered. "The singing I heard tonight. That was you!"

He nodded. "Damiano's a witch," said Gaspare, as though that explained something.

The girl paid no attention. "And . . . and you still look like that," she added, decisively. "Who'd have thought it?"

Damiano could think of nothing to say in reply to this. He wanted to believe it had been a compliment but was not at all sure.

Gaspare shook his sister by her peach-blossom shoulder. "Enough of what he looks like. I want to know why you missed our rendezvous."

Evienne gave him a disparaging glance. "Because there is a lock on the door, of course. I can't go anywhere anymore. Herbert gets so jealous." She was momentarily startled as a monstrous gray head thrust itself under her hand. "Couchicou. You're not supposed to be in the house at night."

"He followed us in," explained Damiano.

"Not much of a watchdog," grunted Gaspare, as he watched the animal fawn over Evienne.

Who giggled weakly. "Couchicou almost tore Jan to pieces that last time he came to visit. Didn't Jan warn you about Couchicou when he met you?"

At this mention of Evienne's lover, Damiano reacted automatically. He reached out and gave the bandog a hearty, approving slap. "Jan did not show up at the Pope's Door either, Evienne."

She caught her breath in unfeigned alarm. "He is dead, then. It is as I feared."

The witch shook his head. "How you are like your brother! No, the Dutchman is not dead; he only decided that it was not politic to fulfill his promise to us."

Evienne's concern hardened into resentment. She snatched a gorgeous emerald robe from its lodging under the covers at the foot of her bed. It was very wrinkled. She thrust her arms through the holes and struggled out of the bed with a certain lack of grace. "Politics, again. Jan never shuts up about politics. What does 'politics' have to do with him and you—or with him and me, for that matter?"

"Wasn't it politics that got you this nice little cubby with the cardinal?" asked her brother. Gaspare was not disillusioned on the subject of Jan Karl; like all cynical people, he trusted implicitly anyone who acted even more cynically. He turned from a hands-on examination of the contents of her dresser table to finger the padded Oriental silks of her garment.

Evienne gazed around her at the crowded little chamber. For a moment it appeared she was going to cry, but instead she raised her arms a few inches and flapped them at her sides, penguinlike. Then she raised her eyes to Damiano, who had withdrawn to the corner of the room and sat sprawled on the rolled bottom of a tapestry which was much too long for the wall on which it hung. His black curly head was bent forward as he examined the bright thing in his hands. Softly, sweetly, he was singing to himself.

Evienne shuffled forward till her hair shone like sunset. "What . . . ? What have you got there? Is it a candle? You'll burn yourself if you're not careful."

"No, he won't," replied her brother in a voice of

authority. "I told you Damiano's a witch now. He's got the rest of the house sleeping with that song of his, and that's why no one's come banging on the door to see what the noise is." As Evienne continued to stare at Damiano's hands (warmly translucent, lit from within), Gaspare took the opportunity to drop into his jerkin pocket one green glass flacon, stained with dried perfume, and a pair of silver earrings.

The girl knelt rather cumbersomely beside Damiano and attempted to pry his hands apart.

He shook his head and pulled away from her. "No, Evienne. It *will* burn. Just sit still and watch." And he opened his hands together, palms up.

It was a little blue hedgehog with flickering, yellow-tipped spines. It ran from his hand heel to his fingertips and then back again, before dissolving.

He shook his head. "It's too difficult to do two magics at once," he sang aloud. "If I'm putting the house to sleep, that's about all I can handle."

Evienne's green eyes were wide as an eight-week kitten's. "How pretty!" she giggled, without any hint of fear.

"Come with us," Damiano said on impulse. "Rocault is no lord, that he can keep you prisoned this way. Neither are you bound to this house like a peasant to his patch of ground."

Evienne sat back heavily and hugged herself. "Come with you? Where?"

Gaspare had turned and was staring at Damiano with as much confusion as Evienne.

"To the Bishop's Inn, for now. Later—when the baby is closer—then we can find you a little house somewhere. We're not so poor as we once were."

Gaspare mouthed the word "baby." Then he exploded. "Baby! Baby. By Saint Gabriele, woman, don't tell me you are pregnant!" The boy gave such a perfect imitation of a brother whose honor is outraged that both Damiano and his sister sat silent for the next few moments.

"Hush," hissed the witch, pointing meaningfully toward the door. "There are limits, Gaspare, to what a spell can do for you."

"Yes," answered Evienne sullenly. "I am pregnant, Gaspare. Is that any of your business, I'd like to know?"

"How'd it happen?" demanded Gaspare, in unreflecting rage.

Damiano beheld his friend's behavior with rising irritation. The only creature more volatile and irrational than Gaspare of San Gabriele was Gaspare when in the presence of his sister.

"Are you going to challenge the Cardinal Rocault to a duel, perhaps?" The question slid away from song and ended in a tone of disgust.

Evienne decided to ignore her brother. "It is because of the baby I must stay. If it's Herbert's, you see—well, I know him enough to say that he'll take care of it very well. And take care of me also."

"And if it's not?" growled Gaspare, as his limber fingers snaked a choker of blue beads into his pocket, to lie beside the earrings.

She shrugged. "Then it's Jan's."

Gaspare mock-spat into the corner. "Tell me how you were such a fool as to get pregnant. You never did before."

"I didn't have any girlfriends in Avignon," she said simply. "What was I to do? Besides, Gaspare, I want this baby. If it is the cardinal's, then it will be my fortune. If it is Jan's . . ." Her face softened, till Evienne appeared about five years old. "I really love Jan. Even when he does awful things, like not coming to see me for seven weeks together. I feel sorry for him, I think. He can be so bad."

Into Damiano's mind came the words of Raphael. "Perhaps the purpose of man is to forgive the Devil." He smiled sadly at the pretty, pregnant girl.

When had he stopped singing? He couldn't even remember. But he was very tired. It had been such a day. And the cloying, close air. And the muffling drapes of woolen. Damiano yawned. He ceased to follow what Gaspare and his sister were saying. He gave his fire to an oil lamp on the dresser.

It was Gaspare who first heard the footsteps. "*Hisht!* Damiano!" the boy whispered sibilantly. "Someone's coming."

Damiano came bolt upright out of a dream in which Saara the Fenwoman had red hair and dog's feet. His heart lurched.

Gaspare was gesturing like a mad consort conductor. "Sing. Sing!" In another moment the boy had given up on

his friend, and seemed to fling himself out of the third-
story window. Evienne was standing with both hands on
her mouth, her green eyes circled by white. Couchicou, on
the other hand, sat with his nose pressed expectantly
against the door, his whip-tail banging.

Damiano could not remember the lullaby he had used
to quiet the house before. He could not remember any
lullaby. Any song. His hands lusted vainly for a staff.

"It's Herbert," the girl said, in a teeny-tiny voice.

Damiano, too, went out the window.

"Evienne—what's that dog doing in here?" demanded a
voice which Damiano, who was hanging by his fingers
from the window ledge, recognized as Rocault's.

"He has been here ever since I got back from dinner,"
Evienne replied. She lied with professional skill. "I have
been too afraid to have him removed. He might get angry
and bite me!"

Male laughter, half contemptuous, half amused, and
the sound of a door opening and shutting again.

"What the hell happened to you?" snapped Gaspare in
Damiano's ear. The two hung side by side, like banners—or
pots of kitchen herbs—from the window.

"I fell asleep," whispered Damiano in reply. His hands
were slowly slipping from the angled wooden sill. He
regripped with his right, causing his left to lose what it had
gained.

He was developing a bad case of splinters in his fingers,
and that worried him almost as much as the fact that there
was thirty feet of air between himself and the ground. Of
course the peach trees were immediately below. They
would break his fall before bouncing him out to the
pavement of the river road. Perhaps he would survive the
fall. It was unlikely, but not impossible that both of them
would survive.

He stared down into the illusory softness of the
blossoming trees. From here he could smell them again.
And out of nothing swam the memory of a sprawling
rosemary bush that at the Fenwoman's command had
snarled his feet in its twining embrace. He heard again the
drone of bees and Saara's clear voice singing words he
couldn't understand.

Then, he hadn't been able to understand. Now—

Well, why not? Though Damiano's special skills were with animals, and his sympathies did not extend to the vegetable kingdom (he ate carrots with gusto), still he would make the effort.

"I'm going to drop," announced Gaspare, "into the peach trees. I'll try to grab the branches to break my fall."

"No." Damiano fixed him with a desperate glance. "Wait just another minute." Then his face went blank with his interior effort.

"Wait for what," hissed Gaspare. "Sunrise? My hands are slipping now!"

But even as he did lose his grip, something hard touched the sole of Gaspare's foot. He fell no more than two feet and then crashed forward, bumping his long nose against the wall itself. Slowly Gaspare rose again, his legs tangled in a wildly expanding growth of blooming peach.

Damiano let the green wood embrace him. He sighed. He blinked unhappily at his wounded hands. "Damn!" he whispered. "Right in the tip of the first fretting finger." He stuck the damaged digit into his mouth.

Meanwhile, Gaspare was kissing the peach boughs with great passion with a face to which the sweat of fear had stuck bruised petals. He swung to the ground, nimble as a monkey.

Damiano followed, favoring his left hand.

Once on the pavement (still shiny with rain) he turned back to his handiwork, scratching his head with his right hand. He had no idea how to properly terminate such a spell.

But Damiano was nothing if not mannerly. "Thank you, peach trees," he called out to the growth. And within five seconds the trees had sucked back into themselves their unnatural extension.

Gaspare swore in awe.

"Everyone is taken care of," sighed Damiano, slumping against Gaspare's shoulder. "Gaspare, Evienne, Jan, the Holy Father, the Devil: everyone.

"Now it's Dami's turn. He's going to bed." And he leaned on Gaspare all the way home.

CHAPTER 11

It was an awkward and lumpy bundle of blankets, clothing, cheese, dried pears and bread. Inside it, like the
golden yolk within an egg, was hidden an exquisite lute.
Wine went in a separate bag; that also for the lute's sake. "It
will hold, anyway," grunted Damiano. "With all that rope,
it will hold."

The constraining rope went from end to end of the
bundle. Damiano slung it bandolier-style, groaned, took it
off, padded the rope with a rag and tried it again.

"Better. And then, of course, the horse will carry it
easier than I."

He had decided to meet Saara in the open, out of the
city. The Fenwoman, after all, didn't like cities, and among
the trees and grass there would be more of what his
euphemistic mind liked to think of as opportunities. He
had no doubt that Saara would be able to find him.

"You look like a fool," stated Gaspare, although the boy
had not turned from his position in front of the window,
staring at the dark street below. "It does your reputation no
good to be seen like that."

Damiano glared. He foresaw this night's mood being
ruined by another of Gaspare's seizures of temperament.
"Well, if that's all that's worrying you, the moon is half-past
full and I doubt anyone will be able to see me at all."

"Another reason to wait until morning."

"Why? I can see well enough by half a moon. Saara can
see excellently at all times. We are witches, remember."

"Heathen," said Gaspare in the same dry, suppressed
tone.

The lutenist, who had a temperament of his own, was
straining to be away. Yet it would be a shame to leave
Gaspare on that word. He stalked over to the boy and spun
him around by the shoulder.

"What is this, Gaspare? Don't I deserve a rest, after all
that has happened in the past month? You, too—you're
always complaining how hard it is to live with a madman.

"That is, when you're not telling me I am not a man at all because I have no mistress. Well, now I have a mistress, and I'm on my way to meet her."

The boy stood with his hands in his jerkin pockets, one hip cocked—an attitude that mimicked carelessness very unconvincingly.

"Go, if you're going already. We'll talk about it if you come back."

"If?" cried Damiano. "If?" A curse issued from the far end of the room, where an early sleeper had had his first rest broken by the noise. With one accord Damiano and Gaspare stepped out of the room and down the corridor.

"If? Mother of God, Gaspare. Do you believe I'm running out on you?" The heavy bundle banged along the narrow hall.

Gaspare cleared his throat and spat. "I believe nothing. It's much safer that way."

Once under starlight, Damiano desired urgently to bolt and run. His mind rebelled at the thought of one more depressing wrangle with the redhead. But he took a deep breath and began again.

"Two weeks at the most, I will be gone. The room is paid up and you have enough money for food till I get back—if you don't spend it on clothes."

"This is not good for your career, you know, musician," said the redhead distantly, peering into the darkness toward the city gate. "In two weeks Avignon can forget. You can't expect to find a job waiting vacant when you come back." Then he looked straight at Damiano. "How can I reach you if I need you?"

Damiano stared back. "Why should you need me?"

Gaspare ignored this. "I am your manager. I must be able to reach you. If you turn into a dove and flap off to Lombardy with that woman . . ."

The dark man leaned back against the white wall, where his hair made a shadowed halo. "Ah. So that's it. I'm not turning into a dove, Gaspare. I feel little enough human sometimes as I am. And a long journey is not the purpose for which I am . . ."

Cursing the limitations of the simple man, who would not be able to locate a friend hidden in the countryside outside the city, who indeed couldn't even find his sister when she was hidden behind a plaster wall, Damiano

stood and cogitated. An idea came: not a good idea, for it
interfered with his plans a bit, but one that might pacify the
boy.

"I will leave Festilligambe with you," he said. "Since he
is a horse and not a man, he will have some notion of
where I am. If you have to find me, just get on him and
give him his head."

In the middle of Damiano's explanation, Gaspare had
begun to shake his head. The movement gained both
speed and power, until at the end it shook the boy's entire
frame. "Oh, no, I won't. The last time I tried something
similar . . ."

"He found me right away, as I remember."

Gaspare snorted. "And almost killed us both. I
wouldn't touch that beast with anything but a butcher's
blade."

That was enough. Damiano's patience snapped like a
lute string, and he turned on his heel.

Already, as Damiano disappeared into the darkness,
Gaspare was beginning to regret the violence of his words.
He was reassured to notice that Damiano left the horse
anyway.

Each rustle was a mystery, and more a mystery as the
witch's ears put a name to it. That rhythmic pinging was
this week's rain, still dripping in a pipe somewhere. It rang
in his head like the music of the spheres. That tiny
interrogative shriek was a bat, chasing insects by the light
of a pedestrian's swinging lantern. The lantern itself hung
by a cord from the man's wrist, and creaked of rust and
leather. The man's breathing, too, creaked. He was ancient.

A second squeaking joined the first, but from below.
This was not a bat, but a rat, making sad complaint about
some rattish problem or other. While passing the next block
Damiano heard a louder sound: a thumping, also rhythmic, from behind an upstairs wall, accompanied by a duet of
heavy breathing. Though recognizable, like the call of a bat
or rat, this sound seemed to Damiano the very essence of
mystery. He stopped still, listening. His hand tightened on
the rope of his bundle.

Finally he reached the North Gate of Avignon, where he
had entered the city less than two weeks ago. As he passed
under he gave a silent prayer of gratitude.

What a clear sky, and what good fortune that three days' rain should have cleared when it did. Even the mud underfoot had been half dried by today's ambitious sun. Damiano nearly tripped over the broad flat road, then, as he remembered that Saara was a weather witch. Could she have worked this change for his sake? Or her own? For both, really. . . . The thought made him blush. He looked about him.

Twenty years ago Avignon had been threatening to burst her gates. The fields beside the road were dotted with small stone huts and large stucco houses, some roofless or without doors, either unfinished or subsequently cannibalized for materials.

All were abandoned now, for who else but a barbarian would live outside of Avignon when there was plenty of room within? They shone like ghosts, rain-washed, moonlit, surrounded by the susurrating new grass.

Two miles from Avignon, Damiano left the road, high-stepping over the soft earth, to look into one of the most imposing of the skeletons. (After all, why hurry when you don't really know where you are going?) This dwelling was in better shape than most; because it was so far from the city gate, no one had yet stolen its roof of tile. It possessed three large rooms through which the wind blew at fancy.

He entered. The stucco walls still stood, though cracked and sea-blue with mildew. The roof did not appear to leak much. Damiano placed his bundle carefully in the driest available corner and leaned out a front window.

No fortress, this, but the house of an ambitious peasant. The windows were square—indefensible, perhaps, but more pleasant for viewing the road. The rooms were big enough that a large family would not bump elbows too often, and the largest of them—the stable—had a loft which still appeared serviceable. Damiano scrambled up and peered down. Then he dropped to the floor and peered up.

He liked the house. He wondered if it were still owned by a man who had plans for it one day, and that was why it had not been pillaged like so many others. It was not too far for a man to live in and work in Avignon—if he had a horse.

Owned or not, the building was still occupied—by a

nest of black snakes, many of whom were spending the evening within, their whip-bodies lumpily satiated. Damiano went over to talk with them.

"Boy, boy, solitary boy." The song approached without noise of footsteps. The hair on Damiano's neck rose. Three snakes lifted sleek heads and listened with their tongues.

"Your playmates are the beasts of the fields."

Outside the window where Damiano had lately leaned stood a shining girl, her loose hair whipping back from her face. Her dress was sprinkled with stars, and her eyes bleached silver by the colorless light of the moon.

"Saara," whispered Damiano, thickly. The snakes all slithered away.

He came to the window, and gently he caught her wild hair in his hand.

"In what way am I solitary, Pikku Saara? And how am I a boy?" He kissed her.

Saara stared vaguely at the rough beams of the ceiling above the loft. "The sun is beautiful today. It would be warmer out there than in here."

Damiano lay beside her, his head comfortably wedged between Saara's neck and her pink shoulder, his knees clasped around hers. He felt perhaps he should be examining himself this morning, assaying both the state of his witchery and the state of his soul, to see what the loss of virginity had cost him. But that seemed such a dreary enterprise. Much more interesting to examine Saara's hair. "That one," he observed, "is coppery-red, almost as red as Gaspare's. And it is straight. But the one next to it is dark, and it has more curl to it."

She giggled, for his breath tickled her ear. "Probably it's your hair."

He grunted. "So it is. But this other one is not—my hair is never so fine—and it, too, is dark. And all around and between you have lemon-pale hairs, and ones of rabbit brown. . . ."

"Don't tell me about the gray ones," Saara murmured, and she cuddled in closer, making her own investigation of his neck.

"Eh?" Damiano gave a scornful snort. "You have no gray hairs. Don't be silly."

One wisp of hair fell across the woman's face. She regarded it cross-eyed. "Not yet, maybe. But it will come. We all grow old, Damiano." She squirmed in his grasp until she could reach his own shaggy head. He bent to allow her fingers in his hair. "What are you looking for, fleas?"

"Whatever," she murmured in reply. "You don't have any gray hairs, which does not surprise me. Nor fleas, either."

"I tell them to go away."

"But your hair, Dami! So thick. If it didn't go in circles, I would think it belonged to a horse."

He smiled and kissed the base of her throat. His head slid lower. "I thought I was a sheep," he said, his words muffled between her breasts.

"You are a thousand creatures," whispered Saara, and then nothing else was said for a quarter of an hour.

"Did I tell you Gaspare's sister is going to have a baby?"

Half his words were lost within a yawn. Saara made him repeat them.

"I have never seen Gaspare's sister, Dami, but my good wishes to her nonetheless."

"It is either the child of a cardinal or a thief," added Damiano, grinning up at his mistress, who was slipping her nakedness into her blue embroidered dress.

(He would dress her in silk satin, and in cloth-of-gold, and buy green velvet ribbons to wind in her hair. She would be the crown of Avignon.

But would Avignon accept a crown that did not wear shoes? There would be no use in buying Saara shoes.)

Her glance held a child's slyness. "Which would be better? I don't know what a cardinal is, but a thief I understand." Saara shrugged an Italian shrug. "If the child is strong and handsome, that is what matters." With practiced hands she braided her hair.

Damiano had a wonderful thought—a thought that made him feel both young and old, which turned him both to stone and to jelly. "Saara. Perhaps we will have a baby?"

Her green eyes darted to Damiano and her mouth opened. "Why—are you worried about that, Damiano? You need not be."

"I would love it," he said, and he laid his head in her

lap, mussing his hair back and forth against her belly. "Nothing could be better."

The northern woman turned her head away in some confusion. "But I thought, Dami, you did not . . . believe . . . in your own future."

He raised his head to hers and there was fire behind his black eyes. "I was a fool," he stated. "But since then I have met the Devil and called him a liar to his face. I am free of his words, Saara."

She said nothing, but continued with her braiding. After a moment his mood softened again and once more Damiano yawned. He let his feet dangle from the edge of the loft and swung them back and forth.

"What a fool I have been, Saara: wrongheaded and self-centered and backward, as well. Everything I did around you was always the wrong thing."

Saara primmed her mouth in superior fashion, but then spoiled the effect by giggling. "It couldn't have been too much the wrong thing, Damiano, or we would not be here now, yes?"

"But Ruggerio . . ."

She put a slim hand on his lips. "Dami! I will bury my dead if you will bury yours."

He kissed the hand and said no more.

"Besides," she continued, "it would be a miserable sort of young man who did not act like a fool now and then."

Saara slid from the high shelf with no more fear than a bird, and landed almost without noise. "Come out, Damiano, and show me what you know about magic."

They lay down in meadow flowers, side by side. "Eh!" Damiano protested. "We are going to get wet if we stretch out on this hill."

Saara laced her hands behind her neck. "So?"

Damiano went up on one elbow. From here he could see the red tile roof of the empty house he had already begun to regard as his, and the reddish ribbon of the road beyond, which his dim eyes could see was busy with people. Easter pilgrimage, most certainly. "All my clothes are new."

She played his rich overshirt between her fingers. "Take them off, then."

"If you will."

She gave him a canny glance and giggled.

They lay down naked in meadow flowers, side by side.

"Now, little witch-man," began Saara, "make for me a cloud."

Damiano only stared at her.

"Come now, Dami. You have all the earth and all the sky to work with. Make one little cloud."

He shook his head. "Show me."

The pretty girl yawned. Idly she knotted her braids together under her chin. "It's easy. First you sing your water out of the earth; there is a lot of it sitting there today."

Saara began to sing, not in Italian (thank God) nor in langue d'oc, but in her own far northern language. "DAH dah DAH dah DAH dah DAH dah" went the rhythm of her verse. It did not seem to have a rhyme scheme, but the sounds of her speech were so limited, and so harsh in his Latin-tuned ears, that he could not really tell.

Damiano flipped over to watch her as he listened. In only a few moments he felt a chill against his damp back, while the hair on his head was gently pulled away from the scalp. He scratched his head.

All around the two witches the air wavered, like that above a boiling pot. The grass on the hillock was complaining in a slow hish and hush as it gave up its glut of moisture.

Damiano opened his mouth to exclaim, and immediately his tongue and palate went dry and powdery. He swallowed and blinked sandy eyes.

Saara's own eyes were closed, and her hands folded on her breast. But her pink, rosebud lips were not dry, and a glistening drop balanced on her chin.

"Then, when you have the water in the air . . ." With the cessation of Saara's droning song, the electric pull in the atmosphere vanished. A wet heaviness settled over Damiano's shoulders, as fog shut their wild hillock away from the world. ". . . . you must send it high into the sky, where it belongs."

It was the same insistent, repetitive melody as before, but sung at least an octave higher. Damiano smiled to watch her, for the Fenwoman singing high in her nose sounded and looked about twelve years old.

Now her green eyes were open, gazing vacantly at the misted sky. Damiano noted a large spot of golden-brown in

her right eye, which he thought quite charming. Water
beaded on the wisps of hair in front of her ears, water that
sparkled like adamant when the sun reclaimed the sky.

Once again Saara yawned. "There." She pointed
straight above them. "See my cloud."

Damiano's bare back fell upon the chilled, sodden
grass. He repressed an unmanly shudder. In the blue
heavens from horizon to horizon there rode only one
cloud: tiny, fleecy, slightly translucent.

And directly overhead.

He commended her. "It is very pretty. The whitest
cloud I have ever seen. But for a little while I thought it was
going to take my teeth with it."

"Keep your mouth closed when someone is making
clouds, Dami. I should have told you that. All Lappish
children learn very early."

Damiano regarded the shapeless wonder in the sky at
some length, chewing on a stem of sorrel. "Is there nothing
to clouds but water?"

"What should there be?" asked Saara. "Fish?"

"Some binding element," he replied, frowning with
thought. "Something to make steam adhere to itself—for
you know that the steam from a kettle doesn't make a cloud
in your kitchen. It merely dissipates and runs down your
walls."

Saara giggled. When she turned on her side her right
breast hung above the left one, almost (but not quite)
touching.

Damiano found this fascinating. He ran a trilobed sorrel
leaf between her breasts. Not quite touching. He had to ask
Saara to repeat what she had been saying.

"I said the sky is all the binding element you need. Take
water high enough and it will be a cloud. And now it's your
turn. I will try to translate the song for you and . . ."

"No," replied Damiano, not raising his head from his
interesting task. "I don't use words in spells anymore."

The Fenwoman's eyes opened very wide. She snatched
the sorrel leaf from his fingers. "That tickles. Well, what *do*
you use?"

"Just . . . song," replied her lover, giving only half his
attention to his words. "One melody or another. Or three
at once. It doesn't seem to matter." Deprived of the sorrel
leaf, he tried using his nose.

Saara scuffed away over the squeaking grass. "That can be very dangerous, Dami. If you have no shape to put your meaning in, you can lose control."

He smiled. Snickered. "I do lose control, Saara. I am losing control right now." He dived after her and bit her gently on the softest part of her belly.

There is no soft part of the belly of a great white bear. Damiano recoiled, skidding down the grass on the slope of the hillock.

"Weren't you the one who trusted yourself so little you kept your magic locked in a stick, like it was a criminal?" asked the bear.

Damiano, who lay naked with his feet pointing down the hill, face on a level with the bear's paws, realized that each of those black-clawed feet was about the size of his own head. He answered the bear very politely.

"I always clothe my spells in shape, Saara. My music has a lot of structure—Raphael has made sure of that. And anyway I find I cannot make up words on the spur of the moment, or even remember ones I knew before. With tunes I have more facility."

The huge, deadly animal sat on its haunches and scratched its side with one front foot in very human fashion. "That is only a matter of practice. First you learn the basic songs by heart, and then you can change them as you need to. There is really very little you make up new."

"Then, with all due respect, Madame Bear, I would rather continue my own way. After all, I cannot have the advantage of a Lappish childhood, and my personal methods, though unorthodox . . ."

The bear rocked back and forth. "You use too many big words," it whined in a deep bass. "And you talk too fast to understand."

"I'm sorry," said the human contritely. "But what other weapons have I against a beast of your majesty?"

"Make a cloud, Dami," begged Saara. "Any way you want to, just get on with it."

Send his song into the earth? No, it was more that his song was the only part of him which remained above as Damiano probed through the soil after water.

Once before he had descended beneath the earth's wrinkled skin: that time after fire. This was a more gentle journey—gentle and permeated with a coolness which could not chill the spirit as it chilled the body. He had to wander far to find water that Saara had missed. He sank down into rock (rock is no barrier to the spirit) and out beneath the rough, silver grass. Here was a river running sunless between two beds of stone, deep underground. There lay a pool where the water had not trembled its surface since the birth of Christ. Everywhere in the deep soil was water bound to stone, bound to rotten wood, or filling the feathery lace within the bones of the dead.

"You are taking a long time, Dami," came the voice from everywhere. It pulled him regretfully from a search which was becoming a goal in itself.

Shape. His magic needed shape, if he was to control it, instead of the other way around. He sang (in his head) a song of marvelous symmetry, in which the two lines of music followed one another at a distance of two bars, like horses in tandem. Then he added a third line, which took round part with the first, while the second line went into a contrasting rhythm. He was no longer pretending to sing. He played in his mind and spirit a lute, and then (dissatisfied with its five courses of sound) an entire consort of instruments.

He called the waters from the ground and led them into the air.

Saara was right. The thin, high atmosphere imposed cloud form on the rising moisture. The problem was structure, of course. He was to be in control, not the vagrant breezes or the roiling weight of water itself. He dictated structure upon his creation.

"Damiano," spoke Saara again. "Is that what a cloud is supposed to look like?" Her words held no criticism, but a vague uncertainty.

He opened his eyes and beheld the enormous, stark-white lenslike formation which covered a third of the visible sky. It was ovoid, regular and pierced in the middle, making a perfect setting for the noonday sun.

"Ah?" He repressed a smile of pride at this, his maiden effort. "What did you ask for? A spell with shape to it will create a cloud with a shape."

In the loft of an abandoned house two miles north of Avignon, there was no light by which ordinary eyes might have seen. But neither the black snakes who curled together beneath the loft or the witches who curled together upon it had ordinary eyes.

It was in the middle of a black hour of the morning before the dawn of Easter Sunday. It was the hour of the soldiers' amazement: the hour of the rolling of the stone.

And Damiano, though he was not thinking of stones, or of soldiers, was all amazed. His mind was lit with a mystery—not the Paschal Mystery—which set him glowing.

"What joy is this," he whispered, half coherently, to his mistress, ". . . that dissolves my body and soul together, so that I lose my name and my voice . . . and though I give all away I am richer in my heart. Though this is called debauchery—though it is called sin—never have I felt more holy nor more hale."

Saara chuckled gently, in part because she did not understand Damiano's words, and in part because she did.

"I did not know I could be so happy," murmured her lover, his lips brushing lightly over smooth blushing skin, ". . . not on this earth. In fact I had been told that happiness was not meant for us; a close friend assured me that misery was our lot, and I . . . I believed her.

"But had I known—had I known before what it would be, to lie with you, Saara of Saami, I would have died years since, with the impatience of waiting."

Saara lay curled against the wall. In her long hair was tangled the stems of clover and mustard and vetch: sweet weeds the witches had plucked together, along with bundles of spring grass, to make a fresh bed upon the rough wooden platform. She cradled Damiano's head on her breast and gazed down at that tousled head with a wondering care.

"It was only yesterday you said to me that you were not alone, Dami. Not a solitary nor a boy, you said."

A smile pulled his mouth wide. With a single motion he rolled from Saara's lap and rolled her on top of him. "I am contradicting myself, bellissima. Nonetheless . . ." and Damiano paused, sniffing left and right. He drew Saara's head to his and buried his nose in her hair.

"Your hair smells a little of pond water, Saara. That's what we get for playing the part of frogs."

"Better than what we might have smelled like by now,

my dear," she giggled. "It is my practice to bathe every day, even when I have to break the ice to do it."

Damiano snorted. "You have strange tastes, beloved. Rose water and a steaming ewer—that I understand, but to immerse one's body . . ."

He combed the offending tress with his fingers. "No more breaking ice, Saara. No more cold beds shared with a pregnant goat." Then his musing smile faded.

"Saara. Your life has been so sad. You have loved proud men, violent men, vainglorious men. I may be a madman—Gaspare tells me so often enough—but at least I can be gentle about it. I will live to make you happy."

The forearms which locked about Saara's breast were very hard and strong, laced with the muscles and tendons used on the lute. Damiano's upper arms and shoulders were less well developed. His body, except for the face and hands, was the greenish olive of dark skin which has not seen the sun. He nuzzled the nape of her neck, rocking all the while from side to side.

Saara was rosy all over, though her shoulders, her nose and the upper surface of her nipples were dusted with bronze from the previous summer. Her eyes were closed, as she relaxed into Damiano's slow, rocking embrace. She leaned back and bit his ear gently, whispering something which made him chuckle as he replied:

"I spoke the truth. I have not been solitary. I have even had creatures I could love, and who would love me in return: not women, it is true, but dogs and angels at least.

"And none of that is wasted. Oh, no, I would be a churl to say it is wasted. . . ." Releasing Saara, he propped himself up on one elbow and sniffed to clear his nostrils of the intrusive dust of the mustard flower. Half mockingly, Saara rubbed his nose with a wisp of grass. He sneezed. She stuck the white globe blossoms of clover into his black hair.

"But this, beloved. To lie here sleepless on rough-hewn boards all the night of the most sacred day of the year, while you tease and abuse me this way—biting me, hitting me with sticks—with no regard for my dignity, my manhood, my comfort . . ." He turned his face slightly, for Saara was now kissing his neck with a predatory passion, and biting a bit harder, ". . . for this I was created. Ah, woman! My queen. My paradise. My great good friend."

For some while now the Fenwoman had not been listening to anything her lover said. Italian was difficult enough, for her, and impassioned Italian of a poetical cast, uttered with a strong Piedmontese accent and half smothered by blankets—that was beyond her. By Damiano's tone of voice she gained enough understanding to make her happy, and in turn she endeavored with a forthright Nordic sort of enthusiasm to transcend her own limited vocabulary. But his last sentence she understood, and it made her laugh.

"Ho! Damiano. I have been called a queen before, by Ruggerio (although he did not really mean it, since he did not usually do what I wanted him to do). And I have been called a friend. But never have I been a friend and a queen together. I think you will have to choose one or the other."

His response was a huge, mauling hug. "No! No, I can't choose. I am Delstrego the madman—just ask Gaspare if it's not true that I'm mad—and I have to have impossible things. You are to be my queen and my heaven, and my friend to love and play games with, and my teacher and my singer and . . ."

His touch quieted into something feather light as he concluded ". . . and maybe the mother of my troublesome children, heh?"

Having the eyes of sight and the eyes of love and the black eyes of a man, still Damiano could not see the look of pain that lashed over Saara's face. She hid her eyes against his shoulder.

He could not see her face, but he could feel her stiffen. "What is it, beloved, what have I said?"

Fear dripped cold in Saara, like blood from a stabbing wound. She thought, He will not want me when he knows. He has youth, time. . . . He has the world, and I am only the first of many. . . .

And though Saara dreaded the truth, she was not tempted to lie. "I can't have your children, Damiano. The children I had are dead: they are all I will have."

The silence that followed was terrible. Then Damiano said, "I am sorry I spoke, beloved. I didn't think. But it is no matter. If we can't have a child ourselves, we will merely buy one."

"Buy one?" Saara nearly hiccuped in surprise.

"Certainly. Of course, such a child would almost

certainly be simple: not a witch. If that would disappoint you too much, then we will have dogs instead."

"Dogs?" she echoed.

"Or horses. Or the big, flat-footed deer your people raise. The important thing, bellissima," and Damiano gave her hand an urgent little squeeze, "is to be surrounded with life, don't you think? Creatures that are young and growing, that look to the future."

Saara smiled in spite of herself, and the cold wound in her heart warmed unexpectedly, as though it might possibly heal someday. "With only you around, Dami, I feel . . . overwhelmed by life!"

She snuggled into the bed of greenery.

By the taste in the air it would be dawn soon. Damiano (in spite of never feeling more "hale" in his life) felt it would not be a bad idea to sleep Easter away. Sinful, of course, to miss the mass, and especially for such carnal purposes. But sin was man's nature, he had been told, and Damiano had a lot of carnal sinning to do if he was to catch up to the human norm.

Besides, he could not really believe there was sin in anything touched by Saara.

". . . has taken my fancy," he was saying. "It is a well-built house, with a good view and at least a rod of flat land on all sides of it. We could do worse than to settle here, at least for a while."

"Mnnh?" Saara was more than half asleep.

"I will go into Avignon to play—for I must play for people, or I will decline—and of course we will use the city as our market, but here we will have both ease and privacy."

"Have what?"

"Oh, we will live very well, Saara, you and I. Between the money I can make from my lute, and that which can be charged for purifying wells and assessing metals (always assuming there is no guild restriction in that area) we can live very respectably."

Damiano felt an impulse to remind Saara that he had begun as a respectable fellow, and of good family. But as he remembered Saara's position as the outraged mistress of his father (which now seemed so poor a reason not to love) he decided that the thing was better left unsaid. Instead he added, "Or we will live respectably once we are married, of course."

He felt her stir in his arms, and her long hair glimmered in a beam of the first light of Easter. "Married? You want to marry me, Damiano? How . . . cute."

"What do you mean—cute?" Damiano was stung. "I offer you a lifetime's protection and devotion and you call it cute."

Saara's eyes were limned clear and colorless in that single intrusive beam. Her lips remained in shadow. "It *is* cute, Damiano. Ruggerio always said that marriage was not courtly, while your father called it the death of love. Jekkinan . . ."

"Shut up about all these other men," snapped Damiano, hot in the face. "Especially my father. If I were not a very mild man, you would drive me to hit you with such talk."

Saara took a deep breath. "Then we would have another battle on our hands, wouldn't we, dear one? The walls of Avignon would shake, I think, if we went to war again. But you must let me finish. My people know no courts, so they don't care if a thing is courtly. I did not cease loving Jekkinan because I married him.

"I think it would be very sweet to marry you, Damiano. It is only that I did not know the men of Italy ever wanted to marry. And also, I don't know what you would do with a wife like me, all stubborn and full of teeth."

She showed him her small white teeth then, and he pretended to be cowed by them. Then he craned his head over the edge of the bed. "What is that?" he whispered.

Saara listened also, with senses honed by wilderness. "A horse," she answered.

Damiano twisted onto his stomach. "*My* horse," he corrected her, full of curiosity. "I know because he comes down especially heavy in front. He has never had a proper training."

He ought to get down from the loft. He ought to wait for Festilligambe by the road: the poor brute wasn't full-sighted, after all, but just a beast with a beast's instinct knowledge. But a strange reluctance to move paralyzed Damiano. He lay poised at the edge of the loft, half out of the blanket, listening to the urgent pa-rump, pa-rump of galloping hooves. Saara put one comforting hand between his shoulder blades. She kissed him on his unshaven cheek.

The horse needed no fuller sight than he had. His hooves left the road at the spot Damiano had, that previous Friday. They plashed heedlessly through puddles and scrabbled over slopes of wet grass. The two in the loft heard a squeal of protest that did not come out of the throat of a horse.

"Hmph. Gaspare. He is stiff as a stick, on horseback," snickered Damiano, but still he did not move.

The horse approached the door at a trot and then stopped. Damiano heard great equine sniffs of nervousness, as the beast passed under the lintel.

"Where the hell are you going, you filth, you sow?" cried the horse's rider between gritted teeth. "I can't see my hand in front of my face in here."

The tall horse stood immediately below the loft. It nickered to its master, who dropped a hand down to the rubbery nose. The horse sniffed the bed of greenery and settled back onto his haunches to reach for it.

Gaspare cursed, grabbing handfuls of mane.

"Up here," whispered Damiano. "We're up here in the loft. Don't let the horse eat this grass—it isn't fresh.

"What's wrong, Gaspare?" he added, though Damiano's tone itself denied that there could be anything wrong anywhere on this dawning Easter Sunday in Provence.

Gaspare choked twice before he could speak.

"Plague, Damiano. The plague has struck Avignon. People are dead on the streets.

"And Evienne—she's gone. She's been stolen."

CHAPTER 12

The walk back to Avignon in the Easter sunshine had not so much the character of an awakening from a good dream as a descent into nightmare. Damiano and Saara hurried south, following Gaspare, whose preoccupied steps tended to weave across the broad, rutted road.

Damiano's belief in Gaspare's words was fragile, for his own personal happiness was strong enough to force the misery of others out of his mind.

But plague. Happiness could not conquer that. Nor love, nor witchery.

I would stop time, he thought. If I could, I would stop time before we reach the city. Before I have to see them die again.

But as Damiano could not stop time, he walked on.

Behind the three paced a winded, halterless horse, whose own progress went by fits and starts: fits of grazing interrupted by explosions of catching up to the humans.

The breeze came down from the north, pressing Damiano's shirt against his back and whipping Saara's dress against her calves till her skin reddened. It was fresh but not cold, its Alpine origins having been softened by hundreds of miles of Provençal indolence.

Traffic upon the road for the most part was heading straight into the wind, as a parade of souls issued from Avignon, dressed not for Easter but for a long journey. Their horses and oxen were burdened and their small children cried. None of those who fled the city spoke to Damiano's company, and he had nothing to say to them.

So the procession he had thought was going into Avignon for Easter was actually going out of it, escaping disease. Yet Avignon was a big city, and these few dozen people hardly constituted an exodus of fear. Perhaps conditions within were not so bad. His memory also told him exactly how stable Gaspare's emotions were and how far his word could be trusted.

Saara stepped beside Damiano, saying nothing, her face unreadably thoughtful.

But there would have been no room for her to open her mouth, had she so desired. Sharp-faced, shaky-voiced, young Gaspare held the floor.

"It was only the day after you left the rumor came, that a man had died all black and swollen. Whether it was the plague that did for him, though, no one knew.

"I myself could have told them," continued the boy with a vicious slap to his own chest, "having seen more of the world than these sheep of Avignon.

"But no one asked me. Besides—who wants to get so near the pest as to diagnose it? Anyway, old Coutelan shut up the inn. No more soirees for the cardinals. Our own hovel, too. No pillow where Gaspare of San Gabriele may rest his head."

"Is it only a rumor, then?" broke in Damiano. "Before you said there were people dead on the streets."

"I said . . . I said"—the boy lost his tongue for a moment in his excitement—"it was a rumor on the day after you left. The day following that it was no more necessary to ask what sickness was making a fellow retch and wheeze and pop out in aching boils.

"Now the vendors are gone from the streets and the shops are boarded. No one goes anywhere except the man with an ox and an open cart. It is just like Pe'Comtois. Chhhaah!" Gaspare spat in the street.

His reedy voice had held a peculiar horrified satisfaction as he cataloged the plight of Avignon. His exophthalmic eyes glinted.

"But Evienne," asked Damiano, trying to put concern behind his words. "How does this affect your sister? Have you reason to believe . . ."

Gaspare's odd cockiness collapsed like wet paper. "I have no reason to believe anything good. I went to see her and . . ."

"How? How could you find your way into the cardinal's house without me?"

Gaspare curled his lip. "How do you think, sheep-face? A sop for the dog and rope with a hook of applewood. The old, reliable methods. But Evienne is gone, and her dresses and blankets with her. They left nothing behind worth taking away."

Saara spoke for the first time. "This is your sister who is going to have a baby?"

"Yes, the slut. They say the cardinal is in conference in the Papal Palace, and I don't know if that means he is in chains or he has old Innocent in chains, but I can't believe he took my sister with him."

Gaspare snorted and his long nose twitched. "Evienne is not the proper stuff for the Papal Palace."

Damiano's head lifted. The soft wind tunneled through his hair. "I hear bells now," he admitted. "Surely they would not ring the Paschal carillon if the city were infested?"

Saara, who could not follow Gaspare's rapid speech,

had been listening to the peal for some time. "No, Dami. There is no joy there. I think those are black bells. They ring because people are dead."

Now the wind shifted and the note came clear. It was a slow, tedious, effortful tolling, and as he listened to it Damiano's last armor fell away from him. He tasted fear on the wind, along with something worse.

Avignon was now a dome of white rising up the hill from the Rhone, scarcely farther from them than an arrow's good flight. The city swam in the morning light, but approaching along the pale pink and busy roadway was the oxcart Gaspare had only just described, driven by a thick and brutish man whose shape Damiano found familiar.

The three people stepped out of the wheels' path, while Festilligambe shied onto the road's shoulder. A great bronze-burnished ox nodded its head solemnly as it passed them, as though to say "Yes, yes. This is the awful truth."

The driver of the cart tugged his beast to a stop before them. As he peered down from beneath the brim of a rough straw hat he sighed hugely.

Damiano was relieved to discover that the man wore neither the features of the Devil nor the mad cart driver of Petit Comtois. Because it was Damiano who regarded the driver so closely, it was to Damiano that the man spoke.

"Turn back, young gentles," he said earnestly. "There is no purpose so urgent it should take you into Avignon today."

Damiano's eyes slid back to the tall solid wood wheels, doweled to their axle, and to the high wooden slats that sided the wagon. "You are certain it is the plague, then?"

At the word "plague," the driver pulled off his woven hat and held it in his hand. "It was fifty dead yesterday, good monsieur. Today there will be a hundred, I am certain.

"Turn back," he repeated, his gaze on Saara's fair face. "For this plague is merciless and it seeks out the young." With those words the driver lashed his ox into movement.

Gaspare, who had stood silent during this interchange, staring with dread at the uncommunicative slats of the wagon, now ran after the man. "Hello, hello! Tell me, have you seen a redhead?" he asked in halting langue d'oc.

The driver mauled his beast to a stop again. "Seen what?"

"A girl with red hair, very pretty," shouted the boy, and as the driver blinked without comprehension Gaspare added, "with a biggish belly. Pregnant."

After a moment the man shook his head. "Going your way on the road there has been no one but you. Or did you mean leaving the city?"

Gaspare grimaced. "I didn't mean on the road. I meant . . ." And then, without another word, he turned on his heel and dashed the fifty yards back to where his friends were waiting. They asked no questions.

The gate stood open. When Damiano expressed some surprise at this, Gaspare only shrugged. "Why not? It's too late to keep the plague out now."

"But to keep it from spreading . . ."

"Is it the business of Avignon to watch out for Lyons?" replied the cynical fourteen-year-old. He made to step under the arch of stucco.

Damiano, stepping behind, felt a cold, premonitory sweat. He grabbed at the boy's jerkin. "Wait a moment, Gaspare. I think it would be better if you returned and waited for us at our house."

"Your . . . house?" Gaspare's lank hair had fallen inside the collar of his shirt. Frowning hugely at Damiano, he pulled it out. "Where do you have a house?"

Saara interrupted. "You are thinking he should not go into the city, Dami? You are right. He is simple, and it would be very dangerous for him."

Gaspare turned from one to the other, insult darkening his uneven complexion. "Simple? From you, sheep-face, that is laughable."

Damiano refused to be offended. "You don't understand, Gaspare. We are witches."

"So you keep telling me. . . ."

"And if we are careful, we will not get the plague. You, however . . ."

Two white patches appeared amid the crimson mottling on Gaspare's face. "Everyone gets the plague. Even Jews get the plague; remember the Pope saying so?"

"Wait for us in the clean air and sunlight, boy," suggested Saara, using what was to her the most pressing argument against Avignon (or indeed any city). "We will bring your sister out to you."

Gaspare glared his scorn upon both of them and entered Avignon.

There was no crowd upon the streets, no press of bodies in the cobbled court before the Bishop's Inn and no one at all sitting at the inn-yard tables, which had been turned upon their ends and now stood ranked against the ground-floor wall.

"This," reflected Damiano aloud, "is not like Petit Comtois, where all was madness and buffoonery. This resembles more my own city, Partestrada, on a fast day with the shops all closed. It doesn't look like plague at all."

"Nonetheless," grunted Gaspare stolidly

Saara stepped lightly over the cobbles. Her toes grabbed and curled, like those of a stalking bird. One slim arm settled on Damiano's shoulder. "Don't be fooled, dear one. This place has evil in it," she said.

And Damiano could feel that. Despite his words, he could feel trouble in the air, and fear in the smell of the bodies hidden by walls all around him.

How odd, to stand in the middle of a disaster which could not touch one. I am a witch again, he thought. I have a power of flame so strong the plague cannot enter in. My lady, too. We could stroll together among piled bodies and suffer no hurt.

And in spite of this knowledge (or perhaps because of it) Damiano felt a surge of hopelessness, almost like despair. He turned to Saara. "We have to help these people, beloved," he whispered, out of Gaspare's hearing.

Her eyes were windows over the sea. "We can't. Years ago, don't you think I tried? In Lombardy, when I felt sickness in the village below, I came down to them. I sang till I became so weak I might have sickened myself. Not one lived who had caught the plague. Not one.

"This plague has jaws like a trap, and those who fall into it, die in it."

"What are you saying to him?" Gaspare whined shrilly, stepping between them and hopping from one foot to the other. "Is it about Evienne? Can you tell me where she is?"

Saara looked down upon him from a height of years. "You should leave this place, boy. You cannot help your sister by dying."

Gaspare cursed. He swore before them both that he

would never leave the trail of his sister until she was found: not for food, nor drink nor rest, and especially not for safety's sake. He kicked the pavement and called Saara crude names in Piedmontese argot. She listened with the calmness of a person who understands so little of a language she cannot be offended in it.

The black horse, who was also out of temper because there was no grass in Avignon, and because he had to step so very carefully over each round cobble, brushed by the irritatingly noisy boy on a search for some growth of green among the stones. Festilligambe found what he sought behind a small garden gate, which swung open at the touch of his nose.

"That's MacFhiodhbhuidhe's gate," murmured Damiano, cutting into Gaspare's tantrum. "He doesn't leave it open." And the dark witch followed the horse through.

The little garden was empty. With some difficulty Damiano shooed the gelding away from a pot of herbs and back into the road. He closed the gate on the animal and then crossed again toward the courtyard door.

Open also. Damiano stepped in, and although his senses told him there was no one within, he called out his presence.

The harper's house was dim and tidy. Downstairs nothing moved. Damiano took the steep, uneven stairs two at a time. MacFhiodhbhuidhe's bedstraw was swept into a corner and his bedclothes were folded. Gleaming balls of brass wire lay in a smug sunny row on a bookshelf. There was no sign of MacFhiodhbhuidhe or of the ancient who did for him. The young witch clattered down the stairs again.

This house gave an impression of age. It seemed all the heavy furniture, neat-dusted and smelling of beeswax, had stood in place unmoved for a long time. Like the harper's music, which probably hadn't suffered alteration since he left his Leinster academy. Damiano once more felt his spasm of irritation at MacFhiodhbhuidhe, tempered by the knowledge that the man was kind. On impulse he crossed the downstairs room. He stopped before the low cabinet to peep again at the exotic Irish harp.

After a minute, he picked up what he found and carried it to the door.

There, in the sunlight, stood Saara and Gaspare, with the horse. Gaspare was looking sulky. So was the horse. Saara had one hand wrapped in the black mane, and she had evidently been bestowing a few home-truths upon both of them.

Damiano came out blinking against the white light. In his arms he cradled three lengths of black wood, wrapped in a twist of brass wires. "It has been taken apart," he announced. "The harp. He said . . . he said to me . . ."

"That he would never take it apart again," added Gaspare.

"Not . . . while he lived to play it."

"He was your friend?" Saara asked gently.

They had been walking with great purpose toward the river for some minutes before he answered her. "I guess so. He was very good to me. I did nothing for him."

Gaspare giggled awkwardly. "What were you supposed to do? He had money and position. You didn't. And we only knew him for a few weeks."

Saara watched Damiano rub his eyes with his shirt-sleeve. He noticed. "Pay no attention to that," he barked at her. "I do it all the time. It means nothing—no more than a sneeze." Then, in an excess of frustrated feeling, he drew back his fist as though he would slam it into the nearest wall.

But as he was a musician and that wall was made of stone, he thought better of the action and hit his fist into his opposite palm. "Curse it all to hell!" he shouted, and then stared wildly from one friend's face to the other.

"Wait for me here," he commanded. "There's something I must find out." He darted down a side street. There followed a disgruntled whinny, and the tall horse followed his master at a trot, a small pot of blooming violets hanging from his mouth.

"He is mad, our Damiano," said Gaspare complacently.

The door was locked from within, the hanging sign was missing, and the windowless face of the jeweler's shop gave no clue to what lay within. Yet Damiano's senses told him that there was someone alive in the shop or above it. He pounded on the door repeatedly.

Finally a voice cried out from a slot window above his head. "Closed! Go away."

Damiano backed into the street. "Ormerin, let me in. It's Delstrego."

"Who?"

"The man with the ruby pendant." There was no answer, and Damiano added, "I swear by all the saints, man, that I am not sick of the plague. In fact I am probably the safest man in all Avignon to let in your door."

After a moment's reflection, the jeweler called out. "What do you want, Italian? Do you want to buy your ruby back?"

"You still have it, then?"

The jeweler cleared his throat. Damiano could see one small brown eye and half a mouth at the burglar-proof window. Ormerin was watching Damiano's horse as the beast tried its black nose into all the ground floor windows on the street. "It's not the sort of thing one sells every week or two. I haven't even shown it yet."

"Ah?" Damiano nodded his head forcefully, as though this bit of information was important. "And your family, Monsieur Ormerin. Your wife and little ones. Are they well?"

Ormerin, who was small and smooth-faced, regarded Damiano with his other eye. "So far, and may God maintain us."

"That is all I wanted to know," replied Damiano, and he ran away again. Festilligambe followed reluctantly.

Damiano returned breathing hard. He had twisted his foot slightly on a stone and walked gingerly. "He hides his lies in a shell of the truth," he gasped. "Like a worm in a hazelnut. You think you have learned to ignore him, and then you find he has struck you in another level of deceit."

Saara stared at her lover without comprehension. She bent down and took his ankle in both her hands. After a few moments the pain departed. "What are you talking about, Dami?" she asked at last.

"The Devil. He told me I was responsible for the plague in Avignon."

Gaspare's gooseberry eyes rolled. He put one arm at the small of Damiano's back and marched him forward. "When was all this?" asked the boy indulgently.

"Last week," replied Damiano, testing his leg.

"Last week there was no plague in Avignon."

The sprain was gone entirely. At the end of the street

the Rhone sparkled, its surface shattered by the breeze. "That was what made him so convincing. He said the sickness came in my ruby, which I sold. But the jeweler is well, along with his family. I think if the ruby *were* a plague stone, they'd have been the first . . ."

Saara's child-pure features expressed anger. "You said you had thrown it away, Dami. You said you believed nothing that he said. . . ."

"No more do I," he replied shortly, and ran his hand over Saara's sleek braided head.

"You did not bring the plague to Avignon." She pulled away from his touch. "It came on a bat, I think."

"A bat?" Gaspare snickered. "A ruby is easier to believe."

"A bat or a rat." She shrugged. "Something with a squeak. Or that's what the earth tells me."

The peach trees were past their best bloom, which is to say that tiny green leaves peeped and pried among the pink petals. The three stopped beside the house, while Festilligambe trotted down to investigate the river.

"Sing us in, my lady," whispered Damiano. "Let's see whether Evienne is missing, or whether Gaspare merely missed her."

The boy cursed under his breath, but made no objection as the Fenwoman opened her mouth in a wailing, foreign chant. Damiano sprang the lock with a word.

Cardinal Rocault's pleasant villa was in considerable disarray. There was broken crockery in the garden, and the chickens were loose. Lying disconsolately across the front stoop was Couchicou, the wolfhound. Damiano stroked him, exempting him from Saara's spell. His tail, heavy as a man's wrist, beat the stone stair.

In the kitchen sat three of the cardinal's servants: two women and the man whom Gaspare and Damiano had met earlier guarding the kitchen door dog-fashion. They were eating the cardinal's cheese and drinking the cardinal's wine. The older of the two women sat on the fat man's lap. They consumed their illicit pleasures determinedly, but none was smiling.

Saara, Gaspare and Damiano passed by with no more regard than they would have displayed passing a public fresco. The dog tarried at the table.

Gaspare was quite correct. Evienne was missing, along with her tapestries and her feather bed. A glance into her armoire revealed that her clothes had likewise accompanied her. In fact, the tiny cubby above the peach trees held nothing which would interest a thief—even a poor thief like Evienne's brother. Damiano's senses told him further that the girl was nowhere in the house.

"Gone," he stated. "But not run away by herself, unless she did so atop a loaded cart."

"It is as I said," insisted Gaspare, searching futilely once more through the empty drawers. "She has been stolen."

Damiano made an equivocal gesture. "Stolen? Say rather taken to a place of safety by her protector, the cardinal."

"Whatever, still we must find her," Gaspare shoved home a drawer with emphasis.

Damiano sighed. "Again?" Saara looked from one to the other.

"Surely that will not be so difficult?" she asked brightly.

"But it's Easter," replied her lover. "Easter Sunday itself. And there are more pressing problems in Avignon than a sister who keeps moving about. And also"—he gave an enormous, jaw-distending yawn—"I'm so sleepy."

He walked into Jan Karl's office alone and shut the door behind him. The blond cleric didn't see him at first, as the table at which he sat with quill and ink faced away from the door, and he was very busy writing a list of names. Damiano gazed calmly at Jan Karl's bald crown until the man turned around.

"Delstrego! What . . ." And Jan's glance darted quickly from his visitor to the paper under his hand and then back again. He covered his script with blotting sand and swiveled his stool around.

"What brings you back here, today of all days?"

"Today of all days?" repeated Damiano very politely. He pulled the only other chair in the room over to the table and he sat himself down in it, lifting his feet up onto the table. His heavy, black mountain boots were pointed at Jan Karl like a threat. "Why is today special, aside from the fact that it is Easter?"

The Dutchman scraped his chair sideways, so that

Damiano's feet were no longer pointed at him. He ran a
hand through his border of silky yellow hair and his long
face drew longer. His mouth made a small moue and he
raised his blue eyes to the ceiling. "Do you see these
authorizations?" he began. "They bear the Holy Father's
own seal. Today I woke up as a lector of the church. An
hour after dawn I became a deacon. Just before you walked
in I was informed that I was about to be ordained a priest
and—by the way, Delstrego, it was a great good thing you
didn't take but two of my fingers back there in that
wretched hamlet in Lombardy. A man without fingers
cannot offer the mass—and as I was saying, I am also made
officer of the palace refectory. Before this day is out, I could
be a cardinal."

Damiano nodded in calm good humor. "Or you could
be dead. Life is full of surprises, especially when there is
plague in the city."

Karl's face froze and he gripped the short arms of his
stool. "The plague is part of the reason for my advancement, certainly. The court has known many losses in the
last few days, especially from among the lower ranks."

These two men who faced one another without friendship were built in quite similar fashion: tall, lean and not
too broad of shoulder. It is hard to explain, then, why the
Dutchman, Jan Karl, gave the impression of having been
stepped on by something large at some time in the past,
and of expecting to be imminently stepped on again, while
Damiano gave a very different impression. The dark Italian
slouched by the window, imperturbable, with eyes of black
stone, looking (had he only known it) like the Roman
General Pardo, when he interviewed young Damiano
himself in Partestrada.

"But it is not only that, of course," continued Jan, as he
poured more sand over his parchment. "It is also the
discovery of Rocault's plots."

Damiano watched the Dutchman empty his sandpot.
The effort seemed less directed toward drying the ink than
concealing the substance of his writing. Damiano considered telling Jan not to bother: that he could never read
script across the width of a table, but Jan's last sentence
stopped him.

"Discovery? Of Cardinal Rocault?"

"Inevitable," replied the blond with a superior shrug.

"Considering how the man was overstepping himself. It was in the kitchen, you know. That is how the post of officer of the refectory has so suddenly become open.

"Oh, there are many new opportunities in the hierarchy now, Delstrego." Jan gave a little giggle. "It is so good to be in the right place at the right time for once."

Damiano rubbed his left hand over two days' growth of beard, making a noise like a pumice stone at work. "Hmmph! I see. The kitchen, was it?" Then he was silent.

Jan, too, had run out of things to say, and stared at Damiano, whom he suddenly seemed to remember was not exactly his friend.

"I, too, once wanted to become a priest," mumbled Damiano, giving the impression of a man deep in thought. "Of course I discovered that a born witch cannot be ordained, no more than a man who is missing his thumb or first two fingers." He scraped his stubble again and peered vaguely at Jan from under a thicket of black curls. He yawned. "And anyway it's just as well, considering what I've been and what I've done."

Then his head was raised an inch and once again the eyes were made of slate. "It's too bad Evienne couldn't also be in the right place at the right time, isn't it?"

"E-Evienne?" Jan Karl stuttered as though the very sound of the name were strange to him. "What has she to do with my ordination?"

"With your ordination? Nothing, I imagine. But with the discovery of Cardinal Rocault's plot . . ."

Jan snorted. "She had nothing to do with that. She hasn't the brain for politics."

Damiano nodded assent. "I agree completely. She has nothing to do with any plot against the Holy Father. So why has she vanished, my dear Jan? Who has stolen her, and where did they take her? Her brother, you see, would like to know."

Karl rose to his feet. There was no expression on his face. "Gone? Did you go to see her at the cardinal's, then? That was dangerous. Too dangerous for me, anyway."

"He went to see her twice. She was locked in her little kennel, like a bitch who is carrying a litter of great value. But now she is missing, and all her furniture is gone with her."

The blond's lips moved soundlessly. Then he said, "If

Rocault had got her locked up, then she probably ran
away."

"With her featherbed under her arm? No, Jan. She
refused to run away, although I offered to help her do so.
She was staying where you put her, like a good girl, and
her only fear was that you had been killed by the
wolfhound, who by the by is waiting for me outside your
door this minute, or that you had forgotten her and would
not return with the glass copies of her jewelry you had
promised to deliver."

While Damiano spoke Jan Karl had turned away and
was staring blankly out the single, viewless window. The
Italian prodded him with a boot. "Heh? Did you make
copies of her jewelry, at least? Mother of God, Jan! That
sweet, stupid little girl loves you!"

Jan Karl shuddered fastidiously. "You exaggerate, Delstrego. How like an Italian you are." He paced across his
square box of a room, his hands folded at the front of his
long black robe. Jan Karl, with his pale skin and dry face,
looked quite spectral in black. "We were friends once,
certainly. But she is the sort of woman who does not
remember things for long. Her senses are earthy and her
feelings very low. I am confident that she no more expects
me to . . . to visit her in her confinement than I . . .
than I expect . . ."

"Than you expect what, Jan?" inquired Damiano, who
was feeling a slow heat of anger spread from his chest out
toward his hands and head.

Suddenly the Dutchman turned at bay, his hands
pressed upon the edge of the writing table. "I expect
nothing from her. I am being ordained, Delstrego. The
affairs of the flesh I have put behind me."

Damiano said, "How noble of you. What a sacrifice."
He sighed, willing his anger into control. "I didn't really
come here to talk about all that, Jan. I think Evienne is
better off without you, myself.

"I need you only to tell me where she is gone. Is it likely
Rocault himself took her out of the city before his discovery, to keep her from the plague?"

There was a noise in the distance, along the hall, of
someone weeping: a man, giving way to deep, hopeless
sobs. The cleric was distracted for a moment, and his brow
creased. He sank back into his chair.

Damiano also listened, and his lips pulled back from his teeth. "Perhaps you may expect another promotion today," he said with a touch of bitterness.

Jan Karl ignored him. He sat biting his lip. "It was Friday midday that Father Lemaître, the officer of the refectory, confessed that he had agreed to offer poison to Innocent in the Easter dinner. He may have been the very first in Avignon to die. He thought the disease was a judgment upon him."

"Indeed? And for what is the rest of the city being judged?" asked Damiano in a low murmur.

"Within an hour the cardinal had been brought into the palace, and no more has been heard of him since. So I don't think it would have been he who gave the order to remove Evienne."

"Then it must have been the Pope himself who took the girl away," whispered Damiano, only half believing his own words.

Jan Karl cleared his throat. "More likely Commander Sforza, if anyone. But I think, rather, she ran away by herself, Delstrego, once she got wind of what had happened."

Damiano shook his head. "No, for then she would have come to you. She has not tried to see you, has she?"

Karl shook his head.

"I thought not. Tell me, where would the Holy Father have taken her—assuming he took her anywhere?"

The Dutchman raised his hands in complete mystification. "He has thousands of troops in hundreds of barracks and dozens of secret cells beneath them."

Damiano slapped his thigh like a man making a decision. "I will ask him," he announced. "That is the only course."

"You will *what?*" yelped Jan Karl, rising once more. "You will ask . . . the Pope himself . . . what he has done with his enemy's mistress?"

Damiano stood also. "Yes. After all, I have met him, and he seemed very approachable. I will tell him Evienne's complete story, and I'm sure . . ."

"You cannot!" Jan Karl's wail echoed through the room, competing with the cries of the unknown sufferer in the distant reaches of the building. "You can't tell him without revealing my part in . . ." He grabbed at Damiano's gold-chased sleeve. "You mustn't reveal my name!"

Damiano pulled away. "One can't go about telling half-truths to the Holy Father," he said.

Jan Karl put his two remaining left-hand fingers in his mouth and bit down on them. "Wait. Wait, Delstrego, before you try anything as desperate as that. I think I know where they might have taken her."

For some minutes after the witch had left, Jan Karl sat beside his writing table, pouring sand from one hand to the other, his fear and his ambition warring with the memory of Evienne's red hair. His eyes gazed unseeingly at the parchment he had been filling, which began: "I have reason to believe that the following men have been involved in the recent and disgraceful attempt . . ." At last he put that sheet aside in favor of one of those which had come to him that morning, took his fingernail and began to worry at a beribboned blob of wax.

CHAPTER 13

It was a strange little procession that wound its way through the rabbit-warren of halls and chambers which was the Papal Palace at Avignon. It was led by Damiano (for only he had been told the way), elegantly dressed in scarlet and gold, his black boots striking the tiles soundly. Saara followed: a sweet-faced and barefoot peasant in a dress bright as some child's painting. Her steps made no noise. After her came Gaspare in finery grown quickly shabby with ill-use. His soft city shoes scuffed a nervous and uncertain rhythm, and his shoulders had crawled up his neck. Gaspare wished they would hurry.

In front and in back, stitching the group together, came Couchicou, the cardinal's wolfhound, who did not know where they were going, but had come along for the company.

The oddest part about this small assembly was the sound emanating from it, for Damiano and Saara together sang a song. They were throwing it about between them, from one throat to the other, as one ran out of inspiration or the other desired to speak. It was not, of course, the same song for Damiano as it was for the Fenwoman, as Saara had her traditions, whereas Damiano tended toward vers libre. But the two interpretations fit nicely, and the main theme of it was to the effect that no one should see them marching toward the palace infirmary, down corridors by torchlight, and through enormous halls whose windows overlooked the Rhone.

Damiano took a breath and let his mistress take over the burden of melody. To encourage her effort, he put his arm around her shoulders. "Jan says that people who show cause to be detained—people of a certain status, that is, such as the cardinal, or cause of a delicate nature, such as that of Evienne—are often put into a suite of chambers behind the infirmary. It is a comfortable situation, he tells me, except for the lock on the door."

Gaspare looked left and spat right. "I wouldn't want to be locked in any rooms, however comfortable, near sick people today."

Damiano's face, which had displayed all the complacent happiness of his amatory good fortune, as well as a good share of the drowsiness which often accompanies such good fortune, grew on the instant grave. He stopped in mid-stride, pulling Saara to a halt with him. "It is as I said before, Gaspare. You should not be here. It is dangerous for you."

"If you catch the plague, child," added Saara, "we cannot help you."

Gaspare balled fists at his sides and advanced upon Damiano. "Stop trying to get rid of me."

The wolfhound, sensing tension in his little pack, weaseled in between the two humans and, with a wiggle and lean, knocked Gaspare against the wall. The boy cursed but did not dare a kick at Couchicou's slablike side.

Damiano turned away. "To get rid of you? I have given that up, Gaspare," he muttered to himself. "Two nations, endless mountains and a plague town were not sufficient for the purpose."

They needed neither directions nor second sight to tell them when they approached the palace infirmary. The stench of sickness informed them of their approach, along with the sight of piles of straw along both sides of the corridor wall, on which the afflicted were placed in long rows.

Damiano had seen plague victims before, and told himself that he ought to be hardened to the sight. Saying that did no good, however, for on the green faces before him, and in their suppurating lesions, pain had been translated into pure ugliness, and death into an unconquerable despair.

"And these are all men dedicated to Christ's service," he whispered, dropping his arm from Saara's shoulders. "It does not seem . . . allowable."

Glassy gray eyes met his, shining from a face made hideous by swelling. They asked no questions, these eyes.

"He can see me," whispered Damiano. "Despite the spell, he can see me. Is that because he is dying?"

Saara took her lover gently by the arm. "Come, Dami."

Gaspare stared straight ahead. His pinched face had gone slick with fear-sweat: Couchicou, too, walked stiffly, pressing his side against that of the boy, and his rough fur bristled along his back.

Moving quietly among the dying were women in white, whose eyes were weary beyond expression, and whose lips moved constantly, without sound. Benedictines, these were. Damiano watched the nuns and wondered, remembering a girl with flaxen hair who once sat in a high loggia, doing needlework under the white north light of the Alps. Carla Denezzi, postulant of the order of Saint Clare: if fortune did not take him again to the high mountains of his birth, he would never see her again.

It might be she was dead now.

Soon they passed the infirmary hall itself, where the stench was overpowering, and the dead lay in stacks covered by sheets. They came to a turn in the corridor where there were no more piles of hay and no more gentle Benedictines, but far off along a tunnellike corridor could be escried a pair of Papal guards, complete with sword and halberd, like those that stood by the main gate of the enclosure. But these pikes did not point to heaven in parallel. They swayed through the torchlight like fir trees in the wind, for the guards were talking animatedly to another, less impressive figure that pointed repeatedly into the darkness along the corridor.

"What?" whispered Gaspare in Damiano's ear. "What's that happening ahead?"

The witch's ears rather than his eyes gave him that

information. For a moment his face went blank with surprise and he grabbed each of his companions by the arm. "By all saints: it's the Dutchman. How did he get here before us?"

Saara said nothing. In the midst of her spell-song, it is doubtful she even understood what Damiano was saying, nor why he pulled them to a rough stop in the middle of an empty corridor. Couchicou prodded them all with his nose, impatient to be going, and then he scented a person he had encountered before now in dubious circumstances. A person of no importance, a person he did not like. The war-dog rumbled like a disturbance of the earth.

Carefully Damiano quieted the dog before he allowed his party to proceed. He suffered a great curiosity to know what was Jan Karl's business.

"It is the seal of the Holy Father himself," the blond cleric was saying. "How dare you impede me in my duty, having seen it?"

It was unfortunately the effect of Karl's Teutonic accent upon the Latin languages that his words came out sounding peremptory at best of times, and when he was excited, quite rude. This effect colored many people's reactions to the Dutchman. Perhaps it was in some measure responsible for the fact that Damiano, whose nature was generally social, could not bear the man's company. Surely it was having that effect at this moment upon the pikemen, who had been already strung to a high tension by the near-presence of plague.

The guard beneath the single wall lamp slapped at the parchment Karl was waving about. He shifted his halberd over one shoulder. "You must give to me the authorization you speak of, Father," he said sullenly, "instead of using it to kill flies this way."

"Father?" hissed Damiano. "Is he a priest already? How could that be, if he was not one a half-hour ago? And if this fellow has no more interest in Evienne, then what is he doing here—getting recipes for poison from the cardinal? . . . I fear there is more going on here than I had thought." And he led Gaspare even closer to the light.

Jan Karl rattled long fingers against the parchment. "What do you want with a page of script, fellow? Could you read it if I gave it to you?" The Dutchman held his breath until the pikeman replied, "No, I cannot read more

than a few words. But I know one man's writing from
another. I am well acquainted with the signature of the
Holy Father."

Jan relinquished the parchment. The guard slouching
against the far wall spoke then for the first time. "What
does it matter whether the signature is the Pope's, when it
is by order of Commander Sforza that no one can approach
Cardinal Rocault?"

Jan's pale eyes widened for a moment like moons. "I
know it is Commander Sforza who has this ordered, but it
is from the Holy Father the commander's orders come," he
stated, his langue d'oc slipping in his anxiety.

Saara herself added her small pushes to those of the
dog. "She wants us to squeeze through," whispered
Gaspare, as though Damiano was incapable of telling that
for himself. The dark witch planted his feet. "Not yet.
There are steps in the hall behind us. Can you hear them
approaching? Something is going on here I think we ought
to understand. Let's hug the wall and wait."

The first guard—the one with an eye for penmanship—
smiled widely. "I believe you are right, Father. The Holy
Father is the master of us all. Yet there is a certain method
in this mastery.

"It is like this: God does not tell the crops to grow with
an edict and a seal, but rather He tells the rain to fall and
the sun to shine and therefore it is done naturally. In a like
manner we soldiers offer our service to the church only
through Commander Sforza, who being also a soldier
governs us as naturally as the rain and the sun. Do you
see?

"And the commander has said that the cardinal is not to
leave his apartments in the infirmary except under the
commander's eyes, and he has also said that no one at all is
to see the cardinal. No one *has* seen the cardinal, in fact,
since he was brought here."

"I have no orders concerning the Cardinal Rocault,"
said Jan Karl hurriedly. "It is only the little Italian girl I need
for the information she possesses, naturally. I was told she
is being kept somewhere down here."

"She certainly is," agreed the guard. "That is if you
mean the little redheaded belle. They are together, for lack
of space. So you see, Father, it would be difficult for you to
see the girl without also seeing the cardinal, and that is

exactly what you may not do." And then the soldier lifted
his head as his less sensitive ears also picked up the tread
of booted feet. "Perhaps here is the commander himself for
you, and your problem can be quickly solved."

But apparently Jan did not want to talk to Commander
Sforza. He shied like a horse and snatched at the parchment still held by the poetically minded guard. The guard,
acting by reflex, hid the document behind his back and put
one hand to his sword hilt. Seeing this, the Dutchman
reconsidered his action and jerked away from sword and
swordsman. In consequence he nearly blundered into the
invisible Damiano, who made his own little dance to the
rear.

Couchicou, the great hound, was not one to appreciate
complex interactions. Neither was he aware that the group
he shepherded through the Papal halls was invisible and
so, unassailable. He interpreted the *pas de deux* as an attack
upon one of his favorite people by one he did not
particularly like. With a bass bellow he sprang, flattening
the unhappy Dutchman and knocking Damiano into Saara
and Saara into Gaspare until all fell down like gamepins.

She hit her head on stone, knocking herself dizzy. The
endless chant was cut off short, and in that moment the ill-
lit corridor became a sudden welter of frightened, struggling, highly visible figures, not the least perturbed of
whom were the Pope's pikemen.

But a terrified cleric being mauled by a dog, and a man-
at-arms with the hair straight up on his head are two
different frightened beings and they behave differently. Jan
Karl curled himself into a ball and rolled, slightly lacerated,
between the wall and the nearest pikeman, who was in
self-preservation holding the wolfhound off with his halberd. The other guard stared openmouthed at the three
people who had erupted out of the floor, and he drew his
sword.

At that moment came a booming hello from down the
hall and a matching pair of warriors sprinted full tilt from
the direction of the infirmary, their studded leather armor
slapping against their legs.

Perhaps because the linguistic complexities of the
situation were lost on her, Saara was first to take command.
She sat sprawled on the flagstones on the infirmary end of
the corridor. The dog's rush had sent both Gaspare and

Damiano sprawling forward, past the guard's station, into the unknown hall. "Run, Dami!" she cried. "Take your Gaspare to his sister. Flee with her. I will follow when I can."

Damiano got his feet under him. He had other ideas. Stealth was a lost cause, certainly, but he still had resources. With a word he summoned flame to each hand and stepped toward the panicked guardsmen, seeking to draw their attention away from his mistress.

But the task he had set himself was hopeless, for nothing as common as a man aflame could pull the men's attention away from the phalanx of monstrous bears, white of fur and white of tooth, which stood shoulder to shoulder and nose to rump, filling the hall between the infirmary and themselves. All four soldiers gasped in synchrony, while the air in the corridor grew very, very cold. The single oil lamp on the wall flickered wildly.

Damiano himself stood in amazement, until all the bears opened their mouths together and said quite clearly, "Don't wait, my dear. Your boy has run ahead. I am in no danger, but Gaspare is."

It was true. The boy was gone. Damiano's quick ears could barely hear his light dancer's steps fading away into the unknown corridor. Cursing Jan Karl and the hound impartially, Damiano followed. Bestial roaring filled the air, along with the *"yip, yip, kiyip"* of an outmatched dog.

He found the boy picking himself off the flagstone floor, wiping a bloody lip. "Can't see a damn thing," whined Gaspare. Damiano gave him five fingers of light, and together they loped on, encountering nothing more except the end of the corridor and a heavily secured wooden door. Behind this door someone was weeping. The witch grimaced at the sound, for he had heard too much weeping lately, and pathos had grown cheap. He shoved open the bar, while the iron locks undid themselves. Damiano smiled thinly, for he took a certain pride from his skill at opening things.

They found themselves in a plush, comfortably equipped chamber that was lit by many wax candles but lacked all sign of a window. There was a table spread for two people's dinner: meat, cheese, wine and bread, none of which had been touched except the wine. There was an ewer for washing and a pot for pissing, both of which had been touched. There was a divan, topped with a familiar shapeless featherbed, and upon that there was a form wrapped in blankets.

But that form was not Evienne, for she herself sat on a hard chair beside the table, with a brocade about her, and she shook with her sobs.

The place stank.

"Gaspare!" she cried tremulously. "Oh, I'm *so* glad to see you. Herbert is sick."

Damiano strode directly to the divan and flipped back the cover. Herbert Cardinal Rocault gazed up at him and whether the feverish eyes recognized in Damiano a lute player he had seen once only in the private chambers of the Pope, there was no telling. After a moment Damiano replaced the blanket more gently than he had pulled it back.

"No one came to take care of him," Evienne was explaining with difficulty. "They just shoved food under the door. There was only me. So much work.

"And now," she concluded, with a whistling sigh, "I don't feel well either. It is so depressing."

Gaspare held his sister's hand in a bone-crushing grasp. He looked at Evienne, recognized that she was tired, and saw no more. Partly this was because Gaspare was simple: that is to say, he had no second sight, and partly this was because he was not a very perceptive person where others were concerned. Mostly, of course, it was because he was Evienne's brother and between them was all the family and all the love either of them had ever known, and he was not able to imagine that his sister might be lost to him.

Damiano was different. He looked down upon Evienne and saw the rosy cheeks of pregnancy mottled with a grayish green, and her smooth throat swollen out of shape. "Oh, dear God," he whispered to the air.

Gaspare may not have been able to understand by looking but he could not escape the meaning of his friend's words. His hand slipped to the floor at Evienne's feet. He shook his head fiercely at Damiano. "No," he said. "No."

Once more he touched Evienne's hand and then turned again to the motionless Damiano. "You. If she's sick you have to *do* something!" he cried.

Damiano flinched. "Wh—what? What can I do, Gaspare? Saara and I—we've both told you already that there is nothing . . ."

Evienne stuffed her whitened knuckles in her mouth and bit down upon them. Then she sniffed. "Are you trying to tell me," she began with a certain rude energy, "that Herbert—that I—have got . . ." and then this spirit failed her. "Is it the plague?" Her frightened breath wheezed in and out, and then she squeezed her eyes shut. "Oh, no, I don't feel *that* bad—just kind of muzzy. And I ache, and it's so hot in here. . . ." Her words trailed off. "I'm going to die?"

Gaspare screamed, "No! No, no, Evienne, you're not going to die, no, never!" And in a single motion he flung himself at Damiano and wrapped himself around the witch's knees, in terrible parody of his action only a few weeks earlier when he had pleaded with Saara for Damiano. "Don't let her die," he cried shrilly. "Please, please, Damiano, don't let her die!"

It was as though he were praying to God.

With clumsy gestures Damiano freed himself and stepped over to this girl who had been so pretty. His large hands were shaking. "Signorina, I don't . . . I don't have any power over this thing. I'm only a man." Awkwardly he touched her hair.

Evienne's eyes were still beautiful, even through fear and disease. Shyly she took hold of Damiano's shirt and whispered, "I am not ready to die. Please understand. I know I must die but not now, for I am young, and this finds me in the middle of my sin. Who will absolve me, if I die here? Herbert? By Mary and all the saints, he's not the one to forgive sins he made happen himself, and he's in no shape to do it anyway. And then . . . and then I have a baby in me. How can I die now?"

"You see?" seconded Gaspare, as though Evienne's words had proven something. Then he hit his sister a weak blow upon the thigh. "Slutty bitch. What have you done to us now?"

In the distance the ursine roarings continued, along with the panicked cries of men. Damiano sank down upon the carpet and hid his face behind his hands.

Why did they both believe this impossible thing—that he could cure the plague? Why did it hurt so badly within him that they should believe this? Saara, who knew so much about healing, knew there was no hope.

His course was clear to him. There was no sense in

suffering the witnessing of this evil he could not help.
Saara had discovered as much a generation ago. It would
only drag down the healthy with it, to madness or suicide.
The only recourse was flight.

Within a week he could be in Lombardy, upon the clean
high hill where springtime reigned all the seasons, alone
among the small high-meadow flowers with an elegant,
barefoot mistress. Within a week, between Saara's magic
and his own.

But Damiano did not move. Wonderingly he watched
himself not moving. His resolution was formed, but he
seemed to lack the power to carry it through.

Was it because Gaspare's red-fingered grip on his wrist
could not be broken? Was it because Evienne was kissing
his hand?

"I am not God!" Damiano shouted suddenly. "I . . .
am not even one of his saints!"

"Not a saint, no, but almost," wheedled Gaspare. "You
are such a good sort of person, Damiano. And you have an
angel, and that means something. Send for your angel,
Damiano, and tell him . . ." And the boy's eyes changed
as he spoke, from his characteristic hysteria to something
unfamiliar to Damiano: something calm and lucid and cold.
"And tell him to send Evienne's plague into me.

"Yes, into me," Gaspare repeated. "Why not? I'm not
anything worth saving. Not even much of a dancer, really.
The only thing I do well is to judge other people's music,
and no one will pay me to do that.

"But it's all the same to the plague, isn't it? Whether it
takes a critic or the cardinal's mistress? And it must be
possible to trade one to the other, too, for Jesus sent a
man's devils into the pigs. Call your angel, Damiano, my
good friend. Remind him of that gospel, if he does not
remember. Please, Damiano. Do it."

Damiano called Raphael then, and the angel came.

It may have been only Damiano's imagination that said
the sick chamber did not smell so bad with Raphael
standing in it, stainless and glimmering. It was certain,
though, that with the first sight of the angel, the witch's
misery became lighter, even though he knew how Raphael
would answer his question.

He asked it anyway. "Seraph. Can you cure the
plague?"

"Oh, no," moaned Gaspare, who blinked about owlishly, as though he might discover the tiny form of an angel in some corner of the room. "Ask more gently, Damiano, or he will never agree to help."

Raphael gazed beyond Damiano to the figure of the terrified girl, who rocked back and forth with her brother's arms wrapped around her and who did not seem to be listening. Then Raphael regarded the motionless form on the featherbed. "Damiano," he said quietly. "If I had power over the plague, no man would have ever died so."

"I thought as much," snapped the witch, and sorrow and frustration made him add, "For a spirit of great reputation, you can't do much."

Blue-black eyes returned their gaze to him. "I'm sorry, Dami. I didn't make my own reputation."

Gaspare only heard one side of this conversation, but it told him enough. "Don't accept any excuses, musician. We have managed so many hard things already—over the mountains at the end of winter, and through Provence starving to death—how can we let my pretty little sister just lie down and die? There must be another way!"

"There must be another way." Oh, Christ! the very words Damiano had used with the Devil, and with Saara herself. And the Devil had nearly had him for his arrogance, and how badly he had hurt Saara, who had done him no wrong, searching for that "other way."

It had been his father's obstinacy in him: that bullish Italian obstinacy which had led him along the odd paths of his life. Stealing witchcraft by force and giving it away in a single grand gesture that did no one any good at all. Making war with the flames of hell as a weapon, and using that weapon against Lucifer himself. Now he was a witch without a staff, singing his spells like a Lapplander—like an infant Lapplander, to be exact.

And no help to his friends at all.

Damiano's lips pulled back painfully from his teeth and he looked away from Gaspare. Had he his staff, he thought bleakly, he would at least try. With his staff he had not been a child in the making of spells. He had known that length of black wood better than his lute, at one time. Though he might fail, with his staff he would at least know how to try.

And then, between one moment and the next, he knew not only how to try, but how to succeed in helping

Evienne. He remembered how, on the streets of Avignon, not far from the Papal Door, he had grabbed at Gaspare himself, as though to use the boy as a living focus for his magic, and then, sensing the danger involved, had drawn back. And he remembered how he had entered the earth and gathered the water from it, leaving only a song to mark his way home.

But he could not claim he didn't know what happened when power went from one person into another. Out of all the witches on the earth, he (and his lady) knew that best.

A witch did not die of the plague, or so said Saara. Not unless he used himself too hard. When he had been simple, he had been in peril of the plague. Now he was not.

Clear and accurate. But that statement was a knife that could cut both ways. And dear God, how it could cut! "What is he saying now?" whispered Gaspare excitedly, for in truth Damiano's attitude was that of one who was very thoughtfully listening to something. Instead of answering, the dark witch glanced over at his friend, heavy-browed.

Then he sank down on one knee beside Evienne. "Go away, Gaspare," he said. "Don't touch us."

Gaspare pulled back with alacrity. "Save her, Damiano. Please save her, " he begged, his voice cracking with tears.

But the face which looked back at Gaspare's was frozen, and oddly pale beneath its strong coloring. "Be quiet," whispered the witch.

He put his right arm around Evienne's waist and she lifted her suffering head. But there was neither comfort nor gentleness in Damiano's eyes as his left hand wrapped her hair and pulled the girl backward, only a great concentration. "Look at me," he grunted at her. "Don't talk."

The stool overbalanced and Evienne lay back in a tangle of skirts, supported only by Damiano, whose hands clenched and clenched, whose arms were trembling. In the girl's eyes despair had been diluted with a strange admixture of terror and hope.

When Damiano had stolen power from Saara, the staff had shown him how. It had felt very good, like wine and sunshine and victory, all together. When he broke the staff, releasing to her half his own soul—what then? What had it felt like, then?

It was not a good memory; it made his head spin, and his stomach tied itself in a knot. Damiano did not want to be simple again, and he did not want to stand in Evienne's position of helpless fear.

Once he had been reconciled to that life of many blindnesses. Once he had been prepared to die. Now he was not reconciled to any loss or limitation on a life grown rich as the orchards of Provence.

And Evienne was such an inconsequential person. Without either morals or aspirations, possessing only a little quick-fading beauty, she mattered to him less than his dog had mattered. Much less.

But being inconsequential did not make it easier to die. And how much he cared for Evienne, or even for her anguished brother, had nothing to do with it. Damiano sought the memory of his defeat, and when he had it, he used it to make a song: a song of fire and of loss. Silently it rang in his head. His lips pulled back from his teeth.

Evienne screamed, buffeted by a flaming wind. She arched her body and threw back her head. She cried for her brother to save her. Then she swooned.

And the girl was drowned in fire—Damiano's fire, a flame of brilliant, consuming color that covered her sweet body over until she looked like a soul in the pains of hell. Gaspare gasped and dived toward her, to free her from the witch's awful embrace. Slack-jawed, gray-faced, Damiano slapped him across the room.

He sang his fire into Evienne, feeling his strength enter all the wounded provinces of her body. He heard the dumb, smooth, insistent beat of her heart and he felt the ugliness of the damage plague had done to the veins of her body and in her lungs. Without thought his fire fed itself upon that evil. The wild bright flame grew hotter. It went white, then blue and sang with a pure and unwavering note.

But Evienne was not a staff or a cup or a cloud. Not a vessel of any kind which could be filled with magic, containing it. She was a living being and simple besides. Damiano's strength flowed into her and out again, running away over the carpet like a fire of oil on water. Again and again he filled her, forcing magic into flesh and soul not created to take it, until, by the time the flame ran quiet within a body revivified, Damiano was empty. He lay half across Gaspare's sister, voiceless, panting like a dog.

Far away along the long corridor, a bearlike bellow

sharpened into a wail, as Saara the Fenwoman sensed her
lover's magic flow out and be lost into the air.

Damiano did not hear her crying, for his attention was
turned within, to where his new emptiness had found
already a thing to fill it, to where within his trembling shell
something unwelcome was finding a home. It was a thing
like a groping hand, but fine as mist. It was mindless and
determined and terribly hungry.

Damiano knew its name, and he had been expecting it.

For a moment he thought he would not be able to rise,
and his hands scrabbled on the slates of the floor. But from
nearby came a helping hand. "The devils into the swine,"
mumbled Damiano to Gaspare. "Strangely, I have never
before thought of myself as a pig." He stood swaying for a
moment and shook his head.

But it was not Gaspare who had helped him to his feet.
Gaspare sat hunched over his sister, who slept now
peacefully, with only a slight flush of the skin to mark her
short visit in the Inferno. It was the fair hand of Raphael
who steadied Damiano, and a white wing wrapped around
him like a mantle.

He put an arm about the angel's waist, just below where
the huge wings sprouted. "One more favor I have to ask
you, Seraph," he whispered hoarsely, staring at the floor.
"And I promise I will then request nothing else."

Raphael asked for no promises. He listened to Damiano, folded his wings around him, and led him away.

Jan Karl burst into the room, bleeding from the shoulder, with his black cassock torn. "Evienne, you idiot, get off
the floor. I have come to release you!"

Evienne woke up confused. These days she always
woke up confused, and usually a little sick to her stomach
as well. But this time her stomach felt fine, at least. Indeed,
she felt fine all over, and quite ready to endure a little
confusion if it meant Jan had come to get her. She flung
herself to her feet, only noticing Gaspare as she bowled
him over.

"Gaspare! How long have you . . ." Some part of her
memory returned to her then. She turned to the bed where
Herbert Cardinal Rocault lay unmoving. A brief glance told
her he would never move again, and she jerked her hand

back, shuddering. "Take me away now, Jan. Death frightens me so."

But at that moment Saara the Fenwoman entered the door, not with the form of a bear but in natural shape. "We have only a minute," she announced. "One minute before they are after us." Her eyes swept the room, resting only lightly on the girl before her, with her red hair and generous beauty.

"Where is Damiano?" she demanded, taut-voiced. "What has happened to him?"

Evienne took a possessive step nearer Jan Karl. She regarded Saara's delicate features with disfavor. "Who's this woman, Jan? Is she with you?"

"Where is Dami, you litter of fools?" cried Saara, and Gaspare, whom the events of the last few minutes had left speechless, rose from the floor.

"I . . . don't know, now," he said, his goblin eyes searching the chamber. "He was here a bit ago. He cured my sister of plague and then I turned . . ."

"He *what?*" gasped Saara, and once more Evienne shuddered wildly and hid her head against her protector's spavined bosom.

"Get me out of here, Jan. I can't take it anymore."

"He cured Evienne of the plague. He set her on fire, and I thought she would burn up, but instead she is better."

Saara stood perfectly still in the middle of the chamber. "I cannot see him," she said. "Nor hear him nor smell him nor feel him. Anywhere."

Through the streets of Avignon walked Damiano Delstrego, with the plague gripping him around the throat. Beside him came an angel who kept his feet from stumbling.

Never had anything ached so badly, nor had he ever been so sick at heart. It was as though there were needles in every joint of his body and hot lead in his lungs. The cheerful sun mocked him with every step.

Prayer behooved him, certainly, but he could think of no appropriate words except ". . . remember us now and at the hour of our death." This phrase repeated itself dreadfully and without comfort in his mind. O God, God, the sick man cried silently, will You remember Damiano, when Damiano has forgotten himself?

"Wouldn't you know," he whispered aloud, "that I would adopt a plague that was already half done with its job? It should take a man a day at least to be feeling this badly."

He walked on, blinking eyes which grew gummier all the time. "It is important," he insisted to Raphael, "that Saara does not find me, for what I have done she could also do, and I am not about to trade my beautiful lady's life for my own—or for that of Gaspare's ridiculous sister."

The archangel did not reply, but his wings contained Damiano in their own corona of light, and his hand rested on the mortal man's shoulder.

Soon they reached the South Gate of the city, which Damiano had never before seen. They passed beneath. "The gates should be locked," commented Damiano. "To keep the disease from spreading. I myself," he added, with a painful and obstructed sigh, "intend not to encounter anyone at all."

Here, close to the muddy banks of the Rhone, the land was broken into small checkers of vine and green wheat soft as velvet. The road ambled down, keeping close to the water. Under an azure sky, even the weeds were all in bloom. "Oh, God, it hurts!" cried Damiano, meaning either the beauty before him or the lancing pain in his body. He broke into sudden violent tears.

Which stopped just as suddenly, and he blundered ahead. "Raphael, you must take care of Saara for me. She has had so little happiness in her life, and she is so kind—do you know that when we were at war and her storm killed Macchiata she took me all unawares, and she might have killed me then, as she thought I had killed her Roman lover, and . . ." He ran out of breath and reeled, but the angel's hand steadied his steps. "Whatever—she could have killed me. She had every chance to do it and she just stood there and watched. I know I said I would never ask another favor, but Saara is a very gentle creature, Raphael, and you must take care of her."

The angel paused a moment before answering. "But she will not let me take care of her, Dami. She doesn't like me very much."

Damiano nodded, and immediately put a hand to his swollen neck. The hand, he saw, was discolored with purplish blotches. He let it drop. "That's true. Well then, you must tell her I said for her to take care of you, Seraph. It will come to the same thing in the end. Will you do that for me?"

"I will."

He found he was no longer walking on the roadway, but through the silky wheat grasses which rustled at the middle of his calf. They tempted him, these soft green mounds. It would be so much easier to lie down here and stare at the afternoon sky—the afternoon sky of Easter Sunday, Damiano realized, marveling. It was only today he had awakened from a bed of grass, drowsy with lovemaking and very near to Saara. . . .

"Oh, Mother of God!" he moaned, as for a moment the sunlight spun in circles through his head. "Saara! How I love her!

"And I don't know if she will ever understand." He lifted eyes that had gathered pus like sand in the corners. "She will not understand why I chose to go with you in the end. She will think I did not care."

"I will tell her," whispered Raphael.

But it was doubtful Damiano heard. He was staggering now, and but for Raphael's help would have fallen with each step. "And what about my pretty lute? Who will get that—or will it wind up in someone's hearthfire?" He winced. "No, it is as His Holiness said. I was not the first, nor will I be the last. The lute will pass to Gaspare, I guess. He deserves it, since he has always cared more for the music than his own dancing." The sick man fixed Raphael with an admonitory glare. "See that he knows what to do with it, heh? Maybe he will have a nephew or a niece to support, if I know the worth of a certain Dutchman."

And then Damiano's head spun like mad planets, and only when the back of his head touched the earth did he realize he was falling. He lay on his back and gasped like a fish on the deck of a boat. "I guess . . . this is far enough. It will have to be."

The sun moved silently and all the birds of springtime made their pleasant racket. Raphael folded his legs under him and sat with wings spread, looking (were there any to see) like a hawk of alabaster over its prey. Damiano lay almost as quiet as the sun, save for the sound of his breath, which came like wind through a tunnel. His eyes wandered.

All was bitter, and the pain bit into his body. But he was glad for the pain, for the moments when it abandoned him were worse yet.

The sun was low already when he turned his head to Raphael. "Water?" he asked. The angel went away and brought some back in his hands. Three times Damiano drank, tasting blood with the water from his cracked and bleeding mouth.

He tried to sit up. "Oh, Christ! Why did this have to be? Not the plague, Seraph. . . ." He then paused, involved with the effort of breathing.

"I mean why did you ask me to live again? I was ready to die, only a month ago. Wasn't that enough? Hadn't I done enough, yet—worked enough, sinned enough, been sorry enough . . . ?

"Saara, too, had to be hurt?"

Gravely Raphael shook his golden head. "I don't know why so much is asked of one and not another."

"It was you!" Damiano cried feebly. "You—cut my hair. You told me not to be a saint. . . ."

"I did not," said Raphael, ruffling worriedly.

But Damiano finished the accusation. "You told me to live."

He glanced down at his hands in the dying light. Their color was nothing he did not expect, but the deepening sky was better to look at. "I think I would have made a good old man," he panted. "We might have had . . . children. Despite what Saara said, she doesn't know everything. Abraham's Rachel had a child. We might have had children." It was dark when next he opened his mouth, and that was to cry out in a panic, "My music! Oh, God, my music! Already now there are two changes to songs working in my mind, and I will never have the chance to try them out. I had only begun!"

Raphael was very near. He bent to kiss the misshapen face beside him, for on this point he understood Damiano very well. But the fever was upon the man: a foreign fire he could not master, but that discolored all his senses. He cringed away from the angel's touch. "Don't. Go away. I stink," Damiano growled savagely. "I can smell myself. Go away, you who are so fond of beautiful things. Go away."

Raphael did not go away, and Damiano, in mad rage, hit him three weak blows on the breast, as he hissed,

"What a fool's game this month has been, pretending I had a life to live, when everything the Devil said came true—even to this. Probably the ruby, too. Probably I carried my own death into Avignon."

Raphael put his cool hand against Damiano's cheek. "Hush, Dami. Don't worry about my brother; even the truth becomes a lie in his mouth, and with my own eyes I saw you defeat him in the streets of the city."

"Defeat him?" rasped the dying man, shaking with the anger of his feeling. "He fled laughing, if he fled at all. Satan has always toyed with me, cat-and-mouse. I think I have found a way to happiness and he closes the door in my face. Always."

Then his red-rimmed eyes widened and his head dropped back against the flattened wheat. "Oh, Christ, to whom do I say this?"

"To me, Dami," answered Raphael, uncertainly. "To me you may say whatever you wish, for I am your . . ."

But Damiano only shrank deeper away. "How you have played with me," he hissed. "Pretending there were two brothers with the same face and different souls!"

"Dami!" Wings of pearl sprang stiffly upward. "What are you saying? Do not be confused between Lucifer and me! You know me, and if that isn't enough, you have seen my brother and me together. It is the fever. . . ."

"Yes, I know you at last, after all these years." Swollen lips drew back from Damiano's teeth, revealing a swollen tongue.

"And there is little to choose between you and your brother. Except that you have the greater hypocrisy. You used me, Seraph. Led me with your pretty tunes and your sermonizing—to be the butt of a joke! And what a joke.

"But for you I would not be here now. But for you I'd be a prosperous burgher-witch in Donnaz, or even back home, in Partestrada.

"But for you I'd not be lying here, perishing like a beast. Can you deny that, Raphael?"

The angel said nothing.

"What is it your brother called me, just this week? 'Bladder of blood and scum. Food for worms.' Yes, very accurate, for my blood is rotting, and already I can feel the worms. Is it fun to play with such toys as me, Raphael?"

The sick man's grimace became a snarl of pain. "Aggh!

To think I was such a clod, dolt, simpleton—O Christ—that I was glad for your attention." His attempt to swallow sent trickles of blood down his chin.

"Well, now it's over, and I hope it was all to your satisfaction. May God curse you to the remotest stinking depths of hell!" With the strength of madness he raised himself head and shoulders off the ground, and his left hand flung wisps of torn wheat and bindweed at the perfect, agonized face of Raphael. "To hell! To hell! Damn you to hell!" cried Damiano, till his voice broke and he sank back into the green sea of wheat.

The angel cowered, as though these airy missiles had power to hurt. Then Raphael shrouded himself in his wings and covered his face with his two hands. His weeping, like his laughter, was like that of a man. He spoke one word: "Why?"

It was a question not addressed to Damiano.

Silence called him out, to find his friend looking up at him. "I am so very sorry, Seraph," the mortal said weakly. "I must have been mad for a little while. I said such horrible things."

Raphael gazed at the dying man and was not comforted. "But what you said was true, my friend. If I had not touched you your path would have been different.

"But please believe me, Dami. If I did you harm it was by mistake. A spirit does badly when he makes changes in the lives of men."

Damiano closed his eyes for a moment, gathering strength. When he spoke it was clearly and after thought.

"If you had not touched me, Raphael, I would not now be Damiano—this Damiano—at all. And I'd rather be the Damiano you touched than anyone else.

"You must know that I love you, Raphael. You should never have let raving words hurt you like that. My teacher. My guide. For whatever you say about your role with mankind, you have always been the messenger of God to me, and by you I have tried to rule my life.

"In fact," and the black, swollen mouth actually attempted a little smile, "I probably should have loved the Almighty more and his music less, but then . . . that's the way I was made.

"Not a saint."

He tried to lift his left arm to touch the beautiful clean

face so near his own, but his hand was tangled in the bindweed, and there was no strength left.

Carefully Raphael freed the long fingers with their broad, knobbed joints, and he lifted Damiano's hand and kissed it.

This time the smile was a success. "I don't hurt anymore," Damiano said. Then he closed his eyes and turned his head to one side. With his free hand he scraped at his face, as though to ward off the tongue of an affectionate dog. "Not now, little dear," he murmured, and gave a quiet sigh.

After that the breath did not rise again.

CODA

All through the radiant night an owl flew above the city of Avignon, blotting the dust of stars with its passage. It might have been hunting rats, so purposefully did it circle, and so low to the ground. But if it was hunting, then this was a bad night's hunt, for never once did the raptor fold its wings and plummet toward a kill.

But the rats of Avignon were not a wholesome food, anyway.

In the third black hour, her heavy talons clutched to one of the teeth of the spire of the Pope's Chapel. Its dry bird's body panted and quaked beneath its plumpness of feathers and its pinions hung down limp as tassels, for an owl is not an albatross, to take its rest in the air.

Saara, also, had not slept much the night before.

No sight, nor sound, nor smell nor touch of him. . . .

She tried not to think, for it was difficult to think and be an owl at the same time. Besides, she had spent the hours before sunset thinking, and it had done her no good.

He had cured the plague. Gaspare said he had cured the plague (which was an impossible deed). That he had burned it out of the red-haired girl with flame. Saara remembered Damiano's sweet fire, extinguished in her presence that day, and she mourned it, not knowing if she mourned the man as well as the magic.

He was not in the palace, for she had searched the palace, even to the piled dead under sheets in the infirmary. That search would have been interesting, had Saara time to care, what with the hidden storehouses and hidden women scattered through the rambling work of stone. There were pictures, both beautiful and curious, and at least one of the Benedictine nuns was born sighted. But she had spent no thought on either the house or its occupants.

No sight of him, no sound. . . .

She had followed the ox wagons, and in the shape of a dog, thrust her nose among the dead. So many. So many.

Too many people here: meaningless, chattering, blind people, whose quotidian deaths meant nothing to her.

The little redhead, too, was a creature that meant nothing. Without brain or bravery, clinging to that wordy bald man who had screamed like a rabbit when the dog bit him. At least they were a pair that matched. Barnyard fowl, the both of them. (She thought, perforce, in owlish images, and opened her beak in what might have been a cruel owlish smile.)

What had Damiano done to himself for the sake of that bit of red fluff? So free with his pity he was, that he might have given anything. She recalled his stricken face when, along the infirmary corridor, one single dying man had seen them pass. She remembered how he had come (a phantom with huge black eyes) to Lombardy, escaping horror and the pain of the lash.

And she saw him as he had been only one night ago, close above her in the dark, soft-eyed, smelling of grass.

The owl's talons slipped against the spire of stone, and her shape wavered, for no owl's body or soul could contain what Saara felt with the image of her young lover filling her mind.

Better not to think. Better, perhaps, to be angry.

At Gaspare's sister? Yes, why not: fat little hen whining, "Death frightens me so, Jan. Take me away from here." Or at Gaspare himself—another squawking chicken, occasionally turning nasty. Had she traveled and studied and suffered and endured and built her art upon experience, for her life to become the plaything of such mannerless infants?

She could kill the bitch. Why not? She had killed before.

The blond unborn-looking fellow would give no fight at all, and Gaspare? To strangle him would be a sizable pleasure.

One heavy, scaled foot scraped flecks of stone from the spire, but then Saara shuddered. Bits of white feather sailed away in the spring breeze, starlit.

She wasn't going to kill anyone. That was the owl talking, not Saara herself. Never again would she willingly kill, and especially not the redheaded girl for whom Damiano had . . .

Better not to think.

Mad orange eyes stared upward, like brass platters set to catch the stars. The only things above her *were* the stars, and the strange dead-tree symbol of the Christian religion, which had been set at the very top of the building.

Damiano (like Guillermo, like Ruggerio) was a Christian. Maybe he was even more of a Christian than the others. Perhaps she ought to ask the help of the Christian elementals in finding him.

Saara did not know the proper incantations to address that symbol of crossed logs. She ground her owl-beak and did her best.

Other wings lighted beside her own. "You, Chief of Eagles," she cried in surprise. "Are you a Christian spirit?"

Raphael was slow in answering. "Among other things."

In the gleam of his plumage and the power of his eyes Saara recognized suddenly that force, greater than her own magic, which had hidden Damiano from her. The owl hissed like a snake. "Take me to him."

"It is for that I have come," answered Raphael.

The rising sun turned the back of her head to red gold. Saara sat upon the damp earth with her hands in her lap, hands curled like an owl's talons. "Didn't you care to bury him?"

These were the first words she had spoken since seeing the body in the wheatfield. She did not turn her head to see whether Raphael was still behind her.

"I didn't think of it," the angel replied quietly.

"That's all right," grunted Saara. "I'll do it. I have a lot of experience at burying people." Then she added, quite casually, "Why can't I cry, I wonder?"

A wind blew from the northwest, making Easter

Monday much colder than all the previous week. Yet the chill could not muzzle the courting birds, nor take the sparkle from the wax-green leaves of the nearby grapes. In the distance a single horse or mule whinnied his presence, answered at great length by an ass in a field nearby.

Saara felt the bite of the wind and huddled against it. She might have slowed the air, or warmed it, but neither seemed worth the effort. "You knew, did you not, when you led him here, that I could have saved him?"

Raphael sat down beside her. Without interest she noted that the spirit did look more like a man to her than an eagle. She was sure it had not always been so, for her people knew the Four Eagles of old.

"I knew it. He knew that also," Raphael said. "That is why he bade me hide him from you."

"From me?" she asked, and then, out of nowhere, the tears came. "From me especially, he wanted to die hidden?"

The angel bent his wings around her and they hung in the air not touching, for his desire to comfort warred with the knowledge she did not want her comfort to come from him. "He knew that to save him, you would have taken the plague in his stead."

Now her eyes swam over, and the angel dissolved in her vision like a reflection of the moon in disturbed water. "Yes! I would have been happy to die in his place. I am old, and he is—was—young. I have had a life: children, lovers, much travel. It was not pleasant, but it was long and full of things. I would have been happy.

"Can you tell me . . ." and Saara took a ragged breath, "that he was happy to die in the place of that . . . sister of Gaspare's?"

Raphael sat still. There was no softness in his face as he said, "It was very hard for him to die. And part of that was because he feared you would not forgive him."

"Not forgive . . . oh, no." Saara threw herself forward on the earth, so that her head was only a few inches from the abandoned thing in its rich clothing, with its face covered with leaves.

But she lay passive only for a minute, and turned then on Raphael with newly minted anger. "Why did you let him do that for her? Didn't you know what such a deed would cost?"

Raphael nodded his head. "Yes, I knew." His blue eyes met hers evenly.

"He couldn't have done it but for you!" she cried harshly, pulling away from the compass of his wings. "But for you I would have found him. But for you, Damiano would be alive now!"

Again the angel nodded.

"Why, then?"

"Because he asked it of me."

"You were his friend!"

Raphael's eyes widened. "I still am."

Saara opened her mouth and cursed Raphael to his face.

His great wings sank in discouragement upon the green wheat. Their pinions lay all awry. "Please," whispered the angel, "try to understand. I did not want Damiano to die. I love him, and all he might have become. But what I did was by his choice, for it was his to choose, not mine. You would have done the same, Saara, in my place."

"Oh, would I?" She could think of nothing to say to this, but after a small pause she observed, "Perhaps spring is not a bad time to die, after all. It is warm, at least, and one is spared the worst of the flies.

"Maybe I will try it out."

Raphael straightened. His wings bowed upward in alarm. "No, Saara. Please don't. There is something else Damiano said, when he spoke of his love for you. He said you were to take care of me."

"Of you? *You?*" Her head snapped up, framed in disheveled brown hair. "Chief of Eagles, have you *need* of anyone's care?"

Then Raphael dropped his eyes. His beautiful hands folded and refolded in his lap, and Saara could see stains of blood and other dirt upon the gossamer fabric of his garment. "I might," he admitted, and then he glanced up at her again with something like embarrassment in his face. "I think it's possible that I will, soon. I am not what I once was."

Drying her eyes, she stared the angel out of countenance. "Yes, I see. You are smaller, I think. Your light is more soft. What happened to you?"

"Damiano," replied Raphael without hesitation.

She grunted, and then a little grin forced its way onto

her face. "I can believe it. Did he come to you with an Italian head full of sad songs, pestering you to do things you didn't want to do, taking no denial, but talking, talking, and talking always?"

"Something like that." The angel smiled.

Then her glance sharpened. "And are you sorry now, after he is dead and flown away, while here we sit all soiled with dirt and crying?"

There was nothing but peace on Raphael's face as he answered, "Not at all."

Saara was weaving a green shroud from grasses the angel picked for her, when she heard (for the second time in as many days) a commotion of hooves in the distance. She raised her head to discover young Gaspare once more clinging to the neck of the black Barb gelding like a monkey. The horse proceeded by leaps and bounds with a clean disregard for property lines. His elegant black nostrils gulped air and his tiny fox ears swiveled independently. At his side ran a hound the size of a pony. They were heading, more or less, toward Saara.

She rose to greet the boy, who promptly slid off the animal's withers to the ground. The dog trotted past her, as did the tall horse.

"I am so glad," began the redhead, with a painful groan. "I had no idea whether that cursed black jackass was taking me to my friends, or to Cloud-Cuckooland. And that impossible dog!" Gaspare turned his head in irritation at the noise the wolfhound had begun: a deep, resonant, heartbreaking howl. "What *is* the creature doing now?" He took a step toward the animals.

Saara put a restraining hand upon him. "No, Gaspare. Don't look. Don't go near. It is deadly for you."

But the dog had uncovered enough. Gaspare had no need to approach further.

"Dam . . ." He fell to his knees, gasping. "Dead? Is he really dead?"

"Yes." Saara stepped away, feeling that another person's grief—especially the grief of a selfish, hysterical child like Gaspare—would tear her apart.

But the boy surprised her with five minutes of kneeling silence, in which he stared blankly, round-eyed, biting down upon his hand. Then he crawled to his feet. "I . . .

have made a very bad bargain," he said in a small voice.
"My great musician for my slut of a sister. It was not what I
asked of him. Not at all."

"It wasn't?" asked Saara, feeling her dislike of the boy
soften slightly.

With a certain dignity he replied, "Of course not. It was
me he was supposed to ask that one . . ." and Gaspare
pointed toward Raphael (who stood in his slightly soiled
robe on the far side of the body, comforting the beasts) "to
exchange for Evienne. Me, not him."

And Gaspare's poor silly face grew longer as he added,
"I have a sense of values, after all."

He blinked the tears from his big pale eyes. "He—he
was . . ." And then he struck his fist into his palm. "I
don't think you really know what he was, lady." His glance
at Saara was once more arrogant. "To you he was a
pleasant fellow to tickle under a sheet, hey? And what was
better, he might make a song about you, glorifying your
name to everyone in Avignon."

Saara had no time to reply to this unjust accusation, for
Gaspare exploded. "But what he was, was the best! The
very best in all of Italy and in France besides!"

"For one year. One little year," Gaspare concluded in a
softer voice. He shrugged. "And that is it, I guess.

"I won't see one like him again." Gaspare gazed down
at the blackened and meaningless flesh that had contained
his friend, until the lights of pearl which were reflected
even over that sunken cheek and dead hand caused him to
raise his eyes.

He stalked over to Raphael. "Hey. Raphael. I can see
you."

The angel was taller than the boy. Slowly he smiled
down at him and gently he extended his hand.

Gaspare took it less gently, in both of his. He did not
return the smile. "You were supposed to give the plague to
me, not him."

The angel did not correct this version of the story.

"You got it wrong, so you owe me something," Gaspare
declared.

Still the angel made no denial, but gazed seriously into
the laughable gooseberry eyes. Gaspare said to him,
"Teach me the lute."

RAPHAEL

First came the seen, then thus the palpable
Elysium, though it were in the halls of hell,
What thou lovest well is thy true heritage
What thou lovest well shall not be reft from thee.

Ezra Pound
Pisan Cantos (81)

For Qui

CHAPTER 1

Two young people sat quite comfortably on the grassy bank
of a stream, leaning against a willow whose ancient body
seemed designed for leaning. Plangent water reflected the
little green leaves of the willow, including even the tiny
round crystals of dew which hung from the leaves, with
only artistic distortion, while below the line of the water
cool fish brooded, wearing coats of bright enamelwork.

On either side of the stream a lawn spread out, tended
by cloudy sheep. Other beasts, too, roamed at their
graceful will across the landscape: the ox and the wide-
horned aurochs, the slouching camelopard, the corkindrill—each animal as fat as a burgher and similarly complacent. None were ragged, none scarred. None raised its
elegant head except in wonder at the sweetness of the air.

Of course there were birds, and even in the lacy mass of
the willow they sang, regardless of the presence of two or
three sleek and platter-faced cats who meditated while
resting upon the largest branches, their white, gray, or
many-striped tails curled below them like fishhooks trol-
ling the air.

Although there were aurochs and a camelopard, and it
has been said that these are wary beasts and unsocial, this
park which contained them had not the appearance of
wilderness. Beyond the copse of fruiting trees on the far
side of the river rose a white palace of intricate shape and
exquisite proportion, though through distance and the
balmy air its exact lineaments were confused. Another,
more homey sort of house rose closer to hand, on the bank
of the stream itself. This edifice was square, three stories
tall, and also white—sparkling white—except for a roof of

red tile and certain tasteful borders of red and gold about the windows.

These windows were large, as though the house had been built without care for winter, and they yawned wide and shutterless, as though no thief had ever been born. From these windows hung pots of divers herbs. A pretty gravel path wound away from the tower and kept company with the stream for a while, before humping itself over on a painted bridge and heading toward the ambiguous palace.

The two young people who lounged beside the path (and beneath the birds, and the cats, and the willow leaves all hung with dew) were both decorative and restful to the eye—of a piece with the rest of the scene. One was a small and delicately made maiden all dressed in white save for a red kerchief which she wore around her neck, hanging down in back. Her hair was not flaxen, but as white as her dress—and yet there was no mistaking this child for an old woman. Her pleasant triangular face was as innocent of wrinkles as it seemed of thought. Her eyes were soft and brown. With a yawn and a stretch this child rolled away from the tree and began rooting about in the grass in the most unladylike fashion, on all fours, apparently searching for something, while she turned those strange, heavy-pupiled eyes on her companion with a mixture of fawning and mischief.

He, too, had large brown eyes, and he was also dressed in white, though upon his glimmering garment there were certain touches (as there were in the square tower) of scarlet and gold. He was not pale, however, but swarthy, and his hair was a mass of lazy curls. He continued to lean against the willow tree while his hands played over the strings of a perfectly plain, perfectly perfect lute. He happened to be seated (in seeming content) on a dead branch, which he took care should not be visible to the girl.

The music he made was like the light which bathed and enfolded this garden without a wall: impossibly rich and simple, too fine-textured for the world of days. And he didn't play alone, for his melody was answered by a descant from the winged sky, while below the grass murmured a sweet continuo.

It was a piece without beginning or end, and a glance at the rapt face of the musician communicated that he was well satisfied with the work. But at some time during that long morning, the musician raised his head and left the music to continue without him. His eyes, like those of the girl, were drowned drunk as though they witnessed something beyond sky, river, leafy tree, and rippling grasses.

As though they witnessed glory.

His eyes were so because he, she, the corkindrill, and all of those who strolled, slouched, soared, or sang their perfection in that crystal air, were the dead—the blessed dead—and this was their realm.

And in truth there was neither stream nor willow, nor leaves of the willow nor dew to hang from its leaves, nor tower nor palace nor pretty gravel paths winding between them.

There was only peace here: great peace, bought with pain, perhaps. Redeemed by love, most certainly. Peace, at any rate, and it had shattered the bonds of time.

But this particular blessed soul (the one with the lute) raised his head and the beautiful drowned eyes squinted, like those of a nearsighted man trying to focus at a distance.

"What is it, Dami?" asked the white girl, and she plumped herself down in front of him.

For some moments he did not respond, but stared past her, and past the stream and the copse of fruit trees and the white palace beyond, into unimaginable or unremembered distance. Then he met her gaze, while his fingers evoked a trickle of emotion from the lute strings.

"I felt, little dear," he said slowly, "as though someone had floated here on the wind from far away, offering me all of heaven and earth to follow him."

She scooted closer, until her soft and innocent (though not particularly clever) face rested mere inches from his. "What did that feel like?"

He sighed. "It felt like a stomachache."

Macchiata snorted and sat back heavily on the grass. "But, Master—Master! You don't *have* a stomach!"

She peered at him sidelong, grinning, and sought again in the grass around the willow. At last she found the branch Damiano had concealed, and she pulled it out from under his legs.

"Hah! There it is.

"Come on, Dami," she wheedled winsomely. "Throw the stick for me again."

He looked into her eyes. "Are you pining for your natural form, little dear? Would you like to be a dog once again?"

Macchiata slipped his gaze and looked hungrily at the branch in her master's hand. "Not pining. I like my girl shape. Especially the hands, which make it easy to pick up sticks.

"Please, Dami. *Please* throw it again."

The greatest of the archangels, Lucifer by name, had a palace as grand as that behind the orchard in Tir Na nOg— the Isle of the Ever Young—though Lucifer's watchful fortress was neither white nor charmingly situated. Atop the square box of it was a small, high chamber possessing four windows. These reached from the floor to the vaulted ceiling, and they stood always open.

One of these windows looked grudgingly toward the clean north, just as one beheld the generous south with due suspicion. The third window kept a wary eye against the wisdom of the east while the last window denied all hope of the west. Despite this eclectic airiness, the atmosphere in the chamber was a bit stuffy and it smelled like a dead fire. A single grayish, dirty fly droned in frustrated circles through the air of the chamber, as though despite all the windows it could not find a way out.

Within the arches of this high room stood only a table and a chair. On the table was placed a small replica of the palace itself, which was as intricate as its original—as squatly heavy and as drear—and only less fearsome because of its size. At the very top of the model perched a tiny cupola of four windows, within which rested two tiny atomies of furniture: a table and a chair. The chair in the model, like that in the original, was empty.

But the owner of the palace (and the model) was returning, ploughing his way through the sky on wyvern's wings. He came not from the north or south or from any other clear direction, but in great, frustrated circles, and he stopped to pant on the black iron roof of this highest chamber before slithering in.

As the light of one window was darkened for a moment by his serpentine bulk, the fly found its way cutely into the model of the palace, where it settled itself upon the matchstick perfection of the tiny table in the highest chamber.

Lucifer sloughed off his hideous wyvern shape and appeared with a sneer upon his elegant carnelian features. He despised ugliness almost as much as he distrusted beauty, but since his own angelic wings had shriveled long ago, he had to take some other shape if he were to fly. He threw himself into the hard chair and scowled out each window in turn.

A long climb and a bootless errand in a place which could not be seen out of any of his watch windows. A place beyond the limits of his dominion. Lucifer was in a foul, foul mood.

Curse the deaf, dimwit shade!

If only Lucifer *could* curse him, or indulge himself in any deed on physical or spiritual plane which could do damage to the object of his dislike. But he could no more sting the little creature than he could sting God Himself, who held it in His infuriatingly careful hands. He could only call it names out loud, not the worst of which was "dago." He stared at his new toy palace, unseeing.

Someone new entered the chamber through the hatch in the floor which led into the rest of the palace. This someone was a small demon, raspberry-colored and raspberry-shaped, with two long feet and a very small head. Observing that its master had returned, the demon waddled over to the table and pulled itself up with its very agile and workmanlike hands.

A single glance at the Infernal Face led it to slip once more to the floor, where with a muted, worried buzzing it started to waddle its way once more to the door hole.

But Lucifer reached out and snatched up the thing, which was named Kadjebeen, plumping it ungently down on the tabletop.

The demon, thus presented, had a strong resemblance to that sort of fat-bottomed toy which has lead weights built into the round wooden base and which cannot be knocked over, no matter how hard or how many times one hits it. Lucifer was very aware of this resemblance, for he had used the little demon in this manner many times. Now he did not strike it, except with a glare.

It had feet longer than its legs. This was perhaps necessary in order to keep its rotundity in balance when it walked. It was not strictly necessary, however, for its feet to curl up in ornamental curlicues at the toes like Turkish shoes. This was a piece of pure individuality on the demon's part, and Lucifer—who was in many ways responsible for the rest of the demon's appearance—ground his predatory teeth at it.

The demon cringed. "Y—Your Magnificence's new palace image is finished," it announced, its voice the timbre of a tree frog's. "D—does Your Magnificence approve?"

Lucifer let his eyes slip for a moment to the marvelous model on the table beside the demon. Then his baleful gaze returned. "There's a fly in it," he stated flatly.

The demon rolled his eyes. (He could do this very well, because they were on stalks.) He examined the work of his hands carefully, and he, too, noticed the insect. He stuck one of his spider-thin fingers into the cupola window and made shooing gestures. A bad-tempered buzz responded.

But Lucifer was no longer paying attention to the image. He had sunk back into his throne with an almost adolescent sullenness, and was biting his fingernails.

"Something isn't right, in all this," he grumbled between his teeth. "From the very beginning, every carefully thought-out plan I made regarding that—that Eyetalian—went awry."

The demon knew better than to ask questions of its master; it merely held one rococo toe in each nervous hand and pulled on them alternately.

"It wasn't my failure, either," continued the twisted angel, as he brooded and destroyed his cuticles. "I led him to me with perfect logic and baited every trap with his heart's desire. I should have had him a hundred times." He shot a pointed look at his servant.

"Not that Delstrego had any importance in himself, mind you. No more than any of that . . . that mortal tillage of mine. But such as he was, he was Raphael's weakness."

Lucifer straightened in his chair and dropped his fist to the table. His face was a sculpture of cold hate, at which the demon stared in a terror of admiration. "Raphael's weakness," repeated Lucifer, gaining fury as he spoke.

"Oh, my sickly sweet, sainted brother!"

The Devil flung himself to his feet. The table was jarred and the intricate, careful palace model skidded over its smooth surface. The raspberry demon flailed and caught it just before it went over.

"Don't do that, please, Your Magnificence!"

"Raphael! Raphael!" hissed Lucifer. His face went from coral to blotched snow and rubies. "After Michael, I hate you more than any created being! And since you've never had the Sword-Angel's hard-headed good sense, you have let events carry you to *me*.

"And you did it all by yourself." And at some sudden memory, Lucifer snickered, as his anger was cut with ugly hope. He stopped before a heavy metallic tapestry which hung between north and east, and he fingered it, following its embroidered story with his eyes.

"Once you were no more than a mirror for Him, like that other sheep, Uriel: beautiful, blank, and . . . and quite safe from influence.

"Now you've become nearly as much a slave to the earth as some sylph of earth's air, brother. You bob right and left as the winds take you, and there is no one down there—absolutely no one, you will find—who can protect you."

And with these words, and the more complex thoughts which went behind them, Lucifer's mood flipped over, from immediate disappointment to eventual success and he looked inward upon a balmy future steeped in revenge.

"You see, Kadjebeen, my playing at dice for the soul of the little witch man wasn't a loss, after all. No—for every time he escaped me, it was by some great expense of Raphael's, until now, after only a little time at the gambling wheels of earth, my brother is near bankrupt."

Lucifer giggled then, and in a moment he had himself convinced that he had never been interested in Damiano Delstrego's soul at all.

"My only mistake," concluded Lucifer, raising his eyes and pointing at the raspberry demon, Kadjebeen, who still sat on the table, clutching his cunning image between his curly feet, "was in trying to use the man as the final bait to my trap now that he is dead and therefore untouch—or rather, I mean, without importance to me. Though as a gesture it would have had such artistic merit . . ."

Kadjebeen folded his hands and stared at his model, lest he be accused of acquiescence in the idea that Lucifer had made any mistake at all. And that he was wise to do so was proven in the next moment, for Lucifer smote his palm with a fist and cried, "Why, by my own powers! Of course. There was no error! He *can* be the bait of my trap, even now."

And then Lucifer strode over to the window of the south, where lay expanses both of desert and plenty. "Woe, my dear Raphael," he whispered, as his blue eyes wandered, making plans. "You have loved well, but not at all wisely."

The baked white earth threw the heat against the baked white wall, which threw it back again. Hidden cicadas produced a tranced droning which was the perfect aural equivalent of the heat shimmer: a sound which a person might ignore for hours at a time before his consciousness came up against it, and which then would become unbearable.

Above San Gabriele the dark hills gathered, looming over the village like large friends who stood too close for one's comfort. Their blackish evergreen slopes promised a relief from the August heat to anyone who had the energy to walk so far.

For the most part, the San Gabrieleans preferred the blackish relief to be found within the wineshop. There, stretched out on the bosom of Mother Earth (the shop boasted no other floor), a handful of men with nothing to do let the sun fry the world outside.

Not that they were all drinking wine. Signor Tedesco, proprietor of the little store, would have been very happy had that been the case. But in all the village of San Gabriele there was not a man who had the money to spend his weekdays in a haze of vinous glory.

One man had a bottle which had been passed around a bit, and another had a half-bottle, which had not. The same fellow possessed a loaf of bread longer than his arm, which he guarded, waiting for the cool of the afternoon to give him the energy with which to eat. Another refugee from the sun had brought his lute, a very fine instrument, bright, sonorous, covered with a paper-thin inlay of mother-of-pearl, upon which he was trading songs with a chitarre player. A second lute, also belonging to the chitarrist, lay on the table unused because it would not stay in tune with the other instruments.

Signor Tedesco regarded his patrons with a jaundiced eye. He had had no intention of creating an atmosphere conducive to the promulgation of the arts. He hadn't even intended for the wine that he sold to be consumed in the confines of his shop.

He knew what an inn was: enough to know his wineshop didn't qualify. He wouldn't mind being an innkeeper, mind you, for he rather thought a man of that occupation might be a little wealthier than a villager who bought twenty casks of cheap red per season and filled bottles with the stuff. But if he were an innkeeper, Signor Tedesco would have tried to keep riffraff like this off his floor.

Especially the redhead in the corner making strange noises on the lute. He was the kind of musician Tedesco liked to refer to as having his ears on upside down. No more than seventeen years old, surely, the young pup bounced his hands up and down the neck of his pretty instrument with great concentration and produced a variety of sounds that Tedesco found quite unpleasant.

(But then, to be fair to the redheaded lutenist, Signor Tedesco had about twenty songs he liked, having known them from childhood, and he liked them played only in certain ways and on certain instruments, and thought the rest of the musical world might just as well go hang.)

The gangling youth pinched a smart octave on the sixth of the scale, then added to it a tenth above, then an eleventh and even a twelfth. Instead of resolving the progression, the musician then damped out the final sound on the beat and called the song complete.

Tedesco didn't know what an eleventh interval was, but he knew how to shudder.

"That's . . . very original," murmured the chitarrist, for although his ears, too, were a bit shocked, he was willing to try to understand. "Why does it end like that? Bomp!"

The redhead had an aggressive chin and eyes of a peculiar pale sage green, in a face which had not yet settled into its adult proportions (if indeed it had any intention of settling). His Adam's apple rehearsed his answer before he opened his mouth.

"That's so you don't fall asleep." Then he shrugged enormously and cast the question behind him. "What can I say? What do you expect me to say? That's how the song came to me."

"Came to you?" echoed the chitarrist, who was a round-faced fellow with a bristling mustache and three fat little babies at home. "You made it up?"

Gaspare drummed his fingers on the soundboard a trifle self-consciously and let his oversized eyes wander out the door as he replied. "Of course I made it up. Everything I play is my own.

"To play another man's music," he added righteously, "is akin to theft."

One who knew Gaspare well—one like his sister Evienne, for example—might have fallen face first upon the dirt, hearing this statement uttered in this tone by Gaspare of San Gabriele. But Evienne was not in San Gabriele but in Avignon, tending her own fat babies, and the villagers Gaspare had left behind some years ago found it easy to forget the scrawny, light-fingered street dancer when looking at this insolent youth with his foreign manners and his exquisite lute.

The chitarrist took this opportunity to run a fingernail down his strings. Signor Tedesco, behind his counter, perked up. But Gaspare had so cowed the round-faced man that he dared not go simply from the root to the fifth and then back again, as he had intended, so his endeavor led to nothing. The chitarrist stared glumly at his finger-nails.

"But what about the master musician of whom you are always speaking, whom you followed from Lombardy to France? I was under the impression it was his tunes with which you educate the village."

Gaspare's eyes did not exactly mist over, for he had not the sort of eye for that, but they expressed a certain feeling. He slumped back, letting his lute lie in his lap like an empty bowl.

"Ah, yes. Delstrego. You know—while I was with him I never touched the lute. Never dared, I guess. And then afterward, though I have had my training at the hands of his own teacher, and it was my idea to sound as much like him as possible . . ."

The redhead sighed. "It didn't work that way.

"And now I see that it could not, and I no longer desire to imitate him, for Delstrego was in a way a soft man. Whereas I . . ."

The bristling mustache stood out like a hedgehog's quills, as the chitarrist reflected on Gaspare's lack of softness. Gaspare himself ignored the smile.

"And when I tried to play Delstrego's songs with my own hands and my own spirit, then they sounded like little birds that had been put in a cage of iron." His long nose twitched and he sat up again.

"So I let them go." The redhead gestured theatrically toward the rough stone doorway.

"Still, if Damiano Delstrego himself were to come stepping in that door out of the summer heat, with his little lute under his arm—then you would hear some music," vouched Gaspare, whose self-importance, though considerable, had never been permitted to come between himself and his admiration for his first friend. "You would hear music more original than mine, and yet music even Signor Tedesco could appreciate."

The proprietor raised his head, frowning, uncertain whether he had just been praised or insulted.

Gaspare, still with his hand raised, stared out the pale shimmer of the open door. Cold water seemed to trickle up and down his spine, unpleasant despite the heat, and he wondered if perhaps he had said something he should not have said.

Behind the wineshop, and behind every other shop and dwelling in their nudging row along this street in San Gabriele, was a straight and narrow alley, which (since the battle of the same name as the town, four years before) led to nothing but a pile of rubble. Without a steady stream of feet to keep the clay packed, this alley had been conquered by grass, which had in turn suffered from a lack of sun. Summer had killed this unfortunate growth and dipped it in bronze, but still it held some value for a gelding who had discovered it in the process of avoiding the sun.

This animal was black and lean. Its long neck was sinuous. Its long legs were . . . well, very long. One of its ears rested malevolently back against its head, but the horse gave the impression that its ill-temper was a chronic condition, not about to manifest itself into action on this stifling afternoon. The horse's other ear made circles of uneasiness. He chewed half a jawful of yellow grass and let the remainder drop.

Under the thatch of the wineshop roof sat a brown wood dove, colored such a pale and desiccated brown that she might have been molded of clay and left to dry in the sun. She was keeping a sort of uncommunicative company with the gelding. She was also listening to the music within.

Doves are for the most part very conservative singers, and do not appreciate any music but their own. This dove, however, was only a dove part-time. She was a witch, and what is more, a singing witch. She listened to Gaspare's lute playing with a quick and educated mind.

It tended to give her a headache.

Bird eyes regarded the stripe of uncompromising blue sky which was visible under the ragged thatch. She didn't know what it was about the heavens which seemed so false, or at least dubious, today. She rather suspected that Gaspare was about to do something he shouldn't. The boy was much wiser than he used to be—the Eagle Chief's influence, if not her own—but still he had a long trial to sled before he could be safely left to his own devices.

Saara could easily imagine Gaspare accepting a challenge to a duel: he who had never held a sword in his life. She could even imagine him challenging some other to a duel. Over some picayune point of music, of course.

Some hot-tempered village maiden could run him through with a pitchfork. Or her father could. At least, being simple (not a witch born), Gaspare could not lose himself in the myriad dangers and seductions that came to a youngster with Sight.

Saara felt a certain responsibility for Gaspare, born out of both friends and adventure shared. She shifted from foot to foot. Because she was a dove, this looked much like a round pot rolling from side to side on the table. She heard the chitarrist in the wineshop make his tentative dribble of sound and, like Signor Tedesco himself, she had hopes. But it seemed fated the man would not continue his plain, confident melody.

The day would not permit.

Festilligambe, the horse standing below, felt the same unease, for he wiggled an ear in the direction of Saara (whom he knew quite well, both as bird and as human) and he stepped out into the unfriendly sun.

That white disk of light bleached the color of the soul,

and it stole the will away. Even Gaspare (bright of hue and mightily determined) ceased playing. The two beasts heard the murmur of his voice seeping through the metallic-hot air. Then that sound, too, died away.

Someone was coming up the hill of San Gabriele, striding long-legged past the ruin of the village wall. The rhythm of his steps, and the regular thumping of his wooden stick, broke the cicada's drone.

He was dressed in black, and his hair was black, and as he lifted his eyes toward the yawning door of the wine-shop, they, too, were black. His face was comely, though the nose was a trifle broad, and in those quick black eyes shone intelligence. From his staff flashed red and yellow, which shimmered, along with the entire figure, in the glare of the sun.

Cold shock crept from Saara's scaled feet up to her bare beak as she watched the form of her dead love approach. Her dun feathers fluffed into ridges. The horse below switched his tail and snorted.

That Damiano, so wise beyond his years, and so hungry for understanding, should walk the scenes of his past like some miser riven from his horde . . . it was unthinkable. And unspeakably sad.

"When I am dead," he had said, "you must let go anything of mine which you hold. The dead should be dead."

But Saara's sadness was reflective and momentary, for she knew that this apparition was not Damiano. For one thing, Damiano did not wear black. For another, Saara herself had taught Damiano to do without his staff, and she did not believe that, once dead, he would go back to using crutches he had left behind in life.

And more importantly, this Damiano shape stood now beneath her, in the wineshop doorway, and was unaware of her very presence. Even in his simple days, Damiano would have known Saara was near.

The horse, who saw something different from that which Saara saw, and from that which Gaspare saw from within the wineshop (with all the hair on the back of his neck rising in protest), made no more sound, but turned his elegant tail and disappeared down the grassy alley.

The apparition carried a lute, Saara saw now, leaning her sleek dove head over the ledge of stone where she sat.

It was a marvelously ornate lute: Gaspare's own lute, in fact. That made quite a paradox, as even now Saara heard the original of this spectral lute thumped clumsily upon the top of the trestle table within.

"Delstrego!" gasped the youth, in tones of mixed joy and terror.

This is how Gaspare is going to get himself into trouble, said Saara to herself, as she launched out from the eaves of the building.

CHAPTER 2

The Devil had his plans. He would work upon the unfortunate Gaspare with his twin needles of guilt and pride. The youth would provide no challenge, certainly, for his haughty and sullen tempers stood out like so many hooks on which the Devil could latch. Raise that hauteur, ruffle that temper, and there Gaspare would be, trussed like Sunday's goose. Lucifer's greatest worry so far had been that he would be required to play the lute as Delstrego had, which was a thing he could not do, having abjured music along with the heavenly choir.

It was not that the prize in this game was Gaspare's little soul; such as Gaspare was merely coarse bread and dry. But his peril was sure to bring Raphael fluttering in, for the angel watched his protégés like a hawk.

So Lucifer was understandably surprised to find himself under the assault of not a hawklike angel, but a small dove, round of keel—at the moment of his subtle plan's unfolding. With not the least peep of warning, this avian flew at his man-shape and pecked it smartly under the eye. Lucifer flinched away from it, displaying very natural confusion and annoyance.

The greatest of angels had no interest in the animal kingdom. The world's furred, feathered, or finny creatures were as much beneath his peculiar temptations as the denizens of Tir Na nOg were beyond them. He was not even very knowing about animal behavior. Did this miserable atom think that Lucifer, wingless as he appeared in his

present form, was yet a sort of greater bird and therefore a
competitor? Did it have a nest nearby? He cast a glance
around him, as the dove swooped to the ground at his feet.

Even as Lucifer perceived the obvious truth, that the
creature was not a bird at all but a human shape-changer, it
had swollen to its full status: that of a woman almost as tall
as he stood in his Delstrego form.

"Liar!" she shrilled in his ear. "Filthy liar!" Curiously
enough, she spoke a barbaric tongue of the far north.

Lucifer had no idea what a Lapp would be doing in a
Piedmont village by the Lombardy border. He was further
piqued to discover he didn't recognize this woman at all.
Perhaps, he considered momentarily, he hadn't given the
tribal primitives of the earth their share of his attention.

In certain ways they were so much like the beasts.

And he reacted to this unknown creature in the way in
which he usually reacted to anything which frustrated him
or set back his plans. He turned color and hissed at her,
and prepared to strike her to cinders where she stood.

But, worse luck, this was not merely a shape-changer,
but one of those unspeakable Lappish singing witches.

He felt her puerile sing-song cutting through his
disguise like a razor through hide. As shape fell away, he
was obliged to grope for wyvern form to cover his
nakedness. He shot at the woman a blast of pure, shrivel-
ing hate, only to see it deflected by a thread of melody. The
malice shuddered sideways and scraped lime off the
wineshop wall.

She dared smile through her teeth as she said, speaking
in heavily accented Italian, "You made another of your
great mistakes when you took the face of Damiano, you
greedy old man. I will crush you for it." Then the bitch's
song actually did try to squeeze him. Though Lucifer
himself was far beyond being hurt by the spell, the wyvern
he wore could not breathe.

With the vision of his spirit, the Devil was very aware of
the round eyes and dropped jaws in the wineshop so near.
Cursing, he gave up his present ambitions toward Gaspare
and rose into the air, determined to escape this constraint
and blast the beast-woman from the face of the earth.

Certainly Lucifer had the power to destroy one silly
witch, once he'd recovered from his surprise and from the
unbearable feeling of having been cheated by this beast-

woman's popping from nowhere. Simple physical destruction was both Lucifer's pleasure (albeit not his highest
pleasure), and his right.

The wyvern circled in the air, persecuted by the witch
who was once more in dove shape. Lucifer snarled at the
bird with the contempt he felt for all simple or straightfor-
ward creatures. Once lured out of human shape, the
witch's ability to sing (and therefore her power) was sadly
curtailed. The wyvern drew a deep breath, gathering fire.

But the bird's anger was so insane as to approach the
maternal, and she seemed unaware of her danger as she
fluttered about the two-legged dragon-thing, pecking at its
eyes.

Lucifer, once collected to himself, was a very clever
spirit, and excellent at drawing together odd threads of
information and making tangles of them. It occurred to him
that there was some connection between this creature and
the matter at hand; after all, it was the shape of Delstrego
that seemed to set her off.

And then he remembered a small interchange with
Damiano on the streets of Avignon in the mortal's last days:
an interchange not comfortably called to mind.

He had dropped a gentle hint that the fellow had
carried the plague with him into Avignon. (Not true, as it
happens, but it very well *might* have been true, given the
dreadful medical ignorance of the populace.) The man had
dared to bray back at him a denial. "We were all clean.
Saara said so."

And when asked who this Saara was, Delstrego had
replied, "Someone you don't know."

Now Lucifer laughed, and ashes sullied the hot air
around him. So even that septic little trading of insults
could be turned to good use.

Someone he didn't know. Perhaps. But such an over-
sight was quite easily rectifiable. He beat off the drab-
colored dove (quite gently) with a wing as hard and as
supple as chain mail, and he peered at her with new
curiosity.

A mascot of some sort? She could have meant little
more, farouche as she was. Pretty enough, in human
shape, but he knew quite well that Italians liked their
woman both clinging and coy. Probably a pet. Whatever,
she was doubtless of some value to his sentimental brother,

and Lucifer was not one to turn his face from fortune. He cringed from the bird and fled upward.

Saara's anger was like a wind which blew through every room of her soul, cleaning it of years of suffering.

Not since she left the fens had she had an enemy she could fight with whole heart: an enemy she had no compunction about hurting. And she had no fear for herself, for after losing two children and three lovers to death, it was a very familiar presence to her. In fact, there was nothing more appropriate which could happen in her life now, after all she had been through, than to be given the Liar himself as target and a clear field of attack. Especially when she remembered the miserable confusion this breath of wickedness had caused in Damiano, both to the man's head and his heart, before cutting short his life.

Along with Saara's slow-blooming happiness. Saara had never thought to ask herself why the Liar had oppressed Damiano so; she knew that too much interest in that demon's mentations only invited him into one's life. But still she could hate him for it.

For she had loved Damiano and loved him still, not with the wise passion Saara had felt for other men in her time, but with the sweet and choking emotion always before reserved for her children.

Saara had neither hope nor plan for survival as she spun about the loathsome, heavy reptilian shape, buffeted by the wind of its wings and suffocated by fumes; survival was meaningless next to the chance to do harm to the Father of Lies. This wild and selfless fury with which a bird weighing all of three ounces flung herself at the Devil he mistook (as he always must) for lack of brain.

Up they went in a flurry of wings, until the air about them grew cooler and lost the flavor of earth, and the sun spun about the sky as a dizzying white disk. Without warning, Saara traded her bird shape for that of an owl, and her talons raked the wyvern in its great yellow eyes. But the owl was half-blind in the light and the wyvern, disdaining battle, escaped it with a bob and dart to the right.

Saara followed, her muffled white wings straining, and for a moment she hung above the wyvern, untouching. Then suddenly the witch flickered and changed shape again, not this time to any sort of bird but to an enormous white bear of the north, which dropped like stone onto the reptile's back.

The wyvern's wings collapsed like sails of paper, and both beasts plummeted toward the earth.

After his first shock at this attack, Lucifer decided to let the bear fall—he could escape the wyvern form before impact: let the witch do the same, if she could. But then he shrieked, for the bear had its massive jaws around the snake neck of the wyvern and those jaws were closing. He suffered a certain amount of pain before he could dissolve his physical form, fleeing Saara now with no more substance than a passing thought, nor any more ability to do harm.

In an instant the bear, too, had vanished, and though it took Saara precious time to pull out of the tailspin caused by this last transformation, the pale dove skimmed the Lombard forest unharmed and returned to her pursuit, chasing nothing more than a nasty glitter in the sky.

There was no hope she could catch a disembodied spirit, however, and furious though she was (with the taste of the Devil's blood in her memory, if not in her mouth), she had half a mind to give up and return to San Gabriele.

Gaspare deserved some explanation, after all.

But against all expectation, she saw the Liar resume his damaged wyvern form in the sky high above her. She flapped harder to catch up, wishing she had studied the shape of the chimney swift instead of that of the dove.

She could not gain on the creature, but neither did she fall behind. Now they were so high above the earth that she was giddy, and her small lungs worked like bellows in the thin air. The wyvern, too, seemed affected, for its wings beat more slowly and blood sprayed in sunlit droplets from its wounded neck. It looked behind it and hissed.

Then Saara's giddiness grew very serious, for down seemed suddenly to become sideways, and the dove lost its purchase in the air and fell sickeningly before righting itself in a different attitude.

Saara looked around her and cursed, for her perceptions had been quite correct; down *had* become sideways, and below her naked tucked feet she beheld a broken regiment of peaks, touched here and there with snow. What it was that had happened to bring her here she was not quite sure, and how to return, if there was any question of return, she had no idea.

But the wyvern was still ahead of her, and that was what counted. She chased the scaly thing down among the mountain peaks; it seemed so weary now and weak from loss of blood that she slowly gained on it.

A spirit could not be destroyed utterly: not even the spirits of little things like mice and frogs, let alone a strong spirit older than mankind. But if she could get over the wyvern again and crash it into the rocks below, then she could do harm to the Liar—oh yes, real, satisfying harm.

With the prize so near, Saara's own weariness dropped away. She saw the wyvern disappear behind the shoulder of a gaunt gray peak, but she found it again in moments. Once more she lost the creature and once more found it.

Now purplish blood spattered the bare stone shelves below as the wyvern snaked its way deeper into the cracks of the mountains. It was heading for one high, solitary cone shape on the horizon. Perhaps there to make a stand.

Saara pressed still harder, for she did not want to encounter this thing on the ground, where even a bear of the north would be no match for the half-dragon. She wanted to drop it from the sky—to smash it to jelly. She was almost upon it.

But the wyvern, with all the appearance of terror, put on a burst of speed and together they approached the face of the mountain, tiny beak to writhing great tail. Saara cried in fury, and the wyvern bellowed back its wrath.

There was a window in the sheer cliff of the mountain: a perfect, tall, arched window, larger than the doors of men. The dove gave one astounded blink and cry, watching the wyvern disappear into it. She beat her wings wildly to the front, but it was far too late to stop her own progress, and Saara fluttered rolling into Satan's watchtower.

Lucifer, seated in his tall chair, caught the bird easily as it skidded across the table. He prisoned her within the compass of his fingers and lifted her, feet upward, into the light for better viewing.

In neither his appearance nor demeanor was there any trace of the wyvern he had been: no scales, no blood. He was in his most usual and comfortable form, that of a king in red (red showed off his golden hair to good advantage), and the family features rested agreeably on his face. He regarded the rumpled dove with a certain curiosity.

But none of this is to say he was in a good mood, or that he had forgotten the jaws of the white bear on the wyvern's neck. Pink flesh showed between the rutched feathers and down of the dove's breast and belly. The little legs kicked, and the head which protruded from between his finger and thumb squirmed right and left. Lucifer felt the tremor of her heart, quick and nervous as a tree of leaves in the wind.

He discovered that when he squeezed the creature, her tiny twiglike beak opened, and when he released the pressure of his hand, it closed again. He amused himself in this fashion for a minute or so, and then he said calmly, "You have a sadly inflated idea of your own abilities, little hen."

Suddenly the dove writhed in his hand, and at the expense of a few feathers, twisted around enough to deliver a sound peck on the skin between his thumb and forefinger.

Lucifer cursed and shifted his grip. He called Kadjebeen, and before many seconds had passed, the small raspberry-shaped demon had erupted through the door in the floor.

"Bring me string," said Satan very quietly. Kadjebeen disappeared once more through the door.

After the demon's disappearance, Lucifer's complacent smile returned. Kadjebeen was his current favorite among the palace staff, being quite handy and even more afraid of him than most. Very soon he returned with a spool of red twine, which he carefully tied around one of the dove's legs.

The other end of the length of twine was attached to one of the barbed turrets of the image of the palace on the table. Kadjebeen bit his lips anxiously as this was done, for he feared damage to his handiwork.

Lucifer was aware of his servant's trepidation, and it gave him a good deal of satisfaction. Throwing the spool of red twine at Kadjebeen's head, he pointed to a far corner of the room, to which the demon retired.

Saara was dumped onto the tabletop, where she lay panting and blinking. After a moment or two Lucifer found the sight of the tied dove less than interesting. He gestured vaguely toward her and her bird shape melted into Saara shape, complete with bare feet and embroidered blue dress, but no bigger than the dove had been.

Saara plucked at the red band around her ankle, but it was so much rusty iron. "Filthy liar," she spat once more, somewhat wearily. "You cannot touch me."

Lucifer giggled. "But my dear little pullet! Obviously I have touched you.

"And you made it inevitable that I should," he added, in the tone of exaggerated seriousness which adults reserve for talking intelligently with children.

And which drives all intelligent children wild.

"If a man gives me the slightest encouragement, I am able to help him hither to my fastness. But you—how lovely it was—came here under your own power, almost against my very will."

"I am not a man," said Saara, sitting with one leg folded and the other knee propped. "And I still say you cannot touch me."

Lucifer smiled wider than was his wont, until Saara could see the serrated edges of his teeth. "It doesn't matter that you are not a man, for 'the male,' (he quoted) 'embraces the female.'" He laughed at his own rather stale wit and poked her belly with his little finger.

Saara had never been to a school in her life and her knowledge of grammar was embryonic. "What on earth are you talking about, you dirty thing? Nobody would embrace you!"

Then the whimsical light went out of his eyes. "Scrawny pullet," he barked, and he ground his teeth at her. "I will derive a great deal of pleasure out of pulling you apart."

Saara looked directly at him, and then through him, and finally turned her back on him and sat staring at the windowless wall of the model to which she was tied.

Lucifer's high color rose higher, from carnelian to the hue of fresh-butchered meat. Hissing, he plucked up the red thread and dangled the woman by her ankle. Her brown braids swung below her head, and her dress crawled up to her armpits. Sniggering, he pulled it off, leaving her to dangle naked. Bestowing this additional humiliation upon Saara did a lot toward restoring the Devil's temper.

Her body was lithe, and blushed like the skin of a peach.

"You know, little insignificant peeper, that you weren't even the sparrow I was out to snare? Not even *that* important."

Saara climbed up her own leg and then up the length of red string until she hung upright by her two hands. She didn't seem to care or notice that she was naked.

"I know," she replied. "It was pretty obvious you were after Gaspare. Well, you won't be able to use that trick on him again, dressing up like Damiano. Gaspare must have seen an eyeful."

The red cord trembled with Lucifer's annoyance. "Have you no sense but to hang there and throw offense at me, savage? Don't you know how I'm going to make you suffer?"

"I know how you made Damiano suffer," was her undisturbed retort. "Yet it didn't get you anywhere, did it?"

The tiny woman's body was spinning around with the natural movement of the twine, and the chamber of four windows passed under her review. She noted it as carefully as she could, especially the vista outside the window by which she had entered.

Obviously they were not really in the Alpine mountains. They were probably in no definite place at all; Saara had enough experience in the realms of magic to know that its geography was unpredictable. When her spinning brought her around to Kadjebeen, squatting in his dim corner, she actually laughed.

"What an unfortunate creature!" she cried aloud. "I wonder how it can manage, looking like that!"

The raspberry-shaped and raspberry-colored demon did not particularly like being laughed at, but he found some comfort in the knowledge that this stranger had immediate sympathy with his biggest problem in life. His Magnificence (who had had a clear hand in the molding of Kadjebeen) had never deigned to express any interest in his servant's consequent plight.

Still Saara spun, coming back around to face the Devil's perfect features and exposed fangs.

"So you noticed little Kadjebeen, did you?" Lucifer snickered, enjoying his captive's dizzying movement. "How would you like to be turned into another like him?"

But Saara had spent too much time as a bird to be made

motion sick. "You can't," she replied casually. "I am not afraid of hunger, so you have no power over my belly or mouth, and I am not afraid of *you*, so you cannot make me shrink like that against the ground. And as for his eyes—well, they must bug out from fear, as well, for he can have no great desire to be able to look back at that face of his!"

"Enough elementary lessons in transmigration," Lucifer growled. He blew Saara into a faster spin.

"There is, after all, a reason I have brought you here."

"*You* brought *me?*" The spin added a peculiar tremolo to Saara's words. "A moment ago you said I came in spite of you."

"Some of each," replied the Devil equably, and losing interest, he dropped the whirling woman to the tabletop. "It is of no account by which way you came. Nor does it really matter that you're not Gaspare of San Gabriele. What matters is that you are a good enough bait to draw my brother Raphael to me."

Saara had landed on her feet, still holding the length of red twine in her hands. She stared blankly at the huge carmine face above her. "Raphael? You mean the Chief of Eagles? You mean the music teacher?"

Lucifer's amusement spread all over his face. "We certainly have the same party in mind, little witch. Raphael the many-feathered warbler, who happens to be my disgusting lesser brother."

The naked woman rolled a coil of twine and sat herself down upon it. She examined Lucifer appraisingly. "They say the eagle is kin to the bald-headed vulture—who also has a very red face, like yours."

In an instant's ungovernable fury Lucifer spat at Saara: spat an incendiary spittle which exploded around her like Greek fire. She barely had time to roll herself into a ball before the flash was around her. To the stuffiness of the air was added the stench of burnt hair.

Saara uncoiled, slightly pinker than she had been and missing most of her braids. Her heart was pounding and she could feel the blood rushing into her face and even through her ears.

But none of this was fear. Instead she felt a mad exhaltation, as it seemed her long life had at last come to some point.

"You picked a bad bait to use, if you want to attract the Chief of Eagles," she said casually, examining a slightly charred fingernail. "We haven't gotten along very well."

"I wonder who you *have* gotten along with, you tusked sow!" growled the Devil, but he was unable to hide the fact that this information displeased him. He drummed enormous fingers on the tabletop (his rhythm was off).

"That hardly matters," he said at last. "Raphael is the sort who would not let a small thing like justly despising you stand in the way of self-sacrifice. He is quite perverse that way, my brother. In fact, a mortal he dislikes may be the better for my purpose." Then Lucifer yawned.

"Likely *any* mortal would have done."

Boredom recalled Lucifer to his own intention. "Why do I sit here communing with this bit of insignificant spleen?" he murmured. "I need only raise my voice now, and . . ."

Suddenly the witch on the table seemed infected by madness. She rose from her stringy chair and began to jump up and down, her round breasts jouncing in opposition to her movement. "He'll blast you, windbag! The Eagle will tear you limb from limb. He'll turn you into a bright-red leather handbag. He'll . . ." and then Saara stopped bouncing long enough to perform an extremely complex and obscene gesture which she had learned in the Italies. When she felt she once more had Lucifer's attention, she began to curse him in earnest.

Forbearance was not the Devil's strongest attribute. Yet his only visible reaction to this torrent of abuse was a momentary tightening of the jaw. "If you didn't believe I could damage this spirit you claim to hate" (Saara actually had claimed no such thing), "you would not be so eager now to have me kill you.

"You will just have to be patient," he adjured the tiny woman, and turned from the table.

Lucifer looked out each of his windows in turn, wasting not a glance on Kadjebeen, who was still squatting obediently in his corner, feeling his mouth with his spidery fingers and staring ruefully at his stumpy short legs.

In the Prince of Earth a fierce emotion was rising: a satisfaction which thought itself joy but bore more resemblance to pride. Like a player of some intricate, slow-

moving board game, he had plotted out a hundred future
moves in this bitter duel with Raphael (more bitter because
he suspected that Raphael was not even aware of it as a
duel) and had decided that he could not lose.

Meanwhile the Lappish curses continued from the little
witch tied to the model on the table. Only Kadjebeen
listened.

"Raphael," called Lucifer composedly, in a voice no
louder than that he had used to call his servant. "Raphael,
my dear brother, why don't you drop by and see me?"

There was a minute's silence. Lucifer knew this didn't
indicate that Raphael hadn't heard him, or that the roads
were bad. Sharpening his very flexible voice, the Devil
added, "I advise you very strongly to make the visit,
brother. You will find you are not my only guest."

Suddenly a wind swirled through the windows of the
chamber, as though whatever barrier had kept the airs of
the world from entering had been breached. It was a
confused wind, as the mint dryness of the Alps met the
breath of orchids, while sand and sandalwood clashed
with pine. But it was very fresh. It made Saara lift her head
and sniff, and little Kadjebeen, in his corner, began to
burble with worry.

The air flickered with a light like sun filtered through a
net of pearls: a soft radiance which rippled and danced. It
was the gleam given off by the white wings of Raphael.

The face was the same as Lucifer's, though perhaps
there was a greater virility in the high, sharp set of Lucifer's
cheekbones. Lucifer's hair, too, was a richer color, to match
the more-than-ruddiness of his skin.

But Lucifer's eyes were a pale and watchful blue, while
those of Raphael were summer evening itself, with stars
shining through darkness.

He was dressed very simply, almost sketchily, in a white
garment which Lucifer called (under his breath) "the same
old undershirt." He was shorter and slighter than Lucifer.
But the thing which distinguished Raphael from his
brother was, of course, that frame of enormous, opalescent, galleon-sail wings: wings which seemed to be nothing more than the radiance of his nature taking on form.

So although Lucifer was striking, Raphael was beautiful, and no creature who had ever had the luck to see him
had denied his beauty, or had come away unaffected by the
sight.

Raphael had never seen himself, nor had he ever had any desire to see himself.

Kadjebeen saw Raphael and his blue eyes yearned forward on their stalks. He regarded the face of light and the brilliant wings—yes, especially the wings—and he thought in his artisanly way that he'd like to build something that looked like that.

Saara gazed at Raphael with an expression akin to pain. She was not considering his face or form, however, but his danger. And as she remembered that Damiano had loved the angel, she also remembered that she had not always been understanding about that. She turned her head away.

Lucifer looked at his brother and flinched; the Devil himself flinched and uttered a strangled cry, for he was as sensitive to beauty as any creature born. It hurt him.

Raphael saw his brother's wincing without surprise. Lucifer always reacted to the sight of him like that. He regarded Lucifer with his own, quite different feelings. "What is it, Satan? What wicked deed is in your hands now?"

Lucifer's great eyes rounded and he lifted his hands in protest, if not to heaven, then at least to the sky. "And they dare to call me cruel! He convicts me of crime without knowing there has been a crime, and though he is kin to me, refuses me my proper name!

"Raphael, you are nothing but a bigot—a narrow-minded and conventional burgher among a similar rabble, fearing to be anything more or less than your neighbor." Lucifer sighed with sad disapproval, but he found his eyes sliding away from that visage of light.

"But no matter, brother. I brought you here only to help me identify a creature. You have always been so interested in . . . animal husbandry.

"See," he proclaimed, gesturing openhanded toward Saara on the table. "It attacked me in Lombardy and hung around my neck halfway home."

As he approached the table, Lucifer waved his hand once more and a buff-colored dove appeared, wings spread and beak open in threat. At another motion of Lucifer's the dove became a snowy owl which blinked, hissing, in the light of day.

At a third command the bird swelled into a white bear which, though miniature, was still large enough to yank

Kadjebeen's model after it as it lunged wildly at the Devil's throat. The demon squeaked in apprehension.

"What do you suppose it is?" inquired Lucifer of his brother.

Raphael stood beside the table. His wings spread out sideways, almost dividing the chamber in two. His face was gentle.

"She is the greatest witch in the Italies," he replied to Lucifer. "Perhaps the greatest in all Europe.

"God be with you, Saara of the Saami," said Raphael to her.

As though she were throwing off a great weight, Saara divested herself of the shapes the Devil forced upon her.

"Get out of here, Chief of Eagles. It's a trap."

Raphael met her eyes, but made no reply. Instead his wings rose slowly to the vaulted ceiling, and he asked, "Why did you do this, Satan? This woman was never any business of yours."

Lucifer's sculpted eyebrows echoed the movement of the angel's wings. "Satan you call me, as though you were some grubbing mortal yourself! And you tell me what is my business . . ."

He strode across the room, his hands locked behind his back and his gaze wandering mildly out the windows. "That is miserable manners even when the busybody is right, but in this case, Raphael, you are quite mistaken. There is in this little female a streak of bitterness and jealousy I can quite appreciate—jealousy of whom, I wonder, brother? But even if there were not . . . even if she were that rare, malformed, or brainless sort of mortal content with everything that befell him . . .

"All mortals are my business and have been so since the plague of them were spawned. They are far more *my* business, Raphael, than yours. In fact, one might almost say that I stand in the place of their shepherd.

"On earth, that is."

Then Lucifer turned in place and regarded Raphael with bored disdain. "But we have had this discussion before."

The angel nodded. "I remember the last time. It was with Damiano. He won the argument."

The delicate, carmine nostrils flared. "He died."

"He won the argument," repeated Raphael evenly.

All the while he sparred with Lucifer, Raphael's wings twitched, keeping time like a steady heartbeat, or like the rhythm of a song. His face was very quiet, but not with a stiffness which suggested he was concealing his feelings. Rather it seemed the angel's feelings were so consonant with his form that they did not disarray his features. He glanced over to Saara on the table, and his head was hidden from Lucifer by a momentary upcurl of his right wing.

He winked at her.

At this little message of reassurance, Saara's fine rage bid fair to desert her, and she felt her throat close in panic.

To perish in combat with evil was one thing, but to die dragging with you one who was greater and older than you: one you had been asked to protect, as well . . .

"Go away!" she hissed at Raphael again, and made ineffectual shooing gestures with her hands. "This is *my* fight, spirit. You can only get hurt!"

But Raphael was speaking to his brother. "What do you think to do with her, aside from burning off her braids?"

"Think?" snorted Lucifer, returning to the table. He stared down at Saara and the air around her once again began to grow very warm. "I *think*, dear brother, that I will keep her a while for observation. That is the accepted course when one studies nature, isn't it? In a jar, perhaps, with straw over the bottom. Of course it might get smelly, and I have no great enthusiasm for catching her natural food . . ."

The Devil scratched his chin reflectively. "But then, after a suitable length of time—say a year, I will make a closer study. Of the inner organs. It will be interesting to see whether they really resemble more those of a bird or those of a bear."

As Lucifer spoke, Raphael's wings expanded up and out sideways, as stiff and smooth-feathered as if they had been carved of stone.

So would an angry hawk have displayed, protecting the fledglings in its nest. And, in fact, one of those stainless wings did block Saara from Lucifer's sight or touch, while the other pushed Kadjebeen bodily out of his corner. The demon stopped to finger a white pinion appreciatively.

It was a figure of Byzantine splendor that confronted the Devil. Pale glory circled Raphael's head and his gown gleamed like the noonday sun. The four winds rose together and swirled about the chamber, lifting ancient dead ashes from the cracks between the flagstones and blowing them away.

Lucifer seemed to have memories of what it meant when an archangel spread out his wings like that, and when his mild face went as hard as justice. For he stepped back, once and then again. His heel touched the low sill of the window ledge and Lucifer put a steadying hand out. A sneer covered his embarrassment.

This was not the vanguard of the Almighty, sent to cast him once more from his heights. This was a single spirit, and one that had undergone change in the streams of earth. Lucifer had planned carefully, and he was in the house of his own power. He was not about to be intimidated by empty show. He was now bigger than Raphael in all but wings, and wings were not weapons of war. He advanced again and stood beside his brother, looking down. He laughed.

Raphael spoke, and his voice cut through the forced and raucous laughter. "I am supposed to beg you to release her, Satan. That is obviously your plan. You, in turn, will refuse to do so."

Lucifer did not demur.

"There are two reasons," said Raphael, "why you might have called me here to participate in this charade. Either you want me to know you are engaged in this cruelty, or you want something from me in exchange for foregoing your pleasure.

"If you only wanted an audience, then I tell you that you have failed. Now that you have brought me here, I will not permit you to harm Saara of the Saami. I will oppose you in any way I can.

"If, on the other hand, you want to bargain—then explain your terms."

Lucifer stifled a laugh. "Well spoken, Raphael. You have condensed what might have been a half hour's stimulating conversation into a scrap of dull prose.

"And I will answer in the same terms.

"Dear brother, you cannot prevent me from harming this mortal. Perhaps once you might have, though I doubt it. But when you might have had the power, you certainly wouldn't have had the interest to do so. Now you can't.

"Let me list for you the reasons why: First, you
answered the summons of a mortal and, not content with
that indelicacy, you stayed to talk to him. And you
returned to him, again and again. You taught him a style of
music and of morals he had no right to know, and in the
end he was unfit for the place and time in which he had
been born. And if he was not what he had been . . ." The
Devil paused and glanced at his brother from under an
exquisite eyebrow.

". . . neither were you."

Lucifer took another step forward, as though to prove
to himself that his retreat had been an accident. "Secondly,
in the wretched village of Sous Pont Saint Martin, you
stood for some seconds on a dimple in the snow. Below
that dimple was an uncovered well, and a mortal man was
forced to walk around you and miss the drop. It was a
quick and smoothly handled bit of prestidigitation on your
part, and I'm sure you thought that since the mortal never
noticed you had saved his skin, perhaps no one else
would. You were wrong.

"Thirdly, in the almost equally wretched village of San
Gabriele, and at the instigation of an unaesthetic and
inconsequential little dog shade, you opened a locked door
and cheated the hangman of his employment."

Another small step. He was almost in touching distance
of Raphael now. Saara shouted a warning.

"Fourthly, you cut a man's hair and tied his horse's
harness in neat little bows. Very decorative, but not your
destined work, I think.

"Fifthly—if there is such a word as fifthly—you committed what even among mortals is a crime. You hid a
dying man from sight for an entire day, preventing anyone
who might have saved his life from discovering him.

"And last of all, the decisive moment came here not
three minutes ago, Raphael, as you announced quite baldly
that you intended to squabble with me over my little prize.

"Could you not feel yourself shrivel as you spoke,
brother? And each time you dirtied your hands in this
mortal muck, weren't you aware of your light dimming?
You have diminished till you are little more than a length of
black wick lying in a puddle of wax."

Lucifer's tone was soft, sorrowful, almost caressing,
and as he finished speaking he reached out into that clear

brightness which surrounded Raphael. He put his hand toward his brother's face.

It stopped, or was stopped by something: some quality of the light or of the shining smooth cheek itself, and the hand clenched empty air as Raphael answered.

"My size and form are whatever they are. I have done nothing to cause our Father pain."

"*He is not my* . . ." The Devil's skin went from red to purple. Both of his hands leaped out at Raphael's throat, but it was as though a wall of glass came between them.

Lucifer swung angrily toward the table. Though Raphael's wing concealed the witch from his sight, the intricate dollhouse sat there, vulnerable. He raised his fist above it.

From the far corner came a squeal of despair, and Kadjebeen hid his face in his hands.

In the middle of his rage Lucifer smiled, hearing the music he loved best. He allowed his fist to unclose and once more turned to Raphael. "You are quite right, Raphael. I do want something of you—something very easily in your power to give, and a generous act besides. And if you give it to me, I promise I will put the creature back where I found it. Unharmed. I further promise to leave it alone in the future: as long as it leaves *me* alone!" Lucifer spared a haughty and scandalized glance in the direction of his captive.

"It's a lie!" shrilled Saara from behind her white screen. "He won't release me, no matter what you do for him. He hates me; I bit his neck.

"And he hates you, Chief of Eagles, worse than he does me!"

Lucifer smiled sidelong. "Just listen to the little shrew. And what a name she gives you, brother. 'Chief of Eagles.' Don't you find it embarrassing?"

"Not at all. I prefer it to being called the Liar," replied Raphael shortly. "Now enough of this tuneless twist. Tell me what it is you want of me."

Lucifer's shrug and smile were a bit coy. "My desire is small and well-meaning. I want to break down the old and unfortunate barrier which has stood so long between you and me, dear brother."

Then his pale gaze sharpened. "I ask nothing of you, Raphael, neither service nor friendship nor understanding (for I know I will get none of these), but only that you take my hand in yours once more."

Raphael stood unmoving, but the feathers on the backs of his wings where they joined the body rutched out, as the hair on a man's head may seem to crawl. And the wings themselves started a barely perceptible tremor.

"No!" cried Saara. "Whatever he says, it is still treachery!"

But the angel was not listening, or at least not to her. He stood motionless, his head tilted slightly to one side, and his dark eyes unfocused. Then Raphael answered his brother. "I want to see Saara sent back first."

"*No!*" screamed the witch.

Lucifer smiled and his eyes grew white-pale. "Afterward, dear brother. I don't trust your decision will remain the same once the motivation is gone."

"Yes, you do," replied the angel, as he shook his feathers into place. "You *do* trust my word, Satan, or you would never have called me. The only reason you would refrain from returning Saara now that I have agreed to your terms is that you have no intention of returning her. Therefore it must be done now."

Lucifer, who had admitted to Saara already that he did not intend to free her, sulked for a moment. "If neither of us trust the other, Raphael, then I guess there can be no bargain, and the woman is sacrificed to your stiff-neckedness."

"It is your bargain, Satan. You offered it, and you must perform your promise first. If this entire scene was set with me in mind, then you should have no objections to letting your bait go free."

Now it was Raphael's turn to close the space between them. "Otherwise it is war between us, and though you are stronger than I and I cannot prevail, you will still not escape that battle unharmed."

Lucifer growled in his throat, but he reached a negligent hand toward Saara, in her concealment behind the wing.

"One moment," called the angel, and the pearly screen lifted like a fan. He leaned toward the woman and spoke. "Saara, when you are home you must forget this and not try to involve yourself with the Liar, neither out of anger nor revenge. Or once again he will have the power to take you captive."

The miniature naked woman ran toward him until the cord tightened against her leg. "Listen to me, Spirit! I don't want my life from your hands. I can't take another sacrifice on my behalf. You and I love the same person and by his own request I was to watch over you. I cannot live with the shame of this failure!"

"There is no shame, Saara," whispered Raphael. "And no failure. Not for you nor for me."

Lucifer found this conversation immensely distasteful. He completed the gesture which caused the tiny shape to vanish.

"She is now back where I found her," he announced.

Raphael's eyes grew a bit vague as he made sure the Devil spoke the truth. Then he glanced once more at the table. "You forgot her dress."

"We didn't bargain for the dress," snapped Lucifer. Then he strode away from the table and let the irritation of this minor defeat disappear in the satisfaction with the great victory it had bought him. He stared at Raphael with an expression of rapt wonder for some moments, knowing he had won. Knowing, despite his own accusation, that Raphael was true to his word and would make no effort to avoid what he had promised.

His. *His*. The beautiful and hated brother, symbol of all that feathered crew who had dared to conspire against him and to stand against him at the gates of eternity with their inane swords aflame! The Devil was trembling as Raphael had trembled, hearing Satan's terms. But it was neither fear nor disgust that caused him to shake, but a lust that was nearly love: a lust to touch once more, in the person of his brother, the very substance of heaven. A broad smile split Lucifer's face, exposing all his unangelic teeth.

Raphael also stood silent. Once again he did not seem fully aware of Lucifer before him. His eyes were almost closed. The angel's lips moved and he nodded, though no sound was audible in the chamber. Finally he came toward his brother. He held out his hand.

But now that the moment had come, Lucifer felt a desire to delay it. "A moment more, Raphael," he whispered. "Let me realize my success." His face was tight, and white patches stood out against his mottled cheeks. His

jaw worked. His cloak of urbanity fell away from his face
and form, revealing the demon tyrant that he was.

"You would have done better to go with me from the
first, brother!" he hissed, and adderlike he struck out with
both his blood-red hands, clasping Raphael's hand of ivory.

A shock passed through the room, sending stinging
pain through Kadjebeen's ears, and causing the little round
demon to go rolling over the floor. It vibrated the dollhouse
palace until its tiny turrets rattled.

Raphael gasped. He fell to his knees. But for the grip
upon his hand he would have fallen flat on the floor. His
face was blank, like that of a man struck by lightning, and
his mouth hung open. Wings beat spasmodically.

Lucifer's face was a mask of lust as he gazed down at
Raphael. His nostrils were distended like those of a pig,
and like a pig his tushes overlapped his thin lips. His eyes
became slits and he whined a bestial delight.

Two outstretched wings beat the floor stiffly, showering
the walls and ceiling of the chamber with glimmers of
pearl. The silvery pinions were twisted in disarray. Then,
ceasing their convulsive movement, they fell twitching on
the stones.

Lucifer grasped Raphael's hand harder, brutally squeezing it, and he panted with the effort of his satisfaction; his
ashy breath fell gray and dismal onto Raphael.

Where the ashes fell the great wings smoked. Their
luster faded to the color of snow, and like snow they
melted away into the wind which scoured the room.

Under that dusty fall of ash the gleam of Raphael's
gown, too, faded, till it was nothing but shabby linen cloth,
and the radiance of his face went out.

With an audible pop the chamber asserted its rights.
The wind trapped within the four windows threw itself
against the barriers and died.

There was nothing on the flagstones of the chamber but
a yellow-haired man lying motionless: his eyes closed and
his lips parted. Already a bruise was forming where his
face had struck the floor.

Kadjebeen emitted a small grunt of unhappiness. He
had really been very interested in those wings. But it was a
small grunt meant for his own ears only. He watched his
master drop the pale hand, which slapped the flagstones
limply.

Lucifer raised his eyes. He found he was still trembling. He paced over to the single chair and sat in it, waiting for the tremor to pass. Unaccountably he was tired—tired and somewhat shaken—somewhat at a loss. As though it had been he himself reduced to a thing of clay and blood, and not his enemy.

But he had his victory, and he stared down at it. Things could hardly be better. Of course Raphael's new shape was still beautiful, as measured by the standards of man. Lucifer briefly considered making alterations.

He could cut off the fellow's nose and ears, or put out his left eye. A hole in the cheek, perhaps, by which the food would dribble out. That would be amusing.

But frowning reflectively, he put away that further pleasure. Anything which changed that face would make him seem less like Raphael to Lucifer, and therefore damage rather than enhance his revenge. It was sufficient that his brother was reduced to the scum over whose interests he had dared oppose Lucifer. That was the main thing. And besides, there would be plenty of time later to add artistic touches.

Let him sing his songs of praise now, and boast of his close relatives in high places. As the Almighty hadn't lifted a finger in defense of his seraph up until now, Lucifer was confident that He wouldn't be quick to reach out a hand to an archangel of human clay.

Now—what to do with the fellow. Lucifer's first idea, when he had solidified his strategy, had been to keep his brother as he had discussed keeping Saara: caged in squalor, under his eye.

But he had had to toss that idea away, for even in the wretched form into which he had been locked, Lucifer didn't trust Raphael's influence upon the palace staff.

Not one of them was loyal, he reflected bitterly. Not a damned one of them, no matter how much he burned and beat them.

Least of all did he trust Kadjebeen, who had trundled out into the middle of the room and stood regarding the man on the floor. Kadjebeen was *too* handy, and inclined to have ideas.

But he was useful.

"Have this thing scourged," Lucifer growled to his servant. "I want him half-killed. Then find . . . find

Perfecto of Granada wherever he is and sell the brute to him. If the slaver has no money, give Raphael to him anyway and tell him I'll collect later.

"He is not to refuse."

As Kadjebeen scuttled (albeit unwillingly) off to set the wheels of torture in motion, Lucifer regarded the fruit of his labor.

The fall of flaxen hair half hid Raphael's features—which were as always, except for the light which had gone out of them. But there was a pale dust of hair on the arm which poked out of the simple white sleeve, and a network of fine lines creased the flesh between the thumb and forefinger. The robe had fallen crumpled to one side, exposing one quite ordinary leg up to the knee. The man's breath came raggedly, and a trickle of blood ran out of his nose.

Lucifer chuckled to himself. "As perfectly imperfect as any on the earth!

"Behold! I have made a man," he whispered aloud, and then he shook his head at his own cleverness. "If that isn't creation," he added, "then I don't know what is."

CHAPTER 3

Dull anguish rolled over him like waves of an untiring ocean, pierced by bolts of lancing pain. But worse than the pain was a nagging conviction which lay beneath it that something was missing; something was terribly wrong. Confusion thwarted all of Raphael's efforts to think; he had no weapon with which to fight it, for he had never before known what it was to be confused.

"I am screaming at myself," he thought wonderingly. He heard the parts of his body—his wounded back, his bruised cheek, and savagely twisted hand—howling their protest against the rest of him. "I know," he replied to the pain. "I know what you are saying, but I can't help it. I can't."

Not for comfort exactly, but for understanding, he threw himself upon mercy.

"Tell me what it is, Father," he begged within himself. "Tell me how to hear this pain rightly. I'm frightened; tell me what it is that is so wrong, which I've forgotten and I know I must remember."

But this message only echoed in his ravaged head. No answer came.

No music, no words. No vision, comfort, chiding, or instruction. No touch of awareness at all. The Other within him was gone as though it had never existed. And suddenly Raphael knew that *that* was what had been wrong—wrong beyond pain and beyond confusion. A dreadful closed emptiness within him.

He flailed his arms, not knowing what the motions were. He made noises.

Lombardy in August could not hold a candle to the heat of the Moorish State of Granada during the same month. In Lombardy the grass was dry, but at least it was grass.

On the brown hills forty miles south of the Andalusian city the ground was crazed like pottery glazing. The midday heat drove even the birds from the sky. Beasts of all sorts sheltered in the shadows of the rocks.

Beside a sheer walled table of stone (a divot laid carefully on the dry dirt) a single iron chain looped in swags through seven iron collars. Seven slaves had spaced themselves out evenly like birds on a fence, seeking their own space in the sliver of shadow left by the table's overhang.

Three of the women were Saqalibah: the pale, broad-faced people who had been slaves to the Moors for so many hundreds of years that they fell in the same class with the Arab horse and other animals of pedigree. Two others had spoken Spanish as children, and one spoke Spanish, Arabic, and Langue d'Ouil, all of them badly, and was uncertain in her muddled memory which language had come first. The last woman, at the end of the chain, was a black, dressed in heavy desert indigo, complete with tassels and coins. She had been put at the end of the chain because she picked fights.

All the slaves were women. The merchants Perfecto and Hakiim specialized in women—women and eunuchs.

* * *

Hakiim gazed sourly at an eighth slave, who writhed over the sandy ground at the end of a separate chain. His partner, Perfecto, had brought him in about an hour ago, slung over the back of a pack horse, and dumped him there on the ground. Neither Perfecto nor Hakiim could bring himself to touch him.

"The currency of that one's understanding has been devalued, I think," Hakiim drawled to Perfecto. "If it is not entirely counterfeit."

Perfecto could do little but shrug. "I had reasons to buy him."

Hakiim didn't want to start an argument, for Perfecto was a man of chancy temper. And he was underhanded (like most Christians), and unpredictable. Hakiim was not a Spaniard, and he had no desire to gain enemies in a country where he had so few friends.

Still, that the fellow should wander off into the dry hills and return with *this*—this piece of damaged property, probably crazy to boot. Perfecto usually had good business sense, at least.

"Saqalibah?" mused the Moor, turning the blond head gently with a boot toe. "Either that or Northman, I imagine. We might as well claim he is Saqalibah; with a eunuch, purity of line cannot matter.

"Were it not for the scars, he would make a good harem boy. Or . . . plaything. Fine face, to be sure, and the coloring is uncommon."

Perfecto regarded his prize with a jaundiced eye. Truth to tell, he liked his prize less than Hakiim did, having been forced to pay good money for him and to act grateful into the bargain.

And he shuddered, remembering the interview during which he had acquired the slave. Perfecto hated doing business with the Devil's crew. His fears ate through him like acid, worse and worse with every summons, and he longed for a graceful way to close the account which stood between the Devil and himself. But it had been almost twenty years now since Perfecto opened this account with a bit of casual homicide, and pay out as he might, the Spaniard always seemed to be in the red.

Perfecto wasn't at all sure what he had been forced to purchase. Was this pretty-faced imbecile a straight bit of goods—some court eunuch who had incurred hellish displeasure, or the slave of some high official who had perhaps made contract with Satan and then tried to recant? He had a splendidly noble face, after all, or would have had, had any intelligence remained behind it.

Or was this but the Devil's bad joke on Perfecto himself, ready to change into a lion or a monstrous adder when least expected? Perfecto had certain nightmares . . .

He answered Hakiim grimly. "He must have been some man's little toy once. But he's a bit large for such cuddles now.

"And of course there will be scars on the back, especially with the way he's grinding the dirt in."

For the blond slave had stopped thrashing and lay quietly now in his much stained linen, directly on the wounds of his back.

Hakiim glanced covertly at his partner's disgusted face. The Moor could no longer restrain himself. "I quite agree! My friend, tell me; why did you accept the creature? Even for free he would have cost too much . . ."

Perfecto's fingers pierced holes in the arid Andalusian earth. Sand dribbled out of his balled fists and his eyes were like little beads of brass.

Hakiim relapsed into silence.

At the far end of the line the black woman began to chant a Berber chant, in the tight-throated, ornate, ululating fashion of the desert. Every time the little company stopped, the black had to do something strange: throwing pebbles at a tree, or covering herself with sand, or swinging her chain back and forth. Otherwise she ignored everyone in the party, slave and slave merchant alike, except when they got in her way.

Perfecto's lips drew back. Now all he needed was trouble from that bitch, who was unfortunately too valuable to bruise.

Hakiim, too, lifted his head. He had more tolerance for the chanting than Perfecto had, for it was familiar music to him. But because it was in the Berber tradition, it unsettled him. The Berber tribes had swept the length and breadth of Islamic Spain a handful of times. They out-Arabed the Bedouin tribes with their narrow-minded asceticism and xenophobia. Even now, under the more urbane rule of Muhammad V of the Nasrid dynasty, Berber warriors made up a goodly number of the forces of the Alhambra. Berbers were not to be found on the end of a chain.

Perhaps it was not only on account of her temperament that Djoura had sold so cheap . . .

Hakiim forced this worry out of his mind. After all— who in the State of Granada knew or cared with what accents a black slave sang her songs? "There's our lovely she-ass again," he sighed instead. "Making her presence known." Then he shrugged.

In Granada they would sell the black. None of the upstart Muwalladun would care what she called herself; to them, all blacks were Nubian, just as all blonds were Saqalibah. Being young, sound, and well-proportioned, she'd bring a good price. In Granada they'd get rid of the entire chain of slaves.

Except, perhaps . . .

But as his glance fell on the eunuch, who lay within two yards of the rug the merchants had spread for themselves to sit on, Hakiim started and did a clear double take.

For the imbecile had lifted himself up by his hands, and he sat bolt upright, his ludicrously fine face filled with wonder as his deep blue eyes sought along the length of chain, until they rested on the ebony face of the singer. He stared intently, swaying side to side with the beat of the chant.

Hakiim almost choked with amusement. Perfecto followed his partner's eye and a grin stretched his features. The imbecile's parody of emotion was just too perfect.

"Look," giggled the Spaniard. "Our eunuch is in love. With Djoura the Nubian, no less.

"At least he can sit up," Perfecto continued. "Maybe by tomorrow he'll be able to walk, and then we can move again."

"He'll walk," retorted Hakiim. "Just let the Nubian lead him, like a goat leads the sheep."

And that quip called forth an idea. "The fellow is a bloody mess and must eventually be cleaned up. Let's give him a real treat in the process. We can bring Djoura to take care of him."

Perfecto looked less than satisfied by this idea. "What if she kills him? What if he kills her? The investment!"

"If she kills him," answered Hakiim, rising to his feet, "then I'll cover whatever he cost you out of my own pocket, and I'll buy her a box of sweets as well. If he kills her—well, I'll crawl to Mecca on my knees."

Then the swarthy Moor turned and grimaced pleasantly down at his partner. "Or do you want the privilege of washing the half-wit yourself?"

Perfecto waved his acquiescence to Hakiim's plan.

Since the black was at one end of the long chain and the only place where the eunuch's collar could be attached was on the other, bringing them together occasioned much shifting, curses, and complaints. None of the women wanted to squat in the sun, so the displaced slaves bickered and poked at one another over a few square inches of shadow, until the chain was folded in the middle, and the unhappy slaves were crowded together with exactly half the elbowroom they'd had before.

Hakiim sat the woman down with a rag and a pot of water. Beside the pot he placed a small lump of lard soap.

"You see that big baby there," he said to her in Arabic, pointing at Raphael. "You pretend he's your baby. Wash him all over. And don't waste soap."

She glared not at Raphael (who had greeted her arrival like the coming of springtime) but at the sky. The Moor stood above them both with arms folded. He scowled, but he was rather more curious than annoyed.

Raphael smiled at Djoura, and he sighed. He put his hand out toward her neck, awkwardly, and when she flinched away he touched his own throat.

"He likes your singing," explained the patient Hakiim.

"Does he?" replied the black dubiously, for no one else in the slave chain had expressed similar feelings. (She addressed her master without respect, indeed without civility, but Hakiim had expected no different). But then Djoura, like Hakiim, had to laugh at Raphael's eloquent expression. "Well, then, he must be a person of very good taste."

She soaked the rag, wrung it out, and soaped it. "Close your eyes," she barked at Raphael and she touched the rag to his cheek.

He started with surprise at the cold contact and Djoura laughed again. She proceeded to lather his puzzled face. "Hah! You poor sieve-head! How pink you are, underneath the dirt!" she chortled. "We'll see just how pink we can make you. We'll get that hair too. Maybe it's pink as well, when all the sand is out of it."

But when she dribbled water onto the blond head, he sputtered and shook like a dog. Perfecto cursed from his spot on the square of carpet, and Hakiim backed off. Both the merchants retreated some yards away.

"Good," growled the black. "Being stupid has its uses. You got rid of them, and if I'd done it, they'd beat me. Or they'd try!"

"I don't like them," she whispered, pouting furiously. "And I most especially don't like the Spaniard. They can crawl in with any of the girls they like, they think—it's their natural right, they think.

"Until they met *me!* I showed them, you can tell the world."

Raphael's head and face ran with thin lather. He squinted his eyes against the sting of soap. Djoura gave him a careful rinse, using as little water as possible. "Sand is better for washing," she instructed him. "It doesn't crack the skin like soap, and doesn't waste good water. We had sand yesterday and I gave myself a good scrub. Hah! You should have seen these ignorant ones look at me, like baby owls along a branch, blinking. They know nothing, being content to stink.

"But here there is not sand, but only dirt. Who can wash herself in dirt, I ask?"

Looking slyly around first, she dabbed the soapy rag at her own face and hands, and then thrust her arm with the rag down the front of her many-layered clothing. As the cool rag swabbed her skin, she sighed in ecstasy. Raphael watched every move with interest.

Having washed down to the fellow's neck and up each arm, Djoura sat back and announced, "Now you have to get up off your hams, eunuch, so we can pull that shirt off you."

But she had no real hope of being understood. She scuttled around behind the fellow and yanked on the garment, but there was too much of it, and his legs were tangled in its folds. "Curse you!" she growled, but without real rancor, for washing the eunuch was the first interesting thing for her since being sold to Hakiim in Tunis. "How you stare at me with those big blue eyes of yours—just like a white cat! I wonder you can even see through them. Well, the shirt's all stuck to your back with blood. We'll have to soak it off."

When the water hit Raphael's back, he stiffened and gasped. Djoura put a hand on his shoulder. "It's all right. It won't hurt forever," she whispered, adding soap. She examined the length and number of the scourge marks with a kind of respect. "Pinkie, you must have done something pretty terrible to deserve *this!*

"I, too, cannot be broken," she hissed into his ear, "though maybe they will make me a sieve-head in the end, like you."

She smiled grimly at the thought. "Or maybe I'll only pretend to be one, and amuse myself laughing at them all."

There were long openings in the back of the eunuch's gown—not whip slices, for they were parallel and neatly hemmed. She wondered at them while she reached her hand through and worried the cloth from the wounds. Perhaps some kind of iron chain or body-collar had passed through these. If so, this eunuch must have been a handful when he still had his senses. Her approval of him grew by leaps and bounds.

"You may not know it," she whispered (as though the hills were full of spies), "but I am a Berber! People think I am not, because I am black, but Berbers are really of all colors." Then she giggled. "Maybe even pink!

"To be a Berber, it is only necessary that you live like a Berber and follow the ways of the Prophet," she added with hauteur, and she crawled back in front of him to glare deep into his eyes. "To be a Berber is to be free!" she hissed, with no thought of the irony of her words.

She threw back her head and all the coins and tassels on her headdress bobbed together.

Raphael listened carefully to the sounds Djoura made. His eyes devoured her color and shape and his skin rejoiced at her touch, even when it hurt him. For her song had broken his terrible isolation, and her chatter kept him from despair. So now, as she at last fell silent, with her brown eyes looking full at him, he tried to give her something of the same sort back.

He repeated the chant she had sung at the other end of the line, word for word, note for note, with perfect inflection and time.

Djoura clapped her hands in front of her mouth. "Oh, aren't you a clever one!"

It was not actually cleverness, or not cleverness in the

sense the black Berber meant. Raphael's repertoire of music was immense, and neither pain nor transformation could steal it from him.

He knew that piece. He repeated it for her an octave down, where he found this new instrument (his throat) was more comfortable, and then to the Berber's amazement, he followed the solo chant with the traditional choral response.

The woman sat stock-still in front of him. The rag she had been wringing fell from her hands. "You are a Berber too? My kinsman? And I have been making mock of you!" She bit down on her lip until the pain of it brought her feelings under control.

Could this pink fellow be a Berber? She had just said there might be pink Berbers.

Well, if he were not, then he *ought* to have been a Berber, between the lashes on his back and the knowledge of the chant.

But how could he have ever lived in the high desert with that silly coloring? Why, he was already sunburned; she could tell because her fingers left white marks on the skin as she touched him.

Perhaps he had not always been this color. Perhaps he had lain in a dungeon some long time. She had heard that years in the darkness could bleach the finest dark skin to white.

She harked to the querulous complaint of the women in the shadows behind her. She reminded herself that they were not alone, Pinkie and she. She listened. Hakiim's reply to the complaint could not be made out, but the Moor was laughing. He laughed a lot, swine that he was. She could not hear the Spaniard. She imagined his hard little eyes watching her.

It was necessary to keep busy, or they would take her back to the far end of the wall and she would never get near this fellow again. "Lie down," she whispered. "Lie down, Pinkie, on your side."

He seemed to understand her Arabic, which was heartening, and further convinced her that her ideas of his ancestry were correct, but he was so clumsy in his movements that she had to push him gently onto his left side. "There. Now we'll get your long legs and your bottom.

"I've never seen a eunuch close up," she added conversationally, "not what he lacks, anyway." But as that thought led to another, she scowled. "The man who makes a eunuch out of a Berber ought to have his own balls torn off and his belly ripped open and both holes stuffed with red ants! He should lose his eyes and his tongue first, and then his feet and then his left hand, and then his right hand . . . and . . ."

As she spoke, searching her imagination for greater and greater punishments to inflict on this nameless castrater, her hand with the rag continued to soap and scrub, until by the time she arrived at the words "his right hand," her own had climbed up the tube of the white linen gown, where it made an astounding discovery.

She popped her head under the hem of the gown to verify what her fingers told her, and then very quickly withdrew it. Out of ingrained habits of concealment, her features adopted an expression of heavy boredom as she dipped the rag once more into the pot of water. She hummed a little tune as she rinsed it out.

The blond man stared at her with bright interest and scratched at the spot she had left wet. The Berber could barely hide her grin. "Don't do that, Pinkie. If they see you playing with that, you'll lose it for sure."

Casually humming, she scrubbed his other leg. And his sickness-fouled buttocks. It must have been the fellow's very foulness, she reflected, that spared him. Hakiim had been too delicate souled to examine him, and Perfecto . . .

Djoura had never granted the Spaniard an ounce of sensibility, but it was he who had dumped the blond among them and called him a eunuch. Maybe he had just been too lazy to look. The black woman leaned forward and put her finger under his chin. She was smiling no longer.

"Listen to me, Pink Berber, if there's a grain of sense left in that poor head. Don't lift your skirt around anyone here except me. Not even to make water. Do you understand me?"

The blond stared back at her.

"Do you understand me?" she hissed in her urgency.

Raphael's clean face sweated with effort. His mouth opened. "I want," he said, slurring like a man drunk on kif, "I want to understand."

She ran her hand over his sleek wet hair.

* * *

"Here's your soap," she said flatly to Hakiim. The Moor drew back his hands in distaste. "Wrap it in the rag."

While she did so he took a glance over at the blond eunuch, who sat gazing vacantly at them, his hands in his lap, as neat and sleek as some mother's favorite child. "Was he filthy?"

The Berber rolled her eyes and deposited the wet rag in Hakiim's hand. "Of course he was. And sick, I think. He cannot be left to himself. You had better put me next to him."

The Moor's jaw dropped. "You *want* to be next to him? My sweet lily of the mountains: the fellow is yours!"

Night fell: Raphael's first night in captivity. He lay on his stomach, trying to look up at the stars.

It was getting bad again. As soon as Djoura had gone away from him—ten feet away, which was as far as the chain would allow—the confusion rose like a mist from the ground, enfolding him.

And the desolation.

His Father had abandoned him. In all the length and breadth of Raphael's existence that had never happened. He would have said with confidence that that couldn't happen. Without His presence an angel should go out like a light.

And perhaps that was what had happened.

He lay with his cheek on bare earth, all his muscles tightened as though to ward off a blow. His eyes closed against a vision of hatred, borne on a face which might have been his own. Why he was so hated he could not recall, nor did he remember how that hate had led to . . . to this. He shivered, despite the sultriness of the night, for he didn't want to remember.

He wanted to remember something good: something which would provide a comfort to him in his misery. He searched in his memory for His Father.

And found to his horror that without His Father's presence in his heart, he could not begin to imagine Him. He couldn't even call up a picture of His face, for all that came to him, unbidden and insistent, was the image of a sparrow on a bare branch, its drab feathers fluffed and its black eyes closed against the wind.

Whenever he moved the iron collar chafed his neck. He

also found his eyes were leaking. That was uncomfortable,
for it made the ground muddy. He laced his hands under
his cheekbone, to keep his face out of the mud.

But the damp earth released a dark, consoling sort of
smell, and he was glad for it. He turned his attention to the
little noises of the camp, where the women were whispering lazily before falling asleep.

The rule of midday had been reversed now; the chain
which had spaced the slaves out at maximum distance to
one another now tinkled in little heaps as six bodies
huddled companionably under five blankets.

Raphael and his nursemaid had been removed from the
communal length of chain and put onto a special little
chain of their own. He didn't have a blanket, and didn't
know he ought to have had one. The Berber had a blanket,
but she also had a lot of clothing on her body, so she threw
the blanket to Raphael.

It was a magnanimous gesture, but as he didn't know
what to do with the blanket he let it lie in a heap, till she
crawled back and reclaimed it.

He heard one of the slaves stagger out of the cluster to
make water, squatting on the dirt with her skirts lifted.
That was also how Djoura had taught him to do it, that
evening. It seemed to him, even in his newborn clum-
siness, that there might be easier ways to go about it.

But all his memories had been turned upside down. It
seemed this human head could not contain them properly—not the important or meaningful memories. He could
recall scattered images of his visits upon the earth: a black
horse, a white dog. A young man with black hair and a
white face.

He remembered singing.

Always Raphael had been fond of mortals. He thought
them beautiful, even when only in the way a baby bird is
beautiful—through its awesome ugliness. Some mortals, of
course, were more beautiful than others.

Finally he had something to cling to. To build on.
Raphael made a song about the baby-bird beauty of
mortals. Turning on his side he began to sing into the
night.

This was better—much better. Here there was consonance and harmony, and even the beginnings of understanding, though he had to work his mouth and lungs to

get it. When singing, it was impossible for Raphael to be confused or alone, or to be anything else but singing.

Behind him came a rustling. Djoura rose from her place, stepped across the ten feet dividing her from Raphael, and stood above him, listening. He raised his eyes gladly to her.

Then she kicked him. "Don't make noise," she hissed, and shuffled away the length of the chain.

In all his existence, no one had ever, *ever* disapproved of Raphael's music. He had no experience with this sort of criticism at all. He curled into a ball of hurt and his eyes leaked harder.

He thought about all the music he had ever made and he found himself doubting it was any good. That foot had been so decisive. He wondered, despairing, if his own creation had been some sort of divine mistake: a piece badly conceived and played.

But if Raphael lost faith in his own music, he did not lose faith in music in general. He had never been too proud to sing the music created by others, so he sought in his memory for a song that might make him feel better: one that had warm edges to it, and that was somehow connected with . . . he couldn't remember.

He sang this song so quietly no sound left the shelter of his huddled knees. It was a very simple song (compared to his own) but it reached out to the things he no longer understood and it gave him strength.

He remembered one little word. "Dami," he whispered, liking the sound. "Damiano."

There was a brush of cloudy warmth over him, lighter than a fall of leaves. Raphael squeezed his eyes to clear the water out and looked up.

Wings as soft as woolen blankets: dark but with a light within like a lamp under smoked glass. A shadow of rough hair framing dark eyes which also had a smolder of light behind them. The face of a friend.

Raphael closed his eyes in rapture and he could still see that face. He crawled onto his friend's lap.

"You should have called me before you started to feel this bad," chided Damiano. "I'm no angel, to be shuttling at will between earth and heaven, and I had no idea where you were."

"I don't know where I am, either," replied Raphael, grateful to be able to talk again without using the slow, awkward body. "And I didn't know you would hear if I called.

"Damiano!" cried Raphael, stricken. "God is gone!"

The dusky spirit started, and its immaterial wings gathered round Raphael's damaged form. "Hush, hush, Raphael, my friend, my teacher . . . Can you hear yourself saying that?

"How could He be gone and I be here, holding you, eh? For what am I, outside of Him?" Damiano took Raphael's head between his hands and forced the frightened eyes into quiet. "Now do you feel better?"

Raphael felt something. He felt the presence of his friend, and for the moment he could imagine nothing finer. But his scourged back picked that moment to communicate a huge throb of pain.

"He's gone," he repeated childishly. "I can't find my Father anywhere."

The sad, sweet face above him (a mere suggestion of a face really, dark on darkness) filled with compassion, and he embraced Raphael gently, as though the poor pale body would break at a touch. "That's what it's like," he whispered. "Yes, that's exactly what it's like."

He brushed the long hair out of Raphael's face. "Don't worry, Master. He is there, and so am I."

"What did you call me?"

The ghost laughed. "Master. You never liked that word. But it's what you are to me. My music master. You must remember you are the Archangel Raphael, and a great person all around!"

Raphael took one cloudy hand between his clumsy ones. "My memory . . . isn't working properly. I think of people and I see baby birds. I think of the Father and I see another bird—hungry—in the middle of winter.

"What does this mean, Damiano?"

"Birds?" The ghostly voice was quizzical. "Well, don't birds sing?" Damiano shrugged heavy wings and gazed intently at nothing.

"It means, Seraph, that God is not missing at all, believe me."

"I will believe you," answered Raphael. "But I have no other reason to believe except that it is you who say it." His shivering had stopped, and without knowing it, he was sinking into sleep. But as the gray shape about him began to fade, he woke with a start.

"Don't go!" he cried out, and even his body's mouth made a little noise. "Don't you leave me too!"

Damiano patted his hand. "But you are a living man now, and must not spend your time talking with ghosts. It isn't good for you, and besides—they will think you are mad as a hare. But I will be with you, you know, anytime you think of me.

"Here—if you think you might forget." The spectral arm reached out and plucked a nondescript pebble from the ground. "I give this to you. If you begin to doubt I am there, take it out of your pocket and look at it."

"I don't have a pocket," whined Raphael, as that fact loomed into an insuperable problem.

The ghost's smile broadened, showing white teeth. "Then knot it into the hem of your gown. Or in your hair. Or keep it in your mouth. Just remember."

Raphael took it into a sweating palm. "But you'll come back like this again, won't you? So I can talk with you. So I can see you?"

"Raphael," Damiano whispered, grinning. "My dear teacher. I am always at your command."

Gaspare was still standing by the door of the wineshop, mumbling and scratching his head, when Saara fell out of the sky.

He knew it was Saara, though he had never seen her naked before, and her hair was hanging in tatters. He winced at the thump she made, hitting the ground.

With his lute in one hand, he slid to his knees at her side. "Lady Saara," he gasped. "Was it really *you* who pecked Damiano in the eye a few minutes ago?"

She lay on her back, but her eyes were closed. Still, she was breathing: breathing rather hard, and her chest rose up and down. He gazed down at it, fascinated.

Gaspare shot a furtive glance around him, to see whether anyone on the street had noticed. But of course there wasn't anyone on the sun-whitened street, and by fortune Saara's return had happened out of the line of sight from within the wineshop.

"Oh, what am I to do?" he mumbled to himself, shifting his lute from hand to hand as though that would help.

Finally he stuffed the neck of the instrument down the front of his shirt, bent down, and picked up the limp woman in his arms.

Thus burdened he shuffled through the dry grass down the windowless abandoned lane. There he encountered Festilligambe, the horse, chewing furiously at the grass in an effort to recover from his earlier panic.

"Uh. There you are," grunted Gaspare. "You can carry her easier than I."

Groaning with effort, he lifted the woman high. The gelding stepped neatly away. Gaspare almost dropped Saara onto the grass.

"Dammit, you bag of bones. This is the Lady Saara. She is supposed to be a friend of yours!"

Festilligambe cocked an ear and his large nostrils twitched. While not disputing Saara's character as a friend, he seemed to deny that it implied such a heavy responsibility. But after a moment's reflection, the horse allowed her to be laid gently across him like a sack of meal.

"Now," muttered the redhead, "let's avoid prying eyes, shall we, horse? I know I have a reputation for being a rake, but the picture we present here is not charming." On sudden thought he removed his shirt and lay it over the naked woman. It didn't cover much.

At the end of the alley was a pile of rubble. Gaspare, leading the horse by the mane, turned left and walked through a gap in a wall and found himself abruptly out of the village of San Gabriele.

Down the grassy hill and into an open pine wood. Not five hundred feet along there was a stream and a clearing beside it where a crude thatch of branches was upheld by rough wooden poles.

This was Gaspare's retreat, where he had lived since the spring made it possible: a mansion perfectly suited to one who liked his privacy and also hadn't two pieces of copper to rub together.

He laid Saara down upon his crackling, piney mattress and regarded her long. When he was done regarding her he dropped the shirt once more over her middle.

Festilligambe, too, peered at Saara, whom he had never before thought of as the sort of creature that rides on a horse. He whuffed her singed hair.

The horse sneezed and Saara woke up.

Her eyes snapped open like shutters caught in a wind. She woke up with jaw clenched and nostrils flaring. Color splashed her cheeks as she sat bolt upright on the bed of branches. Gaspare's shirt fell. She said one word.

"No."

She said it quietly, almost absently, and she said nothing else. But the horse, who had been leaning with herbivorous curiosity over her vegetative couch, leaped stiff-legged into the air and came down running. Gaspare heard his receding hoofbeats but paid them scant attention, for he was lying flat on his back where the blow had knocked him, both hands wrapped protectively around his own throat.

As she sat there rigidly, amid no sound except that of Gaspare gasping and choking on the ground, the red in her cheeks faded to white. The rage which burned behind her tilted eyes faded, so once more they shone like the gold-green of a river in sunlight. She sighed and rubbed her face with both hands.

Gaspare took a long, shuddering, welcome breath. "Sweet Gesu, woman: what did you do to me?" he cried shakily, struggling up from the earth.

Saara became aware of the youth. "There you are, Gaspare." Her regard became awkwardly intense. "What a terrible trouble you have gotten me into!"

His long jaw opened and closed rhythmically. He made fish mouths. "I? Got *you* into trouble? My lady, you nearly killed me just now; I couldn't breathe!"

She waved aside this discursion.

"Do you know who that spirit was, who came up the path in the shape of Damiano?"

He frowned heavily and shrugged. "I guessed myself that it wasn't—wasn't Damiano, I mean. When it turned into a dragon . . ."

"A wyvern. It had only two legs."

". . . when it turned into a scaly monster. Damiano, in all the time I knew him, never showed any signs of doing such a thing. Who was it, then?"

"It was the Liar," and she hid her eyes behind her hands once more.

"Ah!" Gaspare nodded sapiently. "That's better. I had half a notion it might have been Satan himself. After me for my sins."

Hazel eyes popped open again. "But it was. It was the one you call Satan, and he had come for you. For your sins."

Gaspare collapsed again to the earth, and he stuck all eight of his fingers into his terrified mouth. He gave one high, thin wail.

Saara glowered at this lack of discipline. "Don't worry. You're safe. I went instead of you."

"You did what?" He pulled himself toward the cot of branches, a look of dazed gratitude illuminating his ill-assorted features. "You took my sins upon yourself? You went to hell? Suffered for me?"

Saara flung herself to her feet and peered vaguely around for her dress. "I went to his hall, yes, and it was no joke. But if you want to know who is suffering, it is your teacher. Your Raphael."

"The angel?" Gaspare squatted at Saara's feet, growing numb from too many surprises. "Raphael is suffering for my sins?"

Finding nothing around except Gaspare's shirt, she put that on. It did not quite reach her knees. "Sin I know nothing about," she stated. "Just suffering."

She ran her hands through her hair; they snarled among the blackened burned ends of her braids. She looked into the woods about her, as though marshaling unseen forces.

"Let me cut the damage out of your hair, Lady Saara," offered Gaspare, in order to put the conversation on a more manageable level. And he added, half-regretfully, "And then we will try to find you more suitable clothing. After that we will be more in a position to talk about sin and suffering."

She shot him a glance of such coldness he might have been Satan himself, with a voice of treacherous temptation. "I don't have such time! I was asked by Dami to protect your Raphael, and I have failed! I must find what the Liar has done with him—for a spirit cannot be destroyed, you know. The Eagle is somewhere, in a dungeon. Or a jar, perhaps."

"A jar?" echoed Gaspare, uncertainly.

She ignored him. "I will find him and I will bring him away, unless death comes first. This I vow, who have made no vows since leaving the Saami." She raised both her arms into the air.

"Wait!" Gaspare made an expert dive and caught the woman about the waist. "Don't turn into anything, Lady! Tell me where we're going?"

She peered down at the redhead clinging to her, with irritation mixed with surprise. "I am going," she corrected him. "Home, to Lombardy, first.

"And then to Satan's Hall, or Hell, or whatever you call it." Without further discussion, Saara grew feathers and flew.

After she had gone Gaspare sat back into his bed of branches and stared at the scurf of dead needles that coated the ground. Gaspare was thinking about his sins, which he knew to be many. He was thinking about his sins of commission rather than those of omission, and especially thinking about his sins of the body.

Gaspare's sins of this nature had actually been few and exploratory in nature, but whenever he thought of sins, they were the ones to come immediately to mind.

And he was feeling very badly, for though it might be the act of a bravo to follow a giggling girl into the dark, as Gaspare had done more than once (but less than four times), it was the act of a worm to let a pure angel take the blame for it.

He was very fond of his lute teacher, with a hesitant and wary sort of affection which sprang from his knowledge that they were very different sorts of people, Raphael and himself. Without the fortuitous chance that Damiano had been the friend of both, they would have had no reason to meet.

And Gaspare felt, too, that Raphael in his sinlessness never had been able to recognize just how wicked Gaspare himself could be.

And now, unfortunately, Raphael had caught the brunt of that wickedness and was suffering. In a jar, of all things. Gaspare cringed queasily and tried to feel repentance.

What he felt, he found, was resentment. Gesu the Christ had been enough, he considered. What other load of guilt did a man have to bear? And even the Lady Saara . . . (Thinking of Saara as he had just seen her, his thoughts digressed immediately. It was a number of minutes before he could get them back on the subject of guilt.) Even Saara had tried to purloin his sins from him. Surely a woman who looked like that might have some of her own . . .

It seemed the earth was inhabited by posturing heros, with Gaspare of San Gabriele as the only poor dolt among them. Fit for nothing but to be saved from himself. It couldn't be borne!

Well, he *wouldn't* bear it, he decided with a few redheaded curses. He rose to his full height (in three years he had grown prodigiously) and strode off toward the sunlight, seeking his wayward horse.

Lombardy in high summer was a green cathedral, with its constant murmur of clean waters and its odor of shadowy frankincense. On a round hill between spires of rock flourished the wild garden of Saara: a meadow of heavy grass, cut by interlacing streams, dotted with the early blue aster, and wound about with the sprawling late red rose. Not far from the lawn, in the shade of the pines below, she had a little house of sod, built after the manner of her northern people, to which she withdrew only to sleep.

Here also grew rosemary and comfrey, eyebright, and mullein, the vervain which makes the wild cats drunk in the springtime, and orris, for sweetening clothes and hair. Above the meadow, among the feathered birches which crested the dome of the hill, was a stand of hazel also: all plants with uses for the leech, witch, or wise woman.

Saara was all three of these, and on her garden no frost came, though through the winter the high peaks on either side of her hill were painted white.

Under the last full moon of summer she sat, on the round dome of the hill, where the scattered birch striped the darkness with silver, and the fingers of the trees twisted moonlight into chains. She sat tailor fashion, wearing nothing but Gaspare's linen shirt, her brown hair cropped halfway down her neck. Her face, splashed with light and shadow, was not that of a girl.

There is a spell almost all witches know, though some chant it and some read it from books and still others play it through the length of a staff, or scratch it out with the blood of a cock. It is not a complicated spell, only very dangerous, and for that reason it is often learned and rarely used.

Saara, in her long life, had never sung this spell before. When she had lost her lovers, she had refrained. When her children died, even then she had been wise, for she knew the gate of death had its purpose.

But now she, too, had her purpose—a purpose beyond loss or loneliness. Her purpose was rescue.

Through no other means had she been able to find Raphael. He was neither in the wind nor in the voice of the water, and he didn't hear her call—or he could not answer. She hadn't really expected to find him so easily, for she remembered that spinning disorientation in the air and the strange bare peak with a window. That was the place she must find again. For that she needed help.

So the greatest witch in the Italies sat with her hands folded in her lap and her legs bare to the wind as she sang up the dead.

It began with a wail and rose into a chant of four ascending notes, the last of which she held clear and unshaken until her breath failed her. She sang the line again. And again.

There was no expression to be seen on Saara's face, had there been any to see on that dome of trembling birch. She had no feeling in her once the song had begun. And the moon put a severe light upon her features, emphasizing their odd Asiatic cast and draining all color. She appeared neither girl nor young woman under that stained white globe. In fact, there was nothing particularly feminine about the figure on the dry earth. Nothing particularly human. She might have been a peak of rock among those of the Alps nearby, eternally white, cloaked with loud, grieving winds.

The same four notes, building like stairs upon one another. Carving a black path into blackness. They droned on while the soiled moon rolled from the slopes of the eastern hills to its zenith. Untiring, unchanging, they rang over the sparse dome of birch trees and down into the pine-woolly coverts below. At the foot of the hills, beyond the little lakes fed by the streams of Saara's garden, people in the village of Ludica shut their doors and windows, shivering despite August's heat.

And not least of all, Saara's song echoed through the

spaces of her own head, until she was mad with her own singing, and her mind and soul became the pure instruments of her purpose.

And when the moon balanced directly over the earth—directly over the round moonlike dome of the hill—Saara let the stair she had built open, and she spoke one name.

"Damiano," she whispered. She closed her eyes and let the new silence hang in the air.

There was a whispering around Saara, and a rustle like the soft feathers of many birds. "Speak!" she commanded without opening her eyes.

The rustling grew nearer. It grew warm. "Saara," came the sweet, caressing answer. "My beautiful one. My princess. My queen."

Saara's stern face slackened with sorrow, but only for a moment. "Ruggerio," she whispered. "Forgive me. I did not mean to wake you." Her eyes screwed themselves more firmly shut.

"I know, bellissima," the thin, distant voice replied, chuckling, and ghostly lips kissed the very tips of her fingers. "And I do not mean to prove a distraction. May all the saints go with you."

Then the air went thick with vague calls and whispers. Saara repeated the one name "Damiano" and sat as still and unyielding as a rock.

One sound rose among the others: that of a man's laughter. But this was not Ruggerio, though it was a voice she recognized. "The greatest witch in the Italies," it pronounced, and then laughed again. "For a while perhaps. Perhaps stronger than I. But my son was another matter, wasn't he, Saara? My poor, half-blind, mozzarella boy! Who'd have thought it?"

Saara sat as rigid as wood, as stone, and chided her heart for pounding like a hammer. No response she gave to this spirit, and soon it sighed. "Ah. Well, no matter, Saara. God go with you."

And it was gone. Surprise alone nearly made Saara's eyes crack open, but she restrained herself. To think that thirty years of bitterness and fear toward Guillermo Delstrego could lead to this. "God go with you?"

Had the proud, predatory soul of Delstrego bent to that? She had grown to think the man almost the equivalent of the Liar himself in his wickedness.

Her strength trembled and came near to breaking at this touch to an ancient wound.

But now the hilltop was filled with a confusion of spirits and sounds and the witch's guards came up by instinct.

Presences surrounded her like a roomful of smoke rings, half erased by the moving air. These were perhaps spirits who knew her or had touched somehow her long life, or were by some unknown sympathy attracted to the stern, unseeing woman in white linen, who held the gate open and yet spoke to no one.

For though the spell is called a summoning spell, its effect and its danger is that it brings the user very close to that world which is not a world (being placeless and infinite), wherein a living mortal has no business to wander.

And though there was no malice in the vague fingers that touched Saara, or in the soft whispers that questioned her, there was also not one of them without the power to do Saara great harm (should she let them), or to cause her great pain (whether she let them or not).

She took a deep, shuddering breath and her nostrils twitched, as though the air were too thick to breathe. "Damiano!" she called again, this time with a touch of urgency.

There was a moment's silence, and then came a small voice, a sweet child's piping voice, speaking the language of her northern people. "Mama?" it cried wonderingly. "Is it Mama?"

She gave a despairing gasp. "Go to sleep, baby," she whispered into the blackness, while tears escaped the confines of her closed eyes. "Go back to bed. I will come to you soon."

Now it was late and she had almost no strength left to hold the gate and fight the river of innocent, deadly voices. She had a sudden, desperate idea. "Little white dog," she called out. "Little white dog of Damiano's. Spot, or whatever your name was . . . come to me."

"Macchiata," was the matter-of-fact answer, which came from very close in front. Saara held to this spirit and let the rest go. She opened her eyes.

Sitting before her, legs splayed, was a very pretty plump girl with hair that shone silver in the moonlight. Her garb, also, was a simple white shift that gleamed without stain, with a red kerchief which tied about the neck and spread out across her back, sailor fashion. She had little wings like those of a pigeon.

She smiled at Saara with bright interest. Her eyes were brown.

"Some mistake," murmured the witch. "I summoned only a dog. A little white dog which belonged to . . ."

"To Master—Damiano. Yes, that's me." She started to scratch her spectral left ear with her spectral left hand in short, choppy forward motions. She seemed to get great satisfaction out of doing this. "Damiano likes me in this form."

"He does?" Saara exclaimed with somewhat affronted surprise. Then she remembered Damiano's peculiar prejudice toward the human form above that of all animals, however splendid. "Well, I thought the dog looked perfectly fine."

Macchiata was still for a moment, and then resumed scratching. She metamorphosed between one stroke and the next, going from girl to dog, and continued her scratch quite contentedly with her hind leg. "Like that?"

"Lovely," stated Saara.

The deep brown eyes regarded Saara, asking no questions. The white dog smiled with all her formidable teeth exposed and her red tongue lolling to the right. Her fluffy pigeon wings scratched one another's backs behind her.

Saara had not forgotten how last she had seen this animal, frozen like a starved deer in the snow, with her dark master above her, equally frozen with grief. She said, "You died by my hand, dog. But it was not by my intent."

Macchiata pulled her tongue in. Under the spell she had attained an almost lifelike solidity, but still she glowed with milk-glass light. "I remember—I think. You were upset."

"I was," admitted the greatest witch of the Italies. "Upset and afraid, and I struck thinking only of defending myself. Do you forgive me, spirit?"

The dog, in reply, flopped over on her back. "Sure. Why not? Scratch under my left elbow; I can't reach."

Saara obeyed and was surprised to feel warm fur beneath her hand. "Have you fleas, then?"

"No." As the human's hand rubbed in expanding circles, the dog's left foot began a spastic, regular pawing of the air. Macchiata grunted like a pig. "No. No fleas in heaven. Only scratching."

Saara settled back on her heels and looked about her. The moon was descending the western sky; the night was getting old. "Spirit, I haven't much time. Will you help me find your master? I called and he could not hear me."

"He heard you," said Macchiata, flipping onto her legs. She gave a great shake. "Everyone heard you. You called very loud. He just wouldn't come."

Saara felt a cold needle of misery pierce through her. She was some time in answering. "He . . . wouldn't come?"

"No." The dog's nostril's twitched, smelling the salt in Saara's tears. "Don't get upset! He stayed away so you wouldn't get upset. He wanted to come."

Saara swallowed, beyond words for a moment. Finally she said, "I have to see him about Raphael. If I can't help Raphael, I will be very upset."

Macchiata's sticklike tail thumped appreciatively. "I like Raphael. He has never been upset. Never."

"That could change," replied Saara ominously, "unless we help him."

"I'll get Master," announced the dog, and she faded like an afterimage on the eye.

Once Macchiata was gone, Saara wiped her eyes on the sleeve of her shirt and blew her nose into a handful of birch leaves. She had been shaken by every pull on her living memory, and the spirit that had refused to come had shaken her hardest. Had there been some malice in the little creature, to say so brutally "He wouldn't come"? Indeed, the summoning spell was the most dangerous of all spells, to soul and to body, for now that she had done it, she felt hardly the strength or the desire to go on living.

Her children: Could it be they were no more than infant spirits, grown neither in heart nor mind since the day they bled to death with their father on the floor of the hut? Something in Saara, instinct or sense of justice, rebelled at this idea. Was there illusion at the base of the summoning spell? Had Ruggerio not really kissed her fingertips?

Had Guillermo Delstrego not come after thirty years of her hate to say to her, "God go with you"? Something had happened nonetheless, and someone had come to her behind the darkness of her closed eyes. It remained to be seen whether her task had succeeded or failed.

She stared at the disk of the descending moon, and so deep in thought was she that she did not notice the silent approach of one behind her.

"Saara," he whispered. "Pikku Saara."

Saara turned slowly, effortfully, as though a great weight sat on her shoulders. She was suddenly afraid.

Behind her, illuminated by the moon, stood the shape of a man. It was dark, from its rough hair to its booted feet, and a cloud surrounded it like great, soft folded wings. As Saara looked up at the apparition's face the wings opened wide.

Smoky he was, and immaterial: not like the dog nor yet like the spirit who had kissed her fingers. For it was not her spell but his own wish that had brought him this very long way to a hill in Lombardy, in August, and he had little magic with which to clothe himself in flesh. Only the eyes of the ghost were clear to see, and full of tenderness.

"Damiano," she began, and her voice left her as she uttered the name. "I'm sorry to call you. I don't want to cause you pain, when you have the right to peace."

He knelt by her, and she sensed in her witch's soul a hand upon her face. "The only pain which can touch me," he whispered, gently and from far away, "is to see this pain in *your* eyes, Saara. And I will gladly endure it if I can help you. But I didn't think that I could."

"You thought I called you out of loneliness," she stated, and her words held a hint of accusation. "No. I have more love in me than that, Dami, and more sense too. I called you because of Raphael. He has fallen into the power of the Liar . . .

"And I . . . I was the bait used to draw him. It was my fault."

Damiano sank down beside her and the round moon shone unobscured through his spreading wings. Slowly he grew more solid to look upon, as he gazed rapt into her green, tilted eyes. He put his weightless hands upon hers. "How could it be your fault, love, that Satan hates his brother?" He stroked her weathered hands gently. "If it is a matter of fault, then it is my fault that I wrapped my friend so tightly in the bonds of earth he could no longer stand against the Devil's malice."

But the dark unghostly brown eyes reflected no sense of guilt. "There is no fault here at all, Saara, except that of Satan's jealousy. And even that may be borne."

Saara gripped Damiano's large hands. They had become solid and warm. She brought them together and laid them against her cheek.

In another moment he was kissing her and curtains of wing shrouded them both.

"I love you," whispered Damiano, with his head against her neck. "Oh Lady, how I love you!" And then he sighed. "Forgive me, Saara; this does no good, I know!"

So it can be done, she thought to herself. The dead may touch the living in the very manner of life. Her heart raced, burning with the conviction that all vows would be well broken, and the future profitably traded—in exchange for this.

Saara hissed between her teeth and turned her head from him. "By the four winds! How wise I am—how wretchedly wise. Wise enough to put you aside, dark boy, even if you were fool enough to want to stay with me."

When she looked back again her face had hardened. "You see what a woman can be made of, after seventy years of living? I am so strong even you cannot break me, my dear.

"And as for being hurt—what does it matter if I am hurt, Dami? Why should my friends want to hedge me from my greatest desire lest I be hurt? Is it not to be hurt, to have one's desire thwarted? Is it not to be hurt, to be left always behind?"

She turned on the ghost with a sudden, deep-felt anger. "You thought it were better to hide from me and die, rather than risk being saved at the expense of my life. How noble it was of you!

"But would it not have been greater to have given me the chance to prove myself as noble as you? Do you think my own love would have made it less than a joy to die in your place?"

He shook his head, and now the black curls moved with the fingers of the wind. The setting moon haloed his face: large-eyed, ram-nosed, smiling gently. "It would have been a great act, love. I was not capable of it."

Saara was crying, but her voice came firmly. "And Raphael too . . . Walking into the Liar's snare, knowing it was a snare, and I the bait. I told him not to. I told him the truth: that I am old and my life is full-lived. There is nothing which now could please me more than a good death in battle . . ."

"Which you would not get from Satan," replied the ghost simply, shrugging. "But rather pain, confusion, and the shame of weakness slowly overcoming you, like that of an old man who cannot hold his bladder. The Devil has no sympathy with anything quick and clean, and it isn't human death which pleases him, but human misery." He searched her stern face for understanding.

"But in the end it did not matter, Saara, that you were ready to endure the Devil's torment. I believe you have the strength, beloved, if anyone born has ever had it. But Raphael also knew that if he left you in his brother's power, Satan would merely find another mortal tool, and then another, until Raphael could no longer resist him."

Damiano's voice was slow and gentle, and he caressed her hair as he spoke, and when he was finished all she said was, "I love you, Dami Delstrego. We had only a few days together as man and woman, but when flesh is laid aside I will still love you, then and always."

His sad smile widened, lighting all his face. "You are so beautiful, beloved. Like a great song . . . As for me, Saara of Saami, there is nothing left but love. That is why I feared to see you, lest it seem to you another abandonment, when the moon sets and I am there no longer."

She whispered, "I have heard your father tonight. And I have heard the voice of my child. I have heard and seen a great deal in my life and I do not call up the dead to ease my heart, but for help."

"Help?" he echoed, and his wings rose expectantly.

"Help in rescuing Raphael."

Those shadowy wings beat the air in complex, unheeded rhythm, as a man may drum his fingers while thinking. "Of course," he murmured at last. "Knowing you, how could I expect less? But I have no magic with which to help you," he replied at last. "Nor force of arms. I am not a spirit of power."

"You think not?" Saara looked away from his brown, human, dangerous eyes. "But, I don't seek power but knowledge. Once you summoned the Liar—Satan, as you call him."

"Twice," he replied gravely. "I was a fool."

"But I am not," she stated. "And I do not want to meet Satan again. But I must get to his hall, where he has bound Raphael."

Damiano shook his head. "No, beloved. There is no need. Raphael has passed back onto the earth from there."

Her head snapped up. "Where?"

Damiano was slow in replying. "I don't know."

"Have you seen him?"

Once again the spirit smiled slowly, and then he turned his head as though to listen to the rising wind. At last he replied. "I have been to see him. He is in a dry, hot place. He is on a chain. It is a land to which I never traveled. More than that I can't tell you, for even as I look at you now, Saara, beautiful love, I am not here but far away, and there is little besides you yourself that is clear to my eyes . . ." And then it seemed he turned and peered down the hill again.

"For I am neither angel nor devil nor God Himself, to be prowling up and down the living world. Dead or alive, I am only Damiano, and my eyes have their limits."

She snorted, bending to his humor unwillingly. "Then I shall have to steal into Satan's window, as I first thought."

The smile died from his face as the belly of the round moon touched the hills behind him. "Don't try that, Saara."

"I will. I must," she replied. "Look at me, Damiano. Even simple eyes can see now that I am no more a child. This misadventure has aged me. But I am Saara of the Saami; I know what I must do, and I do it.

"Besides, I have sworn that I will find Raphael, so all choice in the matter is over."

Damiano looked into her green Asiatic eyes and nodded his head in submission to the inevitable. "So you will find him. But not this way. Instead comb all the hot lands of the earth first, and all the places where men are kept on chains."

She laughed a trifle scornfully. "No one can live so long! Most of the world is hot, to me, and most everywhere but among the Saami are men kept on chains! No, Damiano. You must tell me how to find Satan's Hall, where someone of greater information may be made to talk."

"That would not be the act of a friend," he said, staring away from her down the wooded hill.

There was a crashing among the trees below, like a deer leaping among the hazel, but Saara was too roused to attend to noises. She pointed a chiding finger at the ghost as she cried, "Was it the act of a friend to help a man die in his own way, when there was another who might have saved his life? Raphael said it was the act of a friend. Do you agree?"

Damiano's eyes were pulled to hers, and breathless spirit though he was, he sighed. "Will you throw me by my own words, Saara? Yes, that was the act of a friend.

"And it is your decision how you will live or die, and your vows are your own to keep. But the pure truth is that I no longer know the way to the Chamber of Four Windows, if I ever did.

"For Damiano is dead, you know." The shadows of his hand touched his own breast. "This is only memory, lent shape by love." As he spoke, his face was growing paler and less defined with the setting of the moon, but the look he gave Saara was an obvious mixture of sweetness and amusement. He raised his hand and pointed beyond her.

"But *there* is one I think might know the way to Satan's palace," Damiano said.

Saara spun in place as the hulking black shadow barged among the birch trees. Above it was a thinner shadow that was cursing continually in a very familiar voice.

"Gaspare!" the witch cried out in recognition.

The horse shied at the sound and Gaspare came nearly off, hanging over the gelding's back by one crooked knee and a handful of black mane. He cursed fluently, sliding down to his feet.

The gangling youth strode closer, staggering and flailing his arms as though blind. He encountered a few birch boles before coming close enough to spy Saara, sitting solid as a point of stone at the crest of the hill.

"Lady Saara!" he began. "I have had the Devil's own trouble finding you. And it's dark here as the inside of a witch's . . ."

Gaspare had a pack on his back and the neck of the lute stuck out of it sideways like an insect's leg. His lank hair hung around his shoulders. Somewhere he had found another shirt.

Saara watched his approach in wonder and consternation. It had been scarcely a week since she had flapped home—a very weary dove—and in that time she had forgotten about the clownish Gaspare. She was not too happy to have him interrupting her ghostly tryst, painful though the meeting had to be. "As the inside of a witch's what, Gaspare?"

The only answer was a mumble and a clearing of the throat, as the youth realized what he had said. Saara turned her attention back to the waiting spirit, who glimmered like ice in the last rays of the moon.

Gaspare, too, noticed Damiano. The young man hissed, drawing himself back, and he made the peculiar Italian magical sign of protection which has been used from time immemorial by men who don't understand the least about magic.

"Again!" he cried in wrath made slightly hysterical by the touch of fear. He scooped a birch branch, complete with withering leaves, from the soil. "Again you try your tricks, Satan! Villainous wibbert, or wyvart . . . wyrven . . ." Giving up on the ungainly word heard only once, he lashed the branch at the apparition, which sat and watched him, wings pulsing slightly.

"Worm!" bellowed Gaspare, slashing his weapon left and right through the translucent form. The colors of Damiano trickled over the thrashing branches like dappled sunlight, while the ghost himself sat placidly waiting.

As soon as Gaspare stopped, panting, to survey his destruction, Damiano spoke again. "Hello, old friend, and God keep you."

Gaspare, leaning on his branch, stared uncertainly. After a few moments, he whined.

"I see you have that pretty lute on your back," continued the spirit, grinning at Gaspare's discomfiture. "I remember it somewhat, though I owned it less than a week. I have heard you play with great enjoyment, Gaspare."

"You? Have heard me play? With . . ." The redhead struggled with the idea that the Devil might like his music. It was almost as difficult for him to believe the alternate explanation. At last he let his leafy weapon fall. "Could it be you are really Delstrego?"

"Damiano Delstrego. Or I was. And I have no one anymore to call me 'sheep-face,' Gaspare. What a shame."

Gaspare blinked away a sudden brightness in his eyes.

He turned to Saara, to find that the witch, like the ghost, was grinning. "Lady Saara," he said decisively, "I think you have made a mistake. I don't think this is Satan at all. I think this is really Damiano."

"Of course it is Damiano," stated Saara.

Gaspare sank to his knees. He yanked the pack from his back and began to pull it apart, until the pearl inlay of the lute belly shone under the moon like the spirit's wings.

"Play for me," he demanded, thrusting the beautiful instrument at the ghost. "Play for me this minute, before you turn to moonlight or I wake up and it will be too late. For my worst fear, old partner, is that I will forget what you sounded like, who were—who are—the finest musician in . . ."

Damiano shook his head, and the gray wings gathered closer. "There is no time left for that, Gaspare. I *am* moonlight; I came with the moon and will fade with it. Besides—the lute and the playing of it is yours. But I will tell you one very important thing—old partner . . ."

Gaspare leaned close to the dimly shining spirit, trying to quiet his ragged breath. Damiano's serious face grew clear, and more intent, even as the rest of him darkened.

"Gaspare. In music, as in everything else, 'best' is an empty word. Don't strive to be best, or you will wake up one day and know yourself no good at all."

Saara's voice rapped out. "Enough! The moon is almost gone! What did you mean, Dami? That he might know the way to Satan's Hall?"

The ghost's smile returned again, ruefully. A ghostly hand laid itself very lightly on Gaspare's bosom. "There." The words came faintly. "He knows it there, for pride calls to pride." Gaspare gasped and shrank away, but the spirit consoled him.

"I am not saying you are wicked, Gaspare, nor that you belong to the Devil's own. Don't be a fool like I was, to let him make you believe that! But you . . . like me . . . may have an understanding of Satan. Raphael wonders if that is what men are for, did you know? To understand the misery of wickedness, as angels cannot. To feel pity for it."

The hand, almost invisible now, rose to touch Gaspare's still unbristly chin. "I'll help you as I can, old friend. I haven't forgotten that you were a very good manager to me."

Gaspare swallowed hard. He wanted to believe he felt the touch of that hand. "And I, sheep- . . . Damiano. I pray for your peace each night—when I think to pray, of course."

"I know," whispered Damiano, and then Gaspare's eyes could no longer see anything.

Saara rose to her feet, her trembling hand raised before her. "Farewell, love," she called to the air.

"Love," came back the reply, or else an echo.

The moon was gone.

"What did he mean?" demanded Gaspare, as the whites of his eyes glinted at Saara.

The Lapp woman subjected Gaspare to an uncomfortable scrutiny. "He meant," she said at last, "that you can tell me how to find and enter Satan's stronghold."

"He meant that?" Both Gaspare's hands clapped to the sides of his head. "I know Satan's stronghold?" His stiff fingers stood up like antlers. "If he knows I know that, then he knows a lot more about me than I do about myself!"

Saara yawned, glancing up at the starlit sky. "That is the first wise thing I have ever heard from your mouth, Gaspare." She walked over to him, somewhat stiff from her hours on the chill earth. She laid her hand on his rather pointed red head and rumpled his hair. "Come now: It's time to sleep. In the morning we can worry at the spirit-puzzles."

CHAPTER 4

The night was more confusing than the daytime. During some hours Raphael slept, forgetting pain, abandonment, and the unpleasant feeling of being cold. But these interludes were interrupted by wakefulness, which, like a prodding finger, reminded him he was lost. And toward morning he was visited by an experience as miserable as wakefulness but different: his first nightmare.

It was the sparrow again, gripping a bare twig with

claws more brittle than the wood, its dusty feathers rutched against a light fall of snow.

It had no song. This vision brought with it a sense of desolation unalloyed by hope.

There was something here he was supposed to understand—he knew that much, at least—and with undemanding patience Raphael was prepared to let the dream unfold until he did understand. But with the first light the slave women began to stir in their chains, and very soon Perfecto (who had also spent a very bad night) was awake and kicking everybody else except Hakiim into rising. His kick to Raphael was perfunctory, for, truth to tell, Perfecto felt an inexplicable distrust of this gift almost amounting to terror.

The new slave did not respond to the urging, because he was not yet finished with his dream. But with the increasing noise and bustle of the camp, the dream finished with him; it flew off, offended.

Still Raphael did not move. He had an idea that if he kept his eyes closed long enough—if he denied the activity around him long enough—they would all pack up and go away. And that seemed very desirable this morning.

He listened to the chatter of the women and the bray of the mules. His throat tightened with unconscious imitation of the noises both made. Stop it, he told himself. Rest again. Make it go away.

Perfecto came back, and the kick he delivered was harder. "Get up, idiot!" the Spaniard snarled. "We're traveling today if we have to drag you by a mule's tail."

The blow hurt, but it certainly didn't induce Raphael to obey. Instead he screwed his eyes tighter.

Make it go away.

And Perfecto did go away.

Raphael was immensely heartened. He curled into a more comfortable ball and waited for sleep to take him again. Hakiim, the Moor, was whispering to someone close by. It was easy to ignore the sound.

The pointy little foot caught him between the ribs and its big toe jabbed and wiggled. "Get up, Pinkie! You get up right now or I'll stuff dirt up your nose!"

It was not the threat but Djoura's tone of voice that smote him. Guilt and remorse splashed through Raphael, all the worse for the fact that he'd no experience with either feeling. He clambered up, tripped in his voluminous gown, rose again, and stood tottering beside her, looking down at the top of her jingling headdress.

The Berber possessed no veil to her headdress. Her excellent teeth shone whiter against a skin as opaque as lampblack as she gave Raphael a wolfish smile. "I knew you just needed encouragement," she said.

Then she walked around him. He gave a yelp of pain as his dress was pulled free of the scabbing wounds on his back. Djoura patted him as one would a horse. "There, there. It's over now. Better quick, I always think."

Again the Berber stood before him. "Well, sieve-head, how are we this cold morning?"

"We are unhappy," he replied carefully in her own tongue. Djoura's eyes opened wide.

"Don't!" she hissed at him, peering left and right from under the folds of cloth. "If you want to keep your . . . don't seem too able, you see? Don't let them know!"

Raphael did not see. He had difficulty following elliptical statements. In fact, his confusion at this point was so great it did not allow him to ask questions.

Djoura, after ascertaining that no one in the little caravan was paying attention to them, continued. "You must hide two things, Pinkie, if you wish to come to a better situation. Your brain is the first, and your bollocks are the second. No one must see evidence of either one but your friend Djoura—do you understand?"

"No," he answered readily, glad to have a question within his ability.

The Berber snorted and shifted from foot to foot. In this manner she resembled a tall, thin tent swaying in the breeze. "I will say it in different words.

"I say to you, Pinkie: Do not show anyone your manhood. And do not speak to anyone but Djoura, and then only when no one else can hear. She alone is your friend. Will you do that?"

"I will do that."

Djoura heaved a great sigh and rolled her eyes to heaven, which she could not see for the row of copper coins which shaded her forehead. "Excellent." Then she brushed her hands together, removing invisible dust.

Hakiim was passing near. Out of habit he put out a hand to slap the Berber woman on her hip. Habit germinated the gesture, but prudence and Djoura's warning stare aborted it. "Now, Pinkie." She spoke in a loud voice. "Last night we practiced pissing. This morning I think we should do some work on eating, don't you think?"

Raphael considered this with furrowed brow. He remembered to wait until Hakiim had passed down the line (to another woman with a more approachable anatomy) before he replied, "I think I would like to practice pissing again."

Watching the eunuch eat was a good joke; it almost served to quell Hakiim's new mistrust of his partner. First there was a problem getting the poor stick to open his mouth. After harsh words and some manual probing on the part of his nurse, Djoura, it was discovered that he had been sucking on a stone. When the black attempted to throw the pebble away, he clawed it from her and locked it in his right hand, from whence none of the woman's strength could release it.

After this he got his face stuffed with cereal.

The slave merchants sat beside their chain of human wares, eating their own breakfast. They had only bulgur in oil and vinegar, the same as everyone else; their condition elevated them by no more than the two squares of silk carpeting on which they rested. Except, of course, that one tended to feel much more elevated without chains upon the neck or wrist.

"Look at him!" cried the Moor in glee. "Such emotion—pathos and ecstasy! Our new boy wears his heart upon his sleeve!"

Hakiim hardly exaggerated, for Raphael's first taste of food brought tears to his large blue eyes. One taste and it was to him as though all the world's jangle and whine were being brought into harmony. Once Djoura put the cool, oily mass on his tongue his mouth took over and transferred custody to his throat, which effortlessly took it down, and after that he was not aware of the bulgur at all, except as a spreading contentment.

He took some in his own hand. (His left hand. Disgusting.) And he repeated the process.

Perfecto watched with an eye which was physically as well as morally jaundiced. "Hugghh! Perhaps the idiot will work out after all."

Djoura's own eyes, very black and very white, flickered from the Spaniard to her charge. She leaned unobtrusively forward. The next time Raphael scooped from the red clay pot and filled his mouth, the little toe of his left foot was violently wrenched.

He choked. Cereal spattered from his mouth and nose. The Berber came forward with her bit of rag. "Hah! See what happens when you play the pig?" she said loudly. Then, in a whisper, she added, "Don't be so cursed independent."

"I wouldn't get my hopes up," replied Hakiim to Perfecto.

The mules of Andalusia were justly famous, being bred from the giant asses found in that country. Hakiim and Perfecto rode two sleek gray animals the size of large horses. Four other mules ambled behind, laden with gear. Beside the mule train, like an attendant serpent, paced the line of female slaves. As the morning was still cool, they were chattering among themselves.

For it had been found impossible to keep seven women (most of whom must not be disfigured in any way) from talking, and the quietest, most orderly solution had been to attach them in linguistic groups. The Saqalibah spoke in a patois of their own Central European language and Arabic. The two Andalusians behind them spoke Spanish and ignored the poor mongrel creature at the tail of the line. They were young, these two Spanish women, and therefore valuable. They hissed slyly to one another without end and shaded their faces with tattered shawls.

On the other side of the mules, proudly isolated, strode Djoura the black Berber, with Raphael stumbling after.

She went fast: as fast as any mule desired to walk. Hakiim watched her without moving his head.

Now there was a valuable property. Perfecto didn't understand how valuable Djoura was, being blinded by the Spaniard's distaste for black skin. But the woman was young, straight, immensely strong, and had all her teeth. And pretty, too, if one could look past her scowl.

Still, she talked like a Berber.

Hakiim was not a Moor of Granada, but a Moor of Tunis, and he knew that in the far south there *were* blacks accepted as Berbers. A few.

I worry too much, he thought to himself. And immediately the eunuch bobbed into view, presenting himself to Hakiim's attention.

Djoura had been very industrious, and now the gangling creature wore not a shapeless gown but a pair of baggy women's pants. Where did she get them? His gaze darted back to the moving tent that was the black woman.

She must have been wearing them, all this time. Hakiim itched to know what Djoura *was* wearing. He had seen her naked, of course, in Tunis. He was too downy a fellow to purchase a woman on the strength of flashing black eyes and a white smile. (No. Snarl.) But he hadn't then paid attention to the dusky pile of cloth on the pavement beside her.

Hakiim itched to know Djoura in other ways, too, but his instincts told him not to scratch. The world was full of women, with most of whom one did not require a club.

That eunuch too. Had he been raised for pleasure? Filthy degeneracy. Hakiim spat sideways, causing his mule's ears—long as the leaf spears of a palm—to rotate toward him.

But that sort of thing was done, and it was none of a merchant's business to lecture the world. And the tall boy, with his pink, hairless skin and his head as yellow as a buttercup: He might still serve for any man who cared for idiots.

Analytically the Moor regarded the eunuch's scourged back. Not bad, really. Not as bad as it had seemed at first, all covered with dried blood and with the gown stuck to it. Pale skin showed scars least. He would have it covered with grease tonight.

If only they had a month instead of two days to reach Granada. Then the welts would have a chance to fade. Perhaps they should farm the creature out to sell later, or cheaper, keep him in a stable until the others were sold and he was ready to leave Granada.

But as Hakiim pondered and watched, the fair slave took a tumble, tripping over nothing at all. Without sense to grab onto his chain, he let it tighten around his neck. Djoura's wrist was whipped back by the force of Raphael's fall, and she rushed back to him, where he lay flat out on the earth, making little gagging sounds and clawing at his throat with his left hand. The right still clutched his pebble firmly.

No, whispered the Moor to himself. Nothing could be worth keeping him another month. Nothing.

Perfecto pulled his steed up beside Hakiim. The serpent of women jingled to a stop. The Spaniard's yellow eye swept over the creature he had purchased, growing more glazed as they stared.

Raphael tottered again to his feet. Djoura examined his knees for bruises and brushed him off. Once more the mule train ambled forward, with the serpent shuffling beside.

"Do you think," Hakiim casually asked his partner, "that maybe our black lily has had children before? She certainly knows how to mother."

Perfecto had an odd complexion, which the sun tended to darken toward orange. He turned his yellow eye upon the Moor. "If she had, she wouldn't be acting this way. She'd have got it out of her system."

Dust deadened the color of what greenery grew beside the road; the berries of the juniper had lost their gloss. To the right of the road the land swept downward, and through the gaps in the stones glimpses of small, summer-blasted pools were visible. Those which were more water than mud scattered a sunflash so bright it hurt the observer's eye.

Dust clogged Hakiim's nostrils and stung his cracked lips. Perfecto must be suffering worse, the Moor thought, in his Spanish singlet and shirt which left the back of his neck and his few square inches of forehead exposed to the sun. Hakiim regarded his partner's squat form analytically. The fellow actually *looked* the part of an ill-tempered man: rolls of fat under his neck burned the color of a village pot, little hands darkening the mule's leather reins with sweat, eyes like those of a pig. Had Perfecto always looked like that? (Had August always been so hot?) Three years the partners had plied their trade together, buying domestics and selling them. Eight times had Hakiim made the voyage to the markets of Africa and returned to Granada with exotics. Eight times had Perfecto disappeared into the wilds of Spain and reappeared with oddly assorted women. It was possible he crossed into Christian lands to gather his merchandise. If so, the Spaniard was ready to risk a lot for money.

More than Hakiim was, at any rate.

Eight times was enough, the Moor decided. Dealing with slaves had given him a certain sense about people, or developed a sense that all are born with. Hakiim could smell when a slave was mad, and when she was dangerous. And he could usually estimate the amount of danger involved.

So with Djoura, Hakiim felt no fear, but neither did he get too close. With the idiot eunuch (not mad, only confused) there was no danger except that of soiling one's clothes.

But Hakiim dropped his mule back behind Perfecto and he watched his partner. Eight times was enough.

Why don't you die, Perfecto silently asked his new acquisition as the eunuch followed Djoura, alternately stumbling and scampering at the end of his iron chain. After a few hours the fellow had learned to hold the links in his hands so that he was not choked every time the black caught him unawares.

If only the creature had curled up and died last night: of cold or of injuries or merely of Satan's malignity. He certainly looked ready to be carried off, with his breath panting and his blue eyes rolling and all the flies on his back. If he had died, then Perfecto would have had the perfect excuse for Satan, and he would not be sitting there now in such a sick funk of worry that his bowels were churning and his collar seemed too tight.

What sort of creature was it? One of Satan's human servants who had failed his task? (Perfecto had never *yet* failed, he reminded himself.) A recreant priest, perhaps? The robe he had been sold in had a clerical cut. The Spaniard shuddered, and his mule replied in sympathy.

He could be anything—even a eunuch. Perfecto had announced him a eunuch, certainly, but that had been only to smooth over the inconvenience of his arrival in the pack train. He had expected Hakiim would discover the untruth of this claim within minutes, upon which Perfecto would proclaim himself ill-used by the seller and would promise to have this mistake rectified in Granada.

But Hakiim had trusted his word. How odd. And Djoura had said nothing. He glanced mistrustfully at the black woman.

Well, maybe Perfecto had told the truth by accident. The demon had not said the man was entire, after all, and Perfecto hadn't bothered to pull off the gore-soaked dress. Why shouldn't Satan be served by eunuchs?

But what if he were neither a gelded man nor entire? It was still possible the noble fair head would blossom into a thing of horror and teeth.

Tonight Perfecto would sleep under a crucifix, if any of the women possessed such a device. If not, he would piece together a cross of some sort, even if only two sticks. Let the cursed paynim laugh! Perfecto was sick to death of Hakiim's sneers and slurs and Moorish pretense. If he had his way . . .

Come to think of it, it might be figured that Satan owed him something for disposing of the blond. (If it was not a trick. If it was not a trick.) Once the lot of them were sold in Granada. Once the money was in his hands . . . It would not be difficult to find another partner.

Perfecto embarked on a reverie which imparted a much sweeter expression to his face. Hakiim was emboldened to speak.

"You know how I call it, Perfecto? You want to hear the order in which they will sell, for how much and to whom?"

Perfecto returned to the breathless, stifling present. "Oh, not that again."

"Why not?" the Moor replied. "Am I not always correct? About both the money and the buyer? I have a knack for these things . . .

"First," Hakiim continued, urging his mount up to his partner's, "the larger of the two locals will go, because her age will make her cheap and yet she is sound. To a miller or a weaver perhaps: some small businessman who doesn't want any fight in his bondswomen.

"The Saqalibah will go next, but not together. As domestics, is my guess: all of them. The little local will sell after that, for a good price and to a peasant.

"The old woman? I don't know, but I think we'll keep her longest. Depends how many households are looking for goosegirls or goatherds this summer."

Perfecto listened to this involved prophecy without a murmur. He didn't give a damn, himself, as long as the sale produced enough gold to take one man (one man) from Granada to some place far away. But it occurred to him that Hakiim had made a large omission.

"What about the black? Don't you think we can sell her at all?"

Hakiim's eyebrows rose and he gestured one finger in the air. "Perfecto, my old friend, you still do not believe in our dark lily's worth! I have no intention of standing her under the sun in the common market."

"Why not?" growled the other. "Can't tan her any worse."

The Moor's eyes shifted under his immaculate headdress. This was better: more like the crude but predictable Perfecto of past years. If only he could rid himself of that prickling down his back when he looked at the Spaniard . . .

"Djoura is a beautiful girl, Perfecto. Strong and young."

"Who'd as soon kill you as look at you."

Hakiim shrugged. "She comes from the desert (Although it would be better, maybe, if we didn't mention that in Granada. At least not around any sons of Islam.) and she has gone from hand to hand, not knowing a steady master. With expert taming, she could be made loyal, and even affectionate. I will advertise her by private treaty only."

Some streak of pugnacity prodded Perfecto to remark, "So why haven't you mentioned the eunuch?"

The answer was inevitable. "I don't believe we can sell him." But the silence which followed this answer had a character which terrified Hakiim. He found himself babbling, "I want no trouble about this, Perfecto. How much did you pay for him? If the price was not exorbitant then I will pay you its equivalent out of my own pocket."

The Spaniard turned in his high wooden saddle. His eyes were set so deep in the seamed and folded flesh that Hakiim could see but one tiny spark out of each. "And then what," he growled. "And then do what with the eunuch himself?"

"Loosen the chain," Hakiim replied.

Despite the jouncing weight of Perfecto's face, it contrived to set in hard lines. "Leave the idiot in the desert? He would die before nightfall."

(How he would love to. If only he dared.)

Hakiim's confusion slid into pure mystification. He had always been the one of the pair whose natural bent had been toward liberality, as long as it didn't cost too much. What was there between the idiot eunuch and Perfecto? A relationship of blood, perhaps? He glanced again at the slave's features.

The eunuch was walking more competently now, and his face bore a very convincing look of deep concentration. His newly washed hair, like silk fabric, fell in waves and folds about his face.

No relationship. Impossible.

"Not in the desert," Hakiim replied to Perfecto. "In a village, secretly. Or at the walls of Granada itself. He will have as good a chance of charity as any beggar—and he can be nothing else but a beggar."

Perfecto turned his body back to the front. He looked neither at the eunuch nor at his partner. "Moor," he announced. "I swear I will sell this boy in Granada. I *have* sworn it. I will shed blood before denying my oath."

Hakiim stared at the back of Perfecto's head. Whose, he wondered. Whose blood?

In the middle of the day Raphael was fed once more of the same cereal and vinegar, and he was allowed a few minutes' rest in the shade of a wall.

This was in a small village, where the houses crowded together as though they had been built in the middle of a city and the city then taken away from around them. The slaves in their bird-flock fashion lined the cool stone wall, ignoring the villagers with the same intensity the villagers ignored them. Indeed, in everyones' eyes, the difference of caste between these tattered Spaniards and the slave women was insuperable. Yet each group felt itself the more respectable, for the slaves took their status (in their own eyes, at least) from their masters, and no one in this congeries of huts would ever own a domestic.

Djoura alone bothered to look at the scene around her, with its naked babies and almost hairless yellow dogs. And her gaze was as removed and disinterested as that of an observer at a menagerie.

Her Pinkie looked, too, of course. Raphael gazed about himself with friendly curiosity, unbroken even when an infant of four years scuttled up and threw a wad of dried cow dung into his lap. The blond closed his eyes and listened to the chatter as though it were music.

Once again life erased its miseries for Raphael and he was free to think about his condition.

It had been terrible, and now was only bothersome. The difference between the two conditions seemed to be connected with what he had eaten and drunk, and when. The time of day mattered too. Cold and dark were unpleasant.

But so was hot sun. And hard stone. And flies that bit. And being kicked or glared at.

It seemed to him he was suspended between a thousand little-understood needs of the flesh and another thousand outside sources of pain. These established his course, as the course of a pebble was established once it was dislodged from the top of a hill.

But that reminded him of his own pebble. Raphael's hand felt sweet relief as he opened his fist and looked at Damiano's gift.

It was such a pretty pebble, all brown and rough with faint white stripes, and it looked as much like a piece of a corkscrew as anything.

Damiano had been a man—he had been born a man. Yet *he* had not seemed to let himself be knocked back and forth between pain and desire, like Raphael was. Damiano had called, "If you have the time, Seraph . . ." very considerately, and had smiled to greet him. Had he been in such misery, then, hiding it all from his friend? Surely Raphael would have seen.

No, it must have been that living as a man was an art which might be mastered. And Damiano, who had done so, was still with Raphael—somewhere, somehow. In a pebble. Flexing his cramped fingers, Raphael stuffed the pebble into the corner of his mouth, beside his back molar.

"I am Raphael," he said aloud, in Damiano's language. "I am not just kicks and heat and hunger. I was before these things, and will be after. I am my Father's musician." He raised his eyes to the southern distance, where sand and dust fell away toward the sea he could not see, the sea they were leaving further behind each day.

Djoura heard these foreign words in Pinkie's voice. Surreptitiously she glanced over, and the blond's face startled her.

He looks as stern as a king, she thought. Praise be to

Allah, could it be my sieve-head's mind is coming back to him?

But if it were so, why didn't he talk sense? She gouged his hip with her muscular toe.

"Hiss, Pinkie! Who are you talking to?"

He shifted the pebble in his mouth before answering. "I am talking to my Father," he replied.

She giggled. "I see. Did he answer you?"

"No," Raphael answered simply. "He doesn't any-more."

Perfecto was thinking, I will accompany him out of the city this time; he will not suspect anything in that. And with all the money I will buy a hundred Masses for protection.

It was an act of grace to kill a paynim. It was holy.

"My uncle will take me in easily, and with this last profit I can buy a small date-palm planting and a couple of boys to keep it. I will not say a word to him, just get on my ship and disappear."

Hakiim's mule swiveled its ears, seeming to reproach him for the plan. "A promise to the infidel is no promise at all," he whispered to the beast.

Djoura observed Raphael narrowly. No longer did he move like a lout, nor roll his eyes like a simpleton. Too much longer and the swine on muleback would realize what they had here, and her new-budded plans would go for nothing. The woman sidled up to Raphael and did her best to trip him.

"The birds in the air," Raphael sang silently, despite his sore feet and scourged back. "The fish in the water, washing their backs in light."

Joy came from somewhere to him: a gift as solid as stone.

CHAPTER 5

The bees were already awake, but then the bees had retired earlier than Saara. She stepped from her hut into the light to find Gaspare stretched on the ground, waiting for her. His orange hair and red face shone like two clashing flames against the green of the bee balm. The young man leaped to his feet.

"I can do it for you, my lady," he stated, biting off his words with force. "Give me two silver florins and seven days and I can do it." His frosty green eyes bore into hers, while his long mouth fairly trembled with intensity.

Saara, who had not slept well, was beset with a desire to turn around and go back indoors, pulling the door behind her. Instead she yawned, combed her hair with her fingers, and replied, "Do what, Gaspare?"

"Go to the Devil," he replied.

Saara lowered herself onto the gray rock which stood beside her door. This rock had a shape rather like that of some quadripedal animal with very round sides and stubby legs. She called this rock her housedog, although the rock had come first, with the house being built behind it.

She considered the possibility that Gaspare were joking with her. He did not appear to be joking, and certainly the boy had had enough stupid ideas in the past, but one could have stupid ideas and still make jokes. Finally Saara said, "I have known men to go to the Devil before without needing two silver florins."

His lips pulled away from his teeth as he answered, "Ah, but without money it takes longer."

Now Saara was certain he was joking. Almost certain. She sighed, wondering once again why Italians had to be like that. "The problem is, young one, that we want to find the Liar, not be found by him."

Gaspare smiled and sat himself down at her feet. His face pulled into a taut smile as he looked across at her. Not up at her, but across. And there was something in his thoughtful expression that prefigured the man that was to be, once all of Gaspare's tempers and gangling limbs had come to terms at last.

Saara felt something like a blow over the heart as she remembered the starved boy Gaspare in ragged clothes who grabbed her about the knees, spouting gallant rubbish, on the road to Avignon, and the same fourteen-year-old who stood white-faced and silent beside the body of his friend.

So she had seen one more boy grow out of childhood, and once again she hadn't noticed it happening.

This cannot go on forever, she said to herself. Everyone growing and growing old and dying except Saara. I do not want it to go on forever.

Gaspare was watching her face attentively. "Don't despair, my lady," he comforted her. "If Delstrego believes I can find old Scratch for you, then it must be that I can."

She shook her head. "It is too great a risk for you, Gaspare. Not only a risk of the body, but . . ."

He flushed to deep burgundy. "What? That again? By San Gabriele, woman, haven't you learned by now that I am Gaspare the lutenist, not some postulant of a cloistered order, to be saved from the contagion of the world!

"Why, Delstrego himself told you you needed my help. Would you throw away the word of the greatest musician of all Italy and Provence—and a blessed spirit besides?" His narrow form swelled with passion and he waved fingers all through the air.

"Delstrego himself," repeated Saara silently. Had Dami become history already, or a legend? What kind of legend died of the plague at the age of twenty-three?

A legend with one believer.

Or two.

But she understood the anger behind Gaspare's words. "No, Gaspare. You are right, and I of all people know better than to protect a person against his own will. If you want to help me find the way to Satan's Hall, I will accept your help thankfully."

Gaspare, who had been building up his emotions in case tantrums were necessary, felt his fury leak away. "Hah? Good, then, my lady."

But his voice still held an edge as he added, "You must remember that Raphael is my teacher. And my friend."

Saara stared at him coolly. "He makes a lot of friends, that one," she stated, and began braiding her damaged hair.

At the crown of the hill stood Gaspare, turning left and right in place. The sun of early morning sent shadows of birch over the ground like tangled lace, while the looming shadow of the larger sister peak to the northeast lapped up through the pines. The morning was impossibly sweet and beautiful, predicting a scorching day.

"Once," the young man pronounced, drawing his brow and scowling fiercely, "when Delstrego wanted to locate a man he didn't particularly like, he walked back and forth through a city, noting when he felt most bothered and irritated. In that manner he drew nearer and nearer, until he could feel the fellow's presence directly."

"It sounds like a good method," replied Saara, who sat with her back against the bole of the tree, chewing a stem of sourgrass. "Of course, *he* was a witch."

Gaspare's overlarge pale eyes pulled away from the horizon to focus on Saara's small face. "Could it be that I am too, my lady, and never have known it? Perhaps that was what he meant when . . ."

"No," Saara cut in evenly. "But I wouldn't let that worry you. Being a witch has its drawbacks.

"Do you feel more bothered and irritated—or perhaps more proud, since it was supposed to be your pride which connected you to Satan—in one direction more than another?"

Once again Gaspare revolved, this time with his eyes closed and hands out, while his cheeks brightened to a cheery red. "I just feel immensely ridiculous," he replied.

The northerner nibbled her tattered leaf thoughtfully. She stared at her bare toes. "Is there any direction in which you feel more ridiculous than another?" she asked reasonably.

"Yes. To the north, where I can feel you watching me spin like a top."

Saara shot Gaspare a quick glance. "But I'm not. Not until now. I haven't looked at you once." Very quietly she rose and stepped past him.

The redhead dropped his hands to his hips, but his eyes remained sealed. "Well, how am I to know if you are or not?" He had a habit of forgetting to call Saara "my lady" when the least bit excited. Saara never noticed.

"I still feel ridiculous when I am facing you."

"Facing me or facing north?" came her voice from behind him. Gaspare jumped and swiveled. He blinked at her confusedly.

"Facing . . . north." His words were almost a whisper.

Saara's smile was slow and drawn. It aged her face. "Good, then. Tell me, Gaspare, if you had to guess, and Damiano had never said a word about pride calling to pride, in which direction would you expect to find the Li— the Devil?"

Gaspare folded himself on the turf beside her, mindful of his skintight hose. "As a child, of course, I believed the Devil lived under the Alps, in the heart of winter. All the babies in San Gabriele are taught that.

"Now, being a man of some experience," (he did not see or chose to ignore the flicker behind his companion's eyes) "I know he is more to be found in the cities of the south, doing his work among men."

Saara lifted her eyes to the green-black southern slopes, out of which the third sister peak rose like a rock from the sea. In the distance the haze was golden.

Then she turned her head (and like an owl, Saara could turn it very far) to inspect the looming, purple north.

"I think we should not be in too much hurry to grow up," she commented.

"What would we do with him?" Saara exclaimed, for the third time. "He is no goat, to bounce over the raw rock . . ."

Gaspare clutched his handful of black horse mane obstinately. "This is the very animal that Delstrego rode through the mountains in the month of November, from Partestrada to San Gabriele and beyond."

Saara ground her teeth together and thought that she would shortly have heard enough about "Delstrego." "That was on a road, I think. If I am right, we will have little enough to do with roads on this journey. And when we reach the Devil's window in the rock (if we ever do), then what is the horse to do: grow wings and fly in?"

Gaspare glared from the restive gelding to Saara. "Then

he will walk home alone. It is no new thing for Festil-ligambe. He's more than half savage as it is."

Saara, too, peered into the animal's aristocratic face. "Why don't we let him decide. If he is to take the risk . . ."

Gaspare snorted sullenly. His rapprochement with the black gelding was too hard-won for him to want to walk when he could ride. And he wasn't sure he trusted the witch, who could pretend to ask and then tell him the horse had said whatever she wished it to say.

But the justice of her proposal could not be denied. "Ask then."

Saara put one little hand beneath the horse's round chin, where spiky guard hairs grew untouched by knife or razor. "Festigi—Festilli—Festie—oh, horse! Tell me, do you want to accompany us north into the Alps, toward that presence we saw together by the wine-shop door in San Gabriele? And will you help us to fight him?"

The gelding's head snapped up into the air. He did an oversized double take, and then, rearing, he spun around and vanished down the hillside.

"Don't feel bad," said Saara gently to Gaspare. "Horses are not meant to be brave."

But Gaspare did feel bad. He felt utterly desolate, and unworthy besides, for he remembered this same cowardly gelding standing foursquare over his injured master, hold-ing off eight men and four whips. In three years he—Gaspare of San Gabriele—had not won the animal's heart. Doubtless he never would.

"It's nothing," he told Saara, looking away. "He always knew I preferred dogs." And he paced heavily down the hill among the birch trees.

Gaspare's few possessions were tied in a square of linen, two ends of which went around his waist and two ends of which went around his shoulders. The lute in its sheepskin case he carried. Saara carried nothing.

The day was fulfilling its high-summer promise, but in the aromatic pine woods of the hill's lower slopes, it was still cool.

"There is a broad road not far north of Ludica," Gaspare was calling to the woman behind him. "It runs all the way from Franche-Comté. In the east it leads to . . . to the faraway east, I think. Once we strike that, we will have easy going, and our choice of trails going into the Alps themselves . . .

"Then we will have to take our bearings again, and I must search my heart for presence of the Devil, as Delstrego said. In fact, I ought to do so constantly, lest we lose our path and valuable time . . ."

Though she knew more about the roads of Lombardy than Gaspare could hope to, Saara let him prattle on. She was used to Italians by now, and besides, she wanted to keep an eye on the shadow in the woods—bulky, black, wary—that was following them.

As Gaspare detailed his plans for self-examination (they involved certain mental imageries of food, drink, cards, dice, and other appealing objects to which he alluded elliptically), this shadow rose onto the path behind, stepping silently on the carpet of needles. Saara faded off the path and let it pass.

For twenty steps the black horse paced behind Gaspare without making his presence known. Then he nudged with his nose.

The gangling youth skittered forward, flailing for balance. Then he turned in outrage and confronted Festilligambe, who stood motionless behind him with muzzle touching the ground and ears flat out to the sides.

Gaspare also stood frozen, though he blinked repeatedly. At last he put his hand on the gelding's bony withers and he sighed.

Since Delstrego had been known to play his lute while riding, nothing could stop Gaspare from doing the same. He did not do so happily, however, for he was never completely relaxed on horseback, and his knees gripped Festilligambe's sides like iron tongs.

But the horse picked its way along the rough ground with egg-cherishing care, for the dove which perched on its pointed head had told him just what would happen if he spilled the lutenist. Slowly the gelding climbed into the fresh air of the mountains, wondering all the while why anyone would want to go to a place with so little grass.

Saara's bird body was breathing heavily. She had shrunk to dove size so as to keep up with the horse without burdening him further, but by the give-and-take of magic, it cost her just as much effort to ride thus as it would have to climb at the gelding's side.

Listening to Gaspare's lute playing was another payment of sorts, for Saara. That the boy had control of his instrument was obvious. His sense of time was good, and his rhythms were highly original. But Saara had been born into a culture where chant was the most respected form of music, and Gaspare's carefully cultivated dissonances upset both her nerves and her digestion.

Yet she said nothing, for among the Lapps (who were all song wizards), to tell a person to stop his music was to tell him to stop his being. She merely wondered if the twigs of the alpine willow would be effective against headache.

Gaspare, who had been raised (or who had raised himself) in the shadow of the mountains, drank deep lungfuls of air scented with evergreens, and he turned his eaglet's face to the stony north. He felt sparks of energy within him like the sparks the horse's feet made hitting stone. Gaspare had only the vaguest idea where they were going, but he had confidence.

Saara did not, for she had no faith in their present course.

It was not that she doubted the words of the spirit, but she knew that there is no translation as difficult as that between the living and the dead, and what Damiano had meant by saying Gaspare knew the way to the Liar's hall might be something completely different from having the boy lead her there.

In fact, would Damiano—who had died rather than let her risk herself—have sanctioned bringing this clumsy young fellow into danger of body and of spirit? If he *had* meant for Gaspare to fling himself against Satan, then the dead were indeed a different order than the living. And though Damiano's suggestion was little more than Saara had protested that same night on her own behalf—that one must not keep a soul from its proper risks—still she found it difficult to extend that liberty to others whom she felt were not fit to meet the challenge. Gaspare, for instance. What could he do against pure wickedness, and how could he survive?

Saara shuddered over the ruthless understanding of the dead.

But perhaps it was all in error. Perhaps he had meant

she would find the path by looking in the boy's eyes, or in some ceremony of their Christian church. She had never studied these Italians' rites. Perhaps Gaspare was right in supposing that the Devil (this time) lay in the south.

Perhaps, perhaps. Doubt, like black water, seeped into her small feathered body and chilled her. She felt old.

She *was* old: old and past her prime. Off on a fool's errand, and caught in a battle of spirits which would have been too great for her strength anytime. She would be trodden underfoot, and Gaspare—he would fly screaming, only to be taken by the Liar and twisted beyond recognition. It would have been better not to have come. It would be better now to turn back. To Lombardy or farther. All the way back to the frozen fens of home.

The dove's heart tripped and pounded. Her vision swam and her wings grew numb. She felt the cold, groping fingers search toward her, impelling rout.

She felt rather than saw Gaspare raise his head from his instrument. He made a noise in his throat.

"Play, Gaspare," the bird cried. "Don't lose the beat!"

Gaspare obeyed out of a musician's reflex, counting silently and coming down heavy on the bass, while Saara retreated into the simple, incorruptible thoughts of a bird. After a moment or two the vile blind fingers passed over and faded.

Saara sighed and fluttered to the stones of the road. In another moment she was human again. She clutched her head in both hands. "Gaspare," she began, her voice quavering like that of an ancient. "Gaspare, young one. You keep your lute handy; it is your greatest protection.

"Do you understand me?" she added, for Gaspare was staring blankly down at her braided head.

He did not answer directly, but asked in turn, "What do you mean, protection? Has something happened?"

Saara herself was shaking. She slid down against a rock and hid her head in her arms. "Yes, of course. Didn't you feel the attack? I can still smell it in the air!"

Gaspare shifted his scarecrow anatomy on the horse's black back. "I feel only that my butt is a little sore. And smell?" He took a deep snort. "I smell the air of the mountains. It's very good."

Saara's hazel eyes pitied his obtuseness. "Nonetheless, young one, there has been great danger here."

She bit her lip. "It is as I feared. All the while we are looking for the Devil, he is looking for us."

She was quite correct; Lucifer was attempting to repair his neglect of the primitives in this world, at least to the extent of locating Saara and dealing with her.

And though he had enjoyed Raphael's misery with good appetite, it was the angel's confusion and sense of abandonment which really pleased his palate. After a little while that confusion subsided, because even in the form of a human slave Raphael could not be kept wholly apart from grace. In fact, the most satisfying waves of desperation in the little drama were coming from the Spaniard Perfecto, and such anguish was a cheap drink and unsubtle.

So now Lucifer was taking the time to seek out ants, which is to say, he was looking for the bothersome Saara. He had not forgotten the teeth of the bear in his neck.

But Saara, though powerful, was not a terribly complex person. She was not prone to greed, and understood neither sin nor sanctity. She had no more shame than a bird on a branch.

Consequently, she was very difficult for Lucifer to find.

He stepped away from his window. "Kadjebeen," he whispered sweetly to the air. "Kadjebeen, I have a bone to pick with you."

The raspberry demon waddled unhappily out from under the table. His eye stalks were wilted as he regarded his infernal master. "I'm sorry, Your Magnificence," he squeaked nervously. "Whatever it was, I will not do it again."

Lucifer's blue eyes flickered. "You won't disarm me so easily, you mountebank. I thought I told you to beat that scum till he was half-dead."

"Yes, well, so I did, Lord."

Lucifer's elegant brow rose in feigned surprise. "You did? Then why, may I ask, can I perceive him from out this window, trotting quite competently down a road in Granada, only four and twenty hours later?"

Kadjebeen's eyes (also blue, like those of a scallop) stared at one another and blinked. They knotted together in thought, and at last the demon replied, "Your Magnificence, it is difficult to know exactly how much of life or death makes half. I thought that if I erred, it ought to be on the conservative side."

"You have always got an answer," drawled Lucifer, frozen faced, and he raised his carnelian hand. The raspberry demon ran (rolled, really) across the floor at great speed, but he was not fast enough.

"What use *is* the stupid beast!" spat Gaspare with childish disdain as he and Saara together tried to haul a scrabbling Festilligambe up the slick bulge of a road-blocking boulder. On the other side of this obstacle lay miles of broad, flat land and a choice of roads, but it seemed that near was no closer than far, for they had been struggling with the horse all afternoon. The gelding's frantic pants left little crystal clouds in the air.

"Do not blame him," chided Saara. "He cannot help that this is no road for horses." With what would have been suicidal confidence in a less stock-wise person, she got behind the horse, next to his dancing hind feet, and pushed. Festilligambe wedged one hoof securely into a crack in the stone and his sweating black quarters rippled with effort.

He was up.

Gaspare, who was still pulling, was knocked flat and overrun. Festilligambe's hooves slipped and skidded around Gaspare's head.

The redhead rose howling, both hands clapped to the back of his head. "Murder! Son of a sow! Bladder full of piss! You touch me once more and I'll knife your black belly!"

Saara put her hand against Festilligambe's shoulder, averting the horse's natural hysteria. She herself was scandalized. "Gaspare! What shame to threaten a fine, useful beast—who didn't even step on you!

"Control yourself, young one. It was you who wanted him to come."

Gaspare did not often remember his mother or her abortive effects to discipline him. As a matter of fact, the woman was best forgotten, but Saara's maternal correction sent him into a rage.

"Wanted him? Yes, I wanted to ride, but the sow's son has dragged his feet for all of a week. He is spoiled meat, and overdue for the whip!

"The whip!" he repeated, snapping his fingers by his right ear. The words had given rise to the idea. But Gaspare didn't have a whip, so frantically he grabbed for the end of the makeshift halter rope.

Saara had no intention of allowing Gaspare to beat the horse. To exercise one's passions on a beast of burden was one of the worst crimes of her nomadic society. She could stop Gaspare with three words sung in ascending melody, and she opened her mouth to do so.

But Gaspare needed no spell to freeze him, for he stood still with the rope end raised in one shaking hand, while the horse rolled his eyes at him. Silence was broken only by the sweet calls of the alpine birds. He shook his head, as though denying something which was being said to him.

And there was something in the heavy flush of Gaspare's face and the shallow glint of his mad eye which pulled a memory from Saara. That carnelian visage, and that cold light of hate . . .

Saara raised her head and sniffed the air. She felt no attack, no approaching hand of despair over her.

It was Gaspare's personal battle.

And it seemed the boy was at loggerheads with himself. His shoulders were hunched and his fists balled, as though he would throw himself at some invisible obstacle. His lips trembled and his hairless chin went slick with sweat. Saara watched with guarded pity, too wise to interfere. What was the Devil's weapon here: pride, as Damiano had warned him, and the anger that it nourished? Saara could not know. Nor did she want to know, for it was none of her business.

Without anything obvious happening—neither change in the light of afternoon nor in the interrogative calls of the birds—the battle was ended. Gaspare straightened. His large eyes softened from steel-white to green, and his hands relaxed. He gave a great exhausted sob.

"Gaspare," whispered Saara. He turned to her.

"Look about you now," she commanded. "And tell me which way."

The young man did not ask for an explanation. With a weary face he peered into the distance first right and then left. Finally he pointed directly north. "This way," he grunted. "There is no doubt."

* * *

Gaspare had not picked an easy path. After a few miles there was some doubt he had picked a path at all. The travelers found themselves in a cleft of round stones between jagged piled cliffs. There were few trees and little grass, though Festilligambe plunged his black muzzle into any damp-looking crevice he saw.

Coming to a crest in a trail which seemed to have been created only by the rain, they found themselves in the reverse of the position they had been in only an hour previously. The ground dropped suddenly by at least six feet, and the fall was almost sheer to bare stone below.

"We cannot take the horse down this," announced Saara. "We must retrace our steps and go around."

"Go around what?" asked her companion, with an ironical lift to his eyebrows. "The Alps?" He gestured from the slab of granite on their left to that of basalt upon their right. Evening light had turned the west to gold, while the black basalt loomed uncomfortably close.

Saara bit her lip. She was not feeling especially confident, and it was late in the day for decisions. "Back to the crossroad then. At least there is flat ground on which to sleep, and some grass."

Gaspare looked at the horse's ribs. "Yeah. He could use it," he grudgingly admitted. He took the animal's halter in his hand. "Although I'd rather be beat by fists than have to endure that upsy downsy one more time."

"Come on, boy," Gaspare said to Festilligambe. "You can't help being a dumb, clumsy horse who can't climb hills."

Festilligambe did not have a speaking tongue, and even after the association first with Damiano and now with Saara, he did not understand Italian.

But he did understand something, for with a twist of his sinuous neck he freed himself from Gaspare's grip. He gathered his quarters under him and threw himself off the little cliff and into space.

Festilligambe was an excellent jumper. He had once cleared an eight-foot wall burdened by two (very skinny) riders. But he had never before flown, so when Saara and Gaspare saw the gelding give a great kick with his hind feet, twist in the air, and disappear, they could do nothing but stare.

Gaspare flung himself face down at the edge. "He's

. . . he's not there!" the redhead exclaimed. "Not running away, not broken on the stones. Where the hell *did* he go?"

Saara, though she stood wide-eyed, was thinking. After a few silent moments she motioned to Gaspare. "Don't worry, young one."

"What do you mean, don't worry? The brute has my water bag on him. He has my *lute!*"

Saara only smiled. "Trust me, Gaspare. Trust me as I trust you. And I do trust you, for you are a true and faithful guide. Take my hand."

Gaspare glared dubiously at the witch, for after all her motherly proddings and botherations he could not believe she had suddenly perceived him as an object of romance.

She was forced to snag his hand by the knuckles. "Now, Gaspare. If you want to find your lute again.

"We go one, two, three, and . . .

"Jump!"

Gaspare had no choice. She dragged him to the edge and leaped off. He could either follow or be pulled head first.

A wrench. White granite blurred and twisted. Black basalt spread over the universe. Down went sideways and he hit on his hip and hands.

It was still evening. Festilligambe stood before him, with Gaspare's bag still safe, though it had slipped over the gelding's neck and hung like a heavy pendant. The horse stood on three feet, resting one hooftip gingerly on the ground. He nickered.

Saara was beside him, climbing slowly to her feet. Her dress was dust-coated up the back and so was her hair. "I am not a cat," the witch stated regretfully, rubbing the back of her neck.

"What happened, my lady? What hit us?" Gaspare inched his knees up under him. They were unwilling, seeming to belong to someone else.

Saara chuckled ruefully. "The edge of the world hit us, Gaspare. For me it was the second time, though it is easier when one is a bird.

"But be glad. It means we are on the right path."

Gaspare ignored all this, for Saara was capable of talking as crazily as Delstrego in his prime. He stood up and stared at a welter of broken points of rock. "It doesn't look the same from down here," he said, and then he shivered.

"From up here," Saara corrected him. "And it shouldn't, for we've come a very long way, I think."

After a short cold night's sleep they were on their way again. Saara took bird form and made a sweep of the bare windy peaks, while Gaspare led Festilligambe along the only path they had.

It was a poor path and the beast was very hungry.

By the time the dove fluttered down again the horse had refused to move. Gaspare, weary of fighting and mistrusting his own temper, was seated on a bare stone. His back was turned toward Festilligambe, while his gaze rested along a gore of the mountains, facing south. There the Alps tumbled away to a low, mauve horizon. He started as Saara spoke.

"There is a tunnel ahead, boy: not natural, I think. The path descends into it."

"Not natural!" Gaspare swiveled to find Saara seated on the horse's back, sidesaddle. "You mean it was made by . . . You mean we have found the doorway into hell?"

"I do not think so, for the hall I entered was high above ground in all its windows. Yet it is significant, I am sure."

Gaspare proceeded on tiptoe, though with Festilligambe's castanet hooves behind him he might have saved himself the trouble. Saara's little bare toes made no sound at all as they gripped rock and gravel.

"Odd," whispered the redhead, "that we've seen no one at all for days. We're not *that* north, are we?"

His hissing voice echoed along the pass, amplified by some trick of sound. The noise continued long after he'd stopped talking.

"I have no idea where we are," answered the witch equably. "Not since we fell sideways off the rock. But I know it's where we want to go."

Now the sound in the air mimicked high wind, though no breath ruffled Festilligambe's mane. Then suddenly it was cut short, and the subsequent silence was even more ominous.

Saara slipped down from the horse, sniffing delicately. "What do you smell, Gaspare?"

The youth snorted obediently, and then again through curiosity. "I don't know, my lady. Sandalwood, perhaps?

"Or, no: What's wrong with my nose to say that? I think it's a stable."

Saara did not laugh at these conjectures. Instead she wrinkled her brow. "More like fresh cut wood than horse dung, I think. But there's something animal in it, also."

They passed between a tower of granite and a sloping drop of some hundred feet, and there before them was white stone with a round black hole cut into it, and it was from this source that came both the odd wind noise and the smell.

Festilligambe balked. So did Gaspare. "We cannot go in there, Saara. It is altogether dark, and may pitch us down a cliff!"

The witch bit her lower lip and studied the entrance. It was regular and very smooth, but round as a foxhole. The rim of it was rounded and full of hardened bubbles, as though the rock were mere dried mud. "Not altogether dark. Unless it is very long, there will be some daylight in it. Give my eyes time and I will see what I need to see.

"You wait here," she said grandly, and she stepped under the arch.

Instantly Gaspare's refusal to continue warred with a contradictory anger at being left behind. He watched her glimmering slim figure fade into the depths. "Gaspare of San Gabriele," he growled aloud, "you ought to be ashamed. Really ashamed of yourself.

"And you too," he added spitefully to the trembling horse.

Dark, dark. Daylight faded much more quickly than Saara had expected. The witch had never studied bat form (not foreseeing that she would one day find herself in the velvet blackness at the heart of a mountain far above the plains of the earth), but she had studied the high art of making do, and she used every one of her human senses to test her progress.

The floor was smooth as a well-made roadbed and round as the sides of a barrel. The walls, scarcely fifteen feet apart, ran smooth. Saara was tempted to give up a slow hands-and-feet approach, trusting the passage to remain level and intact. But Gaspare was right: there might be holes. If this tunnel had been built by the Liar (surely it was built by craft), there would likely be surprises of some nature.

Within, the smell was stronger: musky (like a stable, Gaspare had said) yet tinged with a dry perfume like that of no beast of her knowledge. The hissing wind came louder, and in regular gusts.

Surprises of some nature.

Saara resisted the temptation to change shape. What was the use in becoming a bear before one knew bear qualities were needed? It was hard to think, when one was a bear, and if she were forced to confront the Liar himself, it would be wiser (if anything about confronting the Liar could be wise) to do so in her true image.

On. It was unnaturally dark, though Saara could smell no sorcery around her. (No human sorcery, she qualified, for the deceits of the Liar were subtle.) There was only the musky sandalwood smell, and that grew no thicker, never approaching rankness.

Either her eyes adjusted between one moment and the next, or there was light ahead.

Air eddied roughly in the passage, like streams of water which smash against a stone wall. Saara turned to look over her shoulder at the still blackness she had crossed. Had she had the luck of passing through the tunnel without encountering its heavy-breathing occupant? How, when her witch sense hadn't hinted of any side passage?

Gray day shone on granite, sparking tiny lights like jewels. A dead end?

No, merely a right-angle turn. Saara crawled over something colder than stone. It was an enormous ring of iron, anchored into rock. A chain stretched from it, so heavy she could not budge one of the links which twisted down the tunnel, toward the light.

Sunlight and the smell of cinnamon, sandalwood, cedar: a dry, sharp smell.

The tunnel was not at an end, but here was a cleft in it, a break clean and cruel as though struck by a heavenly ax. One hundred feet away, on the far side of this splash of yellow, the foxhole continued, black and round. But in the middle of the sunlight sprawled the heavy-sighing wearer of the chain.

He was not coiled: not like withies are coiled to make a

basket. His metallic length lay in a sort of G-clef pattern, and though in the sun he glinted in a rich array of red, green, and indigo, his color was black.

Black except his head, which was golden horned, his face framed by a whole series of scaly spiked collars, yellow, scarlet, and indigo, giving him the appearance of a chrysanthemum with a long, bare stem.

He had four legs, no sign of wings, and a crest like little burnished flames which ran from neck to tail tip, some ninety feet in all. His eyes were enormous, gold, slitted like a cat's, and staring down at Saara from great heights.

The greatest witch in the Italies had seen dragons and wyverns before, and would have recognized many fell beasts on sight, but she had never seen anything like this. She stood stock-still while she framed in her mind what might be the greatest power song of her life. Or the last one.

The creature pulled iron-black lips from teeth the blue-white of skimmed milk. Each of these was the size and shape of a scimitar, and his tongue between them was forked. The noise of forges increased. A movement began at the creature's tail and traveled up the serpentine length of him, like the flood crest of a river when the dam has gone.

Yards of gold crest vanished, to be replaced by flat, lustrous belly scales. Four long legs curled up, their etiolated, thumbed paws exposing claws the size and shape of cow's ribs. Last of all the ornate head flipped over and hit the stony ground, until it was gazing madly at Saara, upside down. The eyes were now at her level.

"*Bonjour, madame,*" he said very correctly. "*Comment allez-vous aujourd'hui?*"

She blinked. "I don't speak Langue d'Ouil," she answered in Italian, wondering if the beast's purpose was to distract her, and feeling he had certainly succeeded. "I don't speak any languages but Fennish and Italian."

"Fennish and Italian!" The dragon (if he could be called a dragon) chuckled. "Many people speak Italian. No one speaks Fennish but a native of the Fenland," he stated, speaking that tongue. "Therefore I presume you to be an émigrée of the Fens residing now in the Italies. The north Italies, if your accent is any indication."

Hearing the clear, comfortable sounds of home from

this huge bizarrity struck Saara nearly dumb. But her wit returned to her in time to allow her to reply, "Then you, too, must be a native of Fenland. The south, however, I would say by your accent."

"Lappish is equally familiar to me," the creature replied, shifting his voice more into the nose. His five-fingered paw scratched belly scales reflectively.

"But it would be ludicrous to attempt to convince you that I come from the land of ice and snow. I am merely an exception to the rule I myself stated." Amber eyes hooded themselves complacently, and then the dragon rotated again, in the same direction, so that his jaw rested on the ground twenty feet from Saara's feet, while his body rested quite comfortably with a half twist in it.

"There *are* dragons in the north," stated Saara, taking the chance on his species.

Window-sized nostrils dilated and the creature emitted a huge snort. The dry, woody smell thickened. "Dragons, perhaps, but not such as I," he stated, pique shading his voice. Suddenly the beast flipped to his feet and his neck arced above her, coiling like black smoke in the air (which had grown very hot). "Do I have a barrel like an ox's, wings like a plucked chicken's, breath like rotten eggs, and incrustations both dorsal and ventral?

"Furthermore, have I attacked you with inhospitable fury on the suspicion that you come to rob me of some possession—not that I have any, mind you?"

With a song of seven words Saara created a forty-foot wall of blue ice between the dragon and herself. It was an arduous spell, though quickly done, and her heart was left pounding.

The dragon watched, then casually he leaned over the wall and laced his fingers together. "Really, now, madam. Can you claim that any of the graceless creatures who inhabit their charred holes on the steppes have more than the slightest resemblance . . . I do not mean to sound egotistical, but I am no more like your European dragons than you are like the Emperor's monkey!"

That glittering head full of glittering teeth was now only a few feet from Saara's. She refused to be intimidated by it, and felt some display on her part was called for. "Get back," she snapped, raising a very small hand beneath the dragon's nose. "Get back, animal, or I'll freeze you, crop and craw, into black ice." The sunlight which poured through the cleft rocks trembled and shivered, as hot air met the magic of the north.

The amber eyes grew impossibly wide, protruding like those of a lapdog. "Ugh! Magic," he snorted, turning his head away as though he smelled something foul. The dragon retreated five steps, and then the sight of Saara's set face set him into peals of echoing laughter. Rocks tumbled in the distance.

"Is it my breath, little lady? Or is it the length of my eyeteeth that has swept your manners away like this? I assure you that had I any intention of doing you harm, I would not have waited to address you first."

As the creature backed, so did Saara, from sunlight into obscurity, until she stood at the turn in the passage wall. Suddenly she was around it and running in the darkness.

"Wait," came a bellow behind her. The walls vibrated. Then there was a sharper crashing, as forty feet of ice smashed like glass, followed by the sound of heavy chain being flung about.

"Wait, madam," the dragon called from behind her in the tunnel. "You take my witticism too much to heart!" Then the air rang and crashed as though an iron tower had fallen at Saara's feet. The dragon had reached the end of his chain.

But his voice rose once more. "I really *would* like to speak with someone. I am a long way from home, and it has been years . . ." he said, before the echoes died away.

Ahead was a speck of light. Gaspare was waiting there for her with Festilligambe, if the racket hadn't spooked the horse. Or Gaspare.

But Saara's bare feet slowed, and then stopped. She was half-embarrassed to have run from a creature that had offered no direct threat.

And then the way the beast had spoken. ". . . it has been years . . ."

Saara was not without sensibilities.

But dragons were sly, and talking dragons slyest of all. And *this* beast was in the service of the Liar himself, wasn't it? It was chained there, at least.

Chained. The Lapps chained neither their deer nor their dogs. Saara thought all chains despicable. She turned her face around. "Dragon," she called.

The reply was immediate. "Yes! I'm here." Then he added, "Of course I'm here; what a silly thing for me to say."

Was there a touch of bitterness in his words, of self-pity perhaps? But the Liar dealt in bitterness and self-pity quite frequently.

"Who chained you, dragon?" Saara shouted down the passage.

She heard a gusty, whistling sigh. "It was a nasty fellow with the very inappropriate name of Morning Star." Once again the creature seemed to have regained his composure, as well as his natural loquacity, for he added, "You see, madam, I was seeking after a book: a book which received high praise in certain circles. It is called *La Commedia Divina*, and it was written by an Italian. Perhaps you . . ."

"Never heard of it," replied Saara. "But then, I can't read."

"Ah. Well. I heard rumor of it as far away as Hunan Province, where news of events outside of Cathay hardly ever reaches. By report it contained great wisdom and excellent poetry, and . . . Well, I collect wisdom, you see . . ."

"You collect wisdom?" Saara murmured, but decided not to interrupt. The dragon continued.

"The book was divided into three sections, I believe. The first being Il Inferno; the second, Il Purgatorio; and the third, Il Paradisio." Another sigh-gale wrung through the darkness.

"I think I would have done better to seek after the third section first."

"No doubt." Saara had no idea what the creature was talking about. She wondered if dragons, too, grew senile.

"Why don't you break the chain?" she asked shortly.

There was a rustle. "My dear lady! I have been stuck in this inelegant place for a good number of years now. Don't you think I would have, if I could? It has some sort of disgusting . . ." the voice faded with embarrassment ". . . spell on it."

Saara lowered herself onto the smooth floor of the tunnel, facing toward the great voice and the smell of sandalwood. She sat, thought some, and picked her toenails. "It's not so big a chain," she ventured. "And I have some ability with spells. I think I could break it, if I spent a little time at it."

The rustling stopped. "Well, madam." She heard a self-conscious rustling.

"I swear to you it will not damage my pride at all to have you succeed where I have failed. Please try."

"What will you do if I let you go free?"

This time the silence was longer. "What will I do? Almost anything you should ask. Anything that does not conflict with any previous oath or commitment, of course."

The witch's feet were sore from too much stumbling against rock. She squeezed them as she considered.

Time had taught Saara to have little trust in elementals, let alone monsters. But she had to get by the creature.

And she was definitely not without sensibilities.

"How many years have you been here, again?"

He groaned. "Twenty-two."

"And what have you been eating or drinking in that time?"

"There is a small stream in the passage beyond. As for food—the last thing that passed my lips was a pig, roasted Hunan-style."

"Twenty years without eating?" There was incredulity in her voice. "How is it you are still alive?"

The beast gave a huge metallic shrug. "I am not a frantic mammal, you must understand. And I sleep a lot.

"But I tell you, madam, that twenty years without conversation has been a harder trial."

Saara rocked back and forth thoughtfully. "Well, I'm not one for long conversations at the best of times, dragon, and I don't know whether I believe a word you're saying."

A hollow thump through the darkness indicated it had dropped its long chin on the ground. "Why should you? The world is full of illusion," it agreed somberly.

Saara approached the creature, stepping from darkness into half-light. It lay extended on its side and held one paw—hand, really, with four spidery fingers and a thumb—in the other, flexing it gingerly. From a dull iron manacle on its wrist stretched the heavy chain.

"One would think," it said to Saara waspishly, "that twenty years would teach me the limits of this thing."

"One would think," she agreed. The dragon massaged its wrist.

Saara, standing beside a circlet of iron as large as a hip bath, cleared her throat. "How do I know, dragon, that you won't turn around and eat me as soon as I release you?"

The gold eyes shone with more light than the reflected sun on the stone of the passage seemed to allow. They regarded her with a shade of amusement. "You don't, of course. Just as I have no security that you won't get it into your head to freeze me into a lump of ice. But if words carry any weight with your people (and I seem to remember they do), then it is enough that I say I will not. What is more, I tell you I have not eaten a human creature for approximately five hundred years."

Saara found this statement very interesting, as possibly the dragon intended that she would. It implied that the beast was more than five hundred, of course. (Unless it was a way of saying it had never eaten a human, but then why not just say so?) It also implied some sort of monumental change in the dragon's habit. It positively invited questions.

But Saara refused to ask them. "But perhaps you haven't been this hungry for five hundred years."

The great beast yawned. "I was hungrier ten years ago than I am now. But let's adopt a pleasanter subject, shall we?

"Such as yourself, madam: What necessity brings you to this dreadful, boring place, and how might I be of use to you?"

Saara sat on a chain link. "You be of use to me? I thought it was the other way around."

The dragon's glorious face was turned to Saara, and between the light of his eyes and the heat of his breath, it was like sitting under a desert sun. "Nothing runs in one direction only except water, and that (I'm told) only in its lesser beds.

"I am the Black Dragon," the creature announced, with a strange sort of dignity. "And though you see me at my disadvantage, I assure you that there is little born of earth which is older, or which is my equal in strength." And with that the dragon turned its head to the darkness and gave a short, hollow laugh.

Saara raised one eyebrow. "Well, dragon, I am fairly old

and fairly strong and not tied up at all." And then, with a sudden impulse of trust, she added, "And I'm on my way to the Liar's Hall of Four Windows, to find and rescue the Chief of Eagles, who has been imprisoned by the wicked one."

The dragon started upright. Great writhing coils slammed against the roof of the passage. Its jaw hung open.

The creature hissed like a boiler giving way. "You are what?"

Saara repeated, condensing a long story as best she could. As she spoke the light of the dragon's eyes flickered, and amber rays moved like fish over the walls of stone. The beast itself did not move a muscle.

But when she was finished, it spoke. "This Chief of Eagles, then, is the same the Hebrews call Rafayl, and the Latins Raphael? He is a teacher?"

"Of music," stipulated Saara.

The dragon yawned. "There is only one Teaching.

"I have heard of this person, Raphael."

Then the dragon drummed his fingers against the stone floor, making thunder. He looked neither at Saara nor at anything else in the long gray tunnel, and the light of his eyes faded. At last he said, very calmly, "To hoard or conceal the Teaching is a great crime. Perhaps the greatest."

"To keep a person's spirit imprisoned is greater," she said boldly.

"One and the same."

"Then you will let us go by?"

The long head drew very close to Saara's and the yellow eyes kindled again. "Free me."

Saara felt the beast's will beating down on hers, but there was no magic in it, nor any compulsion she could not resist. Her desire to break the dragon's chain was her own, sprung of pity and nursed by her hatred for confinement of all sorts. She spared one moment's thought to Gaspare, helpless and unaware at the cavern's mouth, and then she put her hands to the cold iron.

But Saara had underestimated the Piedmontese. Gaspare was at that moment inching forward on his hands and knees through what was to him unbroken blackness, cursing as he went. He had heard voices, and he had heard hissing, and he had felt shocks in the earth itself.

He was coming after Saara.

"Too late," muttered the youth as he went. "Too little and too late, may San Gabriele boot me in the behind, but I am coming. No man, woman, or devil may call Gaspare the Lutenist a coward."

That no one save Gaspare the Lutenist had called Gaspare a coward did not occur to the redhead. He comforted himself with the knowledge that he had shown greater bravery than that of the horse, which had bolted at the first ominous crash from within. Carrying all belongings with it. All save the lute, of course, which Gaspare now bore slung under his belly. It banged his hipbone lightly with every jar.

No doubt it was the Devil himself ahead, ensconced amid the quenchless coals. No doubt Saara was long since reduced to a cinder. No doubt Gaspare's own defiance would last as long as it took for a moth to char itself in a candle.

Too little and too late.

Gaspare thought to himself of what it meant to live, and to die. Slowly he stood. He unwrapped his instrument. He walked forward, playing as he went. It was what Delstrego would have done.

From time to time he bounced off the passage walls.

The dragon froze at the sound. He (Saara had ascertained it was a he) lifted his ornamented head. "What *is* that?"

"That is Gaspare," replied the witch calmly. "Playing the lute."

He rumbled deep in his long throat. "I have never heard the like."

Saara sighed. "He is very progressive."

Gaspare thought his eyes were acting up when the faint amber swirls started to play over the passage walls. But he put one hand out and what appeared to be the wall *was* the wall, so he blinked and walked on.

In the center of the yellow light was a shadow, a shadow that grew and came on, with a vague metallic rustling. The shadow grew to be that of the Lady Saara, surrounded by a halo of gold light.

Lute strings faded to silence. "My lady," whispered Gaspare. "Are you in heaven or hell?"

At that moment the halo lifted above the woman, and Gaspare looked up into a shining, awful face.

"Christ!" he gasped, and then his tongue swelled to fill his mouth. His right hand slipped over his open strings with gentle dissonance.

CHAPTER 6

The street hawkers, heard faintly in the distance, called their wares in two languages, or three, if the patois of the Muwalladun was considered. All the flies of Granada droned, and the Sierra Nevada made a jagged rip in the horizon. Hakiim led his customer along a street baked hard as tiles by the sun.

The latter fellow was a man of imposing size and girth, dressed according to Moorish custom in white. Behind him came another, a small person, heavily veiled, who tended to bounce as she walked, after the manner of small dogs.

"Black?" asked the customer, not for the first time. "Black as ink?"

"Black as the abyss," replied Hakiim, and he said no more. It was his custom to maintain dignified silence before such customers as he thought might thereby be impressed. And there was something not altogether orthodox about this potential customer: a shade of hazel about the eyes, perhaps, or a slight fault in speech. Perhaps a converted Christian, or a parvenu from Egypt come to Granada to hide his origin.

Whatever, Hakiim's instincts led him to adopt a haughty attitude and Hakiim's instincts were rarely wrong.

"I've heard that the blacker a girl is, the sounder she is, and the better nurse she makes," remarked the man, as he followed Hakiim with a heavy, rolling step.

"It could well be true," the Moor replied, still without great enthusiasm.

The small person who came behind tittered brightly.

"My little wife had a black nurse as a child. Now that she is . . . now that we are . . . we thought . . ."

Hakiim smiled to himself. Soon, if he kept his mouth

shut, the fellow would reveal every fact and foible of his
household. The Moor did not care, nor was he particularly
disturbed by the idea of the ferocious Djoura as a baby's
dry nurse.

The black's moods were various. Perhaps today she'd
choose to exhibit cold pride instead of homicidal fury. Let
the man look at her and decide; his family's safety was then
his business.

They turned into a door in the blank white wall of a
house: a fine, expensive house, rented by Hakiim for the
express purpose of setting Djoura to the best advantage.
They passed through to the garden courtyard, where
among oranges and tiny cypress the black woman sat,
wearing robes of white cotton, brand-new.

In the corner sat the idiot eunuch, who had been
commanded to sit still, and who obeyed like a dog. The
Spaniard was there, too, crouched unobtrusively in a
corner where the welts on his face would not be visible.
The welts had come from Djoura, as a result of the
merchants' abortive efforts to feed the woman a sedative
dose of kif.

But no such drug seemed necessary, for the black Berber
gave the approaching party only the most demure of
glances before lowering her shy head and lacing her hands
together on her lap.

Hakiim approached. He tentatively extended one hand
which was neither bit, clawed, nor spat at. He lifted the
slave's chin for inspection. She smiled.

"This is Djoura," he said. A shade of question crept into
his voice.

He had expected *some* trouble. He had been prepared
with discipline, explanations of previous ill-treatment,
promises of amendment, offers of help in training . . . He
had set up this entire situation—house, clothing, sale by
private treaty—as an attempt to gloss over Djoura's mani-
acal temper.

What was in the girl's head, to go suddenly all meek
and winsome? (And didn't she look handsome, with her
face not twisted into a snarl?) Hakiim had the sudden wish
he'd stated a higher price.

The customer stepped forward. He gazed down at the
woman from over his white-cased paunch. "Girl," he

pronounced, "I am Rashiid ben Rashiid. I am looking for
an attendant for my youngest wife and a dry nurse for the
baby that is coming. Would you be a good one?"

Djoura batted her curly lashes and smiled at the
ground. Then she smiled at the little veiled face that
peeped around Rashiid ben Rashiid's bulk. She wiggled
from one side of the seat to the other in an agony of
shyness. "I think we would," she mumbled into her lap.

Rashiid liked the girl's attitude. He also liked her looks.
And it occurred to him that the Prophet had ordained that
a man might have four wives, while Rashiid (comfortably
situated as he was) had only two.

No need to think further about that now, however. Now
there was the baby to consider: perhaps his first son. It was
enough that this woman be strong and biddable. Later,
when he was ready to brave his present bride's pique, and
that of her family, of course . . .

But by what strange custom did the Nubian refer to her
lowly self in the plural?

Rashiid ben Rashiid laughed tolerantly. "We, little one?
Are you twins, perhaps?"

A giggle and a scuff of the ground with one sandaled
foot. "No. My brother and I do not look alike."

Hakiim felt his ears prick up. In fact, it seemed those
organs were moving to the top of his head through
amazement. He opened his mouth to contradict the girl—
to assure Rashiid that there was no brother in the case—
when Djoura crooked her finger and the blond eunuch
trotted over.

Obedient, like a dog.

Rashiid stared at Raphael, who returned a blue gaze
free from either shyness or challenge. Then the large man
seemed to puff out larger. He gave out heavy brays of
laughter.

"Merchant of women, what is this?" he gasped, when
he could. "There was no talk of a . . . a brother!"

Hakiim shook his head blankly. "I have no idea. The
yellow-head is of course no relation at all to her, and . . ."

A voice in the corner spoke. "They go well together,"
said Perfecto. "In contrast. Two for the price of one."

Hakiim shot a look of fury at his partner. It was not
customary for Perfecto to speak in the marketplace; he was
not a convincing salesman and his native accent was

strong. In dealing with customers of quality it was the Spaniard's business to keep his mouth shut.

And this . . . this bizarre attempt to get rid of the idiot by making him part of a package with Hakiim's prize discovery . . .

But Djoura took Raphael by the hand, and seeming to gather together slow reserves of courage, smiled into Rashiid's glowering face.

"This is my brother Pinkie, master. He is not a man but—you know—a boy. He is a good worker and does everything I say."

Rashiid found his annoyance melting in this girl's black velvet gaze. "I don't need a boy," he stated, masking confusion with gruffness.

Djoura seemed to wilt, and she gave a long sigh. "Without my brother," she said tremulously, "I must surely languish. Without Pinkie I think I will die." .

Hearing no response, she continued in louder tones. "Without Pinkie I will throw myself into the ocean, I guess. Without Pinkie I will throw . . ."

Hakiim cut her off, feeling her threats were about to extend from suicide to murder. "Don't be silly, Djoura. You've only just met the creature this week!"

Then he turned to Rashiid. "The eunuch, when we first got him, was sick, and Djoura nursed him back to health. I guess they developed some attachment, but it's surely nothing that cannot be forgotten in a few days . . ."

While Hakiim thus held his customer's attention and Djoura watched them with a gambler's blank-faced intensity, the small person stepped out from behind her husband to look at Raphael. Surreptitiously, she pulled aside her veil.

She had thick hair hennaed auburn, and eyes like a doe deer. She was no more than fifteen, and she stared at the blond as though he were something wrought in gold.

Her name was Ama, and as she met Raphael's eyes she gave out a little gasp. She herself wasn't sure what it was she found there, whether pity, understanding, or sheer stainless beauty, but from that moment she felt—like Djoura—that without Raphael she would surely die.

Rashiid was explaining very carefully to Hakiim that it was not that he could not afford either to buy or to keep a eunuch, but rather that his family was small enough that he had no need for a boy, when the small person tapped him on the elbow and stood on tiptoe to whisper something in his ear.

Rashiid accepted the interruption with the exaggerated patience of a man who is humoring a pregnant wife. He listened to Ama's excited whispering.

"That much? You want her how much?"

"Both of them," chirped Ama. "I don't want her to be unhappy."

Rashiid stole a glance toward Raphael, whose hand was in Djoura's, and who watched the interchange with disinterested attention. "Dearest swallow," the householder said, patting his wife on the head, "although your smallest word is law to me, here we must be reasonable. He will eat like a horse!"

"I will sell my jewelry," offered Ama, a little wildly. "My amber necklace, that my uncle gave me, and the gold chains. They are mine, and that will feed him—I mean them—for a long time. Oh, my husband, do buy them."

Hakiim knew enough to back away, lest his own persuasion, added to the woman's, drive his customer to rebellion. Instead the Moor shot a glance at his partner, a glance imbued with all the betrayed fury he felt toward Perfecto. But the expression the Spaniard returned him turned Hakiim's anger into something like fear.

In an effort to save face, Rashiid turned on Raphael. "Well, boy," he demanded. "Why should I buy you? What are you good for?"

Hakiim began, "I'm sorry, sir, but the boy is unfortunately . . ."

But Djoura forestalled him. Squeezing Raphael's hand with desperation, she hissed, "Tell him, Pinkie. Tell him what a good boy you are!"

Raphael lifted his eyes to Rashiid. "I can play the lute," he said in faultless Arabic. "Either *al ud* or the lute of Europe. I can also make music with the Spanish chitarre, the harp, and most other stringed instruments. Winds I have not played so often, nor drums, but I believe I could manage them. I can teach others the mechanics of music. And I can sing.

"There are other useful skills I could learn, probably, but as of yet I haven't had the opportunity." The perfect fair brow lowered as Raphael considered the limitations of the flesh.

Rashiid listened to this calmly stated catalogue of accomplishments with some surprise, for he had assumed that any creature which the slave merchants tried to lump into another sale was worthless. But the customer's feelings were nothing compared to those of Hakiim. Had his mule stood on its hind legs and begun the call to prayer, the Moor could not have been more dumbfounded than at hearing the eunuch talk.

Perfecto, too, was astonished, but his surprise was less pure than that of the Moor, and Raphael's sudden display of intelligence awoke all the Spaniard's nightmares.

"Well, then," Rashiid said equably. "I have not been suffering for lack of a musician any more than for a harem attendant, but if he comes free and has the brain to learn what he is taught . . ."

He snapped his fingers in the air. "Bring the boy a lute."

Hakiim sat in red-faced silence as he listened to Raphael's playing. He reviewed in his mind all the stages of his acquaintance with the blond eunuch, and cursed himself for having at every moment mistaken illness and fear for idiocy.

Why had he never (after the first disgusting day) attempted to talk with the fellow, depending instead on Djoura's word that he was an untrainable idiot? It was always the Moor's wise habit to find the best and most salable skill a slave possessed and to emphasize it, and here he had been hearing the boy sing sweetly (Berber songs, among other unlikely musics) these two weeks and had assumed it was no more than parrot mime.

He shot a glance at Djoura, author of this deceit, but the black sat with her maidenly eyes on the ground, hands folded on her lap. Surely the woman had done it on purpose, but to what end? Had she fallen in love with the stinking creature, after washing the gore and dung from him, and determined that they be sold together?

Well, why not—women did become attached to eunuchs, and evidently there was much more to the blond than had appeared. Hakiim began to wonder how much more; he had never yet seen the fellow undressed. His face was hairless enough, having less mustache than many women, but with certain blonds that meant nothing.

What an error, if they had been traveling with a buck

goat among all his does, instead of a wether! But remedial, of course. Granada was full of barber-surgeons. Hakiim determined to strip the fellow immediately after Djoura was sold off. His eyes roved from the black's to the Spaniard's.

Perfecto, too, refused to meet Hakiim's gaze, staring instead at the eunuch with such an odd combination of enmity and fear that once more Hakiim wondered how the Spaniard had come by him.

Most males in the slave markets were battle captives whose friends or relatives had denied ransom. These were chancy slaves, of course, since they might at any moment claim Islam, and all who took that yoke were supposedly free of all others. A born slave, castrated in childhood, was a different story. The Saqalibah, for instance . . .

But this one hadn't the manner of the Saqalibah.

If the boy was not an idiot (and perhaps not a eunuch), then possibly he was not a slave either. Not legally, at least. Hakiim thought furiously. He wanted no trouble, either with the law of Granada, nor with a kidnapped man's friends.

Raphael, meanwhile, was so happy he had forgotten both where and what he was. He bounced back and forth between the ancient, small-bowled *liuto* that had been borrowed for him, and the beautiful *ud* which belonged to the dusky, somewhat unclean fellow from the bazaar who stood now shifting from foot to foot at the courtyard door. He played a Spagnoletta on the European instrument, then lest the ud be jealous, he improvised upon it a long fantasy which shifted through three classical Arabic scales. The lute spattered like rainfall. The fretless ud sang like a man.

The small wife of Rashiid ben Rashiid cried delighted tears into her veil, while Djoura, equally transfixed by the art of Raphael, was filled with an inchoate pride.

Hakiim thought it time to interrupt. "Enough, Pinkie. You play very nicely, but the gentleman has already told us he has no use for a musician."

Rashiid cleared his throat and turned his bulk toward the slender Moor. "That is not precisely what I said, merchant. I said if he is willing to do other work as well, and as he has been offered free, I would feel it only Allah's will that I give him a home."

Within moments of Raphael's picking up the ud,

Hakiim had evolved an estimate of his value which was roughly three times the value of Djoura. With this in mind he replied, "Your charity does you great credit, ben Rashiid, but there is no need. A good caretaker does not try to sell a horse to a man who wants a camel, nor a camel to a man whose need is for a goat."

Rashiid's deep hazel eyes had a hot glow in them, like those of a man who has been allowed to handle a ruby and whose lust is thereby awakened. Hakiim knew that look well, for it was his goal to produce it in every customer with whom he dealt.

But though it seemed Rashiid was willing to pay full asking price for Djoura, that would not half compensate Hakiim for throwing away the musician. Besides, there were some questions to be asked about that one. Hakiim turned to his partner quite calmly and scratched his left ear, a signal between them which had always meant "back out of this sale."

Perfecto scarcely looked at him. Instead the Spaniard rested his eyes on emptiness as he said quite formally, "We have offered the gentleman a sale and he has accepted."

Now they were bound. Hakiim's lips moved in a curse. "We have offered," indeed! *He* had offered, and now Hakiim was out a large sum of money which might have done much to ease the last few weeks' headaches and speed him on his homeward voyage.

While Hakiim sat with angry eyes averted from the company, regretting monies he had only contemplated having for the past five minutes, Rashiid chuckled complacently and Ama danced her success.

She was a charming little thing and moved her feet most cleverly, despite the handicap of her condition, until she spun around to come face-to-face with the black slave she had just purchased, and whose existence she had completely forgotten.

There was something in the set of that face that called an end to the girl's capers. She backed slowly into the shadow of her husband once more, and peered instead with large eyes out at Raphael.

"I am your mistress. My name is Ama," said the very small and young person, and then with no pause she flipped around on her stool to present the back of her sleek head. "Do you like the way my new maid has done my hair?"

It was a complex arrangement of many little braids which had been then woven together in drooping swags. Gold coins hung at intervals, gleaming against the dark mass.

Raphael smiled at her, thinking that if Ama represented the circumstances of his life as it would be, it would be quite endurable. "I like the style," he answered. "It looks like this . . ." and his fingers echoed the complexity of Ama's hair on the strings of al ud.

"I'm not sure I do." Ama swiveled back, brisk as a sparrow on a branch. "She pulls tight—and the way she looks right *at* me! She is a bold woman. Maybe Nubians are always bold women. My nurse wasn't, though. She was nice.

"The coins are her idea. I had to make holes in the middle of them, so I guess they can't be spent anymore. Djoura said copper, but gold is always better, don't you think?" Her eyes (not bird eyes, soft almond eyes) flitted briefly to Raphael.

"Your hair is even fairer than gold: not like copper at all. So strange! What did you say your name was?"

All this was said very rapidly, as Ama's quick, darting eye looked here, there, and everywhere around the mimosa trees and over the fish pool, resting at last on the musician she had come to bother.

His blue eyes (which Ama thought even stranger than his yellow hair) rose to hers. Had they not been so large, perfect, and deep blue, the little lady would probably not have given him time to answer her question; she rarely felt the need of answers.

But as it was, she felt quite suddenly tongue-tied as he spoke. "I don't think I told you. My name is Raphael."

Ama fitted the name in her mouth as though it could be tasted. "Raphael! Raphael! What a wonderful name. But Djoura called you something else—less wonderful. What was it?"

"Pinkie," Raphael admitted. "To Djoura I am Pinkie."

Ama fingered the red clay beads that bound the ends of her braids. Her sweet child's brow pulled down. "I don't like that. You should have a name as beautiful as you are. I will make her call you Raphael, I think." Then Ama went off into a moment's brown study.

"Or I will have my husband, Rashiid ben Rashiid, make her do it. He likes Djoura, I think. I don't think I do. Do you?"

Raphael opened his mouth to reply, but it was not necessary, for Ama went on, "It is funny, isn't it, that my husband's name is Rashiid ben Rashiid, when his father's name is Pablo? He comes to visit us sometimes and then they speak Spanish. I can speak a little Spanish: Fatima's maid taught me. Until Rashiid bought Djoura I didn't have a maid. Because I am the second wife. In fact, I was almost Fatima's maid, until I got—until we knew I was going to have a baby. That made almost ALL the difference. Now, Fatima might as well be MY maid—but don't tell her I said so or she'll pull my hair for me!

"Sometimes I say bad things in Spanish to surprise the servants. Then I can pretend I didn't understand what I said. I do, of course. Don't tell anybody. Do you speak Spanish?"

In the time it took to draw the next lungful of air, Ama forgot what she had been saying. "Play for me."

Raphael had been attempting to play ever since Ama had joined him on the bench by the fish pool. Now he was given at least a moment to start. The wooden instrument keened under his fingers. He sang, and the words went:

My father is a sparrow in the leaves, in the tangle of leaves.
I hear him in the winter in the bare trees. He calls me.
But I—I have forgotten the language of flight.

By dint of great effort, Ama stayed quiet so far. Then she interrupted. "That sounds classical. It doesn't rhyme. I know what it means, though, because I listen to songs a lot. When you say your father is a sparrow you mean you don't have a father, or that he does not admit to you. And when you say you don't remember how to fly, you mean you are a slave."

Raphael looked startled. His left eyebrow shot up, and it seemed he was about to contradict his young mistress. But instead he replied, "Everyone must take his own meaning from a song, or it would not be a song."

"But I'm glad you are a slave," continued Ama, after pausing to examine his answer and finally throwing it away as a bird will throw away a prize it finds inedible.

"I'm especially glad you are a . . . a boy, and not a man. Or else I would not be able to sit here with you with my veil off and show you my hair. With men, everything is all very difficult. They are strange beasts—men, don't you think? All they think about is leaping on you like a bull on a cow—or I have never seen a bull and a cow, but I'm told it is the same. And so we have to stay hidden all our lives, lest we be disgraced.

"Disgraced!" she repeated, frowning solemnly and dabbling one pretty toe in the water.

"Rashiid, my husband, of course, is not like that. Not exactly like that. He is almost human. But all *that*, you know, is not very much fun." Ama's eyes roved uncertainly from a bronze-backed carp to Raphael's attentive face. "Is it?"

Raphael laid the ud in his lap. He did not pretend to misunderstand her. "I do not know," he replied seriously. "About men with women." Ama snickered.

"Of course you don't."

Her slave's expression did not lighten. "But as life comes from Allah, every part of it must have some beauty in it."

Ama gave a tiny sniff. "Don't talk like a book!"

Then, in the next moment, a spark appeared in her brown eyes. Assuring herself that the garden court was empty except for Raphael and herself, she said, "Let me sit on your lap."

Dutifully the slave put his instrument aside, and little Ama snuggled up to him. Raphael stroked her as one would stroke a cat, and suddenly, for no perceivable reason, he laughed out loud.

Justly he could call himself Rashiid ben Rashiid, for he was a self-made man, come far from his father's mule stud. He had left Granada early, having a dislike for livestock and mules in particular, and made his money in lower Egypt, coming home with a regular income and a new name. Once home he bought a house and planted orange trees (whose fruit was forbidden by law to the infidel) everywhere. But Rashiid had not completely buried Paolo, son of Pablo. For one thing Pablo himself still lived, and for another it was much more profitable to do business with the *giaour*—the Christians. They were less likely to complain to the Hajib when affairs went badly. Therefore the household of Rashiid lived by compromise.

There was a featureless white wall with tile eaves peeping over, which in size suggested a building of Moorish type—facing inward over its central court—and palatial dimension. This was an illusion, however, for most of what was visible from the street was the wall of the enclosed garden, decked out to look like house frontage, with arches, doorways, and little stone steps. The house itself, while sizable, sat huddled in one corner of the lot, revealing its peasant origins in every squat line.

To make up for the limits of the house proper, the garden was scattered with little round and thatched outbuildings which resembled mushrooms springing from the irrigated soil. These, though necessary, looked terribly native.

There were no separate women's quarters, because there was no room for such, and also because Granada (being half Christian) tended to be lax in the observance of the Islamic proprieties. But because Rashiid ben Rashiid did not want to be known as lax in observance, it was necessary for his wives to pretend occasionally that they were not about when they *were* about. For this purpose were maintained certain hidey-holes in various parts of the house to which they could escape in the event of orthodox visitors.

These provisions made life a bit difficult for Fatima and Ama, not to mention the Spanish maids. But the two Islamic women consoled themselves with the knowledge that though they were married to a convert, the very inconvenience they were put to proved that they themselves were still persons of quality.

Djoura (though possessing properties of an entirely different nature) put the closets into similar use. She would retire to them and pretend she was not there, especially when she heard Ama's piping, querulous call. There was one retreat at the end of one of the inside walls of the house which she preferred, for it had a rough, dimpled window through which she could see everything within the walls, from the bondsmen's barrack (very small) to the stable which housed Rashiid's one horse: an immaculately kept Egyptian gray which he never rode. Between these two outposts lay the garden itself, where the orange trees bloomed and perfumed vines twined around the fish pond. This little body of water was perfectly round and sat like a pockmark in the dusty skin of the garden. It had no natural source and had to be topped off daily with water brought in on donkeys (never mules).

It was there that Djoura's eyes were bent, as her chin rested on the thumb side of her fist, which pressed in turn on the clay windowsill. The coins above her forehead rustled like leaves in the day's airs. The white muslin costume which had become Djoura so well had somehow disappeared from the wash, and she was back to wearing her traditional fusty black. With stony, set face she watched Raphael dandle his little mistress on his lap.

Ama was an irritation: a spoiled little fluttering thing and a stumbling block toward certain long-range goals. It was part Djoura's intention to gain a reputation for trust and biddability, and to that end she acted her role before Rashiid very effectively.

Her very contempt for the man—pompous, damp, and fleshy as he was—lent her zest for the part, and the knowledge that he desired her lent her confidence. Yet Rashiid's lust was a danger, too, which Djoura did not underestimate. He was in all ways disgusting.

Ama—curious and willful as she was—could not be dismissed with the same sniff and a sneer. The little woman was ubiquitous, and enough like the black Berber in mind that she could not be readily cozened. Djoura could not feel contempt for Ama. But she could hate her. And she could be jealous.

Look at the little chicken, bouncing on Pinkie's knee—bold as a child on an aged donkey. Wouldn't she get a big surprise if she could see the fellow without his trousers. If she kept behaving so shamelessly, she might get a surprise some day: every man had his limits.

Even Pinkie. Djoura bit her lip, for Pinkie worried her more than Ama did: more than anything else did in this place of rich food and sloth. Ever since she realized that the fellow was no more a half-wit than a eunuch, her concern for him had grown heavier and heavier.

More and more she doubted he was a Berber at all, despite his knowledge of both tongue and music. He sang other songs besides the desert chants, with what seemed to Djoura equal facility: songs in Spanish and songs in languages of which the woman knew not even the name. And the placidity with which he had sunk into this life of captivity was dreadful. What Berber could seem so content wearing the iron collar?

Djoura had never asked Pinkie directly where he had been born or who his people were; first, because it was rare she found the time and privacy for such conversation, and secondly, because she didn't like such questions herself. When the woman closed her eyes at night she would still often see her father's mare scrabbling up the mountain trail toward camp, dragging his headless body by one stirrup. Behind the horse had come the riders of the Bedouin Arif Yusuf, following the bloody trace through the sand.

And then Djoura would be visited by an image of her mother, with veil thrown back, swinging a grass scythe in deadly circles around her head, wearing an arrow through her cheek like an ornament.

A man born a slave had shame in his past. A man enslaved had defeat. It was never good to ask. Yet as Djoura watched Fatima (fat, harmless Fatima, whom even Djoura could not dislike) come puffing out of the middle door of the main house, gesticulating and babbling to Ama in Spanish, she knew she would have to make more certain of Pinkie—since they were going to escape together.

Evidently the first wife didn't like Ama's antics any more than Djoura did, for the two of them were at it now, their shrill, staccato words falling like a shower of stones on the garden.

And here was Pinkie, sent off to the house with a flea in his ear. Now was both time and opportunity. "Hsst! Pinkie!" she called out the window.

He approached, his odd, narrow-featured (to Djoura) face looking as mild as if no one had ever raised her voice to him in his life. "Get in here," she hissed, backing from the rough clay opening.

"Through the window?" the blond asked, and in reply Djoura snatched his hand and pulled him over the sill. He rose from the floor, looking only slightly surprised.

"I didn't want anyone to see us together," she explained. "Enough talk goes on already, you can believe!"

Then her voice roughened and she pointed her index finger at him. "You listen to me, Pinkie, when I tell you to leave that nasty little thing alone, if you value your future."

His eyebrows (and even Djoura had to admit that Pinkie had fine eyebrows) shot up. "Ama? Do you mean . . ."

"I mean the baby girl who calls herself my mistress, Pinkie. If Rashiid (Allah shrivel his big belly) finds out there's nothing but a pair of cotton trousers between his favorite wife and a man's . . . whatever . . . you'll soon be no more than you claim to be!"

His blue eyes shifted uncertainly. "Djoura, what do you mean by what I 'claim to be'?"

Djoura struck her palm against her forehead. "I think you're simple after all, Pinkie. A boy, is what you seem to be!"

"A boy?" he echoed, looking down at his long legs and well knit body.

"A permanent boy. A eunuch," Djoura hissed with ferocity.

Understanding awoke for Raphael. "They think I'm a eunuch? Why? Nobody asked me. Nobody even looked."

She blinked. "Woodenhead! I made sure they didn't! I spent the last week standing in between you and discovery. You can bet I told that oily Hakiim you'd lost your bollocks! Made fun of you for it, too. And I didn't stop flirting with this hog-boweled Rashiid until we were out onto the street."

"Why?" he pressed, as mildly as ever.

Djoura sat herself down on the only stool in the room. "First of all," she pronounced very slowly. "Those two dealt in boys—eunuchs. If you hadn't been one before, you would have been as soon as they found out. And even if they didn't for some reason, no one would buy you entire unless they wanted to put you in a mine somewhere, or out in a field with iron burning your neck and wrist.

"No one. *No one* would have bought you and I together had they known you were entire!"

Two small lines of worry appeared between Raphael's eyes. "But Rashiid has bought me already. If he thinks I am a eunuch, he is wrong, and perhaps I should tell him so."

Djoura hushed him and looked wildly around. "Never! You must never tell anyone or let them know. Not if you want to escape the knife!"

"That is very awkward," Raphael said simply. He laced

his fingers over his knee and sat with his back against the wall. "It is like a lie."

"Hah!" She swallowed a laugh. "Nothing is a lie, if it helps a Berber win back her freedom!"

"It will help you win back your freedom if I let them believe I am a eunuch?"

She nodded decisively. "And yours too."

A look of pain and fatigue touched his fair features and he looked away from her face. In that moment Djoura became satisfied that Raphael, too, remembered freedom. "But he does not believe me," whispered Djoura to herself. "He does not believe I can arrange it." For a moment her own doubts knocked. But the Berber stiffened her jaw, and her ebony hand reached out and touched his.

"Pinkie," she said gently. "You must trust me. I am your only friend."

Raphael looked quickly up. His hand reached down to the hem of his trousers and he felt something that had been inserted between the stitches. "You *are* my dear friend, Djoura, but I have another."

The woman snorted. "Who's the other, then. Ama?"

Raphael's face lit softly. He held a pebble in his hand. "No. I meant someone I have known a while. His name is Damiano."

This was new. Djoura blinked at the news before replying, "And where is Damiano? Where was he, that he was not there to help you when all the sense was beaten out of you and you were sold to a crab louse like Perfecto? I don't call that much of a friend who—"

For the first time, Raphael interrupted Djoura. "He does not live anywhere. He is with Allah. And yet he is a great help to me.

"He gave me this." Raphael proffered the pebble reluctantly, as though afraid she would dash it out of his hand.

Djoura, examining the thing in the half-light which came in through the irregular window, recognized it as the pebble Pinkie had refused to take out of his mouth that first morning in the hills, and had carried all that day locked in his battered hand.

Carefully, she gave it back to him. "Not much of a gift," she said gruffly, but despite her words she was touched.

She let out her breath in what was intended to be a snort, but turned out a rather wistful sigh.

"Who whipped you like that, Pinkie? Your old master?"

He shook his head. "It was my brother who commanded it done. We are old enemies." And after a moment's quiet reflection, Raphael added, "I don't think it is over between us: my brother and I."

"Ah?" This was interesting. It opened up new images of Pinkie. Poor men had less reason to attack their brothers than did great ones. If he were not such a good musician, Djoura might suspect her pale friend of being wellborn. "Your brother betrayed you? Then you had no master, before?"

Raphael's smile was private and gentle. It called out an answering one from her. "None save Allah."

Djoura giggled and placed her head close to his. "'There *is* no master save Allah . . .' We understand that, you and I!"

"So!" The deep voice from the doorway startled them both. "You would teach our boy the *sa'lad:* the statement of faith?"

It was Rashiid himself, and he did not look particularly happy at the words he had half heard. He glowered down at Raphael's head. "Ama tells me your name is actually not Pinkie but Raphael."

The blond rose smoothly. "Yes, that is true."

Djoura blinked in surprise. Having once decided to call her charge Pinkie, it had never occurred to her to ask if he had another name.

Rashiid did not like the response. He felt patronized, and obscurely threatened. In fact, there was something about Raphael that had begun to bother Rashiid: the unclean smoothness of his cheek, perhaps, or the fact that his pretty face stood at man's height and stared at him with mannish directness. Rashiid—or rather Paolo, son of Pablo—was not used to eunuchs, and he did not like standing too close to this ambiguous creature. But it was up to Rashiid to set an example here, in the presence of the girl, so his hand flicked out. "You say, 'Yes, *master*. It is true, *master*."

Raphael's tongue touched a bleeding lip. "Yes, master. It is true, master."

"And I want you to remember, boy: you are no battle

captive, you are Saqalibah. You can say the sa'lad until you are hoarse and you will still be Saqalibah."

"Yes, master," said Raphael very mildly, but his eyes were as unafraid as those of a cat. Those eyes made Rashiid shift from foot to foot.

"You could bow to me, also," the householder growled sullenly. "Never hurts."

Then Rashiid cleared his throat. "I came to tell you that I'm giving a dinner tonight for some very important people. The highest quality, from Tunis, so bring the ud, not the lute.

"And—" Rashiid looked from side to side. He didn't know quite what he wanted to say. How did you ask a slave to be cooperative without showing weakness? He hated to show weakness.

"And don't make me ashamed of you," he concluded lamely.

"I will try not to, master," replied Raphael, and he bowed. Rashiid paraded out.

Djoura touched Raphael's damaged lip. "Raphael? That is your true name?" He nodded.

"That's a silly name, especially for a pink fellow like you." The black's hand was gentle, but her face was as hard as a carving in onyx. "Once we are free," she whispered as she dabbed at his cut with her sleeve, "we will come back and kill that one."

"Now *that* is silly," returned Raphael.

The sea was Hakiim's hope; once he reached the water, temperatures would be temperate and the air moist. But the sea was a very long way away, many days by muleback. Heat had crumpled the airs of Granada so that no line could be discerned between earth and sky, and the air itself smelled like ashes. The Moor had one hand on his mule's girth strap, and was peering into the high distance when Perfecto addressed him.

"You think I'm crazy, no doubt," grunted the round-faced Spaniard. "You must think I'm crazy, after the way I acted with the eunuch."

But Hakiim glanced at his partner's expression, and for the first time in weeks he tended to believe that the man was *not* crazy, for this hangdog attitude was every inch the old Perfecto. The black glint was gone from his small eyes and his fat-shrouded jaw no longer clenched and unclenched.

"I never thought you were crazy," answered Hakiim, with more regard for the amenities than for the truth. "I merely thought you . . . ill-advised."

Silence fell, impossible for the Moor to endure. "It seemed that first you wanted too much for the eunuch, and then, as soon as he was found to be of value, too little. That's all.

"But it is done, and no great loss." He raised his foot to the round wooden stirrup.

Perfecto put one hand on Hakiim's shoulder. "Old friend, I can explain."

Hakiim smiled uncertainly. He no longer wanted explanations, but to be out in the clean air, away from Perfecto and Granada both. "I am to meet a troop of *fursan* outside the Alhambra at noon. They will let me ride with them all the way down to the sea, but I must not be late."

Hakiim's sleek and restive mule pawed the desiccated earth with his hoof. In reply Perfecto thrust one finger at heaven, swaggered behind the house, and returned with his own beast, already bitted and saddled. "I will ride with you to the Alhambra," he said. "That will give us time."

Hakiim was not happy, but he was one of that sort who, while not especially kindly, has a great deal of difficulty being rude. He allowed Perfecto to mount beside him.

The mules danced their first few steps, finding their balance under saddle. The Spaniard coughed and cleared his phlegmy throat. "It has to do"—he chewed his lip silently for a moment—"with a promise I made once. That I would do something for someone. If it needed doing."

Hakiim frowned. He suspected Perfecto of talking nonsense. Like a child. Like a Spaniard. "To do what, and for whom?" He led his animal along a street so narrow that pedestrians darted into doorways to allow them to pass.

Perfecto's animal followed. The Spaniard's reply was inaudible and so Hakiim turned and asked him to repeat it.

"It does not matter to whom I gave the promise, does it? It was a promise and I was therefore honor bound."

Hakiim, as a dealer, thought this attitude was so much dung of the mule. What was more, he was certain that Perfecto had no more illusions than he himself. But as he

turned to say something of this nature, they rounded a
hump in the road, and a white donkey, carrying a man and
two sacks of wood, rammed nose-to-nose into his mount.

There was a great thrashing and hawing, and Perfecto's
innocent mule received a kick in the chest from Hakiim's.
When the incident had resolved itself (the donkey rider
backing his animal along the alley and into a cul-de-sac)
Perfecto pointed urgently along a cross street that led out
of the gates of Granada.

"Here. You will arrive at the fortress at the same time as
if you had cut through the city. *And*, we will be able to hear
ourselves talk."

"I don't want to be able to hear ourselves talk,"
whispered Hakiim to himself, but he turned the mule's
head.

"As to what the bargain—or rather the promise—was,
well, that was to depend on circumstance. As it happened,
it was necessary that I sell this man in Granada."

It was cooler outside the wall, and undeniably fresher,
but Hakiim's mood was unimproved. "Not man, Perfecto,
but boy. And how can you . . ."

Quite calmly the Spaniard corrected his partner. "Not
boy, Hakiim, but man. The blond was never a eunuch."

Hakiim let the reins slide down his mule's neck. For
some moments his tongue forgot speech. "And you knew
it?"

"From the beginning. But I knew that you would be
very unhappy with the idea of selling an entire, so I
thought it better to pretend."

Perfecto, jogging along on the mouse-gray back, looked
more complacent than ashamed.

Hakiim thought furiously.

"I should have suspected something when the Berber
woman refused to be sold without him."

Now it was Perfecto's turn to raise his eyebrows.
"Berber woman? Djoura?"

Hakiim made a negatory wave. "She . . . always
claimed to be a Berber. Pay it no mind."

But Perfecto's little eyes squinted littler. "Are there,
then, black Berbers?"

"A few," Hakiim admitted. "In the west and south. But
that doesn't mean that she is one . . ."

Perfecto gave a heavy sigh. "It would be a dangerous thing, to sell a woman of Berber tribe as a slave, in a land where the Berbers have the sharpest swords," he said.

"You are referring to Tunis?" Hakiim mumbled nervously.

"I am referring to Granada," answered the Spaniard.

The wall of the city rose to their left, gray but gleaming like milk in the sun. Below was a bank of shale that crumbled down to a series of turtle-backed hills. The sprawling fortress called the Alhambra, red walled and white towered, gleamed from half a mile away. Hakiim took a deep breath of sage-dry air and listened to the cicadas in the dust.

But for Perfecto, now, he'd have solitude.

"There is a world of difference between selling a Nubian who *calls* herself a Berber and is not, and selling a man *you* call a eunuch, and who is not. What will happen when Rashiid finds out he has been tricked?"

Perfecto urged his animal close beside. "Tricked? It was not I who told him Pinkie was a boy, but Djoura herself."

Djoura. Hakiim's brow knotted. "Yes! Our black lily must have known. Was she in this business with you?"

Perfecto spat off to the side. "No. Djoura is only perverse.

"And Rashiid can have no complaint to us, since Pinkie did not cost him one shaved copper!"

Hearing an unmistakable jingle, Hakiim turned his head. Perfecto had taken out his moneybag and was shaking it in his hand for emphasis. Hakiim's own profits were kept in a discreet bag-belt which wrapped his body beneath his shirt. It was a heavy belt, but not so full as this moneybag.

A sudden guess made Hakiim blurt, "So you were paid for taking the eu—the blond."

Perfecto laughed, and at this moment Hakiim's mule stopped dead and pawed the black shale with his foot three times.

"A bad omen," grunted the Spaniard. "When a mule does that. Take a good look before stepping onto the ship you engage, old friend!"

Then he added quickly, "No, I was not paid for taking the Saqalibah, or at least not in gold. I told you I did it for someone to whom I owe a number of favors."

Hakiim was getting tired of being told that. "Which makes me suspect the fellow was no more a legal slave than a physical eunuch," he replied. "Tell me, Perfecto. Who puts you under such strange obligations?"

"I will do better than tell you," the Spaniard proclaimed. "I will introduce you."

This was too much. As though Hakiim had any desire to meet Perfecto's low European friends . . . "No time," the Moor said shortly.

"All the time in the world," replied Perfecto, and he laughed.

"Go meet the devil, you damned paynim!" the Spaniard bellowed, swinging his moneybag (heavier than gold), down on the back of Hakiim's neck.

These visitors were so fancy that not only Fatima and Ama had to be hidden but the furniture as well. The normally concealed household bedding, however, was subject to a good deal of attention, as the dining room was strewn with pillows and the spread long ago embroidered by Rashiid ben Rashiid's mother hung dimpled from the ceiling. (This use of her handiwork would have surprised Lucrezza, wife of Pablo, very much.)

Ama found this all very hard, as she perched on a heavy oak table in her hidey-hole at the corner of the house. Since all the floor was taken, she was forced to crawl along the tops of the piled European furniture. Like a cat. And there were no cushions to make her position softer.

Better to be an old drudge like Fatima and supervise the cooking in the kitchen house than be locked up like this, in stifling heat with nary a toy or amusement all evening. Djoura was scrubbing pots, and even Raphael had been taken from the little wife of Rashiid, for he was to play for the guests.

Ama felt a stab of resentment. Wasn't it she who had sensed the value of the musician, when Rashiid hadn't wanted him for free?

And for that matter, wasn't the blond a mere European? Why did Raphael get to attend the party, while her pure Moorish bottom rested on the hard wooden furniture her people despised?

Ama would turn the tables on all of them, she promised herself. Big tables, like the one she sat on.

* * *

Hasiim Alfard, lean and dry-faced Berber of Morocco, looked to go the night without cracking a smile. His two lieutenants, Masoud and Mustapha, sat like dusty shadows at his feet, and unbent no more than their *qa'id*.

Rashiid's reaction to this was a grin like that carved on a turnip-face. He knew such an ingratiating and constant smile displayed a certain feeling of weakness before his powerful guests, and so he wiped the expression from his face again and again.

But it came back unnoticed, and in fact, there it was now, splitting his wide face and revealing teeth of various assorted shades. "You find it crowded in Granada, Qa'id Hasiim, after the tents of your people?"

Hasiim's right hand dipped into the spiced lamb, went to his mouth, and rinsed itself in the crockery bowl before he replied. "I find it . . . dirty," said the Berber. "But then, what can I expect? It is Granada."

The dry man (only his lips were moist, wet with the grease of Rashiid's expensive hospitality) turned slowly away, distracted by the ud player in the corner.

"Dirty?" echoed the heavier man. "Ah, yes. Unfortunately. But you say rightly, my honored friend; it *is* Granada." Rashiid erupted in fruity chuckles. "My own people . . ."

But the qa'id turned back to the food as though Rashiid were not even present. It meant nothing to him that Rashiid had "people," such as the gentry of Granada counted them. In fact, he might as well have admitted to Hasiim that he had been born with the name of Paolo. He would have found himself neither more nor less respected on that account. The city man was not a tribesman of Hasiim's, and that was all that mattered.

The Berber pulled a piece of gristle from the lamb on his trencher. He examined it, frowning hugely.

Rashiid sweated. In all his years in business he had failed to learn that one cannot impress a fanatic any more than one can impress someone else's watchdog. He tried.

"It is so hard," he began, "to maintain the mosques decent and clean in a place like this, in a city where no one knows how to keep Ramadan properly, and infidels wander the streets freely as the faithful."

Once more Hasiim scooped, bit, chewed, and swallowed before answering. "There is no need for mosques," he said, his voice totally devoid of expression. "In our hills there are no mosques."

Rashiid cleared his throat, but said nothing. He had begun to lose hope for this particular gathering. Why had he invited this fellow anyway, with his stiff-necked puritanism and unwillingness to be pleased?

The answer surfaced unbidden: because Hasiim was of very high lineage, and his cavalry was barracked in the Alhambra. These fursan were among the most powerful and fanatic of the Berbers, who were the most powerful and fanatic among the Arab conquerors of Spain.

The man of Granada felt an almost unconquerable desire to sit in a chair. Forty-two was too old to be squatting on the floor like a peasant.

Music intruded into his consciousness. The melody of the blond slave's music soothed his nerves as nothing else could. At least he need have no fear for the quality of his entertainment.

As a matter of fact, Hasiim was listening to Raphael with peculiar, brooding intensity. So were his silent fellows. Rashiid waited until the end of the piece before he spoke again.

"Handles the instrument well for a straw-haired barbarian, doesn't he?"

Hasiim's eyes (brown and shallow set, like those of an Arab horse) flickered. "There is no music worth making except that which glorifies Allah," he stated. "And there is no instrument worthy of praising Allah except the voice of a man."

Rashiid felt a mouthful of eggplant stick halfway to his stomach. His face prickled all over. He turned to Raphael, who sat tailor-fashion on the hard floor behind the guests.

But there was no need to direct the slave, for at Hasiim's words Raphael had put the wooden ud down at his feet. "Shall I sing, then, for you?" he asked, his blue eyes staring directly at those of Hasiim.

Rashiid's terror of nerves resolved itself into a fury, that the boy should dare speak to an honored guest in that familiar voice.

But Hasiim forestalled his discipline, replying, "Yes, of course, if you can do so without impropriety." (For among the things which do not impress a fanatic are manners.)

Raphael closed his eyes. He took a breath, let it out slowly, and then began to chant the same evening song he had shared with Djoura on his first day in chains.

In the kitchen the woman heard him. She raised her head and her hands clenched the handles of the cauldron she was dragging from the fire (black hands, black cauldron). Her eyes stung with tears she did not understand.

In the chamber of cushions, no man spoke until the song was over. Then Hasiim stood up and walked over to Raphael.

"You," he hissed. "Could it be you are a Berber?"

The blond smiled as Hasiim lowered his leather-tough body beside his. "No, I am not. But I sing that song together with my friend, who is a Berber."

"His name?" pressed the other, for Hasiim knew the name of almost every desert soldier quartered in Granada.

"Her name," Raphael corrected him gently, "is Djoura."

Now, in spite of himself, Hasiim Alfard smiled, and his face creased into dozens of sun wrinkles. "And how, in the name of Allah's grace, did a barbarian like you meet a Berber woman?"

"We are slaves here together," the blond replied innocently.

"No, a Berber cannot be a slave," stated Hasiim, as though saying, sheep cannot be green. "Not even a Berber woman."

"Djoura is," Raphael dared to say. "She is cleaning pots in the kitchen right now."

There was a hideous silence.

CHAPTER 7

Saara's second procession through the worm hole was less eventful. The dragon was gone, but Gaspare stepped out into the cleft of sunshine, where that creature had so long been chained, and squinted. And sniffed.

"Doesn't smell bad, considering."

Saara didn't bother to turn. "Why should it, when he wasn't fed for twenty years?"

Gaspare made a worried noise at that, and followed
Saara into the next dark tunnel. "Speaking of which, do
you think we can trust its—his—promise, not to eat
Festilligambe?" His words rang and echoed through the
darkness so that they were barely understandable.

"He didn't eat you," was the Fenwoman's reply, and
then she put her fingers to her lips for silence.

Gaspare didn't see the finger. Indeed, he saw very little
of anything in the deepening gloom, and soon began to
stumble. The witch was forced to take his hand.

It was long, this tunnel, and as sinuous as a serpent.
But like a serpent it was smooth. It became more and more
difficult for Saara to walk cautiously. But the amiable
builder of the tunnel had been chained in the middle of it
since its first construction. The Liar might very well have
made changes; the very regularity of the walls and floor
might well be designed to delude the wanderer away from
caution, so she goaded her ears to hear and her skin to feel.

While feet are moving, time is passing, but neither
Gaspare nor Saara had any sense of time's progression, and
the weariness of their black march turned into irritability.

Gaspare fell, twisting his body like that of a cat in his
effort to keep the lute from striking the ground. The
instrument was saved, but its back-curving neck smacked
Saara sharply on the thigh as it fell. She hissed her
annoyance.

Gaspare himself whispered his curses to the floor, but as
he clambered to his feet again (disoriented in the darkness), he remarked very calmly that a witch ought to be
able to call fire to hand at need.

Delstrego had.

Saara was still massaging her leg, but this implicit
criticism stung her worse than the blow. "I have heard a
little bit too much about Damiano Delstrego lately," she
said between clenched teeth. "And what a great witch he
was. There is a difference between accomplishment and
simple talent, you know. Or perhaps you don't know!

"Of course Damiano could call fire. He had fire coming
out of the top of his head! But it took me to teach him to
make clouds."

Gaspare snorted. "So who wants to make clouds,
except a peasant in a drought?"

Both had forgotten the necessity for quiet and for

caution as well. Gaspare strode bullishly down the corridor, one hand tracing the right wall for support.

Until he fell again.

Saara heard the thunk, followed by a small weary whine like that of a child. All her anger melted away.

"Don't get up," she told Gaspare, and she lowered herself beside the young man. "And don't talk. Give me a minute to think."

Damiano ran through Saara's memories like a bright but tangled thread. Her powers had been his, for a while, and his powers had been hers, for another while. Bodies, too, had shared as they might.

For a short time. Such a short time.

But surely Damiano's favorite magic should be accessible to her. To make a fire without anything to burn . . .

She fished into the unsorted depths of her mind and came up with brown eyes. A lot of curly brown hair, in snarls.

There was a dog, an angel (in all this she mustn't forget Raphael), a girl's face with blue eyes, a wonderful face with braids and green eyes (oh no, put it back, put her own face seen through Damiano's eyes at the bottom of the blackness), a plow horse with raw and pussy shoulders, seen once outside of Avignon . . .

There. There it came, with the image of the abused, fly-bothered beast. Hot anger welling up out of the floor of her mind . . .

"Lady Saara!" yelped Gaspare, scooting across the floor away from the smoldering woman.

"Hush," she chided him, and she turned down all the vents of her emotions. Her dress—last of the two she owned—was discolored, and it smelled of burning hair. She sighed.

But at last Saara raised one hand like a torch.

"There, Gaspare. Behold the world around us!"

"Wonderful," replied the redhead, staring not at the cave but at the flame itself. "Though Delstrego's was blue and did not flicker."

When they found their way under sky again, the sun was already descending. A path worn into the mountainside led away from the tunnel, treeless, grassless, winding up to a broken tooth of a peak above.

So high had they come that the air was thin and it tasted of ice. Gaspare began to shiver.

"There is steam ahead," murmured Saara, who rarely felt the cold. "Hot springs, maybe. Either that or someone is boiling a kettle." She peered narrowly at the single fang above them. It was a bit familiar-looking; seen from farther to the west, it might become quite familiar. She examined it keenly for any sign of entrance. Blood rushed to Saara's cheeks, not entirely because of the wind.

"Does—does not the Devil . . . have cauldrons?" stuttered Gaspare in her ear. "Could it be?"

She shrugged. "If so, it means we have come the right way." With a sigh and a stretch, she strode forward.

The steam wavered in the frozen air. One more rock and they would see it. Hot springs? There was no smell of brimstone in the air. Cauldrons? She herself had spoken of the Liar's cauldrons of steam, but they were part of the world of Lapp children, not of grown witches who themselves had a power of hot and cold.

She stepped carefully around the last rock.

No cauldrons. No hot springs. Just the glistening length of black serpent with floral head and eyes like miniature suns and the hot, moist air of his body hitting the cold.

Something else black was amidst his coils.

"I could not help but notice that you produce fire, too, madam. I could see your spark down the length of the passage. You are a remarkable human in all ways!" chuckled the dragon. He greeted her with a white and steaming smile. "I believe, however, that you left something behind."

It was Festilligambe the dragon indicated. The horse stood spraddled with head and tail drooping, ears flat out sideways, and made no move.

"You found him!" Saara padded up and began to climb over the smooth-scaled sections of dragon. "I didn't think anyone would ever find him again, the way he ran when he saw you."

"He was nervous," drawled the huge creature, revealing his canines further.

Saara came up to the gelding and stared into his black, blank eyes. "Well, he is not nervous now," she commented. "Is he alive?"

"I believe so," replied the dragon, and he, too, turned to examine Festilligambe, but he did not let his armored head get too close.

Saara lifted the horse's unresisting chin with professional interest. "A spell?"

The dragon wiggled, causing Saara to sit down hard. "Please, madam! Do I look to you like a wizard, that I should be casting spells hither and yon? It is only that I am a dragon—that alone produces such an effect on certain animals."

Saara spared him an eye as she got to her feet. "You ask me what you look like quite a lot," she said. "Don't you know what you look like?"

"Mere rhetoric." The dragon used the Italian word, since the Lapps had none fit to the purpose, but he glanced at Saara sidelong, as though he suspected her words to him of having more than the obvious meaning.

Saara put her hand on Festilligambe's withers and shook her head with regret. "I don't know what we're going to do with him," she said. "What good is a horse, for attacking a fortress at the top of a mountain? Especially this fortress."

The jeweled eyes met hers, and in a moment Saara understood what the creature had meant by "that alone produces such an effect on some animals." For a long moment neither the green eyes nor the gold eyes blinked, and at last the creature laughed softly. "I think," he said, "that we should leave the horse here and come back for it later.

"Along with the little flame-head."

"We?" Saara stepped back and sat down on a length of swart tail, moving the spines out of the way.

"We. You and I, woman," added the beast. "Who else has a hope of succeeding against the fallen Star of Morning?"

Saara grinned at the huge, expressionless mask of a face. "And have we a hope, Black Dragon?"

A red split tongue played over the teeth. "Perhaps not."

"Then why do you want to come?"

The dragon turned his head away, to where a tiny and very brave Gaspare was struggling up and over his outermost coil. "Because you freed me. I owe it."

"I release you from the debt," Saara said formally.

The head twisted back along its own neck. "You cannot," the dragon hissed. "It is *my* debt.

"Mine!"

* * *

Gaspare acceded with surprising grace to the scheme, perhaps it was because it was the dragon, rather than Saara, who explained it to him, saying that he should take the horse and explore farther along the road, while Saara and the dragon prowled the air.

Gaspare did not feel comfortable throwing temperaments in front of a ninety-foot-long steaming creature with teeth like scimitars. But he had enough boldness left in him to inquire how the dragon was to fly, lacking wings.

The great creature curled his tongue once around his muzzle before answering. "That is a reasonable question, little naturalist. I don't fly like a bird, you must understand. I swim. I ride the wind. And I can do this because I am hot."

Gaspare frowned thoughtfully into the gaudy, metallic face. Having endured heat, cold, devils, and a shape-changing witch, there was little that one dragon, however well equipped, could do to overawe him. "Delstrego had a power of fire," Gaspare remarked, "but I never saw him fly."

Curiosity lit the amber eyes. "Delstrego? Delstrego you say? Who or what would that be?"

"Never mind," Saara broke in. "If you stay around Gaspare, Dragon, you will hear a lot about Delstrego. But now is not the time. Let's go." In another moment there was only a dun-colored dove on the cold stone path, its wings lifted for flight.

The dragon peered at it closely, as a man might focus on a flea. "More magic," he breathed in tones of disgust, then added more politely, "I fear that in that shape I will fry you without even knowing it, woman of the north.

"Besides, you might have difficulty keeping up with me."

Saara blinked back. "Then how?"

The dragon slid his chin along the ground. Scales rippled in the light of the setting sun. "Behind my head," he hissed.

Using the corona of spikes for footholds, Saara hoisted herself up and looked. There, directly behind the last crimson starburst was a length of smooth neck which did not support a dorsal spine. It fitted Saara like the back of a very round horse. To her surprise she found two small

raised scales with handholds cut into them. She fit her
fingers with difficulty into them.

"You have been giving rides to . . . children?"

He raised his head off the ground. Saara, used as she
was to flight, felt her stomach lurch. "No. Not a child. A
small man. A man of India. A little ugly man with a face
like a frog's."

Coils scraped by Gaspare, not touching. The dragon
oozed a short way down the mountain slope, head
elevated. Saara was no more than one more spine on the
spiny head. Suddenly the air wavered strongly. As the
smell of hot metal reached Gaspare's nose, the beast was
aloft.

It squirmed in the air, like the flecks of paper ash
tumbling out of a chimney. Gaspare's heart was in his
throat as the black tail sliced the sky over his head. The
whip shape in the air loomed even closer; perhaps it was
out of control and would crash with Saara, crushing
himself and the dazed horse in the process.

But no, the writhing of the body continued, but the
head of the beast was stable, erect . . .

Riding the wind.

Warm rushes of air bathed Gaspare as Saara and the
dragon shrank into the blue sky.

"I never was close enough to see the portal itself,"
spoke the beast. Saara felt the deep voice through her legs
and seat. "Lucifer met me on the mountainside, where-
upon I played the part of the credulous fool!

"It had been so long, you must understand, since any
creature had dared attempt mischief upon me . . ."

"I can well believe that," screamed Saara into the wind
that buffeted her face. Her words swept behind her, but the
dragon appeared to hear. "But didn't you sense that he was
evil, not to be trusted?"

The beast snorted a gout of flame. "To which sense
would I be indebted for this information, madam?

"Sight, possibly? I tell you he looked like a man of
substance. Sound? His voice was good enough. Smell? All
mammals—forgive me my bias—smell rather strongly to
me."

Saara only laughed. She was finding the sense of flight
without work quite exhilarating, and the dragon's upwash

made the air around her comfortably warm. "I mean the sense of your power—the magic sense."

A shudder passed along the dragon's length and the scales under Saara roughened slightly. "I know nothing of such, and wish to know no more."

"But you're a dragon!" the woman blurted.

From the splash of flame at his mouth, it appeared the creature had cleared his throat. "I am a natural being," he replied with forced control, "possessing (I have it on good authority) the imperishable essence of truth.

"Magic, on the other hand, is illusion. Delusion."

Saara, feeling an argument in the making, kept her mouth shut, and as they floated up beside the nameless peak of rock, the dragon continued his story.

"He said he could direct me to Signor Alighieri—the man whose teaching I sought—but that it was necessary for me to delve a tunnel through a certain rock.

"Sages have asked their devotees for stranger things, so . . ."

"So you created that hole in the mountain?" Saara was impressed.

"Such as it is, yes. With no attempt at aesthetics, and not with the idea I was to live in it for twenty years, but I did cut it."

Suddenly a wave of breath-stealing heat washed over Saara. "I cut it and then, when the trickster betrayed me, I cut it in two, letting in the sun. But I could not break the delusion that held me there."

And then the dragon laughed, causing Saara's body to tremble on its hard seat. "Trapped in delusion. Such an old story!"

It was intoxicating for both the long-prisoned dragon and his rider: swooping at the gray tooth of rock, swirling great loops in the thin freezing air. But Saara did not forget to watch, either for a tall window in the surface of the peak or for some sign of its deadly householder.

"Perhaps it would be better," she spoke into what she hoped was the dragon's ear, "if we landed and worked from the rock itself. We would not be as easily seen."

"Crawling over stone like a lizard?" the dragon drawled. He wrapped his tongue around his muzzle once again. "All very well if you're not in a hurry." And he continued his sailing progress.

At the top of the peak there was no fissure of any kind in the rock. They worked their way down in great circles.

The sunlight failed and the flat blue sky deepened with that immense suggestion of distance that stars give. Instead of darkening, the peak went white.

Saara felt a touch of dizziness, for though she was used to flying, she was not used to being carried. The long whip-body swung lower and lower, faster and faster. They were almost back to the road.

Suddenly Saara felt it; something bad was below. Something cold and bad. She leaned out over the dragon's neck, hoping she was not about to be sick.

"I see it," replied the great creature, though Saara had not had time to speak. "A bar of light. And more."

Now Saara was horribly dizzy: dizzy as a mote spinning on the end of a string. She felt around her a touch of invisible, filthy fingers.

"It is he. The Liar," she whispered through her nausea.

Beneath Saara the black dragon was like so much steel cable. He said nothing more, but sank swirling down upon the road, not fifty feet from the soft-lit window in the rock. Elegantly, insouciantly, Lucifer stood at the lip of his tall window and watched the dragon's arrival.

They had found him. Or had he found them? Saara knew a moment of worry on that subject.

The Devil had chosen to dress himself in white—white velvet—and his gold hair shone like coins. With both arms crossed over his slender chest, he leaned against the bald rock of the mountain peak and looked the dragon up and down.

"So. The watchdog has slipped its chain." Then, stepping forward on his small (oddly small) feet, he added, "And it hadn't even the wit to run away."

When the dragon opened a long mouth, dim red light suffused the stones. "Base delusion!" he hissed, words muffled by fire. "How fitting that you dress in death's color. You spawn of chaos by error! Begone!"

Then Lucifer laughed outright, supporting his chin in one hand and that elbow against the palm of the other hand.

"This is no watchdog at all, but a parrot!"

Perhaps this was a miscalculation on Lucifer's part, or perhaps it was part of some long and subtle plan of his. Perhaps he wanted to induce the dragon to cover his head of gold curls and his clothing of white velvet in a deluge of liquid flame. But whether foresight or folly, the Devil vanished beneath a molten spew that burned the air and melted rock beneath him.

He vanished and reappeared, rising phoenixlike in a shape that mirrored the black dragon in length, shape, and deadly armament. But whereas the dragon was black, Satan was white: a stainless, powdery white, tipped with gold at every claw and spine.

These two beasts flexed metallic crowns as they stared at one another. The black dragon reared, rising as effortlessly as a bubble in water. So did the white. Together they lifted slowly: two marionettes on a single wire, two heads balanced on serpentine necks which rocked back and forth in time, keeping even the distance between them.

"Clown!" drawled the snowy dragon. "Wind kite!"

The beast of black iron showed its teeth. Saara crouched behind the dragon's multicolored head shield, gripping the pierced scales with all her strength.

She was no more than a flea in a battle of armed and armored knights; invisible, powerless, ignored by both contestants. She suspected that the Devil did not even know she was there.

But she was not forgotten: not by the armored knight who carried her. For as the two dragons rose and the white spewed fire, the black dragon arched his head back, sparing his rider the force of the flaming blow.

At the same time his whiplike tail lashed forward, slicing at the ermine belly of his opponent. The Devil howled and struck again.

Saara closed her eyes, for the heavens were wheeling above her too closely. Her feet slipped from the dragon's metallic sides and there was nothing holding her on except the grip of her fingers.

Whirling, twisting like two strands of a rope, the dragons rose. The sharp peak of granite fell away beside them. The air was lurid.

But though the black dragon was huge and ancient, he was a creature of the earth, with terrestrial limits. He bent back before the limitless onslaught of Lucifer's flame. He threw back his head for a breath of air uncontaminated by his enemy's reek, and at that moment the white beast struck, slashing with scimitar teeth at the iridescent black neck. The black dragon hissed pain and fury.

The floating rope of two strands bent, became a wheel: black-hubbed with a rim of shining silver. The white serpent emitted a blistering laugh and slashed again, using flame and tooth together.

Saara, though she could not see, could guess the deadly situation. "You can't get close enough to use your own fire! Because of me," she shouted thinly into the furnace-crackling air.

"No matter," replied her mount quite calmly, though his mouth spattered flame as he spoke. "There are other weapons at hand." And once more he slashed out at Lucifer, not with his tail alone, but with his whole length, from the base of the neck.

The air cracked like thunder as seventy-five feet of edged violence snapped through it. It caught Lucifer at the crease where his near hind leg joined the body, leaving a sharp pink line which darkened to red. Then as the white dragon pulled back, guarding the wound, the black released his bottled fires.

Blazing acids, not sulfurous but smelling of iron, spattered and stuck to the snowy scales. Wherever they touched, the stainless surface bloomed into whorls of color: red, green, and blue like oil spilled on rock. Then, as the flame went out, the circles darkened.

"Ho, Demon," boomed the black dragon. "You have smudged your funeral whites."

Lucifer coiled and faced his enemy. All was still for a moment, with the two beasts circling each other like twin moons. Then the Devil whispered, "I needn't bother to dress well for *your* funeral, brute."

Snakelike, Lucifer struck. The black dragon twitched back with the same speed, but as he did so he felt the grip of his hidden rider loosening. He slipped back under her but in that moment the claws and jaws of the white dragon found their hold, and the two were locked in awful embrace in the skies.

Saara heard the armor of her champion crack and shatter. She saw moonlight on a tooth as long as her body, before it sank into the black neck not five feet from her leg. She smelled blood.

And the massive head of the black dragon lashed left and right, ineffectually, unable to catch any part of the enemy which was grinding into his windpipe below.

Saara cursed. She released her hold and slid down the shining black scales until the white muzzle (now stained red) was near beside her. She stood, propping herself against the first of the black dragon's dorsal spines.

"Yey! Liar! You fly-blown pisspot! Look here!"

And the white dragon's blue eyes searched up and down, left and right, before he focused on the mite before his nose.

"No matter how long you wash, you still smell like a sick dog, you know," commented the little witch. Then she added, "And though you fancy yourself a trickster, I have found you the easiest dolt in the world to deceive." She let go her hold on the spine and flung herself into space.

Lucifer twisted his jaws around and spared one claw to catch the plummeting human. But no sooner did the black dragon feel his enemy's grip slipping than he himself struck, with a fury of contained hate. Not only did the Devil miss Saara, but he lost his killing squeeze on the black throat, and in another moment his clutching claw was pierced by teeth as sharp as slivered glass.

Meanwhile, the shape plunging in blackness wavered and was replaced by a ball of downy feathers. The owl Saara had become tumbled and lost a few secondaries before recovering in the air, then rose again to soar in wide circles around the battle.

What she saw was a different scene from that she had just left, for the black dragon had a wealth of stored fires and twenty years of stored hate. Once free of the necessity to protect his head, he fought with a savagery that seemed beyond the reach of pain.

He had Lucifer's foot in his mouth and one claw beneath the Devil's long jaw, holding both tooth and fire useless. The white dragon, at the same time, had wrapped his serpentine tail around the black's muzzle and was striking viciously with its edged tip at the other's eyes.

Saara circled, hooting dim, owlish encouragements to her champion, who had now forced his other claw to the Devil's throat and was attempting to strangle him. The white dragon was kicking the black's belly like a fighting tomcat.

Regardless of the dripping wound in his neck the black dragon held on. He caught one of his enemy's punishing

hind feet in his own and twisted the white's lower body
around so that he kicked only air. When Lucifer's front
claws found the tear in the flesh of the black dragon's neck
and worried it open, he not only ignored the pain, but was
not aware of it at all.

Could a mortal creature, however strong or ancient,
destroy a spirit? A great spirit? The dragon considered this
question in a dry and academic manner while his mouth
uttered his rage and talons squeezed and squeezed.

Although the Mahayana philosopher, Nagarjuna, admitted various levels of spirit and matter, nothing among
them was imperishable (except the atman, or breath,
according to certain other Indians). Therefore this dragon
before him (who might contain breath, but was certainly
not purely breath) might well be perishable.

But the Japanese, now, like Dogen, tended to put
change above all, and did not exclude breath from its
dominion. *That* would imply that this white dragon neck
between his claws was susceptible to infinite alteration, no
matter what its spiritual character.

Where does the flame go, when a candle is blown out?

The dragon, deep in such reflections, snapped his
mouth over that of his white enemy, both pinning its jaws
shut and cutting off air. He threw his shoulders into the
cause of metaphysical experiment until the silver throat
caved in beneath him.

The pale body writhed wildly and was still. But a voice
from the air spoke, saying, "I think I am getting bored with
all this."

The white dragon went out.

Like a candle.

The black dragon floated through the air as limply as a
weary swimmer. His fire-washed sides were dull under the
starlight, and black blood oozed down his length, dripping
at last from his tail to the earth far below. His head snaked
left, then right, but his amber eyes found nothing.

Except a tiny feathered shape that darted in above the
lofting heats and sat on his nose. "Quick! There. Follow
while he flees, or it will be for nothing!"

"Follow what?" asked the dragon patiently. Saara
sprang from his muzzle to his outstretched hand. She took
human form and pointed at nothing-at-all among the stars.

"There. The bright shadow. Can't you see?"

Snapping his tail behind him, the enormous beast shot forward, enclosing Saara in a cage of black tines. "Certainly I can see. I see Betelgeuse and Rigel and a host of lesser luminaries, and I see the moon in her half-phase. I see the Mediterranean Alps beneath and I see your little friend disappearing into the window we have sought so long. What else should I be seeing?"

"The Liar! He shines like rotting fish.

"Follow where I point," added the witch, as she saw that the dragon had no more eye for magic than had Gaspare.

"Now up!" she shrilled, and suddenly, "Turn, turn to your left! Sharper."

The dragon obeyed, though growling softly to himself. The earth beneath them reeled repeatedly, with white stone and black pine tilting like beer in a rolling barrel. But Saara was too intent for dizziness now. "Up, up!" she cried ferociously. "Faster or we will lose him."

But the dragon's climb slowed, though his tail beat the air below them so fast Saara could barely see it. It slowed and stopped, and finally they began to fall.

"Too high for fire," whispered the dragon faintly, and they floated, loose as a rope in the ocean, down toward the gleaming earth below.

There were some moments of silence, during which Saara stretched out on the five-fingered hand of iron. "So it is," she admitted ruefully.

They sank, weariness establishing its mastery over both of them. The dragon began to ache.

"That was a famous battle," Saara remarked. "If I were a poet, I would make a saga about it."

The dragon, however, growled glumly. "What does it matter how it went, when I failed you?"

The witch sat up and peered behind them at the black and starry sky. "Failed me? How? Did you expect to split the sky in two? You would have done that before killing the Liar, who was never born."

"Then what were we after?" The yellow eyes, bigger and brighter than torches, looked down at her.

"The answer to a question," replied Saara, who continued to stare into space. "I must find Raphael, the Eagle Chief."

The dragon puzzled. "But we failed in that too. He gave us no time to ask, and now he is gone beyond chasing."

"No," the tiny woman corrected him. "He is not beyond chasing. In fact he is coming back at this moment."

Then the stars spun about as the black dragon swiveled in place. "Where?"

"Coming," repeated Saara, calmly. "He wears no shape." Changing her own shape once again, she darted, a round, fluffy owl, behind the dragon's head spines. "I will tell you where he goes," she whispered, "and what he does."

"He is below you," said the owl. "What do you see?"

"Nothing."

"Then what do you feel?"

The dragon slashed with his tail. "Loathing," he hissed through set teeth.

Again the owl peeped and chattered. "Now he is beside you. Can you sense him?"

The dragon's back scales scraped together. "I feel only . . . disgust," he said, but Saara thought he might have used another word but for pride.

"Now he is abo—" hooted the owl, but at that moment a shape hurtled toward her, and Saara threw herself fluttering to the left.

It was an eagle, and it was shining white. It pursued the rotund owl in the air with a skill equal to her own. Twice it chased her around the dragon's very head, pressing so closely she had not the time to hide herself among the projecting spines.

The dragon craned his neck wildly, but the birds were too tiny and too close for him to touch. Like a hawk mobbed by ravens, he sank away from the combat in the air.

But owls do not give battle with eagles, or at least not for long. One of the eagle's talons struck, taking a handful of feathers from the owl and scattering them. She flapped, off-balance, toward the dragon's protective head. The satanic eagle followed, growing closer.

The dragon saw his chance and took it. He opened his mouth and let the owl flutter through. His crocodilian jaw snapped shut on the eagle. The wounded owl fluttered down on his hand.

"Now I will not ask, but demand," said Saara, whose dress hung in tatters stained with blood. She motioned to be brought nearer the dragon's mouth.

"Liar!" she called. "Now you will take us to Raphael. You will release him from his bondage. Or you will spend a long time in a very dark place!"

There was silence, and the dragon clenched his jaw. Then he gagged, for suddenly out of his mouth and nose was pouring streams of matter.

They were hideous, the white-blue of phosphorescent, decaying flesh, and they crawled. They erupted from the dragon's mouth faster than he could spit them out, and they scrabbled over his body. They came down his hand and claw and reached Saara.

They could bite. They could burrow into flesh. Saara screamed, while the dragon belched helpless fire that lapped his sides but did nothing to discourage the infestation. In a panic of horror Saara watched the scum of pale blue disappear between the dragon's scales.

He writhed like a back-broken snake. In a moment surely he would close his hand and crush her. Saara herself lay in a ball on the black palm of the dragon's hand, clawing at a body that had gone slippery with blood.

Like thistledown the black dragon floated down through the high airs. He touched the stone of the peak and rolled as limp as a leather strap, all the way down to the road.

CHAPTER 8

Where had his pride gone, Gaspare asked himself. He had not felt so shaken since the bad days: the days he tried never to think about, the days before Damiano, when he had been nobody, with bare feet on the streets of San Gabriele.

He watched the Lady Saara ascend into the sky on her serpentine steed, knowing he had been put on a shelf, while she and the dragon were out to confront the Devil. Yet proud Gaspare—man of many tempests—had said

nothing against the plan. Yes, he would continue along the
road, in the unlikely event the Devil had placed the
entrance to his eyrie in plain sight. Yes, he would watch the
befuddled horse.

Truth was, Gaspare was fit for nothing else, for he had
run out of strength. Entering the worm hole had drained
him of bravery in no ordinary manner, while his encounter
with the dragon itself had left him with a dull feeling that
anything might happen next and there was naught that
could be done about it.

The high air (or lack of it) was much to blame for the
redhead's shakiness, but, child of the mountains that he
was, he did not connect the peaks around him with his
intense desire to sit down on the road and shut his eyes.

He leaned against Festilligambe: not a good idea, for the
horse was in no condition to support his weight. "Come,
old outlaw," grumbled the redhead. "Wake up and show
some fight!"

Festilligambe hauled up one ear, but made no other
response to Gaspare's urging. Staring into the gelding's
round brown eyes, Gaspare thought he saw reflections of
amber.

"What has he done to you, ass-face? You look like old
Lucia after her third tankard." The youth twisted Festilligambe's black tail (heavy by nature, thinned by too much
standing near the fire) as though the horse were a pig. A
groan was the only result.

Festilligambe's paralysis conquered Gaspare's. His
spirits rose to contempt for the addled beast. "Snap out of
it, horse. It was just a big lizard, you know. A dumb brute
like yourself."

Suddenly there came a whistling shriek from somewhere above and ahead, accompanied by booming curses
and followed by a great hiss of engines. "Or a brute, at any
rate," Gaspare added with less cockiness. "Come on. We
can't stay here."

To his left rose a slope of rock and rubble, rising to the
sharp tooth of the mountain. On the right the slope fell
again in increasing steepness. Gaspare did not move to the
gravel-scattered edge to look over, for there was an
uncomfortable cold wind.

Ahead of him a spur rose at the right of the road, amidst
the scree, so there would be protection from both sides.

Protection from the wind, at any rate. Gaspare tweaked Festilligambe's ear and prodded one thumb knuckle into his ribs, but the horse did not respond. At last he drew back, cocked his foot, and spun around, landing an impressive roundhouse kick just below the gelding's limply hanging tail.

Slowly the horse swayed forward. Slowly he began to move.

Gaspare entered the protection of the rocks. When the road veered away to the left, following the base of the peak, he clipped the skin of Festilligambe's nostril between two fingers and led him around.

A shrieking roar blasted the rocks. Gaspare gazed up in time to see the dragons, white and black, rise twining into the high air. A horrid glory of flame brightened the evening sky.

Gaspare fell to his knees, not knowing it was Satan himself who assaulted his friend in the air, but knowing it was terrible. "I am useless," he whispered, his teeth chattering. "By God and all His saints, I want to hide!" He hid his face in his hands.

The bellowing faded as the combatants rose farther from the road itself. Gaspare, folding his hands in half-shamed prayer, looked ahead and beheld the yellow light of a lamp.

In front of him, along the road itself, was a window. It extended from the gravel and dust of the earth to a peak at least twenty feet up, and the stone trim around it was as neat and pretty as that of a church. It was the kind of window one could walk through, having neither shutter nor glass. Inside it was a room.

As Gaspare stood perched on the sill, a light spatter of flame licked the stone of the road behind him. Acid hissed and crackled against stone. The youth hopped through, down the two-foot drop to the interior floor, which was tiled quite fashionably in the Italian manner.

"So," he said. "Even as Delstrego described it."

Delstrego had visited the Devil. He had told Gaspare all about it. But the redhead hadn't listened, exactly, because it had been back in the days when he thought Delstrego was . . . well, confused.

But he *did* remember that the Devil's high chamber had been big—so big that a man might sit on a table as large as a ballroom floor. "Not quite as Delstrego described it," Gaspare amended.

Here was a table. Gaspare put his hand upon it. About two arm spans by one-and-a-half, he judged. On it were two things: a rather impressively made model of a fortress, and a bowl of grapes. Besides the table, the only furnishings in the room were a single high-backed chair, various loud and busy scarlet embroideries on the walls, and a red leather bag hanging from the ceiling lamp.

Gaspare's curious fingers played with a tiny steel shutter which hung on one of the few windows of the model. It worked. He peered inside the arched windows on the tiny cupola which topped the model. There was something in it, but he couldn't make out what. By habit he plucked a grape from the bowl and brought it to his mouth.

But there was something about the fruit, something greasy, perhaps, or was it the color which was not quite right? Gaspare put it down again and danced nervously through the room.

No doors, just three other windows. Two of them looked out onto blackness (night fell so abruptly in the mountains). Gaspare peered out of the fourth window, hoping to spy Saara and her dragon.

After a brief glimpse he backed away again, reeling. Gaspare's stomach didn't feel too well. He cursed a prayer, or prayed profanely (from the time he had been a street urchin, the two actions had blurred into one for him), and returned his attention to the toy on the table.

It had no doors either. "No doors," he mumbled. "No way out."

"Go out the way you came in: that's my advice. And do so as quickly as possible," said the red leather bag hanging from the lamp.

Gaspare leaped squealing into the air and his arms flailed. One hand struck the bag, which was soft and saggy, and which began to swing back and forth. Two blue eyes, on stalks, moved in opposition to the swaying. "Don't do that," the bag complained. "You might hurt the image."

Gaspare blinked from the speaker to the work on the table. "I'm sorry," he blurted. "Who . . . what are you?"

It had a mouth, set above the blue eyes. It had a blobby big belly, with sticklike arms and hands tied together behind it. (Tied in a bow. With red string.) It had feet set at the very top of the belly, one of which had been tied with red string to the lamp cord.

"I am Kadjebeen," stated the bag. "I am an artisan."

Gaspare made a discovery. "You're upside down," he informed the bag.

"Yes, I am," replied Kadjebeen equably. "I'm being punished."

"For what?" asked Gaspare, but before the demon could answer, Gaspare had untied the sticklike arms and was working on the knot in the lamp cord. Such was his attitude toward punishment.

The little horror was lowered to the table. It rolled over so that its blue scallop-eyes were upmost. "I was supposed to have someone whipped half-to-death." His small raspberry-colored mouth emitted a sigh.

"What is 'half-to-death'?" Kadjebeen asked Gaspare, but did not wait for an answer before adding, "Life is neither distance nor volume, that I can take out my weights, levels, or my measures and get it exact. What was I to do?"

Gaspare didn't answer. The demon massaged his button head in both hands. "Better to be conservative, don't you think? I mean, one can always whip a little more, afterward, but if the man is dead, one can scarcely whip a little *less*, can one?

"Besides . . . I did so admire those wings."

Gaspare, who had been listening to Kadjebeen's complaint with a certain lack of sympathy, suddenly lunged forward. "Wings? Angel wings?"

Kadjebeen cringed back, hiding his eyes in his hands. (One in each.) "What'd I say? What'd I say? Don't hit me! I'm only an artisan!"

Gaspare repeated his question more moderately.

"I don't know what kind of wings you're talking about. These weren't like regular demon wings. Not leathery. They had feathers like birds'. Whitish."

"Raphael!" cried Gaspare, and when Kadjebeen threatened to withdraw once more, he shook him.

"Yes, yes! Raphael was his name. Nice guy, he seemed. Well put together. Looked a lot like the Master."

Seeing Gaspare's exultant face, he asked, "You interested in wings too?"

"I am . . . interested in Raphael's wings," warbled

Gaspare, dancing another little dance of excitement. "Raphael is my friend. My teacher. We have come from San Gabriele in the Piedmont, looking for him.

"Through cold and wind," Gaspare chanted. "Past dragons and enchanted boulders we have come, and not all the Devil's wiles could stop us!"

Kadjebeen sighed again. "Then he must not have been trying very hard."

Gaspare was stung. "I'm sure he was! If he had any sense he was, because we are justice itself on his trail."

The skin at the back of his neck twitched, as Gaspare remembered where he was and to whom he was speaking. "You . . . *like* him? Your wicked master? In spite of what he did to you? You'll tell Satan I was here, and everything I said?"

Kadjebeen's eyes made independent circuits of the room. "Like . . . the Master?" Then in a rush he replied, "Of course I don't. Who could like him? But I'm sure I will tell on you. He'll torture me till I do."

The round demon sighed. He walked over to his toy and fiddled with it in proprietary fashion. "And then he'll torture me some more, I guess."

Gaspare's courage, working as it did by law of opposition, rose as the demon quailed. "It doesn't matter if you do tell, you miserable insect. We've come for the angel and won't leave without him!" He pirouetted around the table, slicing most gracefully with an invisible sword.

"Well, I'm very sorry, then," mumbled Kadjebeen.

Between one florid step and the next, Gaspare stopped dancing. "Sorry for what?"

Kadjebeen was sitting on the table. He had both hands laced around his middle. Now his color was returning, and he looked more like a raspberry and less like a bag. "Because the Master gave him away."

"Gave him away?" echoed Gaspare. He struck his bony fist on the tabletop. The greasy grapes bounced. "He gave away an angel of God?"

"Watch out for the image," mumbled the demon reflexively. "It's a perfect correspondence, you see, and one has to be careful." Then the demon realized that Gaspare's attention could not be diverted from his goal.

"Yes. He melted off his wings and gave him to one of

his toadies—uh, servants. Perfecto the Spaniard, the man's name is. I imagine your Raphael is in Granada now."

Observing the dusky flush of Gaspare's face, Kadjebeen added, to console him, "The wings were gone by then, anyhow."

Gaspare's impersonal glare sharpened. "You must take us to him!"

The demon squeaked, and drew in both hands and feet, so that nothing but his trembling eyes disturbed his rotundity. "Oh, I couldn't! The Master would never let me! He'd be so angry if he even knew you'd asked!"

Gaspare, whose own fear had somewhere been left behind, strode to the window, where the dazed horse stood placidly, seeing nothing. All sounds of battle had faded, but in his heart was growing a conviction that the battle was already won: a conviction which had nothing to do with Saara's magic, or the length of the dragon's teeth.

"Your master, little insect, is nothing but scum!"

"Oh dear, don't," quailed Kadjebeen, as his ears and eyes rotated nervously. "He is the Prince of the Earth and very sensitive about it."

"He is the Prince of Cowardice," Gaspare declared. "And all his victories are cheats."

He spun theatrically and smacked his chest. "I myself tell you this, you poor deluded slave. And I should know, because *I am a very bad man!*"

Kadjebeen stared at Gaspare with an increase of respect.

"Or I *was* a very bad man. But with the grace of God and the help of His angel Raphael, I am trying. It is hard," added the youth, staring with wide green eyes at the round body on the table, "when you are born with low instincts and have habits both worldly and violent, but it is possible to throw off Satan entirely. Even you could do it."

His gaze on the demon lost certainty. ". . . I think."

"This Raphael person," Kadjebeen thought to mention, "didn't last very long against my Master."

Gaspare frowned, remembering Kadjebeen's part in that deed. "Raphael sacrificed himself," he said with dignity. "For *my* sins, I am told.

"And I . . . I will release him from bondage. I have the greatest witch in all Europe at my side. We cannot lose."

Kadjebeen's stalked gaze shifted to Festilligambe. "The greatest witch in all Europe is a horse?"

"Uh, no. This is Festilligambe. He is probably the fastest horse in all Europe. He is certainly the most troublesome." A glance at the slack-jawed, lop-eared face forced him to add, "He is, however, not feeling his best.

"My companion, the Lady Saara, is at this moment chasing your foolish master's legions from the skies, while I have the responsibility to locate and rescue Raphael."

"He's in Granada," repeated Kadjebeen helpfully.

"So." Gaspare cracked his knuckles, one by one. "Take us to Granada."

"I couldn't . . ." began the raspberry demon, but he changed his mind in midsentence. "I would like to, but I don't see how . . ."

"And you call yourself an artist!" Gaspare's voice, not naturally resonant, rang strangely loud in that stale, tiled chamber.

"An artisan," Kadjebeen corrected him. "I build things. Images. As a matter of fact, I am the greatest maker of images that—"

"Artist, artisan . . . Bah!" Gaspare brushed the distinction aside. "Don't you know that all the arts are blessed, and Satan is their enemy? Raphael is the greatest musician ever created, as well as the most beautiful; it is out of jealousy that Satan has done him hurt. I myself—"

"I myself am tone-deaf," interjected the raspberry demon. "As well as ugly. But go ahead—you were about to tell me what *you* were greatest at."

"I was not," grunted Gaspare, instantly deflated. "I'm not the best at anything, although my old friend and partner . . . Oh, never mind." For to Gaspare's mind came the words the ghost had said at the top of the hill in Lombardy. "Don't strive to be the best, or you will wake up one day and know yourself no good at all."

There was no sound to be heard, except the droning sighs of Festilligambe, who seemed to be waking up. Suddenly Gaspare wanted to be out of this square room with windows that made no sense and air like doused ashes. Even if its owner never returned, it was no good place to be.

"Granada, you say?" He spared a last glance at the demon. "Then to Granada we will go, on the back of the greatest dragon that . . ." Gaspare swallowed.

"On the back of a dragon." He leaped lightly onto the sill.

Festilligambe nickered sleepily. Gaspare dragged him along by the mane. "Come on, ass-face. We have what we came for . . ."

It was black outside, and all noise of combat had ceased. A dust of stars whitened the sky. Gaspare lifted his head, and cold wind caught his russet hair.

Where were Saara and the dragon? Gaspare felt pregnant with news and wanted to communicate it. Surely they had not chased that stranger dragon so far they could not get back to him? All pretty white and gold, it hadn't looked like a beast with much fight in it.

As he stood in the mountain darkness, huddled against a black horse for warmth, Gaspare heard an awkward scuffing behind him.

A squarish black shape was following his trail on spindly pink-purple legs. It looked like a bedding box with the hindquarters of a chicken. For a moment Gaspare's hair stood on end, not out of fear but disbelief, until he recognized the object as Kadjebeen's toy palace, propelled by Kadjebeen himself.

"I'm coming," panted the demon, unnecessarily.

"With that?"

Kadjebeen hugged his masterwork with arms too short for the purpose. His eyes drooped protectively over the top. "It's mine," he mumbled. "I made it. Best thing I ever made. It's an image of the whole palace. Even His Magnificence has never appreciated how perfect a job it is."

Gaspare only sighed. Together he, Kadjebeen, and the horse stepped out of the shelter of the rocks.

There, on the gray-lit slope of the peak itself, lay a long body like a length of rope cast off by some giant. Moonlight glistened on it, for it was coated with some sort of slime, and small, scuttling things went in and out of the great, scimitar-lined mouth, which leaked steam. Yellow eyes shone faintly, staring at nothing.

Caged in one iron paw, undamaged but motionless, was a small shape in a scorched blue dress.

Gaspare stopped dead, causing Kadjebeen to bump into him. The horse reared in panic.

Then Gaspare ran wildly over the rubble and stone, up the slick and gripless slope of rock, toward the fallen dragon with its phosphorescent infection. He reached the black-clawed hand. He squeezed between the bars.

With both hands Gaspare wiped the ooze from Saara's eyes. He wept and cursed together as more came out of her nose and lips. Her flesh looked and felt like wax.

The creeping disease touched Gaspare.

Kadjebeen stood alone on the road, leaning on his work. He was feeling very low.

The fellow had seemed so certain of himself, with his greatest this and his fastest that. It had been a long time since Kadjebeen had met anyone except the master himself who was so self-assured. He tried to remember when and where he *had* met another like Gaspare. His memories were sadly jumbled.

But the raspberry demon was sure of one thing. He really didn't want to hang from the ceiling anymore.

Amid the cries and weeping, as Kadjebeen leaned disconsolately on his image, he heard a familiar sound. From somewhere nearby, his master Lucifer was laughing. Kadjebeen listened, and in his present discouragement he had the idea Lucifer was laughing at him.

Long white wings: light, intricate, craftworthy. Melted like ice.

"No!" He shouted petulantly. Then louder. "No. I'm tired of it. Always the best work is broken and the worst exalted. Always the back of the hand! Well, I won't anymore. I won't!"

And Kadjebeen, in excess of rage, sprang up in the air on his bandy legs and came down right on the cupola of his masterwork—the image of Lucifer's Hall.

He let out an "oof" and an "ouch," for the little object was pointed. But it was also fragile, and it splintered beneath his jelly-shuddering weight.

From the mountain beneath came the thud like that of a slamming door, magnified many times. Kadjebeen stamped. Something shifted in the rock itself. The air popped.

But Kadjebeen hopped again and again, smacking his buboed surface against paper-thin walls. The image gave way.

The fortress of Lucifer gave way. Rock shuddered, deep in the earth. The thin air was loud with broken deceits and the cries of demons with their leashes snapped. The yellow light shining around the corner went out.

A fungoid silvery growth appeared in the black coils of the dragon, as Lucifer dragged himself frantically from the flesh of his victims. His shape solidified, grew hair, was dressed in white velvet.

He hurled himself through the air toward the gate of his palace, at the small figure standing by the shards of delicate stone.

It was not bulbous, not colored like a raspberry. It was a man, or the shade of a man: short, wiry, but not uncomely, with very strong arms and hands. His face was bearded and his eyes round and blue.

"No more, my Master," said the shade, and the voice came to Lucifer from far away. The spirit pointed to its eyes, its body, and to its mouth. "No one is made so badly as you would have them believe," it whispered, and the bearded mouth smiled. Slowly the large, sail-white wings spread behind it and tested the air.

Smiling, the shade raised its strong arms and square, workman's hands. It rose and faded into a sky awash with ihe stars.

Flaming with curses, Lucifer fled away to recapture his scattered devils.

As a half-moon rose from behind the rock-tooth, the yellow eyes of the dragon answered its light. The bladed tail twitched.

And Gaspare, in the pergola of the dragon's upturned hand, held Saara until she was warm again, and her eyes opened.

CHAPTER 9

Though the glassy night was the most comfortable time in late-summer Granada, the servants in their barracks were too tired to stay awake for it and Rashiid and his wives were too well-fed. Only Raphael sat up, crouched half-naked beside the fish pond, and the fish circled at his feet. He was talking with Damiano.

"You look much better, I think," the spirit was saying. "Except for your nose."

"My nose," repeated Raphael. He touched that member for identification and winced at the result. "It hurts. And it whistles when I breathe through it."

Moonlight had bleached the gold from his hair and reduced the glorious color of his black eye to mere shadows. He glimmered as insubstantially as his friend the ghost.

Damiano's cloudy suggestion of a face drew closer and darkened in sympathy. He said, "I can hear it. A very musical sound, as befits a teacher of music. But I know a cure for the problem."

"Tell me!" Though weeks of humanity had taught Raphael some sophistication, his face still reflected his every feeling, and now his perfect blue eyes (one of them rimmed in purple and green) pleaded with Damiano.

"It takes bravery."

Raphael nodded soberly.

The spirit's umbrous wings folded back. He added, "It is not a magical but a musical cure."

This did not seem to surprise Raphael at all.

"Take your hands," began Damiano, "and clap them in your lap." The blond did so, but quietly, so as not to wake the slaves in the barracks.

"Now keep the rhythm and follow me, clapping whenever I clap." The ghost went clap, clap, clap in his lap, making hardly a sound, and then raised his arms above his head and struck his ectoplasmic hands together. Raphael accompanied him in (of course) perfect time.

Three claps more above the knees and three in front at arm's length and three more in the lap and then in front of the face, one, two, and . . .

Perhaps Damiano gave a nudge, or perhaps Raphael, in the heat of the performance, wasn't thinking quite what he was doing, but the third clap came hard and symmetrically down on his injured nose.

He gasped and rose half to his feet. "I hit myself!" he cried aloud, and then, as greater understanding came to him, he added, "You *made* me to hit myself!"

The spectral form wavered, perhaps through shame. "But your nose: How is it now?"

Raphael gave a careful sniff. "I smell blood," he said, with a hint of petulance. "But I think . . . I think . . ."

Again Damiano leaned close. "I don't hear anything."

Raphael, too, listened. "No. Nothing. The whistle is gone."

"And your nose is straight again. You'll be as handsome as ever."

The blond's fine hands were locked protectively around the middle of his face, but his eyes turned to Damiano with sudden interest. "Am I handsome? I never thought about it."

Sadly Damiano smiled. "You've never been a mortal before. Now you'll think about things like that: Are my teeth good? Is that a wrinkle or a spot forming by my eyebrow? Is that fellow a bigger, stronger, better man than I? It's the mortal condition; we don't seem to be able to help it.

"And another part of being mortal, Seraph. Hating. Do you hate your master yet?"

Raphael squatted down again. He lifted his eyes to the stars while the warm wind stirred his hair.

"My master? I feel bad that he hit me. He had never told me I was not supposed to mention that Djoura was a Berber in front of other Berbers. And how was I to know that Djoura's father had been sworn to Qa'id Hasiim years ago?

"And though I know Rashiid had reason to be angry—he felt compelled to give a great gift of money to the Berbers in the Alhambra, as well as losing what he'd paid for Djoura—still, I'd rather not have to see him anymore. Somehow I don't like looking at him or hearing his voice."

"Understandable."

"Is it?" Raphael's left eyebrow shot up in a movement familiar to his student. "I don't understand it. After all, Rashiid will be Rashiid whether in my sight and hearing or not.

"But that is nothing like hate, I know, for I have felt hate. One doesn't have to be a mortal . . . There is one I hate and have hated for a very long time." Then Raphael took a deep breath through his newly repaired nostrils.

"And anyway, this blunder of mine led to Djoura being freed, and freedom was what she most wanted, so I'm glad of it."

"Freedom is what we all most want," murmured the thoughtful spirit, and for a moment he faded into moonlight. When he raised his face to his friend again, there was a hint of fire in his dark eyes.

"Raphael, you must remember who you are!"

The man looked only weary. He turned his head away. "I remember, my friend. My confusion is nearly gone.

"I remember every voice in the choir. And the song, in all its parts—how could I forget that? But my memories are only memories, and don't move me."

The voice of a single frog hidden in the weeds of the pond silenced Raphael for a few moments. Then he said, "More real to me than heavenly music is the fact that my nose hurts, and is dripping blood, and that I know I must dig at the latrines tomorrow, as well as play the ud."

Damiano nodded. He dipped one vague hand into the black pool water, passing it through several little perch in the process. Neither hand nor fish were the worse for it. "You don't talk about God—your Father—anymore."

Raphael's eyes slipped down, from his friend's face to the undisturbed surface of the water. "You mean Allah. Here He is Allah, and the people of Granada use His name in every third sentence. And they all seem to know just what His will is on every issue. All but me, of course.

"Allah and I have not been introduced."

"You are bitter," whispered the ghost.

Raphael smiled and his battered face was transformed. "I'm not, really." He put his hand into the waistband of his trousers and pulled out a little pouch. "I have a pebble, Dami: the one you gave me. I take care of it."

The moon had rolled away and only Jupiter and the Dog Star made light enough to outshine the approach of dawn. In that season and latitude Sirius never set.

Raphael was sleeping like a dog, however, curled against the cold with a protective hand on either side of his nose. Even as he slumbered, the little perch of the pond did not relax their honor guard, and the carp at the bottom hugged the bottom and sides of the tank as though to push their way through soil to the transformed angel.

Soon the dozen men in the barracks would be expected to wake up and be useful. They slept all the harder now in expectation.

But in the main house little Ama was awake; she had had to wake up to vomit, which was her recent custom. As always, concluding this task left her fresh and airy, ready for the day's experience. And now she tiptoed out the white doorway, sure of her path despite the lack of light.

Ama was wearing white. She came sans veil and her hair was undone. She looked more like Rashiid's little daughter than Rashiid's young wife. She found Raphael on the bench beside the fish pond. Finger-length perch darted in every direction.

"Ho, slugabed! Wake up. Wake up and do my hair."

Raphael opened both eyes. He yawned, winced, and touched his upper lip. He chafed his unclad arms.

"Since because of you I don't have Djoura anymore, you must be my body servant," Ama persisted. Then she giggled. "You're much nicer, after all, though you're the wrong color."

She leaned over him and peered closely at his face. "Wrong colors, I should say. How shocking!" Ignoring his incoherent reply, Ama pushed his knees off the bench and sat herself down facing away from him, presenting her abundant hair.

"My husband is a brute; I have always known so. He would hit me, I'm sure, if my family were not so important. I'm glad they are. My uncle is a *nakib;* he has the fealty of two hundred men. But not so much money.

"Why do you sleep outside, Raphael? It gets cold in the morning. It's cold now.

"You know how Djoura used to sleep? Fully dressed, in all those dusty black gowns of hers. Looked like a hill of mud, she did, with her veil over her black face. But she was warm, I bet.

"What did you say?"

Raphael had been about to tell Ama why he slept on the bench by the fish pond: a story which involved his first and only night in the barracks (fully dressed, like Djoura), when because of his humming and his muted conversation with an unseen visitor he had earned eviction. But as he rose from his hard cot he thought of something else to say.

"I don't know how to do your hair, mistress," the slave admitted. "I have never done a lady's hair before."

Ama shrugged and set her small mouth. "You know how to make braids, don't you? Braid it."

Raphael set to work. His hands were good, and he was, of course, an artist. He worked neatly but without great speed, and Ama wiggled. After a few minutes, she wiggled backward into his lap.

"Rashiid is angry with me too. Isn't that absurd? All because I'm the one who wanted the black. How was I to know she was of an important clan? It's Rashiid's own business to know those things; I'm just his wife, after all."

She darted an avian glance back at the blond. "I wish I weren't his wife. I wish I was *your* wife instead!" Then Ama giggled at her own conceit. "The wife of a eunuch! Wouldn't that be an easy job?"

Suddenly the girl spun about on Raphael's knees, pulling her black tresses from his fingers. Her face was inches from his. With her fingers she combed his yellow hair over his eyes and began to twist it about. "Your turn, Pinkie . . . I mean Raphael.

"You'd make such a pretty girl yourself, except that you're too big, of course, and too skinny. But I like your eyes, and your mouth is so sweet. She kissed his not-quite-awake face.

Color had descended from the sky: the green of the pond, the blue in Raphael's eyes, the hidden russet in Ama's hair. "Shall I marry you, Raphael? Shall I forget about Rashiid and marry you? You can be my little wife!"

Ama forced her treble voice down to a masculine growl as she repeated again and again the phrase "my little wife." She had quite a talent for imitating Rashiid, both in word and gesture; Raphael found himself being possessively pawed all over. It was rather pleasant.

"I have only seen one eunuch before," whispered Ama, breaking out of her husbandly character for a moment. "He was the little boy of my uncle's household in Algiers, and he had two red scars in this shape." She laid one finger crosswise over another. "He would cry if we tried to touch them.

"Here, Pinkie. While no one else is watching. Take your trousers off and show me."

Raphael's fair forehead drew down and he prisoned Ama's exploratory hands in his own. "I'm not supposed to do that," he said.

With a force of outrage she yanked free of his grasp. "Not supposed to . . . Who said you're not supposed to?

I'm your mistress and I say . . ." Ama grabbed the waistband of Raphael's cotton trousers and pulled until the cord broke. The baggy garment slipped onto the bare wood of the bench.

Little Ama looked first surprised and then quite confused. She was speechless. Under the intensity of her stare Raphael grew nervous. He also felt quite warm, somehow, though the sun had not yet crested the wall. He attempted to gather the cloth again at his hips, but Ama forestalled him.

"Either a eunuch looks just like a man, once he grows up, or . . ." Her small round eyes rose to his. "Are you a whole man after all, Raphael?"

"Yes," he replied. "But no one is supposed to know that."

Ama rolled her eyes. She edged away from the slave along the bench and folded her hands on her lap. Her feet swung to and fro, not touching the ground. "By the light of Allah!" she whispered, and then, "Rashiid is going to be sooo angry!"

Raphael found he was more nervous than ever, though not nearly so warm. "I did not ever tell him I was a eunuch," he ventured to say to the girl, but she only muttered and shook her head.

Then with her typical unpredictability, Ama squeezed Raphael teasingly in a place he did not expect. "I won't tell," she promised, grinning sidelong. "Not if you're nice to me." Then she turned and darted, perchlike, past the fish pond and away.

In the harbor of Adra, the big-bellied ships bobbed and wallowed in the swell. The longshoremen sang in Spanish and the wind tasted of salt.

Djoura hated it: both the Spanish and the water-laden air, which made her nose run. She despised the whining Northern Arabic of the mariners who warbled and yodeled to each other in the hold, securing their cargo of oranges. She had great contempt for the official Granadan bookkeeper, a sunburned Spaniard who sat on a small date keg by the gangplank, in case the owner of the boat should try to load anything in evasion of the export duties.

Djoura sat behind the gay-striped partitions in the stern of the ship which was to take her across the Mediterranean, and she thought furiously.

It had been a pleasant shock, in the beginning, when the tribesmen burst into the Spanish pig's hot kitchen, scaring his old wife into hysterics and pulling her out of the grease and soot. It had also been fulfilling to see Rashiid babbling apologies—not to her, of course, but to the Berbers he had so grievously offended.

Djoura had not expected these pale Berbers, strange to her, to take such an interest. It was only just—only Berber—that they should, of course, but still, Djoura had lived her life in the real world, and no one else in her five years of slavery looked past her skin color to see that she was of the free people, and that her captivity was an outrage.

And this, besides, was not the manner in which Djoura had planned to regain her freedom. Where did they think they were sending her, anyway? Not a soul had bothered to share with her that information. The black woman knew well she had no living male kin. She had seen her father's headless body, and her single brother—well, if he had lived, he would have found her by now.

Perhaps they would dump her with the first black Berbers to pass through Algiers. Then what would she be? Little more than a slave, again.

As a slave, she had known herself a Berber, and therefore not truly a slave. Now, kinless among her own race, she would be a free but homeless female, and therefore not free at all.

Djoura cursed the pride which had forced Hasiim to "rescue" her—a woman in whom he had no interest, and to whom he had never bothered to speak.

And always Djoura's circle of thought returned to her Pinkie, whom she had groomed for the role of her male "protector" in their escape from Rashiid's household, and who was the unwitting cause of all this upset. How had he suffered for his interference? Surely that greasy swine had not let his loose tongue go unpunished . . .

Poor Pinkie: How long would he be able to hide his secret among that household—without Djoura? He would be a real eunuch soon enough, and with stripes to boot.

Ah, but maybe that would be just as well. Pinkie was so naïve: too childlike even to consider vengeance. And he wasn't much of a man, to look at: pale, beardless, baby-haired. He wouldn't mind as much as some. Assuredly he would not kill himself from the shame of castration, as many men would. Djoura sighed. The wind caused the hangings of her enclosure to flap and billow, reducing it to an unconcealing framework of ropes: a seclusion as ineffective as was this "rescue" from slavery.

Then, between one moment and the next, Djoura knew that she could not leave Pinkie to his fate.

For hadn't she named him her brother? And even as a brother must avenge his sister or die, so must she, Djoura, return for the poor pale singer she had adopted.

Besides, she missed him.

With dignity, the woman rose to her feet. Brass coins jingled sweetly around her ears. A pillar of black, she strode out of her enclosure, ducking under the supporting tent rope.

The bookkeeper with his tally sat on a keg at the head of the gangplank. He looked up with surprise to see the woman standing before him. In faulty Arabic he told her to return to her place.

In response Djoura mumbled something inaudible. She crooked her little finger and whispered again. Rising halfway to his feet, the embarrassed official presented his ear for some petty feminine revelation.

Djoura put one large hand firmly over the man's money pouch and the other firmly against his chest. She heaved.

With a weak cry the bookkeeper fell backward from the keg into the green Mediterranean. Djoura paraded down the plank and into Adra.

CHAPTER 10

"Though heat rises," the deep, pipe-organ voice beneath them intoned, "the upper regions are colder. This is true over all the earth."

Gaspare was not satisfied. He shifted his grip on Saara's waist. (He had shifted his grip so many times that she was developing the horse's trick of swelling her middle whenever the girth tightened.) "I'm more inclined to believe you just haven't gone high enough to find the layer of heat that surrounds the earth."

There was a short silence from the dragon. "I have never read that there is such a layer," he replied at last.

"Stands to reason," attested the youth, kicking the metallic black neck absently.

"I rather think a look at the simple geometry of the situation will explain the phenomenon, youngster."

"Geometry. Is that a foreign word?" Gaspare mumbled distrustfully.

The dragon sighed at Gaspare's ignorance. Saara sighed also, for she had a headache. She had carried it since waking on the mountain's stony side with Gaspare shaking her. She wondered how the dragon (old as he was) could have recovered so quickly.

When Saara as a child had a headache, her mother had used to roll an egg against her head, until the ache went into the egg. Then she would bury it beneath the snow of the yard: egg and ache together.

She wished now she had an egg. She wished she were home.

Home? Yes, and she didn't mean Lombardy, but the far Fenlands, where her Lappish people dug their houses, pressed felt, and followed the herds of sturdy deer through white winter. For the first time in many, many years, Saara the Fenwoman thought of home without remembering Jekkinan and the faces of her dead babies, strewn across the floor of the hut.

Her children were dead, and Jekkinan too. So, for that matter, was Ruggerio, and her old enemy Delstrego senior. All dead and folded away. (Like egg white in a cake. Like an egg itself buried in the snow.) Soon she, too, would be folded into history: that was the rule ever since the Spirit sang earth into being.

Damiano was right; the summoning made the separation of the living and dead worse. Saara felt renewed pain, for she would have liked so much to have shown Lappland to Damiano. He would have liked it, for he liked anything pretty.

If she lived through this, she told herself, she would return to the Fens and see it again—the red autumn, the white winter, the crying geese in the springtime—for the

sake of Damiano Delstrego, and perhaps he would know
the beauty through her eyes.

Padding barefoot down an alley wet with offal, Djoura's
every movement was regal. The night air might as well
have been thick with jasmine as with garlic and piss, for
Djoura's free soul was touching the high winds freighted
with clouds.

For over a week she had been alone among the rocks in
the climbing desert which stretched between the ocean and
high Granada. She had bought a mule and then sold it
again, preferring her own feet for transport. The customs-
man's gold had permitted her to eat well. Now she had
reached Granada.

For the first time in her grown life Djoura's steps had
not been ordained by another. These nights were the first
in her life that someone else had not decided where she
should sleep. She had slept in haystacks and under
upturned wagons. She had slept under the moon.

Tonight Djoura did not sleep at all, but paraded past
mud brick and stucco, through the capillaries of a city she
did not know, toward the liberation of another liberation
besides herself.

The poor were curled dozing in doorways all around
her. Good for them—it was certainly better to sleep in a
doorway than in the rank holes within doors. Djoura
stared down at the sleepers from a great height. Her veil
was back and her hair gleamed with a constellation of
coins. From within one house—a heavy, feverful pile of
mud—came singing. It was bad singing, out of tune and
with strictly private rhythm. But Djoura took it in and let it
add to her own strength; she swelled with power as she
walked.

"I am so tall now," she whispered to the air, "that there
is no chain forged which could span my neck. And should
some clever man forge such a shackle, he would find no
ladder big enough that he could reach up to put it on.

"And if he _did_ reach me, I would crush him in this
hand, for his trouble," Djoura continued. Her black hand
moved invisibly through the heavy shadow. Eyes, teeth,
and coins glimmered. "I grow larger at every moment.

"Like the earth after rain," she murmured on. "Taller

and stronger, stronger and taller." Her round nostrils flared
like those of a high-blooded horse.

"I am Djoura, the black one, the free. The breaker of
chains. I am Djoura: my will is a sword!"

And the walls on either hand fell away from her as
though she had pushed them down. Djoura stood at a
large crossroads, under moonlight. She raised her arms
and made the moonlight hers. Her layered clothing cast a
terrible shadow on the paving.

Even Djoura herself blinked, surprised at the way the
world was acceding to her new-won mastery. The moon
touched her face like a rain of white feathers.

Djoura cupped her hands to the moon. She danced
(with African straightness, lest she spill the moon from her
hands) and laughed, crying, "I am mad, mad with my own
strength! Moon keep me up, for if I stumble, I must knock a
house down!"

And though the woman was far from stumbling, she
did spill moonlight as she spun. Cold light spattered from
the coins on her head over every rough cobble, and her
wide skirts made a shadow like a spinning black planet.

There was one other sharing Djoura's star-washed
stage, though she hadn't noticed him. This was a small
man, long nosed, thin, dressed in Bedouin white muslin.
He sat waiting on the dry fountainhead that marked the
center of the square, and what he was waiting for is of no
importance to us.

His legs were neatly crossed. To Djoura (when she at
last perceived him) he looked impossibly droll, sitting there
so neatly and so still under the savage moonlight, so as she
passed him she reached up one long African arm and
clenched her hand. "I have caught the moon!" she whispered to him, making her eyes round. "I will hide it in my
bosom now, and no one will know who took it but *you!*"

Following her own words, she thrust her hand into her
bodice, lifted it out, and shook her fingers in the small
man's face. "See! I have hidden it. I don't have it anymore!"
She floated away, then, laughing high in her nose.

The man sat without moving. His mouth had gone
faintly sour, and his eyes were fixed on the wall opposite
him. But after Djoura had passed, fading into another dark
alley, he raised his sight to heaven. "There is no God but
Allah," he intoned, "and Mohammad is his Prophet."

* * *

"Yes, a fish," Raphael admitted. "A fish, or a small bird. This orange tree, too, whispers His name to me, but only after everyone has gone to bed."

"His name?" whispered the soft voice that came from the shadow.

"The name of my Father, whom they call Allah: the name I can't remember from moment to moment," Raphael replied. Then he pushed a weight of pale yellow hair from his eyes. "But none of these speaks as clearly to me of Him as one look at your face, Dami."

Either the ghost laughed, or the wind made a rustle in the tree. "Thank you, Seraph. Though I have no more face than the green earth and your memory give me, still that is good to hear."

"The green earth?" Raphael moved closer to the voice of his friend. "I am made of the earth too. This—here—is the earth . . . See?" He lifted one fair arm and clenched and opened the hand. "It is earth itself my desire is causing to move. Flesh is earth, like wood, like fish scales."

"And it is me." The deep blue eyes (not angel's eyes any longer but Raphael's eyes nonetheless) shone with particular intensity. "I am growing increasingly . . . what is the right word . . . *tender* of this body."

Brown eyes, created of Raphael's memory, answered his gaze. "You take your exile well," Damiano commented, his words dusted with soft irony. "But I think you'll get very tired of your body if you sit up every night, talking to ghosts and orange trees."

Like a child, Raphael drew his knees up to his chin and wrapped his arms around them. He closed his eyes contentedly. His form was obscured in a veil of light and shadow: Damiano covered his teacher with dusky wings. "Take it well? My exile? What else should I do? I am bound to this flesh. It colors everything that happens to me, and time does the rest; time is always around me, with the drip of the water clock—plink, plink, plink. Get up, void, eat, work, play for Rashiid, sleep (or try to). Is it time, flesh, or slavery that rules my life? I think if I were not a slave, with someone to tell me at every moment what to do, time would confuse me utterly.

"I do get tired," he admitted. "But it is not because of your visits that I get tired, nor yet from talking to the orange tree. It is because my mistress keeps me awake every night."

There was a moment's meditative silence. "I have heard of men having that problem," Damiano replied finally, in a careful voice devoid of expression. "I have never heard they were to be pitied, however."

The man who had been an angel sighed. "I am not really a simpleton, Dami; I know when you're making fun of me. Without cause, I assure you."

The ghost grinned. Raphael's answering smile was slow.

"It *is* a problem. Ama sleeps during the siesta (which is something I'm not given time to do), and she cannot sleep all night as well.

"She wants to play with me then. She wants to sit on my knee while I comb her hair. She wants to complain about her husband, and she wants me to tell her stories.

"What am I to do? I am her servant, and besides, she is very sweet. But sometimes I'm asleep when I should be doing something else. Yesterday I fell asleep during my master's dinner."

"Did he beat you?" came the concerned question.

Raphael shook his head. Night-silvered hair spilled over his shoulders and cast milky lights on the water. "No. He only threatened to." Raphael gazed upward at the full moon and yawned so hard he squeezed the moon out of his eyes. "I can never predict, about Rashiid."

The spirit also laughed. "So! Sleep now, then. I'll play for you—I'll play especially dull music. You'll have no choice but to nod off."

It was not dull music, nor was the lute poorly played. It was to Raphael very dear music, for he had taught it to his student and Damiano had changed it and added to it until it came back as a gift to the teacher. And Raphael listened in no danger of falling asleep, for he was traveling a long way in his thoughts.

Chained to a framework of bone: prisoned in time. Not miserable, however, even though the damp reached through his cotton shirt like searching roots and his eyes were grainy.

For Raphael's head was full of music: music which took time—man's master—and played with it. It curled around his mortal bones until they shone with light. The walls of

Raphael's prison dissolved under the gentle siege of Damiano's lute.

But his reverie was a slave's reverie and he did not forget that in the morning he would have to help Fatima bake the breakfast breads. Nor that he would then wake up his mistress and attempt the duties of lady's maid. There would be digging, or picking, or pruning, and during the hot hours Rashiid would want his music. Sand the morning's dirty pots, crank the great fan in the north chamber, then dinner and more lute playing (unless there was someone to impress, Rashiid preferred it over the ud). And tomorrow night his sleep would be interrupted or forestalled as it always was, by little Ama, restless as a bird.

He carried all these burdens with him through his joy, like a man dancing with a sack of rocks on his back.

And his sad smile, as he gazed into the darkness where he could not see his friend, was ancient.

Raphael heard a noise through the music. He turned his head to peer over the packed earth of the yard, but he knew already what it was. Ama was coming out.

She walked on her tiptoes, not out of stealth but out of bouncy habit. Somewhere she had found a completely unorthodox, unsuitable scarlet shawl, and she had wrapped this thing around her head and shoulders, making her appear more birdlike than ever. She blundered over a garden rake on her way through the yard.

"Hisst! Hisst!" She scrambled around the edge of the fish pond, calling in too loud a whisper. "Raphael! Pinkie! Where are you? Don't tell me you're not here; I won't believe that!" Her padded skirt caught twigs off the ground. One foot sent a litter of gravel into the water.

Raphael crawled to his feet. He looked questioningly in the direction of Damiano, but the bodiless playing continued. "This is she," Raphael explained, speaking without sound. Damiano made no reply.

He stepped over to Ama. "I didn't say I wasn't here."

She gave out a treble yelp, shied away from him, and slipped one foot into the cold water.

Raphael caught her, and for a moment she struggled in his grasp. Then she was giggling, and she put her arms around his neck and kissed Raphael. She kissed him wherever she could reach: on the left corner of his mouth, his nose, his chin. Her kisses were short and sharp: like bird pecks.

He put her down on the pathway and turned, self-consciously, to the spot the music came from.

"Don't mind me," came a ghostly whisper. "I doubt very much the child can see me." Damiano struck up a saraband.

Ama was rubbing her mouth thoughtfully. "Raphael! Do you know you have a beard coming?"

Confused both by Damiano's and Ama's words, Raphael put his own hand to his face. "A . . . a beard?"

Ama bent him down with a hand behind his neck. She ran her fingernails backward over his cheek with female expertise. "Yes. You're growing a beard." She snickered, came up on tiptoe and poked him under the jawbone. "Well, why not? We both know what you are—or aren't!

"My secret stallion!" Ama bubbled over with connivance as she added, "But how we'll hide *this* from Rashiid I don't know. Unless we pluck them all out, of course."

"Sounds painful," murmured Damiano from nowhere in particular.

The slave, too, made a tentative demur, but Ama was having none of it.

Raphael shot his friend a pleading glance as his mistress dragged him toward the house. The ghost, however, made no move to interfere.

By the light of one candle it was very difficult to find the fine yellowish hairs on Raphael's cheeks. Sitting on her subject's lap was also not the most convenient way to set about the task. But there was only one stool in the women's hidey-hole (now that Moorish visitations had become much rarer) and Ama was used to working in bad light. She was expert with the tiny brass tweezers.

"There's one," she hissed, and the implement hovered closer. The tweezers struck with the speed of a hawk and Raphael flinched just perceptibly.

"Poor Pinkie," Ama crooned, and left a kiss on the spot she had stung. The kiss took much longer than the plucking.

Raphael looked around at the candle-dancing clay walls.

"Perhaps I should simply tell Rashiid that I am not a eunuch at all," he ventured to suggest. "It is the simple truth."

Ama drew her breath in in a hiss. "Raphael! Then you would *be* a eunuch for certain. Do you want that to happen?"

He squirmed in his seat, considering the question. "No," he replied with some decision. "I don't know quite why, but that is a very repellent thought."

"Or maybe he would merely kill you in his rage!" Ama's dark threat dissolved into a giggle. She plucked and kissed three times in succession. Then she kissed three times more. "My dear Pinkie. You're funny, with your 'simple truth' and all!"

Ama was so small and warm and cuddly that Raphael found himself hugging her. Her hair was against his lips. He stroked it. She lifted her face to his.

The only other woman who had ever touched him had had hands less soft than these. Black hands, which had bathed him and combed his hair. Hands that smelled like sun and sand. Raphael heard Djoura's rich, brocaded songs in his ears as he held the little Arab girl.

His embrace grew tighter, with an urgency that seemed imposed upon him from outside, against his will. Ama pressed her round, fragile body against his. The last kiss did not end, but wandered from her mouth to her neck. Raphael's flesh was singing like the strings of a lute struck all together. So this was lust, he thought to himself.

This beautiful thing. Lust. A grin stretched tightly across his face.

"Why aren't you looking at me?" hissed Ama in his ear. "Why are you sitting there smiling into space like that? Don't you like to kiss me?"

Raphael had to swallow before talking and still his voice was thick. "I do," he said, smiling shyly. "And I don't know why I was staring out; I just was."

"Then kiss me again, and keep your eyes closed," she insisted. Raphael obeyed his mistress, and she in turn took his hand in her smaller one and placed it where she thought best.

The stool Raphael had been sitting on had gotten lost somehow. They were sinking to the floor. And the floor was warm. It was as though the earth were turning soft and silky: like flesh.

But behind his closed eyes the flesh he stroked was not amber, like that of Ama, but ebony, and the mouth that touched his was heavier. And more proud.

"I want you to be my husband," Ama crooned, burying her face against Raphael's breast. "You are so beautiful. So gentle!

"I don't love Rashiid; I hate him! He is a bear. A stupid pig! I want *your* love."

Raphael's blue-black eyes clouded over. He struggled up from the floor, pulling his mistress onto his lap once again. He nestled her sleek head beneath his chin.

"Poor Ama," he whispered. "My poor, dear Ama."

Ama struggled free. "What do you mean, 'poor Ama'? You are supposed to say, 'lovely Ama, beautiful, generous Ama'! Are you not my slave, after all? Is it not I who am conferring honor?"

She stood, and thus was slightly taller than he was, seated. Her taper threw a writhing shadow on the wall behind. Raphael saw a small candle flame in each of her shining brown eyes.

"I . . . I called you poor Ama because you said you were unhappy," he said simply.

Ama settled her clothes, like feathers, into place. She leaned forward to him, hands on her knees, and kissed the tip of his nose. "Ah, but you can make me happy!" she whispered, and her ready grin was back.

"See this?" She let the brilliant shawl fall about her face. "Isn't it terrible? Spanish. I wore it for you!"

Raphael took the fabric in his hand. He didn't think it was terrible at all, even if Spanish. It suited Ama's olive coloring very well. He thought it would look good on Djoura too.

"How can I be your husband when you already have a husband?" he thought to ask.

"If Rashiid will be angry to learn I am a man, will he not be much angrier to find you want to . . ."

Ama cut him off with a grimace. "Rashiid is not to know, mooncalf!"

"This is Rashiid's house. You are Rashiid's wife, and I am Rashiid's slave." Raphael folded his hands between his knees and let his head hang forward. For a while he watched the play of shadows on the tile floor. "I may be a simpleton, as everyone says, yet I know we cannot act *that* part for long here without the master discovering us."

There was total silence from Ama, which lasted until Raphael lifted his eyes to see she was crying.

He opened his mouth in incoherent apology, but Ama spoke with trembling voice. "Don't you love me, my Pinkie, my Raphael? I have loved you since the first time I saw you. It was because of you I made Rashiid buy that nasty black Djoura, and . . ."

"Djoura isn't nasty," he began, but seeing Ama's expression, immediately took a new tack.

"You are very dear to me, mistress. You are my closest friend in this place, and . . ."

"You have closer elsewhere?" Her dimpled chin jutted forward.

Raphael was not allowed to reply, for Ama found her own answer. "Djoura! That's why she wanted you sold together; she said you were her brother, but what she meant was quite different, I'll bet! I'll bet you lay together every night you could!"

"That isn't true," he said, but as he spoke his mind filled with unbidden images, with the Berber's song all mixed with Ama's warm skin and the divine irresponsibility he had just learned to call lust. Therefore his words did not carry authenticity to his mistress's ear.

"I'm going to tell Rashiid you attempted to force yourself on me!" the girl declared.

"Please don't," Raphael said weakly.

"Why not? Why shouldn't I?"

"Because it's not the truth."

This plain response seemed to daunt Ama. "Well, I'll just tell him you're a whole man. That's the truth, and will be the same in the end."

He reached out a hand to her, but hers hid behind her back. "But you said he would do me harm."

Ama snorted and looked down the length of her nose at the fair face before her. "A moment ago you were the upright one: the one who wanted to tell him. And you a mere Christian—a giaour! Trying to make me feel low. Well, where's your courage now?"

The entreating hand dropped to Raphael's lap. "I never said I was courageous, Ama. In truth I am not very brave at all."

He blinked confusedly and rubbed his face with both palms. "Nor very clever, I don't think.

"But I do know this; if I lie with you, mistress, it will lead to great unhappiness, maybe death, for us both."

His blue eyes gazed so steadily that Ama turned her head to one side. "I'm not afraid."

"I am," whispered Raphael.

Ama ground her teeth. "Then be afraid of this, Pinkie. Unless you're a lot . . . nicer to me by tomorrow night, I have every intention of telling Rashiid what I know about you."

Ama snatched the candle and stalked out of the room.

He sat with his forehead propped on his spread fingertips, his elbows on his knees. "How have I gotten myself into such a sticky web, when to my best understanding I did nothing wrong at all?"

It was the sort of question a man asks of the air, but in Raphael's case the air replied. "Know your own duty; that's all that's asked of you, and it's simple enough, isn't it?"

Raphael lifted his beautiful, offended face. By the velvety movement of a shadow it seemed his friend was standing just outside the window. "No, it is not! Simple? How can you say . . ."

Damiano's vague form wavered, shruglike. "That's word for word what you said to me once."

"I did?" The slave hoisted himself out of the window again, and took a calmative breath of night air. "How dared I open my mouth about mortal concerns, having never been a mortal of any sort?"

There were the stars, up above his head in a Spanish sky untainted by clouds. There was the full moon. Unaccountably, Raphael thought of Djoura. "A mortal of any sort," he repeated, lamely, to those stars.

"Yet your advice was always of the best," Damiano chuckled, in a voice as soft as the wind. "You told me to dress myself to attract girls. You cut my hair becomingly. You even won over my sweetheart, who felt she had reason to hate you.

"In fact, Raphael, mortal or no, you have always known how to please the ladies."

The blond turned to stare at Damiano, which was difficult, since he had no clear idea where he was. "You were listening!" he blurted aloud. "To Ama and me!"

There came a soft rustling, not like that of orange leaves but like that of a man shifting from foot to embarrassed foot. "Yes, I was listening. Shouldn't I have been?

"After all, I hadn't said I was going away, had I?" Then, in tones airy and droll, he added, "Perhaps I should write you a note to tell you when I'm nearby. I remember someone suggesting that policy to me once."

The ghost's voice had taken Raphael to the garden wall. He slumped against it, feeling its coolness as a relief more than physical. "Don't make fun of me, Dami. If I was officious in the past, you can console yourself with the knowledge I'm wretched enough now."

Damiano stood beside him in an instant, perfect from his rough hair to his large mountaineer's boots. His square hand (nails cut blunt on long musician's fingers) rested on his friend's shoulder. "I'm so sorry, Seraph," he said. "I was only trying to make you laugh.

"Is it what your mistress said that disturbs you? Is it her displeasure, or do you fear your master will really do you harm? I have some advice on that point, if you'd care to listen."

As Raphael opened his mouth to tell Damiano that he was quite definitely afraid of what Rashiid would do, another answer came to his lips. "It's not any of that."

The cicadas were droning like a headache, like sleep. Rashiid's unused mare moved restlessly in her confined quarters, kicking at a board.

"When Ama . . . embraced me, I really wanted to . . . to . . ."

"Of course you did," said the ghost.

"No, you don't understand. I wanted to . . . replace her with someone else. And make love to her instead."

This statement hung between them in the air for some moments before Raphael added to it. "I miss my friend Djoura."

"Ah." Damiano's voice held understanding, but he could not resist adding, in the next breath, "Wasn't she the one who used to kick you at night to make you stop singing?"

"She only did that once," the slave replied with offended dignity. "And I understand now. Her whole plan was to keep everyone from finding out. That I am not a eunuch."

A ripple of pigeon gray against the white of the wall showed that the spirit had ruffled his wings. "Well. That leads us back to the original problem. The fact that you are not a eunuch."

Raphael, feeling very uncertain of himself, listened in his friend's voice for clues. "Is that what you think, Dami? That the problem is simply that I *ought* to be a eunuch? Perhaps, then, I should allow my master to . . ."

There was an explosion of immaterial feathers. Damiano's twin sails snapped upward, hiding the moon and stars. "Seraph! Teacher! Raphael! What are you saying?

"You must not permit yourself to be so maimed! Nor, for that matter, should you continue as a slave. Nor languish without your lady friend.

"And *that's* the advice of Damiano, the intrusive spirit. Take it or leave it," he concluded, less passionately.

Raphael couldn't help casting a furtive eye over the dark garden, even though he knew Damiano's outburst had made no sound another could hear. "But Rashiid is my master," he answered. "Under the laws of man. And Djoura—she is freed and gone from here."

The ghost allowed his smoky wings to sink back again, until they obscured his outline, but a pair of quick Italian eyes darted from the wall to his friend's wan face. "Laws of man," he echoed, rumbling in his deep, mumbling, Piedmontese accent. "Hah, for the laws of man!" A complex, obscure gesture accompanied the words.

"Raphael, you know me for a witch, don't you?"

The blond's eyes (not quick; not Italian) deepened in memory. "I know what you were in life, my dear friend."

Damiano lifted one eyebrow and one wing, in unconscious imitation of his teacher. "Well, Seraph, alive or dead, I'm about to work a great magic for you. To help alleviate this problem."

Raphael managed a smile. He let his back slide down the smooth wall until he was sitting on the turf. "Which problem, Dami? That of my freedom, or of my . . ."

"They are linked," the ghost replied shortly. With a face so full of gravity it wore a scowl, he floated back from Raphael.

Great dusky wings stood out sideways, as stiff as heraldry. Two rather large hands were lifted in front of Damiano's breast. He raised his flashing eyes to the heavens. "Habera Corpus!" he intoned. "Ades, Barbara, Ades!"

His shadowy hand was lit suddenly and only for a moment. The air smelled of lightning.

"Witness," cried Damiano, pointing inexplicably at the top of the garden wall. "Witness my power."

Raphael looked, saw nothing, and gazed confusedly once more at the spirit.

Who completed the ruination of the effect by winking.

But at a sound Raphael's head turned again to the wall, just in time to see Djoura, bareheaded but draped in her numerous garb, put one foot and then the other over the top and drop to the dry garden earth beside him.

Raphael's welcoming embrace was oddly hesitant and awkward, for the juxtaposition of what he had imagined with what he had never dared made him shy. But the black woman was too full of her own mission to notice.

"Don't ask questions," Djoura hissed into his ear. "I have walked all the way across Andalusia to rescue you, so you just follow me."

With a glance back toward the spot where he had last seen Damiano and another at the figure of the boy who lay snoring at the bolted garden gate, Raphael did follow Djoura, up and over the garden wall.

Now I am a renegade, he thought, crouching in the obscurity of the roadside, looking back at the pale height of clay he had just scaled. Just like Lucifer: a renegade.

Not quite like Lucifer, he qualified, as a firm dark handhold pulled him on. Lucifer would never let anyone lead him by the hand. The snores of Ali the doorkeeper faded in his ears.

For five minutes he scuttled after his liberator, along alleyways he did not recognize, passing squares where even now in the second hour of morning they encountered people who had risen already for the next day as well as people who had not yet been to bed.

He was prodded to walk upright. He was made to stroll. Djoura, stepping meekly behind him, twisted her bony knuckle into the small of his back to induce him to behave. "You are free, Pinkie! Walk like a free man!"

Raphael was walking the only way he knew to walk. On impulse he turned on his heel and came round beside the woman. He laid one arm over her shoulders.

"If I am free, then this is how I please to walk," he replied reasonably. "And if I were wholly free, I would not walk at all, because I need so much to speak with you, my dear Djoura."

The Berber wiggled out of touch. "None of that! What are you thinking, man? You'll have us both pilloried, holding on to me in public."

Raphael smiled ruefully, feeling not very free at all. But he trotted along, talking over his shoulder, while Djoura drove him from behind.

"Did the magic pull you from your Moroccan home, Djoura? Or were you still on the sea when the call came?"

Djoura puzzled at his phrasing. "I escaped from the ship before it sailed the harbor. I tossed a customs man into the water, took his wallet, and walked down the gangway an hour before sailing.

"Pah!" She spat dry and catlike upon the street. "That ship was like a prison, and I've had enough of chains. And I have no family left in the south.

"Besides." Her voice dropped in timbre and her eyes snared moonlight. "I had to come back for my pink Berber."

A grin spread over Raphael's face: a shy grin as tight as a shrunken suit of clothes. All he could say was, "I missed you, too, Djoura." But that smile and the warmth which accompanied it dissolved as he thought further.

"But if I am running away from my master and you are running away from your home, then where are we going to?"

The black woman snickered. "How about your home, Pinkie? Don't you have one, somewhere, with a mother who would be glad to see her little boy again?

"Along with his charming friend?"

Raphael stopped dead in the exact middle of the street. He made no answer, nor did he glance at Djoura, but stood with his hands clenched at his sides and his head bowed. He bit his lip. Djoura was standing before him, a concerned look in her coffee-colored eyes. "I know already that you are not a Berber," she said diffidently. "It was the music you play that confused me. But I have heard you play the music of many places, since, and that doesn't matter."

"It doesn't? You came back for me anyway?" They were quite alone on the street. Raphael touched her face. The look she gave him back was haughty, as though to say the reasons she did the things she did were hers to know.

"Djoura, I don't know how to find my home anymore. My memory has been . . . damaged. But I know the earth is filled with pleasant places to live. Come with me and we will find one we like."

"That is for me to say," replied the woman, shooting him a glance over a lopsided smile. "I am the one with the wallet," she added, letting coins tinkle softly beneath her clothes.

But she let him kiss her in the darkness that came after the moon's setting.

CHAPTER 11

The great military entity that was the Alhambra was not about to bestir itself in the cause of the wounded pride of the Qa'id Hasiim Alfard: not though he had a thousand horsemen under his command. But Hasiim had also within his regiment a few dozen men tied to him by blood: tribesmen and sons of subordinate tribes. These had allegiance of another order.

Days before Djoura arrived back in Granada, Hasiim was aware of her escape. When the fursan courier relayed this message to the qa'id, he did nothing but shrug. But Hasiim's many eyes and ears were opened.

Djoura led her blond companion through a tangle of sleeping streets. There was no indecision in her step, for what is the use of indecision when one does not know where one is going? Raphael, too, followed without hesitation, for it was all one to him. The light (hardly more than symbolic) iron ring about his neck had been hidden beneath swaths of fabric.

Black fabric.

"In the north," murmured Djoura over her shoulder, "it will be necessary for me to pretend to be giaour—a Christian. You will show me how."

Raphael considered this silently, while he gazed down at the uneven street in front of his bare feet. "I'm not sure," he said at last, "that I can do that convincingly."

"Because I am black?" Djoura countered, with rising belligerence. "Or because I am too much of Islam?"

Raphael shook his head. "Because I myself don't know

how. There are so many dogmas *and* sacraments, and one
need only do or say one word wrong to get into a great deal
of trouble. I have not ever studied . . ."

The Berber woman snorted. "Yet you yourself are a
Christian, and have managed."

"I am not a Christian," he stated, and for easier
conversation, Raphael fell back beside the woman. "That
much I *do* know. There is a ritual called baptism which one
must undergo to be a Christian, sometimes by immersion
and sometimes by sprinkling. I have never been baptized."

"That you remember . . ." chided the black good-
naturedly. "But you don't remember much."

She took his hand. "Ho! You are so cold, Pinkie. Is it
because of your weak skin?"

At her touch (And it was not cold at all. No, underneath
all her tentlike layers, Djoura was very warm.) Raphael had
begun to tremble slightly. He turned his hand beneath
hers, and moved his sensitive fingertips over the surface of
her palm, her thumb, her wrist . . .

And he said nothing at all.

Dawn was near, but the darkness now was almost
complete. Djoura stopped in her tracks, suddenly indecisive. "We'll give you another shawl, Pinkie. That will keep
you warmer."

He allowed her to drape another musty garment over
his shoulders. "Djoura," he whispered, when all was
arranged to her maternal liking. "Could you call me
Raphael?"

She stiffened and barked a laugh. "That again?" When
he neither moved nor responded she continued more
seriously. "That is a very important name in the desert,
Pinkie. A fearful name. Raphael is one of the great djinn,
which a good Berber—a good Muslim—must never bow to
worship."

Then it was Raphael's turn to laugh. "I don't ask you to
worship me, dear one, but only to call me by my name."
And when Djoura didn't reply he took the opportunity to
kiss her softly upon the lips.

Djoura stood still for a moment, then made a very small
noise in her throat and turned her head away. Stepping
back, she protested, "I don't want to be pawed around by a
simpleminded man!"

"I am not simpleminded, Djoura," he replied with no hint of offense. "Only new here.

"And I love you. When you left the household . . ."

"That was *your* fault, with your big mouth . . ."

"When you left I missed you terribly, and then when Damiano brought you back . . ."

"When *who* brought me back?" the woman almost wailed. "You *are* an idiot, Pinkie." Djoura caught her tongue, then, and with unexpected consideration corrected herself, "Raphael. I came back by myself, with no help from anyone!" She turned on her heel and paraded forward again, going nowhere in particular with great determination. Raphael took hold of her skirts so that he would not lose her in the dark. "I'm glad," he began again. "Either way. That you came back for me."

She sniffed. "You are my responsibility."

The man's steps slowed. "That's all? Your responsibility?" His fingers slipped their hold. Raphael came to a disappointed stop in the middle of an empty street.

Djoura, feeling his absence as quickly as she had his uncomfortable presence, turned around again.

"Curse it all, Pinkie! You only think you love me because I wiped your ass for you when you were sick and pushed food in your mouth."

Raphael had one hand resting on each of the woman's shoulders. "What is the difference," he whispered softly, "between thinking you love someone and loving them? I love you because you are kind and hate to be known as kind. Because you are brave . . ."

"Brave, huh? Because I kicked you?" Her voice held a shade of embarrassment.

"Ah, but you won't kick me again, will you?" His grip slid down to the woman's elbows. He took her hands.

Djoura was suddenly aware that Raphael was taller than she was. And the awkward, gangling Pinkie of her memory had to crumble before the presence before her, that held her hands in a grip no longer cold.

"And because you sing, Djoura," he continued, as though he had not been interrupted. "When I was newly a . . . a slave and I tried to refuse this life, I heard you singing."

In a small voice, very unlike herself, Djoura said, "I only did that to bother the woman sellers."

"You did it beautifully," Raphael insisted. "It was the voice of . . . of Allah, to me. It still is."

Once more Djoura snorted, but she allowed Raphael to slip his arms around her. "I have grown very bad at hearing *his* voice, Djoura, except through others.

"But what does all that matter? In the end I don't need a reason to love you, except that you are Djoura and I am . . . myself. Whatever you call me."

The Berber woman allowed her head to rest against his collarbone. She rested her hand on his shoulder. Although she was no less uncomfortable, she felt no desire to move. "Ah, Pink—Raphael. I know you are no simpleton. In some ways you are as wise as a scholar. And my singing is like a bird's peep next to yours.

"If only you weren't . . ."

"Yes?" His voice was tender but worried. "Weren't what?"

"Weren't such a funny color!" Djoura burst out, and then she giggled. They both giggled together. It was a laughter that grew almost rowdy and then was cut off knife-sharp.

They stared at one another, mouths still open, silent.

Raphael pulled her closer. "You can't see my color in the dark," he murmured close into the woman's ear.

The arms Raphael and Djoura wound around one another were hard through labor. It grew very warm on that tenebrous windy street.

"I think it is getting hotter, even up here," stated Gaspare. Saara had one hand gripping the dragon's pierced scale while the other held the young man's hands together in front of her waist.

He leaned out over the dragon's side and the updrafts of the great beast's movement caught his red hair. Nothing but Saara's grip held him on. "This is a long mountain range, dragon," Gaspare observed idly. "What comes after this?"

"Granada," replied the black dragon.

The first light was miraculous but frightening, for although it enabled their feet to move with careless speed, it exposed them to the cruel, awakening world.

How white was Granada, where the sun had bleached

even the urine-stained walls to fairness. And how large, for they had been shuffling through half the night and had never reached the north city wall. It was as though Djoura's stern leadership had taken them in circles.

The odor of lamp oil and that of candle wax floated out of the bare little windows along the street. Soon sandaled feet and bare feet trod the cobbles and the clay beside theirs. Raphael was once more pushed out in front. Djoura's eyes sank to the earth, doelike, submissive. She prodded her leader with one concealed knuckle.

"I don't know where I'm going, Djoura," he said amicably. "The street keeps curving to the left."

"It can't do that forever," the Berber woman hissed. "Tell me what you see."

Raphael cleared his throat. "I see . . .

"A shop with a brass cup hanging out in front. Another with a wheat sheaf (very dry) impaled above the door. I see a man in trousers striped with red."

"Keep walking as you talk."

Raphael strived to obey. "I see a crack of the sun, along that cross street. Shall we take it?"

"The sun or the cross street?" countered Djoura. They giggled together—again.

"Now the sun is gone again. I see an ass pulling a cart of sand—get over to the side, here. And I see three women with very large bottles.

"Children. More women. A black man in the doorway, with green-striped trousers."

Djoura had to sneak a glance. "A eunuch," she announced, flat-voiced. "Nothing to me."

"Now the sun. Another ass. Watch the man lying in the street."

"Drunk." Djoura stepped carefully around.

"Two more asses. A man on a horse." Raphael was panting with the effort it took to speak while picking their way along a street where every house was vomiting forth its inhabitants.

The street *did* continue to turn left. It seemed to be a circle. What use was it to travel in a circle like this? And why would anyone build a circular street?

Raphael was about to suggest they turn at the very next cross street, and go right, toward the outside of the circle. Instead he stopped dead.

"I think you should raise your eyes, dear one," he whispered.

Djoura lifted her eyes toward the odd-dozen black-robed men on their little desert horses who were sweeping arrogantly along the street, sending men, women, and the tiny donkeys fleeing toward doorways.

In front of them came a small fellow, mounted bareback on a horse he was having difficulty managing. Djoura recognized him at the same moment he recognized her, and she saw him pointing and heard him say, "That is her. The black infidel who worshipped the moon before my eyes!"

But Hasiim the Berber did not need such identification. He spurred his mare forward.

Raphael was watching the man come, followed by a mass of pounding hooves which could smash human flesh into the clay of the road. Had Djoura not snatched him by the hand, he might have stood there until overtaken, for he had no experience in running away from things.

Nor was running a very useful endeavor, for the horses were faster than any barefoot man, let alone a woman wrapped in heavy skirts. But Djoura slipped around a corner of the street and pulled him into a doorless entryway.

"Fly-caked pigshit!" she hissed violently. "Infidel, am I? Well, this infidel is going to split him like a fish!"

Raphael heard horses racketing toward the narrow corner. One came through. Another tripped—slammed the sun-baked wall. A man screamed and the beast went down.

Toward them danced an hysterical Arab horse, with its light bit clenched firmly in its teeth. It tossed its head while the small citizen of Granada bounced unhappily up and down on the animal's withers. His right hand held a cavalry scimitar out in the air, where it wobbled dangerously. His left was caught in the horse's mane. He did not look at the fugitives at all.

Without hesitation Djoura struck, pulling man from mount and the sword from the hapless fellow's grasp. The freed horse bolted forward along the alley, leaving the shouts and screams of the inhabitants in its wake. The disarmed warrior crumbled into a ball before Djoura, also screaming. She lifted the scimitar above her head, then stopped still, an expression of disgust on her face. Finally she kicked the fellow out of the way.

Raphael stood next to Djoura, watching the struggling mass of fallen horses and riders which blocked the alley entrance. One animal urinated in its panic: the air grew sour.

In the sunlit street a small white mare whirled. The black robes of her rider billowed as she was spurred toward the congested corner. Then lifting into the air like a deer she leaped the whole mass and came down perfectly balanced in the alleyway only fifteen feet from Djoura.

Hasiim reined his mare expertly and her hind feet pulled under her. Dropping the reins along the mare's neck, he lifted his sword in a practiced hand.

Djoura hefted hers like a club.

The white mare sprang forward. At that same moment Raphael stepped out into the alley between Hasiim and Djoura. He raised his empty hand toward the beast. "Dami!" he cried. "Old friend, help us! Help us if you are near. If you can. Remember the horses in the pass of Aosta!"

There was nothing to see. No shadow more or less haunted the alley. Raphael's hope shrank and he chided himself for expecting too much of a friend who had, after all, passed beyond earth's turmoils.

But the horse—Hasiim's war mare—stopped dead in her tracks. Hasiim was slammed hard against her neck. She lowered her head. Nickered softly.

In the moment of the Berber's amazement, Raphael was up behind him. He took Hasiim's sword arm in both of his and struck it against the alley wall.

Hasiim cursed his mare's infidelity. He cursed enchantments. He dropped the sword.

Raphael took it in both hands and was off.

Outside the alleyway and in the wider street beyond, the desert horses stood locked in a pleasant dream. Neither spur nor quirt led to more than a fly switch of the tail. The horses who had fallen now climbed to their feet and stood together, completely blocking the entryway.

The townspeople of Granada remained where the onslaught of the fursan had driven them, watching from windows or huddled in black doorways, and what emotions this humiliation of the Berber cavalry raised in their several Muslim or Christian breasts were theirs to cherish.

Raphael passed the sword from one hand to the other, until suddenly its weight settled in his grip and he knew what to do with it.

THERE WERE FOUR OF US: MICHAEL, GABRIEL, URIEL, AND MYSELF. WE DROVE HIM OUT—HIM AND ALL HE HAD DELUDED TO STAND WITH HIM.

Raphael darted back to Djoura, and their two swords faced the light.

"What was that?" hissed the woman. "What happened to his horse?"

Raphael opened his mouth, but hardly knew what to say. "A . . . deed is redeemed: a deed done years ago, in the high mountains of the north. It is my friend who has helped us—he of whom I told you. The pebble."

"The pebble?" Djoura's startled eyes shifted from the danger ahead to the strange fellow beside her.

"Off your horses!" Hasiim spoke in the hill Arabic of Morocco. (Down the darkened alley Djoura heard him and cursed in the same tongue.) "Off your horses and after me!"

A more slender shape appeared among the equine silhouettes blocking the corner. One man squeezed through. Another.

With no other coign but a bolted doorway from which to fight and over a dozen swordsmen slipping toward them, the fair man and the black woman turned together and fled down the alley.

It was dank: the cobbles both slippery and odorous. Djoura ran with a focused, arrowlike urgency, like a person who knows refuge is just ahead. Raphael followed her in similar fashion, not because he believed there was such a refuge (no, he knew it was only Djoura's unquenchable confidence which led them) but because he did not want to lose her. The woman's dusty black skirts were hiked, and her scimitar bobbed in her hand. This weapon scattered once more the mothers, children, and men without employment who frequented the alley. Again shrieks and bellows.

The fugitives passed the small man's horse, the runaway, as it was being led by eager dirty hands through a doorway of clay daub toward some illicit fate. The sound of foot pursuit echoed behind them, giving wings to their own steps.

Then they were out in the morning sun again: first Djoura, whose clothes drank the brilliance and gave nothing back, but whose head flashed with coins, then Raphael, wound—no, tangled—in shawls over his striped household trousers, his fair hair flying like a horse's mane. Their eyes watered in the light and before them rose a wall: the north wall of the city of Granada.

It was impossibly high, and here and there the poor had built mud-wasp huts of clay against it, narrowing the street to a mere donkey track. Djoura turned to the left and as she bolted forward she shrieked, "The gate! We must find the gate!"

Raphael's breath rasped in his throat. He felt his nose bleeding again. He pressed behind Djoura through a blockade of dirty children, while a dog with pointed ears and a curling tail barked sharply at the confusion.

Was that a gate ahead, round arched and trimmed with tile? It was: the north gate of the city, as high as a house, and the wall around it was ornamented with lapis cut into the words of the Koran. Djoura sprang toward it and stopped, for in its shadow were framed five swordsmen, with the Qa'id Hasiim in the front.

Raphael crashed into Djoura from behind. He put one arm around her shoulder and glanced about them.

On their right the city wall, far too high to climb. On their left, a potter's shed. The street was littered with clay pots and with broken fragments of clay.

What had this wild flight gained them, besides burned lungs and a head full of panic? No matter. Djoura was not about to flee again. She backed against the white wall, where a buttress stood out a few feet. There she was as obvious as a fly on sugar, but there was no longer hope of hiding. Shouts from left and right told her she was surrounded by her enemy.

But then was there anyone on earth who was not Djoura's enemy? Not the people of her home, anymore, nor the Spanish giaour who stared at her now from buzzing clumps in the street. Only Pinkie—Raphael—with his weak skin and strange eyes as blue as a blind man's, who stood by her now, back to back, with his scimitar fluttering in his hands lightly as a bird. She pressed against him.

Hasiim's men erupted into the sun and when they spied their quarry at bay they gave out a noise like hounds. They came with the fury and undiscipline of men who are not used to fighting on foot.

And they slid to a confused halt, for there was no flaw or opening in the defense of the blond European who stood with back against the chiseled wall. And the black woman beside him, with her weapon held up rigidly like a headsman's sword . . . All knew she was mad, and in league with spirits besides, but who knew what strange arts she possessed to do harm?

Hasiim then came forward, for he was a pure Muslim and without superstition, and he had a wealth of injured pride to avenge. He glanced from Raphael (with only professional interest) to the black Berber. He was armed once more.

Raphael shifted his balance so that he faced Hasiim and stood slightly to the front of Djoura. He caught the warrior's eyes with his own and held them. Djoura, seeing that her Pinkie knew more of this business than she did, took one step back. Then Hasiim struck: a feint toward the black woman which ended as a stroke at Raphael's wrists.

He met steel, and the blond flexed his blade in a tiny circle. To Hasiim's immense surprise he felt his weapon loosen in his grasp. The scimitar hit the earth. Hasiim flung himself back.

To take a breath. To consider. To demand another scimitar from his milling followers.

Raphael did not drop his eyes from Hasiim's. He saw the Arab blink, shift from foot to foot, breathe a prayer to Allah.

Him and all he had deluded to stand with him. Satan himself had given back before four angels. What hope had a mortal warrior, however skilled? Raphael looked at Hasiim and knew he could destroy the man. He stepped out from the buttress, his scimitar drifting like a leaf in the breeze.

The Berber's eyes widened. Raphael met those eyes.

And Raphael was lost.

This man was not Satan nor had he been bought by him. He was a stubborn and prideful mortal—a man not to Raphael's taste. A dangerous man. But Raphael gazed at Hasiim and felt a peculiar painful pity.

This hesitation gave Hasiim—who felt no similar emotion while glaring at Raphael—time to strike another sweeping cross-hand blow. Raphael countered, but did not press the advantage.

With a strident ululation, another tribesman stood beside Hasiim, sword at the ready. In this man's face Raphael read plain fear, mastered by the desire to please his commander. This second warrior slashed fiercely at Djoura, who raised her blade against the attack. But the swordsman feinted away and licked in beneath the woman's awkward guard.

Raphael snapped the man's blade in two. Djoura opened his face.

Hasiim, losing patience, shoved his subordinate aside and rushed his opponent as though he himself were still on horseback, slashing in even diagonals as he came. Raphael flung himself down on one knee before Djoura and his scimitar flashed broadside, clashing against Hasiim's weapon. Then he sprang up again and knocked the qa'id backward before he could disengage. Taking the swordsman's wrist in his own, he twisted the hilt of the weapon, trying to pull it from Hasiim's grasp.

They fell and struggled, breath hissing into one another's face. Next to Raphael's head a sword struck the ground and sparked. Hasiim's eyes shifted. He cried a few words in his Berber dialect and the attack was not repeated.

Only a few inches above Hasiim's face hung that of Raphael. It was pale under its sunburn, bearing no sign of anger or outrage, but rather the sad concentration of a tutor with a very slow pupil. And from Raphael's neck dangled, like some rough piece of jewelry, the iron slave collar. Hasiim grabbed it in one hand, while the other hand dropped his blade and fixed itself against Raphael's neck. With one hand he pulled, while the other pushed, crushing.

Arching back, the blond put his knee against Hasiim's chest, while he worked his two arms between his opponent's stranglehold. He made no effort to use his sword against Hasiim. His breath came in a choking hiss. His vision sparked.

He broke the hold.

Raphael stood above the fallen Hasiim, who looked up

with fanatic indifference, expecting death. He did nothing, but his sword twitched like a cat's tail, warning off the fursan who had witnessed this crude duel.

A voice was calling out to Raphael. He didn't understand at first. "Drop your sword, giaour. Look up and drop your sword."

Raphael did look up. Around the frosting-white tiled wall, behind the Berber fursan, stood a semicircle of humanity. Raphael stared from face to face.

There shuffled a poor Spaniard with confused, rolling eyes, bearing baskets of fish and of peppers. Next to him stood a proud Moorish householder in silk and muslin, his hands upon the jeweled hilt of a scimitar which had probably never seen use. Here was a woman so veiled neither her age nor race could be guessed at, another woman with tawny hair, sans veil but with the ring around her neck. Two teenage eunuchs, well dressed, who stood carefully not touching anybody. A dark peasant ignoring the squirming horned kid in his arms to stare, stare, stare . . .

Each casual figure engraved itself into Raphael's stunned brain, as though within the astonishment, fear, or unholy excitement expressed in these faces he would find the clue to every mystery. But finally his eyes found (as they were meant to) the five soldiers who stood with their legs braced, their wicked small bows drawn and aimed at both Raphael and Djoura.

The woman did not move. Neither did she drop her weapon. The steel of her sword sent glints of silver over the white mosaic wall, joined by the spark of gold from the coins in her black hair. Her face not black now but suffused with a ruddy blush, and when she spoke to her companion her voice held a furious elation.

"When I cry out, Raphael, then we will go forward together. We will give them reason to fear us!"

His face filled with pain. "But they will kill you, Djoura!"

She snorted in her habitual arrogance. "What are these but dogs? They will kill us anyway. This way . . .

". . . is freedom." She took one step forward.

But Hasiim, who had risen cautiously to his feet, heard her fierce whisper. He replied not to Djoura, but to Raphael. "My men are not dogs. I say they will not kill you:

neither of you, unless you make it necessary. The woman I have promised to return to her own people and I will do so.

"You . . ." He stared at the fair figure. Raphael's borrowed clothing had all fallen off and he stood now wearing nothing but his eunuch's trousers. The scars on his back were visible around his sides and shoulders like the tendrils of red clinging vines. "You we will return to your master, and what he may do to you for this scandal is none of our business.

"Though I say," and here the Moor paused. "Though I say that if I thought I could buy your loyalty with your sword arm, I would trade ten good horses for you."

Raphael said nothing in reply. Slowly he lowered his blade. Djoura turned upon him a look of infinite bitterness.

"It gets hotter and hotter," observed Gaspare, shifting his sweaty seat from side to side. "If we have to go much farther south we'll all burst into flame!"

The black dragon smiled: an action which caused Saara's thighs and knees to tickle. "That is mostly my own personal heat. It is actually quite cool at these altitudes, even in the south.

"I could cool down by going slower, of course . . ."

"Don't listen to the boy," snapped Saara, who felt she had been sharing this aerial perch with Gaspare for too long entirely. "I'd rather have the speed. I feel time is pressing."

The dragon's sigh was more disturbing to the riders on his neck than his smile. "I won't ask you why," he drawled. "It's probably some sorcery and I'd rather not know about it . . ."

Saara opened her mouth to say it was not sorcery at all, but just a feeling she had, but the dragon was not finished.

"Besides, if I'm not out of my reckoning, that white shimmer where the mountains slope down is Granada itself."

Gaspare craned over Saara's shoulder. It seemed they had finally reached the bottom of the Sierra Nevada. Good. Mountains were nothing special to Gaspare. "Even if that is not Granada," he called into the black dragon's ear, "I think that the horse has to do something."

"I know, I know," came the lugubrious hiss.

* * *

They set down to discuss plans upon a rock rubble only a few miles north of the city. Since the dragon was quite capable of firing any house or dry field he touched while at flight heat, it required some thought how to rescue Raphael without setting all Granada ablaze. The horse was released to gather what nourishment he could find.

But instead of offering suggestions, Gaspare stretched himself out with his back against a stone while he played the lute. Saara only paced.

Both of them heard a terrific racket, as though boulders in the nearby landscape were being crumbled into powder. Gaspare started up. It was the dragon, giving himself a good scratch against the rocks.

Gaspare's rhythms were almost as hard to listen to. Saara could not rest. She could not even sit down.

"He can alight on a tile roof," stated the witch. "That way, even if he does set the timbers ablaze, he can knock the house in and contain the fire."

"Fine by me," mumbled Gaspare. "Of course the inhabitants of the house might disagree . . ." He raised his eyes and seemed to see Saara for the first time.

"What's wrong with you, my lady? You act like you have ants. Can you feel Raphael's presence from way out here?"

"No," Saara said shortly. "I don't know *what* it is I feel." She shot Gaspare a glance under lowered brows.

"I told you, didn't I, that I was going to go home after this?" Gaspare lifted a surprised face.

"What else should you do, lady: stay in Granada?"

Saara grimaced. "I mean home. To the Fenlands. If I live. Home to my people, the Lapps."

Gaspare put both hands around the neck of his lute and corrugated his young brow massively. "By sweet San Gabriele, Saara, why do you want to do *that?*"

She took offense. "Don't speak of my home in that tone of voice, youngster! You've never been there to judge it."

With a single gesture Gaspare discounted that fact. "I know it is not civilized," he replied. "And so no place for the greatest witch in all the Italies. And Spain."

Saara's ire dissolved in Gaspare's predictable flattery. She produced a nervous grin. "It is a peaceful place, Gaspare, where the greatest enemy is winter. And beautiful, too, for in the autumn . . ."

". . . all the grasses and moss turn a scarlet red, which covers the steppe and shines against the blue sky or the gray clouds like sunset," said the voice, the familiar soft, deep voice which was not that of the dragon. "And the snows in winter take the color of the curtains in the sky, so bright that the dark time grows light enough for one to walk about and marvel."

"Dami!" cried Saara, and her voice caught in her throat.

"Here," he replied, and there he was, clear and only slightly shimmery, sitting on the hard ground between the witch and Gaspare. His storm-cloud wings were scarcely visible behind the mortal image.

Saara put her hand out, but stopped before touching. "I . . . wanted you to see that. I thought about you and the russet time . . ."

"I know," he whispered and gave her a very comfortable little smile. Then he turned to Gaspare and let him share the wordless joke. Then he stood up, wings rising behind him.

"Listen to me, my friends. I am here to interfere in the affairs of the living, as doubtless I should not!"

Damiano's amused smile faded into seriousness. "If you wish to be of service to Raphael, you must go into the city now. Move quickly. South of the central square you will find a broad avenue linedwith orange trees. On this street is a house with a carved gate of cedarwood in a white wall. Enter in.

"There are also within Granada right now some fine horsemen riding fine horses very slowly. These are a sample of my interference, and as such may be of interest to you. But finding the house with the gate is more important.

"Go now; you are needed." The ghost did not fade; he was simply not there anymore.

Gaspare rose as though on a string. He filled his considerable lungs with air. "Dragon!" he bellowed. "Come quickly!"

"A ghost?" repeated the dragon.

"The ghost of Delstrego," replied Gaspare importantly. "And he said to hurry."

The black dragon took to the air lithely enough, springing off his coiled tail, but he refused to be hurried in speech. "I wish I might have seen that."

Saara had to chuckle. "I thought you would disapprove terribly. Magic being delusion, and all that."

The great beast considered. "There is that. But spirits have their place in the natural order. If I disapproved of spirits in general, why would I then be adding my small energies to the rescue of one?

"Besides, madam: if this specter had knowledge to communicate . . . real wisdom, perhaps . . . What is it he said again?"

Gaspare repeated Damiano's message, word for portentous word.

They came to the city and passed over the wall. The dragon swooped down in a stomach-twisting dive in order to inspect the place more closely. With its regular low rows of daubed buildings and crowded streets (smelling even up here in the air) it looked like—first, a hive of bees, and then like a hive of disturbed bees. "People can see you," shouted Saara. "They're terrified!"

The dragon writhed contemplatively. He slowed his progress so as to examine the length of one avenue broader than its fellows. "So it seems," he murmured silkily. He rose a few yards higher.

"That edifice just beyond the city," he explained for his riders' sakes, "set like a pearl in the red sand. That is the Alhambra, military center of the State of Granada, as well as the residence of Muhammad V, lineal descendant of Muhammad ben Yusuf ben Ahmand ben Nasir, who founded the present dynasty. It is generally accepted to be one of the most beautiful constructions in the world, and into its stones have been set the words of Ibn al-Khatib, that most martial of Islamic poets . . ."

"Fly!" shrieked Saara, whose sense of urgency had become almost overpowering. "South!"

"I *am* flying," declared the dragon patiently. "And hysteria will make me fly no faster. Besides, if we went faster, I should have missed what I now see below—that small force of either Bedouin or Berber cavalry, whose horses plod with their little teacup muzzles scraping the dirt of the road. Did not the sage spirit speak of such?"

"But he said the house on the street of oranges first, the cavalry after!" Gaspare insisted. "I heard him distinctly."

Still the dragon, hanging high above the street, vacillated. "Yet we *have* the cavalry, while the house on the street of oranges is theoretical only. And the prompting of spirits is a very subtle thing. Perhaps we should first investigate . . ."

"I've had enough of this," said Saara, and without further ado she turned into a dove. Gaspare, left without a handhold, squeaked and grabbed for the dragon's coronary spines. "Me, too! Take me with you, Saara," he bawled.

Unruffled the dragon said, "Youngster, I am more than willing to set you down."

CHAPTER 12

The dove scouted, dipped, and led the horse on. Gaspare clung like a monkey to the lean black back, with nothing to restrain Festilligambe but a tattered rope bridle. But the young man's cross-continental ride on a dragon had burned away all the nervousness he had once felt around horses.

They passed the central square—a little plot of green, cleverly irrigated and tended with immense labor—and found the avenue that was edged in fragrant orange trees without trouble. This way was wide and fairly empty. The few people they did pass were dressed well in Saracen style. They failed to notice (or pretended to fail to notice) the sight of a horse chasing a little brown bird along the avenue. Gaspare, not knowing which of these strollers might have had a hand in Raphael's imprisonment, cursed the overfed lot of them equally.

He sought the house with the white wall and carved wooden gate. Odd. ALL the houses had white walls and all the white walls had wooden gates. They were almost all carved, too, with inscriptions in Arabic, meaningless to a young man not even literate in his own language. The words of the dragon flashed into his mind. "The promptings of spirits are subtle." Damiano, too? Gaspare had clean forgotten that the ghost had specified cedarwood as the material of the gate they were seeking. But then, neither would he have been able to recognize cedarwood if he had remembered.

Saara, however, fluttered straight toward a gateway of mottled yellow and orange, which was set into a feature-less wall surmounted by red tile.

She stood beside Gaspare. "It's bolted. There's some-thing going on inside: I hear voices and the sound of a bellows. Can he jump it?"

Gaspare turned Festilligambe and trotted across the street. Then he stared at the looming wall of wood and daub. "Sweet San Gabriele," he whispered. "Never."

In his frustration he turned on Saara. "He's only a horse, you know: not a Cathaysian dragon." Then an idea occurred to him.

"Delstrego—Delstrego could have made a flame to burn this door away from in front of me!"

Saara, who had been about to return to bird form and dart over the wall, found herself stung by Damiano's name. "Oh, he could, could he? Well, Gaspare, you stand right there and you will see what I, whom yourself have named the greatest witch in all the Italies *or* Spain, can do!"

Gaspare waited nervously.

The desert horses were aware of a presence in the air before their riders. Their dreams of honeyed grass dis-solved into the terror of rabbits beneath a hawk.

The black dragon's interest in the beasts, however, was only aesthetic, for he had recently consumed both a large fat mule and several wild Andalusian cattle (scrawny, but serviceable), and dragons do not eat as frequently as men. And neither did the Berber riders interest him greatly, for he did not see among them any select individual whom a spirit might have thought worth noticing.

There was the little fellow who, once thrown from his horse, waved a spindly sword into the air . . . But the dragon was hoping for something more flamboyant.

And his sun-bright eyes noticed very soon that the little troop, which had been riding south, toward the Alhambra, held a prisoner—just one. A woman whose ebony skin gave off the same rich highlights as his own scales, and who wore a corona of gold tips (again like his) in her hair.

The dragon chortled with delight at this exotic find. He

plucked her from among her captors with the care a collector will give to blown glass.

Simon the Surgeon stared from Rashiid to the cup in his hands. "It is the common practice," he observed. "Without the draught many more of them die. Since he is full grown and unwilling as well, there is a good chance that this one might."

"Indeed he might," said Rashiid, with rising inflection. "Indeed he might." The rotund householder's eyes were shining; his hands were knotted fists at his sides.

Rashiid was angry. Being awakened to take delivery on a runaway slave that one had not yet noticed was missing—that made one angry.

It also made one feel a little bit of a fool.

Stripping the boy for flogging only to discover that he was no boy at all but a man intact—that added to both the anger and the foolishness in no small way.

But sending for the local surgeon: saying to the functionary, "Come," and having him come, and saying to the assembled household, "Stand," and having them all stand—that was a thing to comfort one with one's own power. Rashiid's mottled hazel eyes were gleaming with that power, and the assembled household shifted from foot to foot, its many subservient eyes turned to the sky, the pond, the white garden wall . . . Anywhere but to Rashiid.

Anywhere but to the man tied to the hitching post.

Raphael, too, stared past his master, to the white clay wall of the house. But his eyes were not focused on the house. His head was turned slightly, as though he were listening—listening to something important, yet expecting interruption at any moment from a fellow who tended to interrupt. Who had a reputation for interrupting important communications.

Who was a bit of a fool.

"He very well might die," Rashiid repeated again, for emphasis.

Simon shrugged and put the cup down on his workbench. He was neither overawed nor afraid of Rashiid, for Simon was a free man employed to do a job. Since the greatest part of his work was done at the market, where buyers of young beasts wanted them castrated before taking them home, this wealthy cityman was an unlikely source of business. His tempers could not do Simon harm. The surgeon considered telling him not to get in the way.

No—Rashiid was the employer, and there was no use borrowing trouble. Simon put the cup down.

He signaled his apprentice to step up the bellows pumping.

Some practitioners castrated with hooks and some used clamps and a few used a loop of shrinking leather, but Simon the surgeon had a curved knife with a handle of wood, and this served for almost any occasion from gelding to bloodletting; one could even shave with it. He thrust this blade into the coals so that its single stroke would both cut and cauterize.

The second wife of Rashiid had been standing with her older housemate: soundless, white-faced, one knuckle between her cupid's-bow lips. Her round eyes had grown more than round, watching Raphael bound to the post. Watching the coals laid and the fire draw up. Now a waft of hot, metal-scented air came to wrap around her where she stood. The fire spat back at the bellows and the blade itself made a noise as it heated.

Ama fainted into Fatima's arms.

Rashiid saw his wife crumple. He subdued an impulse to go to her. It was first pride that caused him to ignore the incident—the unwillingness to break this moment of power with softness of any kind—but then a horrible surmise entered his brain and Rashiid's face went hard as stone. Let Ama give thanks to Allah that she had been discovered to be pregnant *before* this boy who was not a boy arrived.

Raphael's blank eyes saw only the face of Djoura at the last moment he had seen her, before they had bound him and thrown him over a horse. Her scorn withered him still.

For Raphael had no great confidence in the choice he had made; perhaps the mortal-born woman had been right and they should have died together under the blue and white tiles of the wall. Now she would be taken back to Africa, where she did not want to go, and he . . .

Raphael heard the knife moan in the orange coals and he knew dread—dread of loss and further shame . . . Dread of a life compassed by drudgery and by whippings, played out to a dull rhythm of days. Dread of simple pain.

Surely Djoura had been right.

But though the song was of pain and fear, still Raphael's body was singing. That body had a will of its own, and he heard it telling him what it feared most was to die.

Raphael listened to the voice of his body with his head turned slightly to one side and on his face was a distant, concentrated expression. But when Ama slumped into Fatima's arms he saw and he opened his mouth, as though he were on the point of saying something.

Had he spoken, it would have been to tell her that he knew she had not betrayed him to Rashiid. That he did not blame her for his fate. But Rashiid, Ama's husband, stood between them, so Raphael said nothing at all.

The knife came out of the fire, not red-hot but hot enough to twist the air around it, turning morning mist into steam. Simon approached Raphael and peered appraisingly into his eyes.

In shock already, the surgeon said to himself. Bad risk. Aloud he called, "Bend him back."

The calloused hands of the head gardener came around Raphael's neck and shoulders and stretched him back over the hip-high wooden post. One hand covered his mouth. Another squatted behind him and held his knees.

He could see nothing but the hairs on the gardener's arm. He heard the man's heavy breathing. He felt his own body stiffen and he wondered at this, for he had not told it to do so.

Next came a fearful deep noise like wind and a great thudding and crashing. Raphael did not know what caused this, whether with the gardener's shoulder against his ear, an accident with the surgeon's coals, or his own body's confusion. But the howling continued and suddenly he was released, reeling at the end of the chain which bound his hands to the post.

The household of Rashiid was scattering like so many birds and crying in a dozen voices. The surgeon's terrible knife lay abandoned on the ground. Rashiid himself was waving his arms wildly and his face was contorted.

In the middle of this uproar a horse plunged and reared: a black horse. Upon his back was a tall, gangling rider with red hair. He was shouting something inaudible, and so was Rashiid. A flutter of feathers sank down by Raphael's feet and rose up again as a woman.

She sang a word and his chains fell open to the ground.

* * *

The horse seemed to be moving all its legs independently, like a spider. It sailed over the threshold like a leaf in autumn.

Gaspare wondered if he were going to stay upright at all, for the vicious cold wind sucked him along willy-nilly. He spun over packed ground, narrowly missing the wave-lashed surface of a pond, with his hands full of horse's mane and rope. He lifted his eyes.

It was Raphael and yet it wasn't Raphael whom Gaspare saw: naked, squinting with confusion, gape-mouthed, lost in the middle of all the screaming Saracens. There was the angel's hair, perfect face, slender figure—but all pinched out of mere human clay. Gaspare sat the capering horse with unconscious expertise, his eyes locked on Raphael's confusion. He saw his teacher fall to his knees. Rage filled Gaspare, mixed with nausea, that he should have to see Raphael reduced to this. With a choked scream he threw Festilligambe into the tumult.

Raphael blinked at the horseman almost half-wittedly. But then the naked man's eyes focused on the head of the lute projecting beyond Gaspare's right shoulder, and memory awakened. "Hoa!" shouted Gaspare, and he pulled on the reins.

But the horse had his own memory. His black ears swiveled to the human beside his withers. He nickered uncertainly. Then Festilligambe lifted his fine dry head and bellowed like a stallion from joy.

Raphael, grinning at this salute, hoisted himself up behind Gaspare.

There was another hand on the bridle: the same calloused hand that had held Raphael only a minute since, the hand of the head gardener. Gaspare kicked at it and the horse attempted to rear. Rashiid, seeing this, ran from the doorway where Gaspare's first rush had pressed him and put his own white-knuckled hand on the headstall. Festilligambe threw his head futilely from side to side. His tragic large eyes rolled, showing white all around.

Gaspare dropped the reins and took instead two handfuls of the gardener's hair. Dragging the man half off the ground, the redhead bit him in the ear. His uneven teeth ground together until the gibbering fellow dropped his hold. But in the time it took to accomplish this action three more men had taken hold of some part of the horse's anatomy. One grabbed Raphael's bare leg and began to pull him to the ground.

Saara had not been idle. Though weary from her wind summons (but she *had* to show Gaspare) she had scrabbled over the turf among fleeing feet and horse's hooves. Now she came up with Simon's bitter-edged knife. Hands dropped away from Raphael. From the horse.

Rashiid, for whom the capture of the horse had meant victory won from defeat, turned at the disturbance and did not see the knife at all, but only a child-faced woman with brown hair in uneven braids and a dress which did not cover her legs. She reminded him a bit of Ama, and Rashiid was not pleased with Ama. With a cold sneer he released his right hand from the headstall to cuff her across the mouth. With no expression on her face Saara released his other hand from the reins by slicing it off at the wrist.

Rashiid sprang back, stiff-armed, pumping blood like a garden fountain into the air. The whole household went still.

Simon the Surgeon had taken no part in the melee, but had flattened himself against the house wall as soon as the horse blew in through the gate. He was paid to do a job, after all, not to get himself killed. But as Simon was a surgeon he knew what was necessary when a man had lost a member, so he took Rashiid, tripped him, dragged him to the overturned brazier and pressed his spouting arm against a coal. The householder's shrieks reached deafening proportions.

Faces appeared—cautiously—at the gate. They disappeared again. There came the sound of a horn from without. It echoed along the street and was answered by another.

Gaspare looked at Saara. So did Raphael. Saara glanced from one end of the suddenly motionless yard to the other. She shifted her knife nervously.

Then the smell of hot metal and the horrible smell of Rashiid's seared hand stump mixed with another smell of burning. A lacy, twisting shadow descended. The carefully watered grass withered and steamed as the dragon set himself down. Djoura squatted within one enormous claw, her hands firmly over her face.

Lantern eyes took in the yard, the pool, the cowering

humans. They lighted on the horse, with its double burden. "So! It seems you didn't need me at all!" the dragon said brightly.

Like a caterpillar with fluffy spines the dragon rode through the air, the gyrations of his body pushing first Djoura, then Raphael (who held to her), and then Saara (who held to *him*) upmost. Saara was at the end of the line because she had the least to lose by falling. Gaspare rode on one of the monster's upturned palms, to be nearer his horse.

"He did well, didn't he, dragon?" asked the redhead, not for the first time. "He cut into that mass of Saracens like . . . like . . ."

"Like a black dragon," prompted the black dragon.

Gaspare thought maybe the dragon was making fun of him. "I am serious. Festilligambe showed the real, heroic soul of a horse down there, regardless of fire, knives, screaming . . ."

"Horses . . ." the great creature rumbled meditatively, "have very different souls, one from another. So have men. Have they not, Venerable Sage? And dragons, too, of course."

Venerable Sage let the wind toss the fair hair from his face. "I certainly cannot deny that." Then Raphael added, "Could you speak in Arabic, please, so that Djoura can understand?"

"Certainly," the dragon replied. In Arabic. "The language of Mecca, or of the south, perhaps?"

"The south."

An enormous long throat was cleared. "The young man has just noted, Child of Beauty, and I have agreed, that horses, men, and dragons are quite various. Within each species, I mean—the other is obvious."

Djoura shifted her three-finger grip at the handholds in the dragon's neck scales. "Men are very different from one another, of course. Some are pink."

Then she lifted her head high and rested back in Raphael's arms. "But that difference is of no importance."

It was a beautiful morning over the foothills of the Pyrenees, with scattered soapsuds clouds over the pelty meadows. The dragon writhed for the sheer feeling of it.

"Where exactly am I taking you all?" he asked, first in Arabic and then in Italian.

"Lappland," answered Saara promptly. "If you are going that far." Gaspare groaned from below.

"I think you're a fool, my lady. But Lombardy for me, *signore*. Where else?"

"The land of lights is not too far at all," stated the dragon. "And Lombardy is on the way." Again he shifted language.

"And you, Venerable Sage—where would the lady and yourself like to be ferried?"

Raphael was silent. He threw back his head and regarded the blue, uncommunicative sky. "I don't know. All the earth is beautiful, and I'm sure it is my fault that I cannot feel myself to belong to it. It is just that I never expected . . ."

He shook his golden head. "Never mind me. Take us any place we might find a welcome, Djoura and I."

"Lappland," said Saara, who caught the meaning of the exchange through the foreign words.

"Lombardy," insisted Gaspare, who had done the same. "A very civilized place, as Raphael well knows. Besides, I need my lessons."

"There is always Cathay," added the dragon with studied casualness. "In Cathay they know how to respect sages. And spirits."

The blond smiled. "And am I either?" Then his expression softened.

"What can we possibly do for you—uh, Venerable Dragon? I and all my friends owe our lives to you. Perhaps many times over."

The black dragon chuckled steam. "No matter, Venerable Sage. I have a great respect for teachers."

"Do you want me to teach you, then?"

The creature gave a tiny shiver then, which every passenger felt but none understood. "Can you teach me truth?"

"No," replied Raphael gravely. "Just music—the lute, primarily. But in the study of the lute you may find more than you expect."

"Music?" The dragon emitted a long, serpentine sigh. "Truth through tuned strings, instead of through privation, paradox, or long silence? I've never heard of *that* approach."

It was Raphael's turn to chuckle and he gave Djoura a little squeeze. "That is not to say it won't work, however."

The dragon held up one five-fingered obsidian, clawed hand. It was the one that held Gaspare. "It would have to be a rather large lute."

"Very well. You can learn to sing instead," said Raphael equably. "Every type and every individual created has its own music."

Once again the dragon cleared his throat and bobbed diffidently through the sky. "To sing? The thought makes me very awkward . . ."

Raphael chuckled. "The thought makes everyone awkward. But that tension can be overcome. You will find . . ."

"What's that I see?" called Saara from behind them all. "Straight ahead. Coming fast?"

They all looked, but only the dragon's eye saw, and with an organ-pipe whistling he humped and turned in the air.

Saara clung to Raphael who held to Djoura tightly. The Berber locked her fingers in their grips.

In a few moments they could all see.

It came in the form of a white dragon. It came in the form of a writhing, legless wyvern. It came in the form of a phosphorescent, myriad plague.

It was destruction, dread, the death of hope, and it was coming fast.

"What is it? *What is it!*" cried Djoura, craning her neck around. But she did not need the stricken faces of her fellows to tell her it was terrible. "Why is it chasing us?"

For a moment no one had the heart to tell her, then at last Raphael spoke. "It is Satan—Iblis—whom Saara calls the Liar. It is my brother."

Then Lucifer swept over them. He came between them and the sun, huger than a cloud. His shape was that of a king in rich robes, with a visage of blood.

The black dragon sank crazily toward the earth.

Saara felt the shadow touch her, with paralysis and despair in its wake. She laughed—laughed at the naïveté of her plans for the future. She had no future. But with that single laugh the paralysis passed Saara over, and her despair turned into unbreakable resolve. She let go of the man she had tracked across Europe and took to the air.

"No!" shouted Raphael, as he felt her go. "Saara of Saami! This is not your battle anymore!"

And indeed, as she flung herself at the breast of the hideous king, it vanished in front of her, leaving nothing but cloudless sky. The dove fluttered wildly before an iron hand struck her and sent her falling.

Gaspare screamed.

The dragon vomited fire at the apparition. He grabbed the falling woman with one hind claw. Flicking his snake's tail he flung himself toward the broken hills.

The sound of cruel laughter was all around them. It turned the air poisonous to their lungs. All eyes dimmed.

But the black dragon touched the earth again, searing the autumn grasses at his feet. Gently he shook off his living cargo.

Lucifer alighted before them, and his towering size reduced the Basque hills to clods of dirt. His colors were bright and monstrous. He wore a crown of gold and the face of Raphael.

"Haven't we done as much mischief as we possibly could?" he inquired jovially, looking carefully from Saara to the dragon to Gaspare. "Haven't we?"

The dragon coiled around his tiny dependents as dragons coil around their hoards. His corona of gold and scarlet stood out stiffly from his head. His eyes gleamed as white as an August sun. "Delusion!" he hissed. "Puffed, empty delusion!"

Lucifer regarded him thoughtfully. "It is no delusion that you are going to die, snake," he said, grinning horribly.

But a small black hand gripped one of the dragon's coronal spikes. Djoura's face appeared next to it. She had a stone in her hand. She stepped out.

"No, child!" The creature moved to guard her. "You don't know what it is you are facing."

She opened her lips, which were whitened with fear. "I know," she said. "I have faced slavery," Djoura whispered almost without sound. "I have faced swords. I have faced *you*, great dragon.

"*And*," Djoura found her voice at last. "I have stolen the moon. The moon! Did you know that, Iblis?" And with a mad laugh, the Berber woman flung her stone at the Devil.

It soared its futile course. It might have hit the apparition's knee. But instead the small missile hung in the air and grew, until it became the image of a black man in blood-caked robes. His body was hewed and his head struck off before them. The open eyes of the head wore an expression of idiocy.

Djoura shrieked her incoherent rage, and she would have flung herself at Lucifer, armed with nothing except her black robes and her fingernails. But Raphael, wordless and set-faced, came up behind the woman and restrained her with his arms.

Again Satan laughed. He reached a long arm out. The black dragon swelled dangerously, like an adder in the grass, as the hand of Satan came near.

"How is our little woods dove, then?" A gout of acid flame passed through his arm harmlessly. "I know her from before, I think. I have a weakness, you know, for the small songsters."

Saara lay white-faced where the dragon had put her down, her head against Gaspare's narrow breast. She watched death approaching and she said, "You never touched me, Liar. You never will."

Gaspare, too, watched the hand descend. Because he was seventeen years old and Italian besides, he rose to meet it. Because he was Gaspare, he unslung his lute and began to play. He shouted, "Here is a small song, then, from a small songster."

The hand hovered, seemingly more from amusement than fear. "Gaspare of San Gabriele," said Lucifer. "You are miserably out of tune. As always."

"Out of tune, certainly," replied the redhead. "But in time, you must admit. I am told that is more important. And besides, Satan, if you do not like my lute playing, then I will be forced to sing for you, instead, and many find my voice even harder to take."

Then Lucifer tired of the game. His hand swept down . . .

And found itself between the lance-toothed jaws of the black dragon. Fire spouted from its nostrils and between its buried teeth. Both the dragon and the red king hissed.

Lucifer fit the fingers of his other hand around the

dragon's throat. The tiny human atoms fled away—all but one that stood motionless as a tree on the bare hillside.

Toad-flat, baleful, the dragon's head steamed. He ground his teeth into Lucifer's hand. Ninety feet of black iron struck the ground like a whip. Lucifer lifted the creature, still locked in his hand, and struck again, this time at the speck that was Djoura.

A writhing whip, however, is not an accurate weapon, and he missed. Frustration flushed the perfect face purple. He exposed a swollen mottled tongue as he lifted the dragon again.

"Stop!"

It was Raphael who had stood still on the smoking hillside, regardless of the titanic war around him. "All of you. Satan—leave him. Your business is with me."

Lucifer turned his mountainous head. The gold of his crown shone in the sun.

"You?" he said. "You, little ball of clay: half-witted animal?" His mouth split into a sly snarl.

"You are the only one among these in whom I have no more interest. What more could I do to you, after all?"

But as Lucifer spoke so, he flung the dragon away from him. Like a thread in the wind, the dark length swirled.

Djoura was stalking toward Raphael, her eyes locked on the mountain of dread before him. Saara came up slowly on his other side.

But Raphael stepped forward, putting them both behind him. In his sculpted face was neither confusion nor doubt. "It is not what you could do to me which is at issue. It is what I can do to you. I know you fear me."

"*What*?" The air around the robed shape wavered. It burst into flame. "Fear *you*? What you can do to *me*, you bag of offal? You are helpless!"

Raphael, weaponless and half-naked, stepped toward the mountainous form. "You have no idea what I can do, Satan. You have never known, and that is *why* you fear me. But I will tell you what I can do.

"As you took my hand, Satan, so I can take yours."

Lucifer watched his brother approach, one arm stretched out before him. "Maggot! We both know you have no power to . . ." But the red king seemed to shrink into himself as he spoke, growing smaller, or perhaps farther away.

As he walked Raphael was whispering, though neither his brother nor the friends who stood silently on the hillside behind knew what he said.

He came to the brooding apparition on the hill.

With a hand pierced and bloodied, Lucifer made to push Raphael away. They touched. And at that touch the red king collapsed like a sheet full of wind, and Lucifer and Raphael stood face-to-face: of equal height, two images of the same creation.

"You do not know me, brother," Raphael said quietly. He reached forward. "But now you will."

His fair hand lifted toward Lucifer's face.

Lucifer recoiled. "No!" he cried, and he flinched away. Raphael smiled patiently. He reached out again.

"No! I won't have your tricks! You insipid, cunning toady, it's not you but *him* in you! I won't stand it!"

Lucifer backed off, his voice cracking, but still Raphael walked toward him. The Devil reached out fending hands which became claws. Raphael slipped past them. Satan had turned to flee when he felt Raphael's touch on his shoulder. In blind panic Satan took the man by the neck with both hands and he shook him. Then convulsively he threw him off, smashing Raphael against the ground.

So quickly the fight was over, for Raphael's human body lay motionless at his brother's feet, its mouth bloodied, its neck at an ugly angle.

There was stillness on the rolling hills, and the only sound was that of the smoldering grass.

Saara stared transfixed at the defeat of her last crusade. Gaspare, beside her, held the neck of his lute in both hands and his lips were pulled back from his teeth. He opened his mouth to ask a question of someone, but no sound came out.

Djoura, too, stood without moving for a terrible minute. Then with a thin cold wail she flung herself down at the very feet of the Devil and bent her head to the broken body.

But oddly enough, Lucifer, too, stood paralyzed, staring at the shape of flesh he had himself created. His lips drew back from his teeth in an expression that was not a smile. He lifted red eyes to the sky.

There was a crack of fire in the air above. All looked up to see the black dragon swimming back toward his enemy, flaming along his entire length. In the beast's yellow eyes gleamed no more intelligence, but only bestial fury. Where the dragon passed, the earth smoked beneath him.

Lucifer saw him coming and his hands clenched at his sides. His eyes searched distracted over the hills, almost as though in search of hiding. He took once more to wyvern shape and fled upward.

Ebony jaws closed around the wyvern's serpentine tail. The wyvern shape wavered and a flayed form dripping with pus flapped its wings against the dragon's rococco head. Slipping free in its own mucus, it fled, with the dragon giving chase.

Flame ate through the membrane of one loathsome wing. The dragon caught Satan again, and now it was a creature of many boneless legs which wound vinelike around the black dragon, and pressed a sucking, platterlike mouth against the scales of his neck. The dragon spun, and bit, and burned the lamprey-sucker to dry leather. Both beasts howled.

But the sky around the combatants changed suddenly, deepening and growing more clear. The furies in the air faded to shadows. Their cries were muted.

All the stars came out.

Saara lifted her head to witness the sun and moon shining at opposite ends of a sky grown glorious. Gaspare gazed at the heavens mutely, holding to his little lute as though to a lover. Miles away, a panicked horse slowed his flight, blowing clouds of bloody froth onto his lathered sides.

Only Djoura the black Berber missed the miracle, for she was alone in her world of grief, rocking and sobbing above the cast-off body of a slave.

In the middle of this indigo splendor, one star grew brighter than all others. It swelled to rival the moon. It flickered in shape like the shadow of a bird in flight.

Silver light entered the mad eyes of the dragon, and he let his enemy go.

The Archangel Raphael shone in the sky like truth revealed and in his hands was a sword. "Come, Satan," he called, and his voice was sun striking a field of ice. "See what your malice has bought you."

The wyvern took to wing again but the brilliant air

rejected him. He sank to the earth and his stiff wings fell from him to lie like the wings that ants shed in their season and that one finds in the morning grass, covered with dew.

As Raphael descended, Satan rose once more as the red king—King of Earth—and he shouted, "You interfere! Again! It is unfair! It is not your right, Raphael, for the earth is *mine* and all upon it!"

Still the angel descended. The burned hillside grew bright as crystal. "I do not interfere, Morning Star. I am sent against you.

"For not all upon the earth is yours, nor ever will be."

The sword of light struck once and the Devil's gold crown went rolling over the turf.

Lucifer lifted his arms in defense. "I am given no weapon against you. It is not fair!"

But the angel made no reply. His blinding wings drew forward and round his brother and encompassed him. "Go!" cried Raphael, and once more, "Begone from this place, and torment these children no more!" and he touched Satan with his hand.

The Devil was not there.

The heavens lightened slowly and the glory went out of the sky. Gaspare drew a breath that rattled along his throat.

Saara looked about her at the daylit plain, and she saw Raphael as she had seen him many times before, a figure of alabaster and feathers, no larger than a man.

"Chief of Eagles," she greeted him gravely.

But he did not reply, for he had not heard Saara at all, nor seen her. Raphael's eyes were on the keening Berber woman, and the body she had covered with her tattered clothing.

He stepped over to her and went down on one stainless knee beside her. "Djoura," he whispered for her ear alone.

Through her grief, that was the single voice which had the power to reach her. She stiffened. Turned to him.

Her sloe eyes widened as she took in what he was. Who he was. "Djinn!" she gasped. "The great Djinn."

And after a moment. "Raphael?"

He cupped his hands around her face. "Your Pinkie. Always." He lifted her to her feet.

Djoura blinked around her. Her eyes were tear-blind. She seemed to wonder where the Devil had gone. Then she glanced at Raphael again and lowered her eyes.

She turned away.

"Isn't that like me," she mumbled to herself. "One man I can stand, out of all the cursed world. One silly pink fellow is all, and he turns out . . . turns out to be . . ." She shook her head till the coins in her hair rattled. "Well, not for me, anyway." She sought again the body of her friend, but it was not to be found, but only the black shawl with which she had covered it.

She kicked the crumpled fabric. She took a step. Another. Tears streaming down her face, Djoura strode away from the scene of battle as though she were beginning a journey which promised to be long.

But Raphael was beside her, and in his face was a loss which did not belong on the features of an angel. He trapped her hands in his and she was forced to raise her head. "What, then?" she said roughly. "Does the great Djinn want Djoura to wash pots for him?" And she laughed at the idea. Harshly. Like a crow.

Wings flashed back with a sound of cymbals. Raphael threw his arms around the woman and pressed his head to hers. The angel gave a short, sharp cry like that of a hawk and the wings plunged forward, crashed together.

Raphael was gone from under the sky.

So was Djoura.

After a few stunned moments Saara, Gaspare, and the dragon crept forward. There was nothing to be seen on the Pyrenean hill, neither angel, nor devil, nor black Berber woman.

There was nothing to see but burned dry grass. Nothing to hear but the call of a horse in the distance.

"Well," commented Gaspare, fiddling nervous fingers over his tuning pegs. "It's not everyone's idea of court-ship."

"No," replied Saara wearily. "Not everyone's. But as long as it suits . . ." She ran her hands through her heat-damaged hair.

The dragon cleared ten feet of throat. "Madam, I would like to suggest we catch our missing cattle and leave this place—before anything else untoward happens."

"Nothing else will happen," Saara replied, wearily but with great conviction. "And if it did, they wouldn't need *our* help!" She let Gaspare help her onto the broad black back of the dragon.

EPILOGUE

Two men walked up the hill toward San Gabriele. This village was surrounded by a bank of dirt and stones which might once have been a wall, but was now reduced to a mound that harbored grass and wild alpine pinks. Beside the road leading into the village rose a single oak tree, much the worse for wear.

The old man, dressed loudly in vestments of Tyrian purple, with sleeve bobbles picked out in silver, stopped to lean against the tree. It was an action appropriate to both his years and the difficulty of the climb, but his attitude, along with a certain hauteur in his lean face, gave the impression he had halted only to gaze out over the tilled valley below.

The younger man, perhaps twenty years of age and dressed demurely in black, felt a prick of guilt at having used his great-uncle too hard. His neat, smooth-shaven Provençal face darted a glance at the other's bitter features. But how to apologize, when old Gaspare would never admit he had felt tired?

Great-uncle made it difficult to feel sorry for him.

Now the old man's fierce green eyes rested on his companion. "Why do you call yourself Caspar, when you are supposed to be named after me?" he asked. His leathered mouth pulled sideways, as though he tasted something foul, and two white points appeared on the bridge of his nose.

The story was that Grandmama and Great-uncle Gaspare were the illegitimate children of some Savoyard nobleman. It had always seemed silly to Caspar—the sort of story any bastard might make up—but looking at old Gaspare, he found it more credible. From where else had the old man come by that hawk face and those obnoxious manners?

"Caspar is the same as Gaspare, *grand-oncle*, and comes easier to a Provençal tongue."

The ancient green eyes narrowed. "I didn't want you to

be called Gaspare at all." Caspar scratched nervously under his skintight black jerkin and wished once more he hadn't come to visit, namesake or no. "I wanted you to be called Damiano."

Caspar hit one hand with the other and snapped his fingers in the air. His gestures were Provençal, not Italian, and Great-uncle Gaspare regarded them with suspicion. "That's it! The name my grandmother keeps forgetting, of the lute teacher you had as a boy."

Gaspare, through the years, had grown quite a set of unruly gray eyebrows. He raised them both. "He wasn't my teacher, boy, but my good friend. And your grandmother has no business to forget his name. Not with what he did for her."

Caspar's eyes slid to the packed earth beneath the tree. Again that business. Caspar himself would rather have come from a family of no pretension, conceived between lawful sheets. "You mean that Grandmama Evienne and he . . . that he might be my . . ."

"NO!" spat Gaspare, glaring at his namesake's small, very French features. "Your grandfather was Cardinal Rocault, certainly. Almost certainly."

The old man flung himself away from the tree and proceeded with great, gasping energy into the village. Caspar followed, drumming his fingers against his thigh uncomfortably. He heard his great-uncle mutter, "I could only wish . . ."

Since there was a hint of softening in that voice, Caspar humored the old man. "You told me about that one when I was a little boy, hein, *grand-oncle*? He was the one who talked to animals, yes, and God sent wounds of flame into his hands, and an angel comforter? He tamed a wolf that had ravaged the village."

Gaspare's look of incredulity settled into scorn. "That was Saint Francis."

"Ah. So it was," Caspar replied equably. "I am mistaken. But I heard so many stories, you must understand, and as a child I believed them all."

The old man's lips drew back from his imperfect teeth, and his angry hand made the swordsman's instinctive gesture toward the hilt of his sword. This surprised Caspar, as well as daunted him, for to the best of his knowledge, his great-uncle had never worn a sword in his life.

"Delstrego was a man of our times—of *my* times, at least. There might have been much of the fantastic about him, but he was a *real* person, boy. Born a few days' ride west of here in the city of Partestrada."

"I rode in from the west," replied Caspar readily. "But . . . I can't recall a city of that name." Then, realizing he had not spoken diplomatically, he added, "This is not to doubt you, *grand-oncle*. There are many ruins."

Gaspare winced. "Yes, no doubt. Ruins.

"It never really *was* a city, of course. Except to Delstrego. A market town.

"Ah! It means nothing, boy. Forget it." The look of defeat on Gaspare's ancient face might have melted the young man's amiable heart.

But he never saw it, for his great-uncle had turned his head away. "And forget the stories you heard as a child," the old man growled. "About dragons and witches and angels and . . . whatever. It was just to entertain you: not to be believed. If you could remember only that the man was the greatest musician of his day . . ."

Gaspare gave a dry snort and smoothed his fashionable, threadbare, trailing purple sleeve. "Or perhaps even that is too much. Yes, I'm sure it is. It . . . it has been a very long time, boy, since I have seen an angel." He turned at the stairs that led to his rooms, and, though he would have liked to rest before assaulting them, preceded his grand-nephew up.

The cynicism of this last reply heartened Caspar. He did not believe, whatever his family in Avignon told him, that Great-uncle Gaspare was mad or senile. He was just old and angry (as old men often were), and had his own kind of humor. Caspar sat down at the other side of the table and gazed at the old man's incredible lute while Gaspare poured him a mug of rough cider.

Such an instrument. Covered with inlays of shell and ivory, it was almost too pretty to be taken seriously. But Gaspare had plucked it for him, and he had perceived that it was of the highest quality, with a true tone clarified by age to bell-like sweetness. "That is the lute Pope Innocent gave you?" Caspar asked, a touch of awe in his voice. He smiled the smile that everyone in Avignon found so charming.

But Gaspare was staring out the window. "The Pope

gave it to Delstrego. I inherited it only." Cold green eyes wandered through the room, and though they touched Caspar's brown ones only for a moment, the younger man was abashed.

"It seems I was born too late," Caspar said.

Old Gaspare's eyes widened, looking at the other's sleek exterior. Remembering the plague. Remembering hunger.

"Too late for Avignon," Caspar qualified. "Since the papacy has been in dispute, most of the good patrons have removed to Rome. And so has the . . . the thrust of the music."

He shrugged and touched both hands to his breast. "So. You see me on my way to Rome. Following my art."

Caspar quailed as his great-uncle's face went red, then purple. It clashed terribly with his purple jacket. The old man's aristocratic hooked nose stood out white in relief. "What do you say, boy? You are going to Rome—after the music?"

"Yes," came the answer. "Oh, I know it must sound absurd to you, as it does to my own father (since I am guaranteed a place in the guild at Avignon, and that is a thing a man may seek for a lifetime), but . . ."

Gaspare had turned from his namesake and was staring fixedly again out the window. His hands, laced together, were white-knuckled.

"Following the music," he mumbled under his breath. "Without a sou, I suppose."

"No." In truth it had been part of his plan to ask his great-uncle for provision during his stay, but one look at the old man's worn foppery had caused him to put that matter quietly away. His innate honesty forced Caspar to amend his answer. "Not quite without a sou."

Gaspare cast one taut look in his direction. He gestured at the lute on the table. "Play it for me, boy."

Caspar had been longing to play ever since seeing the lute. But the voice held more challenge than invitation, and besides, old people never liked his music.

Yet it was old Gaspare who taught his father to play the lute and Caspar had learned from him, so Great-uncle had a right to hear. Caspar cleared his throat. "I am more used to an instrument of six courses," he qualified, lifting the lute from the table. It was almost weightless.

"Six!" cackled Gaspare. "Why, boy, you have only five fingers to play them with!"

Caspar's smile twisted under the expected witticism. He found the lute in very close tune.

Gaspare listened to a Provençal folk tune done in very pleasant, antique style. In a very few seconds' listening he had granted the boy technical competence. But he cut him off roughly before the song was done. "Don't humor me, Nephew! God's bollocks, I'm a musician too! Play your own music for me! Play to your limit!"

Caspar's eyes rose startled and he glared back at his great-uncle.

Everyone at home thought the world of Caspar and he did so *like* to be liked. Here he'd come eighty miles out of his way to visit the old man only to be treated like this! Unremitting hostility and scorn.

Of course what Gaspare said was quite true. Caspar *had* been humoring him. He ground his teeth together and flexed his fingers over the hand-tied frets. "Very well," he snapped at his great-uncle. "I'll play what I like best. But don't bother to tell me you don't like it!"

Caspar played. His left hand spread like a spider on the broad lute neck. His right hand bounced. He played seconds against one another. He ended lines on the seventh chord. He played melodies that chased each other impudently in and out of a music where structure threatened to dissolve momentarily into chaos. The lute sounded like a guitar, like a harp.

But though there was virtuosity in Caspar's attack, it was not mere show, for the technique worked in the service of feeling, in a music with much soul and a very playful rhythm. His unobtrusive chin (nothing like Gaspare's chin) jutted out as he played, like that of a man who speaks and does not expect to be understood.

When he was done and not before, he glanced up at his great-uncle. He was prepared for coldness, and half-expected an explosion. But to the Provençal's horror, the old man was weeping. Tears spattered onto the black wood of the tabletop. Caspar was stricken. "Great-uncle! Forgive me. It is dissonant, when one is not accustomed to it, certainly. But I had no inten—"

But the young man was no fool, and he read the truth in his great-uncle's face.

Gaspare reached over the tabletop, shoving pitcher and mugs to one side. "Boy," he whispered. "Don't apologize. Never apologize for being what you must be.

"And pay no mind to me, for I can't explain it to you. It's just the music, when I'd believed it to be all lost.

"But nothing is lost, you see? Nothing. Not even if his . . . his city is lost, and no one remembers his name."

Caspar's quick brown eyes narrowed. "I don't understand, *grand-oncle*. But have I finally done something right in your eyes?" Caspar asked, half touched by the old man's tears, half still-resentful of his tempers.

"You have," replied Gaspare, grinning at his greatnephew. "Of course you have, boy. You have shown me an angel."

THIS IS THE LAST OF THE TALES OF DAMIANO AND HIS FRIENDS I WILL WRITE. BY NOW I IMAGINE THEY ARE ALL RATHER TIRED.

I KNOW I AM.

BUT NO CONCLUSION IS FINAL, AND THE READER IS WELCOME TO CONTINUE THE STORY IN ANY DIRECTION DESIRED. AFTER THREE BOOKS, HE OR SHE KNOWS AS MUCH TO THE PURPOSE AS I.

Bertie MacAvoy